About the Author

Nottingham born, 'Baby Boomer', Michael Heath obtained a master's Degree for research in Kidney Transplantation and a PhD for work completed on Rheumatoid Arthritis treatment, whilst working in Pathology Laboratories within the UK National Health Service. He later moved into the commercial pharmaceutical sector, in the Clinical Development of new drugs, working globally and for a time living and working in Italy. In his writing he draws on experiences gained during those times and first tentatively put pen to paper in 'novel form' ten years ago. He is married and has two daughters, two granddaughters, and one grandson.

Dedication

This novel is dedicated to the whole of my family, who have put up with me so patiently during the writing of this book, and particularly to my grandchildren. May this book in years to come successfully stabilise a prized table with one leg shorter than the rest!

Michael Heath

SEEDS OF EMPIRES

AUSTIN MACAULEY PUBLISHERS™

LONDON ∗ CAMBRIDGE ∗ NEW YORK ∗ SHARJAH

A CIP catalogue record for this title is available from the British Library.

ISBN 9781528966627 (Paperback)
ISBN 9781528967068 (ePub e-book)

www.austinmacauley.com

First Published (2021)
Austin Macauley Publishers Ltd
25 Canada Square
Canary Wharf
London
E14 5LQ

Acknowledgments

I would like to thank the team at Austin Macauley Publishers for steering me through the 'publishing maze' in such a friendly and patient way.

Chapter 1

It was a bleak grey dawn. The early February wind, having given up a couple of degrees to the threatening icy waters of Liverpool's river Mersey, cut through the light-weight hospital issue jacket like a freezing scalpel. The jacket's wearer, hunched against the icy blast, grimaced, pulled it tighter and set his glowing nose like a beacon in the direction of the obstetric unit. He kicked at an empty food carton caught up in the Siberian gust and broke into a trot as he covered the last few yards of the gravel path, which terminated at the service entrance to the unit. He fumbled in his pocket momentarily for his identity swipe card, which would gain him access to the unit and provide escape from the arctic morning.

He extricated the photo identity card from the other items in his pocket, an almost empty cigarette packet and a couple of crumpled lotto tickets, and stared down at the photograph of a man who might have been his son or much younger brother, rather than the tired and worn out Mersey Shore Hospital porter now staring down at what used to be his own face. The face of Bert Scarfe.

Jesus! he thought to himself. *Ten years in this shit-hole has really done me in.*

And he was right, for he had been a reasonably good-looking man in his early 30s when the photograph had been taken. Reasonably good looking and with hopes for the future. But that was before Edith and the empty, loveless, childless marriage, not to mention his increasing dependence upon alcohol to get him through the day.

Before he had the time to pass his identity card through the locking system, the early dawn was pierced by a wail from within the unit, which sent the flocks of crows and gulls huddled on the frost covered grass cursing as they lifted up into the icy wind where they responded to the pitiful cry with those of their own.

As Scarfe entered the dimly lit corridor, he allowed himself his first and only smile of the day as he trudged off along the trail that he now knew well. That path took him to the foul smelling storeroom that was, for this particular extra-curricular journey, the repository for "pathology specimens for collection".

Chapter 2

Max Hart gazed out of the window of his 10-by-10 feet corner office on the fourth floor of the Clinical Development Building, at the snow covering the roofs of the nearby buildings and which, overnight, had covered much of the "World" campus with a white virgin carpet. In the best World practice, the roads and pathways had of course been cleared very early in the morning from the fall of the very first snowflake. The sun was a frozen orange suspended in the sky, whilst below it the white clouds reflected the pale orange glow.

Hart's PA entered the room carrying the morning mail. Janet Blane had been his only PA since his arrival at "World Pharmaceuticals", New Jersey, from the UK seven years earlier. These had been enlightening years for the grey-haired widow of some sixty plus years, who had taken an instant shine to this outspoken, often brash, but always amusing English physician. She had somehow grown accustomed to his frequent outbursts of rather blue language, the kind of language which she had traditionally found so unpleasant in others. She had never tired of listening to his daily anecdotes about what he called 'my previous life', spent firstly in the health service as a physician in the UK and then in a series of pharmaceutical companies based in the UK, but also working on secondment in Italy and Germany. His roles in the pharma industry had given him huge license to travel extensively on business in Europe and the Americas, always staying at good hotels and eating and drinking fine wines at some of the best international restaurants. The international travel and gourmet education came with perfect timing, coinciding with his marriage, which nursed like a sick animal for five years, eventually passed away.

'So, Janet, how are you today?' he asked.

'I am fine, thank you, Max. I thought I'd better remind you that you have the meeting with Doctor Halle in thirty minutes.'

Hart grinned at her, looking younger than his late thirty odd years.

'Thanks. Ah yes, my appointment with the famous Doctor Halle-bloody-tosis. Still, with things really looking up now and development plans coming together rather nicely, I shouldn't be bad-mouthing him, should I? Or, should that actually be bad-breathe-ing him? You know, Janet, this could be the dawn of a new era for me and the team in this company that we love so much,' his voice heavy with sarcasm.

The last few months had been hell for Hart and subsequently for the development teams that he led. He had been set unattainable targets for improbable drug developments with impossible timelines and ridiculously small budgets. However, such was his determination, professionalism and above all leadership qualities, together with the dedication and loyalty of his team, that together against all odds, they had done the impossible and brought their primary drug within striking distance of submission to the US Food and Drug Administration. Hart's arguments with senior management had often been heated, often actually incendiary in intensity, but now it seemed that common sense was about to reign all around with the likelihood of sufficient budget and resource being made available for him to orchestrate the final push to achieving the goal of FDA approval of what was an exceptional drug. A drug which not only offered a treatment for the pain and the modification of the actual symptoms of rheumatoid arthritis, but which offered a real once-and-for-all cure from the crippling disabilities inflicted by the disease. It was the first ever drug reported in the public domain with these particular efficacies and together with its surprisingly good safety profile, it was consequently a potential source of billions of dollars to the company. The final hurdles for the drug consisted of a series of extended toxicological studies in patient volunteers. These trials alone had almost caused the meltdown of Hart's team as a result of the predicted difficulties that would be experienced in finding patients willing to volunteer for these crucial studies. For even with such an excellent safety profile, the reputation for these treatment types was bad, both with prescribers and patient groups alike, not to mention with external ethics committees.

The stresses and strains in reaching the current development position were not just confined to Hart's on-site relationships with higher management. On occasions, they had unfortunately also spilled over into certain of the international meetings they had sponsored with key rheumatoid arthritis opinion leaders. Traditionally, "professor famous" was always pandered to with a level of sycophancy that Hart had always excelled at. That was until recently, when Hart had taken particular offence at not just the behaviour of one particular expert and the way in which he addressed other members of an international expert meeting Hart had organised, but also in some of the extremely unethical proposals which he had put forward with respect to patient populations and toxicological studies. At that time, Hart had let off what he later called 'a little re-directional steam to put discussions back on course' but the steam had caused more than just one set of eyebrows to be raised. In fact, Hart had been led to understand that delicate discussions were still taking place between some of the opinion leaders and his own senior management to rebuild some of the bridges burnt during his outburst.

The fateful occasion had been an advisory board meeting attended by a group of European opinion leaders in rheumatoid arthritis who had flown in from Holland, France, Germany, Spain, Belgium and Italy, and a couple of people from Hart's own US team. The meeting was sponsored by World Pharma and held in Prague. It had started well enough with excellent input from many of the board, but had suddenly turned to mayhem when it had become clear that certain opinions held were actually cast in stone and would be defended to the death. Some of these opinions, with respect to patients' treatment, were grossly unethical and in many cases at odds with the patients' human rights. Hart, as chairman of the meeting, rather than calm tempers down as they flared had actually fanned the flames, himself arguing violently with the German spokesman. Peace eventually broke out following the intervention of the Dutch representative, but by then, the damage had been done. The German professor, with battered ego, not being accustomed to such violent opposition took no further part in the discussions and the meeting drew to an embarrassing close with little valuable outcome. Complaints to World's most senior management were certain to follow.

Whilst most of the European experts beat a hasty return home, the Dutch rheumatologist and latter 'fire-fighter', Paul-Peter Timmerman, stayed on and accompanied Hart to dinner, whilst Hart's colleagues from World made their own dinner arrangements. Dinner was not surprisingly, a quiet affair taken in an historic cellar restaurant close to the Charles Bridge, with Hart clearly embarrassed by his earlier outbursts at the meeting.

It was after leaving the restaurant, walking through the cobbled streets, that Hart finally said,

'Look, I'm really sorry about the way I handled the meeting this afternoon. I should have facilitated it properly rather than getting drawn into a fight with that Nazi Muller. If you hadn't been there, I would still be fighting with the prick. You know this phase of our studies is particularly fraught. How we are going to get patients on board for the tox' studies is anybody's guess at the moment and Muller's insistence that we use braindead patients on life support machines was just too much for me.'

The Dutchman looked at Hart, concern on his face.

'Yes I know, Max, but my worry now is what steps Muller will take, for as you know he and your boss, Halle, are close friends and he is bound to make some official complaint.'

'Ah fuck them both!' Hart spat. 'I've been working eighteen hours a day for the last two years to get this drug to where we are now. It's revolutionary in what it offers arthritis sufferers and there is no way that the World board will want to rock our boat at this critical stage. What I need to do is to present to the board the latest study data. Then whilst they're calculating the undoubted profits which will flood in after launch, I will tell them that to achieve this goal this year rather than the next year, or the year after that, I will need an adequate budget and additional personnel. At the same time, I shall have to drive out the wild ideas of Muller, with respect to his "braindead volunteers", which have already been presented to some members of the board by his chum Halle.'

Timmerman patted Hart on the back.

'Well, my friend, I wish you the best of luck in those endeavours. It will not be easy.'

However, as it turned out, from Hart's viewpoint, it *had* been relatively easy. He had met with the board, presented as he had outlined to Timmerman the week earlier and walked away confident that all his requests would be met by these senior executives so obviously outwardly elated with the data he had presented, and inwardly doubly elated at the prospects of what these data bore in terms of future sales.

And so today, he stood in his office talking to his PA, just thirty minutes away from the meeting, which would reveal exactly what the level of increases in budget and resource would be to enable him and the team to complete the development program. Inwardly, for the first time in ages, he felt thrilled and excited.

'I'm pleased to see that at least you are wearing a tie today, Max,' smiled Janet.

'Yes indeed! I even considered wearing a pair of trousers. The truth is, Janet, I'm only wearing the tie to string myself up with if I don't get the red carpet treatment,' he continued.

Janet laughed and pointed towards the door.

'It's time you made your way to the meeting room in H3, best not be late...just this once.'

'Right then.'

Hart picked up his briefcase and headed out of his office to the elevator which would take him to the ground floor, from where it was a five-minute stroll past the executive car park to the senior executive building, in which meeting room H3 was on the third floor.

Within seconds of him summoning the elevator, it arrived. Its doors opened to reveal Judith Paris-Cregg, standing there in usual statuesque fashion, wearing the etched-in frown which Hart had never seen her bereft of at any time since his first day with the company.

Sod it, he thought to himself. *I thought she travelled everywhere by broomstick.*

He gave her his best hypocritical smile and stepped in.

'Good morning,' and nodding towards the elevator floor buttons, 'You going down?'

Without breaking the frown or smiling, she nodded in the affirmative. This man had been responsible for her disproportionate irritation with his every action from his very first day with World, when it was clear to her as senior personnel assistant that this new employee had a weird and diverse personality, far from the norm aspired to by human resources at World. However, more senior people than herself saw this as an eccentricity perhaps born of his outstanding brightness and held the belief that perhaps he represented a long overdue breath of fresh air in the company. Since that first black Monday, his constant flippancy had made her feel at times the need to exact some kind of violence upon him. But retribution, she had discovered, need not necessarily always be of a violent or physical nature.

There was, gratefully for them both, no further conversation as the elevator continued its journey down. Upon leaving the elevator, as he reached the door leading out of the building, he became aware that she was just a couple of steps behind him and she remained there as he progressed on his way to the senior executive building.

Chapter 3

Not another word passed between Hart and Paris-Cregg as they made their way in single file to the executive building, him holding his briefcase and her clutching a crimson folder in her hand.

To enter the executive building was to enter a different world. Open and airy, it was all chrome and glass with sumptuous carpeting and acoustic tiles covering the ceiling, so it was also very quiet. Although Hart had been inside this building several times before, it always looked different, mainly due to the monthly rotation of the expensive expressive artwork and ornamentation which adorned the place and also the masses of flowers which were replaced the moment any blooms began to fade.

H3 was the smallest of the half dozen boardrooms situated on the third floor. Hart walked over to the elevator, which was already waiting with doors ajar. As he turned to select the button for the third floor, he was surprised to see that his follower was still close on his tail, the quality of the carpet muffling the sound of her footsteps.

'Which floor, Ms Paris-Cregg?' he asked.

'The third,' came the even more surprising reply.

They were on a collision course to the same meeting. The elevator stopped directly in front of the huge double mahogany doors of room H3 and suddenly the importance of the moment dawned on Hart. The excitement and anticipation he had felt in his own office earlier came surging back. His mouth felt incredibly dry and he experienced a slight dizziness. He saw this meeting as being likened to winning the lottery, considering the reward he was about to receive. But this was no more than he deserved considering the vast amount of work he had put into the project and the long nights he had spent pouring over data and study protocols. He took a large intake of breath and knocked on the door.

'Enter!'

It was Robert Halle's voice which did the bidding.

Hart opened the door, motioned Paris-Cregg to enter ahead of him and went in behind her, closing the door firmly as he went.

The small boardroom was laid out in a similar fashion to the other parts of the building with sumptuous carpet and expensive artwork and even flowers. In the middle of the room was a large table of the same mahogany as the door. Hart was a little taken aback by the seating arrangement at the table, which comprised three chairs on one side, two of which were occupied, with a solitary chair on the other side facing them...interview style.

Robert Halle rose as they approached the table. Although he was almost within the same age range as Hart, he had a more mature and distinguished look about him and was considerably more formally dressed. He was a tall man, around six feet two and his tanned face harboured a neat black moustache, similar in colour to his short rather too black hair. Looking at Halle, Hart in his irreverent way decided that if the going got tough, he would look at that moustache and think of it as a leech (a twist on the old "imagine them with no trousers on" ploy). Halle looked every inch a senior executive in his navy blue "power suit", complimented by a white shirt with button down collar and an expensive plain red silk tie. Hart would not be fazed by a single thing.

Just think of the leech, he told himself.

'Good morning, Judith; good morning, Max. Judith, will you sit over here please.'

Halle indicated the seat on his side of the table next to the other occupant.

'Max, please take the seat there if you will.'

He indicated the seat which was in the interview position.

'Before we begin, let me introduce you to Doctor Spencer. Doctor Spencer is the head of Discovery Medicine at our Boston site, but he will be spending some time with us here at Mount Olive and I thought it would be useful for him to be at this meeting.'

Then, turning to Spencer he said,

'And here we have Judith Paris-Cregg of our human resource department and of course, Max Hart.'

What, no title? thought Hart. *Remember the leech, Max. But why is this Spencer guy here anyway?*

Halle now seated, continued,

'Right then, let's get started. Over the last few months, Max, you have put in a tremendous amount of effort, along with your excellent team, in taking the development of our leading drug for the treatment of rheumatoid arthritis to its present well-advanced position. In addition, you have argued at length and determinedly with regard to the shortage of both budget and human resource for this project, which as we well know is a key area of development for World.'

Too bloody right it's a key area, thought Hart.

'As a result, it has been decided at the highest levels, Max, to increase the available budget to the project by one million dollars per annum for the next three years and to make a suitable adjustment to the level of staffing on the project as soon as Judith has confirmed the figures you have passed on.'

She nodded in agreement.

Hart flushed with excitement. 'Halle-bloody-lujah,' he said under his breath, and smiled as the unintended pun on Halle's name registered. It wasn't so bad after all then that Paris-Cregg, the wicked witch of the East Coast, had parked her broomstick here.

'In making these additional resources available, the board do need to see that they are value-enhancing to the project and we...*they*, have made certain decisions in this respect, which I will now present to you.'

Somewhere in Hart's head, a distant alarm bell started to ring. There was no such thing as a free lunch and he was about to discover the cost.

Just remember the leech and stay calm, he recited silently in his head.

Halle continued, 'In addition to your lobbying for the additional resources, Max, you have also argued quite forcefully over your concerns relating to certain proposals which have been made, proposals calculated expressly to overcome the toxicological study issues of the drug in the shortest and most cost effective time.'

Hart now had an inkling of where this was leading and it disturbed him.

Halle went on, 'I'm talking here about the problems you describe as being of an ethical nature with respect to some of the more innovative solutions suggested by our colleagues in Discovery, supported might I say by some powerful external expert opinion.'

Suddenly, the leech under Halle's nose lost some of its effectiveness in controlling Hart's calm state and he blurted out,

'Let's not beat about the bush here, those proposals were—'

He was cut off by Halle's raised hand, but in that instant, he suddenly remembered who Spencer was and he now understood why he was at this meeting. Spencer was a "novel ideas" man and it had been him who had first raised the possibility of using braindead patients in some of the trials which posed greater difficulties with patient recruitment, and Halle had pursued and supported this line of research.

'As I was saying, Doctor Hart,' formality suddenly creeping into Halle's demeanour, 'it could be argued that your ethical concerns have impeded the progress of the work to its final conclusion and taking that argument further, that this has therefore cost money in terms of lost revenue because of the necessity for a later drug launch date.'

'Now hang on there,' broke in Hart. 'That's bullshit and you know it. You've already accepted the fact that we have all worked our balls off over the past six months and—'

'I haven't finished yet. Please hear me out before you respond any further, Doctor Hart.'

Halle was now in cruise control as he continued, 'The board has now decided that we should press ahead with Doctor Spencer's proposals for the toxicological program.'

The mantra that Hart had been clinging to suddenly felt unimportant as his anger washed over it in a torrent. *Fuck the leech!* he thought and the floodgates opened.

'Are you telling me that you are proposing to get approvals from the distraught relatives of patients being kept alive by mechanical life support systems? Braindead patients? I thought we had confined this bloody stupid idea to the bin ages ago. It's unethical, and more than that, it's totally immoral.'

His voice was getting louder and the earlier flush of triumph imparted to his face was now replaced with the redness of anger. Spencer and Paris-Cregg looked down at the desk, embarrassed but not surprised at this predicted and calculated reaction from Hart. It was the reaction that Halle had been counting on, and raising his hand to silence Hart once more, continued,

'Doctor Hart, these are not mere proposals any longer. They are approved actions to be taken, approved at the highest level within the company.'

Hart wasn't going down on this point without a fight.

'To do this, you will have to obtain the support of international opinion leaders and then the FDA. You will never find anyone stupid enough to support you, Halle. Anyone supporting this would have to be totally out of their mind. And what about me and the team, how do you propose to motivate us to follow this bloody stupid plan through?'

Halle never changed his oily tone or emotionless face once…unless it was to allow a small smile to briefly touch the corners of his mouth.

'But Max,' informally once again, '*au contraire.* The project will be supported by Professor Wummer, the highly respected professor of rheumatology at the University of Munich, in Germany. Tomorrow, he will be seconded from his university position there to begin a twelve-month period with us here at World, as senior consultant for the whole rheumatoid program. Obviously, World will be making more than adequate monetary compensation to the university and its research department for this secondment. Whilst he is in post here, he will be assuming the title of "Acting Head of Development". In other words, Doctor Hart,' (now back to formality), 'he will be your project leader, and we expect you and your team to give him your fullest co-operation.'

'The man might be regarded by some of his pals as an opinion leader, Halle,' Hart fumed, taking a dig at Halle's known friendship with the professor, 'but to most others, he's regarded as a bloody bombastic idiot. He was present at a European advisory board meeting we held in Prague recently and his behaviour was outrageous. He was professionally inept and socially appalling. He managed, totally unaided, to piss off the whole of the delegation.'

Halle didn't rise to this minor jibe.

'Not everyone held him in that regard. In fact some of those delegates you mentioned supported the formal complaint he made to World with regard to your own outrageous behaviour at that meeting.'

For once, Hart was out of his depth and he failed totally to recognise the gravity and the scope of the scenario that was developing around him and he careered on blindly. Letting his heart totally over-rule his head, he plunged into the trap that had been so carefully laid for him.

'That man is a prick! His clinical ideas are pure science fiction. He has the social skills and diplomatic abilities of Attila the Hun and there is no way that I am prepared to work with him.'

On the opposite side of the table, Spencer fought hard to hide a smile. At his side, Paris-Cregg's lips tightened even more as she re-considered the thoughts she had had upon first meeting Hart at the lift on her way to the meeting, *Retribution need not necessarily be of a violent nature.*

Halle continued,

'Being as you have brought up behaviours, Doctor Hart, let us spend a few moments looking at some of your own. Judith, could I have the folder please?'

Judith Paris-Cregg passed him the red folder that she had carried to the meeting. Hart stared at her intensely. Halle opened the folder for the prosecution, read silently for a few seconds and then looking up began.

'I don't intend to go through this list item by item, Doctor Hart, but I will select just a few of the misdemeanours at random which we have down here.'

Hart sat in total silence as Halle ran his finger down the page and continued,

'I see here that "Doctor Hart is prone to frequent comments of a sexist and politically incorrect nature, often constructed with overt sexual innuendo." Moving on I also see that that "Doctor Hart habitually overspends on hospitality, particularly with respect to restaurants, wine and hotel bar bills."'

This was ludicrous thought Hart.

'Look, Halle, wining and dining important opinion leaders is part of the job. They expect it, for Christ sake. As for political incorrectness and sexual innuendo, that's ridiculous.'

He still hadn't totally grasped the gravity of the situation, as Halle continued,

'Of course, we also have here recorded your many episodes of sarcastic insults and foul language. The final reference I will make here is to your outrageous and unprofessional behaviour at the annual company meeting last year when you caused gross insult to our eminent guest speaker and embarrassment to the whole of World's senior management.'

The incident Halle was referring to was now part of the folklore of World Pharmaceuticals. It was the gaffe which had raised Hart's image to iconic levels amongst most ordinary World staff members, but which had placed him in (boiling) hot water with senior management. He was fortunate, in fact, to suffer no more than a written warning instead of the instant notice of dismissal that others at today's meeting would have been far happier with.

The incident in question occurred during the keynote address by Professor Marc Le Blanc, a "professor famous" from the Hospital Saint Germaine in Paris, France. Hart was due to speak directly after Le Blanc at this important meeting and was, thus, connected up with a "remote microphone" clipped to the lapel of his jacket. The controversial rheumatologist had been pontificating for forty-five minutes on 'the effects of being overweight and obese on the outcomes of treatments for rheumatoid arthritis' and eventually he brought his mind-numbing presentation to a close by saying,

'So if I may borrow a famous quotation to end my presentation, please remember "man is what he eats".'

At this point, as the trickle of applause began to circulate the room, Hart whispered to a colleague seated next to him,

'Le Blanc must eat arse-holes then.'

Unfortunately for Hart, the microphone on his collar had been activated, ready for his own following presentation, with the result that his whisper was shared by the whole audience.

But that was then. Now, today at *this* meeting, Hart's temperature was still rising. He still had things to say, even as the trap predictably closed upon him.

'You know, this company makes such a big deal of diversity. People are sent on courses where they are instructed that the company needs diverse people to help provide a different approach, one which will put us one jump ahead of the competitors, but the truth is that this company loathes anything or anybody who dares to stray from the company's idea of what is normal, the boring, the middle of the road, the bloody anally retentive! A charisma by-pass is not essential to work here, but it bloody well helps most of you. What you really want are clones. Clones of yourselves, without any personality or any ability for lateral thinking.'

At this point, he redirected his glare to Paris-Cregg, who reddened and lowered her eyes to stare at a point on the floor in front of her chair. He was on a roll now.

'This pathetic list you present is totally irrelevant to this discussion and the three of you know it. The bottom line is the disastrous effect that your Professor Wummer will have on the project we have worked so hard on and come so far with. His control of the development program will destroy it and I'm not prepared to let that happen and I repeat, there is no way I am prepared to work with this unethical idiot…and that is final!'

Throughout this tirade, Halle had remained calm, but the killer punch was on its way! He waited for what seemed like an eternity and then fixing Hart with a steely stare, said through smiling lips,

'Your outburst has underlined all the points I've just recounted to you. I see that there can be no compromise for us here, Hart. Therefore, in view of your total lack of acceptance of Professor Wummer, your determination not to work with him or support him at any cost, and added to that your total disregard for, and abuse of, senior members of staff, I have no alternative but to tell you that as from this moment, you can consider yourself no longer an employee of World Pharmaceuticals.'

'What! You're firing me?' spluttered Hart incredulously.

'No, Doctor Hart,' returned Halle, 'let us say that your employment has been terminated by mutual consent. You will be paid eighteen months full salary, as severance. This amount will be rescinded should you make any attempt to fight this legally. I can assure you that our legal department has already run over this in great detail and we are acting well within our rights. Your comments and actions here today have been witnessed by senior members of the company at this table and a report of this meeting will be made available to the senior executives of World Pharmaceuticals and our legal section later today.'

Hart was on the canvas. The referee could have counted on to one hundred and he would still have been out. He could not mouth a single syllable.

'Your desk will be cleared for you, Doctor Hart. In some minutes' time, a car will arrive to take you off the campus.'

There was a knock on the door.

'Wait! Any personal effects will be forwarded to you and HR will shortly be in touch with you to explain fully the arrangements of our *mutual agreement* and also to tidy up any loose ends there may be relating to your displacement. Doctor Hart, you may not go from this room to any other part of the campus other than to the car which now awaits you outside.'

He turned to the door,

'Come in, Roberts! So, please place the keys to your car on the table, and Mr Roberts here will drive you home.'

Roberts was not one of the company's regular chauffeurs. He was an "outsider"…and large with it! Clearly, Halle had expected a little more physical fight from his opponent.

Meekly, Hart stood, turned and followed the "driver" out. Halle walked over and closed the door. There was a certain degree of shame written on the faces of both Paris-Cregg and Spencer but neither spoke. Instead, it was Halle who said,

'I would like to thank you both. Hart was so wonderfully predictable. Give him time to leave the campus and then get his team in here please, Doctor Spencer. Judith, I would like you to be here also for that meeting.'

He turned to one of the ornate mirrors in the room, adjusting his already perfectly knotted tie and treated himself to an unusual bout of humour.

'Yes! I feel much better for that "heart to Hart" conversation, ha, ha, ha.'

In the back seat of the car, Hart was a forlorn figure. He was whupped. And whupped good! He had been a lightweight in the ring with a heavyweight champion. A trap had been set and he had rushed blindly into it. As the campus receded rapidly behind the black, funereal limousine, all he could think of were his ironic statements made earlier in the day before the debacle of a meeting,

Janet, this could be the dawn of a new era.

And what else had he said? Ah yes, he had said that he would hang himself with his tie if he wasn't given the red carpet treatment.

There's no bloody chance of that, you bastards, he thought.

His defiance was trickling back, but it was much too late, the contest was over.

Chapter 4

By now, the members of 'O' Club, Rio de Janeiro's exclusive sporting and leisure club, had become accustomed to seeing the fifty-something-year-old priest with the shock of black curly hair, slightly greying at the temples, with bag and rackets and flowing cassock dashing through their ranks either on his way in or on his way out of the centre. Either way he was always dashing. The clue to which direction he was taking was to be seen in his face. Sweating on the way in, and profusely sweating and bright red on the way out.

Twice weekly, he would rush from his place of work and worship, sprinting the four hundred metres which separated the church of prayer from the "temple of health and fitness" where he played squash. On Tuesdays, he played "just for fun, fitness and cardiovascular exercise", so his run took him directly into the changing rooms, where he would change into his off-whites, play for forty-five minutes, then shower, change back into his work clothes or rather his "uniform" as he liked to put it, and then at a slightly slower sprint than his inbound journey jog back to his office in the cathedral. He always arrived back after his game feeling exhilarated, but always red-faced, hot (no matter how long he extended his cold shower at the club) and as wet with sweat as if he had showered with his clothes on. The one pause he made between the end of play and dressing was to take a long drink of his favourite glucose energy elixir, which he had opened and stood in a small basin of ice so that it could attain as low a temperature as possible whilst he was playing. This was his routine and it was cast in stone.

On Thursdays, he played more competitively, taking part in the club's league or ladder matches, where despite his advancing years, he was still able to maintain a good standard and consistent high placing in the tables. In fact, such was his level of competitive play that this very year he had easily won the veterans knockout tournament.

Whilst other club members referred to him generally as the "flying priest", not too many of them realised that Claudio Santos was in fact Archbishop Santos, or more accurately Archbishop Claudio Cardinal Santos. He was a friendly and sympathetic man and well liked amongst both colleagues and congregation. Within the confines of his profession, he was identified by many purveyors of "the true word of God" to be a man, although quite young to be in his present position, who was a star still rising, especially in the eyes of Rome. He was perceived as a moderate, a moderniser and an outspoken advocate of human rights.

But today was Tuesday and as he changed into his almost worn-out kit and pulled on his ancient sneakers, he was able to relax mentally and anticipate eagerly the next forty-five minutes of cardiac exhilaration. In accordance with his strict routine, he opened a bottle of his favourite energy drink, took a couple of gulps and then wedged it between the cubes of ice in the bowl, to be savoured later.

As Jesus Christ was at the core of his profession, so were the same words at the core of any particularly arduous game he played on court. He was always quick to call upon the almighty to give him that extra metre in his play and also to call His name when his racket flashed at thin air in missing the ball. His game nearly always drew fascinated onlookers, who would peer down from the spectator gallery, eagerly waiting for his curses and expletives.

This particular day's game had gone well with Santos narrowly defeating his younger, more agile, opponent by just the odd few points, and then like clockwork it was back to the regime of drink, shower, drink again, dress, finish the drink and finally leave the club at a gallop. Other members, well accustomed to his regime, stood back and cleared a passage for him on his rush to the exit, bag in hand. Not breaking his speed, he descended the dozen steps leading from the club entrance and as usual hit the street running. He particularly enjoyed the run back to the cathedral after his games, often commenting that the return run was the most important few minutes of the whole sporting exercise in terms of that extra morsel of fitness now required in larger portions with his advancing years.

Today seemed a little hotter than usual though. The air was heavy and its quality poor. Somehow, it was more difficult to force the oxygen into his lungs. In fact, it was difficult to breathe at all. As he ran, the street ahead suddenly became a blur and as he gasped for more air. A searing pain shot through his chest and quickly ran down his left arm which carried his bag. Then all went black and the "flying priest" crash-landed on the hard pavement, his game well and truly over.

Another apparent club member, who had today paid particularly close attention to Santos and who had earlier watched him swallow the final drops of his glucose drink, was the first person to reach the prostrate body. He checked for pulse and heartbeat. Nothing. Taking out his mobile phone, he first called for an ambulance for the deceased priest and then made one other call.

'Si, this is Miguel. It is done. It was as you said, he is…he *was* a man of great regularity. Si, I watched him swallow the whole drink and I have checked just now and can confirm that the priest is dead. My job here is done.'

Chapter 5

Hart sat motionless in the back of the limo feeling numb, but not numb enough not to realise what a bloody fool he'd been to play into Halle's hands with his threats of resignation.

The journey home took thirty minutes. The driver cum-all-in-wrestler had been pre-programmed with perfect instructions with respect to the route to take from the office. There were no words spoken throughout the whole delivery.

'Thanks,' Hart finally mumbled as he dragged himself out of the vehicle and received the predictable response as the driver pulled away.

'You're welcome. Have a nice day!'

He took his door key from his pocket, *Thank God, it wasn't kept on the car key ring*, and found the keyhole at the third attempt. He walked through the hall into the sitting room and dropped into an armchair. Looking at the ceiling, he asked aloud to no one in particular,

'What the hell do I do now?'

After an hour of being hypnotised by a crack in the ceiling, he decided to go outside and walk to the small lake, which was part of the residential suburb in which he lived in this comfortable rented residence. It was in walking multiple circuits of this, "Tiger Lake", that he had often gained inspiration when beset by problems, be they clinical, technical or just personal. Such was his life up until now that he reckoned that over the last few years he'd probably walked far enough round the lake to have reached the moon. After an hour of walking and kicking leaves, he suddenly realised that the temperature had really dropped and he was freezing cold, and he beat a hasty retreat to his house. Having spent one hour in walking meditative contemplation, he had come up with a two-point action plan. One, to make a list of actions as soon as possible, and two, to get back to the house. *Get bloody warm and then get pissed* (which was actually four actions in total, but who was counting?).

After a long hot shower and a change into T-shirt and jeans, he felt a little better. As he approached the sitting room from the bathroom, he was startled by the ring of the telephone.

Perhaps it's Halle ringing to tell me it was a huge mistake and that they really want me back, but on double salary!

He picked up the phone and speaking in as bold a voice as he could muster,
'Hello?'

'Max, its Janet. Do you want to talk… Are you in any *state* to talk?'

She had known him long enough to know that his likely destination in circumstances such as this was a voyage to the bottom of a wine bottle, but she was surprised at his clarity.

'Janet, thank you, I'm fan-tastic. Fucking fantastic.'

'Well, that's good, Max, at least you're still able to string a couple of expletives together.'

She was genuinely pleased to hear his abrasive response.

'After you left, the whole team and I were taken over to H3 where we were told what had happened.'

'So just what were you told, Janet, and by whom?' Hart interrupted.

'We were spoken to by Doctor Halle and Judith Paris-Cregg. Doctor Halle told us that we had all done an excellent job under what the board had recognised as difficult and stressful times with respect to the inadequacies of the head count and budget, but that this was being redressed…as of yesterday. He told us that Professor Wummer was coming on board, to the great appreciation of senior management, but that you felt that you were unable to work under his direction and, therefore, by mutual consent, it had been decided that you would leave the company as of today. He went on to say that despite your occasional lack of total support to the company, and I quote him directly, your "frequent deviations from preferred company behaviours and best practices", you had been offered and had accepted a very generous termination package. He ended the meeting saying that if any of these issues were discussed elsewhere outside of the boardroom, "the Company would reluctantly have to let those transgressors go as well".'

'The bastard!' Hart exploded. 'And what did Paris-Cregg have to add to his speech?'

'Nothing, Max. I think that she was there only as a witness and silent support to Doctor Halle. When Doctor Halle had finished, we just went back to our offices in shocked silence. It wasn't until sometime later that we all got together and translated what Doctor Halle had actually said.

'The new organisation of the team under Professor Wummer will be announced in a few days. You know, Max, that none of us believed for one single moment that things had happened as Doctor Halle had said. We know that you have always supported the team to the hilt and we were all sure that something very nasty must have taken place in that room earlier.'

'Janet, I really appreciate this call, even though I'm feeling somewhat pissed off and severely wounded at the moment. I can't go into the details of the meeting I had, suffice it to say that I was totally stitched up by Halle and his cronies, and to my own discredit, I walked right into it. I behaved exactly as Halle wanted. He must have been planning this move for some time. Look, I want to thank you, Janet, for all you've done for me over the last few years. I guess you got used to my occasional use of the odd expletive and my occasional political incorrectness. It's just such a pity that I missed my own leaving party!'

'You are a comedian to the end, Max. Your swearing was in fact one of the things Halle kept returning to in the lecture he gave us. You should work on it.'

'Thanks for the tip, Janet, I'll talk to you again soon. Bye for now.'

'Bye for now, Max, and we'll talk again soon I'm sure.'

Minutes later, the phone rang out again.

'Oh, who the fuck now!'

Hart really was in no mood for any more callers, but nonetheless he picked up the receiver.

'Yes!'

'Max, it's me.'

Hart should have guessed who it would be. Ken Rogers was Hart's support physician on the clinical projects and probably the nearest to what Hart could call a friend at World. His voice was grave and almost apologetic.

'Jesus, Max, where do I start? We're all shattered—'

Hart cut in, 'Look, Ken, forget it for now, I can't handle any sympathy at the moment, but thanks all the same.'

'But what are you going to do, Max; surely, Halle can't just steamroller you like that?'

'You're talking to a very *flat* man, Ken. He just did! I guess I'll think it over a few times, but I'm pretty sure that I will be contacting a lawyer or three over the next day or so.'

Rogers moved into concerned friend and adviser mode.

'Yes, you do need some legal advice, but be aware that Halle is close to Mondo himself who must list several big-name lawyers on his list of friends, who he would swing into action at the drop of a hat in the event of any large-scale legal battle.'

'Oh I'm sure I'm much too small a fish in the pond for the old Sicilian to worry about, Ken.'

'I wouldn't be too certain of that. Mondo has been publicly doing some major moving and shaking recently. Rumour has it that he is involved in some extremely delicate negotiations with members of certain African governments regarding medicines in Africa. He's also been seen rubbing shoulders with some very high-ranking church officials in New York. Again, rumour has it that the two are in some way connected, and anything, small fish included, that rocked the Mondo boat now would bring the whole of the Mondo organisation thumping down on them. On you, Max.'

'All these rumours, Ken. I'm surprised that you hadn't picked up on one about my departure from the company?'

Rogers protested vehemently, possibly a little too vehemently because far from dispelling Hart's comments which were said in jest, he actually left a mote of suspicion in Hart's churning mind.

Hart continued,

'I'd not heard of Mondo's love affair with these groups of people though. I guess I should read the papers more often.'

'You should, then you'd know that Mondo has recently made huge contributions of money, both company and personal, to the Catholic Church and its charities. The company is on the verge of providing Christian scientific scholarships and funding Christian universities with some serious amounts of money.'

'But he's Italian isn't he, so why shouldn't he give to the Catholic Church? It's probably a case of him ensuring some "pizza pie in the sky when he dies".'

'Possibly, but you know his younger brother is archbishop of New York?'

'Bloody hell, what a complex web,' Hart replied disinterestedly.

He was getting tired now and there were far more important things to consider. Rogers was a nice guy but was inclined to be boring at times. Hart had to end the conversation and get him off the phone.

'Look, Ken, I'm going now. I need to get my mind thinking about my future. You know there's a possibility that I could be blacklisted from other pharma companies as a result of this. I can't exactly see Halle giving me much of a sparkling reference, can you?'

'Of course you'll get another job, Max. You'll walk into one.'

'At the moment, in my present state of mind, I'm thinking the only vacancy applicable to me will be on some bloody Arctic survey post. Still, free food and accommodation and as much ice for the margaritas as you could wish for. I understand that some of the penguins are really quite good looking too.'

'Antarctic.'

'What?'

'Antarctica. Penguins live in Antarctica, Max, not the Arctic.'

'Fucking Hell! Goodbye, Ken, I'll call you in a couple of days.'

Hart hung up the phone not waiting for Rogers' adieus.

Chapter 6

That same evening at 57 East 57th Street, New York, a glittering event was taking place in the candle-lit ambience of the Cosmopolitan Suite of the Four Seasons Hotel, a sleek monument to New York sophistication towering some 52 storeys over Manhattan's premier shopping and business districts between Madison and Park Avenues. This event starred many of those players briefly discussed by Ken Rogers in his telephone conversation with Hart, including regional church leaders, politicians, civic dignitaries and heads of local academia, this whole orchestra of movers and shakers together with their partners brought together and conducted by *il maestro,* Alberto Mondo. The glitterati were indulging themselves in pre-dinner champagne and cocktails in a side room. The main room itself, with its 12-foot ceilings, elegant suspended lighting and backlit onyx panels was set out for 80 people who would be dining at 10 circular tables graced with fine mauve linen table cloths and napkins and laid with ornate silver cutlery and fine bone china tableware. Each table was beautified by a central island, composed of yellow and mauve tulips and enhanced by the glow of 3 elegant long narrow mauve candles set in crystal holders and positioned at 3 corners of the floral island. A small stage lay along the far wall of the room occupied by six young angelic-looking young women, who filled the air with haunting music from the six gilt harps they were playing. These angels were seated on gilt high backed chairs surrounded by a sea of the same yellow and mauve tulips that adorned the tables.

The music wafted through the rarefied atmosphere into the pre-function suite, where Alberto Mondo was holding court in the centre of a group of elegantly dressed World Pharma sycophants, who were listening intently to his wisdom relating to future company philanthropic possibilities. Mondo was proud of his association with philanthropy, but this was not new, for his family history was rooted in it and the resultant respect and esteem in which the company was held was now widespread not just in the community at large, but also in certain corridors of the White House itself.

As one of the acolytes in the group took a rare opportunity to espouse his own particular views on some world issue, Mondo allowed his thoughts to stray and drift back to where it had all begun. Not for just himself, but for his Mondo antecedents way back in the 1800s in Sicily and specifically to the founder of what had been an essentially family business up until its flotation on the New York Stock Exchange. Francesco...Francesco Mondo.

His reverie was disturbed by Franco Negri, his close friend and ally, who was now moving in the heady higher circles of the Vatican but tonight he was here with Mondo, embracing him smilingly. Mondo's mind switched from the past back to the present with a rush and he returned the priest's embrace warmly.

'Alberto, there's a young man here who wants a word with you.'

Negri stepped aside to give way to the smiling face of the robed priest that was Peter Mondo. Alberto and Peter embraced. Still holding his brother in his arms, Peter Mondo smiled at him.

Peter, or Pietro, Mondo was, at 45 years, one of the youngest "pending" cardinals ever to be nominated to that lofty position. His handsome tanned face and shock of black hair, together with his statuesque sportsman-like build gave him the air of some celebrity film star, and these looks together with a faultless charm had certainly not held him back in his rapid rise in his chosen calling. There was certainly a family trait here as Alberto Mondo himself was a decidedly distinguished-looking man, looking much younger thàn his 68 years with his full head of white hair, swept backwards, crowning a classically handsome Sicilian face.

'Ciao Alberto, where were you just then? You seemed a million miles away?'

'Ciao Pietro,' he smiled in return. 'No, not a million…a few thousand perhaps. You're looking wonderful, how are things?'

'Things are fine, Alberto, grazie mille, and tonight, I believe that you will make me even more proud of you and our family heritage, yes?'

He glanced around the room momentarily.

'But who else is there that I should meet and talk to amongst this elite gathering you have brought together before we dine?'

Albert Mondo looked around the room to a small group of seven men, three white Americans and four black Africans, two of who wore clerical robes.

'Well, you could help out Robert Halle over there. He might need a little support I think. He's actually talking to two African bishops who you might be acquainted with. The other two Africans are important politicians from their region. You know, we are hoping to sponsor a little of…what I shall be announcing tonight.'

He paused and tapped the side of his nose in a knowing but secretive way.

'As you know we hope for World Pharmaceuticals to be involved in actual drug development in Africa soon, where we hope to inaugurate our first African research facility and distribution point in Angola. I don't have to tell you that Africa is a huge and largely untapped market for pharmaceutical companies, but I hope to change that even though there is so much poverty there, for part of my vision is to strive to make healthcare freely available and accessible to all.'

Peter Mondo placed a hand on his brother's shoulder.

'You are a good man, Alberto. I will go over to them and try and sound intelligent.'

He gave a short laugh and with a smile on his face crossed the room to join Halle and his small group. Negri looked on, his face etched with seriousness.

Peter Mondo's traverse of the room was interrupted by the arrival of an ostentatiously dressed "Master of Ceremonies". He carried a large gilt staff topped off with a gilt crown, which he struck three times on the wooden floor. As the blows rang out, silence fell upon the chattering crowd.

'Ladies and gentlemen, will you now be pleased to take your places for dinner.'

A ripple of applause passed through the throng, who obediently filtered into the dining room to where their named places awaited them. At the tables, they were able to peruse the gold edged set of menus, which highlighted the fare that was to be presented to them whilst drinking a fine prosecco served to them by an army of waiters.

Alberto Mondo himself had chosen the menu, which he had based on a rather spectacular evening he had spent some months previously in London, where he had had the honour and pleasure of joining a gathering of similar "captains of industry" at a royal banquet held at London's famous Guild Hall, where the evening had been presided over by Her Majesty Queen Elizabeth II. The theme for that evening had been "Medicines for Africa", a theme not too far from the program set for this particular evening.

Looking down from his position at the head of the top table, Mondo was able to drink in the atmosphere of the occasion unfolding in front of him and to focus here and there upon not just particularly important guests, but also amusingly on some of the more pompous attendees and their antics.

Almost item for item the menu mirrored that of Mondo's memorable dinner with British Royalty those months earlier. Even the wines were matched, both by name and by the vintage. The port was a different matter though. Being one of the British royal family's own labelled vintages, it had been a nightmare to obtain in the volume required for this evening's extravaganza, but being a "Captain of Industry" does give one certain privileges.

The menu read as follows:

MENU:
Roast Fillet of Sea Bass with Wild Mushrooms

Breast of Duck with Bigarade (citrus) Sauce
Braised chicory
Snow peas
Rosti potatoes

Salad

Caramalized Pear Tart

On a separate menu, not available to the guests was a list of the wines to be served with appropriate courses:

Wines:
Prosecco (Veneto, Italy)
Sauvignon Blanc – Cloudy Bay (Marlborough, New Zealand)
Pinot Noir – Mount Edward 2001 (Central Otago, New Zealand)
Orange Muscat and Flora – Brown Brothers 2003 (Australia)
Port – Royal Vintage 1960

After a few non-denominational, multicultural words of grace and thanks, presented by Peter Mondo, the very serious business of eating and drinking began.

Chapter 7

As the final traces of the final course of gastronomic delight were whisked away by the omnipresent staff, the angelic music from the stage drew to a close with perfect timing. As the musicians exited gracefully from the stage leaving their harps in place, a projection screen glided down from the ceiling to almost the floor level of the stage. At that moment the handsomely costumed Master of Ceremonies once again gained the attention of the gathering with three strikes of his pole on the floor and then in crystal clear tones boomed,

'Ladies and gentlemen, please be ready to receive Mr Alberto Mondo.'

There was a ripple of applause as the MC stood back and allowed the passage of Mondo onto the stage. He paused for a moment to ensure he had everyone's attention and then with a nod and a smile moved into the speech he'd been rehearsing relentlessly for the last few weeks.

'Esteemed guests, gentle ladies and gentle men,'

There were smiles and restrained laughter from the floor.

'I do not intend to make a long and boring speech here tonight. In fact, I have no notes prepared,' he held up his hands like a magician would, 'there's nothing up my sleeves.'

Again polite laughter.

'I intend to say a few words solely from my heart.'

He placed a hand over his left breast.

Behind him, the screen came to sudden life with the appearance, via background projection, of the World Company logo.

'I welcome you here tonight as head of World Pharmaceuticals on behalf of the company. You know we are not exactly a corner shop,' smiles from the tables, 'but we do see ourselves as a family business. In fact, we see all our people as members of one large family.

Our company was founded over two hundred years ago by my ancestor Francesco Mondo in Sicily and I am very proud of that heritage. We have always prided ourselves on our charitable and Christian ethics and particularly the importance of the closeness of the company to the general public. Our first aim has always been to serve the public as best as we can.' Polite applause filled the room. '…and I am very proud of our company vision.'

Behind him, the company vision or more accurately its mission statement came up. The way in which the slides came up on cue for this "unprepared speech" was truly a psychic experience for the projectionist.

'Indeed, at World Pharma, we truly dedicate ourselves in the first instance, to humanity and the quest for longer, healthier lives. To this end, we strive to ensure that our products are made available to all, whatever race, class or income capacity. We do this through the continual development of ethical, innovative drugs in our various cutting edge research facilities.'

Another slide came up on cue, this time an aerial photograph of the New Jersey research establishment, followed by similar photographs of other World's international installations.

'Our second aim is to make for better communities through local investment and employment.'

A slide showing building works and floating dollar bills was rapidly followed by one of groups of happy smiling workers walking into a World establishment. If any of the audience had twigged the anomaly of his "unprepared, unrehearsed" speech with the slick slideshow taking place in perfect harmony behind him, they weren't showing it. The tables were full of nods of approval and spontaneous applause from this august body of politicians, churchmen, leaders of academia and community dignitaries. Mondo raised a hand to quieten the applause and continued,

'Finally, of course, we aim to secure an equitable return for our investors.'

He continued,

'As a Christian company, there are additional things which are important to us. This includes the provision of academic centres of excellence where student scientists can be developed in our field of research in an atmosphere essentially wrapped in Christian values and fellowship. We would wish to nurture and strengthen the faith of the students as well as develop their scientific minds.'

Again a slide came up on cue showing smiling students on campus with the outline of a church in the background. This was met with vocal approval from the audience and a sustained round of applause, especially from the robed and dog-collared guests.

'I am delighted to announce to you, therefore, that World Pharmaceuticals is to contribute the sum of five million dollars to the New York College of Pharmaceutical Sciences towards a new science facility which will offer both academic and spiritual support and guidance—'

He was cut off by loud applause which he waved away once again before continuing,

'But also...' dramatic pause, 'But also, we will sponsor 200 new students each year.'

This time, he permitted the waves of applause to break across him before continuing,

'And this is just the beginning, for at the same time, we are examining the details of bringing similar projects to other centres of learning excellence, both in the United States,' a slide containing a cascade of other major cities in the US flashed up, 'and importantly in key areas of Africa,' the appearance of a slide of the "Dark Continent" brought gasps of admiration and further applause, '...which will benefit from improved employment, education and above all improved healthcare.'

He directed his stare at the African Angolan contingent in the audience who beamed back at him and applauded enthusiastically.

'And that's really all I have to say, ladies and gentlemen, except that is, to pay my thanks to my brother Peter. Perhaps I should say Archbishop Mondo?'

He laughed and was joined by parts of his audience.

'For Peter has been not just instrumental in the decisions which have been taken, but has been the light to which, like moths, we have all been drawn. It is his inspiration which sowed the first seeds of an idea within World, which he then nurtured through our board of directors to the point of the decisions we now have today.'

All eyes in the room now fell on his handsome brother who gave an embarrassed smile and nodded. On the stage, with the final slide projected behind him, containing the words "$200 million: New college; Scholarships; African investment", Mondo the elder rounded off his most polished "unrehearsed, off-the-cuff, presentation".

'And so, friends and colleagues, my many thanks for your most gracious attention and of course for your precious attendance here tonight, and I will now give way to beauty in the form of our lovely musicians.'

The angelic group returned to the stage amid rapturous applause for Alberto Mondo.

As the music began, Mondo re-took his seat at his table next to his beautiful wife, Barbara, and nodded his appreciation to the audience.

Chapter 8

'God bless you and thank you for your help, Father. You have truly brought me back from the edge of lost reason. You are so kind to make the journey all the way up here just to talk to me.'

The attractive dark-haired woman, seated in a wheelchair, held out her hand, which was taken and shaken very gently by Joao Guedes. Her life-threatening depression and loss of faith following the horse-riding accident, which had confined her to the wheelchair, together with the fact that her family had over the years contributed so much financially to the Andalusian churches had seemed to be more than sufficient reason for Archbishop Guedes to respond to her urgent cry for help. As archbishop of Malaga, his responsibilities spread out from that city to cover the whole of Andalusia. This was a particularly beautiful area and so it was really not too great an imposition for the priest to make the scenic journey to the expansive single-story home of Maria Gonzalez on this particular errand. He had driven to her home in the Galician mountains through the plains of Catilla-Leo, which were open to the outside world only through the valley of the Sil to the southeast. He had arrived at the little town of La Horra and then proceeded steeply upwards along and around the twisting road known locally as "The Serpent's Pass" until finally arriving at the Gonzalez residence.

But now, his meeting with Maria was concluded and God's mission, for that day here at least, was completed. This aspect of his work was unfortunately now taking up a major part of his time, due in the main to an increasingly questioning and challenging population, but at 51 years of age he still had a boundless zest and energy which enabled him to fulfil God's calling in the most exuberant way. He would often say to colleagues and friends who pleaded with him to reduce his round-the-clock availability,

'I am here to carry out God's work…and God does not sleep.'

His efforts and dedication had been recognised however, and although still young in church terms, he was already cast as an archbishop. Furthermore, rumour had it that he was now on the short-list to receive the red hat, or "zucchetto", of a cardinal.

But he did live his chosen lifestyle in an Olympian mode, pursuing an almost 24-hours-a-day routine of praying, eating and official duties appropriate to his position, as well as fitting in a daily four-mile run. This "running priest" never failed to complete his four-mile jog, even when his duties took him away from his beloved Andalusia, which was often these days. On a recent visit to the Vatican, when he was honoured with an extended audience with the Pope, he had raised more than a few eyebrows with his daily runs through the Vatican grounds.

He smiled kindly at Maria Gonzalez as he released her hand and said,

'Maria, it has been my pleasure to serve you and to bring you back into our fold. Everyone is important in the eyes of God and you, especially, are particularly important to our Andalusian Church. Please, if you have any further need of my services, do not hesitate to contact me.'

With that, he turned and climbed into his car. Maria Gonzalez smiled to herself as he pulled away and drove out of sight around the bend. He would not be required again...

'But it would have been an interesting challenge to obtain "his services" between the sheets.'

Her mind briefly went into overdrive at the thought, as she nimbly alighted from the wheelchair and proceeded to walk to the veranda of the house, where she poured herself a large glass of red Riocha, which she raised in the direction of the departed priest.

'Salute!'

Reaching down, she picked up the phone and dialled the number which was written on a small pad at the side of it. It rang just once before it was answered.

'*Si?*'

'He is on his way.'

'*Gracias*,' came the reply.

She hung up.

Joao Guedes was content as he began his drive from the Gonzalez property. He felt he had had a positive effect on the wavering faith of the woman feeling that he had re-established her faith in both God and the Catholic Church. As he commenced the twisting, turning track of the "Serpents Pass", he marvelled at the stupendous panoramic view of the mountains and valley laid out before him. Way down at the foot of the mountain, he could just pick out the rooftops and white walls of La Horra, where he looked forward to a lunch at Pablo's in concert with an ample volume of chilled fino sherry, served as was the tradition, in a shaped copita. As likely as not the fino would be followed by perhaps one or two glasses of the local red Riocha. If he had one weakness in life, it was his inability to say no to a final "one for the road" Riocha, and as often as not half of this would be spilled down his front during his involvement in the animated good humoured arguments and discussions which were as much a trademark of Pablo's as was the tapas. He checked the time on his watch, it was 4.15 pm. By 5.00 pm, he should be seated, tulip-shaped glass in hand, in the restaurant awaiting his lunch. Five o'clock was by no means late for lunch, as typically in this area lunch never began before 3 pm and one was lucky if dinner was served much before midnight.

Engrossed in the wonderful vista God had fashioned before him, he began to sing aloud. He was hitting the top note of his song as he approached one of the many steep bends in the road. As he came out of the blind bend, his top note of 'ahhhhhh' suddenly became a higher note 'aghhhhh', as at the last minute he saw in the road directly in front of him a small flock of sheep, which had found themselves forced by some unrecognised hand from the green of the mountain side down onto the black tarmac of the pass. He turned his steering wheel and braked violently to avoid the leading sheep, now just yards from the front of the car. There was a sickening thud as sheep and metal made contact, accompanied by awful bleats of pain from the injured animals. The outcome of the impact was to project two bloodied animals up over the car hood and crashing through the car's windscreen. As the shocked priest fought for control of the car, the damaged vehicle ploughed through the simple retaining fencing, the only barrier between the road and the abyss, or more likely between this world and the next, bounced once and then cart-wheeled over and over down the shear mountain side. Moments before exploding in a fiery orange ball, the priest's body was catapulted through the space once occupied by the windscreen onto the mountainside, where it bounced and rolled before coming to rest against one of the larger projecting rocks. The orange ball quickly became blackened with smoke, but none of this was observed by Joao Guedes, whose now sightless eyes stared blankly out from the twisted and lifeless body of which they were once the windows.

The priest's watch had stopped at 4.18 pm.

He would make neither lunch nor dinner, but even in death, the usual post-prandial red stains down his front were in evidence, albeit of a different source and nature.

Chapter 9

At the end of dinner, with guests milling around both the dining room and the outer rooms within the Four Seasons Hotel, Alberto Mondo left the noise behind him and took temporary cover in the anteroom, where he sat sipping his wine and reflecting on his grand performance.

At the sound of footfalls, he looked up to see his old friend Franco Negri approaching him once more.

Negri was no simple village priest despite his humble Sicilian background. In his position in Rome as "Prefect of the Congregation of Bishops" and unusually also Camerlengo to the Pope, he was regarded as a formidable character. Sitting as close to the Pope as he did, his role enabled him to advise the Pontiff on Episcopal appointments around the whole world. However, in addition to this, after a series of successful short-term secondments in Brazil and Mozambique as a Vatican diplomat, he had been appointed deputy to the secretary of state, giving him a key role as the Pope's chief of staff. Above all of this though, he was friend, confidante and personal adviser to the Pope. Indeed, he was his friend's adviser on far greater reaching issues than global Episcopal appointments.

Negri was looking less intense than before dinner and for a second time that evening extended a hand to Mondo, which Mondo shook firmly.

'Congratulations on a stunning performance Alberto. Something for everyone, *si*? The church, the universities, the politicians and even something to make the ladies smile. All of that straight from the heart, no?'

Mondo smiled. 'Of course my friend, of course, bu…'

He rose from his chair took Negri by an elbow and led him to a far corner of the room where he continued in lowered tones,

'But how fares the Pontiff in Rome? You know I worry every day that he is now on his life's last lap.'

The previous smile had gone from Negri's face as he replied,

'The Pope is clearly dying, Alberto, but I believe him not yet to be, to continue your metaphor, in the finishing straight. He is very tired and thoroughly worn out, both by his illness and his burden of duties which take more of his life source every day, but he is treated with the best and most appropriate medications for his condition, as you know. I do believe, however, that his physician would be quite surprised if he were to grace us with his presence for much more than another twelve months.'

Mondo nodded his head.

'Ahh Franco. That is too soon for his departure. There is still so much to be done under his benign leadership, so far to go. He himself has many tasks important to all of us before he leaves us, for despite any wish he may harbour to be released from this world, for him, heaven must wait.'

He glanced around the still empty room.

'But what about his medication? I am assuming that the supply is regular and of the desired quality and that there are no problems with its administration …medically or politically?'

Negri nodded affirmation adding,

'There are no problems in Rome, Alberto, but I have heard that elsewhere our colleagues are becoming stretched to deliver the medication we require in sufficient amounts to meet the increasing demands we place upon them.'

'Franco, you are right, but things are in hand. You know that there are many other advanced neurological disorders that we are treating, not only Parkinson's disease, and there are many who will pay premium amounts of money for these treatments, always in a private capacity and we are striving to meet these demands also. We are increasing pressure on our suppliers of the raw materials all the time and this is not without risks. But come, that is my problem not yours and not so great a problem. The important thing is that il Papa receives whatever is necessary for his continued survival and we will work towards that. However, the memory of the Tornay situation back in 1998 still makes my blood turn cold. It was nearly the end for us then, when for one stupid action our delicate house of cards nearly fell around us. Such a thing must never happen again.'

The event that Mondo was referring to was the scandal around the mysterious deaths within the Vatican's Swiss Guards, which was investigated internally with the conclusion, much to the general disbelief of the rest of the western world, that a young guards' officer was murdered by the hand of his senior officer in revenge for the discovered relationship between his wife and the younger man. The senior officer then went on to take his own life. Mondo, however, was well aware of the true facts of the case, which had connections running deep into certain secret affairs of the Vatican and into the darker, even more secret side of World Pharma's activities there.

'Don't worry, Alberto. Although the Pope has many physicians in attendance, the leading and most important prescribing physician is well aware of the particular situation and is quite supportive of it. The Pope himself has been fully aware of his medical condition and its prognosis for some time now and has accordingly been setting the house in order so that when he is finally taken, only the most suitable of my brother cardinals will be in the position to participate in the final ballot for his successor. He already regards Pietro very highly you know, and your latest pronouncements which, of course, the Pope was circulated with well in advance of tonight's speech, and especially those comments relating to the proposals for Africa, which Pietro has been so involved in pursuing within World, has increased the brightness of his light immeasurably in the Pope's eyes. I believe that it was indeed a masterstroke of yours to focus the attention for the African phase of your strategy in Angola where his Holiness was born and where with his increasing infirmity his thoughts and memories spend much time.'

Mondo puffed out his chest proudly.

'This has been a long game, Franco. Some might say if they were aware of it, that it is a game worthy of a chess grandmaster, but this game in which we have seen bishops as major players, with the inevitable sacrifice of lesser pawns together with the occasional higher-ranking pieces, is not yet concluded. If the Pope dies before the key players are in their essential positions on the board, then the game is lost and my "Great Plan" fails. But this should not be a gamble Franco, for we...I...control the pieces and, therefore, the game completely. *Your* job is to ensure that the Pontiff remains in this world.'

He smiled once again at Negri,

'Your job is to make heaven wait a little longer for the divine presence of il Papa.'

Chapter 10

It was some days after Hart's untimely ejection from World Pharmaceuticals, aka 'World Pharma', before he finally got round to arranging to meet Ken Rogers for dinner and then at the last moment, he cancelled it, not yet feeling able to go through the recent events face to face one more time. Thinking of his finale at World, one thing was certain, at being a big time loser, Max Hart was definitely a big time winner.

In the end, he had agreed to spend some time in friendly discussion with Rogers on the telephone, but already despite the earliness of the evening, he was rather drunk having raided his wine cellar. The phone rang and Hart picked it up, eager to put it down again, but began the pleasantries anyway.

'Hi Ken, you're late as usual. So then, Ken, as a new retiree, I'm relaxed, wearing jeans and T-shirt, but I expect you're still suited and booted and wearing a fetching silk tie, yes?'

There was a pregnant pause, Rogers being somewhat taken aback by Hart's strange start to their conversation. Hart proceeded to fill the vacuum.

'Do you know what they call a man in a suit back where I come from, Ken?'

'You'll tell me I'm sure.'

'Indeed I will. We call him the bloody "defendant"! But anyway, where have you been all day, I did try to contact you several times earlier? Not up in front of a judge I'll be bound. No, if I'm thinking correctly, you will probably be wearing an interview suit?' Hart joked.

Again there was a too long embarrassed silence on the line, during which pause, the penny dropped for Hart.

'It *is* your interview suit! You've been for a bloody interview, haven't you?'

'Well, actually, Max, I *was* invited to a discussion with Doctor Halle this afternoon. I was going to tell you anyway if you had given me half a chance.'

'And what pray might that have been about? Tell you what, I'll write my guess on a piece of paper and we'll see how much of a clairvoyant I am.'

'It's no secret, Max. Doctor Halle was talking to me about my career and my future with World and—'

'And what?' Hart cut in. 'Let the clairvoyant guess. You have been offered my fucking role in the company, haven't you?'

'Look, Max, I have been offered a more senior role in the company, yes, but it's not—'

'And you've accepted it, haven't you?'

'Look, I couldn't turn it down. The package was so much better than the one I'm getting at present, but don't think that it's *your* old—'

Hart interrupted. 'So what does that make you now then, bloody Judas or bloody Brutus? Either way as I see it, it makes you a fucking traitor.'

Hart's friendship with Rogers was now in severe question.

'I really am sorry, Max, but I felt I had no choice.'

'No choice, my fucking arse!'

'Max, that's totally uncalled for, I think you owe me an apology and actually it wouldn't hurt if you used a little less of the foul language; it's totally unnecessary. You do know that it has become something of your trademark at World?'

Hart drew a deep breath and held it for a few moments before responding,

'Yes, Ken, I apologise once again. I will say just one more thing and then you will not hear me curse again during this entire conversation. I need to educate you a little I think. You see, you have to remember where I come from and the culture associated with that background, swearing was as common as breathing. In fact, both were part of the same process. Swearing was an integral part of the vernacular and to remove it would have been akin to removing a vital organ. Now, as a prime example before I zip up the curse purse, I will take you back to my days as a junior houseman at my first hospital. I remember as if only yesterday, an ambulance driver complaining about his vehicle of which he was finding the engine very difficult to start up. The way he put it, using the local vernacular was,

'"This fucking fucker's fucking fucked!"

'There, you see, a totally understandable sentence using a single definite article and four grammatical cases of the same profanity. Brilliant! It's so economical in words and yet so positively explicit. Could Shakespeare himself have put it any better?'

The two men laughed but the situation was now extremely awkward and Hart decided to end the conversation as soon as possible.

'I contacted a couple of key lawyers today to see what kind of legal action I might be able to take against World.'

'And?'

'And nothing. The bloody…' he checked himself, 'The useless buggers were more like "lame ducks" than "legal eagles". It seems that I have been made a reasonable monetary offer of termination by World and their recommendation is that I should forget any aspirations of unfair dismissal and take the money and stay quiet. Otherwise, the likelihood is that World would counter my charge using a basis of unprofessional conduct becoming a senior medical adviser etc. etc., with the result that I might get nothing at all.'

'So?'

'So I will take the money and run. I'll take the money from the bastards and go back to the UK for a short break. You remember those friends of mine, the Barnes? I worked with Jason Barnes back in Leeds when he was an aspiring anaesthetist. There has always been an open invitation for me to spend some time with them if ever I was back in England in Nottingham. Jason is a consultant anaesthetist now at the main teaching hospital in the city, so I called him earlier today and arranged to have a short stay with them.'

'Sounds like a good idea. Have you been reading the newspapers this week?'

'Ken, the only reading I've done this week has been the labels on the numerous bottles of wine it's been my pleasure to dispatch. Why do you ask? Has somebody tried to shoot Halle? They'd have to hit his arse to get anywhere near his brain, that *is* for sure.'

'No, but earlier this week, Alberto Mondo held a rather splendid "do" at the Four Seasons for a large group of academics, politicians and clergy.'

'Shit! My invitation must have been lost in the post.'

Rogers continued unabashed by Hart's interruption.

'According to the press, he made a particularly well received speech about a huge donation to help Christian students find both academic and spiritual fulfilment.'

'Fantastic! He wants to build a stairway to heaven using money from drugs launched on the backs of tragic braindead patients. What a bloody hypocrite!'

'Hang on, Max, there's more. Next, he plans to spend major bucks in Africa on a research institute, whilst at the same time providing free, or low cost at least, healthcare to the poverty-stricken indigenous population.'

'That man's a bloody saint, Ken, no doubt about it. But, Ken, I'm tired and a little drunk and I really need some sleep, so I'll say goodnight to you.'

'Oh, goodnight then, Max.'

But Hart had already hung up.

Chapter 11

Hart let several weeks go by before he finally pulled himself together and "firmed up" his intentions to travel to Nottingham with a call to his friend Jason Barnes. During those weeks, he lay low and out of contact with a single US soul, other than the staff in the local restaurant and those at the supermarket. In the end, he bit the bullet and booked a business class flight with BA flying from New York's JFK to London Heathrow.

Hart never slept during transatlantic flights. Instead, he preferred to catch up on the movies and eat and drink. It was no surprise, therefore, upon arriving at Heathrow Airport, that he felt as if he had been awake for a week. However, he effortlessly passed through passport control and baggage claim and rather than taking the Heathrow Express, headed for the taxi rank where he took a cab directly to St Pancras Station. It was a long and expensive alternative, but eventually he was boarding the Midland Mainline train for Nottingham. Within minutes of boarding, he was fast asleep.

As his train began to brake, slowing down for Nottingham Station one hundred sleeping minutes later, he stirred and looking up saw in the distance the welcoming sight of the illuminated Nottingham Castle. Within fifteen minutes of arriving on the station platform, he was "cabbed" and on his way to his friend's house in Wollaton, with just one stop-off on the way to purchase a couple of bottles of quality champagne.

He'd arranged with Jason Barnes to stay with them for a maximum of two weeks. Two weeks of rest and recuperation. Anything longer and he would seek accommodation elsewhere.

When Barnes told his wife, Alix, of Hart's intention to move in with other friends if he extended his stay, she laughed.

'I didn't think he had that many friends who were still talking to him. What time will he get here?'

'He told me around 7.00 pm. Tell you what, Alix, we should make some arrangements for evenings or days out while he's here. Why don't you contact Vicky and ask her to join us in town for lunch on Saturday?'

'That sounds like a good idea. I'll call her later and fix it up.'

He picked up his black valise, gave his wife a peck on the cheek and headed through the front door to the black VW Polo parked on the drive of their Wollaton home, just 15 minutes from the hospital where he worked.

Chapter 12

As the taxi pulled into the road in the leafy Wollaton suburbs in which stood the Barnes' five-bedroomed neo-Georgian house, he paid the driver, grossly over-tipping him by UK standards, and exiting gingerly approached the front door and rang the bell. His small suitcase in one hand and two bottles of champagne precariously held in the other. It was precisely 7.00 pm.

After the third ring, he heard running in the hall inside, and the door was finally opened by Alix Barnes.

'I was beginning to wonder if you had seen me coming and changed your mind,' he smiled as they embraced.

'Max, it really is wonderful to see you again. Come on in.'

Jason Barnes hot on his wife's heels, smiled and grabbed Hart's free hand tightly, shaking it warmly.

'Max, it's great to see you after all this time. How was the trip? How are you feeling—'

Hart didn't give him time to complete his sentence.

'Like shite actually, but it's a real tonic to see you both.'

'Come on, Max, I'll take you to your room and Alix will make us some coffee. Give me that case.'

'Hang on a sec'.

Hart reached down and retrieved his case from the drive.

'There you go,' he smiled as he handed the champagne to Jason. 'One for each of you.'

They laughed as Barnes handed the two bottles to his wife and then directly led Hart up the stairs to the room that was to be his place of meditation for the next couple of weeks.

'Here's your room, Max. What do you want to do, have a sleep, something to eat, or just have some coffee?'

'Just give me five minutes or so to sort myself out and I'll be down and join you both,' Hart replied as he slipped out of his jacket.

'OK, see you in a bit.'

Barnes turned and descended the stairs to the kitchen where Alix was making the coffee.

'He'll be down in a couple of minutes, perhaps then we might hear a little of what's been happening to make him look so ill. I know he's jet-lagged and tired, but Christ, he looks really washed out and depressed.'

Chapter 13

Two hours later, Hart now looking fifteen years younger, joined the Barnes in their lounge.

'Sorry, folks, I must have been more tired than I thought. I only closed my eyes briefly and off I went.'

Having unpacked, showered and changed his clothes, he felt almost human again. Alix Barnes indicated a small table in front of the sofa.

'Look, Max, I've prepared some slightly stale sandwiches. I'll get us some coffee and perhaps then you can tell us of your recent er... adventures.'

Hart smiled.

'Adventures. That's one word for it certainly. Where's your daughter by the way?'

'At Grandma's,' volunteered Jason.

Over the next two hours, relaxing in the comfortable lounge, they recalled their "salad days" until finally the conversation turned to Hart's life changing experiences at the hands of the World organisation and also in part to his own tendencies towards self-destruction. Hart held very little back as he described the traumas of recent weeks, relating in full his incompetence and general lack of astuteness during his final meeting with Halle et al. before his "premature ejection" from the company. The end of his tale was met with silence, until a grim faced Jason Barnes responded,

'That's a real horror story, Max. I think that even the most sanguine of people would have been near to exploding in those circumstances, let alone someone of your...let's say...sometimes incendiary nature. Still you're here now and you're welcome to stay as long as you need.'

'You're really kind thanks. Both of you. As I said before, I'll sort myself out over the next week, or at most two, and decide on some direction forward.'

'In the meantime,' Alix Barnes joined in, 'Jason has a house key for you so that you can come and go much as you please. By the way, Jason and I have arranged to meet an old friend of ours for lunch tomorrow in town. Fancy joining us?'

'I'd be delighted; it's some time since I've seen the old place. I expect it's changed somewhat.'

The Barnes' withdrew, dirty pots in hand, to the kitchen leaving Hart alternatively slurping coffee and sipping red wine. Ten minutes later, cups, saucers and plates draining, they returned to the lounge to find Hart semi-reclined on the sofa sound asleep and clutching a glass of the red wine to his chest. Jason started forward and made to lift the glass from Hart's fingers. The somnolent

Hart offered staunch resistance even in sleep however to this potential loss of alcohol. Barnes tried to lever the fingers away from the glass's stem and base.

'Bloody hell, its rock solid! We either wake him or break his fingers.'

The couple laughed and deciding to chance their luck and leave him there, they went on up to bed, leaving Hart caressing his wine.

Hart awoke at 4.30 am, with not a single drop of his cabernet spilled. He emptied the glass in a single gulp and headed for his bed feeling slightly drunk, but for the first time in weeks, feeling really relaxed, both mentally and physically.

Chapter 14

The following day at around noon, the trio climbed into the Barnes' black Polo and headed off to Nottingham. The constant chatter in the Polo did not distract him in the slightest as he soaked up the sights of these former happy hunting grounds. There was obviously considerably more traffic here now than during his last visit, and a tram system had materialized too, but the overall feel, even through the car's windows, was just the same.

'So tell me a few things about Vicky before we meet her, such as what work she does etc. etc.? You can start with what she looks like, tall, short, fat, thin, ugly, beautiful...'

The Barnes responded in unison, 'Meg Ryan!'

'...And she works as a research scientist at the Queens Medical Centre,' added Alix.

Hart smiled. 'That will do nicely. Thanks.'

Jason parked a few minutes' walk from the Cock and Hoop pub where lunch had been organised. As they moved past the bar into the inner pub recess, Hart stroked his hand over the solid pewter bar surface and smiled. Although he loved living in the "States", he did miss the more early period and aged architecture and buildings of his native country.

He followed the Barnes down a short flight of stairs, scanning the tables for the famous...yes...there she was....Meg Ryan's younger sister!

After the obligatory air kisses between the Barnes and Victoria Crosse, Alix Barnes made the introductions.

They sat and during the polite chatter and questions and answers that abound on such occasions, they perused the menu.

The quartet ordered food and drinks, and very soon, they were laughing loudly and at length at some of Hart's more risqué tales.

At 2.00 pm precisely, Alix Barnes checked her watch.

'Jase, we should go now,' and turning to Crosse and Hart, 'I'm sorry guys but we have a prior appointment with a solicitor and we really have to fly. Max, we can meet you later if you like, or you can be a really big boy and come back home on the bus when you're ready.'

'Don't worry about me, Alix; if Vicky doesn't mind, we can have another drink and then perhaps take in some of the sights if she has the time? If I get lost, I have your address on a tag around my neck.'

Crosse smiled and nodded her approval.

The Barnes said their cheerios and duly departed leaving, Crosse and Hart together.

'So, Max, what is Max actually short for? If short for anything that is.'

Wearing his totally serious look, Hart responded,

'Well, some say that it's short for "Maximum-pain-in-the-arse", but actually it's just short for Max, but what about "Victoria Crosse"? That's quite a medal. Was it ironic humour on the part of your parents or just an unrecognised chance choice so to speak?'

'They just liked the name Victoria. The medal thing never crossed their minds until the Christening would you believe.'

Over the next hour, they skimmed the surfaces of what were their current lives, including talking about their respective jobs. It was during this session that Hart divulged to her some of the details of his demise at World, details that had already been imparted to her by Alix Barnes prior to their meeting. By 4.00 pm, they were getting on like a house on fire but then Crosse checked her watch.

'Max, I have to leave in a few minutes to meet a friend who has a really serious hang-up which he wants me to advise him on. It's a real tragedy actually, but before I go, you might be able to help me bit with it. Would you mind?'

He smiled at her whilst thinking to himself, *Jesus, I've only known her for five minutes and already she has me doing an "agony aunt" spot.*

'Be my guest.'

'OK, see what you think of this… This friend of mine, who lives quite close to here, recently arrived home from his office to find his wife, another friend of mine, lying dead on their upstairs bed. She had taken an overdose of prescription anti-depressants, which I believe she had been hoarding for some time as part of some plan she had made to possibly take her own life at some stage.

'The reason for her depression was the loss, or rather, the miscarriage of a baby which the couple had tried for years to produce. After years of her failing to become pregnant, she and her husband approached "The Paddocks", a private fertility service at a clinic situated at the edge of the county. She subsequently became pregnant some four times, but on each occasion, she lost the baby at a very early stage of its foetal development. However, her final pregnancy was looking to be going well with the unborn baby seemingly doing fine. Then out of the blue during a visit to the clinic, she appeared to spontaneously miscarry. Of course they lost the baby and she never really recovered from the grief and subsequent despair. They moved house to a place here in The Park to try and shake off the terrible depression that haunted her every waking minute…and that even haunted the few minutes each night that she was able to sleep.'

'That's terrible. Her husband must be suffering terribly.'

'Yes he is, but the thing is that Denis, that's his name, is totally hung up on it. He started to go to group counselling sessions in an effort to get some positive form of help and where, to his surprise, he very soon came into contact with others who were receiving counselling for the premature loss of unborn babies at this very same clinic. Looking for additional explanations for the death of the unborn child and his wife's subsequent suicide, he became inordinately suspicious of the standards of practices at the clinic. He really has got a bee in his bonnet now and has in fact gone so far as to hire an investigator to look into this place together with other associated clinics. There are several of these I believe; one of them, its so-called "sister clinic" based in Liverpool, has the same high rate of miscarriages as this one and I can tell you that both are way above the national average for this type of incident. My friend Denis is convinced now that there is some huge malpractice on-going which he is bent on exposing. Of course, because of my scientific background, he regards me as his scientific confidante and has invited me round today to advise him on his next moves, but how can I possibly do that? It's totally out of my scope or understanding?'

Hart considered her comments for a short time before responding.

'Let's look at each scenario in turn, Vicky. It's not in my scope either by the way, but we can at least apply a little logic to it. Firstly, the miscarriages. Once it has been established that someone fits into this high-risk group then further occurrences for that person must be expected. This friend of yours…'

'Ruth. Ruth and Denis Williams.'

'OK. Once Ruth had been identified as being in a high-risk group with respect to miscarrying, her subsequent outcomes could actually be considered as being expected. In fact, for her *not* to miscarry could have been the most unlikely of the two possible scenarios. Secondly, the counselling. Obviously all the attendees were there through the same or similar reasons and so clearly would have similar experiences to relate. I don't see anything sinister there. Finally, the sister clinic. Presumably dealing with the same patient group, this clinic would almost certainly be bound to have similar outcomes to those at other places, especially dealing with such a high-risk patient group. As for the national average, once again the fact that these patients belong to such a high-risk category, together with the fact that these clinics actually concentrate on these difficult cases, means that their success rate generally is bound to be below the national average, even though they have particular expertise. The statistical probability can be assessed and I'm sure that the probability of more miscarriages occurring at these particular clinics would be significant.

'I can give you an example. I once worked in a renal transplantation unit which had one of the worst records for post-transplant kidney survival in the UK. The reason wasn't that the physicians were inept or that the unit itself was inadequate; it was that this place accepted many patients for transplantation who had been rejected, pardon the pun, from most other centres. The reasons for their rejection at other units usually included their age, in that they were too old, or their ethnicity, but at this unit, there were few rules in this regard. Probably the main defining issue, however, was that at that unit, kidneys were transplanted mainly just on the basis of them being able to match blood groups between donors and recipients rather than the more commonly recognised tissue typing. So you can see that these patients, like your pregnant women, started out in the unit with a far greater chance of failure than would have been expected in other units, where of course, they probably wouldn't have been considered for treatment in the first place. Does that help a bit?'

She nodded appreciatively but still looked pensive and concerned. Hart had anticipated her next move but rather than volunteer himself, hung back waiting for her to make the anticipated request. After all, there was no point in volunteering if volunteers weren't actually being looked for.

'Max, Denis is going to find it really hard to accept these explanations from me. What he is really looking for is my support in his witch-hunt. I know we've only just met but…'

She was having difficulty putting words together now, but Hart still hung back….just in case. Then she came out with it.

'You wouldn't consider coming with me, would you, and putting forward what you've just told me, as a sort of external, non-connected semi-expert?'

He didn't hesitate in replying,

'I'm certainly no expert, Vicky,' and smiling, 'but as I've nothing else to do, I'll be happy to come with you.'

'Oh, Max, thanks a million. I was dreading going alone. Denis is quite a wealthy man and is prepared to waste a lot of money unnecessarily on this, what with private investigators and the like. We can walk to his place from here; he lives just five minutes away in The Park, near the castle.'

With that, she gave Hart no further time to reconsider his offer, emptying her glass in a single gulp and standing as part of the same movement.

'Let's go while I still feel positive about it.'

Hart raised an eyebrow at the rapid premature ending to their lunch and likewise hastily drained his drink and then together, they climbed the stairs and walked out into the street.

Chapter 15

Whilst to the majority of people alive today, the Vietnam War conjures up famous iconic images relating to the involvement of the United States of America. The involvement of France, predating that of the US, is rarely apparent in various sections of the modern media. The French defeat at Dien Bien Phu was, up until that time at least, one of the most notorious single failures of 20th century regular troops to defeat irregular nationalist insurgents. But for many years after the war had been lost by America, much of the land still remained as "no go" areas, a legacy of the various fighting forces who had laboured there. Much of this legacy came in the form of unlisted, undetected, unexploded landmines.

Nguyen Duc Manh had looked forward to this moment for many years now and had spent much time and effort in bringing his dream to fruition. The effects of the indiscriminate laying of landmines during the conflict were still visible in the throbbing, pulsating streets of the towns and villages around Dien Bien Phu. After all these years, crippled, limbless and blinded local people still haunted these streets for all to see. But now the whole region was on the verge of a famous declaration. Over the next few days at a series of official ceremonies, the various regions around Dien Bien Phu were to be proclaimed officially clean of these remnants of war and, therefore, officially safe. After all those years, the final remaining landmines had been removed and once again, the land could be returned to the people, safe in the knowledge that they could travel, build homes and grow crops without fears of a premature explosive end to their activities. A single item taken from the scrapheap of recovered explosive ordinance and labelled, "The last mine", had itself taken on an iconic form. Transported across the country to be seen and cheered by people in their thousands, it had been promoted to a status fit to rival the famous US Liberty Bell, now resting in permanency in Philadelphia, Pennsylvania.

Tomorrow, Archbishop Nguyen Duc Manh would lead the procession out to the newly erected monument in the centre of what had until recently rejoiced in the name of "Sector C", where he would lead the multi-denominational blessings and thanks. But today, he had chosen a time-out for himself in order give his own very personal prayers of thanks. As he walked slowly across the ground where the ceremonies would be held, he breathed in deeply the clean air fragrant with cherry blossom, inwardly rejoicing at the glorious backdrop that was the setting sun in a beautiful red sky. Upon reaching the plain obelisk, which had been chosen as both the final memorial to those who had died and as a permanent reminder of man's brutality to man, he knelt before it. As he prayed, he permitted his eyes to remain open, straying upwards to the deep red and pink hues of the setting sun, variously reflected off the scattering of small white clouds. His ears strayed to the sounds of the vast variety of neighbourhood birds, having their final conversations and arguments before the fall of night. He smiled in appreciation of these wondrous God-sent gifts and making one final sign of the cross climbed to his feet. With a last look at the magnificent sunset, he made his way back down the track which would lead him out of "Sector C".

Suddenly, the priest was rudely shaken from his ambulant euphoria, startled awake by the myriad of birds, which, leaving their roosting places in universal panic, flew chaotically into the air, their calls taking on an urgency that only they themselves could translate. Seconds later, in the former stillness of the falling night, a huge blast tore across the open ground, instantly receiving back multiple echoes from the hills beyond. The dissociated bloody airborne remains of Nguyen Duc Manh temporally melded with the crimson background of the sky before returning earthbound to land in dismembered disarray around the base of the obelisk.

From a vantage point on a hill overlooking the field, Kiem Nguon Dung smiled. He permitted himself a smile infrequently but today was an exception, for he was well pleased with his work. The remote detonation of one of the series of landmines he had placed along the track had been perfect, and with advance knowledge of the priest's intention to make this personal visit to the monument, it had been simplicity itself to plant the seed of his extermination almost at leisure. He removed a cell phone from inside his tunic and made his call. Then, within minutes of the priest's dispatch to places unknown, he had mounted his bicycle and was pedalling away from the scene in the opposite direction to the local town, from where crowds would no doubt now be rushing.

The local "Dien Times" newspaper would soon report this latest tragically ironic death in an area of recently assured safety. Several thousand miles away, the "Vatican Times" would also eventually report the death of yet another "young" high-ranking priest from the list of considered future candidates for the Papacy.

Chapter 16

Even *further* westwards on the globe than Italy, a third incarnation using the title of the "Times Newspaper" lay open. This time it was the New York Times, lying open at a page far from that containing the banner headlines of the day. Tucked away at the bottom of page 38, in the international news section, was a short paragraph reporting the sad death of a Vietnamese Catholic Cardinal who had been blown to pieces by a landmine on the eve of the day he was due to give blessings and thanks for the completion of the total eradication of landmines in that area.

Its reader had left it there, while he paced the room, impatient and anxious for the telephone call that was just minutes overdue. Suddenly, the stillness of the room was pierced by the shrillness of the phone's ring. He jumped slightly, even though he was expecting the call, and quickly plucked the handset from its base.

'*Si, pronto?*'

The familiar voice of Negri at the other end of the line was loud and clear, considering the distance it had travelled.

'*Ciao.* Come *stai?*'

'I'm well, thank you. Despite your lateness with the call!'

There was a brief pause at the other end as the caller strove successfully to hold back his own irritation at the welcome he had received.

'Yes, occasionally certain things must take precedence. I'm afraid His Holiness needed me for a moment,' his tone was unusually cold.

'Ah good, so then you will be able to give me a latest update on his health.'

The caller passed over the recipient's callousness and continued with the medical update.

'He grows very weak. Yesterday, he suffered a sudden setback and the doctors' previous estimations for a further twelve months of his life are now looking rather optimistic.'

'That is unfortunate. You will have heard, no doubt, of the sad demise of the Vietnamese cardinal. His death was planned on the assumption that the Pope would have at least twelve more months remaining before passing over. Our game of chess is at a critical stage of play. The disposition and status of the pieces on the board are governed totally by the health of il Papa. I need you to speak to our doctors and then tell me what is necessary to re-set the clock to twelve months. I don't care what it takes, but report back to me soon. Is that clear?'

'Perfectly.'

'Then *ciao*, let us speak again very soon.'

'Cia—'

The caller's farewell was cut off abruptly as the man in New York slammed the phone down onto its cradle.

He poured himself another glass of red wine and stared out of his New York office window. He had come too far to be undermined now by useless Vatican physicians still living in the dark ages. If there was no improvement in the Pope's condition over the next couple of days, it would be necessary, through the offices of his friend in the Vatican, to send in his own small team of specialist physicians and that would be both diplomatically and logically very difficult, despite his friend's elevated position in the Vatican. But the Pope's survival for a further twelve months was absolutely critical to his *Great Plan*.

Chapter 17

Crosse and Hart ambled through the centre of the City of Nottingham, embraced by the winter sunshine.

Eventually, the couple were walking up the gravel drive of Williams' beautiful-looking home. As Crosse rang the doorbell, the tension was evident in her face. At the sound of the door chimes, the door was answered almost immediately by a dishevelled middle-aged man with pallid skin and sunken features, looking as if he hadn't slept for weeks. Crosse gave him an unconvincing smile followed by a hug.

'Denis, I hope you don't mind but I've brought along a colleague to join us…' (A colleague of at least 3 hours!). 'This is Max, Doctor Max Hart.'

Hart extended his hand, which was taken and gently shaken by Williams. Hart felt a sudden shock as his fingers closed around what was like the hand of a physiology class skeleton. Williams' limp hand appeared to consist of almost fleshless bones, covered in semi-translucent skin.

'Max is a physician who has spent the last few years working in the pharmaceutical industry. I thought he might be able to shed some light on your theories and perhaps volunteer a few ideas of his own.'

Hart delivered an unconvincing smile and Williams smiled briefly in return, beckoning them both over the threshold.

'Yes, thank you, Vicky. Please, both of you, come in.'

He led them into a sitting room and indicated them to sit down. They seated themselves in expensive, comfortable deep leather armchairs and then straightway, Crosse got down to the business in hand.

'I've already given Max a little of the background detail, so we can go straight ahead with what you began to tell me on the phone the other night if you like.'

'Yes of course.'

Williams began, somewhat nervously it seemed, in response to Crosse's invitation. As he began to talk, his fingers intertwined and released, tightened and relaxed.

'…and since Ruth passed away, I have been receiving bereavement counselling. As part of this, I have been attending self-help group sessions, which are available here in town. It's rather like alcoholics anonymous I expect, only *we* sit and drink tea and coffee and talk about the tragedies that have brought us together. Driven us together in fact. On my second visit to the group session, I met a couple who had also lost a child during the early stages of the wife's pregnancy. The week after, I met two other couples who were there for the same reason. This went on week after week and always with one over-riding common theme. All these couples had received treatment for the same conditions at the same unit of the clinic as Ruth had. Furthermore, all of these women had actually been present at the clinic at the time that they had lost their unborn babies. Not a single one of them had suffered a spontaneous abortion anywhere else. Not at home, not out shopping, not at friends…only during visits to that place.'

Hart cleared his throat and raised a finger as Williams paused and looked at him.

'You know, Denis, your wife, and I expect all these other women, were being treated at this clinic because each of them had a particular problem with respect not just to fertilization but also to sustaining or maintaining the life of a foetus. Therefore, they were already in a very high-risk group of patients with respect to actually losing their babies. Did the consultant not discuss these risks with you and your wife during your first visit, even before she became pregnant?'

'Well, yes, of course he did but—'

Hart interrupted again and continued in a clinical, unattached tone that made Crosse wince (*perhaps inviting Hart had not been such a good idea after all*).

'…and I would expect that similarly these risks would have been described in some detail to the other prospective parents?'

Williams rose to the question and was clearly irritated at Hart's directness.

'Yes, of course, we all knew that there were certain risks, but following initial physical examinations and laboratory tests, we were all told quite clearly that our overall chances would be improved significantly by proceeding with the treatment and care offered by the unit. They weren't exactly giving it away for nothing you know! The fact is, Doctor Hart, that following initial screening tests, we were all led to believe that our chances of success would increase dramatically, and what happened in the end was that we had no chance, no chance at all. Not one of us had a successful outcome. Only tragedy.'

'But that was the reason that you all met in the first place at these counselling groups. You had all met with similar tragedies. You would never have met otherwise. Certainly in those circumstances, you could never expect to meet those couples who had been successful at the clinic. I guess the clinic must have had *successes* there, otherwise you wouldn't have gone there in the first place, surely?'

He opened his mouth to continue but this time it was Williams who interrupted.

'Listen, Doctor Hart, in the first twelve weeks or so after the death of Ruth, I met fourteen other couples who had lost unborn children in similar circumstances at the same unit. Through these couples, I was directed to over twenty other distraught couples, again wracked with the same tragedies, and I have a list of more…more! I've done my homework, Doctor Hart. I've not just looked up the statistics for ordinary non-risk women at other units. I've been able to obtain the statistics for a whole group of women at risk elsewhere, women similar to those at The Paddocks but treated at other specialist units in the UK, and do you know what, Doctor Hart, do you know what, the incidences of spontaneous abortions at The Paddocks Fertility and Obstetric Unit are twenty times higher than in comparable units elsewhere! That's twenty times, Doctor Hart, not just two or even five, twenty!'

There was almost triumphalism in his voice as he finished his sentence.

Crosse said nothing, hoping Hart would respond with a reasonable argument, for the case Williams presented whilst not compelling, was certainly very persuasive. Hart didn't disappoint her.

'That certainly is a big difference, Denis, but I can think of several explanations which I would like to put to you.'

Williams shrugged and Hart continued. He began by outlining his experiences in the kidney transplantation unit in Leeds that he had discussed with Crosse earlier, drawing on similarities between the backgrounds and case histories of fertility and renal transplant patients and emphasising that many patients had likely been taken on and treated, who would most probably have been rejected at other units due to their low likelihood of success. When he had finished, he looked at Williams with a more kindly and compassionate eye.

'So, Denis, does that give you any slight cause to doubt your suspicions?'

A slight smile played across Williams' lips and he nodded slightly.

'That's a good parallel, Max…but what if I told you that there was another hospital, just *one* other hospital in fact in the whole of the UK with almost identical outcomes to The Paddocks? What if I told you that this hospital, which is in Liverpool for what it's worth, is run and owned by the same consortium as The Paddocks, with physicians who rotate on a regular basis between the two hospitals? I know this for a fact from looking at official documents of the consortium's assets, which are freely available, and also from reports provided to me by a private investigator that I've employed who has been privy to information that is not usually freely available, but which is not totally confidential either.'

Hart tried to be as kindly as his increasing exasperation would permit him.

'But don't you see, Denis, that just underlines what I've been saying. The Paddocks is treating patients who would not be taken on by most other units and likewise so is the clinic in Liverpool, which you yourself say is part of the same consortium and which, therefore, will be governed by the same principals, criteria and standard procedures for accepting and treating patients. The fact that some of the staff are rotating their duties between hospitals and, therefore, exercising those same criteria in both places confirms it even further.'

Crosse saw the obviousness of Hart's argument and looked sympathetically at Williams. But Williams was not finished.

'OK, I do see where you are coming from, Max, but there is more. My investigator has turned up other interesting information. He has spent time talking off the record to certain of the staff at both clinics and for sure there are very strong rumours at both places that all is not well. Members of staff are aware that a select few of them are earning a considerable amount of extra money through additional work done in the clinics. The nature of this work is a tightly guarded secret amongst the earners, but nurses, porters and other sections of staff are turning up in expensive clothes, driving fancy new cars and taking holidays in the sun in places which were previously "somewhere over the rainbow" to them. He's an expert, this private investigator of mine. He has also been able to do background work on staff members who have been identified as being on this "special extras list", which has included gaining access to certain bank accounts. Very illegal I'm sure, but also, and this time quite legally, he has been talking to neighbours of this privileged few. It is very clear that they have all started to come into a lot of additional money, money that they have made no real attempt to hide, other than what they have had to do to earn it of course.'

Suddenly Williams' logic wasn't looking quite so distorted and extreme, but he had to come to the point of what he would like from their meeting, his mind seeming to have already been made up on some course of further action. Crosse cleared her throat.

'Denis, what are you going to do now? What is it that you think I can do to help at this point in time? Surely you should lay the facts you have before some appropriate authorities, somebody who can take some proper action?'

Williams' body tensed as he looked at the couple sitting before him.

'I need to know even more of what is going on first. Don't you see that as soon as I make any complaint, whatever committee or body that I submit my grievances and suspicions to will quash it almost immediately as the ramblings of some unfortunate but disturbed loser in the healthcare system? My complaints and observations will be lost in paperwork and despite them making a limited show of understanding my grief, there will be a gentle but outright denial of any wrong doings.'

He looked directly at Hart as he said,

'And more than likely, if they can be bothered to offer any form of explanation, they will probably use the line that Doctor Hart has given me. Before you protest, Doctor Hart, I know for a fact that the health service looks after its own in matters like these. I can even see some limited need for it. I started my own working life working in it, for Christ's sake, before setting up my own business! But I repeat, I must know more of what's going on. I would be failing Ruth if I didn't persist in this and certainly I would not be able to live with myself was I to throw the information I have so far gathered into the rubbish bin.'

Hart looked at Williams closely. He was a man on the very edge of reason. One small push and he would fall into the abyss of a total nervous breakdown. Despite his own reasoned arguments against Williams' theories, in the back of his mind lurked the seed of a nagging doubt. Despite his eloquence to Williams, there was in fact a huge difference between the two scenario pictures he had painted. The kidney transplantations had been performed within the National Health Service, where the treatment had been free, gratis. In the case of these fertility treatments, however, this was an entirely privately funded affair. Williams, and others like him, had invested a hell of a lot of money with these two clinics and had been promised a better chance of long-term success. Surely, it was not in the business interests of the hospital consortium to knowingly permit anything that would inevitably lead them to the worst outcome record in the country? The life-blood, and, therefore, the income and reputation, of clinics offering these services must surely be outcome success? That being the case, then his own arguments were critically flawed.

Finally he spoke.

'So, Denis, you must have something in mind? You must have thought of some additional way forward on this before you would consider informing the authorities?'

Williams was silent for some moments and then turned his haunted eyes to Crosse.

'Vicky…Vicky, I want someone to attend the Paddocks clinic and get some impression of what really is going on. I guess I want a dummy patient, if you like, to look over the place with a damn sight more openness and focus than Ruth and I did when we were there. We were totally intent on our own problems and took in not a single glimmer of any activities that might have been out of the ordinary.'

Crosse's eyes widened as the realisation of what Williams was saying hit home to her.

'Bloody hell, Denis, you want *me* to do it, don't you?'

He looked down at the floor briefly in embarrassment, but then swiftly looked up directly into her eyes.

'Yes, I think I do, Vicky. In fact I know that I do.'

Crosse was suddenly on her feet.

'No, Denis. No, no, no. You know I would do almost anything for you, but I just cannot do that. I wouldn't know where to start or what to look for. I don't know what's supposed to be normal in this type of hospital situation. I work in a hospital, but I'm a bloody scientist for God's sake, not a physician or a nurse or whatever!'

But then another voice piped up…

'But I *do* know what's supposed to be normal, Vicky. I am a physician remember.'

Both Crosse and Williams stared at Hart in utter amazement as he continued,

'I know hospitals very well. I also know how their supplementary services operate, such as the pathology and X-ray departments for example.'

He paused momentarily and then,

'I'll do it for you, Denis. But I can't do it alone. I'll do it on the condition that Ms Crosse agrees to accompany me on an expedition for just *one* day only. Of course, she will have to accompany me as Mrs Hart. Doctor and Mrs Hart would have to visit The Paddocks as either prospective customer/patients or as family visitors, or as both of course, but in any case, I can only do it if you help me, Vicky.'

Hart suddenly heard a pin drop across the other side of the city!

Chapter 18

It was a beautiful sunny day outside the confines of the old red Ford Fiesta car as Victoria Crosse drove with Max Hart squeezed into the passenger seat, to the exclusive Paddocks Hospital on the Nottinghamshire/Leicestershire border.

The meeting at the home of Denis Williams one week earlier had left her feeling somewhat stunned and very uncomfortable. Hart volunteering to undertake this "mission ridiculous" had stunned both Williams and Crosse alike, his offer coming just minutes after he had delivered his cutting critique of Williams' suspicions, actions and conclusions relating to the activities of this hospital. It had seemed at the time that Hart's comments were truly the coup de grace for Williams' proposals, but then had come his total about-face.

Now Crosse was driving him to the hospital as co-conspirator in this "make it up as we go along" activity, a position which left her feeling nervous and somewhat traumatised.

Hart's crackpot plan was that they should visit the hospital and under the wafer thin cover of being family visitors, tick the boxes of items and questions that he had put together, which he believed could settle the business for Williams once and for all. These items included a reconnoitre of the fertility unit and likewise the pathology area (although this latter would almost certainly be out of bounds to visitors) and generally take in the ambiance of the unit. If possible, he wanted to talk to appropriate patients, especially in the fertility and obstetric sections, in as a relaxed way as possible using the guise of being fellow patients/customers. Hart believed that his skills at joining just about anyone in conversation, no matter what their social position or job, would be an asset in his plan to spend time also talking with nurses and porters. He guessed that mealtimes and outdoor smoking breaks were ideal for this activity and the "non-smoker" Hart had even purchased a pack of cigarettes, especially for that scenario.

'You can't beat proper project planning, using proper props.'

He had told Crosse, holding up his cigarettes.

The most difficult thing by far, however, that Crosse found herself able to agree to, was Hart's suggestion that they should arrange an appointment in the fertility clinic with the physician who had dealt with the Williams. At the end of a lengthy, often heated, discussion, Crosse decided to defy the "timid wallflower" accusation Hart levelled at her and against her better judgment, she had agreed to meet Doctor Sumaris. With an appointment in the late afternoon, this would give them a double-reason to be in the hospital and provide them with plenty of time to hunt around and tick the other "must dos" on Hart's list. Visiting a non-existent relative plus an appointment with Doctor Sumaris would fit Hart's bill nicely. However, in order to meet Doctor Sumaris, a referral from either a general practitioner or hospital consultant would be necessary. Secondly, VC, as Hart had now taken to calling Crosse, was distinctly uncomfortable with the plan for she was sure that come the crunch, she would not be able to bluff or lie her way through any appointment with the specialist. Another problem was that of the cost, for there would surely be a price to pay for the appointment with Sumaris.

Hart, oozing the confidence of a second-hand car salesman, eventually nipped all three of these problems in the bud with some ease. For the patient referral, he called his friend Jason Barnes outlining his requirement and rather than asking Jason himself to refer VC and himself, asked if he could get another colleague or friend to do it. Jason actually had a GP friend who owed him a huge favour and eventually after some persuasion, the GP complied with his request and organised a letter for an appointment for a couple who were seeking additional medical help at "the internationally renowned Paddocks Fertility Unit". A copy of the completed referral letter was in Hart's hand within two days of him dictating its preferred contents to Jason. As for the cost, Williams being a man of some wealth, had happily offered him an open chequebook.

Hart decided that they should not use their own real names for the visit and decided, much to his own amusement, that Mr and Mrs T Hanks had that certain "ring" to it. This irritated Crosse who identified it as yet another example of Hart's flippant approach to this serious business, but once again with Williams in mind, she kept the peace and went along with it. As special icing on the cake Hart decided that the name of the referring physician should not be that of the GP, but rather that of Doctor Robert Halle.

The plan was so good that Hart almost believed it himself. There was just one other thing he asked of Crosse for their visit.

'In case I need a disguise at any stage to gain access to areas which are out of bounds to the public, could you bring me a white lab coat from your place at the QMC, and better make sure that there's no label or anything in it that could tie it in to your own department?'

Crosse had agreed.

On the day of the visit to The Paddocks Hospital, when Crosse had pulled up at the Barnes' residence, he was there waiting outside, smartly dressed, and holding a large orchid plant in a pot. As he climbed into the car, he looked at Crosse and smiled.

'An orchid for my sick granny. She'll love it. Andiamo!'

Chapter 19

As Crosse drove the old Ford through the leafy lanes on the way to The Paddocks, despite his apparent confidence, Hart was far from it, but realising Crosse's condition, he had to perform according to his own words of advice and encouragement he'd given to her.

'You can do almost anything if you relax and brazen it out, even run a clinical trials program without being fired,' he had added with irony. 'You know what an Italian friend of mine used to say, "Always have the brass neck in all things. Have the brass neck and people will believe anything".'

'Where is he now?'

'Oh, he was fired for incompetence. He stuck that neck out too far, once too often. Too much brass and too much bullshit by far!'

The pair laughed.

'So, Max, what exactly are your true feelings now about Denis's concerns and about this mission?'

'As I said to Denis, I really do think that there will be a reasonable explanation for his suspicions. I do believe that what I told him about the rate of spontaneous abortions and their likely reasons will prove to be correct. You know in this age of registers and quality audits, not to mention government inspections, the kind of conspiracy that Denis is suggesting just cannot exist. It's impossible to hide the data and the patient histories. This whole area of medicine is constantly under the microscopes of the various safety and regulatory agencies, although I have to say that my own most recent experiences are in the good ol' US of A rather than here in the UK, but nevertheless, I'm sure that the audits and external checks will be very similar in both countries.'

'So what are we looking for? I mean if there is something very irregular going on, what could it be and how on earth on this simple visit are we expected to detect anything? I know that Denis has his data and figures but I just can't believe what he is suggesting.'

'To be perfectly honest, Vicky, I really don't know what we are looking for; we'll just have to see what we can see.'

'But you don't think there's anything in it, do you, Max?'

'No I don't, although I admit that there's a tiny nagging suspicion at the back of mind.'

'But why would they do that and risk their excellent record?'

'That's the concern I have as well, but at the end of the day, it could come down to the "root of all evil".'

'Sorry?'

'Money. Unless that is, these internationally respected experts have come up with some new experimental technology which isn't firing on all cylinders yet, but which they have sufficient confidence in to convince them to include these riskier patients in their programs. I think the answer to Denis's suspicions lies somewhere within this scenario.'

'So what are your other possible scenarios?'

'Well, if my first suggestion is off target, my second guess would have to be connected to staff competencies. In other words, staff employed in these units might be at best described as "not being up to the job" and at worst "downright incompetent". These people will have the correct qualifications I would guess, but little or no "hands on" experience. If this is the case, then Denis is probably correct with certain of his theories and something considerably more official than our "fly on the wall" examination must be set in motion.'

'OK. So what is option three then?'

'I'm afraid that number three is clutching at straws and straight out of some science fiction movie. It surely wouldn't stand up to any proper discussion, let alone there be any possibility of us finding evidence of it.'

'I don't understand. What are you talking about?'

'Hang on to your seat then. Live foetal material could be being obtained through induced early terminations of pregnancies in this high-risk group of women and used at other institutions for further experimentation or even as treatments in some particular disease areas.'

'My God! I see what you mean. Let's stick to your options one and two, shall we? I'm not up to the stuff of science fiction!'

'OK, Vicky, let's go through the plan one more time. How long before we get there?'

'About twenty minutes.'

'Right. Feel free to bring up anything you don't feel comfortable with, OK?'

'Like being here…period? Sorry, go on.'

'So… When we arrive at the hospital, park the car somewhere a little unobtrusive. You know, not bumper to bumper with any Porches, BMWs or Mercs that might be taking up most of the parking area. If we are here as prospective fertility patients, the assumption should be that we are not short of a little money, and to be honest, VC, your car doesn't really cut the mustard in that area.'

Crosse looked flabbergasted.

'Perhaps you should park it where they put out their rubbish,' he joked, adding insult to injury.

'So then we make our way to reception, me with the plant and you with the white lab coat tucked in your bag. If reception is busy, we just breeze past, hopefully unnoticed, and go about the job. If we have to check in, however, then we say that we have an appointment with Doctor Sumaris later in the day. That much is true at least. We say that we have arrived early in order to kill two birds with one stone in that we are also here to visit my poorly granny who is a patient on whatever ward.'

He held up the plant and beamed.

'Every base covered, eh?'

'What if they ask for the surname name of your granny? You will need the name of a real patient for that, as they will no doubt check their listings. Got that one covered?'

'Shit! Good point.'

He paused in thought for several moments.

'OK, Plan B. When we arrive, I will go in ahead, say ten minutes before you. I'll take the plant, to which I've now become very attached by the way, and if challenged first, ask urgently where the toilet is. If no challenge is forthcoming, I will take a stroll, but for either option, I will get hold of a patient's name from somewhere. There may even be a patient list on a board at reception. We'll see anyway. Then, armed with a patient's name, I'll return to reception in time to meet you coming in. Yes, that should do it. We will then check in as per Plan A … Mr and Mrs Hanks etc. etc. … with an appointment with Doctor Sumaris etc. etc. … but also there to see Granny Hanks, or whoever, before she's eaten by the "big bad wolf". Having registered with reception, we will be bona fide visitor/patients. The next thing to do will be to get directions to the fertility clinic, the path lab and the restaurant.'

'The restaurant?'

'This is likely to be a long day, my lovely, and refreshments will be needed at some point. Probably most importantly though, the restaurant should be a good place to make social contact with other visitors and staff. Denis told me that many of the staff eat in the staff section of the restaurant, so we can listen in to their conversations if we sit close enough to them. Who knows we might get some idea of what, if anything, is going on from that source. You know people relaxing and off-guard?'

He shrugged his shoulders.

'So…for one final time, we check in, theoretically visit granny, but in fact, check out our locations of interest and then speed to the fertility unit where we generally nose around and pick up any literature, etc. If we can, we will try and join any of the couples, or patients, there in conversation. You know, "Have you been here before?"… "How many times?" … "Is it good?" … "Is Sumaris a nice guy?"…and a bit more difficult, "What problems, if any, have you had?" You know the sort of stuff, VC, just talk to them.'

Crosse was looking a little distressed again.

'Do you really think that people will want to discuss their most intimate problems with strangers though?'

'Normally, perhaps no, but this is a specialist clinic situation and my experience is that many patients are often actually eager to talk about their histories. It's almost like therapy for them to able to share their problems. You know the saying "a problem shared…" It would be excellent to get patient feedback, but I'm really hoping to be able to get hold of some staff feedback, such as staff attitudes, dissatisfactions, etc. They're bound to talk over tea and coffee, and hopefully we will be able to pick up on something. While you are in the clinic, I will go on a little detour and see what's to be seen at the pathology lab. If this hospital is the place of science fiction as per my unlikely third scenario, then perhaps pathology, or more specifically histopathology, could be the place to check out. It will certainly be off limits to visitors, but people are always accidentally wandering off piste, if you get me. You never know, that white coat of yours might actually come in useful.'

'Have you any idea what you will be looking for if you actually do trespass into the lab?'

'No, is the honest answer, but certainly my roving eyes will suck in everything in sight as quickly as possible. I'm sure if there's anything suspicious, I'll be able to pick up on it.'

But in truth, he wasn't in the slightest bit sure, and the more he talked, the more he was convinced that at the end of the day, they would return to Williams with no information at all.

'I don't actually think we will find a single thing out of place here, VC, but at least when we say "hasta la vista" to The Paddocks, we will be certain that we have done all we can for Denis. Who knows, he might then let this thing rest once and for all? By the way, if I do make it to the labs, I think that you should wait for me in the restaurant. I propose that to do a complete job, for the sake of our consciences, we should set our stall out to be here most of the day. Now our appointment with Sumaris is at 4.00 pm, so we leave fifteen minutes ahead of that time and I cancel it from your car on my cell phone.'

He looked at his watch.

'I make it that we will have almost 7 hours to really get the low-down on the place. What do you think?'

Crosse looked doubtful.

'Seven hours is a hell of a long time. Don't you think that somebody might eventually get suspicious of us, two people walking around the place like health inspectors or something? I thought the idea was to be as invisible as possible. You know, slip in and slip out, job done?'

'I think we will be fine, Vicky. The clinics I'm used to have patients and visitors waltzing around all the time. It's not unusual for patients to have to hang around for the most of the day, even at top of the range private places like this. You know, waiting for X-rays, laboratory reports and so on in between seeing various specialists. No, I'm sure we will be fine.'

'That's good then, Max…because here we are, The Paddocks Hospital.'

Crosse turned the battered car into the hospital drive and proceeded towards the car parks.

'So which car park area shall we use, Max, visitors or patients?'

'The most inconspicuous one I think. As I said before, keep this jalopy away from the finer pieces of automotion. Look!'

His hand went up.

'Over there on the left, park there. There's plenty of space and I don't see any CCTV cameras.'

Crosse felt suddenly weak with nerves as she killed the engine, but Hart seemed to be aflame with enthusiasm.

'Right! I'm going in. Follow me to reception in ten minutes. Say goodbye to the plant then!'

He smiled as he manoeuvred himself and the plant though the car door and headed off to the sign-posted "Reception".

Chapter 20

Hart purposefully strode the thirty yards from where Crosse had parked her decaying red car to the main hospital entrance, buoyed-up by his pep talk to Crosse moments earlier. The dodgy used car salesman had just bought a used car from himself!

There was no time to pause or rethink as he neared the doors.

Just go for it...and keep the "brass neck" well polished!

The doors slid open with a double sigh to reveal a lush surround of dark-green foliaged plants, china blue walls and a deep pile plain navy blue fitted carpet. The whole area was illuminated by a series of small, art deco chandeliers. Quite a place! Directly in front of him was the solid teak reception desk behind which a rather flushed and flustered blue uniformed receptionist was present, obviously embroiled in a difficult phone call.

As the conversation at the counter continued, Hart checked his watch. He had to get a move on otherwise Crosse would be in alongside him. He leaned gently into the counter and giving his best Sunday smile to the receptionist in sotto voce,

'Excuse my interruption, but I've been on the road for the last four hours and I would be really grateful if you could direct me to the bathroom?'

He finished the sentence with a sham wince of pain on his face.

The receptionist smiled and stabbed her finger down the corridor to the right.

Hart waved a thanks and proceeded in the direction she had indicated.

The corridor curved to the left and looking back over his shoulder as he approached it, saw that the reception area was now out of sight around the bend. He increased his pace walking past the door marked "Gentlemen" and forward towards two overhead signs he had been hoping for further down the corridor. As he neared the signs he saw that "Charnwood Ward" was straight on and "Kegworth Ward" was to the left. Another sign indicated that to the right, one would find "Obstetrics" and "Gynaecology" and also "Pathology". He smiled at the additional sign for the Department of Cytology, as happy memories of his time spent in such a department some ten years before came to mind and he murmured to himself,

'Ah "cervix with a smile".'

All he had to do now was to find a suitable name with which to label the fictional granny. Luckily, he quickly arrived at the nurses' patient name boards containing the list of female patients on Charnwood Ward. A quick look and he identified an aunt rather than a granny, Mrs Elizabeth Scott, a day patient for an endoscopy on Charnwood Ward. That was as much information as he needed.

Mission completed. He took in the directions for the fertility and gynae units on his way back to reception, together with those of the pathology laboratory. He arrived back at the reception area at the same instant as Crosse stepped through the automatic doors.

She smiled with relief as he looked at her and winked.

'We're visiting my aunt, Mrs Elizabeth Scott, on Charnwood Ward if asked.'

He took Crosse's arm and led her to the smiling receptionist.

'Hello again. How can I help the two of you?'

Chapter 21

Hart delivered his well-rehearsed speech to the beaming receptionist like an old stagehand and as he'd anticipated, there was not the slightest suspicion that there was anything unusual or untoward about his and Crosse's potentially long stay in the hospital during the day. The receptionist duly pointed out the locations of the wards and the obstetric unit and indicating the direction of the restaurant, which was on the other side of the hospital, was at great pains to point out the excellence of the new a la carte menu in their newly refurbished Sherwood Restaurant. When their orientation lecture was over, Hart directed Crosse towards the restaurant and cafeteria.

They decided to take the opportunity to collect their thoughts over coffee in the cafeteria, which was next door to the restaurant, Hart feeling that this was a good place and time to get a first glimpse of any hospital staff taking an early morning break. Within a few minutes of leaving the reception area, they arrived at the oasis. As Hart pushed open the cafeteria's double doors, they were instantly met with the tinkle of music.

'Ahh the hills are alive with the sound of Muzac,' Hart joked as they approached the counter. The song playing was Tony Bennett's, "I left my heart in San Francisco", and Hart couldn't resist an ironic comment to the young girl behind the counter,

'I hadn't realised that they did heart transplants here now.'

The comment flew un-noticed some ten feet over the confused girl's head, who replied,

'I really don't know, sir, but our information desk will be able to assist you I'm sure.'

Laughing, they ordered coffees, which they took to a table in the corner of the room opposite the door through which they had entered.

'You're going to tell me now that sitting here, we can see all who come in and leave, whilst at the same time keeping our backs covered,' smiled Crosse, now showing none of her early almost paralysing nerves. '*I've* seen that movie too.'

'Thatsh right, shweetheart,'

Hart replied with his stock impersonation of Bogart, which was interchangeable with his impersonation of Sean Connery, both being similarly awful.

'I ushed to come here wid Lassie. Did you know that she wore the shame coat in every movie she ever made?'

Crosse laughed as her cup came up to her lips, blowing some of the froth on the top of her cappuccino onto the end of her nose.

On the far side of the room, one-half of the wall was given up to floor to ceiling glass sliding doors, which opened out onto a patio. Beyond the patio area, lawns and mature trees and shrubs rolled back to a lake in a woodland setting. In the far distance, the hills of east Derbyshire were just visible.

Whilst the cafeteria was well posted with "No Smoking" signs, there were, however, directive arrows to a smoking area located through the glass doors and to the right of the patio. Hart tapped his jacket pocket.

'I would guess that the best places to talk to staff and other visitors are over a table like this, or out there on the patio by the smoking area, or in fact by the drinks machine in the corridor outside. Although I don't smoke, I'm quite happy to join the smokers out there and pass one around if necessary. I might even consider a bit of personal lung abuse if it seems worthwhile.'

With empty cups and an empty cafeteria, it was decided that a walk to the fertility clinic might be in order. Accordingly, they left the warm comfort of the café and strolled in the direction of the unit, which was central to this whole disturbing business. The signs pointed them in a direction away from the reception area, which they were both grateful for.

Hart spoke first,

'Let's see how things are at the unit. It may be a good idea to take a seat and just observe the place. Who knows we might even get the chance to pass the time of day with a patient or two.'

'Fine, but what if we are approached by a member of staff? I suppose we could say that we have a later appointment and thought it would calm our nerves to arrive early and see what the place was like.'

Hart smiled. 'We'll make a spy out of you yet, VC.'

After several minutes walking, a suspended sign indicating that the pathology laboratory was off to the left loomed up. Just past the turning was a restroom. Hart slowed to an amble and gently took Crosse's arm at the elbow.

'I need to take a quick look at the path lab and now might be good time to do it. It will be interesting to see if it's out of bounds to the public. I'm sure it will be. You can either come with me as a "lost couple" looking for the fertility clinic or you could perhaps wait for me outside the restroom. That's always a good excuse for hanging round.'

'I'll go with you, Max. I think your "lost couple" option would be more believable if we were apprehended by anyone.'

'Right. Off we go then.'

They took the left turn as directed by the overhead sign and almost immediately the characteristics of the corridor changed. Gone was the plush deep piled carpet, which was now replaced by one of a more industrial quality. Gone too were the rows of pictures which had so far adorned the walls during their passage through the visitor/patient areas. In their place were occasional staff notice boards and posters relating to forthcoming hospital events, which included both social and educational items. The couple quickly scanned the notice boards but saw nothing of relevance to their enquiries, just a forthcoming staff trip to a seaside resort, updates on the latest lotto draws and a few personal articles for sale.

As they moved on, a series of doors came into view on each side of the corridor. Crosse slipped her arm through Hart's as they walked on, nervousness now encroaching upon her. Hart squeezed her arm in encouragement but he too was feeling unusually nervous. Or was it excitement? In rapid succession, they passed doors which identified the interiors as those of Haematology, Clinical Chemistry, Blood Transfusion and finally Histopathology. Opposite the Histopathology room was a much smaller room with a small opening window, which was obviously part of a specimen drop-off arrangement. The door was to this room was open. It hadn't escaped Hart's notice that apart from the histopathology drop-off room, the doors to each of the pathology areas could only be opened by an appropriately coded swipe-card. Lights were visible behind the half-frosted glassed doors and white-coated people were obviously moving around doing their jobs within. Suddenly Hart came to a halt.

'OK, VC, I've seen enough for now; let's head back to the main corridor.'

As the relieved Crosse opened her mouth to respond, the door of the histopathology department opened and a man emerged, dressed in the dark-grey uniform of a hospital porter. He eyed the couple who nodded and smiled at him weakly.

'You lost or something? This area is out of bounds for visitors.'

Crosse accepted the proffered excuse gladly.

'Yes, we seem to have wandered away from the main corridor. Can you direct us back to it, please?'

George Henson pointed back down the corridor from whence they had come.

'Go straight down there, follow the bend and its straight in front of you. This is a staff-only area!'

He added this in case they hadn't heard it the first time, not permitting himself even a fraction of a smile.

Hart could feel Crosse trembling on his arm. Back on what Hart had called the "yellow-brick road", it didn't take them long to reach the sign indicating "Fertility Suite". They paused momentarily and Hart looked at Crosse.

'Still up for it, matron?'

Crosse nodded rather reluctantly and gripped Hart's arm a little more tightly and as "brass" replaced his own jangling nerves, he pushed open the clinic door. As they stood inside, still at the threshold of the clinic, Hart added,

'We just see what we can see, OK? If we feel comfortable, I suggest that we sit for a spell and just observe the comings and goings of the patients.'

He nodded in the direction of a series of couples seated around the waiting area.

'If we get the chance to fall into conversation with any of them, let's do it. It would be excellent if we manage to find out what any of their experiences or even their expectations of this place are. If you think we start beginning to appear suspicious, and I don't see why we should, these folk look more nervous than we are, we will leave and perhaps return later when perhaps a new batch of them has filtered through. What say you, VC?'

71

'I agree. I don't want to stay here one second longer than is necessary, even if we are not rumbled. Still we do have a bona fide appointment and you're right, these people look about as nervous as I feel.'

'Excellent.'

As the couple moved into the waiting room, wading through the deep luxurious carpet, they took in the room's opulent décor. Twenty or so low teak tables were placed symmetrically around room, each one having two accompanying deep, low-backed velvet armchairs. The whole room was done out in a variety of shades of green. Extremely restful and tranquil shades of green in fact. Light was provided by equally spaced wall lights, which emitted a soothing cream glow.

Each table was adorned with an elegant standing spotlight for those who could challenge their nerves with a touch of light meaningless reading. Magazines and home and gardening books were presented in a series of table-matching teak bookshelves, which hugged the walls at various points around the room. A good number of randomly spaced tall, green potted plants added to the room's ambience.

Crosse nodded towards what clearly was a reception area at the far end of the room. Standing behind what looked like a church pulpit was a tall, young, dark-haired receptionist who locked eyes with them and smiled. With renewed confidence, Crosse took Hart by the elbow and purposefully approached her.

'Hello. We have an appointment with Doctor Sumaris later today but are taking the opportunity to also visit a relative who is a patient in one of the surgical wards here. This is our first time here and we're feeling a little nervous so we decided to have a glance at the clinic before coming back for our actual appointment.'

'Of course, that's no problem at all Mrs...?'

'Hanks.'

The receptionist ran an elegant, long, slim finger down the diary.

'Ah yes, Mr and Mrs Hanks. Please feel free to come and go as you will. Do whatever makes you feel the most relaxed. There are magazines around the room and fresh coffee and boiled water for tea at the other end of the room.'

The elegantly long fingers left the diary and indicated a table at the far end of the room set out with all the required paraphernalia for taking a very civilised cup or two of tea or coffee, along with a selection of fine chocolate biscuits and Scottish oatcakes.

'You might also be interested to read the pamphlets we have over there', again her hypnotic fingers pointed the direction, 'which describe the Paddocks Hospital and what we offer. There's also a particularly good item there on our particular unit here.'

Hart couldn't believe his ears. This was going to be a piece of cake. In fact, several pieces of cake and a couple of chocolate biscuits.

'Marvellous!'

Chapter 22

As Hart and Crosse sipped their coffees, they took in a little more detail of the room's other occupants. There were a half a dozen couples seated at the tables amongst the foliage. The place was as quiet as a morgue, with very little communication taking place between the nervous attendees. Hart exchanged nods and smiles with those nearest, who were not too well camouflaged to be seen and then began to thumb through the information packs he had picked up on their way to the refreshments.

'Let's sit down over there, VC, and peruse these pearls of wisdom.'

He held up his collection of pamphlets and moved towards one of the small oases where, once seated, he began to read them in earnest.

'Hey look at this "most wanted list".'

Hart handed Crosse a sheet of high quality embossed paper and she squinted as she focused her eyes on it in the semi-gloom of the room.

It was an organogram of the fertility unit staff complete with their photographs and condensed curricula vitae. There smiling up at her, she saw the good-looking, olive-skinned and black-haired image of Doctor Sumaris. Other faces in the gallery included nursing staff and the other unit physicians. One smiling face instantly recognisable was that of the receptionist. Meanwhile, Hart read through the booklet entitled, "The Paddocks – Your Hospital".

The first few pages outlined the hospital in general with its objectives and history and a list of services it now provided. The services covered IVF, medicine and surgery, a strange item called "matched lifestyles" and geriatric care, with a new geriatric, or rather "healthcare of the elderly", residential unit in the process of development. Eventually, Hart reached the chapters in the brochure dedicated solely to the fertility services. Again there was a short historical preamble which was followed by a large section outlining the global expertise that had been developed there. This was accompanied by a similar "rogues gallery" of photographs of the personnel. Suddenly, Hart's flagging attention was enlivened by a section headed "Unit Success rates". Here, care had been taken to outline clearly some of the possible pitfalls and problems, which could be associated with fertility treatment but interestingly the main thrust of the piece was a confident overview of the successes at the unit, which "were amongst the highest in the Western World". This was supported with a wedge of confusing statistics, but the final paragraph was clear... "the unit prides itself upon its globally acclaimed expertise and integrity. To this end we retain the right to be selective in accepting patients where necessary, to ensure realistic and acceptable outcomes."

In other words, Hart thought to himself, *if you only have an outside chance of success, we will dump you. The income may be good, but the success rate seems more important.*

He then thought back to the afternoon in Denis Williams' sitting room when Williams had presented to him and Crosse the post conception high failure rates at both this unit and its sister unit in Liverpool. He thought too of his own half-explanation that the units were most probably taking on the difficult and most-likely-to-fail cases that other units would reject and he gave an involuntary shiver. If Williams' information was correct, and he had supported it pretty well with documented feedback from his "outside sources", then this brochure was speaking with "forked tongue". Still, it was early in the day yet and Hart and Crosse still had the best part of a full day ahead of them.

'See anything of interest, Max?'

'Take a look at this and tell me your immediate thoughts.'

He passed the brochure to her, holding it open at the page he had just read.

'Forget the mug shots and hype. Just read that last paragraph where my thumb is.'

He watched her read it, and then,

'Now go back and look at the statistics on the previous couple of pages.'

'These results look a damn sight better than Denis was telling us, Max. Either he has been led up the garden path by his informants, or this falls somewhat short of the truth. If that *is* the case, of course it blows your theory right out of the water.'

'Don't abandon ship just yet, Vicky. If you look at the small print, it also says that "figures are correct at time of going to press". However, I see from the cover of the booklet that this is a fairly new edition.' He turned to the front cover, 'Printed only 6 months ago. That's well within Denis's timeframe of events.'

'What now then?'

'It's too early to jump to conclusions yet, VC. Let's hang around here for bit, say thirty minutes, as we planned and get a feel for the place. We can then regroup in the Paddocks famous restaurant and perhaps indulge ourselves in one of their Michelin starred "nose-bags". And stop looking so bloody nervous!'

'We don't all have PhDs in Bulshitology, Max.'

'Ouch!'

He placed a hand over his heart and grimaced in mock pain.

As they sat and observed, the proceedings laid out in front of them, it was obvious that the couples were being ushered to consulting rooms located to the rear of the waiting room area, but suddenly it became not very obvious where they went from there. It was Crosse who first made the observation.

'Max, have you noticed that the patients are not coming back this way after seeing their consultant? There must be an exit beyond the reception desk.'

'Great minds, VC, my thoughts exactly. We should try and check out where the exit is before lunch. It would be interesting if we could get some look at patients after their meeting with the physician. You know, to see how they look emotionally? Elated, delighted, distraught or distressed. What do you think?'

Before Crosse could respond, Hart noticed the male partner from one of the waiting couples break out of the foliage and make his way to the refreshments area. In rapid succession, he was followed by one of the other males, obviously keen to break the monotony.

'Hang on, VC, its time I had another coffee, but this time with the chaps.'

'Fine, I'll stroll over and check out that exit. I see that receptionist has left her post.'

'OK, I'll meet you back here in fifteen minutes or so.'

Chapter 23

The three men stood around the coffee machine behaving like perfectly polite English gentlemen, or in other words smiling in perfect silence. Hart hadn't been living in the US for the last few years to let this go on for too long and decided to break the ice.

'This is my first visit here. I think the dentist is much more preferable.'

'Oh it's not that bad.'

One of his companions on the ice replied,

'When you've been here as many times as I have, it's not much different to being in any other boring waiting-room, apart from the terrible background music that is. A television would be much better.'

'It wouldn't work. The trees would block out the reception,' Hart joked, indicating in the direction of one of the groups of potted plants.

The man laughed but was not joined in his mirth by the second man, who instead carried on from Hart's opening comment.

'Actually my wife and I find it really quite depressing. There have been so many failed attempts.'

Hart decided to try and bring the man out a little further.

'Still, it's good to read in their brochure that they have such a good success rate overall, don't you think?'

The man took the bait.

'Don't you believe all that you read there, or anywhere else in this place as far as that goes. We've been coming here for five years now and in that time, we've met lots of couples in the same situation as us. There are lots of us, who, despite what they say in their bullshit brochure, don't make it. So why do we come, I hear you ask? Well, because it is recognised as being one of the best clinics of its type, not just here in the UK, but also abroad. I do think the figures they churn out in that brochure are bollocks though, but even so they are still probably better than anywhere else and despite everything, we still feel that our best hope lies here. Anyway, I'd better take this coffee back to the wife or else I'll be in even more trouble.'

He gave a half smile to Hart and the first man who both nodded as he left them. This first man was clearly in no hurry to return to his leafy area and poured himself a second cup.

Hart took the opportunity to continue the conversation.

'My wife and I are worried that when she does eventually become pregnant, we could lose the baby before it reaches term. We're having nightmares in fact over that,' he lied shamelessly.

After a short pause, the man replied,

'That's one of the main reasons we get depressed coming here. We know that a lot of women have succeeded with this IVF, but have then gone on and lost the baby during the early weeks of their pregnancies. I can tell you there are many more than these booklets will tell you. Just remember that the details they give are generally for IVF success alone in producing a fertilized egg, and not for those that go on to full-term live delivery.'

The comment hit Hart like a sledgehammer. Of course! Why had he been so stupid as to miss it? Publishing fertilisation success rates was a far cry from publishing completed term success rates. He could not believe that he had not queried this himself.

Shit! he thought.

The man wasn't yet done.

'Recently, it seems that every time we come here, there is someone who has lost a baby. That's why nobody talks to other couples in here. No news is good news, if you know what I mean! You might have noticed that the exit from this area is not very obvious?'

He looked at Hart who merely shrugged his shoulders, but his pulse was racing now with expectation.

'That's because it's on the other side.' He nodded past reception. 'It's a clever way of hiding the fact that a lot of upset people leave from these consulting rooms and it doesn't do for new customers to be put off now, does it? In fact, sometimes you can even hear cries of disappointment from some unlucky customers. Yes… "customers" seems to be the operative word here. There is behind reception another area which is like this but smaller and not so…well decorated. It's a kind of recovery area for distressed couples. You know, so that they don't leave here, looking all doom and gloom? So why are my wife and I also here? Well, we are here for the same reason as the other guy. We think this place holds the best chance for us.'

He drained his coffee.

'I'm sure we'll meet again soon. Good luck!'

He smiled and beat a retreat to his patient wife, embarrassed that he had let his emotions get the better of him, but for Hart, this incident had been perfect. He waved at the man's receding back and looked around for Vicky Crosse.

Crosse emerged from behind reception and made her way to the excited Hart.

'Look, Vicky, we need to take that time out right now. Our man over there has been very forthright with his descriptions of this place and its workings, so let's go to this famous restaurant.'

Chapter 24

Upon entering the recently refurbished Sherwood Restaurant, they were picked up immediately by an eager young *maitre d'* and ushered to Hart's choice of a table for two by the window. As well as providing clear and open views of the landscaped gardens and the smoking area outside, their seated positions also lent them to a panoramic view of the restaurant itself. The waiter handed them each a leather-bound menu and handed a smaller matching wine list to Hart.

'Would *madame* and *monsieur* like a drink whilst they are looking at the menu?'

Crosse looked at her watch. It was dead-on mid-day.

'I wouldn't mind a glass of white wine actually, what about you, Max?'

'Fine by me,' he replied. Then to the waiter, 'Do you do a New Zealand sauvignon by the glass?'

'Yes of course.'

'Then we will start with those please.'

Hart raised a quizzical eyebrow towards Crosse.

'Sorry, Vicky, you happy with that?'

'Perfect, thank you.'

The waiter disappeared as quickly as he had arrived.

'Max, I'm amazed at this place,' Crosse was almost whispering, 'I can't believe we are in a hospital. This place is fabulous.'

'I've travelled a lot and stayed in some pretty decent places, but this is well up with the best of them. But let's see how we get on with the menu and the food. Let's get something ordered and then talk turkey. There's none on the menu by the way. Turkey that is.'

'This is amazing. It sounds stupid but it almost seems immoral in a hospital setting.'

'Morals have nothing to do with it, VC, its money, pure and simple. At the end of the day, we all go either of two ways, down in the ground or up in smoke, it's just that this makes it more comfortable in between, and especially if you're just visiting.'

A waitress, seeing the couple talking, assumed they had chosen their lunches and promptly approached their table.

'So have madam and sir chosen?'

'Just about,' Hart replied with gravitas, 'but tell me, can we be assured that the meat has not come to the kitchen by way of one of the surgical wards?'

'Oh no sir I can assure…'

Her sentence trailed off as the weak humour dawned on her.

Hart couldn't help himself, but the waitress wasn't impressed at all. She'd seen too many of these "bloody well-to-do smart arsed people and had had too many of them taking the piss in their condescending way". She was a natural for her job!

They both ordered the Thai green prawn curry, which when it arrived was indeed delicious, and which they ate at a snail's pace to allow maximum use of their time for observation of the restaurant and the outside garden areas. During pauses for air in between mouthfuls, Hart updated Crosse on his conversations with the men in the fertility unit. Crosse took in the information eagerly.

'So Denis could be right after all. Does that mean that we can finish lunch and go?'

'Hold on, VC, all we have is the hearsay of one or two patients. There's nothing at all that Denis could do with the information we have that he can't do with what he already has. In a nutshell, that amounts to zero. He still has nothing concrete to act upon.'

'So what else can we do?'

'I don't know. At least we should sit it out for the rest of the day and see what else we can turn up. What Denis then does with our information is entirely up him. There are hospital agencies he could approach. Anyway, let's get ourselves an excuse for a little more monitoring. I suggest we take a dessert and then some coffee. We should have had a starter you know.'

Dessert was duly ordered and the eating of it progressed at the same slow-motion pace that had propelled them through the main course. Over the course of the meal, there had been few fellow lunchers in the restaurant, joining them in the "pan-Asian delights", and none of them seemed in the slightest bit emotional or distressed...apart from the effect that an over-cooked scallop had on one of the diners.

However, partway through the sliced pineapple with grated ginger, topped off with creme fraiche, Hart caught sight for the first time of some of the other hospital employees outside of the confines of the haute cuisine. Two uniformed porters had stepped out from the employees' restaurant section and had taken up positions in the outside smoking area. Upon closer inspection, Crosse was sure that one of them was the misery who had spoken to them during their trip to the histology lab earlier. Hart removed the napkin from his knees and wiped his mouth.

'OK, VC, I've got no option but to whip one out!'

Hart's huge store of double entendres had returned to him at about the same time as his appetite. Crosse looked non-plussed.

'What I mean is, is that I'm going to have to step outside and join those two chaps in a cigarette. It might be useful, but first I have to learn how to smoke convincingly.'

'Just don't inhale and you'll be fine.'

Hart wandered over to the exit and headed for the smoking area where the two porters he had spotted were deep in both earnest conversation and a double-cloud of cigarette smoke. They looked up as he approached and he smiled and nodded as he took the new unopened packet of cigarettes from his pocket. He fumbled the cellophane wrapper from it and took out a cigarette. This was his first ever packet of cigarettes and he felt very awkward in his actions. In fact, he put this performance so far on a par with his past efforts to assemble a small piece of flat-packed furniture. Amateurish and pathetic!

'Excuse me, could I beg a light from you please?'

His begging was met with stony silence but several seconds later, one of the men tossed him a cheap plastic lighter. He caught it and turned his back while he went through the pantomime of lighting the thing squeezed between the thumb and forefinger of his right hand. Miracle of miracles he managed to light it at the first attempt drawing the smoke into his mouth and then immediately expelling it, not permitting it to pass down his throat and thus expose him, through convulsive coughing, as a "first timer". Crosse smiled to herself as she watched his self-conscious show through the window.

'Thanks,' he said, handing back the lighter and moving far enough away from their cloud base to avoid their smoke, but close enough to hear their conversation.

The men were discussing the weekend's sports results and the fates of their particular favourite teams quite loudly, but eventually there was noticeable lowering of the volume and Hart really had to strain his ears to hear. He moved over to a trashcan and deposited the cellophane wrapper in it, returning to a spot a little closer to the porters' huddle where he could hear a little better.

'Any action today?'

It was the porter from histology who Hart and Crosse had met earlier who responded.

'I'm getting bloody fed up with waiting.'

His rather rotund companion placed a finger to his lips, in a silencing manner, and moved his eyes in the direction of Hart.

'Keep the volume down for Christ's sake. Look, I've been told that there could possibly be something today. You'll just have to be patient, but in any event, be ready just in case.'

'Stuff that, I can't sit around all day and bloody night. I could really do with some extra cash right now. The bleedin' horses have been running like cows!'

'Look, things have to be just so. You should know by now that the time has to be just right, otherwise the shit could really hit the fan and where would we all be then eh? Just cool it, will you?'

The second man's conversation was suddenly interrupted by the sound of his cell phone, which he placed to his ear and walked to the far side of the patio. When he returned some moments, later he was smiling.

'Looks like your luck's in. Stand by for a pick-up call up later today.'

'Great! Do you know around what time? I need to fit in my tea breaks you know.'

'I don't know exactly, but it sounds like it could be around 4.00 pm this afternoon. You gonna be all right regarding the freezin'?'

Hart was deliberately looking the other way during this conversation and puffing enthusiastically on his cigarette.

'Yeh, its fine. I've had the dry ice ready for friggin' days now. I had to almost get down on my knees and beg for it from that little shit in the lab. Told him it was for a series of urgent biopsies.'

'Nice one. Looks like the missus might get that holiday she's been chaffing about after all. You'd better get back in case it comes early, otherwise Sumaris will really be pissed off, you know what he's like.'

'OK. By the way, you aren't 'alf putting on weight, you fat bastard.'

'Didn't I tell you? I'm sleeping with your wife, and every time I shag her she gives me a chocolate biscuit. Those calories soon mount up.'

'Fuck off!'

The two men laughed and left the paved smoking area, walking around the perimeter of the restaurant.

Chapter 25

Hart returned to the restaurant table and took some minutes to restore his composure after his first ever smoking experience, after which he went through what he had heard outside.

'I couldn't believe my ears, VC. Either something extraordinary is about to go down here today, or I'm putting two and two together and coming up with five. What I heard could have been connected with anything in any part of the hospital, up to the point that is when one of the guys mentioned that the secretly guarded job was for a certain Doctor Sumaris.'

'My God! What exactly are they going to do for him?'

'It wasn't too clear. I guess they could have been talking about placing a bet on the horses for him or fixing him up with the rather attractive blond nurse on the ward or whatever...'

Crosse's face took on a look of acute disappointment. But it was only temporary as Hart continued,

'But dry ice and transportation of biopsies were mentioned, so we can rule out the horses...and the nurse, unless Sumaris has some yearning to seduce her in some swirling mist of liquid nitrogen vapour.'

'So what do we do next then?'

'All we can do is to return to the unit and wait it out. Sit and perhaps roam around a little and hope that we bear witness to whatever they are up to. It's a long shot, but I can't think of much else. What do you think?'

Once again, Crosse was sounding confident and eager.

'I agree with you. We could perhaps venture into that area *beyond* reception, the unit that seems to be where patient dramas might be most evident. Sometime either side of 4.00 o'clock sounds about the time from what you say the porters said. One thing's for sure though, we must leave here before we are called to our appointment.'

'Indeed, but let's not get too excited yet, VC, this might yet turn out to be just a small piece of petty thievery or something of that order, and nothing at all to do with the business we are looking at here.'

'There goes that bucket of cold water again, Max! Come on, get the bill sorted and let's get back to the unit.'

Crosse looked at her watch,

'Jesus, it's almost three o'clock! Let's get a move on.'

Hart signalled for and paid the bill, which arrived almost immediately.

Chapter 26

Within minutes of leaving the restaurant, Crosse and Hart arrived in the fertility suite waiting room. The room was empty apart from a solitary couple waiting for their consultation.

'Well, there are certainly no alerts or alarms going off here at present, are there? One thing we must be aware of is that if things are as quiet as this right up to the time of our appointment, we may just get called in early.'

'Oh my God, I hadn't thought of that! Now I'm really nervous.'

At that moment, their attention was drawn to the sound of the consulting room door closing. As they looked on, a lone male figure walked slowly back to the waiting room and dropped heavily into a chair, where he sat staring at the floor.

'Bloody hell! He's one of the guys who spilled a few beans to me over coffee when we were in here earlier. He's the one who said that it had taken them five years, but now his wife was well and truly pregnant and actually doing well. He doesn't look too well himself though, does he?'

The man looked thoroughly miserable and dejected and, therefore, probably pretty vulnerable. Hart turned to Crosse.

'This could be the change in ambience we are looking for. Wait here while I go and have a word with him.'

He walked silently across the room, his footsteps absorbed by the thickness of the carpet, to where the hapless man was seated and took a chair opposite him. He spoke gently to him,

'Hi, remember me? We spoke at the coffee table earlier. Are you all right, you look terrible?'

The man looked up, his face grey and lined with worry.

'It's my wife,' he murmured, 'they think that she could lose the baby.'

Hart checked the time on the clock on the wall. It was hovering around 3.30 pm.

'Can I get you something, a tea or coffee perhaps?'

'Thank you, a tea with milk and two sugars would be nice.'

'No problem.'

Hart walked quickly over to Crosse and whispered in her ear. She immediately stood up and went over to the refreshments area where she prepared the tea and took it to him.

Hart crossed the room purposefully to the receptionist.

'I think the chap over there has just had some rather bad news and he's not looking too well at all. In fact, I think he may be on the verge of either passing out or vomiting.'

A look of concern filled her face. She could do "passing out", but "vomiting" was totally off her "can do" list.

'I'll get a nurse in here,' she said urgently, picking up one of the telephones.

With the receptionist engaged on the phone and the man in the care of Crosse, Hart took the opportunity to pass behind the reception station un-noticed into the additional waiting area of the consulting rooms, "backstage", quickly looking for somewhere that he could remain as inconspicuous as possible. This room, or the "Distressed Room" to the unit staff, although less ostentatious than the room he had just left, nevertheless, was furnished quite similarly. Hart quickly picked out a particularly secluded seat at the far end of the room with good vision of the consulting room doors and sat down carefully scanning all around him. As he screwed up his eyes in concentration, he saw a light behind the section of frosted glass in one of the doors and heard voices coming from beyond it. As stealthily as possible, he approached the door and placed an ear to it, taking care not to let his outline be seen through the glass, and listened. From within the room, he could pick out a whimpering female voice, which suddenly increased in volume and anxiety.

'It's gone, it's gone! My baby...!' This was followed by terrible, body wracking sobs.

Then came the consoling voice of another female in the room.

'Try not to be too upset, Mrs Simms. Come on, Janice, we now know the exact requirements for a positive outcome from an IVF for you. You can become pregnant again very soon, next time with a far greater chance of success with what we have learned this time. Isn't that right, Doctor...'

As she completed the doctor's name, Hart's gaze simultaneously read the same name on the consulting room door... 'Doctor Sumaris'.

'Janice, I'm going to get your husband back here. Is that OK?'

Hart leapt back to the far side of the room and took up a position behind a tall plant, at which point, the door he'd just been listening at swung open and a white uniformed nurse emerged accompanied by the sounds of Mrs Simms' heartbroken sobs. Within a very few moments, the nurse returned leading the very distraught-looking husband back into the room.

As Hart pondered his next move, a door further down the corridor abruptly opened and the porter from whom he had taken the light for the cigarette earlier emerged and made his way with some speed to Sumaris' room. Hart retreated further but the man was too intent on the job in hand to let his eyes stray away from his chosen path. He knocked twice on the door, which immediately opened just a crack. A crack wide enough, however, to admit an article that Hart was unable to make out. As the porter turned and retraced his steps, Hart was able to see that what he had been handed was a grey cardboard kidney dish covered with an inverted version of the same. As the porter disappeared through the door from which he had made his first entry, on impulse Hart made to follow him.

'Shit!'

The door was locked, entry beyond possible only by using an appropriate swipe card.

'What now? ... Of course!'

He turned and made for the outer reception area where he'd left Crosse. His rationale was that the porter would probably have to return with the carton to the histology lab, where its contents would have to be dealt with in some way. As he re-entered the reception, Crosse was in conversation with the young woman behind the desk, but broke off as he approached them.

'Are you feeling better now?'

She winked as she asked him the question. Then addressing the receptionist, 'He looked terrible a few moments ago, almost as bad as that other gentleman.'

The telephone range and the receptionist spoke monosyllabically to the caller.

'Yes...yes...OK...right...bye,' and then she turned her gaze and beaming smile upon Crosse and Hart.

'I'm really dreadfully sorry but there has been an unexpected emergency back there and Doctor Sumaris will have to cancel your appointment for today. There simply is no way that the doctor will be able to meet you I'm afraid.'

'No problem, we will check our diaries and call you tomorrow.'

The couple turned round and Hart promptly ushered Crosse by the arm to the exit.

'Unexpected my arse! I think they must run a bloody acting school here as well...and a pretty bad one at that.'

They pushed open the door and stood momentarily in the corridor.

'What's going on, Max?'

'The lady back there has just lost her baby, Vicky. And right on the time accorded by our two porter friends earlier.'

'Jesus!'

'I've just seen one of the porters pick up something from the unit and dash off with it. I tried to follow him but couldn't get through the security door. My guess is that he has taken it back to the lab. I'm going back to the lab, the way we went earlier, and see what I can see.'

'Why don't you take this?'

Crosse removed the white lab coat she had brought with her from her bag.

'I'll carry it just in case I can use it, but that porter guy knows I'm only a visitor so it would look odd if I suddenly turned up "in uniform", unless you've a false beard and glasses in there too that is? You go back to the car and wait for me there.'

'You won't have to say that twice. You be careful now and I'll see you soon.'

'I should be out in thirty minutes tops.'

Chapter 27

Hart proceeded with some speed to the corridor area which would give him access to the various divisions of pathology that he was after. He didn't want to spend a moment longer than was absolutely necessary here now.

The histology section was his best guess as the destination of the returning porter from the fertility suite and he headed directly there. As he followed the pathology signs, it dawned on him that his trek would more likely as not be pointless, as once again the rooms would be guarded by the swipe card entry mechanism he had encountered earlier and despite his increasingly nervous state, a feeling of premature disappointment welled up inside him. Suddenly, the "Histopathology Department" door loomed up, and as he had anticipated, the door was equipped with a swipe-card mechanism.

'Shit!'

But his eyes were diverted away from the door to a second door further along the corridor. This door bore the sign "Specimen Reception/Preparation" and he suddenly remembered it from their first foray along the corridors. As he approached it, he could just see through its semi-opaque windowpane, the profile of the porter he had followed. The man turned and moved deeper into the room working at something that Hart was unable to make out from this distance and angle of vision, and then he exited through another door at the back of the room. As Hart was about to deliver another semi-audible expletive, he noticed that this outer door on his side, unlike the other doors, carried no security lock.

With the room, temporally at least, devoid of people, he felt reasonably safe to quietly enter. He rolled up the lab coat he had been carrying on his shoulder, stuffed it inside his jacket, and gingerly opened the door. He quickly traversed the room and peered carefully through the window of the second door, checking that his quarry was not returning, then feeling slightly more at ease looked around, taking in as much as his limited time allowed. There were free-standing refrigerators and deep-freezes at various points around the walls and the spaces between them were bridged with benching. The benches contained various items for blood sample preparation, including centrifuges, pipettes, empty sample tubes and a series of bottles of chemicals no doubt required for specific treatments of specimens for various assays. On one wall was a large system of wooden pigeonholes labelled with the names of various hospital wards, no doubt the repository of blood and urine specimens together with their accompanying test request cards.

'Bingo!'

His eyes lighted on what appeared to be the grey cardboard kidney-shaped bowls, one seated on the other, previously picked up by the porter in the unit. With another quick look through the door to confirm his safety, he approached the containers, gently flipped off the upper one and peered inside. Empty!

Suddenly there was a noise behind him and a female voice.

'Excuse me.'

His heart stopped beating! A nurse had entered the small room through the same door as he himself had some minutes earlier. He turned and smiled at the young nurse standing there, who blushed and continued,

'I was told to drop these specimens off here,' she held up a large tray, 'have I come to the right place?'

'Yes, that's fine. If you leave them with me, I'll sort them out.' He managed a smile back.

The nurse handed him the tray of samples and exited the still partly open door.

'Bye then.'

'Bye, thanks.'

His response was a hoarse whisper. He had to move quickly and get out of there.

He placed the tray on the bench and once again peered through the window into the room beyond. This time, as he looked, the porter came into view and Hart involuntarily shrank back. But there was no need for panic, for the man was too intent on the process he was performing to notice any other goings-on. He was now wearing thick insulated gauntlets on his hands, in one of which he held what Hart was able from his hospital days to identify as a specimen transportation box, and in the other a metal bowl. The bowl was apparently steaming, but its contents weren't hot, they were cold, very cold. It was in fact dry ice, used for maintaining constantly low temperatures for sensitive or delicate specimens during transportation. The porter rummaged in the box, ensuring the specimen was lying in the correct position and then having checked that his protective gloves were nice and tight, proceeded to pack the dry ice around it. The procedure that was taking place was crystal clear now to Hart. The recently aborted foetus collected by the porter was now being prepared and packed in dry ice for transportation elsewhere. But to where? Although desperate to escape from this place, Hart could not consider doing so until he was sure of where this specimen was being sent for the next stage of whatever process it was destined for. However, he noted with some despair that the completed package was now being placed by the porter into a section within the inner room which was clearly an outgoing specimen pick-up area. Whoever was collecting the box would have to ask for it directly from someone inside that room…a room he had no access to.

That was it then. He had gone as far as he could. All he could do now was to return to Crosse in her car and think of some quick strategy by which they might learn the destination of the box, or should he stay on here longer? The decision was instantly made for him, for as he looked up the porter was just feet from the door and on his way out having left the specimen at the collection point. Not to leave now would mean his being exposed, so Hart had no option but to beat a hasty retreat from the room back to Crosse, waiting in the car park. As he approached her rust-red car, he checked his watch. He had been inside the laboratory areas for forty minutes!

Chapter 28

Seated in her car, Crosse was giving birth to her third set of kittens. Forty minutes! What should she do if Hart failed to turn up? Go back inside, call the police…what? This chain of thought was thankfully broken as she saw him emerge from the reception and make his way towards her car. Her high anxiety instantly turned to anger as the smiling Hart climbed inside.

'Where the hell have you been? I've been worried sick!'

'Whoaaa, hold on a minute while I get my breath back! Now then…'

Hart related the whole of his story up until the time he left the specimen preparation area with the packaged specimen, carefully packed in dry ice, waiting on the other side of the inaccessible door.

'So there we have it. The specimen is sitting waiting, obviously to be picked up, but by who and for why we don't know.'

'What next then? We can't just leave things in the air like this.'

Crosse was impatient now. With so much done and so much adrenalin spent, she couldn't face the prospect of returning to Williams with the final piece of the Paddocks jigsaw missing. They had witnessed a tragic event in the fertility unit just moments after Hart had overheard two porters talking about "some action" that afternoon. Furthermore, one of the porters had been summoned to the unit to collect a specimen almost to the minute of the time Hart had previously heard them discuss. However, whilst much of the knowledge they had gleaned that day was only circumstantial, for example the stories of other patients' experiences related to Hart by the patient's husband, details of the processing and collection of the specimen could be actual hard evidence.

As they sat in silence pondering the situation, their attention was drawn to the sound of wheels spinning on the gravel drive leading to the rear of the hospital building. As they looked, an orange van sped past them and out of sight.

'Bloody hell! Look at that!' Hart pointed at the disappearing rear end of the van.

'What? It's just an orange van.'

'Is it buggery,' Hart replied excitedly. 'Didn't you see the writing on the side of it?'

'No, I was too busy looking where the gravel was flying. It chips the car bodywork paint really easily you know.'

'Jesus Christ, Vicky! The van had WED on the side in huge black letters.'

'So?'

'So...sod the rust bucket! WED is Worldwide Express Delivery! Don't you see? The van has come to collect the package and the driver is late. That's why he's in such a hurry.'

Hart opened the car door and stepped out.

'What are you going to do?'

'I'm going to follow him and try and get the address from that package. Give me a pen and paper!'

Crosse swiftly gave him what he wanted, then he pulled on the white lab coat, put the pen and paper in his pocket and then broke into a run in the direction taken by the WED van. As he turned the corner, he saw the van up ahead. It had slowed and was now configuring a tight U-turn, presumably in readiness for a rapid departure. As the driver left his cab and approached the unit door, Hart returned to greyhound mode and partially hidden by ornamental bushes, sprinted unseen up to the door which was now still slowly closing from the driver's entry. Another few seconds later and Hart would have been locked out, once again. The lock on this door was operated from inside. Entry was by identification via an intercom set into the wall, but no identification was necessary for him as he slipped through the diminishing crack of the closing door. He straightened his white coat, buttoned it and proceeded at a more suitably dignified pace down the corridor, following the signs for "Pathology Specimen Reception".

He stopped abruptly at the sound of voices ahead, before slowly edging his way forward once more. He peered around the corner of a turn off in the corridor, where the voices were coming from, and his pulse quickened. There was his "friend", the porter handing over the easily identifiable box to the uniformed WED driver. Signatures were exchanged by the two men on their respective clipboards and with a grunt the porter turned and moved back to the door to the laboratory area, but then turned and shouted to the retreating driver,

'And next time try to be on bloody time, will you, or I'll start using a different courier!'

The driver raised an apologetic hand and headed past Hart to the door he'd recently entered by. Hart's mind was racing.

What to do? What to do?

The driver was out of the building and back in his van before any inspiration came to him. Then suddenly he had it! He spun on his heels and darted to the exit, which he sprung open using the rapid release mechanics, passwords, swipe cards or codes being necessary only for entry to the building. As he emerged into the waning sunlight, he was aware that the van driver had started the van's engine and was going through his Le Mans wheel-spinning routine prior to lift off, music blasting out of his open window. With a rush, Hart launched himself in front of the orange blur waving the driver to stop, which indeed he had to do or else run completely over him. As the van skidded to a halt with Hart pressed closely up against its front, the incredulous driver leaned out of his window and at some considerable level above the dulcet tones of Mick Jagger shouted,

'You fucking idiot! What the bloody hell is going on? I could have killed you!'

Instead, he killed the music and Jagger's voice disappeared down into the radio's speakers.

Hart pushed himself away from the van and smiling went round to the open window where he met the blazing angry glare of the red-faced driver.

'Sorry about that,' he gasped, 'bit of an emergency I'm afraid. I'm Doctor Halle from the unit… That's my package in that box you have there. I think I may have cocked up the address on it.'

The driver's face had returned to its original unhealthy pallor and in a somewhat apologetic tone of voice said,

'Not worth dying for though, mate. Here have a look and check it out, I can't afford to make any more mistakes with this delivery job.'

He reached back and flipping open the transport box, lifted out the object of Hart's desires. He swung the medium sized package into the eagerly waiting hands of Hart who stared long and hard at the delivery address.

'Come on, mate, is it bloody right or wrong? I've got a couple of more pick-ups to do yet today.'

Eventually Hart responded, trying hard to take the address to mind.

'Yes, it's correct after all. Thanks anyway…better safe than sorry though, eh?'

He handed the package back to the impatient-looking driver.

'Right. Can I go now then?'

'Yes of course. Have a safe journey.'

The driver hit the van's gas and the radio volume control at about the same time. As sharp gravel sprayed up, stinging Hart's leg, the van lurched away, ironically now to the blaring radio tune of "Bat Out of Hell". Hart removed the notebook from his white coat pocket and scribbled a reasonable facsimile of the correct address onto the empty page:

Prof. Doctor. Gerhard Roscher Schmoller Institute
Greifswald
Walther-Rathenau-Strausse 477
17487 Greifswald
Germany

'Perfect!'

He was elated, but suddenly struck with an overwhelming urge to leave this place. He hurried back to Crosse's car and scrambled inside, fighting his way out of the lab coat and shouting happily,

'Got it! Let's vamoose, amigo…and bloody quickly please!'

Crosse did quite a fair impersonation of the orange van as she urged her almost terminally ailing vehicle to kick up the gravel and speed towards the car park exit. Free again at last!

Chapter 29

As Crosse steered the "rust bucket" back to sanity, well Nottingham at least, Hart sat and smiled.

'For God's sake come on then, Max, don't just sit there grinning like a bloody Cheshire cat, what have you discovered?'

'Well, basically, I have found out where the specimen is being sent to. The package is now on its way, by WED courier to a place called Greifswald in Germany, probably for further or final processing.'

'Never heard of the place.'

'Oh I have. In fact I've been there on several occasions. It's a town on the Baltic coast of what was East Germany, close to Poland. I also now have a theory of what might be at the bottom of all this.'

Before he could continue, Crosse butted in,

'Stem cell harvesting for stem cell research?'

'Exactly.'

'Or some stem cell derivative at least,' Hart added. 'We will have to think carefully about how to advise him on his next steps, for clearly he will want to pursue this matter with even greater energy now. Another consideration of course is that this is no longer solely an issue within the UK. The fact that the package is now speeding to Germany would indicate that this is an international issue. It could even be a global issue.'

'Look, Max, he will want to know straightaway, so I think we should go for it and deal with whatever reaction he has as best we can. One thing's for sure, I want off this case totally after today even though I'm really fond of him.'

'OK, driver, let's do it, and don't spare the horses, or in the case of this car, I guess that "don't spare the donkey" would be more appropriate!'

Chapter 30

The solemnity of the man's evening ritual with the red wine from his family's place of origin was irrevocably disturbed by the trill of his personal cellular phone from inside his green velvet smoking jacket. Ordinarily, he would have been angered by the disruption of this lone personal ceremony, but this was his own very private telephone, the number of which was known to only three other people, one of whom had already telephoned early that morning, and he knew for sure that the male Italian voice he would hear this time would bear important news. He pressed the button to receive the call.

'*Pronto.*'

'*Ciao*, it is I.'

The voice, coming from Rome, was faint and slightly distorted

'I have news for you.'

'Tell me.'

He could tell from the tone of his contact's distant voice that this was not going to be the bad news from the Vatican that he had been half-expecting, but praying against. The distant voice continued,

'I have three things to tell you, but I need to be very quick and then I must go. First, his Holiness the Pope is actually now improving in health slightly. Second, I have been in touch briefly with our Church in Africa. The brother I spoke to confirmed that it has emerged since his meeting with other members of the Church Council there and governmental officials, that the building program will be approved to proceed immediately. With that, permission will follow without doubt for the approval and use of your company's medications extensively throughout the country, bypassing many of the usual bureaucratic committees. Included in this approval will be a general permission to proceed with the battery of clinical trials your people have presented to the health authorities at the major hospitals, including our own missionary hospitals of course. There does not seem to be any limits on which types of drugs may be trialled there and I think, therefore, that it is safe to conclude that you have la carta bianca for the use of your company's current licensed pharmaceuticals and importantly for the study of your new drugs in very early phase clinical trials. There will be clearly no shortage of available patients for these. My last news is that the Pope has been discussing Pietro at length with some of our senior brothers here in glowing terms and certainly Pietro is now seen as a bright guiding light in this new generation of young cardinals. This is also very important for it makes him a very well supported and credible candidate now.'

'*Bravissimo*, that really is excellent news! Really excellent news! *Grazie mille* for this and of course for the great work you are doing on our behalf.'

'No problem my friend. *Ciao. Ciao*, my dear friend.'

'*Ciao mio caro amico.*'

There was a distant click and the line went dead. The ecstatic gentleman returned the phone to his pocket and leaned back in his chair. Such wonderful news! He reached for his glass and raised it, offering a silent toast to his favourite personal saint and took a large gulp of the wine.

'Ecstasy indeed.'

As he savoured the wine, he considered his two most recent calls. This latter call from Rome had been very important indeed, but for different reasons to the earlier one. His earlier call had been from a person who was in total contrast to his friend in the Vatican. That young lady was the fire to his Vatican contact's ice. The "fire" was the young and very beautiful Claudia Volpe.

Chapter 31

As Crosse pulled up on Williams' drive, his haggard face was instantly evident to the pair in the car framed in the downstairs sitting room window and before they had even the time to release their seat belts, Williams was out of the house and onto the drive eagerly opening Crosse's door.

Williams ushered them inside the house and into the room where they had first come together. It was Hart who kicked off and led the feedback session, firstly asking Williams to hold back on too many questions until they had completed their report. Then, over the next forty-five minutes, Hart went through the day's events in detail with Crosse filling in any gaps and adding to it details of her own personal activities during Hart's absences. True to his word, Williams kept his questions to a minimum as Hart and Crosse proceeded, but his face became grimmer and grimmer as Hart approached the finale.

As Hart finally completed his account, Williams stared at the floor, then suddenly leaping to his feet and striking the palm of his hand with his clenched fist he cried out,

'I knew it! I just knew it! The bastards! It was so obvious that something was going on.'

He paused briefly and then, staring at Hart, in almost a whisper said,

'What type of research will the foetuses be used for do you think? Who could be behind all this?'

Hart glanced at the uncomfortable-looking Crosse. There was no way she could respond to this, even if she knew the answers.

'Ah, well, in for a penny… Vicky and I talked briefly about this on the way back here, Denis. It looks like, well at least this specimen today, is being sent to a place in Germany. Really what is done there we can only guess, but we think it could involve stem cells.'

'Of course!'

Williams sat down heavily in his chair, where his white skeletal fingers fiercely gripped the chair arms.

Hart continued,

'Well, it may be stem cell research, or it could be that specimens are being regenerated directly into some form of direct treatment or medication for conditions that we'll go into later. It could be both of course. This place in Germany that we've mentioned might be where all the necessary processing is occurring, or it might only be a sort of staging post where the specimens are appropriately treated in some way before being sent off elsewhere. That way it would certainly help cover their tracks from the UK, if not actually covering them completely. But listen, VC is an immunologist. Come on, girl, and help me out here!'

Williams' sad eyes met those of Crosse.

'Please, Vicky, I know nothing about stem cells other that what I read in the tabloids occasionally.'

'OK, Denis. Where shall I start?'

The question was rhetorical, for Crosse had presented on this subject many times before to medical students and Williams did have a distant medical background. She cleared her throat and went into "best presentation mode".

'Although stem cell related medicine still smacks of the stuff of science fiction, especially in the tabloid press, there are good theoretical and proven experimental grounds for concluding that these cells are the root of all cures for all diseases, not to mention their potential as a source of eternal youth! Some recently published research has indicated that there could be as much value in cells obtained from the amniotic fluid surrounding the foetus whilst it's still in the womb, but for now, embryonic stem cell research remains at the cutting edge, with great expectations for these treatments. There are still many bodies of course, including governments and especially the church, who see the whole stem cell concept not so much as a moral maze, but more of a totally amoral philosophy.

However, even detractors from stem cell research would likely agree that this area of scientific investigation could indeed potentially lead to "miracle cures" for diseases which at present we can only hope to control the symptoms of.

Take Parkinson's disease for example. This is a disease with no known cure, the current treatment being aimed solely at controlling the disease symptoms. Public awareness of the condition, with its very visible emotive symptoms, has increased greatly through the press coverage of the long list of famous people who have suffered from it. There is certainly no class discrimination when it comes to Parkinson's patients, who range from ordinary folk in the street to members of various royal families, film stars, politicians and high-ranking members of the church.'

Williams added his own contribution,

'Yes, I remember a couple of film actors who have it and weren't Yasser Arafat and Pope John Paul also fellow sufferers?'

'Indeed they were. It has been a very hot potato for some time now, especially in the realms of politics. In August 2001, somewhat surprisingly to many onlookers, the then President George W Bush announced that federal funds could actually be awarded for researching human embryonic stem cells. Not so surprisingly, the church at large, in all its varieties and flavours, has very divergent views on it. It is unlikely that there will ever be a general consensus on the subject as opinions and ideas are in a state of constant flux.'

'The taking of unborn foetuses for research has to be totally and unquestionably immoral and illegal! Stuff the medical reasons for it!'

'Relax, Denis. Let's hear the whole story before we get totally pissed off with it. The work Vicky is talking about is, in the main, carried out within the very strict confines of existing laws in licensed laboratories, which will have full regulatory approvals for the work.'

'The thing is, as Max has just said, research of this nature is tightly controlled and is not illegal under those prescribed conditions with written informed consent being obtained from contributors of foetal material where necessary. That is from parents. Probably two in every thousand of the population suffer from Parkinson's and stem cell research would appear to be able to promise successful treatment for it eventually. There are many other diseases though that could potentially benefit from some form of stem cell treatment. There's Alzheimer's, spinal cord injury, stroke, heart disease, diabetes, osteoarthritis, rheumatoid arthritis, burns even. The list of potentially treatable diseases and conditions is almost limitless.'

'And all of these use cells from embryos?'

'No not all. I mentioned amniotic fluid earlier, but stem cells can be derived from other sources also, for example from adult cells and from umbilical cords and human placentas that are discarded after birth.'

'So why then are these bastards killing live foetuses?'

'However, Denis, despite these other sources of stem cells, those derived from embryos seem to have unique potential above all other sources. The reason for this is that these particular cells have the potential to develop in all tissues of the body so that their areas of influence are very wide and, therefore, they have the possibility to have an effect on all the diseases I've mentioned. However, having said all of that, this miracle of cures has not yet lived up to early expectations. Who knows why? Perhaps those initial expectations were too great? Perhaps too many desperate people were hoping for a miracle? That said, embryonic stem cell research and treatment still offers great promise and depending upon one's particular outlook, great perils.'

'Tell me about the market for this type of treatment, it must be potentially huge. Do you have any idea what it might be worth to the pharmaceutical industry? Also, what about the legality of it? Surely, there has to be some illegalities in the system?'

Williams' question was one for Hart.

'There is obviously a fantastic commercial market for successful pharmaceutical companies in this field. Off the top of my head, I would guess that the neurology market alone is worth in excess of ten billion dollars a year. As with all research, however, much of this research is very expensive.'

Williams smiled and nodded cynically.

'You may smile, Denis, but I can tell you that it currently takes something in the order of two billion dollars to get a drug to the market place successfully, and remember that only one in ten candidate drugs gets anywhere near obtaining a license. In fact, I'm rather out-of-date now with those data, but from my experiences at World, I could guess that that the success figure has shrunk to almost one in one hundred by now! Of course, in this big bad commercial world of investments and investors, pharmaceutical companies also have to ensure that their investors, or shareholders, receive what they commonly call "an equitable return on their investment". Before a drug can turn a penny of profit, all this expense has to be met. Consider also that these drugs only have a limited patency life of twenty years, probably eight years of which is lost in the clinical research of their efficacy, their activity dose ranges, adverse events and the general toxicology of the compounds and lots more things besides, after which any other company so desiring can make and sell their own generic varieties of them. You can estimate roughly, therefore, that a company only has some twelve or so years, maybe less, in which to recoup all the research costs, make a profit and provide acceptable returns to their investors.

'Now one obvious question around this research is, "is there a great enough supply of embryonic material to support all the on-going and planned programs?" If the answer is "no", which is likely, then we should ask how this shortfall is being met. Certainly not legally I would bet. A relatively small volume of research material could be derived theoretically from such activities that we possibly now suspect at the Paddocks, but importantly can't currently absolutely confirm, but something on a far greater scale would be necessary to support the level of research that I suspect is ongoing worldwide at present. Where do you think the raw material is coming from, Vicky…the third world?'

'I wouldn't think so. Not for direct treatment at least, for whatever treatments are being given they must surely require stringently controlled processes, not to mention obtaining adequate quality levels of the materials themselves, even though they might be operating illegally.'

It was Hart's turn to smile cynically now.

'You're wrong actually, Vicky. In this business, unscrupulous companies will attempt to get away with whatever they can, especially if there are huge dollar signs flashing over their project.'

'OK, Denis, I'll wrap this up now.'

'No, please, Vicky, finish what you started. Tell me how these cells work, I'm interested. I feel I've a vested interest in them in fact.'

He smiled a wry smile. Hart too smiled.

Crosse finished by lecturing him on the current knowledge of the cells' modes of action, most of which clearly went over Williams' head.

'So where does this fit in with the Paddocks and the activities we think are going on there. It was just my confident supposition before, but I'm bloody certain now that things there are very wrong. Do we all agree…?'

Hart responded carefully.

'It would seem to me personally, from what you and others at the clinic have told us and from what we *thought* we witnessed, that all is not as it should be there. Certainly, it needs some more formal investigation by the appropriate authorities.'

Crosse seemed to nod in agreement.

'Hang on then,' Williams continued, 'let's just finish this feedback and then you can tell me what to do next.'

Hart began to protest; he was not in a position to answer the "what to do next" question. Vicky had done really well that afternoon buoyed up by himself, but he had counted at least one half a dozen occasions when she had asked the same question, "what do we do next", or "what do we do now" and to be honest, he had been winging it, making it up as he went along using the famous "brass neck". However, his words were drowned out as Williams went on.

'Finish the story please, Max. What do you think happens after the tissue has been stolen?'

'Well, there's not a lot I can add really, but what I would say, and Vicky please correct me if I'm wrong, the cells have to be grown or cultured. The foetal tissue has to be transported to a suitable laboratory if one is not present at the source, maintained in suitable conditions such as temperature et cetera, otherwise the cells, which by the way are often referred to as "regeneration seeds", will deteriorate and beak down. Usually, I would expect that a temperature as low as minus seventy degrees Celsius would be necessary for this type of tissue.'

He glanced at Crosse who nodded affirmation.

'It goes without saying that it is not possible to extract stem cells from living embryos without first destroying them. Legally stem cells can be generated from human embryos which have been created in the lab, usually through in-vitro fertilisation.'

Williams was nodding. This was the process Ruth and he had been through at the Paddocks. For every line of explanation, he had another question,

'I was wondering where one could draw the line between bona fide and illegal research, but it's now patently obvious to me that these people are committing murder. But how do the regulators and guidelines cover this type of work? How do authorities know that these institutions are sticking to the rules? What about the church's opinions on this?'

Crosse beat Hart to the punch by a spilt second.

'Companies are bound by law to have all such research approved by suitable ethics committees. These companies obtain their human tissue from fully informed and consented donors, but that tissue is the in-vitro fertilised product, placental or from amniotic fluid. I'm not sure what happens outside of the UK, but here companies must follow the Polkinhome report, which describes exactly how human foetal tissue may be obtained and used. As for the church, Max covered this earlier, but the Catholic Church would seem to hold the firmest views on this. The Vatican considers all research using stem cells from human embryos morally unacceptable, a view shared to different degrees across most other religious denominations.'

There was a slight pause and then Williams spoke again,

'Thank you very much, both of you. I think I now have a fairly full picture of the events and of the issues around them. So what do I have to do now to nail the bastards, go to the toothless authorities?'

Hart took up Williams' question.

'You could report all of this to the authorities, Denis, but I'm not sure that it would get you much closer to a final resolution. This may well be an international organisation, and closing the unit for example at the Paddocks would be like taking a wilting flower off a vigorously growing bush.'

'But both you and Vicky have been there and seen it—'

'Look,' Hart interrupted, 'if you did go to the authorities, and I'm not really sure who exactly these would be, letters would be sent, phone calls made, appointments kept and the clinic visited, but following the first contact, the clinic would make damn sure that there would be no evidence come any enquiry. There's no way in which a proper legal visit could be made covertly as we did, so when a visit *was* orchestrated, you can bet you're your boots that everything would be in apple-pie order.'

'But what about the press? I could go to them.'

Williams had very quickly moved from being relieved to being desperate once again.

'I'm sorry, Denis, but I don't think the press would be interested in this either. It would be too difficult. VC and I were really very fortunate to be able to penetrate the place and come away with what we did. You can imagine what would happen if the press blundered in, the alarm bells would be heard on the moon.'

'But what can I do? I *must* put a stop to this somehow!'

Crosse left her chair and moved across the room to Williams and put a hand on his shoulder.

'I don't know, Denis. I really don't know.'

Hart suddenly realised that he was under the gaze of two pairs of tearful eyes. It was clear that both Crosse and Williams were now tentatively looking at him to suggest some way forward. Finally he spoke,

'I don't think the ultimate conclusion to this business lies here in the UK and I don't really think that there is anything else we could pursue here. At present, any reporting by us of the events we have witnessed, or of the information you have collected, Denis, would more likely than not only cause the perpetrators to shut up shop. At least for the time being anyway. With the information we have, it would be in my opinion at least, virtually impossible for any authorities to penetrate the goings on and emerge with any concrete evidence, no matter how great their suspicions might be. What is needed is harder and more detailed evidence. I think there is one more step we can take, or at least that I can take... and that is pay a visit to the specimen's destination.'

'To Germany you mean?'

Crosse was incredulous at the suggestion.

'Exactly. To the place indicated on the courier invoice where the next stage is carried out. This could be the further treatment and extraction of these "generation seeds" or it might indeed be where some form of actual direct patient treatment is carried out. In any case, if we don't follow it up, we will probably never know.'

'Surely, you're not suggesting you should go to Germany, are you, Max? But if indeed you were, then I would be very happy to finance whatever you feel is necessary, but in no way do I want you to put yourself in any danger.'

Crosse looked on in stunned silence.

'There would be no danger I'm sure, Denis, and after all, I do have time on my hands to follow this up for you. Also, I actually know this town of Greifswald slightly. I've been there on several occasions before during a short spell with another former pharmaceutical giant. More importantly though, I have an old friend in Munich who travelled with me there on those occasions and who would, I'm sure, be very pleased to see me again.'

He paused momentarily,

'But being temporally unemployed, I would unfortunately have to take you up on your offer for the costs of travel, accommodation and food, Denis.'

Williams was fit to burst with enthusiasm.

'Absolutely no problem, I'll sort out everything. Max, I'm so grateful, what can I say? I never expected this.'

'Me neither!'

Finally Crosse spoke, her words heavy with irony,

'You didn't mention any of this during our discussions in the car on our way here!'

'No, VC, it was plan B. I hardly knew it myself at that time, but look folks, if I'm going to do this trip, then let's discuss it properly. First of all, I go alone.'

He paused waiting for the dissention. None arrived!

'What you can do to help me, VC, is to get your hands upon all the latest info on this stem cell stuff, publications, international meetings, leading pharmaceutical companies in the field et cetera, you know the sort of thing I mean. And I need it ASAP please. Secondly, Denis, you are going to have to provide me with the funding and some plastic means of payment, also ASAP.'

Williams didn't hesitate.

'No problem. I'll put a lump sum into your own bank account, and within a day or two, I will be able to let you have one of my company's credit cards.'

'Excellent. I'll get things rolling with my old German friend. Can we talk tomorrow and try and get this thing sorted by the end of the week?'

'Of course. Bloody marvellous! Thanks a million!'

'That's that sorted then. Come on, Vicky, let's go. If you could drop me at the Barnes' place, I've got some calls to make. I'll call you tomorrow, hopefully with a more detailed plan.'

'Max, I'm staggered. Out of the blue you decide to make this German jaunt. You must be crazy. You've no idea where this shot in the dark is going to lead… probably nowhere!'

'You're right, but to quote the late great George Harrison, "when you don't know where you're going, any road will take you there".'

Chapter 32

Within one week of the meeting at Williams' house, following his visit with Crosse to The Paddocks, Hart was seated in a cab on his way to Birmingham Airport.

In his carry-on bag, he had return flight tickets to Berlin's Tegel Airport and a printed e-mail confirmation for a two-night stay in the Quality Hotel, close to the airport, although he hoped that one night there would be enough. Things had certainly moved swiftly since he volunteered to take the investigation to the next level. A call to his old friend, Klaus Grille, in Munich, a contact from long gone days when working with a previous pharma company, had resulted in the decision for Hart to travel out to meet him not in Munich, but in Berlin where Grille had business that day.

The day before his departure, Crosse had called him and told him excitedly that she had remembered being sent, some weeks before, details of an upcoming stem cell symposium in Venice, Italy. The early program notification had she thought, indicated that most of the leading companies pursuing research in the field would be there sponsoring the events, and there was an excellent looking preliminary scientific program listing presentations by many of the leading lights on the subject. Hart had told her to get the meeting details and costs and to run them past Williams. In the event of his German trip revealing any additional valuable evidence, a visit to the Italian symposium might add some tasty icing to this increasingly interesting cake.

Three hours after leaving Nottingham, he was belted into his preferred aisle seat on board the Lufthansa flight bound for Tegel Airport in Berlin. Two hours later, as the plane made its final approach to Tegel Airport, having gone through the details of the business numerous times, he was content that he now had the events of the case clear in his mind, sorted into a mental list of the next steps that were necessary to bring his activities in this depressing saga to a final close.

As he folded his newspaper and wedged it into the elasticated pocket in the back of the seat in front of him, he failed to notice a short paragraph in the 'World News Section'. There he would have read of the recent tragic, but somewhat ironic, death of a Roman Catholic priest killed outright in an explosion in a reclaimed former minefield in Northwestern Vietnam on the eve of his much publicised ceremonial blessing of the now "clean area".

With the plane finally at rest at the terminal building, he retrieved his hand luggage from the overhead compartment and made his way off the plane, warming at the thought of meeting his ex-colleague and friend Grille once again.

Grille was a man in late middle age. A serial adulterer, he was to Hart's knowledge now with his fourth wife at least, his rather ordinary looks and gentle manner giving no hint of the fire which clearly burned within him. When Hart had been based in the UK in his former company, Grille had been his German contact and their friendship had blossomed quickly during Hart's regular six-weekly visits to Munich and hospitals further afield, where they were taking part in Hart's particular German clinical trial projects. Site visits with Grille from Munich to Berlin, Cologne, Manheim and yes, Greifswald, were a common occurrence, which Hart enjoyed immensely.

He felt sure that following his appraising Grille of the situation, a visit to Greifswald would be almost certain, but they would first meet that night and discuss the issues in more detail. One thing was for certain, Grille would be only too pleased to accommodate Hart's need for information and as he was still working with clinics within the Greifswald area, he would undoubtedly be able to manufacture a suitable case for a visit there on business

Once free of the airport building, Hart took the almost embarrassingly short taxi ride in the large cream coloured Mercedes from the airport to the Quality Hotel on Hollander Strasse.

He checked in at the art deco fronted Quality Hotel and was immediately given a message from Grille, "Arriving 18.00 hours, see you in the bar at 18.15".

Hart smiled. Beer was always very high on Grille's list of priorities no matter what the agenda or circumstances.

At a few minutes past 6.00 pm Hart, freshly showered, was propping up the hotel bar drawing on his second medium-sized light beer when a hand descended heavily upon his shoulder, causing a quantity of the "amber nectar" to spill over the side of the glass.

'Make mine a very big one, please Max!'

'They only serve beer here, Klaus. You'll have to go into town for what *you're* after!'

Chapter 33

After an hour rooting around the various untidy drawers in the shared office where she worked at the QMC in Nottingham, Crosse finally laid her hands upon the Italian stem cell conference details. The meeting was indeed scheduled for a Venice venue and had the impressive preliminary title of "Stem Cell Regenerative Medicine: Commercial Implications for the Pharmaceutical and Biotech Industries". A read of the advanced program confirmed that this would be perfect for their current needs. The program header read, "The most comprehensive stem cell meeting you will attend this year!" The full meeting was provisionally programmed to commence with a keynote address by Renee Hanotin, professor and director of the Program for Development and Regenerative Cell Biology, at the Pompidou Institute in Paris. This opener was followed by a series of presentations by medium to heavyweight academics and industrial scientific experts from all over the world. Topics included the harvesting of stem cells, latest advancements in the treatment of Parkinson's disease and applications in brain repair and spinal injury. Probably of greatest interest to Hart would be the list of sponsoring companies who were providing money for the meeting, but who in return had the chance to demonstrate their science and products at an extensive trade show running concurrently in an exhibition area in the same building. In addition, the more major companies had their own hospitality suites where suitable invitees from the scientific fraternity could be served with food and drink whilst being updated with the companies' latest publications and clinical study outcomes.

A quick scan down the alphabetical list of sponsors revealed the name she'd hoped for, the Roscher Institute, Greifswald, Germany. Another look down the list of presenters revealed that old man Gerhard Roscher himself was due to speak during one of the sessions. Better and better!

'Jesus, he must be about two hundred years old by now.'

With all the details in hand, Crosse returned to the "bleak house" that was the Williams residence and presented him with the printed information and costings. Without a single query, he took the bundle from her.

'Thanks, Vicky, I'll get my travel people to firm all this up for the two of you and make all travel and hotel arrangements. If Max returns empty-handed, we can always cancel.'

Chapter 34

Grille took Hart's hand in both of his own and shook it until Hart felt it might become unattached to his arm. His pleasure at meeting Hart after so much time was enormous, a feeling reciprocated entirely by the man with the numb arm. Grille and Hart had been a great team when working together on German clinical study projects and their totally opposite personalities and ethnically driven humours had resulted in some extraordinarily good times together, although much of Hart's humour had sailed some miles over Grille's head.

'So Klaus, it's great to see you again…and you look so well after all this time. Still married to number four? If so, she really seems to suit you?'

'Max, great to meet you too. You look just the same,' he lied, 'and yes, I am still married to Greta. I think she might finally be the one.'

'I should bloody hope so after all this time, here take this.'

The barman placed a large foaming Steiner of light beer on the bar, which Hart, with an effort, handed to Grille. They clinked glasses, uttered a simultaneous 'Cheers' and drank deeply.

Hart gave Grille time to take another large gulp before continuing,

'There's no restaurant in the hotel, Klaus, only this breakfast room cum bar, but there is an Italian restaurant just a few minutes' walk down the road. What do you say, we sit down here for an hour or so and then amble down to la Madonna del Castello" for dinner?'

'Ya perfect, Max. We have much to talk about.'

The next hour was fully taken with talk of the old times and times spent in between then and now, interrupted only by the barman who kept their throats and voices well lubricated by a constant flow of the excellent local beer. Grille was drinking litres to Hart's halves. Hart covered his demise with World with a dismissive, 'It was time for a change,' and eventually brought the reason for his visit into the conversation. It took him thirty minutes to describe the events up to his flight, including a graphic description of his visit with Crosse to the Paddocks after which the wide-eyed Grille nodded his head and blew out an extended beery breath.

'Max, this story is amazing.'

'The thing is, I believe that there is a strong possibility that live embryos are being removed or aborted from their mothers for their stem cells, probably at various places in the UK and then sent to this laboratory or whatever it is in Greifswald. Similar activities may be happening all over the globe as far as we know. It could be purely for research, or it might even be that research has moved on to actual early treatment regimes, I don't know.'

'Max, this is a terrible thing and if you are correct, a very dangerous game for you to be playing in …'

(*Shit! He's going to pull out. He's a lovely guy, but he was always timid and nervous and never ever prepared to take any risks. Bollocks!*)

'But,' Grille continued, 'we will make our visit to Greifswald tomorrow, no? I will show you this research place.'

Hart was amazed. 'Terrific!' Grille had come through.

'Max, I have seen this place during my visits there. The Gerhard Roscher Schmoller Institute is quite famous in that region, not only for respected research but for what you call, "the cutting edge treatments". But you must have a clear idea of what you need to find or do when you arrive there. It is no good just sitting in a car outside and watching. Tell me.'

'First, let me say thanks a million for the offer, Klaus. What I want and what I will probably be able to get are very different things. What I would like to take home with me is the knowledge as to whether or not this institute is the final destination for the embryos, or is it a possible staging post?'

Grille looked blankly at him.

'You know, an intermediate destination where the material might undergo further treatment before being passed on to a final treatment place? It seems clear to me from what you have said already that one of my questions is answered at least, in that both research and treatment happen there.'

Again, Hart felt that Grille might wobble and change his mind, but whatever the effect of Greta on his old friend, he was now made of far sterner stuff than before he had married her. Or perhaps it was the numerous litres of beer he had consumed that were bolstering his courage? In any case, Grille was resolute in his intent. He slapped the arm of the chair,

'Max, we will answer all your questions. Believe me!'

'I appreciate your sentiment, Klaus, but the problem will be that when we arrive, I will need, somehow, to get inside the institute. Will that be straightforward do you think?'

'Ah, that will be very difficult, Max. Probably impossible. You see all have to have permits to enter. There is even a special check-in entrance for patients, so it will not be possible for you to walk in like in a normal hospital for example. However my friend…'

'Come on then, you've got something up your sleeve, haven't you? What is it?'

Grille smiled and looked at the ceiling, milking his moment for all he was worth.

'Well, Max, you must have a special pass to enter the unit, that is for sure, but let me tell you for a moment about my wife's brother.'

'Ahh Jesus, Klaus, can't that wait?'

'No, listen to me for a moment and you will understand. My wife has a brother Ernst…' Hart's eyes rolled up in the direction of the ceiling with bored impatience, but Grille continued, '….who was diagnosed with cancer of the prostate, which caused much distress in the family, as you might imagine. Well, I was working with an oncology trial around that time and I was able to get Ernst enrolled through his local hospital onto the treatment arm of this new drug. In the end, it worked and he is now really well and working fine again.'

'That's really good news for you all, Klaus, but how does that help me with this little venture?'

'Well, Max, he now owes me a great favour.'

'Excellent! But, how can working in Munich be of any help here though?'

'Max, I never said he lived or worked in Munich. In fact, he lives and works in Greifswald!'

'Shit! I'm sorry, Klaus.'

'You will be even more sorry yet my friend, you see his job is as security officer. Security officer at the Roscher Institute! Is very good news now, ya?'

Hart's arms shot skyward and he punched the air, 'That's brilliant news! I can't believe it.'

'Please believe it. I have taken the liberty of already phoning him and he has agreed to meet us both tomorrow in the town…'

'Excellent!'

'… But it may be that he might need a small…inducement though. It depends on what he has to offer.'

'That will be no problem I'm sure, Klaus…as long as he doesn't ask for a new car or a house.'

'No, no for sure he won't. Come, Max, please, let's eat now I'm starving.'

The unlikely couple made their rather unsteady way to the Madonna del Castello restaurant where they dined very well on copious German-styled Italian food, Hart preferring to accompany his meal with an Italian Chianti, to the litre of beer chosen by Grille.

As they relaxed at the table after devouring the meal, Grille outlined the plans for the following morning's departure.

'We will leave the hotel at 06.00 hours…'

'Bloody hell, is that really necessary?'

'To continue, we will leave the hotel at 06.00. It is necessary to leave at this time as we will travel to Greifswald and back to Tegel for your flight home all in one day. I have an appointment in the hospital in Greifswald, the one where Ernst was treated in fact, to check on their progress in a current trial we are running there, sometime during the early afternoon. We will meet Ernst at mid-day in a small bar on the outskirts of the town where he will talk to you about the institute and clinic, where of course he works. Remember the tip though, eh?'

'No problem, Klaus.'

'So Max, listen please. It is important for him not to be seen talking to you or else he loses his job. The clinic is very sensitive about security and confidentiality. He will even have to get special permission to leave the place for lunch, as normally they must all eat on the premises. When you speak to Ernst, you will have to decide what you want and how much you want to know. I expect the "tip" will depend upon what extra you will need to know and to do further. For your cover, whatever you do, I have with me some extra folders containing information of my trial and study reports which you can carry. If anyone asks, you may say that you are from the UK seeing this important trial blah, blah. You can think of the rest to say.'

'You really have thought of everything Klaus and I'm really grateful. How do you think your relative will react to me getting access to the clinic?'

'Access? What, go in? I think only Ernst will know the answer to that. He might only want to talk about the place. There may not be any way for him to let you enter the clinic, it could be far too dangerous for him and his job, but we'll see.'

'OK, let's see what tomorrow brings then.'

Hart was sure he would need to gain some sort of access to the institute and Grille too believed that this would be what Hart would be keen to run past Ernst the next day, but for now, both men preferred that particular topic of the conversation to end there. The two went back to old times and old faces they had known until finally Grille checked his watch.

'Max, it is almost midnight. We must go to bed.'

'Bloody hell, Klaus, we've only just met! What sort of a boy do you take me for?'

'Ha, ha, always the joke, but tomorrow we must leave on time or else you will not take your evening flight. And that will be no joke, no?'

The "odd couple" returned to the hotel under a bright starlit sky and full moon. The air was still and there was no wind, but for sure somewhere a mighty storm was brewing.

Chapter 35

For once, Hart's "wake on demand biological clock" failed him and the harsh ring of his bedside phone shook him rudely from his slumbers.

'Jesus!'

He fumbled for the receiver in the darkness.

'Yes? Hello.'

'Max, come. You have over-slept and it is time to go.'

'Rubbish! I've been out for my usual early morning run. I'll be with you in five minutes when I've changed out of my running gear.'

He leapt out of bed and quickly took a shower and completed his other necessary ablutions. Outside, the dawn chorus of birds singing in perfect German seemed deafening. Luckily, he had decided upon what to wear for the visit to Greifswald and possibly the clinic, the night before and laid the clothes out on a chair. Within minutes, he was dressed in casual business jacket and trousers. He pushed his remaining clothes and his wash bag into his holdall and after quickly checking around the room for any left items, he exited and descended to the waiting Grille in the lobby below. It was now thirty minutes since the bell of the telephone had exploded in his head. Not bad.

'Come on, Max, come on!'

Grille was impatient to hit the road and forestall the inevitable battles with the early morning traffic.

'OK look, I'll check out at reception while you get me a coffee and a Danish from the buffet to take away. Is that OK, Klaus? Thanks!'

Five minutes later, he had checked out, cancelling his additional night, and was following Grille to the car park, coffee and a half of one Danish pastry in one hand and bag in his other hand. Grille found his black Audi A4 and opening the trunk, took Hart's bag, which he dumped unceremoniously beside his own and slammed down the lid. At last he smiled.

'Is good. Now we can concentrate on the journey and our meeting with Ernst. Take a seat please.'

He fastened his seat belt and when he had confirmed that Hart had done the same, he started the engine and carefully moved off. After a white knuckle ride through the streets, he finally hit the signs for the autobahn that would take them most of the way to Greifswald.

'Max, we want autobahn number 11 first and then route 109. Then we can relax and talk.'

'OK partner, there, there, go left, go left!'

'Oh shit! Sorry Max.'

The car veered to the left missing a bicycle by inches and touching the edge of the pavement as Grille squeezed between a van and a lamppost en route to the sign-posted autobahn. Eventually, they picked up route 109 and both of them visibly relaxed. The "Wacky Races" were over for now and they could cruise the road which would take them some 230 kilometres in a northeasterly direction away from Berlin, all the while hugging an imaginary line parallel to the Polish border some 40 kilometres to the east of them.

Grille was finally able to relax and talk.

'This mission you are on is a serious one and quite dangerous in potential Max, but we are good friends and I am happy to help you.'

'Thank you, Klaus, that's very kind, thank you so much. I shall be interested to hear what your brother-in-law has to say and how far he is prepared to go to help me when we meet him.'

'Well, he is no Einstein in intelligence, but he is clever in other ways...'

'Like in getting money?'

'The joke again, eh? No, he is alert enough to be wise to the comings and goings at the institute. Shit! Look at that car! But my big concern, Max, is you. You did well this morning not to be like the "sore thumb sticking out" with the clothes, but I am a little worried that you have no German at all.'

'Surely no problem that. I'm with you as a visitor from head office, so I'm not expected to know any German. The English only speak English you know.'

They both laughed and Hart once again closed his eyes thinking of the journey and the task ahead.

'I see there's been no improvement in the road surface, Klaus.'

He shouted over the noise of the tyres on the rough road surface.

'You are right, Max. If anything at all they are even worse now in parts.'

Conversation was almost impossible and so for the next hour and a half pleasantries were few and Hart sat back and tried to enjoy the view, but eventually the body parts, mechanical and human, had to be checked and reorganised and Grille shouted,

'Max. Would you like a sausage?'

After a brief pause, Hart shouted back,

'I thought I had told you last night, Klaus, that I was not that kind of boy!'

Grille considered this and then the pfennig finally dropped.

'Sometimes you are funny ha, ha, but more often you are funny in a strange way, Max. Is this a normal Anglo-Saxon humour or are you a little disturbed? Listen, there is a service area a few kilometres ahead at Pasewalk. I will stop there and you may decide what you want. I want at least a pee.'

In due course, Grille pulled the Audi into the car park at the rear of the café and whilst he took a pee and a sausage, Hart spent the time walking around the car flexing his arms and legs whilst taking in the view of the rest of the car park. Grille returned shortly with both hands full of sausages and cardboard cups of coffee and they both re-entered the car, where they dispatched the food with due haste.

'Now come on, Max, we still have some way to go and we meet Ernst in a couple of hours.'

Just over one and a half hours later, they were driving past the open fields on the outskirts of Greifswald. Hart was suddenly aware of a silence in their journey, almost like a sudden deafness. It wasn't deafness, however, but rather the sudden absence of road noise, for after all those miles of bone shaking, the rough road had finally given way to something approaching a decently smooth surface. To the far left, Hart could discern the higher steeples of the town's churches and then as they drew closer the Gothic, Renaissance and Baroque architectural styles which on previous visits he had so much admired. To the right was the huge non-Gothic nuclear power station which fed the town with its energy.

With a sudden lurch, the Audi made a late turn off the autobahn and onto a slip road.

'Shit! Sorry Max, I almost missed it. The inn where we meet Ernst is just ahead.'

The Audi sped along the slip road and made another sudden right turn in the direction of an inn straight out of Grimm's Fairy Tales in appearance, which suddenly loomed up at them and Grille swung the car into the car park where he stopped in a cloud of dust. Hart breathed a deep sigh. Whilst Grille had started the drive as a pale imitation of the great Michael Schumacher, he was obviously feeling more the part now, driving with more abandon than care and Hart was pleased that their journey was almost complete. Grille swung his head from side to side taking in the other cars in the parking area.

'We are here, but I am not yet seeing the car of Ernst. He will be here though, so let us wait inside and sample a little of the hospitality.'

He smiled at Hart who responded,

'That's the name of the famous beer here is it, Hospitality?'

It was clear that Grille was eager to wash down some of the journey's dust, or at least some of the dust he had just stirred up in braking to such an abrupt halt.

'Come, let's go inside and get a couple of beers. Ernst will be very nervous at meeting us so we must find a seat in a quiet area if possible. They are so strict at his work and he must, therefore, be very careful. That is why he suggested this out-of-the-way inn.'

They entered, Hart taking up a position behind Grille. The bar room was simple enough, with heavy beamed ceilings and walls, and with substantially built wooden tables and chairs spread casually around the room over the stone flagged floor. Apart from four what appeared to be farmers, seated together and involved in an animated conversation, the place was empty of clientele. Grille approached the bar and ordered two large light beers from the blonde, rosy-cheeked, buxom barmaid. Lapping the froth off the top of his selected drink, he ushered Hart to the farthest table from the farmers, where they sat and sipped their beers.

'Ah the beer is very good here, Max, yes?'

'Very good, but don't ask me to finish it. Jesus, I can barely lift it!'

Chapter 36

Peter Mondo had dined well that evening at his brother's home, and now the two of them sat feeling completely relaxed in deep leather armchairs close to a crackling log fire in Alberto's study, alias the "Cypress Room". It was a very traditional looking affair with all the usual paraphernalia of huge wooden desk and padded wooden swivel chair, but the difference was that all the major wooden items in the room were fashioned from wood from the Italian Cypress tree native to southern Italy. The cypress panelling of the walls was interrupted frequently by tall bookcases all made from the same variety of Mondo's favourite wood, (which brought back so many memories of his original birthplace) and all filled with leather bound books…which had remained unopened since their day of their delivery. But these were for decorative purposes only, as were the numerous original artist pictures of cypress filled landscapes and occasional hunting scenes, which lined the wall's spare spaces. The surface of the wooden floor was broken by the deposition of occasional Turkish rugs, the pattern in each rug telling an Ottoman story, which was totally lost on their current owner. The lights were subdued and the atmosphere wonderfully restful as both men sipped on their twenty-year-old Grappa and stared into the almost hypnotic dancing and flickering orange and red flames from the crackling logs in the fireplace. It was Albert Mondo who broke the silence.

'Pietro, this is a wonderful honour that the Pope has bestowed upon you. You should be very proud. Of course it goes without saying that we your family are overjoyed at your success in your chosen path.'

Peter Mondo smiled at his brother, older by some years.

'I am very happy at my elevation to Cardinal and yes, I have to say it, proud of the honour which I believe it brings to our historic family name.'

'Bravo Pietro. Bravo. Do you have any plans as to what you want to achieve in your position? I know already of course of your caring for the poor and sick of the world and indeed of some of your more progressive thoughts on the Catholic Church itself.'

'I will have to wait and see how best the Pope wants me to grace the church, but as you rightly hint at, I am a liberal in viewpoint and there is much I would like to do. Of course, I will be very new in the post and so any changes I can bring about will have to be done stealthily and gently…at least in the first instances. I would like to change some of the directions the church is moving in and as you say, of course there is my great interest in Africa. I feel that I must try and make headway into poverty and untreated disease there which still haunts that vast continent.'

'The Pope must indeed be impressed with your calling in that area, Pietro, especially as it is on his "own turf" so to speak.'

'Possibly, but I think a major aspect here, Alberto, is the way in which World Pharma is proving its Christian charity not just in fine words but now in fine deeds. Provision of healthcare and medicines for those unable to afford them is a previously unimaginable thing and it must make you the enemy of every other pharmaceutical company on God's planet?'

His brother smiled. Their futures looked good.

What Mondo Senior saw was the incredible opportunity, for the first company who possessed the balls, to take on the Dark Continent, and he had the balls. The cost of "the free medicines program" was miniscule compared to the benefits which would realistically be gained from it. One area to benefit would be clinical research, where huge clinical trials programs would be possible at a fraction of the cost of that in the rest of the world, trials which would be impossible to carry out elsewhere not only because of the costs but also, and of increasing importance to him, because of the inability elsewhere to obtain the necessary ethical approvals essential for the conduct of the trials. In other words, the door would very soon be opened to him for a far less ethical approach to clinical research. This was just the tip of the iceberg for World, for the research went much further than mere clinical trials. In fact, with the virtual ownership of a population bought with free generic medicines, access to the people's minds and particularly their bodies would surely rapidly follow. It was almost incalculable just how far desperate people would be prepared to go in assisting medical research and drug development in return for a handful of "pink placebos", but Alberto Mondo had a very good idea of just how far it would be.

Peter Mondo, the man of God, was in glorious ignorance of both the African potential and his brother's unholy intentions, for his own focus was on goodness and charity. This ignorance and naivety were not items limited to him alone however, for a major section of his fellow cardinals had also been dazzled by the light of Christian charity and aid generated by his brother and World Pharma. This light had even travelled as far as the Pope himself. In the short time that Peter Mondo had been at the higher levels of ecclesiastical society, the admiration for him from his peers had swelled at a significant rate, aided of course by the workings of his brother's most charitable pharmaceutical Company. But Peter Mondo had many attributes of his own, and already at this early stage of his cardinalisation, he was being cited by some as 'the one to watch', as the state of the health of their leader fluctuated daily.

Promotion to the highest position in the Catholic Church was a million miles from Peter Mondo's ambitions and aspirations. His brother, however, had no such elusions and was already progressing with an agenda which he believed would place the two of them at the global pinnacles of their respective professions. An empire for each of them!

Chapter 37

Hart and Grille sat at the inn and drank. They had been there an hour. People drifted in and out, but there was still no sign of Grille's brother-in-law and Hart was showing obvious signs of nervousness, which didn't go un-noticed by his companion.

'Don't worry, Max, he will be here. Trust me. If there were any problems he would have called my handy.'

Hart took a moment to register the word "handy", it was German-speak for "mobile" or "cell" phone, and he nodded unconvincingly taking another sip at his beer. The door suddenly opened and five agricultural workers strode in noisily, followed by a middle-aged man who was on his own. Hart glanced at Grille.

'Ernst has arrived, Klaus.'

Grille looked up and squinted across the room.

'You are right. But how did you know?'

'It's obvious that here is a man trained for surveillance. He has that particular walk and ambience of a well-trained and experienced security officer, and…'

'Max, I'm very impressed with your powers of observation.'

Hart continued, '…but I believe the biggest clue to his identity is…the cap and uniform he's wearing, which has his ID and security badge on it. He's obviously here under cover!'

'Always the joke, but remember, no jokes with Ernst. He is very serious and will not be of great help if he feels you are not serious or that you are taking the piss. Is correct, taking the piss?'

'Perfect.'

The tall, uniformed, middle-aged man with dark hair, greying at the temples made eye contact with Grille and unsmiling crossed the room to their table. Grille and Hart stood up as he approached and Grille extended his hand, shaking Ernst's vigorously in greeting. He then introduced Hart to him in English. Hart smiled and shook his hand, inwardly wincing at the vice-like grip.

The three of them sat down around the table and with Ernst having refused Grille's offer of food or drink, the question and answer session began, Grille acting as translator.

'OK, question number one. Is he sure he doesn't want any food or drink?'

'No thank you. He cannot risk the smell of beer on his breath and in any case, his time here with us will be short.'

'That's a shame, I was thinking how healthy he looks.'

Grille gave Hart a hard stare.

'Sorry Klaus. So then, where exactly does he work and how long has he been there?'

'He works as a security officer at the GRS Institute in Greifswald. That's the Gerhard Roscher Schmoller Institute, and he has been there for the last five years.'

Hart aimed his next questions directly at Ernst rather than looking at Grille

'Who owns the clinic and who is in charge?'

He continued to face Ernst, as Grille translated his answer.

'The clinic takes its name from the founder who still sits on the board and who is still a big name in scientific and medical circles. Ernst believes that he still owns a major share in the clinic, but there are rumours of a recent buy-out, or take over, by a much larger pharmaceutical company.'

'What's the word on the grapevine? Which company is in the frame?'

'Pardon me, Max, could we go back to English please, my American slang is a little out-of-date.'

'Sorry. Who is rumoured to actually be the new owners now?'

'It is a difficult question, but the rumour is very strong that the institute has been acquired by an Italian company based somewhere in the very south of Italy, but that company is rumoured also to be a subsidiary of a much bigger international organization. More than that that he does not know.'

'Good. OK. So what is the nature of the work done at the institute and clinic? Is it research, or actual treatment of illnesses, or perhaps some of each? Also, what are the disease areas that are being worked on?'

'The clinic was founded purely on research. People around the city are very proud of the history of the unit. Over the years, very good work has been published by the institute in top scientific journals. Let's get this clear though, Max, there is the institute where research takes place, and there is the clinic where people are treated with drugs presumably based on, or coming out of, that research. I personally have heard of and read about some of the major works done here. It has a great reputation for high quality work done in the areas of injury to the spine and in neurological…is that how you say it…diseases?'

'Do you mean diseases such as Parkinson's?'

A little excitement crept into Hart's voice.

'Yes exactly. Ernst believes that there might be some treatments of this disease there as he has recently seen patients, many obviously neurologically disturbed patients, with their families around the place. You know Parkinson's is not too difficult to identify, even for a security officer. Well, Max, I think we getting close now to closing and costing this little conversation, no?'

'No, not just yet, I have one really important question first and then we can talk about payment. I already know that the institute or the clinic receives specimens from other places outside of Germany, like the UK for example. These may sometimes be specimens that require special methods of preservation at their source, such as freezing. My question is, does the institute or clinic ever send materials of their own away to other places, laboratories for instance, for further testing or processing. This too might require special treatments such as freezing, or the use of special containers for transport?'

The pauses for translation and discussion were getting longer as Hart's questions became more involved and difficult.

'To Ernst's knowledge, some specimens *are* sent to other clinics and laboratories, and he thinks to some place in Italy, and yes sometimes they are in strange-looking containers, but he has no knowledge of what special treatment of the specimens might be needed. Max, he is only security, he is not a bloody scientist. As a security officer though, he knows that specimens arrive from outside of Germany, and he has seen UK before on labels. In this time now, he is responsible for giving couriers permissions to deliver samples directly to the special reception and dispatch place; it is the same place within the institute for all such parcels. He can confirm also that parcels leave from that same point for other places. Again, as security, he has to be there to meet all couriers, but what is inside the parcels he has no idea or in fact no particular interest. The people who work in that area should have some idea though. And now, before going any further, I think you should show a little appreciation by way of some money, don't you think? Trust me he will work much better for you with some paper stuff in his pocket at this point.'

'Yes of course. You're the boss.'

Hart had no idea at all what the going rate should be for this kind of information and reaching over the table pushed some euros into Ernst's hand. Ernst looked down and did a rapid count. One hundred euros! His eyes lit up.

Bollocks! Hart thought to himself. *I've given him too much, should have tried fifty. Ah well, its only money, and not my own anyway!*

Grille smiled and spoke quickly to Hart.

'Max, that is too generous.'

Hart smiled back. 'Well, I can't take it back from the poor bastard now, can I? Just think of it as a carrot. The information he has given me so far has been useful, but I do need to know positively whether specimens are being rerouted elsewhere from there or if this is their final destination. Some stuff is clearly being sent away but it's not obvious what that is.'

'But how can you find this out, I think that Ernst has told you all he knows?'

'I believe you are right, so what I need to do is see for myself. I'm fairly sure that if the specimens we are interested in are sent on elsewhere, then some additional work has to be done on them and they have to be transported in some special way. I need to see what the containers look like and also see the labels on them if possible. The package I saw which was sent from the Paddocks Clinic in the UK was very clearly labelled. This type of package would stand out a mile if I saw anything like it here. I really do need to know at the end of the day if this is the last stop for the specimens or whether their final resting place is somewhere else and if so where? Ask Ernst if and how I might see what type of specimens arrive and what are dispatched from the institute. Tell him there will be an extra two hundred euros for the right response.'

'I will ask him but you are asking too much of him I think.'

For the next few minutes, Grille and Ernst were embroiled in a particularly lively discussion accompanied by much raising of eyebrows and shaking of heads. Eventually, Hart picked out of the conversation the mention of euros and immediately there was a softening in Ernst's facial expressions as he took on a more conciliatory look. After what seemed like an eternity, Grille turned his attention to Hart.

'It is very difficult. Very, very difficult. You see there are cameras both inside and outside the facility and all people, including visitors, patients and family attenders must have security passes. It would be too much a risk to Ernst's job to supply you with such passes, but—'

'Shit, Klaus, I only need five minutes around that dispatch area!'

'Wait, wait, wait! But…there may be a way that you can get your five minutes.'

Hart's sinking hopes suddenly found a lifeguard

'Tell me!'

'The dispatch area is close to the clinic entrance where people must check in. At around three o'clock in the afternoon, there is always a crowd of visitors and new patients crushing around getting passes from security and it could be possible for you to slip in as part of this crowd if Ernst can arrange to be on duty. He will be able to turn the blind eye as you go in, but you must be sure to return to the same entrance when you want to leave. Please remember that you will likely be in the view of cameras all the time, even when you are outside the building. Obviously, it must not be apparent that Ernst is part of your deception. He suggests that you take a seat in the waiting area close to the dispatch area and sit with a book or magazine and wait until 3:15. Longer than your five minutes yes, but that is the time when specimens are picked up by couriers. This is your only chance, Max, just one shot. If there are no specimens there, then you must leave. If they are there, you should be able to obtain a good look at the way they are packaged et cetera and see if they stand out to you in any way.'

'Klaus, that's great; tell him I'll give him the extra two hundred euros.'

'I told him, Max. Unfortunately, the price is now four hundred!'

Hart looked shocked, but in fact couldn't care less about the cost.

'Bloody hell, he's some businessman, this brother-in-law of yours. OK, he's got it, it's a deal.'

'Good Max. One more thing, to help us you must carry that small folder of documents I have brought for you. As I told you before, these are related to the trial at the nearby hospital that I am here to check out. If for any reason you are questioned, then you are a stupid Englishman who was here with me at the hospital but who has wandered away from me and lost himself. Here is my card so they can call my "handy" to support your story. We must meet by 3:30 back at my car so you really do have to be quick.'

'I promise. I promise too that I will make a very good stupid Englishman if needs be.'

'That will be indeed the easiest thing for you, Max.'

So the plans were laid. In accepting the money, the grateful but still unsmiling Ernst in a sudden rush of conscience had volunteered to try and obtain copies of specimen transit documents, which might be revealing. The three plotters left the inn, Hart lighter by five hundred euros and Ernst heavier by the

117

same amount and went their ways ultimately to the same car park, which doubled, or rather trebled, for the institute, the clinic and Grille's hospital.

Chapter 38

In the Department of Research Immunology at the QMC in Nottingham, Victoria Crosse was feeling somewhat pleased. She had managed, at this late stage, to enrol both herself and Hart for the imminent Stem Cell Research Congress, this year located not in Venice as the advance information had declared, but in Padua. Finding suitable accommodation, however, was a much more difficult task for Williams' travel people, as Padua was almost four times smaller than Venice, whilst supporting a similar-sized local population. To make matters even more difficult, the city's hotels were often used by delegates from conferences in Venice, as it was just 45 minutes away by train. In the end, it was Crosse herself who was rewarded after one hour on the internet and a couple of direct calls, with two late cancellation rooms at the Hotel Al Giardinetto in Padua. Denis's travel people could rest easy.

Interestingly, the GRS Institute based in Greifwald had a stand in the exhibition hall where numerous posters would be present containing recent newly published works, and they also had a hospitality suite on the first floor of the convention centre where interested parties could get further topped up with development and scientific information and also buffet food items, all washed down with the odd glass or two of wine or other drinks of choice. Turning to the last few pages of the conference literature, Crosse was interested to see that down the alphabetic list of conference sponsors was one, World Pharmaceuticals and Healthcare. It was only a few weeks since Hart's untimely departure from that company and Crosse had no idea whether Hart would warm to this piece of information or not, the chance embarrassing meeting with ex-colleagues possibly being a fair reason for Hart to decline the visit.

She would hold this news back until he had confirmed his intentions to travel out with her as this visit was too important to be upset by a bout of prima donna foot stamping.

Chapter 39

At exactly 2.00 pm, Grille eased the black Audi into the car park. To the left was the hospital and to the right the clinic. Entrances to both buildings were a mere thirty-second stroll away. Grille turned to Hart and set the game afoot.

'Right, Max, I will go to my appointment now at the hospital.'

He pointed in the direction of a smart, four-storey redbrick building.

'I will see you back here at 3.30 pm precisely. Here is the spare key to the car. If you fail to meet me at that time, I will come to the clinic to find you. To have to do that, however, would be very embarrassing for me, so please, Max… be here!'

Hart was feeling a nervous thrill in anticipation of what were his next options.

'OK, Klaus, I'll see you later, hopefully with some information which will make this trip worthwhile…other than the opportunity of eating a sausage with you again of course.'

'Just go, Max, and be back soon. We will joke later.'

With that, Grille got out of the car and made his way to the hospital entrance. Hart's plan was to mingle with visitors to the clinic and gain entry mingling with a group suitably large enough for him to be able to maintain his "incognito" status. His first disappointment was that the only other visitor at present seated at the outside entrance was a remarkably fat black cat and he, therefore, took the decision to go walkabout until things became a little more active. He locked and left the car and took the footpath which led to the clinic entrance, but some metres short of the doors, he diverted down an adjoining pathway towards a green park area. He decided to let a few minutes slip by, whilst waiting for the patient-visitor "rush", and sat down in the now very pleasant sunshine on one of the park benches, his briefcase of German notes and clinical trial information by his side.

After ten minutes, he stood up and walked purposefully back towards the front of the clinic. As he rounded the front of the building, his eyes widened. What had previously been an empty entrance area had become a seething entrance to Wembley Stadium on cup final day. The fat black cat no longer sat on the mat!

Chapter 40

The antique gold carriage clock on the mantelpiece of the Adam fireplace in the ornate office of Albert Mondo tinkled rather than struck 10.00 o'clock, on a still wintry New York morning.

The man himself was engrossed in his regular weekly telephone conversation with Italy, on a call which had come through on his private number some thirty minutes earlier from Franco Negri's own private number in the Vatican.

'...so in summary, Alberto, all is well. Better than expected in fact, for he is almost a new man looking to be able to complete at least twelve more months. Pietro is in a good place and already being talked of in the highest terms. You should be well aware now, Alberto, that happily there is a considerable groundswell within these walls favouring a new more liberal approach to things which have previously been completely set in stone.'

'I am very pleased, Franco, but will you be able to attend our meeting in two weeks' time in Padua? I myself cannot be there and it is so important to have high level representation, especially as our colleagues from Sicily will be there along with Robert Halle.'

'I will, Alberto, but as you know, this type of thing is a long way out of my comfort zone and I must be very careful, for as you are aware for a man of my office to be seen in high profile at such an event would be extremely controversial. How do they say over there, it would be like taking tea with the devil, no?'

'I understand perfectly, Franco, but it *is* necessary for you to be there and I want it. Claudia will also be there, of course, and you know how difficult that could be for her. Just be careful, that's all. *Both* of you must be careful.'

'Yes of course, Alberto, but now it seems that I will be taking tea with not just the devil, but with his wife also!'

Chapter 41

As Hart watched the "Wembley Way" of people queuing in the true continental fashion of everyman for himself, he mentally ticked off his imminent actions before joining the scrummage. His main challenge was to obtain names and destination addresses for any biological materials which were to be collected by a courier service. Ernst had given him the necessary information and it seemed that if no specimens were evident at between 3.15 and 3.30, then he would have to leave. As he eased towards the throng, he picked out the surveillance cameras situated high up on the clinic walls, one each side of the entrance doors, taking in the activities below and instinctively lowered his head in a vain attempt to become invisible and then dived in.

The water was lovely! He certainly didn't look or feel out of place in the crowd which contained a fair number of similarly dressed business types, many also carrying briefcases, and for the first time, he noticed that there were several patients being pushed in wheelchairs and several walking stick and crutch assisted patients.

Pushed and bustled, he found himself at the heels of an elderly red-faced man who was accompanied by a very plump fraulein, who he was pushing in a wheelchair. The frail-looking man was sweating profusely and was clearly in some distress. As the crowd moved forward, Hart felt a change in his step and realised that he was now being herded up a ramp to the doors. The ramp was there for the ease of wheelchairs, but in this instance, a ramp too far for the old man and his charge. The old man staggered slightly and then went down on one knee. Seizing the moment, Hart moved quickly and took hold of the handles of the wheelchair, allowing the old man to recover and climb to his feet. Then, as the old man called out to the crowd ahead to let them pass, the trio were able to move forward almost unhindered through the grudgingly parted wave of people, right up to the security gate. The security man at the gate addressed the old couple and was clearly asking for either identification or the required pass for entry. Hart's stomach started to tighten and his mind raced contemplating quite how to deal with this imminent situation. Where the bloody hell was Ernst?

The pressure of a hand on his shoulder caused Hart to turn his head and the burly security man nodded as Hart felt a hand go into his pocket and something drop. Ernst then quickly moved away, leaving Hart to show the pass he had just been given to the guardian of the gate who nodded him through without even looking up.

Inside, Hart was immediately accosted by the old man, extremely grateful for his act of chivalry and he pumped his hand vigorously whilst telling him what a good egg he was. Of course Hart couldn't understanding a single word of the man's profuse thanks but nonetheless, he smiled and nodded…fluently in German.

He clipped the security badge to the lapel of his jacket and looked around for the dispatch room that Ernst had described, and there it was, exactly as foretold. He checked the time on his watch.

'Shite!'

It was already 3.15 pm. Where *had* the time gone? He was here just about in time. Fingers crossed he wasn't too late. The crowd was thinning now as the people filed off in different directions heading to their appropriate therapeutic area departments. Hart found a free seat in direct visual line with the dispatch room and sat down, eyes fixed on his quest. Within minutes, there was activity within the room and Hart's heartrate increased, as through the plate glass window, he saw what could be his holy grail. On the sill behind the window, close to an access hatch, had been placed a silver heavyduty polystyrene box some two feet square in dimensions. The box was evidently there for collection by a courier as Ernst had predicted.

Hart left his seat and wandered over to the window craning his neck in an effort to read the dispatch address.

'Bugger!' he muttered under his breath.

The address was on the opposite side of the container facing inward to the dispatch room. In that instant, a young man clad in dark-blue trousers and blouson jacket bearing a large red and blue striped badge was buzzed into the room through a door from the carpark. Hart directed his gaze through the dispatch room and out into the car park, where a red and blue striped van bearing the same insignia as the young man's badge was parked. The insignia of a winged-ankled Hermes was a good enough clue for Hart to realise that this was a courier. His mind was racing. *What to do to get that address?*

Meanwhile, the rather handsome young courier was increasing the heartrate of a frosty middle-aged woman in a white dress-uniform and nurse-like white lace hat, whose small empire over which she ruled with an iron hand was this confined space of the dispatch room. Her face, capable at the very least of turning milk sour, if not to the full gorgonzola, cracked into a gushing smile. It was there for the taking and, take it he did, but it was the silver polystyrene box which found itself in the courier's hands and the rejected welcoming face quickly returned to milk souring mode.

As the courier headed back down the corridor to the staff only exit, a jacketless clinic official in white shirt and two-tone green-striped tie, with a security badge clipped to his shirt pocket, strode purposefully up to him and flashed him an additional photographic ID, whilst holding up his hand for the young man to stop. The official took the package from the courier and turned it so that the address was visible, then with a nod and a quick 'Good', he smiled, turned and retraced his steps down the corridor. The courier feigned a slight shrug and continued his exit of the clinic. Once back in his van, he revved the engine noisily and with tyres screeching sped away with his "guaranteed 24-hour delivery" item.

Inside the clinic, the official put his jacket back on and returned the out of date Princeton University Medical Library Identification Card, bearing a younger portrait of himself, to his pocket. Hart smiled at a job well done and was about to make his own exit from the building when the door re-opened and the courier returned, silver box in hand.

'Oh shit! What now?'

But wait, this was a much older courier, albeit dressed identically to the former, and heading in the opposite direction away from the dispatch room. Outside in the car park, a van bearing the same livery as the earlier caller sat waiting. Now at this point, Hart should have been more than happy with the outcome of his meeting with the first courier and made his way back to the relative safety of the Audi, but he was intrigued by this second arrival. With his adrenalin levels still high from his recent success, he impulsively turned and made to follow the package and its bearer down the corridor deeper into the heart of the clinic complex.

The man, given a head start, was now out of sight and Hart had to pick up his pace to try and catch up man and parcel. Ernst, now waiting for Hart at the visitor exit looked on in alarm as the stupid Englishman disappeared down a side corridor. What should he do, wait here as planned to safely see Hart off the premises or make some effort to head him off from whatever new mission he had embarked upon?

Travelling at double time along the corridor, Hart turned a corner and came to an abrupt halt. He had reached a T-junction in his pursuit. Should he turn left or right? He decided that the package he was attempting to trail now was probably totally unrelated to what had gone before and, therefore, this was a totally foolhardy action.

In his time honoured foolhardy fashion, he quickly made two decisions. The first decision was to take the left turn. This decision was based upon the presence on the wall of a red circle with a red bar across its centre. No entry for non-clinic personnel! The correct way of passage for visitors was clearly and effectively indicated every three metres by way of a yellow arrow set in the white floor tiles. This was fool-proof for the average visitor/patient, but unfortunately not idiot proof for inquisitive Englishmen. His second decision was to discard the security pass as soon as possible, and a nearby bin helped him complete this. His rationale here was that in the event of his being reeled in by some other member of security or clinic staff there would be nothing to associate him with Ernst. A group of visitors coming up behind him finalised his decisions and propelled him forward into his red-alert left turn, as they themselves took the right turn following the officially advised yellow brick road. He smiled to himself as he strode out, in time with the Muzak drifting out from speakers somewhere above him, pleased with his bold decision. A smile incidentally shared by the overhead security cameras which picked him up the instant that he transgressed in his journey.

At the next junction, with the courier not yet in sight, he turned right working on the assumption that a left turn would bring him in a circle back to where he started. He continued forward at speed, still the unknowing star of the hidden cameras.

At the next bend in the corridor, it suddenly opened out into a much wider thoroughfare. On both his left and right sides were a series of glass fronted rooms, some glazed from floor to ceiling on the other sides of which were working white-coated technicians and scientists all too busy with their various duties and functions to notice the "trespasser" in the corridor beyond their immediate domains.

As he briefly locked eyes with one of the workers, in looking quickly away, he finally caught sight of one of the corridor security cameras.

'Shit!'

Spoken through clenched teeth, but with an ever-smiling mouth.

'Smile, you're on Candid Camera.'

Acting totally unconcerned, he continued along the corridor, if anything a little more relaxed, taking more time to look into the various laboratories and even nodding and smiling at anyone who glanced up. Most of his smiles were one way however.

It must be the special type of smile absorbing glass, he smiled to himself.

It wasn't the first time that jokes had been cracked on board the Titanic. Steady on there…disaster ahead! The iceberg still ahead, however, was of the human female variety.

Suddenly in one of the half glazed labs to his left, he caught sight of his quarry. He hung back peering for as long as he could remain undetected into the room where three scientists clad all in white and wearing white rubber boots and white caps worked on the package delivered by the man in the blue uniform. He watched as one person removed what appeared to be a type of vacuum flask from the polystyrene box and proceed to unscrew the lid. The whole activity was shrouded in a white vapour which emanated from the box, which no doubt contained dry ice. The release of the lid of the flask resulted in more white vapour rising from inside the container. Hart guessed that the temperature inside the flask would be around minus 20 or 25 degrees centigrade if it did indeed contain biological material.

A second of the trio took a pair of forceps from inside a steriliser and reached down into the flask with them. When he withdrew the forceps, they were gripping a smaller flask which he placed very carefully into a rack appropriately shaped to hold it vertically and securely in place.

The third member of the group removed the lid on the smaller flask and using a second pair of more delicate forceps (removed from a second sterilising unit), probed its interior for a few moments before removing a single item from inside, which he duly paced onto a regular-sized Petri dish.

At this point, Hart moved closer to the glass in order to try and obtain some idea of what this item was. It was difficult to see exactly, but it was certainly reddish in colour and definitely tissue of some sort. Crosse would have known what it was instantly, of that he was sure.

He had seen enough. There was no way that he would be able to get a more definitive look at the item of the scientists' engrossed interest.

In the side room to the laboratory, the courier was taking the final signatures on his receipt invoice and would very soon be back out in the corridor. Hart decided that he would take the opportunity presented by the departure of the courier to tag on behind him, presumably back to the clinic exit, his curiosity satisfied. The camera above Hart's head had now changed from its flashing orange colour as he had entered its zone of vision, to flashing red as the programmed time allocated for outsider presence in any single camera's range was finally exceeded by Hart's continued presence.

As the man in blue proceeded to the exit, Hart, tucked in not far behind, couldn't help but feel pleased with his venture into espionage. He felt a certain satisfaction at having been able both physically and mentally, to enter this secure building and have this brief look around. He would be even more satisfied though when he was breathing fresh un-recycled air again on the outside.

By the time the two exiting men reached the part of the complex, where the corridor narrowed, leaving the laboratories at their backs, Hart was right up to the shoulder of his companion marking time with him in footfalls. As the pair neared a door in the corridor, it suddenly swung open towards them as a worker exited carrying a box of washed and sterilised laboratory glassware. The two men, startled and avoiding this sudden potential collision, actually collided with each other, each man scattering his documents onto the white tiled floor. Hart's documents included the hospital notes given to him earlier by Grille, which he had recently removed from his briefcase in an effort to display a more bona fide image whilst in the red zone. For the even more startled courier, the spillage included his recently signed invoices and delivery details.

The two men apologised profusely to each other in their respective languages and set about retrieving their spilt documents from the floor, each man passing to the other their own respective pieces of paper. Then with a nod and a smile they proceeded on their way, Hart once again falling in behind the courier, but this time a little further back.

The minor collision over Hart decided to change down a gear, steadily falling further behind the courier. But still the iceberg lurked to starboard with Hart heading towards it, totally oblivious of its presence and of the danger it offered. …And the band played on…or at least the canned Muzak continued to filter through the background sound system.

At a junction in the corridor ahead, the courier turned left. On reaching that point, Hart realised that the patient-friendly yellow arrows indicating the Klinic Ausgang (clinic exit) actually went to the right, and so to the right (starboard) he steered.

Suddenly, Hart's passage appeared not as straightforward as it had at first seemed and his confidence and inner bravado of some minutes earlier evaporated in a rush. Approaching him along the corridor side by side, were two extraordinarily large, black uniformed, peak-capped security men. Disconcertingly, he noted that each carried a large baton suspended from his belt and then even more disturbingly he spotted their holstered firearms. If ever there was an occasion for a "Gulp!", this was it.

He met the situation head on.

'Pardon me, I'm English, is this the correct way out?'

126

Both of the security men looked anything but friendly, but one of them looked rather awkward and uncomfortable with the confrontation. It was Ernst. Hart's immediate intention now was to try and extricate himself from this situation whilst not indicating in any way his acquaintanceship with the "good cop" and concentrate on placating the "bad cop".

Ernst's companion spoke briefly into a hand radio he carried and then to Ernst. It was in fact Ernst who spoke first to Hart.

'English?'

'Yes, and I'm sorry I have no German,' Hart responded smiling. 'I seem to be a little lost here.'

Ernst gripped Hart at the elbow.

'You must come with us.'

He turned and still holding Hart's elbow directed him down the corridor until the three of them arrived at a door labelled in dual languages, "EINFAHRT": "PRIVATE", which he opened and entered with his captive. His partner followed, closing the door behind him. Ernst seemed to be the one in charge here and Hart was wondering how this would play out, Ernst obviously nervous that Hart might let drop their pre-acquaintance of a few hours before. Ahead of them another door opened and Hart was pushed forward into a windowless room which contained nothing but a wooden desk with a chair either side of it, a comfortable one for the interviewer, and one less comfortable for the interviewee. The walls and ceiling were painted a dark-grey colour, the only light source being a naked 60-watt bulb hanging from the ceiling, directly over the desk. The door closed behind him with a clunk. His collision with the iceberg was imminent.

Behind the desk sat his interrogator, with head bowed looking at a report, no doubt of Hart's transgressions since leaving the path of righteousness way back along the clinic corridor. The blonde-haired female slowly raised her head. As she did so, Hart caught his breath.

'Bloody hell, it's Doris Day!'

Doris waved Ernst to leave the room, which he briskly did, leaving his colleague and Hart with "Her who must be obeyed". Clunk!

Hart tried out his best indignant look and started to speak in an effort to get his retaliation in first, but he was silenced by a suddenly raised hand and a steely glare.

'Please sit down!'

Hart nodded and sank onto the unpadded plastic backed seat, taking in more fully now the interrogator's appearance. His first thought was how someone so attractive could show such obviously poor dress sense. The attractive thirty-something blonde had closely cropped hair and wore a high-necked olive green blouse, abetted in its crime against fashion by a shapeless brown tweed jacket. He wondered about her lower half of dress.

Hart began to speak once again, but Doris's impeccable English interrupted him in mid-flow.

'You were in an unauthorised area for thirty five minutes. But first, what is your name, please?'

127

Her Mont Blanc fountain pen hung poised over the document on the desk in front of her. She continued before Hart could respond.

'You were found in the most sensitive and confidential areas of our establishment and I need to ask you certain questions before deciding upon how to proceed with your case. Now, you are an American I presume?'

Hart's chance had finally come. He had to decide on a persona, chastened and apologetic or ballsy and outraged? The coin came down for outrage.

'Actually, I'm English and I totally resent the way I have been brought here like a criminal,' he blustered. 'I arrived here with a German colleague, who is working with some of your colleagues on a clinical study, and went for a walk while he's in discussions with your medical people. I got a little off course in looking at the really interesting surroundings and have now been brought roughly here as a virtual prisoner by a couple of gorillas in uniform! Now, you begin to ask me questions without even the courtesy of telling me your own name. It's a disgrace and I aim to make whatever official complaints are at my disposal.'

Not a bad starter for a defence. She looked at him in icy examination, clearly weighing up whether his righteous indignation was real or assumed. After a brief moment, the iceberg melted slightly.

'My name is Frau Arben. I am head of security at this clinic, which is at the forefront of certain medical research and technology. As a result, we have much information which would be of great value to our competitors or to those agencies which act as intermediate purveyors of such information to interested companies. So please be kind enough to give me your name now.'

'(*Que Sera!*) My name is Hart, Max Hart, and as I said before I am from the UK.'

'Good. Thank you, Mr Hart.'

She wrote quickly on the document.

'Now, next I must ask you to please empty your pockets onto the desk.'

She saw Hart's indignation about to boil over again and continued,

'Because of the secrets we have here, I have to ensure that you are not leaving us with a little more than you arrived with.'

For the first time, she allowed a small smile to dance across her lips. Stunning!

Hart shrugged his shoulders and smiled back, deciding that having scored with indignation he should now go for the conversion, and maximum points, with charm.

'I understand your situation and have no problems in doing as you request, but I must emphasise that this is a total misunderstanding and I am totally innocent of any misdemeanour other than that not being able to read German. I have nothing to hide see.'

He proceeded to turn out his pockets and place the contents plus the trial details from his small briefcase onto the desk. He also removed his Raymond Weil wristwatch and placed it with his other items. There was indeed very little for Frau Arben to examine; his wallet and passport, a set of keys, a cheap pen, a toothpick, some coins of both European and British denominations, his mobile phone and a comb. She stood and began to examine the clinical study documents briefly. Hart had been correct in an earlier assumption; her skirt was the same cloth as her jacket and accompanied by thick green woollen stockings. The fashion crime at least doubled in its seriousness!

'Of course that clinical trial information you are looking at is itself confidential, and by the same token as your own research you are now at risk of breaking that confidentiality and the laws that govern it. I have to warn you now as you have warned me I'm afraid.'

At these comments, Arben abruptly left the trial papers alone and concentrated on the modest items from Hart's pockets. Hart suppressed a smile. She lifted the cheap pen and looked closely at it.

'That's a ten cent ballpoint pen,' assisted Hart, 'it's not as beautiful as your own of course, (interesting that a woman with such terrible dress sense should have such a high quality pen) and of course it doesn't take photographs or fire darts.'

Arben continued, not deflected by the strange attempt at humour.

'No, Mr Hart, but the "handy" I see has a camera facility.'

Hart smiled at the "handy", mobile phone terminology, and at the sudden look of anticipation in Arben's beautiful pale-blue eyes. (*Doris Day with Paul Newman eyes. Incredible!*)

'I never use it for that purpose, Frau Arben. You can see for yourself by pressing the photo recall button.'

Frau Arben dutifully complied and true to Hart's words confirmed that no photographs had been taken. She nodded in acceptance, but passed it to Ernst's even larger colleague for further examination. She then spent some minutes examining the remaining items in an extravagant fashion, as if indeed the comb might contain a stiletto knife, or the key ring a special key which would open the vault to all her clinic's untold secrets. She lingered a little longer with Raymond Weil but soon satisfied herself of his particular individual innocence. Sitting down, she made eye contact with Hart and continued her questions.

'You have confirmed that you understand that this is a confidential unit, but I am worried, Mr Hart, over how you managed to enter the unit in the very first instance. You must have been aware of the need for identity cards at the entrance?'

'Well, not exactly, you see there were so many patients crowding out there and...'

'Yes, yes, of course that is another aspect of our work here. We develop some very novel and innovative drugs here, again the natures of which must remain very confidential. Many of our patients are very ill when they come here, another reason why observers such as you should not get involved or mix with them.'

'Hang on. I had no intention of, as you say, mixing with any of the patients and I can assure you that other than help to push a patient in a wheelchair through the entrance that is the only contact I have had. I expect that as the whole area was so chaotic the guard, sorry the *security* man, assumed I was with the patient or missed me completely and it never crossed my mind to enquire about obtaining a pass, especially as I do not speak any German at all.'

Hart was almost convincing himself again, but there was no reaction from the iceberg.

'Mr Hart, could I see some form of identification please.'

It was a demand rather than a request.

'You already have my passport there on the desk and also my wallet which contains my drivers' licence. Other than that I have this birthmark…'

He feigned as if to undo his trousers.

'That will not be necessary,' Arben quickly interjected, 'the passport will be fine. Please note, Mr Hart, that in terms of confidentiality, I have particularly not looked into your wallet.'

'That's a shame, there's a wonderful picture of my cat in there,' smiled Hart.

Arben frowned and opened the passport. For a brief moment, she looked closely backwards and forwards at Hart's photograph and his real-life face.

With a final slap together of the passport pages, his interrogator sighed and took on the steely ice-maiden look she had worn upon his arrival and spoke,

'Mr Hart. I am not convinced entirely with your story and—'

As she spoke, Hart's spirits began to sink, but her sentence was interrupted by the telephone ringing on her desk. Clearly irritated by the interruption, she answered the call. Minutes later, her face like thunder, she replaced the receiver with some force and turning to Hart continued…but not quite at the point she had left off.

'I think you should leave now, Mr Hart. Your colleague, Doctor Grille, has now confirmed your story and is waiting for you in the car park. You are either a very stupid or lucky man, Mr Hart.'

The lifeboat had arrived! Hart collected up his items, including his "handy" which Frau Arben's huge colleague replaced on the table and replaced them in his pockets and briefcase, greatly relieved at the sudden turn-around.

'Thank you, Frau Arben, it has been…*interesting*…to meet you,' he beamed, 'and I'm sorry if I have spoilt your day, but these things do happen occasionally.'

Arben frowned even more, crossed the "interrogation chamber" and opened the door. Outside, Ernst was waiting, apparently on guard. He stiffened as she walked out and barked a few words at him. She turned to Hart.

'This man will show you out. Your English humour has not been appreciated here today, Mr Hart. In other words, as you say "we are not amused", and if I see you here again under any circumstances, I can assure you that it will become a police matter!'

As Hart opened his mouth to form a response, she spun on her heel and went back inside the room slamming the door behind her. The final CLUNK! Later, she would replay this recent interview, along with Hart's other afternoon exploits as captured by the close circuit cameras.

Chapter 42

Ernst continued with the charade and spoke no further as he led Hart to the exit. Hart had not given him away and he would prosper from the way in which he had handled this intruder, not that he hadn't already prospered to the tune of a fair number of euros! Ernst couldn't dare ask now, but he was intrigued to learn how and why Hart had cleverly managed to dispose of the pass that he had procured for him at the start of this awkward saga.

As Hart emerged from the clinic, he immediately saw Grille who was now parked as close to the unit as he could possibly be without actually being inside the building, a look of grave worry etched upon his face. Hart walked the couple of metres from the clinic to the Audi and climbed inside, smiling slightly. Before he was properly seated, Grille started the car and gunned the engine. As he let out the clutch and surged forward, the rear wheels squealed as they fought for traction on the tarmac. Remaining patients and visitors looked up nervously, most of them unable to move at more than a snail's pace even if called upon to do so in the event of any emergency, as the car tore out of the car park.

'Phew, Klaus, I do believe we finally have lift off!'

'Max, for God's sake! Why on earth did you go inside the research area, are you completely insane? That was never the plan.'

'Impulse I'm afraid, Klaus, pure impulse. I'm really sorry if I put the wind up you.'

'Vind? You put a facking hurricane up me! Just remember that I have to come back here as part of my proper job.'

Grille was furious, and was getting madder by the minute. The madder he became, the more his English eloquence disintegrated.

'Und Gott knows vat vill 'appen to Ernst?'

For the first time since escaping the clinic, Hart felt guilty about his selfish departure from the carefully laid plan, although he was finding it very difficult to suppress a smile at Klaus's failing English under pressure.

'Look I'm really sorry, Klaus, but I had no option but to trespass a little further into the clinic, or our trip here would have been a failure,' he lied. 'I had to follow a courier to get the information I needed.'

'Und did you get it? I expect you just asked the courier outright, ya?'

'Well, actually I sort of did,' Hart smiled at him.

'Jesus! Vell come on, tell me!'

'I saw packages which resembled the one I had seen in Nottingham and simply asked the courier if I could check the address, and before you remind me that I don't speak any German, I didn't have to. I just excused myself and took

131

the package from him and read the address. He didn't object. I showed him my library ID card and he thought I was part of the staff.'

At the mention of the library card, Grille looked blank, but deciding to ignore it, pressed on.

'But the important question, Max. Vere does the parcel now go?'

'To someplace called Basiglio in Sicily. I have the address written down.'

'And what else did you find? I hope there is more to make it worth my blood pressure to rise like this?'

Grille's humour was slowly returning and with it his reins on the English language tightened somewhat.

'I walked along corridors, past laboratories where everyone was seriously working away, but it didn't mean much to me and—'

Grille's blood pressure was on the increase again.

'Vat! You got nothing from it! Incredible!'

'Hang on, Klaus, give me chance! As I was saying, all looked as a lab should look to my untrained eyes, but then I saw another courier who had *delivered* a package to the unit. The first one was picking one up for delivery elsewhere you remember. So I followed him, hoping to find the exit, but we had a sudden collision—'

'Bloody hell!'

'—a sudden collision trying to avoid an opening door. Both our papers fell to the floor in a heap, so we helped each other pick them up...'

'Your good deed for the day, eh, Max?'

'....and by some mistake I ended up with this.'

Hart triumphantly held up a yellow sheet of paper and waved it in front of Grille, who appeared underwhelmed.

'So?'

'So, *mon ami*, I only have the delivery docket for the package he just brought!'

Grille leaned over to try and make out what was written on the form and in so doing almost left the road.

'For God's sake, look at the road will you, Klaus and let me tell you! This is a delivery note and it tells me that it has come from a particular hospital in Liverpool in England, one of the hospitals outside of Nottingham where similar events have probably been occurring to those at the Paddocks. Of course the rest is German and means nothing to me.'

Grille snatched the form from Hart's grasp and quickly scanned it, again almost leaving the tortuous autobahn.

'Ah, Max, you should learn some German. If you did, you vould now know zat not only did zat package arrive indeed from Liverpool in the UK, but also zat in two days' time the contents vill continue further on their journey. Yes, Max, you haf been very fortunate, for in two days' time ze journey for zat specimen will be completed at a place called Basiglio. And vhere is zat? Of course, it's in Sicily!'

With his total immersion lesson in English (squeezed into two days) almost over, Grille had now for some reason reverted to a version of the English language usually seen to be spoken by ze Germans in ze comic books.

Hart punched his open hand.

'Yes!'

'So Max, tell me vat your conclusions of today are.'

Hart paused to collect his thoughts, and then,

'Well, I have seen specimens taken from here and sent to wherever this place is in Sicily. My question all along has been whether the samples sent from the UK remain here to be used for whatever, or whether they are subsequently moved on, perhaps following some intermediary chemical or biological process in the lab, and we have certainly resolved that one. My venture beyond the entrance back there and the obtaining of this receipt shows that specimens arrive here from other dubious places, i.e. hospital units, in the UK and then continue on their journey from here using the same courier to Sicily. Quite a trip! I would expect that the courier arranges the onward journey by air as speed will be essential for human materials of this type.'

Grille nodded and smiled.

'Ya Max, zat has been a good vork.'

The trip from Greifswald back to Berlin's Tegal Airport was completed without the need for any stoppages. Hart's plan was to take the late BA flight from Berlin to Birmingham airport in the UK, leaving Grille to replenish the car, now running on vapour alone from an all but empty tank, with fuel before returning it to the rental agency. By the time Grille had cursed his way through the Berlin traffic to the airport, Hart had just 45 minutes to change his flight ticket and catch the plane. As the car screeched to a halt at the "No Parking" area outside the departure building, Hart leapt out followed almost as quickly by Grille and the two men shook hands warmly.

'Klaus, you are a great doughnut with a cream filling.' (A reference to an old joke of theirs relating to JFKs famous "I am a Berliner" malapropism many years before during the Cold War whilst on a visit to the city.)

'Und Max, you are a vonderful condom (Grille's own reference to a verbal gaffe by George Pompidou, or rather by his translator, during a visit to London by the French president years before), and I look forward to our next…less frenetic…meeting, when perhaps ve vill just eat and drink, ya?'

They laughed as Hart collected together his belongings and then made his dash for home, waving a hand behind him as he went. It had been two excellent days for both of them, both in terms of investigative outcomes and in the rekindling of a great relationship.

On the plane, Hart dozed for most of the flight to Birmingham, noticing through bleary eyes on the back page of the newspaper of a fellow passenger that Manchester United had come from behind to beat Barcelona in a key European football match the evening before, but missing a brief article on one of the inside pages relating to the recent accidental deaths of two relatively young (by Vatican standards at least) Catholic cardinals in somewhat unusual circumstances.

Chapter 43

It was after midnight when the British Airways Airbus A180 dropped out of a moonless rainy night and landed at Birmingham Airport. Hart took his bags and wearily followed the line of fellow passengers off the plane into the terminal building. Thirty minutes later, he was sprawled in the back of a black cab being bounced the sixty odd miles back through the now torrential rain to Nottingham, feigning sleep in order to avoid conversation with the eager Asian driver.

His time spent on the return flight from Berlin had afforded him the opportunity to dozily consider not just his agenda for the following day with Victoria Crosse and Denis Williams, but also an outline plan of where next to take this complex business. What was obvious to him was that this was indeed a potentially very dangerous adventure into which he had apparently thrust himself and for him to progress his, no *their*, interest any further would almost certainly make life even more dangerous. He decided that tomorrow, he would meet Victoria over lunch if she was available, and fully brief her on his eventful German trip prior to them meeting Denis Williams. Certainly before their meet with Denis, it would be essential to get some semblance of logic of what he believed was happening. As for the next steps on this crusade, he would definitely attend the forthcoming international stem cell congress in Venice, and more specifically, make an attempt to spend as much quality time as possible around the various company trade and scientific stands at the meeting, as well as pulling in any appropriate scientific presentations in order to glean as much information as possible as to how, when and where biotech and pharma companies were proceeding in this area.

One thing was for sure, he needed to discuss with Williams the essential next steps forward in involving the legal and medical authorities in this business…if indeed there were any steps that could be taken in these directions. With those things in mind, he adjourned his tired mental deliberations and drifted into a genuine sleep, which despite the raucous symphony of the cab's irritating aged diesel engine notes, the sounds of the outside traffic, the strains of old tired and inadequate windscreen wipers and the rain beating on the windows and roof, together with his continual side to side movement on a seat polished slippery smooth by the daily presence of a hundred backsides, came quickly and easily.

He awoke only the when noises that had cushioned him for the previous eighty minutes disappeared and he found himself in the cab outside the Barnes' house. It was 2.00 am and the rain had finally poured itself out. He paid the driver the small fortune that was the cab fare registered "on the clock", plus an additional payment for having travelled beyond the cab's normal operating zone and added a reasonable tip and dragged himself into the street looking at the receipt.

'Bloody hell! The flight to Berlin was cheaper!'

He turned his key quietly in the lock of the front door to the Barnes' house and tiptoed directly to his bedroom. So far he had not talked too much of Williams to them, but he would remedy that in the morning.

God...it is the morning!

Chapter 44

Hart was up, showered and dressed by around 11.00 am. He called Crosse, who couldn't make lunch, and, therefore, briefly outlined the events of the previous day to her, leaving the details for that afternoon when she would pick him up at around 4.00 pm and ferry him to the Williams' place. He then called Williams and updated him as he had done Crosse some minutes before and ended the call with the arrangement to see him sometime after four o'clock. He next sat and mentally prepared a form of agenda for the coming meeting, realising that he must check that Crosse had made the logistical arrangements for the Venice congress.

For the rest of the day, up until Crosse picked him up just after four o'clock, he sat with an endless supply of percolated coffee, re-living recent events and focusing upon what would be the best options to follow to ensure that some serious positive action would be taken by appropriate authorities. When he felt he had sorted things into some kind of order, he took his notebook and his "50 cent biro" and transferred his conclusions onto paper.

When Crosse arrived, it was immediately clear that her mood was one of seriousness and concern.

'Max, are you really OK? You know I'm worried that perhaps we may be biting off more than we can chew and that we could already be in really deep waters.'

Hart smiled at her.

'Victoria, please do not hesitate to mix your metaphors whenever you feel the need. I've been having some blue-sky thinking and although we are likely to be standing on a burning platform, I feel that our glass is half-full in terms of bringing a suitable outcome to our job in hand. Or should that be *our* glasses *are* half-empty?'

'No seriously, I think that at present we are OK, but we do need to talk to Denis with regard to our next steps before opting to call it a day. By the way, did you manage to make my arrangements for the Venice trip?'

'Yes I've done it, it's now Padua rather than Venice, but let's discuss it when we get to Denis'. Come on, we should go.'

As previously, upon their arrival, they were met by Williams before their feet actually touched the tarmac on his drive. He quickly ushered them into his house, a starving man hungry for information.

'Come, come.'

Williams eagerly showed the pair into the room at the front of the house where they had held their previous meeting and where Hart immediately began his update.

For the next hour, Hart described all he had seen at the Greifswald Clinic and threw in, in typically Hart fashion, all the peripheral details including his "Doris Day experience", concluding with a flourish when he revealed to his intent listeners what he had contrived to "lift" from the startled courier at the clinic. Throughout his revelations, Crosse and Williams had sat silent as it became more and more evident to them that there was indeed some veracity in Williams' desperate concerns and along with this probability came the realisation of the seriousness and the likely danger to them of having detailed knowledge of this business, let alone by actually interfering in it. At the end, Hart had expected a deluge of questions, but his audience merely sat in stunned silence until he finally broke the silence himself.

'So there you have it. Today we have to decide upon what next steps, if any, we should take. For example, do we pass on the information we have gathered to more suitable bodies at this point or do we continue to follow it up ourselves to the next stage, whatever that might be, bearing in mind that we may be moving into personally dangerous waters?'

Despite his bravado, Hart had many misgivings about going deeper into the business. He had been genuinely afraid at times during his visit to the German clinic, especially when "caught in the act" by the security chaps, followed by his interrogation by Frau Arben.

It was Williams who reacted first. Clapping his hands together, he looked at his visitors and said through clenched teeth,

'We have no choice but to continue, especially now that we have this latest information that Max has obtained. What do you think, Victoria?'

Crosse grimaced uncomfortably and nodded her head.

'I'm surprising myself, Denis, but I do actually tend to agree with you, *but* should we also consider notifying some appropriate official body as well?'

'Like who?' Williams quickly responded, whilst looking at Hart.

Hart took up the cue to speak.

'Well, folks, as I see it we actually have three options. Option one is to present our findings to whatever or whoever those appropriate authorities are. It shouldn't take too much effort to come up with some suitable suggestions…although God knows how effective they might be? Option two could be to take this one step further by ourselves and only contact officialdom when we have gone as far as we can, or at least as far as we dare. The third and final option is to totally forget about the authorities, be totally fearless and plough on regardless until we reach whatever the end point might be.

It was Williams again who spoke first. He had finally come to see, through the red mist of despair and revenge, the many dangers and difficulties which would be associated with the progression of this quest, and when he spoke, the nature of his words came as some not insignificant surprise to Crosse and Hart.

'I'm now happy to go along with whatever your preferences are. I do finally realise what could lie ahead for both of you if we go forward and I really would not want to put your safety at risk in any way. Obviously, money is not a problem and I am happy to spend whatever is necessary, but your safety does concern me.'

'Thanks for that, Denis.'

It was Hart who took up the discussion.

'I've had a couple of days and a couple of journeys which have given me the opportunity and time to consider the whole thing in some detail. Being scared to death at least once has certainly focused my line of thought! If we take option one and present our findings to an appropriate official body, whilst being a weight off our shoulders, well mine at least, it will be all too easy for the door to be closed on this permanently. In any case, any ripples arising from this option would clearly serve as a warning to whatever criminal perpetrators there are. I believe in terms of outcome that nothing in effect would happen other than to warn them off for a time. Jumping to option three, this is obviously the gung-ho approach. Shooting in the dark or peeing in the wind, we would possibly ruffle feathers; like VC, I just love mixing my metaphors, and we might even learn many of the truths, but to prosecute an outcome the inclusion of some official body at some stage will be essential. This leaves option two. We continue with our probing, getting information from wherever we can, but we keep an eye on who might be the best official organisations to have on board, and as soon as we feel that we have a case to act upon, we turn them loose. Release the dogs of war! Denis, I can give you some leads on this, but this is something you could do yourself for the team. Find out which people we will eventually want to get into bed with. So as your starter, and I have to tell you that I am going to be totally frank and earnest with you...'

He looked at Williams who nodded seriously.

'...that's Frank when I'm in New York and Earnest when I'm in New Jersey...'

Crosse's eyes rolled upwards towards the ceiling. It seemed impossible for Hart to be anything other than maddeningly flippant at all times, whatever the situation.

Hart continued, disappointed at their response to his joke,

'Taking the complaints process in sequence, the first point of complaint should be the doctor or with members of the hospital ward staff. However, this will be like water off a duck's back to them, and in any case, people generally and also patients are too easily blinded by science and diverted by hospital protocols and other bullshit to make any worthwhile inroads into obtaining suitable explanations.

Next, one could approach the relevant local ethics committee, or the hospital trustees or management team. The problem here is that these people will most likely make the right noises and give you agonised apologies, but at the end of the day, all the apologies and half-assed explanations in the world will not make for one effective jot of consolation to you. Although cages might be rattled behind the scenes, and a certain limited number of procedures changed, the overall result will be a whitewash. Whistle-blowers are still very few and far between I'm afraid when it comes to medicine, and when there's any possibility of expensive litigation, these bodies will do whatever they can to smooth everything over. Top quality plastering! Of course once you have taken these steps, there is no reason to believe that any possible miscreants will not be tipped off by "friends in high places" and then their own medical defence will trip into action. The same negative outcomes will occur whether the hospital is private or state run, there's no difference, all of them will have similar defence mechanisms. The next step you could consider taking, if you are still pissed off by all the bullshit is—'

'Pissed off by bullshit is an interesting grammatical concept, Max, worthy of Shakespeare himself.'

'Glad to see you are still awake VC…'

'…I repeat, the next step, if you are fed up with the bull*ship*, and that's an intentional concession to gentility, is to contact the General Medical Council. *Now* we're getting serious! I would also advocate contacting as many official high-ranking committees and bodies as possible, even though they may be irrelevant to the case. The Royal College of Physicians is one example. Letters to the Lancet and British Medical Journal might be additional considerations, although I'm not too sure about that. Don't stop there though. Contact your Member of Parliament, and even better, the Government Minister of Health, and why not push the boat right out and contact the Prime Minister himself? The thing is if you can create enough ripples, eventually you will achieve a wave and hopefully some interest from people who really can make a difference. These first ripples though have to be large enough to take on any safety mechanisms that are tripped. I hope that makes sense. And how about using investigative journalists as well at this stage? But remember that we are dealing with amoral criminal activities here and therefore police authorities of some flavour should also be contacted. What flavour they are will have to be your own decision, Denis. Do some research on it, but it does have to be a high-ranking organisation rather than just the local police force at the end of the road. One other really important thing to remember, Denis…these are only *my* recommendations. I have no past experience in pursuing events of this kind. I may be entirely wrong. However, at least the medical contacts I've given you are correct, but it's your choice and you must choose wisely. There's no reason of course why you shouldn't contact all of them, but it's worth remembering that as soon as your first shot is fired, the bad guys ears might be the first to hear it.'

'Just one question to you, Max. Are you *really* prepared to continue to help me with this, bearing in mind that things could possibly get nasty in ways we cannot yet be aware of as we move forward, especially if you find yourself embroiled in the sort of situation you found yourself in whilst in Germany?'

'Yes, Denis, I *will* do it…but don't worry *too* much, because if the kitchen does get too hot, my feet won't touch the floor on the way out!'

'Then let's do it. Vicky, Max, let's bloody well do it! But come on follow me.'

Williams led the way down the hall and paused in front of a closed door. Placing a hand upon the doorknob, he turned it sharply and threw the door open.

'Welcome to the "War Room", my friends!'

He stood aside and ushered his astonished visitors inside.

The room was small, some twelve feet square and windowless. Against one wall was a large table on which was a state of the art computer, a printer and a fax machine. Laid out neatly on the table were various stapled pages of printed paper. Hart lifted one and skimmed over it.

'Logs, or diary entries if you like, covering our thoughts and activities as we've progressed towards this point today,' Williams explained.

Alongside the table was a large photocopier.

On the walls were details of staff lists from the Paddocks Hospital, together with photographs of key personnel including that of Doctor Sumaris. In addition, there were graphs depicting the total number of miscarriages and terminations recorded on a monthly basis over the last five years for the UK NHS institutions and alongside of these equivalent details for the Paddocks and the Mersey Shore Hospitals.

Williams had also attached a large map of the UK and an even larger map of the world to a wall, on which he had pinned small red flags in the areas of Nottingham, Liverpool, Northwestern Germany around the area of Greifswald and what appeared to be Venice.

Bookshelves adorned other walls in the room, filled with a large variety of scientific and medical reference and textbooks dealing with subjects relating to pregnancy, stem cell research, motor neurone disease and a host of other disease and related therapeutic areas. In one corner stood an easel containing a flipchart, with a neat row of variously coloured felt-tipped pens waiting in anticipation on a sill below the chart. Williams had already taken tentative steps to indicate some sort of flow diagram on the top page, "Paddocks... TO... Greifs... TO... Venice... TO... ??"

Hart was impressed with just how much Williams had done to make this into what he had aptly described to Hart and Crosse as his "war room'" and decided that it must have been therapeutic to Williams in his turbulent mental state as well as helping their cause.

Hart smiled.

'You can add to that, "Final specimen destination LaboratorioVita, Basiglio, Sicily", the fruits of my German labours.'

Chapter 45

When the meeting with Williams concluded, Crosse and Hart retired to sit down comfortably and discuss Hart's travel arrangements for the meeting in Padua, in the bar of the hotel at the end of Williams' road. A swiftly taken glass of prosecco each and they were ready to start talking again. Hart blew out his cheeks on putting his empty glass down on the table,

'Phew, I don't know about you but I was ready for that…and a couple more besides I think! Right, down to business again. Have you sorted out for my trip to Padua, VC?

'Well, it's all sorted, but slightly differently to how you wanted it.'

'What do you mean? It's not Padua then?'

'Yes, of course, it's still in Padua! The big difference is that I'm coming as well.'

'What? It's not necessary, Victoria, and it could be bloody dangerous.'

'I'm going, Max, and that's all there is to it. You forget that I am a pretty well qualified and published scientist in my own right, particularly well informed and with no little level of expertise and knowledge of the very clinical area that we are investigating. Besides, which you will need a second pair of investigative eyes and ears if you are to make this trip anywhere near being remotely worthwhile. And you know what, we've not yet even discussed what the objectives of the trip are yet!'

Hart smiled and finally got a word in, 'You are actually correct on both counts, VC. I relent. I would love you to accompany me. Is Denis OK with the expense?'

'Well, actually Max, my department at the QMC is paying, has paid in fact, for my own registration at the conference together with the travel costs. Denis will just be paying the hotel bill. Talking of hotels, I have to say that Padua is basically full up and it has been really difficult for me to find a hotel that is above fleapit standard, but we have been very lucky and I have booked us in at a hotel conveniently placed for the conference centre in Padua.

We fly to Venice on Thursday next out of East Midlands Airport, which you may remember is just 45 minutes from Nottingham at the most. We arrive at the Marco Polo Airport, Venice, from where we take a train or taxi directly to the hotel, the Hotel Al Giardinetto, Padova, which is apparently some sixty minutes from the airport. I actually managed to get us in there, not via the internet but by phoning them direct. I was really lucky as they had had two cancellations only minutes before I called. The conference is at the Sheraton and runs over three full days, the main events being the keynote scientific papers and lectures, interspersed with the poster presentations. There will be the usual pharmaceutical company stands and exhibitions of what they are currently up to in this particular field, which also means that there will be the usual hospitality lounges where you will be encouraged to eat, drink and think pharma.'

'I *have* been to quite a few of these events before, you know, VC.'

'Sorry, Max, I'm just making sure you have all the details. Now then, I've already had a long look at the advanced program and you will be very interested to note that there is a keynote paper being presented by a certain Doctor Muller of the Gerhard Roscher Schmoller Institute, Greifswald, Germany. Originally, Gerhard Roscher Schmoller himself was booked to speak, but it looks like he's dropped out now, probably due to his advanced years. The company which runs out of that institute also has an exhibition stand, and probably hospitality suite I would guess at the conference centre. Here you are here's a copy of the advanced program.'

Hart took it from her.

'Good work, VC. Has Denis seen this yet?'

'Yes, I gave him a copy of it as well.'

Hart nodded and began to scan through it rapidly, a skill he had perfected long ago in his pharmaceutical days, when he routinely became an instant expert following a quick scan of the latest scientific publication. A quick look at the opening summary of any scientific paper followed by a similar look at its conclusions and he had absorbed enough of the manuscript into his head to be able to appear expert on the subject.

Without looking up from the text, he said,

'It looks very interesting. Scientifically that is, but it will be of extra benefit to us if we are able to take a browse around the stand of the company who are supporting that German institute and see what else they are up to. We could even accept a piece of hospitality at their hospitality suite, time and invitation permitting. Umm, I see they haven't indicated the name of the Sicilian sponsoring company yet.'

'Max, what I thought we might do is to divide the meeting between the two of us. When we have the final full program, we should highlight those presentations which would seem to best fit our enquiries and try and ascertain where the key research work is being performed and by whom, and if they have any links to the contacts that we have already identified—'

Hart completed the sentence, probably erroneously,

'—and hang around the hospitality suite, take a little of what's on offer, a little champagne, a few delicious canapés, and try and see if there are any big fish biting at the same time. The only problem with that scenario though is that I'm not sure whether or not I would know a big fish, even if it jumped up and bit my nose!'

Crosse smiled. 'That's another reason for me to be there, Max. I actually do know many of your so-called "big fish", certainly by name and several of them by sight.'

'Excellent,' Hart beamed, 'and you know these days it is common practice for delegates to take as many photographs as possible, such as those of key scientific posters when copies are not readily available, and if we work it right, we could pull in photographs of people we feel might be these elusive big fish as well. All we need are a couple of decent cameras as well as our cell phones.'

He looked at her questioningly.

'We have indeed got cameras in the office very suitable for that purpose, but you know mobile phones have great camera facilities on them these days. We just have to be a little sensitive and ensure that we are not being observed as industrial spies or members of the legion of scientific paparazzi. There is a lot of sensitivity around data being photographed or poached, but data from published papers and abstracts should be fine to photograph. It's just the unpublished, possibly cutting edge stuff that people get nervous about people copying. For any big fish photos, we will have to pretend to be snapping a poster or something and "inadvertently" include them in the shot.'

'That sounds like a very reasonable plan of action, VC. Now, we'd better drink up before all the bubbles are gone.'

Chapter 46

It had been quite some time since Hart had driven on UK roads and apart from feeling the claustrophobia of being boxed in by traffic all around and continually placing his right hand into the door pocket when groping for the gear change lever, he was getting used to it again. However, his previously good intentions of regulating the number of expletives used in his everyday language had been completely blown within the first five minutes of setting out behind the wheel of the hire car. It wasn't a one-way road of expletives though, as for every "effin idiot" he aimed at fellow drivers at least ten were aimed back at him, often with interest!

He would probably have fared better in the soothing company of Victoria Crosse, but he had chosen to take this solo venture from Nottingham to London rather than to East Midlands Airport so that once in Padua, at the end of the conference, he could take a train on to Milan, where he would spend a few days in the company of his good friend Gianni Bossi with whom he had worked in Milan some years before whilst on secondment from his then UK company. It would be excellent to meet Gianni again and to perhaps revisit some of the haunts he had frequented in his earlier life there.

As a result of the Milan diversion, it had been necessary for Hart to book a flight out to Venice from a London Airport and the return from Milan to Birmingham. On this occasion, he was flying out from Gatwick Airport, some forty or so miles south of Heathrow, itself nearly three hours' drive from Nottingham and he was struggling. He had given himself a maximum of six hours to reach the North Terminal of the airport and to wait out the obligatory two-hour pre check-in time. Consequently, in order to ensure that he made it to flight BA2584 to the Marco Polo Airport in Venice, he had had to rise even before the "early bird" and set out in the early morning darkness.

In contrast, Crosse only had a one-hour road trip to Birmingham Airport where she would take the Alitalia flight to the same destination.

After what seemed like one week, Hart finally arrived at the car rental office at Gatwick Airport. With the car returned to the agents, he took the shuttle-bus to the terminal and checked in for his flight. Thinking about his return flight to Birmingham already, he had decided to take the bank-breaking taxi ride back to Nottingham rather than spending another white-knuckle ride behind the wheel of a hired car. As was his general rule, Hart had opted to travel light, taking all his clothing and personal items in a small, wheeled suitcase which fulfilled BA's regulations relating to size and weight and which, therefore, allowed him to carry it on board the aircraft. He also carried a leather satchel, in which he had placed his passport, glasses, scientific notes, conference information and details of his itinerary.

Feeling tired after his arduous journey, he headed straight for the business lounge upon emerging from baggage check and passport control.

At about the same time, Crosse was taking coffee in the standard passenger lounge at Birmingham Airport prior to boarding her plane. Like Hart, she had packed lightly, enabling her to carry her bag on board also. Her slight concern was how she would manage her return with all the additional paperwork, pens and general freebies. Still, no problem, there was always the "complimentary conference bag" to put the key selected items into and the "complimentary conference bin" in which to "file" the rubbish.

Both of their flights were called on time and both of them initially relaxed back in their seats, assessing which of their fellow passengers were delegates destined for the same meeting, whilst at the same time contemplating what the next few days might impart. Soon into their flights, however, as discussed previously, they both scrutinised the conference program along with advanced meeting scientific abstracts which they had been able to download from the internet.

By the time their respective flights were descending into Venice Marco Polo airport, whilst Hart had gained an overall perspective of the meeting, Crosse had been more specific and had identified the key presentations and lectures she would aim to attend. She also had gained a good idea of the layout of the areas assigned to appropriate poster presentations and the commercial stands, together with companies' associated hospitality suites, a prime target for many less scientifically keen attendees who tended to spend a good deal of their time there taking advantage of the seemingly limitless flow of gratis drinks, food and goodies.

Hart had decided that his main area of interest once there would be those sections relating to the commercial aspects of the sciences, including symposium sponsors and individual specific stem cell related works. One particular item of detail he noted, however, was the location of the stand belonging to his "friends" at the GRS Institute in Greifswald.

Hart's flight touched down a little over two hours after leaving London and with just his "carry-on" case and satchel in the overhead luggage compartment to worry about, he was soon exiting the plane and heading through passport control. Within twenty minutes of landing, he had both cleared passport control and emptied his rather full bladder. Now feeling comfortably lighter, he was able to zig-zag his way through the thronged airport in his quest to rendezvous with Crosse at the allotted official airport meeting point. He found the blue "meeting point" sign, which rose some 20 feet above the masses with ease. Crosse was due to arrive 30 minutes ahead of him, but there was no sign of her. He looked around and saw a staircase which climbed away to a bar and small shopping area and he ascended it taking the stairs two at a time. Upon reaching the summit, he scanned the army of travellers below, noticing that many of them were already "badged up" for the conference, but Crosse was nowhere to be seen. He turned on his phone and checked his messages. Nothing.

Suddenly, standing out from the seething masses below, he saw her. She too held her carry-on suitcase and gripped the perfunctory meeting related journal under her arm. He felt unusually excited at seeing her and briefly considered the best way to gain her attention in the crowd without attracting the inquisitive eyes of the whole ensemble below. In the end, he pinpointed her position, skipped down the stairs and waded through the "Brownian movement" of the gathered travellers. Thankfully, she had stayed at the spot where he had previously picked her out and he was able to "home in" on the Meg Ryan lookalike with surprising ease.

'Good journey? God, this is all so frenetic!'

'Actually, my flight was bloody awful,' complained Hart. 'Full of delegates and their bloody flickering laptops…and the white wine was warm!

'Mine was fine thanks! I was actually able to do a bit of work…which I will show you in the taxi.'

'Talking of which,' Hart interrupted, raising his rolled up meeting agenda and using it as a pointer, 'we need to go through those doors straight ahead.'

Ahead of them lay the ranks of "ground support carriers", the drivers and meeters and greeters holding up placards on which were emblazoned various company and delegate names, standing there smiling and looking hopefully at all the arrivals. With heads down, Hart and Crosse skirted these expectant ranks and headed for the exit and the sign indicating "Taxis". Although the train would have been quicker, Hart had no inclination to re-join the throng at the Venice railway station and had instead opted for a taxi. Had Hart been a little more observant, he would have noticed one welcoming placard which would have been very interesting to him. Still, who wants to ruin an appetite just minutes after arriving in one of the best kitchens in Europe?

The automatically opening glass doors gave them immediate access to the taxi rank, which at this point was still relatively quiet ahead of the tidal wave of oncoming delegates behind them. Within a couple of minutes, they were seated in a taxi under the enquiring eye of the driver.

Crosse called out the hotel name and address in Padua and the driver shot off like a rocket, his command of English exceptional as he asked the duo if they were attending the symposium and then continued, informing them of his love for Manchester United FC.

'So what can you tell me about Padua, Max?'

'Not a great amount to be honest. It's certainly a very old place and had a lot of contacts with ancient Rome in early times. What I do know is that the university of Padua, founded in the 1200s, is the second oldest in Italy. It was, I believe, the place of the very first medical school…at least in Europe. That's probably why the city was chosen, although by default, for this meeting. The thing is though that the size of everything here is rather restrictive in terms of holding a decent-sized meeting.'

'But, Max, this is a relatively new emerging science and whilst there's a great deal of interest worldwide, the amount of work being done globally in this area is still relatively small. The fact that as yet there's not much of a commercial outlet for it is also a major factor affecting the size of meetings such as this.'

Despite the driver's estimate of thirty minutes for the journey time from Marco Polo Airport to the Hotel, they were "Italian minutes" and it was exactly one hour after departing that they actually pulled up outside. They immediately alighted from the cab, dragging their light luggage out with them and Crosse took the few steps into the hotel main entrance and on to reception where she proceeded to check in. As Hart, still outside on the pavement, flipped through his wallet and sorted out the fare. He paid the driver giving him a hefty tip on Denis and after a handshake and an *'arriverdici'* entered the hotel and made for reception where he saw Crosse waiting, having now checked in.

He looked around expecting to see many delegate faces in the lobby and bar, but it was quite calm and he proceeded to introduce himself to Nelli, the classically dark, attractive receptionist, whilst at the same time handing over his passport and reservation confirmation.

'I expected there to be more people around the hotel,' he added.

'No, there was in fatto a big chaos around the hotel this morning when many people arrives and again this afternoon, but now is tranquil,'

Nelli replied, flashing large brown eyes and displaying a perfect set of teeth, set in a beautiful smile.

'But I will expect another big chaos tomorrow morning when even more peoples arrive for the conference,' she added.

Hart completed the registration card and presented his credit card, which was duly swiped through the machine "to cover any incidentals taken during your stay", and then compared room numbers with Crosse. He was in room number 206 and Crosse in room number 218 on the same floor.

One hour later, showered and changed they were treading the cobbled street to the small trattoria which Nelli had recommended, both armed with agendas and notepaper, where they dined on antipasti followed by spaghetti alle vongole washed down with a local red vino della casa, the house wine. A quick double espresso each, during which Hart had just enough time to explain to her the "crime" of taking a cappuccino after 12.00 midday, then a quick payment in cash, with compliments to the chef, and despite their previous decision they were out of the restaurant and on their way on foot to register at the Sheraton Conference Hall.

Upon arriving outside the hall, Hart indicated an empty bench seat close to an illuminated fountain. Once seated, Hart indicated the image of a man staring out at them with vacant eyes from a recess within the fountain, his long hair illuminated by both the fountain's strategically placed lights and the illuminated halo above his head.

'That, VC, is Saint Anthony, Padua's very own patron saint. You got your purse? He's the patron saint of lost articles. You know there's a patron saint of just about everything, even one for the health of your television! It's true, in fact it's Saint Clare, or Chiara, of Assisi. She probably ensures that it is correctly tuned in and focused. Not so much parental control as "saintly control", so beware of those naughty adult channels, eh? Right, you up for registering then?'

Crosse smiling, and for sure there had been a lot of that this evening, responded.

'Come on then.'

And holding aloft her meeting brochure,

'I've highlighted here the presentations I really would like to attend and get a feel for. In fact one or two of them are actually being sponsored by our friends in Greifswald and Sicily. While I'm sitting in on those, you could perhaps spend some time checking out the posters in the exhibition hall?'

Hart relieved her of the brochure and quickly scanned the meetings she had marked. There was the opening keynote presentation from a US professor, currently widely regarded internationally as being the top researcher in the field, "A Biological Perspective of Stem Cells", and then a series of other talks and presentations by speakers from such diverse European countries as France, Belgium, Germany, Portugal and Greece, talking on a range of subjects that included: stem cells and the FDA, current issues with stem cell intellectual property, spinal cord injury, brain repair, Parkinson's disease and interestingly, one entitled, "An ethical cost for true recovery?"

'I think I may do the keynote presentation as well and also this one on "Ethics versus potential outcomes", and then most probably go walkabout and see how much hospitality I can obtain at some of the sponsoring company hospitality suites. It could be interesting to see who turns up there, if I can recognise anybody at all that is. I'll also do as you suggest and do a *passeggiata* of the poster sessions. It's some time since I last did a gig like this, so I really must remember to try and look intelligent at all times, Vicky, and I expect a nudge from you if my mask of pseudo intelligence ever slips.'

Crosse laughed. 'Don't worry, Max, I promise to be on "dope alert" at all times. So we're agreed then. We will both do our own thing in the main so as not to appear to any interested bodies to be working as a team. You know I think we may be getting a little paranoid here. Who on earth would be interested in us? Who knows what our business is here and how could anybody know anyway? I think we should lighten up and go with the flow a little. We don't have to meet up once off our starting blocks unless something of real note arises and we can keep in fairly regular contact via text. But phones on vibrate mind you as any ringing will surely draw attention to yourself and will almost certainly get you ejected from a meeting.'

'Got it.'

'Right then, it sounds like we have a plan. Let's go in and register.'

It was getting late in the day for registrations and only a few delegates were in the hall, walking around absentmindedly, each clutching their fake leather "meeting bag come folio", the item de rigueur at all meetings of this type, containing important details of what was being presented over the course of the next days and where it was happening, together with appropriate scientific papers bound into "the meeting journal", which made note taking a rather redundant process. However, because most attendees would scribble down masses of their own notes and comments during the meeting there were also notepads and an array of ballpoint pens bearing the names and logos of various scientific and medical sponsoring companies.

They both headed to the left of the hall, Crosse to a booth labelled "Names A-C" and Hart to one labelled "Names F-H", where both were handed their conference bags together with pre-printed name-cards assembled as lanyards to be hung around their necks. Without these, they would be unable to gain admittance to any of the events. Saint Anthony might yet come into his own as the meeting proceeded and delegates became less formal and less protective of their belongings being drawn more into the traditional party spirit that accompanied many of the sponsors' "hospitality events". With all items on board, the pair crossed the hall and outside into a star-filled night.

As they strolled in what Hart only guessed could be the direction of their hotel, he looked up.

'This is perfect. Here in Padua, nicely dined and now walking under a Van Gogh "starry sky".'

'It is indeed, Max, but I think you'll find it's actually a Van Gogh "starry night",' corrected Crosse.

'And I think that you will find that I was exerting a certain poetic, or should that be artistic license, O Pedantic One! What I think we should do now is to retire to our rooms for the night and have a thorough read of the folders Denis has furnished us with.'

By this time, they had completed the short walk from the Sheraton and had arrived back at their hotel entrance.

'That's a very professional approach and a good idea to boot. I'm surprised at you, Max! In fact I'm off now! *Buona notte caro.*'

'*Buona notte*, and I'll see you at 8.00 am for breakfast. We can make final tweaks to the day's agenda then, before setting off.'

They nodded, smiled at each other and each with a wave, retired to their respective rooms for the night. Hart decided that he would not attempt any sleep that night until he had both read and taken in all the information in Williams' file, and until he had decided upon a serious plan of action for the next day, for despite his constant show of flippancy with Crosse, he was deeply worried as to what the morrow might actually bring.

Chapter 47

Once in his room, Hart threw off his jacket, retrieved the "Denis File" from his battered satchel and flopped down into a very comfortable equally battered armchair. He opened the file and began to read.

The contents of the file were essentially reduced-size versions of everything that Williams had presented to them in his "war room" back in Nottingham. There were photographs of key staff from the Paddocks Hospital and also several snaps of what Williams had considered to be appropriate staff members from the Paddocks' sister hospital in Liverpool. There were also very accurate summaries of Hart's visits to both the Paddocks and to the clinic in Greifswald. Finally, after the four pages in which Williams had reproduced the bones of the brainstorming that the three of them had done, there was a virtual "route map" cum flow diagram which attempted to link together Liverpool, Nottingham, Greifswald and Sicily. There was also a bulleted list of questions that required addressing where knowledge was absent and needed to be gained, the biggest one having been placed against the Sicilian arm of the network:

- **Sicily...Which company?**
- *Who owns it?*
- *Is it a multinational company?*
- *Where are the company headquarters?*
- *Who runs it?*
- *Important people associated with it?*
- *Is it just a front for clandestine research?*
- *If so, what is its 'actual' area of research?*
- *Health aspects, biological sciences, drugs???*
- *How does it fit in with the other hospitals identified?*
- *Are there any patients resident at the other hospitals receiving their drugs?*
- *Are there any outpatients there?*
- *What are the patient diagnoses?*
- *Age range and gender of patients?*
- *Confirm relationships/link-ups between UK, Germany and Sicily*
- **What is the study that is most likely to be responsible for the death of Ruth Williams??**

Hart was a little stunned by Williams' final bullet point, but understood the sentiment of it totally. Overall he was impressed with the effort Williams had put into devising and supporting this piece of work he expected Crosse and himself to complete, but one thing he decided for sure was that upon completion of this trip, although he had enjoyed his role in it, whether they were successful or not in ticking any of Williams' boxes, it would be time for the pair of them to pull out gently and wish Williams "good luck" and "adios amigo". All they could do was to present Williams with a report of their observations and findings to add to those that he already had, and direct him for one final time to report the whole thing to the appropriate authorities.

Having come to that final conclusion, Hart felt satisfied. He checked his watch. It was 2.30 am (1.30 am in the UK) and he went to bed, where he slept fitfully until finally stirring at 7.00 am.

Chapter 48

Over the last few months, Peter Mondo had forged a close friendship with Giulio Falcone during his increasing number of activities around the Vatican, which were now regularly taking him out of America. Like Mondo, this fellow priest was young and fit and popular amongst other cardinals there. The pair of them shared very similar views on the way the church should proceed into the future and were seen by many of their contemporaries as beacons of light in that progressive movement. It came as no surprise, therefore, when the two priests were selected to attend a seminar in Caserta, a city some 40 km north of Naples.

Both men looked forward to this honour immensely, realising the great opportunity it gave them both to cross swords, in discussion at least, with many of their older more conservative peers. Mondo was particularly looking forward to the debates and discussions on contraception, abortion and the new medical technologies, the ethics of which were taking up an increasing amount of open discussion time at various meetings, where he was growing skilfully and happily into the role of chief "shockmeister" and "Devil's Advocate".

Mondo also looked forward to taking his daily morning 10km run in temporary new pastures, as did his running mate, Falcone. This had become a great event between them both, each one pushing every day to edge past the other at their "virtual" finishing line. Mondo put his recent run of victories down to the two new pairs of black Nike's he had brought back with him from the US and which he now wore continually. On this particular morning, they discussed Mondo's newfound victory streak and lifting his cassock, Mondo baited his friend in giving a nodding approval to the black Nikes, with the bold gold tick, that he was wearing. Falcone looked down ruefully,

'For sure, if I had those on my feet, I would be eating breakfast every morning before you were even in sight of the refectory.'

'Don't kid yourself, Giulio, it's my perfect stride pattern that beats you and it will beat you every time. I'll prove it.'

Later this particular day, they were travelling together by metro, bound for Rome's central station, la Stazione Termini, from where they would take a train to Caserta. As usual, their conversation was energetic, wide ranging and self-challenging, covering not just the ethical issues that both felt passionately about, but also less important items such as football, basketball and food.

In leaving the metro and heading for the ticket office in the station to collect their return tickets for the direct train to Caserta, Mondo halted his stride and taking Falcone by the arm said to him,

'Giulio, please wait a moment, I must get copies of the Washington Post and the New York Times from the newsstand back there if they have them. I'll just be a couple of minutes. I'll let you look after my bag, but be careful my extra pair of Nikes is in it!'

Unfortunately, the newsstand was unable to meet his requirement for American newspapers and he was directed back towards the station entrance to a larger store, which he found easily and bought his papers. He glanced at the headlines and then at his watch as he ploughed back into the crowd, suddenly feeling a little disorientated. And then he saw his friend at the same instant that Falcone spotted him. Both raised an arm...

The ear-splitting blast ripped through the concourse demolishing all kiosks and buildings in its path. There were screams and blood and torn away body parts floating seemingly in slow motion wrapped in a swirling, dense, black plume of acrid smoke. Masonary fell like rain smashing down to the ground taking with them many of those bodies that had been lucky enough to survive the initial thunderous explosion. As the dust began to settle, the scene resembled the site of some ferocious battle. What survivors there were, were now staggering randomly around, confused, concussed and choking on the thick foul smelling and tasting smoke and dust which hung like a bloody curtain suspended from some 20 feet up and hanging down to the now excavated ground below. Masonry was still falling, bloody body parts were still falling and people were still screaming as they groped their way through the acrid filthy curtain and crawled over the bombed-out floor.

Suddenly there was a tidal wave of people, many disfigured, all dirty and bloody, some dragging others, charging towards the exit in a state of total blind panic. Blind too because of the dense smoke and still falling debris. People stretched out arms and hands in front of them as they ran, bloody and torn. Somewhere emergency sirens were sounding, but these meant nothing to the sea of lemmings heading for the exit. Gas main or bomb? That was the question on the minds of anyone who could yet think in the total bloody chaos.

The priest stood there in absolute shock. He was relatively uninjured apart from a few scratches, but his eyes hurt like hell and he could barely breathe. As his senses slowly returned, his overwhelming thought was to find his friend and companion and impulsively he surged forward in the direction of the crowd, but it was against the general flow and he soon found himself travelling in totally the wrong direction, carried along by the surging mass. As he was transported on the human tide towards a corner where a kiosk, which had been selling espressi, latte, machiati and cappuccini ten minutes before, had been ripped away leaving a crevice in the corner of the wall, with a great effort, he broke out and pushed himself into it forcing himself against the jagged bricks of the wall, watching as the panic-stricken mass of commuters and travellers fled past. Slowly his eyes turned to the debris and rubble on the battle theatre floor: metal, stone, wood, plastic, blood and bodies in various stages of disassembly.

The torrent of people finally abated to a stream and then a trickle and at that point he went out to try and locate his friend and colleague. Picking through the corpses wasn't easy, either physically or mentally, but eventually he reached the point where he thought he may have seen the waving hand immediately before this particular world came to an end. It took no time at all. There in front of him covered in a mountain of masonry, rocks and timbers was a single body part that brought him instant recognition. It was a lower leg part and a ripped piece of black material that had once been part of a cassock. The foot was still attached to the leg and there in all its gory glory was a black Nike shoe with a golden tick.

People in trance-like states recognised the priest's uniform and gathered round him for help and solace, but at this point, he was the same as everybody else on that concourse, shattered, confused, afraid and totally distraught for his friend. There was no place for religion here...not just yet anyway.

Chapter 49

Crosse and Hart met as arranged for breakfast, with Crosse arriving some ten minutes later at the table, which passed rather quietly. They did, however, exchange one or two comments relating to their agreed plan of action, but generally confirmed with each other that it would remain basically as they had decided previously.

After a low-key breakfast, they retired briefly to their rooms, re-emerging 30 minutes later carrying all the documents that they would require over the course of the day tucked nicely in the fake leather folio each had been given upon registering their names at the conference centre the evening before.

'Remembered to bring your war room stuff as well as the symposium stuff VC?' Hart asked a little officiously.

'Yes, thanks Max, I also remembered to put my shoes and trousers on,' came the sarcastic reply.

According to the concierge, it's a 20-minute stroll to the Sheraton. I can't remember how long we took last night, but there's no pressure on us getting there too early anyway. I can't remember the route, but there are bound to be others following the same route, all with name badges I expect.'

At this, he fumbled in the folio where he eventually found his lanyard containing his name badge and hung it around his neck. He hadn't noticed but Crosse had arrived at breakfast with hers already in place. As if on cue, as they walked out into the morning sunlight, they merged into a line of some 40 other delegates, sounding sufficiently boring not to be confused with tourists.

'Come on, VC, let's step out and leave these people behind before they send me back to sleep. I'm almost sleep-walking as it is.'

As they quickly turned the corner at the end of the hotel driveway, they stepped out into a different world, where their senses were immediately assaulted by the noise and the rush of the morning traffic, not to mention those rushing on foot.

'At least it's almost fresh air at last,' gasped Crosse.

She hated the manufactured atmosphere that existed in air-conditioned hotels and was always relieved to breathe the "real stuff" even though it was probably high in toxic traffic fumes. The traffic really was frenetic, with brakes squealing and horns blaring, all cars apparently in the hands of would be Formula 1 drivers, although "drivers" was not strictly correct as hands were mostly either on horns, using mobile phones or gesticulating wildly at other motorists. Hart pointed to a black BMW whose driver was approaching a set of traffic lights whilst speaking on his phone, gesticulating at everybody in sight and with an open newspaper perched on his steering wheel. Crosse smiled happily.

'You know, Max, I really love all this. The noise, the smell, the outrageous driving behaviours, it really makes me feel that I'm...abroad.'

Hart agreed. 'I just love Italy and the Italian people. They enjoy life so much. I get the impression that even the not so well off enjoy a great quality of life.'

'Yes I agree with you for sure.'

Hart leapt out of the way as a moped sounding like a very large mosquito mounted the pavement to dodge around a line of waiting cars. The 16 or so year-old, very attractive rider, laughed and threw Hart a wave, flicking back her dark hair across her helmet-less head.

Her arrival and departure signalled a veritable cloud of other giant "mosquitos", which followed in her wake around the stationary honking cars. This shoal of Aprilia and Piaggio mopeds and Vespa and Lambretta scooters was a fine touristic sight and had both Hart and Crosse beaming.

They laughed at the gesticulations and Crosse shouted above the traffic noise, 'They say that if you amputated an Italian's hands, he would be totally unable to speak.'

'He'd still bloody drive though!' retorted Hart.

The 20 minutes' walk to the Sheraton Padua Conference Centre once again turned out to be 20 "Italian minutes", and so 40 minutes after leaving their hotel, they were crossing Corso Argentina and arriving at the imposing entrance of the Sheraton. Looking up at the sound of billowing flags, they saw along the extensive frontage of the rooftop the flags of many nations signalling a truly multinational conference and below these a single large expanse of plastic sheeting advertising the event now ongoing inside: "International Congress of Stem Cell Regenerative Medicine", along with an accompanying logo constructed out of the letters ICSCRM and a representation of a human cell in the process of multiplication.

Hart nodded at the sign,

'If you're going to have an acronym, you should have one that spells something out that's pronounceable, or at least have a bloody short one. Who's going to remember that mouthful, and the logo-cell-thing is ridiculous?'

There were fewer people shuffling around the vestibule of the conference centre than Hart had anticipated, but Crosse assured him that by noon the place would be as tight as a tin of sardines. Hart suggested a seat and a coffee before starting proper and Crosse agreed. They found a table and a couple of chairs in a small refreshment area and armed with a couple of gratis cappuccini, proceeded to investigate in detail once more the contents of their folios. Hart gave a deep sigh,

'There's so much rubbish here, VC. I really need to get rid of at least 90% of it before walking round. I can't carry all this tosh around all day, or I'll end up with arms as long as a gorilla.'

Crosse smiled. Hart was such a drama queen, but at least, he seemed a little less nervous than she thought he had appeared earlier. She was glad that the major part of the day would be spent on her own as she might actually learn some science. Within 15 minutes of sitting down, it was time for them to get up again and follow their agreed plans to head off in opposite directions and then meet up again for a bite to eat and to compare notes at 1 o'clock. Crosse headed off to take in a series of scientific presentations that she had highlighted in the program, whilst simultaneously obtaining some idea where possible of any obvious relationships between representatives of scientific institutions and the pharma company folk. This was a difficult assignment as there is an automatic almost natural incestuous relationship between those two groups, which *has* to exist for their own individual survival with each one feeding off the other symbiotically…both taking care not to over eat.

As soon as the starting pistol was theoretically fired for Hart and Crosse to hit the scientific trail, Hart immediately disbanded his plan to take in the presentations and instead opted to walk around the poster stands and observe both the poster details, the poster minders, and like Crosse for any obvious particularly heavy incestuous relationships between science and pharma. It was also a chance to get handfuls of freebie pens and paper, patisseries and more coffee. The conference centre had 15 multi-functional rooms, all equipped with the most modern presentation facilities. Live presentations from staged areas were split between 10 of these rooms, which varied in size according to the anticipated size of the audiences. Two of the rooms with sliding doors had been metamorphosed into a single unit and it was here that the first session of posters were being exhibited. Posters of varying physical quality, mostly of A0 size and laminated, were pinned to a series of free standing movable notice boards in a labyrinthine fashion which meant that having entered at one end of the labyrinth one had to progress to the distant end, unless turning back and retracing one's steps. Below, each poster was a pile of smaller A4 versions for punters to take away with them.

Hart accepted a "plastic glass" of freshly squeezed orange juice from a smiling female attendant and proceeded to walk the maze, taking in the general gist of the posters on view either side of him. Coming from a medical background focused generally on sterile, unemotional clinical scientific research, it was a strange experience for him to view the sensationalised scientific publications around him, some of which appeared to be more akin to semi-biblical pronouncements, with titles proclaiming such findings as "Foetal Injections Cure Early Diagnosis Paraplegia", "Severed Spinal Cord repaired" and "Parkinson's Defeated After Just one Month". There were also satirical pictorial cartoons representing Lourdes-like vistas. He didn't read the articles in any depth feeling that there was bound to be a massive hole somewhere in the scientific procedures but bore in mind that these articles and the others would have to have undergone some form of proper peer review to reach this stage of publication. Had he leaned in and read a little, however, he would have learnt that these articles were indeed the product of an over-zealous imaginative mind and were presented only to demonstrate how sensitive one should be in reporting on this very emotive branch of research.

Further on down the line where the genuine publications began, reading between the lines of some of the scripts it was clear that on the one hand semi-religious evangelical nuances were sometimes in play and on the other hand write-offs of all things religious through *man's* successes at manipulating his own biological future. By this time, Hart had woken up and smelt the coffee and it depressed him how science appeared to be being manipulated to further religious and anti-religious doctrines. He was wrong though, as he would soon discover as he wandered on and he gradually became more engrossed in some of the science on show. Much of the research on show was serious and based upon watertight scientific principles. He would later see, in company breakout refreshment rooms, how the future of this very special branch of science was being meticulously devised and planned.

Hart remembered a previous comment of Crosse, that 'whilst there was tremendous excitement being generated by some outstanding ground-breaking work in this scientific field of research with some truly significant validated outcomes, in many instances the big breakthroughs after many years of potential and promise, were yet to happen', and it sobered his thoughts as he read quickly as he progressed down the maze. It also brought his thoughts back around to exactly why they were at the conference, the tragic circumstances which had brought them here and what their intentions were over the next couple of days…and that sobered his thoughts even more.

He stopped briefly at a poster entitled, "Commercial Implications for the Pharma and Biotech Industries".

'Ahh the sweet smell of money,' he muttered under his breath. 'I wonder what the price of a miracle is these days.'

Whatever the cost or the price, there was obviously no mention of such associated treatment details in the article. What there was though was a list of companies together with their visions, mission statements and current policies relating to their engagements in human embryonic stem cell research. As Hart scanned through the listed companies, he suddenly caught his breath.

'Bloody hell!'

There, before his very eyes was printed the stem cell research policy of a company he knew very well….World Pharmaceuticals. This had taken him totally by surprise. He had always prided himself on keeping his ear to the ground whilst in employment with World Pharma, apart from in the instance of his own demise of course, and he felt that very little would take place in their various fields of research and development at least without him getting a gentle whiff of it. He returned to the beginning of the article and this time concentrated properly on it…having initially sped over the opening few lines:

'…. blah, blah, blah, and World Pharmaceuticals recognise that the use of human embryonic stem cells is a very sensitive political, religious and general public issue, being the subject of much on-going ethical debate. The World Board of Directors believe that it is their duty to make every effort to deliver ethical, new, novel, safe and innovative medicines to the global population and to carry out research using human embryonic stem cells offers the possibilities of delivering those exciting opportunities. World is actively monitoring all such developments within these novel therapeutic areas with the intention of engaging in appropriate research in these areas, both within our own research and development facilities worldwide and through collaboration with suitable external ethical companies and international institutes of excellence. This company would like to state formally that it is neither involved nor interested in research involving human reproductive cloning. This company will only utilise stem cell lines that are compliant with the following criteria:

- The stem cells used must have been derived from a fertilized egg that has been created for reproductive purposes
- The fertilized eggs must no longer have been required for reproductive purposes
- Full and total informed consent must have been obtained/given by the donors for the use of the fertilized egg for scientific research
- No financial inducements to any person or organization must have been provided for the donation of the fertilized egg.'

Hart picked up several of the A4 copies of the poster and added them to the others that he had accumulated since entering the poster maze. He looked again at the poster still shocked that his former company had, totally unknown to him, embarked down this scientific route and he made a mental note to call the US and talk to…talk to who? Which one of his ex-colleagues would be prepared to openly discuss company research issues? Certainly not his old friend Ken Rogers, even though it had been Hart who had given him his first break in pharmaceuticals when Rogers had become terminally disenchanted with working in the public health service. No, since Hart's departures from World, Rogers had apparently found that the "Emperors old clothes" fitted him very comfortably indeed as he proceeded at a great rate of knots to sail up the promotional ladder in Hart's old clinical development area.

No, it would have to be Janet. Good old faithful Janet. It was time he called her anyway, if only to see how she was. He would call her that evening. Now what was the time difference? Yes, six (or was it seven?) hours, so he could call her at any time within reason after 3 pm Italian time. For now though, it was a forward march through the poster labyrinth, and over the following two hours he visually scanned and picked up abstracts and full copy A4s of all that he believed to be of interest, both of the published and the pre-publication science which was related to the various stem cell therapeutic areas on display.

Towards the end of his voyage of learning, one poster leaped out at him and despite his previous briefing by Crosse of what to possibly expect on his voyage, his heart rate skipped up two gears at the sight of the poster:

"The Effects of Embryonic Stem Cell Treatment in Patients, Identified in a German Population, with Parkinson's Disease".

Schmoller G.R, Lehmann P and Rolfes S.A

The Gerhard Roscher Schmoller (GRS) Institute, Greifswald, Germany

Hart moved close to it picking up the smaller copy whilst keeping his eyes fixed to the text reading quickly but intently, to the end. In reaching that point, his racing heart surged even more when he read the closing remarks,

'We would like to express our thanks to our sponsors in this study, World Pharmaceuticals, without whose dedicated support this ground-breaking research would not have been possible.'

'World linked to GRS! Bloody hell!'

Hart was stunned, but still this probably didn't mean too much since at least 90% of the work published here has been sponsored by pharmaceutical companies of one kind or another. For some strange reason, he found himself trying to find excuses for his old company. Such loyalty!

Hart's impatience at not being able to call Janet in the USA immediately was almost unbearable. He checked his watch. Whilst too early to call the US, it was in fact time to rejoin Crosse at the "Meeting Point" for their planned "spot of lunch" and updates. As he hurried past the final remaining posters, he glimpsed reports of cosmetic studies where skin cells had been cloned from subjects and then re-injected into the donor. The reported outcome shouted "instant youth", but Hart was unimpressed. What probably appeared as Shangri La to many appeared more like some sort of Dante's Inferno to him.

As he left the room and headed for his rendezvous with Crosse, he thought of how he had managed to therapeutically disassociate himself from World over the last weeks, but suddenly within minutes, all self-repair had been reversed and memories of his last few fateful days working for World had come rushing back.

Chapter 50

The citizens of New York who awoke to CNN News on their televisions were the first in the US to hear of the devastating explosion at Rome's major railway station.

Alberto Mondo had prior knowledge of his brother Peter's planned rail trip to a weekend seminar on that same day and when the news was broadcast, he became immediately frantic to hear any news at all of his brother's situation.

The news had been generous in its description of the dead and injured, amongst who were many children and other members of the public, certain of who were nuns and priests.

Had Mondo been aware of the actual events unfolding at the station, he would have been mortified, as once the dust and smoke had settled and some of the light debris had been moved away, bodies were being detected everywhere in and around the devastated station concourse. As searchers moved around looking for the injured and the dead, suddenly a cry went up, 'Body found,' and other helpers converged onto the scene. What they witnessed at this scene, were the legs and obvious cassock of a priest protruding from a pile of masonry. The lower parts of the cassock in view were dirty and torn, as were the socks visible from the totally untouched black Nike trainers sporting a large golden tick. To the side of the lower part of the body was a sports bag. One of the searchers reached down and pulled at the name tag attached to one of the handles and read out the name to his fellow helpers,

'It says Mondo. Father P. Mondo. He was a priest.'

He made the sign of the cross and lowered his head to his chest in respect. His associates did likewise.

Two hours later back in New York, Alberto Mondo was still pacing his office, worried sick, when suddenly the telephone rang. He stared at it for just one moment before snatching it to his ear.

'Yes!'

It was his PA,

'I'm sorry to disturb you sir, but I have a call for you from Rome...'

Chapter 51

Crosse saw Hart first as she waited at the "Meeting Point". As he drew up to her, she nodded in the direction of his bulging folio and his armful of re-prints and papers.

'It looks like you've been shopping already,' she said with a smile.

'We have to talk, VC. I've come across something that's really interesting and to be honest, a little shocking for me. Can we find a place where we can sit down?'

'You must be joking, Max, its chaos here; we'll have to go outside.

'OK then, let's move out of here. Conference food is shite anyway. I noticed a small bar on the way here on Via Manzoni, across the way. Let's go there.'

'Are you all right, Max, you seem a bit…'

'Strung out and tetchy? Well, yes and no. Let's just say an old wound was re-opened back there, but more importantly, I do have something very interesting to tell you which may or may not have any bearing on the mission we are on, but you know I just don't believe in coincidences of this type.'

The two of them moved away from the hall and outside into the bright sunlight. With Crosse leading the way, they proceeded back the way they had come earlier. Via Manzoni soon came into sight and they crossed the busy road to it, dodging and weaving through the stop-go traffic, horns blaring all the way. Although just 10 minutes on foot from the conference centre, it was clearly enough distance to separate them from the herd of meeting delegates. Crosse saw the bar ahead and entering headed straight to the back where she found a table for two in a corner. Hart dropped heavily into one of the wicker chairs set around an aluminium table, covering one area of it with his pile of papers and his folio. Crosse lowered herself into the wicker chair facing him expectantly. He let out a long sigh.

'That's better, I feel as if I've walked a marathon already this morning.'

Before he could add anything further, the waiter, lying in wait like a lion at an African waterhole, pounced. The pair quickly scanned the menus which were thrust in front of them and each ordered a ham toasted sandwich, and a medium-sized beer.

'Enough of the drama queen now, Max, what the bloody hell have you come up with!'

Hart raised an eyebrow at Crosse's unusually stern tone of voice and responded in a surprisingly serious manner.

'You know, VC, I've had some really disturbing thoughts and feelings this morning. I spent most of my time wandering around the maze of research posters as we previously agreed, looking at work that has been carried out and the names of the various researchers involved in it, in an effort to catch sight of anyone or anything which could remotely be connected to the reasons we are here. Whilst the majority of the work presented was scientifically sound, with proper statistical analyses and fair conclusions, a good part of it would have been more appropriate for presentation at Brother-Lee-Love's Salvation Show. So depressing! Some of the work presented had replaced science with tabloid newspaper-like spectacular unconfirmed or dubiously witnessed almost hysterical individual claims. Virtual miracle cures for inoperable brain injuries, Alzheimer's disease, severe spinal injuries, Parkinson's, et cetera, et cetera. You name it and there were miracle cures presented for it. There was almost a religious fervour surrounding some of the presenters…and you know how much I love that! However putting that that to one side, when I got over my initial depression and arrived at the section containing posters presenting the possible resultant commercial implications for the pharmaceutical industry, I was staggered to find a proclamation from a major scientifically serious company who were until quite recently quite dear to my heart.'

His face took on a very bitter and rueful look and Crosse decided that silence was the best option of the moment for her. After a brief pause, he continued,

'Yes, I had absolutely no idea of this but World Pharma now have a very keen interest in stem cell research. Perhaps they've had it for some time and I was unaware of it, but in any case, up on the wall back there was a whole article sponsored by them on their philosophical and active research stance in that particular therapeutic area. That was the first major surprise to hit me today. The second was a very well written presentation of the outcomes of the treatment of Parkinson's disease in a German population, based in…guess where? … Yes, Greifswald!'

The level of Hart's voice rose and Crosse simultaneously raised her eyebrows whilst placing a finger over her mouth to indicate him to keep his voice down.

'And I've not finished yet, because the biggest surprise of all was to read the acknowledgement at the foot of that poster thanking World Pharma for their continued support and sponsorship! I've brought copies of the shite for you and Denis somewhere here in this pile.'

Once again, Crosse indicated for Hart to lower his voice,

'So, Max, what does this actually mean? You know very well that sponsorship is essential for the very existence of small companies, let alone supporting their very expensive research programs if they believe the science and the therapeutic objectives to be sound and worthwhile…and ultimately profitable to themselves of course. It's just a fact of research medicine life. Somebody had to do it for the German crew and perhaps just coincidentally it was World.'

Suddenly, as if arriving by transporter beam, two sandwiches and two medium beers arrived on the table in front of them and the bill was squeezed under the ashtray.

'Let's eat, VC, and then I suggest we have a re-cap on what we now know and then agree on where to go from here, if indeed it is any different to what we have already agreed to. OK?'

Crosse nodded her approval and lunch was taken. Fifteen minutes of concentrated eating, drinking and simultaneous silence later, they were ready to discuss the mission once more. Hart patted his mouth with his napkin and cleared his throat.

'OK, let's do the recap then. We are aware for sure that human embryonic tissue is being illegally gathered at hospitals in the UK, and who knows where else? We also know that at least a part of this tissue is being sent out to the GRS Institute in Greifswald because I've been there, done that and got the T-shirt...almost. In addition, we know that this tissue is being *possibly* part-processed, but almost certainly being re-sent from there to "Vita Pharma" in Basiglio, Sicily. From today, we are now aware that World Pharma is providing whatever scientific help and financial resource is necessary to paint a wider and possibly more pharmaceutically ethical face on the GRS Institute. It seems obvious at the moment, therefore, that we try and establish exactly what the link is between the three organisations, especially that with Vita Pharma of which we currently know very little. I don't think we are quite at the place yet when we can hand over our findings to Denis and tell him to contact appropriate authorities, the case is currently much too thin. I have in fact been searching for any references to Vita Pharma on the posters I've scanned, but so far no luck.

'I'll call Denis tonight and give him an update. I also intend to call my old PA back at World in the States and see if she has any info on World's links to GRS. If not, she might be able to dig something up through the old PA network there.'

He drained his glass and smiled at Crosse.

'I feel a lot better now, VC. Sorry if was somewhat tetchy earlier, unusually stressed I think. Dolce?'

'No thanks, I'm full, but you have whetted my appetite for further information and I really want to get back for the early afternoon presentations. Who knows, Vita might crop up in one of the studies on the agenda? What about yourself?'

'There is a totally new set of posters going up this afternoon which my eyes are just aching to see. I'll keep a close lookout for any reference to, or mention of, Vita Pharma as well. I also noticed earlier that GRS has a hospitality lounge for the punters. Anyone can go in and use the facilities without any formal invitation I think, so I might crash in there as well. It might actually be useful for you to crash it with me, if only for a glass of champers and a couple or three canapés.'

'Sounds fine. What time would be best do you think?'

'Tell you what, why don't we meet again at the "Meeting Point" at say 4.00 pm and then go on together?'

'OK Max, I'm going to set off back now, are you coming too?'

'Actually, VC, if you don't mind, I think I will have a stroll back via the scenic route, whatever that is, and pull in some of the local sights. To be honest,

I really do need to clear my head a bit after this morning's shocks to my system. I might also scribble a quick list of questions which I will give to my old PA Janet when I call her later. Who knows she might even know how many other pies World could have their sticky fingers in.'

'Right then, I'm off. See you later. *Ciao*.'

'Ciao Bella.'

Chapter 52

'...Put them through.'

When it came to matters of business, Alberto Mondo could be a very hard man indeed. In fact to some, he was regarded as somewhat of a bare-knuckle fighter, not very sophisticated in the ring, but often brutal and able to go the full distance. It was common knowledge that he would be prepared to skirt normal acceptable behaviours and regulations and possibly even the law, to do whatever was necessary in order to emerge as victor in any clash in business, but the current events had rendered him powerless. For the first time, he could ever remember he felt utterly drained and useless, for in this turn of events, he was completely unable to exert any influence, fair or foul, on the outcome.

'Yes?'

'Alberto, how are you?'

Mondo was completely taken aback.

'Peter? Peter is that you?'

'Yes of course it's me, why who were you expecting?'

'But I have seen the terrible news on the television from Rome. The death of the priest at the station. I thought...I thought...'

'You thought it was me, yes? Well, it's not, but very sadly it's my very good friend and colleague Giulio, Giulio Falcone. I was with him until five minutes before the detonation of the bomb. I left my bag with him while I went to buy American newspapers, during which time he went into it and put on my spare pair of trainers. I don't know why, but I guess it was as a joke following a conversation we had had earlier in the day. Then when his body was found in the rubble, they found the bag with my name on it next to him and of course the trainers on his feet. They put two and two together and unfortunately made five. I would have called you sooner, but I have been so stunned and in shock since the explosion, and also so very deaf, that it just was not possible. Apparently, some terrorist organisation have claimed responsibility in retaliation for Italy's clampdown on refugees from North Africa.'

'No problem, no problem, caro Peter, the main thing is that you are alive and I thank God for that. I must go and quickly inform other people here of your deliverance from death, but I will call you later. *Ciao caro e un grand abbraccio.*'

Alberto dropped the phone back onto its cradle and slumped into his chair. He poured himself a large brandy from the decanter sat on the table at the side of him and staring into the fire took a long deep drink and closed his eyes. The end of his world had just been averted.

Chapter 53

Hart paid the bill to the cashier standing by the till at the bar and exited into the glorious afternoon sun. He looked around for a moment and then decided upon Via Manzoni, which he casually wandered down, folio and papers clutched in both of his hands.

'*Ahh, la dolce vita,*' he whispered to himself.

Within five minutes of walking, he came across a litterbin and quickly looking through the publications and documents he had picked up at the conference centre dumped most of them inside it. Those not "recycled", he put into the folio. His intention was to walk nowhere in particular, as long as he didn't get lost, and just take in the Italian ambience. The cobbled pavement was a little uncomfortable in his newish loafers, but the ambience was wonderful. Occasionally, there was the not so wonderful aroma of the Paduan sewers, but that was all part of the experience. He loved simply everything about Italy and Padua lived up to all his expectations, and certainly after the shocks of the morning session, this was exactly the therapy he needed. At the end of his few days in Padua, he would definitely take the train to Milan where he would meet his old friend and eat in his house with his family and all in the world would be *almost* perfect. Denis would have to wait.

As he strolled past a small open park area, complete with tinkling fountain, he decided to make use of one of the unoccupied wooden benches and sit back and concentrate a little more on what he and Crosse had decided to do. Greater delving into the activities in Sicily of Vita Pharma was essential. Perhaps Denis could do this and e-mail any relevant details back to them. One thing foremost in his mind was that his time on this project was almost up. The upsets of the morning had clearly demonstrated to him that the business was still too stressful for his improving rehabilitation, but also it was possibly potentially too dangerous. Yes, after this week, he would retire from "the case" and decamp to a sunny beach in Greece for a couple of weeks.

He suddenly became aware of the laughing voices of small children and opened his eyes in time to see their mother ushering them away from the presence of the likely drunk who had fallen asleep on the park bench. He laboriously raised his arm and looked at his watch. 'Jesus!' It was almost 4.30 pm! He had fallen asleep and was now late for his rendezvous with Crosse. He stumbled to his feet, tripping and going to ground in one ill-elegant movement, creating an even better impression of a drunken man. Standing with some difficulty, he then hurriedly retraced his steps to the conference centre, where he headed directly to the "Meeting Point". He arrived looking very hot and bothered as Crosse was impatiently pacing in the opposite direction. He tried dusting himself down and straightened his shirt collar.

'Hi, VC, sorry I'm a bit late, I got really engrossed in this particular research paper and the time simply flew by,' he lied.

'Don't worry, I've only just arrived here myself,' she returned the lie. 'It looks like you were reading the article in a sand pit!'

'Tell you what, Vicky, just in case we need an invite to the GRS hospitality suite, let's head over to their poster, which I read earlier, and get into conversation with one of the authors if one is there. That way our show of interest is bound to lead to any necessary invitation.'

'OK, we might also hint at some future collaboration or even sponsorship from the University of Nottingham...' added Crosse, '...if we want to get his juices flowing a little more. Perhaps we should also take another look at the suspects' mug-shots that Denis put together for us before we go, just in case.'

Five minutes later and "mugged up", they were swiftly picking their path past the first section of the posters, giving themselves little time to take in much of their contents. Hart noticed that a change in the ambience now pervaded the posters, for whilst many of the morning's efforts were dedicated to the tabloid newspaper sensationalist headline format, the afternoon presentations were more of a serious scientific nature. He approved of the change, this being more like the serious clinical presentations that he was used to.

'I hope your man is still there, Max.'

'Yes, so do I. Hang on that's him there, the tall blond chap with the glasses and the bright orange shirt.'

'Ouch! Far too much carotene I think!'

The couple moved up to the relevant poster and looked intently at it, whilst feigning serious conversation relating to its content.

The owner of the loud orange shirt smiled at them.

'If you have any questions, don't hesitate to ask and I will try and give you an answer.'

Mr Orange possessed a German/American accent, but his English was spot on.

Hart under his breath, said, 'Yes, where the hell did you find that terrible shirt!'

Crosse burst out laughing, but immediately worked hard at straightening her face.

With straightened face, she faced the orange man,

'Yes, thank you, this is very interesting work. Unlike much of the work on show I see that you had quite a large number of subjects taking part in your study.'

The delighted presenter moved closer, 'Yes indeed, we had 200 patients, all with Parkinson's disease and mostly from the northeastern areas of Germany. That is from Greifswald and surrounding areas. The others were still of German origin but spread rather further afield.'

'And I see that half of the patients received placebo,' continued Crosse.

'Yes, but placebo patients were allowed to continue with their normal medication throughout the entirety of the study. It was a double-dummy, double-blind, comparator study, with the placebo identical in appearance to the active drug. Of course, those patients who benefited from the active treatment will be allowed to continue with the treatment for as long as they wish once the trial has finished.'

Hart felt the need to join in.

'That's very impressive, Doctor...?'

'Freidel. I'm Doctor Freidel. It was a beautiful study with outstanding efficacy demonstrated by our compound,' he beamed.

'Thank you. Yes, very impressive, but I don't see very much detail relating to the safety profile of your new compound. What about adverse events? I am aware that this class of drugs can have somewhat disturbing side effects on certain patients.'

Freidel commenced the case for the defence.

'Of course there were adverse events, but these were only of a minor nature and it was concluded that only one of them was significantly attributable to the active study treatment.'

Crosse for the prosecution,

'But nevertheless, there is no evidence of that presented here. You really should have given more space to adverse events in the discussion. I don't feel totally convinced,' and turning to Hart, 'what do you think, Professor?'

Hart placed a hand under his chin,

'Umm, I think you're right, we will perhaps have to have a re-think before considering this drug for our patient outcomes study, in any case at least until we have more convincing safety data available. You know, Doctor Freidel, our study is extremely large and is planned to recruit five thousand patients globally.'

He looked at Crosse.

'This represents a huge financial lay-out to your company Doctor *Crasse* and we would require greater convincing safety data for this drug before we gave it further consideration.'

Behind Freidel's back, Crosse briefly stared daggers at Hart for his deliberate uncomplimentary change of her name. Hart gave her a quick smile in return as Doctor Freidel wrung his hands and looked at his poster.

'A five-thousand-patient study?!'

The colour of Doctor Orange's face was now competing very well with his shirt for that particular end of the colour spectrum. Despite *Professor* Hart's comments, he was nevertheless bursting with enthusiasm. Crosse had earlier talked of the possibility of getting presenters juices flowing and here it was, *orange* juice by the litre.

'Look, we have much more data on file in our hospitality suite which I can show you. I could even copy some for you if it helps. Oh, here is my card by the way.'

'Thank you, Doctor Freidel. Do we have time, Professor?'

Hart looked ruefully at his watch,

'I'm not sure.... but yes I think we may have. This does look like a really ground-breaking treatment and I would hate to leave without a proper insight into its true potential.'

Doctor Freidel almost passed out with simultaneous relief and pleasure at his catch.

'Good, good. Please follow me, I am sure you will not be disappointed and while you are digesting the data perhaps you would also like to digest some of our excellent canapés along with a little champagne, yes, ha, ha, ha?'

He turned away from the stand with Hart and Crosse close at his heels. Hart looked at Crosse and winked. 'Ha, ha, ha!'

Chapter 54

Crosse and Hart accompanied Freidel towards the imposing room that was the GRS Institute hospitality suite, located on the first floor of the conference centre. The hubbub of the chattering throng faded behind them and from the top of the stairs they had a panoramic view of the various meeting rooms and registration areas.

Once inside the suit and still smiling, Doctor Freidel turned to them and encompassing the tables with a wave of his outstretched arm said,

'Please help yourselves to any drink or food that appeals to you. I apologise for the slight mess, but you know what it's like. I will disappear for a short moment and return with the safety details that I promised you.'

Crosse and Hart smiled and nodded in reply as "agent orange" then threaded his way across the room disappearing through a closed door and into a room recessed at the back of the main area. Craning their necks after him, they saw the sign on the door indicating, "Strictly GRS Personnel only". When he finally re-emerged carrying a wad of papers, he was followed by one of his colleagues, which kept the door ajar a little while longer. Before the door clicked shut, they were able to see that that room was somewhat larger than expected. They caught a glimpse of a series of filing cabinets, at least one photocopier, a large table with chairs and an array of computers. Before Freidel reached them, Hart turned to Crosse and quickly said,

'Look, VC, can you deal with our host while I go and take a look at those other posters on the wall opposite? I'll have a general nosey around and you can catch me up when you've done with the doctor.'

'Thanks a lot!'

Before Crosse could protest anymore, Hart slipped away into the crowd. He began his patrol close to the back office from which Freidel had recently emerged and began taking interest in the posters on the wall. These were certainly of a better quality than those downstairs, with well-designed studies, proper statistical assessments and reasonable conclusions. The wall was pretty much filled completely at eye level with presentations of studies completed at the Gerhard Roscher Schmoller Institute. As he moved along the line, his attention was suddenly drawn to a voice, which had risen above the others from somewhere across the room behind him, a voice that he almost recognised. Almost, but not quite. Unable to place it he moved on once more, eyes sprinting over presentation after presentation, until suddenly his eyes widened...and then widened again! In front of him was a presentation of what appeared to be the trial that had worked as their boarding pass to this room but which on closer scrutiny, whilst similar, had several differences. For instance there were fewer patients taking part in it and it was a far simpler set up in terms of treatment arms. However the phrase that had caused the dilation of his pupils stated, '…and our thanks to our collaborators in this study, Vita Pharma, Sicily,' and there followed a short list of names of the Vita personnel who had collaborated, '…and also colleagues at the Paddocks Clinic, Nottingham, England.' Once again there was a short list of people. Furthermore, to add insult to injury, beneath the lists of collaborators was a photograph of a smiling group of people standing under the fronds of an exotic tree in some Mediterranean location. The photograph title read, "HOPE Study Research Teams meet in Tenerife." As for the poster session downstairs, beneath the posters on tables were size A4 copies of them. Hart swept a few of them up.

Suddenly there it was, a definitive link between Germany, Sicily and the UK, with a photograph for additional proof, but what about World? How could they possibly be linked to these other contributing countries? At that point, Hart wasn't exactly sure of what his feelings were, excitement, anger or even elation, but for sure, his heart was racing once more and he wanted nothing more than to escape from this place, where the walls had suddenly begun to close in on all sides. He tried moving to return to Crosse, but his legs would not work, he was completely rooted to the spot.

Standing there, Hart could do nothing more than stare down at the smiling faces in the photograph. The tanned faces with dark hair were a giveaway for the Sicilian contingents, but what about the others? Bingo! Amongst the others smiling in the sun he recognised at least two of the people from Denis' mug-shots, reviewed with Crosse less than an hour ago, and yes he remembered seeing them during his visit to the Paddocks. He felt sure that given a little time with Denis' checklist he would be able to identify a good many more of the northern European faces at least. Then in a sudden instant, he recognised one additional face, one which he knew haunted Denis' sleep. It was one he had passed over as being part of the Sicilian contingency, but now he realised it was none other than the olive skinned Doctor Nicos Sumaris, Ruth Williams' consultant at the Paddocks.

It was then that the voice that Hart had heard some moments before above the voices in the crowded room came drifting back, and coming closer. He knew very well that it was a voice he should remember…but who? The owner of the voice was very close now, in fact so close that he brushed against Hart's shoulder and in that instant, the recognition exploded in his brain and he was filled with hatred and perhaps even a little fear. The voice cut into him like a knife.

'Doctor Sumaris, how very good to see you again. I do hope you are well.'

'Yes indeed, very well, thank you, Doctor Halle.'

Hart's head was about to explode with anger.

Fucking Halle!

'And how goes our current little study, Doctor Sumaris? I understand that there have been some small problems in recruiting suitable…..er subjects?'

'Yes, but I am sure that we have overcome that now and I believe that the team are very happy with the material we are collecting for them. Your own personal intervention and recommendations have been very welcome, thank you.'

'Not at all, there is too much at stake to permit sentimentality to steer us off our course. I look forward to our meeting later this evening, when we will be joined by our colleagues from both Germany and Sicily. I believe also that the redoubtable Signorina Volpe will also be joining us, an occasion I'm really looking forward to.'

Suddenly there was nervousness in Sumaris' voice,

'Oh really, that will be a great pleasure, but does that mean that there are more problems with the work in hand?'

Halle lowered his voice,

'Now is not the time to discuss this. We will cover everything at our meeting later.'

He suddenly turned away from Sumaris, the audience was over. His voice rose in volume once more,

'Ahh, Professor Mancini, how good to see you again, and looking so well.'

Mancini, a brittle white-haired old man of some 80 years, standing on the perimeter of an effusive group of young acolytes nodded and sipped his red wine. Thus, in this way another round of "schmoozing" the international opinion leader began, leaving Sumaris looking rather like a chastised schoolboy.

Hart stood there still motionless, in fact in a state of paralysis still unable to put one foot in front of the other or in fact raise an arm now. Right then, the cavalry finally arrived and broke the spell. Crosse approached him from the side, took his arm and pulled him away from the schmoozefest, whispering to him,

'Come on, Max. I've got all the data that we didn't need from Doctor Friedel and all for the price of being bored totally witless for the past 20 minutes while you did your thing. I hope it was bloody well worth it. Hang on, you look so serious. What's wrong, somebody die or something?'

Hart looked her in the eyes and very deliberately said in a low voice,

'Look behind me to your right and across the room. Can you see a tall, distinguished-looking man with black hair, greying at the temples and sporting a moustache? I don't know this for sure, but if history is anything to go by he will be wearing grey flannels, a navy blue blazer with silver buttons, with a handkerchief in its breast pocket, and wearing a striped tie. I can't hazard a guess at the shirt unfortunately.'

'No, I don't think so…hang on…wait…oh yes, he's chatting to a man who looks to be about 100 years old and who keeps spilling red wine everywhere.'

'Now, VC, can he see me from where he is standing?'

'What? Why?'

'For Christ's sake, Vicky, just answer the bloody question, will you. Can he see me!'

'Sorry. Well, on and off.'

'For fuck's sake!'

'Look, Max, in the main, he can't see you, but when people move around I guess he could if he was looking this way. Anyway he has his back turned towards you at present.'

'Now listen, I'm going to walk around the perimeter of this room and leave through the doors where we came in and I want you to walk between me and him in his direct line of sight so that I'm invisible to him at all times. Got it?'

It was clear to Crosse that something serious was afoot with respect to the blazered, moustachioed man and now she was worried.

'OK Max, trust me. Keep your face turned to the wall and your back turned as much to the centre of the room as you can and I will cover you from the man. Right, he's deep in conversation, let's go, now!'

It seemed to Hart that it was taking forever, but in truth in just two minutes they had (almost) completely traversed the sum of the squares on the other two sides of the room, in such a manner that Hart had remained completely out of sight of the man causing him so much grief. Out onto the landing of the first floor and quickly down the marble staircase, with Hart tightly gripping Crosse's arm, they found themselves in the expansive lobby where they were able to mingle with the few conference remainders. Hart didn't stop there but ploughed on until they were outside the building completely and round the corner into Via Manzoni before he finally let go of her arm giving out a great sigh of relief as he did so.

'I'll have bruises there tomorrow. What the hell is going on?'

'Let's walk up the road, there's a park where we can sit and I'll tell you everything…and there's a lot to tell I can assure you.'

Hart was calmer now, but he was still very watchful as they made their way to the small park where delegates were few and far between. He drew a deep breath and began his tale of his experiences at the centre. He confirmed with Crosse the links that he believed they now had to all parties they had identified in the UK, Germany and Sicily and now finally the USA courtesy of World Pharma. He told her of the photograph of all the protagonists together at some "jolly" somewhere in Tenerife and then he narrated the horror story of his near miss encounter with Doctor Robert Halle, his adversary from World who had effectively ejected him by the seat of his pants from that company.

'By the way, Vicky, thanks for getting me out of there. You know I actually froze to the spot at one point and if you hadn't popped up, I would still have been there trying to force the walls and ceiling back to their original positions. So claustrophobic…but I'm fine now. It was clear to me listening to Halle's attitude and posturing during his conversation with Sumaris that World must be the real powerbrokers here.'

Crosse studied the seriousness on Hart's face.

'Are you afraid of this man, Halle, Max?'

Hart hedged. 'By the way, you've not mentioned it so I assume I was correct in my description of him? He was famous at World for always wearing the same style of clothes, right down to his tie. Rumour was that he had a special set to go to bed in. Silk of course. No, really, VC, I'm not physically afraid of him. How could I be afraid of a chap who sleeps in a silk blazer with silver buttons, wearing a tie for God's sake? I'm actually incandescent with anger at him still for the way he treated me at World. He's a bastard of the highest order. Trust me…I'm a doctor. I do want to see him go down though if at all possible, although quite how we accomplish that I don't yet know

174

If I'm afraid of anything, it's the sheer size of the organisation he works for and the resources they have at their fingertips. You and I are just a couple of irritating fleas on an elephant's back and I'm just hoping it doesn't decide to scratch the irritation. One other thing of importance which I heard via Halle's conversation is that there is a meeting planned somewhere this evening at which all will be present. There's going to be Sumaris, the Sicilians, the Germans and of course Halle himself. What I wouldn't give to be a fly on the wall of that meeting room.'

'Come on, Max, after your reactions just now do you really think that you'd be up to being a fly on their wall, or even a flea in fact?'

'I'm fine now, Vicky, it was really just the shock of that bastard standing shoulder to shoulder with me. What I would really love to do now, and what would probably signal the end of this current escapade, would be to get back into that room at the back of the hospitality suite where Freidel retrieved that data from, and really give their filing cabinets a first class going over. By that, I mean systematically going through them division by division.'

'I don't think I can support that idea, Max. You can't just walk in and help yourself to what could be their most sensitive trial documents. What I think you should do now is what you said you intended to do this morning, that is make your call to Denis, contact your friend Janet in the States and then call your friend in Milan, pack your case and leave. Leave tomorrow morning and give yourself a few days of relaxation in Milan as you originally planned. I'll go on making the most of the science on show here and finally return to the UK on the flight I'm booked on.'

Hart stared into space for a long moment and finally said,

'It's a big "yes" from me to almost everything you've just said Doctor *Crasse. Yes*, I think you should continue with the congress as per our agenda, but from now on, forget the sleuthing and only pick up on stuff that is of interest to you and to your job at the QMC. *Yes*, I will give Janet a call in the US tonight and *yes* I will call the Jolly Hotel Presidente in Milan and book a couple of nights there. Oh and *yes* I will also call Denis tonight. Now then, was there a "no"? No, just one final "yes" and that is that I will go back to the conference centre and try at least to have a good look around that back room before I leave this city.'

'Max, no. We have done all that we can here and I think that it is time to call it a day. It has to be up to Denis now to make what he will of our findings and bring about his own resolution to this business. It really is getting too involved and heavy now. Who knows how dangerous it might be for us to keep going?'

Hart felt incredibly sympathetic to her concerns. She was a scientist not a private eye for God's sake, and it was unfair of him to expect her to get involved any further. Still, he wasn't a private eye either, but now he felt compelled to take it one step further before retiring from the case. Earlier in the day, he would have agreed 100% with Crosse's suggestion, but now there was another thing to consider, the catalyst that had brought this visit to boiling point. The arrival of Halle on the scene was the catalyst of a hate that Hart could not bring himself to quench and he really did need to go one final extra yard. But that would be alone. Crosse must decide how to make the most of the conference now for herself and return home totally at her own time and pace. But for now, he needed one more piece of the jigsaw, that being Halle's relationships and standing with Vita, the GRS Institute and the Paddocks.

So there it was the bottom line. Hart, despite his earlier paralysis at the mere sound of Halle's voice, would make one attempt to gain entry to the room at the back of the GRS hospitality suite and interrogate as many of the filing cabinets as he could, if possible making photocopies (he had noticed what appeared to be a copier in the room previously when Freidel had passed through its door) of whatever appropriately important documents caught his eye. He would make just one attempt that evening and then if he failed he would indeed "go quietly" as Crosse had implored. He smiled at Crosse.

'Right, VC, this is my final decision. You have done more than enough in this enterprise and it's time for you to take an early retirement I think. Thank you,' he feigned a salute to her. 'As for myself I'm going to try and get one last look inside the office within the hospitality suite. If for any reason at all, it seems an impossible task once I get started, I will also take my gold watch and retire immediately, OK?'

'Actually, Max, it's not OK. If you are going to do one more bloody stupid thing, then I insist on doing the bloody stupid thing with you. Now is *that* OK?' She smiled and rolled her eyes in mock frustration.

It was obvious to Hart that she was immoveable on this issue…and time was tight.

'Right then, Vicky, your gold retirement watch goes into mothballs until the completion of just one more sortie behind enemy lines. If you really want to give me one final hand, here's what I would like you to do. At just before lights out, I'm going to try and peek inside that office, but as I've said previously, only if it's safe to do so. I obviously can't do it if Halle or anybody from that team is around, remember they have a meeting together somewhere this evening and it really would be sods law if I barged in while they were in full flow. What I would like you to do if you are still up for it, is to accompany me back to the suite and spy out the land ahead of me. Look around and ensure that the coast is clear, with me a few paces behind you and hopefully out of sight of anybody in front of us on our route. If we make it to the suite and it is open, we go inside. You will then check out if the back office is locked or open. If open, you will peep inside and see if there are any people in there. If there are, it's a "whoops sorry, are the drinks finished now" or "sorry I'm looking for Agent Orange?" Then give me the yea or the nay to proceed. If it's a "yea", I go in and you retreat and we meet back at the hotel. If it's a "nay", we both retreat at bloody double time straight back to the hotel and pack. How's that sound?'

'I warn you, Max, I'll be as nervous as hell, but yes, all right I'm game. But this really will be the very last time! When do you want us to return to battle?'

'Right away if possible, but I *would* feel better if I had my trusty satchel with me if there turns out to be lots of goodies in the suite for me to copy or to take, rather than this delegate folio tack. How about we take a walk back to the hotel and then return to the hospitality suite when I've picked up my satchel and dropped off this folio thing?'

Chapter 55

It was shortly before 7.00 pm when they arrived back at the conference centre from their hotel. Hart's radar was tuned to maximum sensitivity as they entered the building for there were very few people left around the area now, only stragglers picking up the last copies of the reprinted posters. The official end to the conference day was 7.15 pm, the final staged presentation ending at 6.45 pm, so Hart had assumed that this would most likely be the best possible time to go into action. The most vulnerable part of their passage to the hospitality suite was the climb from the main area of the poster presentations up the marble staircase, when they would be exposed to whoever was coming down the stairs, or looking up from below. Crosse had Hart covered at the front but there was nothing she could do about him being seen from downstairs. He was confident, however, that nobody here at this time would know him well enough to be able to identify him by the handsome contours of his backside. They arrived at the top of the stairs outside the hospitality suite unnoticed. The only other person they came into direct contact with was a cleaner vacuuming the carpet directly outside the door of the suite. Whilst Hart hung back, Crosse strode purposely forward at the same time that the cleaner opened the door and went inside. If her intention was to clean the floor in the room, then their intentions would likely be brought to an abrupt end, but no, a brief call out to Francesca her workmate who was finishing off her duties here, resulted in both of cleaners leaving the room together.

Crosse was about to turn and leave in order to give Hart the all clear when two young females emerged from the back office. They were clearly part of the GRS "front of house hospitality staff", dressed in the suite uniform of yellow skirt and matching jacket, with white shirt and brown knotted silk scarf. Crosse had to say something at least to them to allay any suspicions. She quickly racked her mind and what emerged was,

'Excuse me, I arranged to meet Doctor Freidel here to go over some trial data, but I'm afraid I'm a little late. Is he still around?'

The girl whose nametag revealed her to be Emma smiled a knowing smile at Crosse.

'I'm sorry but he has returned to his hotel. We are closing here now. When we leave, the cleaner will lock up for the night, but I could give you the name of his hotel if you wish. In fact we are going there now if you want to accompany us?'

'Not on your bloody life!' translated as 'No thank you, I will come back tomorrow,' and she left the room to find Hart, who was now standing behind the slightly ajar door of the Gents/Signores WC where he had a good view of both the hospitality suite door and the stairs. She heard the two "hostesses" behind her and rather than seek out Hart from wherever he was hiding, paused and feigned to forage in her bag until they had passed her.

'*Buona sera signora*,' called Emma and Lucia in unison. 'Have a good evening,' added Emma causing a stir of laughter between the pair.

'*Buona sera…*' replied Crosse to the backs of their heads. '…and up yours!' This time under her breath.

Hart stepped out of the "convenient" toilet.

'Is that it? Is the coast clear now?'

'Yes, that's the last two company personnel gone. There is just one final cleaner who will return soon and lock up…so it's all yours if you think you have the time…and still have the nerve!'

'Excellent! Thanks, VC. If you now return to the hotel, I will do my thing here as quickly as possible and catch up with you there later. I don't intend to be here for a minute longer than is necessary.'

'I could wait for you outside if you like, Max?'

'No, if this goes pear-shaped, I don't want you caught up in any part of it. One of us at least has to remain innocent, so off you go before the cleaner arrives. Thanks anyway.'

He smiled at her and kissed her on the cheek.

She gave him a hug, "take care", and descended the stairs.

Hart turned and walked quickly to the suite, observing as he went that the cleaner was still working down the corridor. She looked up as he made for the room and he made an extravagant show of raising his arm and calling '*buona sera*' to her. Once in the room, he made directly to the back office, which was thankfully unlocked. He paused on the way to pick up a couple of the poster copies, just in case he needed a "prop" or two in the advent of any tricky meeting. Spying a row of company uniform jackets hanging from wall hooks, he removed one of the name badges and duly pinned it to his own jacket. "Frans Voigt" was now ready to go to work.

One of the first things that met his eye, standing in the centre of the small office was a large photocopier and luckily it had been left switched on. Hopefully, he would find something that would be worth using the machine for!

He suddenly heard a noise in the outer room. He walked through gingerly only to find the cleaner helping herself to a plate of sandwiches overlooked by the previous cleaning lady. She looked somewhat guilty at the sight of Hart. Caught in the act! He nodded and raised a thumb to her, not for one minute expecting her to understand English,

'*Va bene*. It's OK. *Buon appetito*.'

She nodded and smiled in gratitude.

At this point, Hart thought it wise to bring out his "props" and removing the two rolled up posters from his pocket, walked over to the wall, and finding some tape attached them, both to the nearest space on it. Suddenly, he realised that it was on this exact spot that Halle had materialised this afternoon and he was surprised that he felt absolutely no emotions at all. Fear, anger and nervousness were all gone. Perhaps they had cancelled each other out in the thrill of the moment? He now felt that he had done enough to ensure that the cleaner was on side should he need her in any way before he left.

He returned to the annexed office and began to check out the filing cabinets. There was a row of six of them, each unit containing four sliding drawers. He placed his fingers in the handle of the top drawer of the first cabinet…locked! He then tried the second cabinet…also locked!

'Shit!'

The third, fourth and fifth cabinets were likewise locked and each received the same expletive. The sixth cabinet, however, he found to be unlocked,

'Geronimo!'

He carefully pulled out the bottom drawer. Empty! Then the next drawer up…also empty! The third drawer up was also was totally vacant. He placed his fingers through the final drawer handle and slowly inched it open, almost afraid to look inside it. When he did peer inside he found it… Empty!

'Shit! Shit! Shit!'

He pushed it back in a little harder than necessary and heard a faint metallic tinkle from inside. He gently slid the drawer open again and there he saw lying on the bottom of the otherwise empty compartment, a collection of six small silver filing cabinet keys attached to a single circular key ring. He clenched his fist in jubilation,

'Yes!'

At that moment, he became aware that the cleaner was standing framed in the office doorway, and she was making it clear through the art of mime that she had finished checking the work of the previous cleaners and that she must now lock up the whole of the suite in two minutes' time. First, however, she mimed that she had to lock the door to the room adjacent to the hospitality suite further down the corridor. Hart also indicated, using similar mime skills, that he too was about to leave in two minutes. He watched her leave the suite and enter the corridor to the room further down. When she reached the door of that room, he stepped over to the doorway and called out to her 'buona sera signora'. Absently, without looking back at him, she replied in similar vein whilst attending to the door lock.

At this point, Hart ducked back into the suite quickly passing through to the back office, where he doused the lights and crouched under the computer table pulling a chair in front of him and waited. A couple of minutes later, the cleaner returned. She glanced around the suite and peered briefly into the darkened office, then satisfied that all was in order she exited the suite turning off the lights as she went. Hart waited a moment until he heard the sound of the key turning in the lock and then rose from under the table. He was locked in, but he had already noticed upon his arrival to the suite that the lock was similar to that of most hotel rooms in that whilst it could be locked from outside and be impregnable without the right key, from the inside a simple turn of the door handle was sufficient to operate both the locking and opening mechanisms.

He removed the keys from the top drawer of cabinet number six and systematically worked through them until he had identified the correct key for each cabinet, which he then inserted into each lock. It was time to see what the cabinets would reveal, if anything, to assist his and Crosse's mission.

The drawers of cabinet one were virtually empty apart from random commercial pamphlets and non-specific odds and ends, a virtual waste bin. Cabinets two to four contained reprints of papers, folded AO posters, A4-sized posters and various papers describing and discussing the science of stem cell therapeutics, with some devoted to discussing the ethics of that branch of science. There was nothing of note there that could not be found on the internet or in the actual compendium of papers and posters presented at this symposium.

Cabinet five, however, was a different kettle of fish, offering him a much richer seam in his mining for data and information dedicated to the clinical trials, one of which had most likely been responsible for his attendance with Crosse here in Padua. Before getting too involved in rifling through all the documents in front of him, Hart decided that the best way for him to stay focused on finding answers to the questions they had put together with Denis was to consult Denis' list, of which Hart had a copy folded in his pocket. It was the same one he had studied in his room when they first arrived at their hotel:

CONFERENCE ANSWERS TO CONCENTRATE ON:

- **Sicily…Which company?**
- *Who owns it?*
- *Is it a multinational company?*
- *Where are the company headquarters?*
- *Who runs it?*
- *Important people associated with it?*
- *Is it just a front for clandestine research?*
- *If so, what is its 'actual' area of research?*
- *Health aspects, biological sciences, drugs???*
- *How does it fit in with the other hospitals identified?*
- *Are there any patients resident at the other hospitals receiving their drugs?*
- *Are there any outpatients there?*
- *What are the patient diagnoses?*
- *Age range and gender of patients?*
- *Confirm relationships/link-ups between UK, Germany and Sicily*
- **What is the study that is most likely to be responsible for the death of Ruth Williams??**

Having quickly revised the questions that they were there to try and answer, he put away the list and started looking through the file's contents in earnest.

It was clear that the documents in all four compartments of the cabinet were in alphabetical order, which was good news. The bad news, however, was that it was the German alphabet of titles.

Of course, it's going to be in German you bloody idiot, it's a bloody German company!

His earlier elation went down and like a punctured Zeppelin. With documents written in German, in not having any of that language in his armoury there was no way he could read their contents. All he could do was to photocopy all the documents en masse and hope that he struck gold somewhere amongst them, but that would take forever and it would be an incredible imposition on him to try and carry all the copies away from the suite. His gloom was lightened, however, upon closer scrutiny of the papers, for it suddenly became obvious that each file document and title was accompanied by an English translation running alongside. Half of the page was in German and the other half at the right side of the page was English.

'Hallelujah!'

Hart could now rapidly visually scan all titles and abstracts, pick out what appeared to be the most relevant ones to their cause and copy them on the photocopier at the centre of the office floor, which was patiently waiting and already warmed up by its previous users...once he had checked and confirmed that the machine was not hungry for more paper in its tray of course. He hoped that he would be able to reject most of the papers, which would cut down both on the time taken to produce the copies and on the resulting weight of his industry.

What he found, using his rapid reading skills, were published papers completed in stem cell research both by workers at the Gerhard Roscher Schmoller (GRS) Institute working alone, and joint papers between the GRS and Sicily. Interestingly, he discovered that Vita Pharma in Sicily were also listed under another name (clearly another Sicilian subsidiary or a department within that company itself), and one that he'd come across before, that of Laboratorio di Scoperta Fondamentale. On a couple of papers names of people at UK clinics stood out at him, for example Doctor N. Sumaris. There were other organisations also who had assisted in various clinical trials with GRS, but so far all the material he scanned was not actually confidential, being already in the public domain and freely accessible through scientific journals and the internet. Nevertheless, he decided to quickly scribble down the list of contributors to the work and the journal names. He looked around and saw on the computer desk a box of headed writing tablets and pens which were destined to be handed out to delegates. Whilst in "help yourself mode", he also took a couple of laser pointer pens, which he clipped to his jacket inside pocket...just for hell of it!

Moving on to the next drawer proved to be more interesting. Going through the files, he came across a country-by-country list of all the clinics, hospitals and institutions that GRS had previously worked with and those currently involved in ongoing research studies. Hart considered that this information could likely turn out to be more valuable to them, since it was possibly more likely that here would be represented partnerships rather than just investigators and opinion leaders taking part in their clinical trials. As he scanned the documents, sure enough in the section headed United Kingdom were listed the Paddocks in Nottingham and its sister hospital/clinic in Liverpool, together with listings of all personnel there who were part of their research program. At this point, it was apparent to him that Nottingham and Liverpool were not the only two sites in the

UK currently signed up, there being four others in England and one in each of Scotland and Wales. He wondered about Northern Ireland's absence from the list of contributors and whether it was perhaps due to the Catholic Church's influence there. A thought for later he decided.

Moving on, he came across lists of clinics and hospitals in France, Germany, Switzerland, Italy (strike that previous thought relating to possible influences of the Catholic church!), Spain, Scandinavia, etc. etc., and then South and North America and Africa. He pulled out all the documents he wished to copy and loaded them onto the waiting machine and then gleefully pressed the green "start" button. It was very noisy but very quick in producing the copies he wanted, which were shooting out into the collection tray at a great rate of knots.

In no time at all, he had lists of all GRSs global contacts. He had no time to re-file the original documents in any sort of correct order and so pushed the pages back into the files randomly. It was at that point in his endeavours that he noticed printed at the foot of many of the document pages, "The Gerhard Roscher Schmoller Institute, an affiliate of World Pharmaceuticals International". Q.E.D! A problem for Hart now was that he had a massive telephone directory size pile of photocopied information which he fully intended to leave with. His trusty satchel, however, was very yielding and allowed him to squeeze every last page of his booty into it leaving room for just a little more. He returned to the cabinet and the final drawer.

The final drawer, he found, was divided into two sections. To Hart's delight, the first section was labelled "Vita Pharma", and the second, "Africa". So engrossed had he been in his clandestine work that he suddenly became aware that his time of remaining undiscovered in that area must surely now be running out. At that point, he made the decision that without paying too much attention to the papers' contents he would pull out all the "Vita" documents and copy them all. Whilst the copier raced through this latest load, he went back and focused on the "Africa" section. He expected the contents here to be of a similar nature to that being presently copied, but not so, for instead he saw that these consisted of publicity handouts and agendas for forthcoming African meetings, together with trial work completed, ongoing and proposed. Various photographic pages showed smiling African bodies in white coats shaking hands with similarly smiling white bodies wearing summer weight suits and in the foreground were positioned very large boxes of what were clearly marked medicines and drugs. In some of the other shots, appropriately dressed church dignitaries were shown in similar poses shaking hands with white men in suits, whilst surrounded once more by huge stacks of boxed medicines.

Hart made mental notes that: a) there were a lot of clinical trials on-going in Africa, b) GRS, or more probably World, were making drugs available in the poorer areas of poorer African countries, c) this looked to be happening through the good offices of not only local African leaders, but also of local church organisations and d) A question: how are all these trials obtaining the proper regulatory permissions to proceed?

Hart promised himself to transfer his list of mental notes to paper as soon as possible. There were in fact too many of these latter publications to copy and so he decided to take a handful of them, rather than copies and just hope that nobody noticed come the following day. Of this he was confident, once the hurly burly of the day's provision of hospitality got underway.

He added these latest items to his bulging bag and squeezed in the final hot copies as they emerged straight from the copier. All copying achieved successfully, he pressed the red "OFF" button and put the wonderful machine to bed for the night. He was happy. Content in the knowledge that amongst his veritable library of papers, still emitting heat in his bag, were the likely answers to all the questions Denis, Crosse and himself had posed at the outset of this venture and almost certainly much more besides.

He checked his watch. He had been in the small office room for over one and a half hours. It was time to beat a hasty retreat and relax in the hotel with Crosse, with a glass or three of well-earned prosecco.

He closed each cabinet drawer fully and locked each drawer of the first five cabinets with the appropriate small silver keys before returning the bunch of six keys to the bottom of the top drawer of the sixth cabinet. He looked around taking one last look before departing and on impulse snatched another copy of the photograph from the wall of the GRS study team standing under the palm trees in Tenerife, pushing it roughly and angrily into his trouser pocket.

He picked up his bulging, heavy bag, extinguished the office lights and made for the main door of the suite…and freedom. He was sure that the door would unlock from the inside without a key in the way of hotel rooms, but nevertheless, he was still nervous about this final test.

As his fingers were about to close around the door handle, his heart momentarily stopped.

Somebody was turning the handle from the other side of the door!

Chapter 56

Hart quickly tossed his bag, full of what he hoped were evidential reprints, towards the wall behind where the door would open, flicked on the lights and quickly traversed to the other side of the door in the direction of the wall posters whilst ripping the previously "borrowed" name badge from his lapel and pushing it into his top jacket pocket. His hope was that his explanation of remaining in the room to catch up on as much detail of the studies as possible, which was in many ways certainly true, would hold some water with whoever was on the threshold of entering. He turned smiling at the room entrants,

'Hi, I'm still working here. There's no end to it is there. It's not all champagne and oysters you know?'

'This room is officially closed now and out of bounds to all delegates. You still being here is a very serious matter, as there are many important and confidential documents here.'

Hart's surprise at his recognition of his discoverer was matched equally by his discoverer's own surprise. Hart's instant thought was,

Bloody Hell! It's Doris Day.

Doris Day, aka Frau Arben from the Gerhard Roscher Schmoller Institute in Greifswald, frowned and looking somewhat stunned herself continued,

'I know you. We met under similar very suspicious circumstances at the Institute in Greifswald... Mr Health.'

'Hart. My name is Doctor Max Hart. I remember you too.'

He decided upon a brash response to his discovery and extended his hand for a handshake. The handshake attempt was ignored.

'Nice to see you again. I'm sorry but I arrived here quite late and was so engrossed in these excellent reports,' he waved at the wall, 'that I completely lost all sense of time. It's all quite innocent I can assure you,' he beamed at her.

It was then that he looked over her shoulder at her companion. It was none other than the very large mean-looking man who was there when they had last met. Unfortunately, it appeared that Ernst had probably been left back home in Greifswald. He considered trying to lighten the moment by injecting some humour into the occasion, but then quickly decided against it. The only thing that would likely amuse this man mountain was ripping Hart's head from his shoulders.

'Well, goodnight then both of you, I hope to see you again tomorrow.'

Hart moved to go out of the door, but quickly realised that the only way out was either through or over the mountain.

Frau Arben spoke a few abrupt words to her colleague who spun Hart around, pushed him against the wall and began patting him down in search mode.

'Hang on there, I've nothing to hide. I don't even have a briefcase so it must be obvious to you that I am only looking at the documents. What do you think I am some kind of industrial spy?'

Hart was trying to sound his most hurt and indignant now.

'You are trespassing, Doctor Hart. For the second time, you are trespassing.'

Arben's partner stopped his search at Hart's trouser pocket from which he lifted his cell phone, which he passed to Arben.

'Feel free to put your number in it if you like Frau Arben and I can call you when you're off duty,' Hart quipped.

The attempted joke was totally lost on his interrogator.

'For all we know, Doctor Health, you could indeed be a spy, working for a competitor company. We will check your "handy" and if we detect that you have sent any photographs or messages within the last hour, we will assume that you are indeed here on false pretences.'

A few more abrupt words to her colleague and he began to manipulate the "handy".

'Who are you working for, Doctor Hearth?'

'It's Hart for Christ's sake. Hart! Why would I want to steal anything that was freely available on line and through published papers? As far as I can see, there is no original work here at all. What I have told you is completely true.'

Hart knew that what he said made sense, but only a half-wit would totally fall for his basically cock and bull explanation. But what could she do? He had nothing incriminating on his person, there were no messages on his phone and he had clearly been looking at posters when they entered.

'Were you reading in the dark, Doctor Hart?' Arben gave a sly smile. 'The light was out when we arrived at the door and only came on when we began to enter.'

'No, I had finished and was just about to leave, so I turned out the light. I turned it on again when you arrived. It's no big deal I can assure you.'

Arben spoke once again to her colleague and he headed into the back office where he proceeded to attempt to open the filing cabinets. They were locked of course apart from the empty one.

Thank God I took the trouble to re-lock them, thought Hart, his confidence now failing.

Arben's henchman called back from the office, indicating that all looked well and that the cabinets were untouched. She nodded, obviously pleased with the response. Had she finally come to the conclusion that Hart had indeed only spent time with the posters on the wall? If so, there was absolutely no reason why he shouldn't walk away…and right now. The unfortunate thing about that was that he would have to leave his bag of plundered documents behind, which was not a good thought after all his efforts to fill it in the first place.

Arben approached him.

'So it would seem that there is no evidence of any theft or intent to steal confidential papers. However, Doctor…Hart, it is clear to me that you are a very suspicious person and a person I am unable to trust. I have said already that this is the second time you have been apprehended in questionable circumstances and so…'

She paused for a moment during which time she said a few words to her colleague who nodded in agreement.

'…and so, we will leave you as we found you. We found you in this locked room, trespassing…'

'Hang on a minute, you're not the bloody police you know. You have absolutely no right to keep me here or in fact to continue to interrogate me in this way. Be sure that I will make the strongest complaints about this to the conference organisers and also to the conference security, whose role you and your colleague seemed to have totally usurped!'

Hart really was angry now and had almost convinced himself that he was indeed an innocent man caught up in a complete misunderstanding. Arben raised a hand to silence him.

'Do not worry yourself about informing security doctor, for when my colleague and I leave this room, leaving you locked inside it, I will personally contact security and strongly suggest to them that they speak to the police as a matter of urgency relating to your break-in and attempted theft of intellectual property. My colleague Herr Alpen,' (That was the first time Hart had been made aware of the "gorilla's" name and he apparently wasn't a primate after all, he was a bloody mountain!), 'will remain on the other side of the door until someone in authority arrives, when you will be able to give *them* your rather weak and pathetic explanation. He will ensure, Doctor Hart, that you will not escape, believe me. Here returned to you is your handy, would you prefer the lights to be left on or off? Ha, ha, ha, good evening, Doctor.'

With that, she turned, smiling at her little joke, and flounced out of the room. Mr Alps trundled after her, closing and then locking the door securely from the outside.

This was an outcome that Hart had neither expected nor allowed for in his plans. Unless he could find another way out of these rooms undetected, he was to use his own words, "totally stuffed", and for sure, Max Hart was no Harry Houdini.

Chapter 57

He was sitting in his usual favourite place, in his usual favourite chair, in front of the blazing log fire, his favourite cognac at hand. Age brought with it few genuinely agreeable moments, but for him this was one of them.

Recent events at the Rome train station had left him shocked and had increased his awareness that his long-game strategic plans were so very fragile and susceptible to being rendered worthless by the many chance or random occurrences that he found impossible to completely mitigate for. The telephone rang and he lifted the receiver.

'Yes?'

'It's me. I have the news as promised from the bishops' agenda meeting ahead of the USA Congress of Bishops. The meeting finished a short time ago and was loud and ill-tempered.'

'As we expected then.'

'Yes. The large majority of my colleagues there were very much aligned against any thoughts or deeds relating to embryonic stem cell research, so treatment using such materials was a total non-starter. Being so close to the Pontiff, I really had a conflict of interests and therefore said very little, but I observed a lot. My big surprise was the lack of valid argument from the younger bishops.'

'I am not surprised, but it doesn't alter a thing in respect to our plans for the future. The key thing is the health of the Pontiff and we must take whatever steps are needed to ensure his continuance both in life and in office. What is his current state of health?'

'As you know, he was very sick for a long period as his Parkinson's became much worse, but when we introduced the new treatment he improved quickly and very noticeably so. But just as quickly, presumably as the treatment wore off, he slipped back again although not as far as where he had been at the start. We adjusted the doseage accordingly and once again there has been an improvement, but we are confirming that we have no cure here, only management of the symptoms and it will be necessary to re-adjust the treatment upwards as we move forward.'

'And how is his personal physician taking on the ethics of giving this treatment? Are there any problems?'

'No, no problems with the physician, the problems lie with the nature of the treatment material itself. As you know at best, this is a dangerous form of treatment, and I'm talking in terms of health rather than eternal damnation. I'm not a scientist of course, but I am told that the treatment requires a specific form of embryonic stem cell material from highly specific foetus types and that a very particular and difficult method of cellular extraction is necessary.'

'Things should improve once our African friends come on board, which should be very soon.'

'You know I increasingly worry about the moral issues of this, not just the ethical ones.'

'I know how you feel, but science is at the threshold of a major advancement in this field and most importantly we need to ensure the short to medium term future of our Pontiff. We have to ensure that Pope Gelasius actually does have a medium-term future and you well know the reason for that. That has to be our major effort and concern and when we talk of his eminence's condition, I feel that the need to press ahead becomes even more urgent. We cannot change our direction and we cannot reduce our pressure on the work underway, of that I am totally convinced. But now I must go as I am waiting for another important call, so goodbye, my friend.'

Chapter 58

Hart stood rooted to the spot as the door to the room closed feeling totally stupid, exposed and worst of all outsmarted. At the crucial moment, his famed forte of quick wit and repartee had been outdone for the second time by a German woman who most probably thought that a "joke" was the yellow stuff in the centre of an egg. What should, or more to the point, what *could* he do now? Here he was, a virtual prisoner waiting for the arrival of the conference security people and also the local police.

He tried the door in the vain hope that all had been bluster and empty threats from Frau Arben, but indeed, it was securely locked with a key left in place, and as he turned the handle, he heard a deep throaty cough from the other side. Her sentry had been posted. He began to run through scenarios that might arise during any interrogation by police or security people and soon decided that to go down that route was potentially far too much of a gamble. He had no option, therefore, but to spend time trying to fathom out a way to escape from this place of detention.

A quick reconnoiter of the main room and the inner office quickly revealed that there were no exit doors that he had overlooked earlier. It became evident that the only opening to the outside world from there was a window high up in the back office, and that was too high to reach. There was a single table and chair close to the window and he dragged the table below the window and using the chair as a step climbed onto it. Still too high to be adequately examined, he lifted up the chair, placed it on the table and stood on it. The window was about one metre wide and 40 or so centimetres in height and was fastened shut by a mechanism which was operated by a ring-pull. It might just be possible for him to squeeze his body through the aperture of the window, but what sort of landing would he have on the other side, especially with a bag of hard-earned documents in one hand? He put his forefinger inside the ring and pulled it down sharply. It opened smoothly, revealing an aperture that would likely be wide enough to allow his body to pass through. He looked beyond it eagerly.

'Shit!'

Although he was in a room on the first floor, the paved area below the window, set in a small quadrangle with the hotel walls on all four sides, was at least three stories down. Clearly there were rooms at levels -1 and -2, and to add to his aggravation, there was absolutely no means of attaining those depths other than by the possibly suicidal means of a plastic-looking drainpipe, a full arm-stretch and a half away from the window ledge. Descent *was* possible but probably only in freefall. No, defenestration was not an option.

189

He climbed down onto the floor, knowing very well that time was running out for him, leaving the window open and the chair in place.

'Come on, think. Bloody think!' He felt a sense of hopelessness rising inside him.

So, there were no doors and the only window was an invitation to a swift fall onto a concrete paving. He began to walk around the perimeters of both rooms looking for ideas of escape and even for possible hiding places, but to no avail. Disillusioned and worried, he ambled back into the outer office and sat on one of the plastic chairs, where he let his eyes roam around the walls and "that bloody window", and eventually the ceilings.

On focusing his gaze above, he became aware that the ceiling in the inner office was different to the one in the outer suite. This outer office ceiling was, like in the other public places in the hotel, ornate with elegant plaster cornices and coving at the junctions with the walls. The inner office on the other hand was a modern business afterthought, constructed in the modern way in order to accommodate the latest computer and printing facilities which were a must for converting a palatial suite into a functional office and conference venue. Consequently, in the back office, the ceiling was bereft of any fancy decorative mouldings, but instead covered in two-by-two foot square white ceiling tiles, no doubt suspended from some type of light aluminium framework, but certainly a good deal lower in height than the ceiling in the main outer suite. He jumped to his feet and did a couple more circuits of both rooms talking in all aspects of the different ceilings.

Walking to a set of four tables, positioned under a vent in the inner office, which was clearly part of the air conditioning system, specifically incorporated to maintain a constant cool airflow to the bank of computers, he vaulted onto the tabletop. He pulled up one of the four chairs set around the tables from the floor and stood it on a table. In order to inspect the ceiling more closely, he stepped onto the chair and slowly raised both arms. Then with fingers stretched he tentatively placed his finger ends near the centre of the nearest ceiling tile. Holding his breath in hopeful anticipation, he gradually applied increasing fingertip pressure to the tile, which held itself in place briefly and then completely lifted from the aluminium frame that it was seated in. He peered through the gap into the exposed roof space. Nothing!

Too bloody dark!

Mobile phone.

He took out his mobile phone and turned on the "torch mode".

Rubbish! The usually bright light was no more than a fading candle glow and totally useless for the job at hand. Clearly, the phone's battery was almost exhausted. But then, he remembered the laser pointers that he had acquired a little earlier and put in his jacket pocket.

Keeping the tile raised with one hand, he fumbled in his pocket and finally withdrew one of the laser pens. Turning the beam on, he pointed the laser into the ceiling space. *Yes!* He was now able to see the inside of the space, albeit only in a bright red pencil of light. Moving the beam around, it was clear that the aluminium framework in place for seating the polystyrene tiles, was quite flimsy and would be totally unable to support any kind of weight other than the white squares currently in place. However the pencil of light also picked out what was clearly a narrow more robust horizontal gantry, obviously there to accommodate the weight of an engineer for servicing and repairing the AC unit and its myriad of pipes and electrical cables and no doubt also to help in repairing any damaged tiles when necessary. He raised the red beam and could see the gantry leading off into the distance, where it branched at its current level, but then stepped up as it moved into and above the elegant plastered ceiling in the suite next door.

Geronimo!

Hart finally had a germ of a plan which could at least take him from the confines of the rooms below the ceiling space, but additionally might hopefully lead him towards an eventual escape further along the gantry in another room or corridor. If not an escape route, it might at least provide a hiding place for the imminent future. However, his plan required careful stage management to mis-direct the eyes of his captors and would-be prosecutors away from his ceiling exit and towards the open window. This was essential, for the last thing he wanted was to be pursued within the confines of the ceiling space.

He descended to the floor once again and stood back, viewing the scene of his hopeful misdirection.

He returned to the table beneath the window and ensured that the chair he had placed on it earlier was in place. He looked up and checked that the window was fully open. One thing he needed to do to complete his stage management once inside the ceiling space, was to return the other chair, used as a step on the set of tables, to a position back under the table in symmetry with the other three chairs there. For this, he needed something hook-like and long enough to enable him to lower the chair to the ground from ceiling level. He had seen an umbrella stand earlier and headed for that hoping to find a largish umbrella with a crook handle.

Bugger!

All were of the straight variety with not a crook in sight!

And then he remembered the ringed opening device on the window. This must surely require a pole of some sorts with a hook on the end of it to enable the window to be opened and closed adequately from floor level? Looking desperately around, he suddenly saw it, leaning up in a corner of the room, partially hidden in shadow.

Perfetto!

He quickly arranged the set of tables neatly in their square and tidied the piles of papers spread around them. Dashing back into the suite, he picked up a filled water jug and four glasses and duly placed them neatly in the centre of the tables. He was ready to vanish, hopefully in true Houdini style, but wait! He suddenly remembered Frau Arben's final words to him,

'Would you prefer the lights to be left on or off?'

Taking one of the blank pages of paper and a pen, he wrote a brief few words on it and sealed it inside one of the envelopes laying on the table, on the outside of which he wrote in large letters, "FOR THE ATTENTION OF FR. ARBEN". He then placed this in an upright position on the sill beneath the open window.

He quickly returned to his elevated position on the chair standing on the square of tables and carefully raised the ceiling tile, which he now pushed to one side leaving a two-by-two open entry space to whatever lay above. Returning to the floor, he placed the window hook upon the chair in a reachable vertical position from within the ceiling space and standing back surveyed the whole stage that he had set.

Shit! My satchel!

He quickly traversed the two rooms and retrieved his satchel from close to the room's main door and then returned to the tables. Very carefully, he mounted the table and then the chair, ensuring that in his excited state he didn't move any of the table's contents of papers, pens, water jug and drinking glasses from their positions of symmetry. He placed his precious satchel through the aperture onto the gantry in the roof space above him and then taking hold of the convenient handles on the gantry pulled himself up into the ceiling space. It took a lot more effort to do this than he had anticipated, but the "flight or fight" activity of the adrenaline now surging through his system easily overcame his shortcomings in the upper body strength department and he soon found himself laying prone and panting on the gantry, staring down through the space previously occupied by the tile. Just four short jobs left to do now. The first, to reach back down and take the window hook; the second, to hook the back of the chair on the table and carefully lower it down to the floor and into position under the table using a slightly swinging motion; the third, to either toss the window hook back towards the wall under the window or pull it into the roof space and leave it laying horizontally there. He chose the second of the two options and finally to return the white tile to its place in the aluminium frame, ensuring above all else that it fitted exactly and snuggly and did not appear to be out of place to any slight degree when viewed from the floor below.

Four out of four! With the tile in place, his new prison cell was quite dark and reaching into his jacket pocket he retrieved the laser pen. Turning it on, he was delighted to see that it now gave an even brighter red pencil of light in the greater darkness. With the pen between his teeth and his bag under one arm, he was now ready "to boldly go, where for sure *he* hadn't ever gone before". As he took his first crawled movements forward along the gantry, he thought of the few words he had left for Arben in the sealed envelope and smiled. Would she see it as joke or egg yolk? Would he have the last laugh after all? His short message read,

"FR. ARBEN: I HAVE ASSUMED THAT *YOU* WOULD PREFER THE LIGHTS TO BE LEFT ON!

Regards MH"

Chapter 59

By the time members of the conference security staff had arrived outside the door of the hospitality suite, along with a translator fluent in Italian, English and German, Hart had cursed his way quite some distance along the gantry, getting caught in various wires and AC hosing as he went, but at all times taking great care not to transfer any of his weight from the gantry onto the fragile tiles and frame, inches below him. He soon learned that to ensure this, he had to put his satchel's shoulder strap over his head, using the area of the back of his neck to take the heavy weight of copied documents, whilst leaving both arms relatively free to help him move forward relatively safely. So far he had travelled the whole length of the office and had turned a 90-degree corner, away from that dreaded place, passing now above a corridor outside and away from the suite.

Upon the arrival of the security staff and the translator, there was a brief conversation between themselves and the man-mountain prison guard Herr Alpen. The female hotel member of staff seconded to the role of translator acted immediately in translating, after a fashion, German to Italian and vice versa. Alpen's report of a break-in to the locked room, accompanied by associated noises of papers being rifled and drawers being opened and closed was sufficient to convince security that higher officialdom was required and they promptly called the local police, who arrived on the scene, via their blue and white Alpha Romeo with full lights flashing and claxons blaring, within 15 minutes (there now being a quiescence in activity since the televised football match had finished).

Once they all had been updated on events, the scene was set and the troops ready to move in. Alpen unlocked the door and threw it open, and the police charged in pistols drawn, followed by security and Alpen, with the translator tentatively bringing up the rear. It was Inspector Clouseau at his finest. The police each dropped to one knee raising their firearms in the way of the "good policing manual", whilst shouting out instructions to whatever miscreant was in the room to immediately come out and surrender. Their barked Italian instructions were followed after a pregnant pause by a quivering, trembling, barely audible translation into English by the hotel staff member.

Nothing!

After a few minutes, the front line troops exchanged quizzical looks and seeing that the room was empty of further human life proceeded to check gingerly behind sofas and under tables, pistols always at the ready in their outstretched arms.

Again nothing!

They also noted that despite the report of general mayhem, with sounds of papers being thrown around and drawers being opened and closed, in fact all was totally neat and tidy. In phase two, they moved in on the back office area, again with pistols raised and at the ready. Once again, they barked out for the interloper to give himself up and once again a pregnant pause was followed by the almost whispered trembling English translation, courtesy of the member of staff.

Still nothing!

More exchanges of quizzical looks between the policemen as they entered the pristine office, briefly looking around the tables and chairs and filing cabinets. Finally, they holstered their weapons and turned to the red-faced security staff and the bemused Alpen. It was at this point that Arben returned, the temperature of the room immediately dropping by several degrees.

Alpen looked at her through dog-like eyes and shrugged his shoulders.

'The room is completely empty, Frau Arben. He's no longer here. I have no idea of how he got out, but for sure he didn't come through the door or pass by me. I've been here every minute since you left.'

One of the "Clouseau duo" of policemen had jumped up onto the table by the window and gaining access to the opening via the conveniently placed chair reported to the room.

'If there was anybody here in the first place, he might have gone out through the window, but that looks very difficult to me. To be honest, I'm not sure that there actually was anybody in here at all.'

The translation of the policeman's assessment into German, brought Arben rapidly from simmering to boiling point, but the room still remained iceberg-cold.

'Of course he was here, I spoke with him! You're useless!'

This was translated from German into Italian by the embarrassed interpreter/staff member.

'Very well, I see no reason for us to remain here any longer,' responded policeman two and turning to the hotel security people, 'you will be hearing more of this from my superiors.'

Again, the translator moved into action, translating into German for the benefit of Arben and Alpen, more confident now but she was becoming more embarrassed at the charade by the second.

Then, having been joined by his colleague, arriving at his side down from the table-top, the pair of policemen marched stiffly out of the office and the suite and returned to their flashing car.

Arben considered the situation for a moment and decided upon discretion, and addressing the two security people smiled painfully and said in English,

'I'm very sorry, but there seems to have been a terrible misunderstanding here, but thank you for your help,' and she indicated with her hand towards the exit, summarily dismissing them.

The translator's final piece of work was to translate Arben's English into Italian for the sake of the security men, had they not understood her.

Thankfully they were also too embarrassed to make any more of the issue and made their swift exit together with the young translator. Arben strode through to the suite and slammed the main entrance door door shut.

'Surely, he couldn't have gone through the window, Frau Arben? There must be some other exit somewhere.'

Suggested Alpen nervously, following close at her heels.

'Of course, he went out through the bloody window, you totally useless article, where else could he have gone? Into thin air!'

She returned to the inner office bursting with anger and frustration and as she began her bitter tirade at her Alpine colleague, she suddenly saw the envelope leaning up against the wall on the windowsill where Hart had placed it. She lifted it down and putting her forefinger under the sealed flap ripped it open. She pulled out the piece of paper which nestled inside and read it. Alpen stirred himself for some heavy fallout as her face turned a bright crimson and her mouth twitched in spasm. He was clearly about to feel the full force of her highest level Volcanity Eruption Index, the initial indicative tremor being a massive,

'*Scheisse!*'

But by now, Hart was too far advanced along the ceiling tunnel, swathed in the red aura of his laser pen, to pick up any of the blue vibrations from Arben back in the inner office. Unbeknown to him, his escape ruse had comprehensively succeeded in its aims.

Chapter 60

Hart was over the elation of his escape now and becoming concerned as to when, where and how he should alight from his current space. Half-blinded by dust and airborne insulation fibres, his full concentration was on the positioning of his limbs and ensuring that the satchel remained securely hanging from his neck, for one misplaced hand, knee or foot, or the satchel hanging too low could literally bring him straight down to earth. It was essential that he kept on the strengthened service track, or gantry, built mainly alongside but sometimes above or below the main AC venting system. As for headroom, there was effectively none at all to spare, causing him to keep as low as possible and almost crawl along the gantry, completely flattened out at times, which made the positioning of his satchel difficult. Despite all of this, however, he had made really good progress and the longer he crawled the more skilled and agile he became. However, his skill and agilty didn't impress him much at this point, where he just wanted out of the ceiling space and his cramped confinement.

Thinking back to where he had entered the overhead tunnel in the back office of the GRS hospitality suite, he was considering that a likely place to emerge would again be close to one of the AC vents, which probably meant splashdown in another room rather than on a corridor, so his plan now was to soldier on until he arrived in said place. His eyes, when not stinging, were growing quite accustomed to the darkness, but his aching teeth, still holding the laser pen, were telling him that he should be considering giving them a rest. He decided to listen to his teeth! Removing the pen from between his incisors was a huge relief, although now of course he had jaw ache to contend with. With an effort, he turned off the pen and clipped it into the top pocket of his jacket.

As his eyes accustomed themselves further to the dark, he gradually became aware that he was occasionally able to pick out an illuminated edge between some of the tiles and the frame that they were seated in and he guessed that this was low energy light coming from the hotel corridor. His sudden hope was that when he eventually arrived over a meeting room, provided the lights were on in there, the light bleeding between the edges of the tiles would become more intense, indicating a possible landing place for him.

At last he saw, in the near distance, the level of light bleed through the edges of the tiles that he had been thinking would be a good indicator of a room below. He edged towards the light source, slowly and ultra-quietly now, as any mistake at this point could be catastrophic. Suddenly he picked up the sound of murmuring voices coming from somewhere below, just up ahead. In addition, he clearly heard the clinking of crockery and then, pervading the dusty atmosphere of his confinement, the aroma of freshly brewed coffee.

The light intensified as he inched forward and he noticed a grill of about six inches square between room and ceiling through which light was almost flooding. Excitement rose in him. Suddenly someone in the room below clapped their hands together re-calling the meeting to continue. Clearly time had been taken out for refreshments.

'Ladies and gentlemen, or should that be *lady* and gentleman? Can we take our seats again so that we may continue please? I think we should be able to complete our agenda within another 15 minutes or so and then we might retire to the bar?'

'Hear, hear,' came a voice from the meeting.

Hear, bloody hear, came a voice from inside Hart's head.

Hart tried his best to peer through the grill at the assembled group below, but the angles of the slats in the vent were such that he could only see one small area of the room, that being below and in front of him, where the chair at the meeting table was empty.

And then the earlier voice became a little nervous,

'Err please, Claudia, if you could take your seat now, we will continue. Thank you.'

There was a sudden blur of green and a scraping of chair legs on ceramic tiles as the vacant seat at the table below him became taken. What he saw from above was a head of wonderful long, red hair which cascaded onto a pair of shapely shoulders clothed in a green jacket of sorts. He just couldn't help himself and found another inch of space in front of him from where he was now able to gaze down on the most magnificent pair of suntanned breasts, barely covered at all by the tightly fitted black buttoned, green jacket. Feeling like some "Peeping Tom", but not really caring, his eyes travelled down the beautiful form to the short green skirt which, with legs crossed, had moved upwards to reveal glorious black fishnet stockings. Hart knew that they were stockings because the short green skirt had risen far enough up the leg to expose the lace-stocking top and beyond that a couple of inches of bare leg.

God, I've got the best seat in the house, mused Hart to himself. *How long did he say until the end of the meeting, 15 minutes? I'd better do my best not to fall asleep.*

There was a cough from an obviously nervous chairman, out of sight to Hart, and then he announced,

'Right then, we have two more items on the agenda and then we will adjourn until tomorrow. So then, Doctor Halle, will you now give us a brief update please on our status and progress in the various countries on the African continent and also a little insight into our new areas of development.'

Hart's blood ran cold. Once again he was just feet away from his arch-enemy, albeit from a different position in space this time, who would most probably be either standing or sitting right below him, no doubt sporting his famous signature blue blazer with silver buttons, a jaunty pocket handkerchief, grey trousers and white or striped shirt accompanied by his striped company tie. This was clearly a very confidential meeting of World Pharmaceuticals staff at least, but most probably also research scientists and/or research management from her sister companies, GRS and Vita Pharma and why not from the medical centres at the Paddocks, the Liverpool Hospital and who knew where else? Oh yes, there was also the stunning (but so far faceless) Claudia, in view below him. There was the screeching of chair legs on the tiles once more and just audible footsteps followed by a clearing of the throat. Obviously, Halle had risen from the table and walked to some presentation position at the front of the meeting and was now about to speak to the room.

'Thank you, Maurice. Because of the importance and obvious confidentiality associated with our efforts in Africa and the recent attempts at this very symposium by outsiders, most probably industrial spies, to gain greater insights into our achievements using certain clandestine methods…'

Bloody hell, that must be me he's referring to.

Hart strained his neck to try and see more of the faces in the room, but without any success. *Arben must have reported back to him already.*

'…I intend to only speak today. There will be no supporting slides or documents and no handouts. Instead you will all be copied with an authorised copy of the meat of my presentation by e-mail once the conference has ended, but don't worry, there will not be a test at the end of my brief update.'

The attempted joke received just one or two nervous laughs. Clearly, Frau Arben was needed to drop out a few of her amusing one-liners!

'So…we now have 25 hospitals in four African countries who are engaged in our projects, with three more countries lined up on that continent and a possible resulting further 30 hospital sites. We also have six universities who are keen to become involved in our stem cell program. Greater details will follow in the e-mail I promised you. However, most importantly, the number of clinics which are now screening and entering patients into our African studies has grown to 450.'

A collective gasp of surprise and admiration went up from the audience.

'The actual number of patients who have consented to take part in our African clinical trials is now in excess of 4,000.'

The admiration kept on flowing from the floor. Hart too couldn't help but be very impressed with the figures Halle was presenting. He himself had been involved in directing many international clinical trials and he was fully aware of the often-huge difficulties in recruiting suitable patients for them.

'But what of the cost I hear you say, or at least I expect you to think. I'm a pretty good mind reader, you know, these days.'

Another well-rehearsed ad-lib trotted off his tongue.

'I can confidently tell you that the cost to World, and that includes drug and other biological materials costs, ethics and safety committees payments and payments for the investigating doctors and their staff my friends…amounts to peanuts!'

Hart winced. He loathed that smarmy, pompous, self-satisfied, self-congratulatory voice. It had not changed one bit in the weeks since they had last crossed swords; in fact, if anything, it had got worse. Hart was so totally pissed off that it was all he could do to remain on his perch and not go crashing down through the ceiling to "punch the bastard's lights out!" Clearly, a cause for him to get a grip on himself and remain as calm and unmoving as possible, although his blood was rushing so loudly through his pounding ears that he was thinking for sure the crew below would be able to hear it. Halle smarmed on...

'You see the majority of the doctors and nurses involved in our studies are working in impoverished hospitals and clinics and are content to just take advantage of the medications we are placing at their disposal, even though much of it is only placebo, albeit not labelled as such. That said, we do have an important program of issuing free medications in certain areas and in those situations, of course, the medication on offer is often out of date, always out of patency and license and is usually generic in nature, which also make for very low costs. You may ponder the ethics of such activities, but I tell you that we must do this as a means of being able to continue in staging our clinical trials program when other companies are failing. Failing miserably I would add! We can be confident that World is now the major pharmaceutical company, in some areas the *only* pharmaceutical company, with such a major presence. A presence I may say that is also greatly appreciated at governmental levels in these countries. It is fair to say that through our charitable work, we have been able to oust our competitors in these regions almost totally. Of course, we have been assisted greatly in these achievements by our close ties with governmental agencies, as I have mentioned, and equally importantly our close ties with local church leaders on the ground, with connections stretching upwards to the highest levels of the local predominantly Catholic Churches and even further, back to Rome itself.'

His own flow was suddenly interrupted by a nervous hand which was raised in the audience. Halle gave the apparent questioner a hard stare.

'You have a question, Doctor?'

There was the sound of people moving in their chairs to look at the brave soul who was prepared to enter the lion's den. When it finally came, the nervous male voice, speaking in English, had a distinctly Italian accent.

'Yes, sorry, but I worry that there seems to be a low level of certain ethical behaviours exercised in some of the activities that we are progressing so well in. For example, in re-labelling placebo, and also what about drugs that are well past their recommended expiry dates being given out? I do understand very well, however, the need for us to be close to the government ministries in these actions.'

Eyes that had been turned to this colleague now abruptly turned to the front of the room, the rest of the doctor's international colleagues being suddenly very keen not to be associated with him in any way and certainly not observed to be offering him any support. Looking at the red-headed Claudia below him, Hart was very aware by the rotation and of her head that she was assimilating the reactions of every other person in the room to the hapless doctor's comments. His card had been marked! His eventual support for the local governmental initiative did nothing to quench the fire in Halle's eyes as he responded, hardly attempting to hide the menace in his tone.

'I am very sad that you have a problem here and I do hope that nobody else here is similarly troubled.'

He scanned the room looking for other potential volunteers for his withering glare, but all were quiet and straight-faced.

'The placebo issue is not an actual issue in truth. All such placebo medications are given a common brand name and there is no hiding it from medical staff or licensing bodies that they do not contain active ingredients. In fact they are, therefore, in no way harmful. As for out of date re-labelled drugs, I can tell you that they too are not harmful to patients; in fact, the opposite is true, as their time-degraded active ingredients have even less opportunity to cause adverse events or minor side effects. It's a matter of semantics. At the end of the day, the physicians and medical staff are happy, the patients are certainly happy to receive treatment that for so long remained completely out of their reach, the church is happy to have more contented and perhaps healthier congregations and the politicians are very happy to have more contented voters. It's a win-win situation, my friend. Look, if you are so badly troubled, I will ask our colleague, Claudia Volpe, here to speak to you later and arrange for you to leave the program. It is not a problem.'

(Hart was amazed. *I'll buy that used rust bucket with no engine!*)

Claudia nodded her agreement as backsides shuffled uneasily on chairs around the room. Daniel rose to leave the den, but Halle raised a hand.

'No, please remain; Claudia will discuss things with you at the end of the meeting, perhaps in another room. I was about to add, before the interruption, that in working in Africa, we are very close to the Pope's own ethnic roots and he is, therefore, very keen to see the African countries raised from third world medical status as soon as possible. It is for this reason that I will not be joining you at tomorrow's meeting, as at that time, I will be meeting someone who is very close to the Pope in the Vatican and who has an excellent rapport with him, especially when discussing ways of improving people's lots in the poorer African townships and villages. So to sum up, because of our relationships with governmental and medical agencies, we have no problems with ethics committees and we are, therefore, able to push our studies forward. Our current success in Africa, and we are still only at the beginning, has proved to be far beyond our initial expectations and, in fact, we are way beyond expectations in our Western scenarios also. Africa is currently a blank canvas for us, my friends, and the picture that we can paint on it is entirely of our own choosing.

'Now I said there were two items I wanted to talk to you about. The second is our very exciting regenerative tissue program…'

Hart's brain was going into overload. He was now aware of the scale of World's global plans, especially those for Africa and presumably there would be confirmation of at least some of these within the documents he had in his bag, and now he was about to learn details of their stem cell program of research. What he couldn't understand, however, was what had happened to Halle since he had worked with him at World. He was viewed by all, apart from the usual "brown nosers" and of course the bitch in human resources, as a pompous, self-righteous, stiff bastard, but for all that, to Hart's mind, he had always been totally professional and ethical in everything he did. The only thing he was famous for within the company was his consistently boring mode of dress, which spoke more of his total lack of personality than his gregariousness…and of course his infamous bad breath. He was Doctor Halletosis to many within the lower echelons of World. Hart could not reconcile the particular version of Halle he was now witnessing with the upright "straight as a die Halle" he had known, but who he would forever hate and despise for the way in which he had manipulated and orchestrated his "retirement" from the company. Surely, there must have been some turning point in Halle's life, some extreme event which had given rise to this Jeckyl to Hyde conversion?

The day would come when all things would be made clear to Hart…by the man himself.

For the moment though, Hart's attentions were drawn to the lady in green below, who was valiantly trying to re-cover the exposed area of her naked upper thigh, caused by her almost microscopic green skirt riding "onwards and upwards". He watched her as she raised her thigh from the seat and pulled hard on the skirt's hem. Sadly for Hart, it eventually yielded and once more her modesty was restored. Unfortunately, because of this distraction and also due to his lapse in concentration whilst analysing Halle, Hart had missed the opening words of his second agenda item, but with a shrug of the shoulders and a shake of the head, he re-tuned to Halle's address to the troops below.

'…for we have an almost inexhaustible supply of human foetal tissue and looking towards our African developments, this will only increase the tissue at our disposal. We will rule the pharmaceutical world for years to come.'

He smiled as he cast his gaze around the room lingering momentarily on the representatives from Germany, England and Italy.

'We, at World, owe all of you a huge "thank you". However, I have to mention that at this stage of our research, it has become evident that there are certain genetic differences in the foetal tissues we are working with. These are not great or insurmountable differences, but ones which currently prevent us from advancing as quickly as we would prefer, but for sure, this will be resolved very soon. This means though that for the present, we have to continue with the human tissue from our current, that is *your*, sites here in Europe. So that's it, my friends, please keep up the good work, World Pharmaceuticals is depending on you.'

He smiled graciously as once more, his face skimmed the audience, finding time to turn his smile to a blistering frown as he passed it by the Italian doctor who had spoken out earlier about ethics, and who was now persona non grata with his colleagues in this room with his research future in grave doubt. In fact, his future, period, was in grave doubt and likely left in the hands of the glorious Claudia.

'In rounding off today's meeting, I would like to invite Claudia Volpe to step up to the dais and say some final words. Claudia, please.'

Unusually for the upright Halle, he beamed an "in your pants" smile at Volpe, who left her seat, pulling down the misbehaving skirt, and replaced him at the front of the room. All Hart saw of her disappearance was her head going forward and her backside rising…and then she was gone. But not far. She smiled her gorgeous smile at the audience and the whole of the audience, seduced by it, smiled back. Sadly, this was all out of Hart's visual range. She gave a slight cough and then began to speak. She spoke in a rather deep throaty English, heavy with an intoxicating Italian accent. The audience was in the palm of her hand…and so was Hart, and he had not yet set eyes on her face! This lady was very special indeed. She continued at the point where Halle had left off.

'As Doctor Halle has said, we must continue to process living human stem cell tissue from all of our European sites. It is true that Africa is not yet a complete solution, but it will be very soon, but until then, Europe must press on. We are, in many ways, being held up by our own success with the result that we need more and more tissue for processing into medications for the treatment of severe medical cases where we are successfully beating back crippling and debilitating disease. Our major problem now is that we are having to increase the doses of the treatment regimens in order to maintain these medical improvements and this has resulted in the need for us all to increase our levels of production of the tissue extracts. Of course, that includes the obtaining of the tissue at source.'

At this, the audience paused from eating out of her hand, and audibly groaned. Volpe raised her hand and the groans subsided.

'You know we have many important and wealthy people now being treated by our revolutionary tissue medication in many different countries. These important people have reached the point where they have a greater need for increased doses of our drug to actually keep them alive. Ordinarily, they would have died months if not years ago if not for us and so we, therefore, have no choice but to do all we can to preserve their lives further. I must, therefore, tell you all, no, *encourage* you all,' she smiled a brief ironic smile, 'to take whatever steps are necessary to increase the capture and delivery of the foetal tissue to meet our expanding requirements. Doctor Sumaris, you seem to want to make some point.'

To the annoyance of those around him not wanting to be caught up in the spotlight of any further dissent, Doctor Sumaris, sitting near the front of the audience, had raised a hand. He began shakily,

'Yes. In the UK, we are working to full capacity already. I know now that there are times when we come under suspicion from our patients and I feel that it would be dangerous for some of us to try and increase the number of tissue samples. National records of stillbirths are kept and made available to the public and sooner or later, alarm bells are going to ring somewhere and we will be inspected by government inspectors. I have seen inspections by both the Medicines Control Agency in the UK and the American Food and Drug Authority several times and I assure you that they leave no stone unturned. The people who are sent into sites have a vast knowledge of the appropriate sciences and they delve very deeply into all on-site standard operating procedures.'

Hart smiled to himself thinking, *Don't worry, chap, those bells are ringing loud and clear already and soon the relevant people will start to listen to them.*

Sumaris' voice held a note of panic in it and he was all but pleading with Volpe to untighten the screws, but the beautiful woman was having none of it. She looked at Sumaris coldly.

'That is *your* problem, Doctor Sumaris. I must remind you that you have entered into what from your point of view is a very profitable contract. A contract from which you have already been paid a considerable sum of money and the bottom line is that you are expected to continue to deliver. Any problems relating to meeting our requirements are yours and yours alone. I'm afraid that you passed the point of no return a long time ago. In fact, many thousands of US dollars ago.'

Her voice became more menacing.

'You will deliver. There is no argument to be had and neither is there any room for negotiation at this stage. You know that the consequences of breaking our contract would be dire for you, and that applies to *all* our colleagues here today.'

This latter came as an afterthought and she looked around the room at all the faces to underline the point. Within that room, there was not a single person who would hold her stare. Instead, eyes looked down at the floor and bodies moved uncomfortably on their seats.

'Is that perfectly clear to you, Doctor Sumaris? Is that perfectly clear to everyone else in this room?'

Sumaris nodded, looking crestfallen and rather ashamed. He spoke not another word. The rest of the audience too remained silent and in that silence one would be able to hear a pin drop. From his lofty position, Hart could sense the fear in the room below and wondered just how this stunning woman could raise such trepidation in the mostly male audience. She certainly was in possession of great power over her "colleagues"... and still he hadn't seen her face!

The uncomfortable silence was finally broken by Maurice, the meeting chairman.

'Very well, ladies and gentlemen, that will be all for today and I look forward to meeting everyone again at 10.00 am tomorrow here in this room. Everyone that is, except Doctor Halle, who will be ensconced with the high-ranking person from the Vatican at that time. I believe that you will be taking lunch at the Hotel Torino, Doctor Halle, which is a little too far from here to enable you to catch the end of our meeting. Can I just remind our Italian colleague who spoke at the beginning of Doctor Halle's session to meet directly with Claudia on the way out? That just leaves me to say thank you once again for your attendance and attention and I will see you all tomorrow. Good evening.'

Chairs were pushed back noisily and the room cleared quickly, some delegates desperate for some fresh air, whilst others were more in need for an urgent visit to the WC. It's amazing what a meeting can do to the bowel movement! Hart breathed out heavily, his cramped position now beginning to tell on him when suddenly he finally saw the face. Claudia Volpe had left the dais and returned to her previously occupied seat when she suddenly flicked back her head and using the palms of both hands, smoothed and massaged the skin around her neck. Clearly, she too was feeling the stresses of the meeting. Hart froze! Was she looking straight at him? Could she in fact see him at all? In fact there was no need at all for him to worry, for as she stroked her neck, her eyes, formerly visible to him, became firmly closed in relaxation. It was then that Hart saw the full features of her face. She had the most beautiful face he had ever gazed upon. Large (now closed) brown eyes, delicately aquiline nose and wonderful full lips, all expertly cosmetically addressed and absolutely perfect (in fact like a young Sophia Loren's *even* better-looking much younger sister!), and together with the hair, the body, the legs and the voice she was at that moment to Hart, Miss Total Universe.

Three people remained in the room after the others had left, Halle, Maurice and Frau Arben. Claudia Volpe had suddenly left the room chasing the "colleague" who had had the temerity to consider leaving the team, but who it seemed had not had the courage to stay behind and be "counselled" by her.

Halle spoke.

'Frau Arben, what exactly was the problem earlier with the intruder?'

'Oh it was just some minor matter, Herr Doctor Halle. It is completely resolved now.'

'That's good. Perhaps we could discuss security in general a little more over coffee when I return after lunch tomorrow? Without wanting to sound paranoid, we really have to tighten up our security procedures from now on, especially as we are at such a sensitive time in our program.'

'Of course, Doctor Halle, I will look you out in tomorrow's afternoon. Until then, goodbye.'

As Arben exited, Halle turned back to "Chairman Maurice".

'Yes, Maurice, it is essential that we keep a very close control of all security matters from here on in. You know I can't help but find the attitude of our UK colleagues somewhat disturbing. Now is certainly not the time for cold feet and I think that theirs are…ahem…dropping in temperature to say the least. They will need some close observation I think.'

'Yes, but don't worry too much, Claudia's team have already been briefed on the matter and things are in hand…one way or another.'

'That's excellent; thank you, Maurice.'

With his arm around Maurice's shoulder, the pair left the room, Halle first extinguishing the lights and then Maurice closing the door behind them. Hart was alone at last and in the dark, he decided to wait at least five minutes to ensure that there were no returners to the room before attempting any touchdown from his confinement into the room below. With nobody returning to the room after five minutes, he decided to take his chances and descend.

Whilst waiting, he had reactivated his laser pen light and scoured the void along the AC gantry for a service access point similar to that at his original point of entry. He didn't have to look very far, for just six feet further along from his vantage point of the lovely Claudia, he detected the service-ceiling tile which was large enough to permit him entry to the room below.

Getting down was, despite the aches and pains he now had as a result of being cramped in the tunnel for so long, far easier than getting up there in the first place what seemed like hours ago.

Having maneuvered himself forward, he lifted the tile and placed it to one side. Directly below the opening he had created, he was able to identify with his laser pen one of the meeting tables onto which he dropped his priceless cargo, the satchel of documents he had so lovingly kept hanging from his now aching neck over these past hours. Quickly finding the service handles attached to the support gantry, he took hold, one in each hand, and easing his body through the open space now, let his weight be taken by his locked out arms. From there he lowered himself to within two or three feet of the table top, whence he finally let go and dropped squarely onto the table landing surprisingly perfectly balanced. Gaining the floor in one short jump, he reviewed his situation and decided it would be best to return the tile to its former resting place just in case it set alarm bells ringing when noticed by the returning delegates in the morning. Running on pure adrenaline once more, he hoisted a chair onto the table and climbing first onto it and then onto the chair he reached into the ceiling void and carefully worked the ceiling tile back into its position in the aluminium frame. A descent to the floor and a re-positioning of the chair under the table and it was "job done".

He picked up his bag and advanced to the door, where he was suddenly struck by the thought that like the previous door, this one too might now be locked from the outside and he would be forced to undergo the same agonies again. He listened at the door for sounds of voices or footsteps in the corridor outside for a full minute and then, assuming the coast to be clear, confidently turned the door handle. The door opened. He quickly looked both up and down the corridor, and seeing that at this moment it was free of any people he made his exit from the meeting room. Upon emerging, he almost immediately saw a sign with an arrow, indicating the direction to the exit… "*Uscita*", which he quickly followed. He was slightly worried that the sign would direct him past the room he had earlier escaped from but no, quite soon in his quest for freedom he was directed down a minor staircase to the hotel lobby where his nostrils were suddenly filled with the smells of the night air. He breathed them in deeply and headed straight out into the street where his senses were immediately hit with all the sights and sounds associated with a typical Italian evening *passeggiata*.

Surprisingly, he immediately recognised where he was in relationship to his own hotel and headed directly back to it at a steady *passeggiata* pace, his heart pounding with the excitement and the exhilaration of the evening's events. He couldn't wait to meet Crosse and relate his experiences and discoveries to her. She must be wondering where the hell he was by now.

It seemed that in the end all had turned out rather well for him…but he would certainly have to do something about his suit; it was a total mess!

Chapter 61

It was now four large glasses of cognac since he had received the recent call from the Vatican and one more glass would be enough to bring an end to his productivity and clear thinking for the remainder of this particular day. The log fire still flickered in the hearth, still producing the myriad of ever changing shapes and images holding his gaze almost hypnotically. He was just about to pour himself this one last drink when the telephone rang out. He had been expecting this call for some time, but even so he jumped slightly at the first ring. At last! He reached forward and picked up the receiver.

'Yes.'

'*Ciao*, it is Claudia. I'm so sorry to be late with my call but things went on a little longer than anticipated at the meeting.'

'That's no problem, Claudia, you're here now. Where exactly are you by the way?

'I am still at the conference centre in Padua. There were a few things that needed tidying up at the end of the meeting, but all is sorted out now.'

'I hope things went well, Claudia. As you know, we cannot accept any backing out, cold feet or refusals at this important stage of our program.'

'Trust me, I know exactly what is needed and the lengths to which we have to be prepared to go to achieve success. I am very happy to do whatever is needed to ensure a quick and positive outcome to our plans. Today there was indeed some complaining and a little whining from a minority of our overseas colleagues, worried about the possibilities of them having regulatory inspections, but by the end, they were content to press forward at a greater rate.'

'That's excellent, I did expect you to tell me that some colleagues were requesting a greater rate of pay for their efforts.'

'No, no, the discussion of money did not arise. There was just one of our researchers, from Sicily I'm ashamed to say, who I think would like to leave the program.'

'That is impossible, Claudia. It would be too dangerous for anyone at this very sensitive stage to leave the program. We would be far too vulnerable.'

'Do not worry about a thing. The good doctor will indeed leave the program very soon, but he will not be in any condition to involve any outside regulatory people…if you follow my line of thought? This will also be a good sign to others in the trials not to consider going down the same route.'

'Very good, Claudia, you are an excellent partner in this business and I trust you implicitly. I will support whatever action you have decided to take.'

'Thank you so much; it is getting late here now and I have to mix with just a little more with our other partners, so I must say *buona notte* to you for now.'

'*Buona notte,* Claudia.'

He hung up the phone and settled back in his chair, taking up where he had left off, reading the images in the flames of the fire. Dozing there, his mind drifted away from the room he was in and back to Sicily and Claudia Volpe, her background and her rise through the ranks of her organisation. For such a beautiful young woman, hers was a story of heartbreak, retribution and frequent savagery in her role as *Capa di Capi* of all the Sicilian mafia groups. She was perfect for the role!

Chapter 62

Crosse was frantic with worry. It had been more than three and a half hours since Hart had returned to the hospitality suite with no word at all from him during that time. *Surely a phone call shouldn't have been any problem? What could have gone wrong?* The only explanation she could think of was that Hart had in some way, at some stage, been apprehended and was currently languishing in some local police lockup. A worse thought was that he had been caught by those he had set out to expose and was now going through some terrible interrogation at their hands. Should she call the police? Should she walk back to the conference centre and carry out her own search for him, in which case she might miss him turning up at the hotel? She decided that all she could do was to wait…for now at least, and hope that he would turn up before she had to make a decision as to what to do next.

Hart arrived back at the Hotel Giardinetto feeling breathless and very relieved to be "home". The hotel lobby was pretty frenetic, filled with conference delegates in their various groups waiting to be met and wined and dined by high-rolling pharmaceutical company personnel.

He smiled and nodded variously as he excused himself through the throng on his way to the elevator, acutely aware of the stares and long glances he was receiving during his passage. He arrived at the lifts and entered the vacant one, pressing the ascend button to his and Crosse's floor. He turned and faced the lift's mirror.

'Bloody hell!'

The reason for the stares was now very apparent, for as well as the creased and dirt covered state of his suit and shirt, his face was also covered in streaks of dirt and dust and to top it all off, his head was crowned with a wonderfully intact spider's web.

Eventually reaching Crosse's door, Hart knocked abruptly on it.

The door was opened almost immediately by a frantic-looking Crosse.

'Chimneys swept, *signorina*?'

'Where the hell have you been, Max? You look bloody filthy!'

'I'm fine thanks. Thanks for asking! Sit down and I'll tell you everything. You'll find a lot of it utterly unbelievable I promise you.'

He swung his arm holding his satchel forward and dropped it onto the bed. He then opened it and tipped out all its contents onto the overlay.

'These are going to need a lot of sorting out eventually, but first let me tell you everything.'

He began, starting from the moment he first entered the hospitality suite, having just left Crosse, and continued with his story telling all, including details of his experiences relating to being locked in the back office and of his travel through the overhead ducting. He described the important meeting he had overheard and his final touchdown and escape from the conference centre. He covered the details of the trials and personnel involved as far as he could remember them and the information he had picked up relating to the vast global scale of the project, including the African countries. Crosse's responses fluctuated between wide-eyed incredulity and deep-frowned concern. When he finished, Crosse, who had fired various questions at him during his telling of the tale, just stared at the bed unable to speak, unable to even know where to start.

'So to conclude, VC, Halle seems to be the main man here, but this Claudia person with the shock of red hair,' he failed to mention the breasts and the legs, 'also seems to be very important in the scheme of things. She has this aura of strength and she certainly put the fear of God into the folk assembled there. I think I should go to my room, take a shower and put on a change of clothes and return here and make an attempt to sort out these documents, some of which I'm sure will be totally irrelevant. After that, I propose, we ring Denis and briefly update him, but certainly confirm to him that his suspicions have been totally correct. These goings on are globally huge and break all the rules in the book when it comes to medical and ethical regulatory issues and probably a lot more when the legal aspects are examined. It's all incredibly serious. I think we should then fax as much as the relevant documents as we can directly to him. There's a business suite here in the hotel so that should be straightforward. It was clear to me whilst listening in from the crow's nest earlier that some of the physicians involved in the collection of foetal materials are running very low on foetal resources and are in fact getting very cold feet about it. This has pissed Halle and Claudia off to a huge extent and I feel that Claudia was there to put the frighteners on them.'

For the next fifteen minutes, Hart regaled Crosse with what he believed the international stem cell retrieval business directed by Halle was about, but in the end confessed that other than great profit he couldn't see anything else that appeared to be an additional reason for the project that was sufficiently important to encourage such risks.

'You see, VC, the potential profits are really enormous, but if the house is built on the sands of corruption and illegality, it will certainly fall very quickly. There has to be some other reason, some grand plan, that at present is totally outside of my comprehension, but which is possibly the main endpoint for all of this. But what is that endpoint? At some stage, legality and proper ethics will have to return to the processes surely, to give the project longevity and to ensure that it's all not just a fly-by-night operation?'

'In which case, Max, there should come a point when all illegality has to cease so that the actual grand plan can run to fruition unencumbered by these prior wrong doings? Is *that* the way it is do you think?'

'Yes probably, but it is definitely time for us to disappear off this particular map and back to normality. In other words, I will leave for Milan tomorrow as we discussed, and you should leave tomorrow for the UK. Let's get the hell out of here for God's sake.'

'But you've not said who Halle is working for. Presumably, he's just a cog in a much larger wheel?'

'Look, you will see amongst these documents references to work being done in Asia, Europe, Africa and the Americas, the scope is huge and whilst Halle is clearly a key member of the team pushing it, I honestly think that in some way, he is working under the instigation of something else very large. Running low on adequate foetal material and the associated risks of increasing the supply must be a major headache to them. I get the impression that things have not gone straightforwardly in the foetal cell/stem cell production area. Possibly the volume of material they've been getting has been enough only up to the point when it became apparent that there are genetic differences in the possible uses of the cells, for example reading between the lines of what Halle said to the assembled team they could have found to their great chagrin that at present, for whatever reasons, not all Caucasian patients can be treated effectively with stem cells from donors from just any genetic or ethnic background. It might be that Caucasian patients require Caucasian donors only. He didn't go into any detail so I don't know whether the same applies to non-Caucasian patients. So pack your bag and let's leave tomorrow. It's been fun but *arrivederci* Padua.'

'Hang on, Max. Surely, even World is a far too large ethical and respected company to get dragged into something like this?'

'Don't be too sure, VC, corrupt and unethical activities have been pursued in the past by other pharma oligarchies.'

'So you know everything you need now?'

'There's just one thing I would like to confirm and that is the connection between World and Vita in Sicily. The name of Laboratorio di Scoperta Fondamentale, also based in Sicily, came up in certain of the documents. What a mouthful! However, I get the impression that Vita Pharma are the more important of the two. We can definitely link all the other players in the game together. I've been threatening to call my old secretary Janet in the US, so I think I'll just make that call. So to conclude this little session, we sort the documents, we call Denis, we fax Denis and I'll call Janet and then we bugger off.

'Actually, Vicky, you know I keep banging on about you leaving on a jet plane tomorrow? Well, there might just be one final favour you could do for me, or rather us, but only if you feel up to it. You know, you must put yourself first.'

'OK, Max, what is it, put my head in a lion's mouth or something else equally innocuous?'

'As I said, Vicky, this is only if you want to do it and indeed only if it fits in with your flight schedule tomorrow. When I was in my concealed ceiling place back at the conference centre, I heard Halle say that he was unable to be at a meeting tomorrow with the rest of the ensemble as he had an important meeting lined up with some guy in the Hotel Torino. For Halle to miss out on another occasion for beating up on these guys, he must be meeting somebody really important. What I do know though is that it is a person of import from the Vatican.'

'So?'

'So, as I have just said, only if you feel like it, I'm wondering if you could stroll along to Halle's place of rendezvous with me, find a suitable place out of sight from wherever Halle is and let's see just who he is meeting. The meeting in the conference suite that he can't make because of this more important one begins at around 10.00 am, so we should aim to be secreted somewhere discreet in the Hotel Torino from about 9.30 am I think. We really should pick a spot where he can't see me so that makes it more important to try and get there before he does...if you're game that is?'

'OK, Max, I'll do it; after all, you're the one that everybody seems to be pissed off with, not me, but let's make it 9.00 am just in case he's early. Nobody knows me so I'll be fine staked out in the open. I might even take a couple of touristy photographs if the surroundings seem appropriate and accidently catch Halle and friend on them as well.'

'Excellent! Right then, I'm off to shower and change out of these rags and I will be back in thirty minutes or so. We have a lot to do this evening and we will probably have to have room service for a bite to eat I'm afraid, as it's unlikely that we will find any time to dine out.'

'Fine, but one last thing, Max.'

He looked at her quizzically.

'Make sure you remove that bloody spider and its web from your head before you come back.'

Spiderman smiled and left...through the door rather than the window.

Showered and dry and cosseted in his hotel "courtesy bath robe", Hart began to think more of the direction he should follow from here. For sure he would be on a train to Milan tomorrow, where he would relax for a few days in the company of his Italian friend and family, but he was thinking beyond that. He felt sure that he had most probably done all he could to help Denis expose whatever was going on, certainly in Nottingham, which had been the centre of his wife's demise, but globally he was not so sure about it. The possibility that he might be able to bring down the vile, Halle sent his adrenaline surging once more, but until he had phoned Janet and hopefully been able to get some more of the background to Halle's and World's activities, he would have to leave all thoughts of total vengeance on the back-burner. He filed those thoughts and smiled as he thought of the next few days he would be spending with Gianni Bossi in Milan, which reminded him, he had not yet booked his hotel there. Another item to add to the ever-lengthening list of things to do.

Chapter 63

Thirty minutes later, but a little behind schedule, he was in Crosse's room where she had already made a start on sorting through the documents, trying to put together those that looked to be associated with each other in some way in the same piles, and others which she thought might be valuable only to the rubbish bin, together in separate piles. He quickly finalised and approved these various piles she had started and tossed the rubbish pile into the bin.

'You've done a really good job there, VC. Why don't you go down to the hotel business suite and see if you can fax these documents to Denis while I call him, he does have a separate fax number. Oh and don't worry if the cost of faxing seems exorbitant, Denis will be happy to cover it if it means he will get the information ASAP, but in any case, put the cost on my room number, OK? I also need to call the US and then Milan to book a hotel.'

'OK, will do. Give Denis my regards.'

She scooped up the relevant document pages and left for the business suite, which she knew would be open all night if necessary to allow delegates to contact their home bases at whatever times it was at their "homes".

Five minutes later, Hart called Denis on Crosse's room phone. The telephone was answered almost at first ring. Williams must have been virtually sitting on it.

'Hello?'

'Denis, hi, it's Max; how are you?'

'Max, it's so good to hear you. More importantly how are *you*? Oh, my fax machine has just started to spew papers out and it looks like they're from Victoria. It looks like you've been busy.'

'Busy is not the word. Listen, and no questions until I've finished please...'

'Go ahead.'

Over the next fifteen minutes, Hart retold a summary version of his day's events. There was a short silence when Hart had finished, during which time he wondered whether Denis was still on the line, then...

'My God, Max, this is really major. I mean it's huge and has to be much too big for us to take on any further now. We must surely have enough details to start a really effective fire under these bastards?'

Hart was greatly relieved to hear Williams acceding to the opinion that they had gone far enough and done all that they could. It had taken some time, but now Williams had realised completely not just the scale of the thing, but the levels to which the proponents would likely go to evade discovery and capture. Murder could clearly not be ruled out in this respect and he suddenly became very nervous and guilty at the danger in which he had placed his old friend Victoria and his new friend Max.

'So then, Max, where do we go from here, or more appropriately where do *you* go from here? I really want you and Victoria to leave there as soon as you can. You've done a great job and I don't want you to remain in any danger for a moment longer.'

'No worries, Denis, both Vicky and I totally agree with you. We have one minor thing to complete tomorrow and then Vicky will be on a plane home and I will taking a train to Milan for a few days of "rest and recreation" with an old friend. Are those faxes still coming through?'

'Still coming. I must have a pile the size of a telephone directory here. I'll let you go now, Max. Take care the pair of you.'

'It's OK, Denis, I won't do anything stupid…I've already done that! One final thing though. Could you go through the list of agencies and institutional bodies that I put up on the "war room" board and get a definitive list of their addresses and telephone numbers please? I want you to re-copy all the info that Vicky is faxing to you, split it, and assemble it to be re-sent to each of those addresses please. When I return next week, I will add a report of my own to each document set, and then we can courier them to all and sundry. If you have their telephone numbers, you might want to call each agency and body and get hold of the names of the most appropriate people there to address them to. Make sure you include as many overseas institutions as you can, you know the roots of this organisation stretch out all over the world.'

'Yes of course, I will do that, Max.'

'OK then, Denis, good to hear you, I'm off now.'

'Bye Ma—' but Hart had already put the telephone down.

After speaking to Denis, Hart immediately called the concierge and then reception. The concierge was able to tell him that on the following day there were fast trains from Padua station to Milan, stopping only once or twice, leaving at 7.00 am, 12.00 mid-day, 4.00 pm and 6.00pm. There were also "stopping trains" that required changing in Venice, with several more stops then on up to Milan. Hotel reception was able to put his call through directly to reception at the Jolly Hotel Presidente in Milan, where he'd stayed before. He made a reservation there for three nights without resorting to speaking English once.

'*Perfetto Dottore,* Hart. *Ci vediamo domani sera.* See you tomorrow evening.'

Perfetto indeed, in his mind's eye he was on holiday already. Checking his list, it just remained now for him to call Janet in the US and then his friend Gianni Bossi in Milan to confirm his planned arrival time there. He checked the time. No problem. With the time difference of minus seven hours, Janet would still be at work in her New Jersey office. However, he decided upon calling his Milanese friend first and using his own mobile phone, in order to reduce his (or rather Denis's) hotel costs. He dialled his friend's number, which quickly went into "please leave a message" mode. After leaving his message, containing details of his train and the time of his arrival in Milan and also the name of his Milan hotel, he waited until the clicks in the background of his call ceased, which he believed

213

confirmed that his message had been successfully left, and hung up. Then using the *room's* phone, he promptly punched in the numbers of his old office contact at World. The ring tone sounded far away as it rang out, which of course it was, and he was overcome with a strangely poignant feeling as he waited for someone to pick up the phone at what had been the centre of all his considerable activities for those years before his unceremonious ejection. Suddenly he lost his nerve and had the urge to slam the phone down. He would have done too was it not for the unmistakeable voice which came down the line to him,

'Clinical Development, Doctor Rogers' office.'

'Doctor Rogers' office.'

Hearing that hurt him more than he could have imagined, but after these weeks what was he going to say to break the ice?

'Hello, Clinical Development, Doctor Rogers' office, remember an old ex-employee?'

There was a small gasp at the other end of the line,

'Max! My God how wonderful to hear you. Your voice is unmistakeable, although you do sound more English now than when we last talked.'

'Ahh, I must have picked it back up from the natives. Does that mean that my Cary Grant accent has morphed into a Michael Caine one? Anyway, how the devil are you, Janet?'

'I'm fine thanks, Max, but I've decided that life is too short to spend it all at work and so I plan to retire at the end of the year. Your own departure and the way it was manipulated rather convinced me to finally retire. But what about you, are you back working in pharmaceuticals?'

He was touched by her comments on retirement. He knew that she had indeed lived mainly for work (and also for her husband up until his fairly recent sudden death) and the pleasures she gained from it, so things must have changed a whole lot for the worse in the months since his departure to cause her to bring forward her retirement date.

'Well, Janet, I'm actually calling you from Padua in Italy.'

'Wonderful! Are you there for work or for pleasure?'

'I'm doing some pharmaceutical consultancy work for a short time with some old acquaintances in the UK, but when I finally get my head screwed back on properly I'll be back over there to terrorise some poor sods I'm sure. But I note that Brutus Rogers has stepped into my old sandals and toga.'

'That's right, but these days Ken is different. He's become a real 100% company man.'

'There you go, Janet, I leave him as a beautiful butterfly and as soon as I'm gone, he metamorphoses into a company maggot! That's a life-cycle in reverse.'

'A lot has changed here, Max. There's no fun anymore.'

'Look, Janet, when I'm back, which will probably be soon, I'll get in touch and wine and dine you a little. How about that?'

'That will be lovely, Max, but tell me, what big favour are you about to ask of me?'

'You've always been able to read me like a book. I don't want much, Janet, on this occasion, just a few bits of general company information.'

'Max, I can't talk about the company from here on the phone, it's too open. Give me your number and in a few minutes, I will get back to you from a quieter desk. It doesn't matter that it's Italy, as making long-distance telephone calls is the one thing that the company is still pretty lax about.'

Hart gave her his telephone details, or more accurately Crosse's room details, and hung up. Seconds later, the door opened and in walked the beaming Crosse.

'All done and dusted. Everything went through without a hitch. Have you made your calls?'

'Yes, I'm waiting for a response now from my old PA Janet, it should be any minute.'

Right on cue the telephone rang out, making 'the sound of a couple of skeletons making love in a biscuit tin', to quote one of Hart's famous one-liners.

'Janet? Hi. The thing is I'm doing some background publications work on stem cell research and development and treatments and I'm checking out the competitors in the field. As you're the font of all knowledge at World, are you aware of anything that *they* are doing in that field these days?

'I'm not aware of anything directly, Max. As you know the various clinical research and developmental trials that are on-going are made fairly open to everyone here. In any case, all our studies have to be registered on the FDA website along with all other company's studies, so there's no reason for any secrecy from that point of view.'

'Yes I'd forgotten about that, I'll give the site a try. What about partnering with other companies for certain studies, or buying specific biotech companies, or pushing through acquisitions of institutions and companies outside of the US. Anything ring a bell there?'

'Hang on Max, I can easily access the company's own internal website and see what's on there. Hang on.'

Hart heard the tap, tap of the keys of a keyboard and he waited. For a couple of minutes, it was silence apart from the occasional additional *tap, tap, tap*, then,

'OK here we go. I have here a list of affiliates and international marketing companies related to ours. We seem to have involvement in most European countries, with various affiliated companies as well, for example World Italia et cetera. Certainly, I see listed several African-based companies. It looks like World is big in Africa and growing rapidly. Hang on again Max,' *tap, tap, tap…* 'Right. Here we have a list of recent acquisitions. Wow! Somebody sure has been busy, I never realised that—'

'Sorry to cut in on you, Janet, this is good stuff, but can you focus on Germany and Italy, particularly Sicily for me please. Anything recorded there?'

'Indeed there is. There must be a dozen or so acquisitions here in most European countries in fact and wait…yes, last year World acquired a set-up in Germany in a place called Greifswald. It's called the Gerhard Roscher Schmoller Institute, or GRS.'

'Yes!' Hart looked at Crosse and gave her an aggressive thumbs-up.

'And you mentioned Sicily, yes, around the same time, we acquired a company called VITA Pharma and an associated laboratory complex called, and forgive my Italian, il Laboratorio di Scoperta Fondamentale. Phew, that's a bit of a tongue twister for a good ol' Jersey gal! Actually that's quite interesting…'

'Why's that?'

'Well, that's where World Pharmaceuticals was born so to speak, in Basiglio, Sicily way back. In those days though it was called "Mondo".'

Hart nodded and gave Crosse another thumbs-up, this was music to his ears.

'One other interesting thing, Max, is that our glorious leader and company owner has a brother who's a priest, in fact he's a cardinal now, living and working most of the time in the Vatican, although he does still commute to New York when necessary. Rumour has it that he's quite high up in Vatican circles and could even be a chum of the Pope, if the Pope actually has chums. Seems he carries a torch for Africa and has lobbied variously for cheaper if not totally gratis drugs to be made available by pharmaceutical companies in the poorer regions. It seems that he is truly one of the good guys.'

'Fantastic, Janet, that's all quite an earful and I can't thank you enough. My word is my bond and I promise that I will wine and dine you at the place of your choice, sod the cost, when I come over to the good ol' U S of A.'

'That will be wonderful, but make sure you come before I retire to Florida! Stay safe. Bye for now.'

'Bye Janet, it's been great talking to you again and thanks a million for the information.'

He gently returned the telephone's handset to its cradle and in a quiet tone of voice continued,

'There we are then, Vicky, we can now show that World is linked to every other organisation that we've come across in our travels whilst working for Denis. We just have the one thing on our agenda tomorrow morning and then it's "hi ho Silver away" from here. So then, what time is it now, we certainly have finished quicker than I had anticipated? Oh hang on, I made some mental notes of things to follow-up on whilst over in the back office of the hospitality suite, relating to Africa, the status of World with these other companies that keep cropping up, and what the church involvement in this might be, but I believe all my questions have been pretty much resolved by Halle's presentation, what we have in these documents and what Janet has told me just now. That's it then… and it's bang on ten thirty. Fancy popping out for a quick pizza or something?'

'Only if we can wash it down with a suitably large amount of the local vino rosso.'

'Molto bene. A quick meal and then some shut-eye. We should meet at 8.00 am tomorrow for breakfast before our little jaunt to the Halle rendezvous. How does that sound?'

'It sounds fine to me. You know things have gone rather well today…in the end that is. I wonder what sort of an evening your friend Halle has been having. He would have severe indigestion for sure if he knew what was afoot here. Let's go out and eat pizza, pardner.'

Chapter 64

A few hours earlier, a stately looking man in a blue blazer with silver buttons formally summoned over the waiter in one of the bars at the Sheraton Hotel da Vinci. The young waiter smiled at the moustachioed customer and his female companion.

'Madam, sir, would you like to take a drink?'

Halle answered for the pair of them,

'Yes, my colleague will take a glass of Riesling and I will take a glass of your Amarone, please, and I will pay in cash.'

There were no smiles from the man or his companion and as the waiter turned to depart, he could almost feel the cold radiating from the couple. Arben shifted nervously in her seat. There were a thousand other places she would prefer to be rather than here this evening, here no doubt for interrogation by Halle. It was Halle who finally broke the awkward pregnant pause in their conversation.

'So then, Bettina, tell me. What was that "little problem" you had earlier which caused you to miss the start of our meeting?'

'Really, Doctor Halle, it was nothing of importance, just some delegate dawdling in the hospitality suite when we were about to close.'

'So who was this delegate, Bettina? Did you speak to him?'

'Yes sir, it was just some university person working for another company who was looking at our posters and publications. He was quite complimentary about the work. In fact, I met him some weeks ago in Greifswald. He was with a colleague there on some clinical audit at the research centre. There is nothing to concern you, Doctor Halle; in fact, I have his details in my folder. I even have a photograph of him from the CCTV. She finally allowed herself a smile.

'Here, take a look for yourself.'

She picked up the manila folder lying on the chair beside her, took out the A5 sized photograph and held it up in front of Halle. Arben handed Halle the rest of the file, which he rapidly skimmed through before giving his attention to the photograph still being held aloft by Arben. He couldn't help but be impressed with this show of efficiency, for inside the folder was a complete list of minor incidents and offences committed mainly by her own staff together with the names of the perpetrators of these "crimes" together with their personal details. When his gaze finally did land on the photograph, his face suddenly hardened and his lips tightened. He was shocked and angry. Very angry, and Arben could see this and she became quite fearful. He snatched the photograph from between Arben's fingers and glared down at it. Grinning up at him from the photograph was the image of the man he had labelled a "foul-mouthed loser" on the day he

217

had conspired to finally get rid of him from the company. Hart haunted him, even though Halle had had the last laugh in getting him fired, although it was officially recorded by human resources as "leaving by mutual consent", for he truly hated Hart and at the sight of him here his blood pressure rocketed and his face became very florid.

'Is there a problem, Doctor Halle?' Arben's now tiny voice was also a little unsteady.

'I know this man very well. Too well!'

He raised his voice considerably on his second statement and simultaneously struck the face in the photograph with the backs of the fingers of one hand.

'This man is trouble, always trouble. Tell me exactly what he even just *might* have done. I want to know everything, from your first meeting with him in Greifswald to you meeting him again here at the congress. I cannot tell you, Frau Arben, quite how pissed off I really am to see his face. I really *am* pissed off!'

It was very unusual indeed for Halle to resort to expletives of any kind, no matter how minor they were and how great was the cause, such was the effect of Hart's grinning image on him. Arben related a sanitised version of the events at Greifswald followed by the Padua incident, reducing them to minor co-incidental instances, but indicating that she had organised a telling off and a warning to him from the in-house security and the local police.

'I'm not so convinced, Bettina. This Hart is a slippery eel, good at misdirection and at lying, but he's intelligent and not to be underestimated. If he is working for a competitor, you can be sure that he will always get them something a little extra for whatever they are paying him. Give me the photograph and leave it with me. I'll discuss it with Claudia and decide what will be the best way to deal with *Doctor Hart*.'

He emphasised Hart's name in taking the photograph from Arben, who now felt a little better seeing that some of the initial shock and anger seemed to have had receded from Halle. He hadn't quite done yet though.

'Did you process his cell phone? Check for messages and photographs?'

'Yes of course. There was absolutely nothing relating to us.'

'Very well, Bettina, take these incidents as a good lesson for you, but expect no more trouble from that quarter. You will hear no more from Hart I assure you!'

Chapter 65

After completing their relatively quiet breakfast, mainly due to their crushing hangovers following the more than liberal consumption of wine the night before in celebration of the imminent end to their mission, Crosse and Hart checked out of the hotel but left their bags with the concierge for picking up later. In their fragile conditions, having looked at a map, they decided that a walk to the Halle rendezvous at the Hotel Torino would be just the thing to blow away the cobwebs...of course for a second time for Hart, following the previous evening's events! The hotel was easy to find by following the sign-posted route to the Basilica of Saint Anthony, located as it was less than a stone's throw away from that monument.

Crosse sensed some tension in Hart as the hotel came into sight and felt the need to offer him some encouragement.

'Right then, Max, this is the really easy part. All we have to do is take a suitable pew in the lounge here and wait for Halle to hove into view. You can stay totally out of sight if you like. I think I would recognise him anywhere, if only for the blazer and moustache. When you've had enough just say the word and we will remove ourselves from here and make our way back to our hotel and then onwards to our respective points of departure. I can smell the fish and chips already!'

'You got the camera, VC?'

'Absolutely.' She patted her shoulder bag.

If at all possible a photograph of Halle's Vatican contact would prove useful to the bank of information that they accumulated, but they had already agreed that personal safety had to come first and if snapping a picture revealed either of them to Halle, then they would certainly forego this layer of icing on the cake.

They entered the hotel, Crosse taking a slight lead, but both on red alert looking for any sign of Halle, or in fact signs of anyone else who looked as if the Vatican could be their home, which possibly meant someone wearing a cassock or similar garment. The extension to the lobby that they entered was expansive, with tables and chairs set out for formal breakfasteers or just people en passant wanting to watch the world over a cappuccino or espresso coffee. Liberally arranged between the furniture were large pots containing very healthy looking palm plants and trees of varying heights and ages to the degree that sitting discreetly, and in the main unobserved except for the ever vigilant waiters, would be absolutely no problem. They hovered momentarily and were quickly picked up by one of the waiters, ready to usher them to a table, but Crosse paused looking around the room.

'One moment please. Yes, I would like the table over there please. The table for two.'

'Certainly, *signora*, please follow me.'

She had scanned the room intelligently looking for a table which was particularly well screened from the others, whilst offering a clear view of the entrance to the area and also being close to an exit, should a hasty retreat need to be beaten.

'Excellent table, VC, well done. I'd never have thought to take the table most suitable to all aspects of our job here. We have discretion, but with a good view of the customers and the perfect means of slipping away. Anyway, I think coffee only will suffice for this little exercise, don't you think?'

The waiter raised one eyebrow in anticipation of Crosse's order.

'Yes, I'll have a cappuccino please.'

'And I'll have the same, but could I have a double shot of coffee in it, please?'

'*Grazie*,' the waiter responded and with a small bow sped away.

'OK, Max, here we are. Eyes peeled and scanning.'

'It's clear which one of us is most on the ball this morning, Vicky.'

The time was 8.15 am and there were few people in the room at tables. Those who *were* there were taking breakfast. Suddenly Hart caught his breathe as a flash of crimson flashed between the fronds of a potted palm across the other side of the area. Someone had left their table and was heading purposefully towards the exit to the main lobby area. Hart recognised the legs, the breasts, the hair, the mouth, indeed every beautiful thing about the young woman. It was Claudia Volpe, now wearing very similar clothes to those he saw her in yesterday, but this time the green had been exchanged for crimson. Her look was devastating!

'Are you all right, Max, you look as if you've seen a ghost?'

'Not a ghost, Vicky, an angel. The lady in red just about to exit this area is the infamous Claudia Volpe. She must be staying at this hotel and presumably is now heading out for the conference centre for her morning meeting with the cringing minions.'

'I see what you meant last night, Max, she certainly stands out in a crowd.'

As she finally made it to the lobby, she almost collided with an elderly man who scurried past her without looking. Or did he? Wasn't that a wink of an eye of recognition? He was dressed in a black cassock and wearing a black three quarter length overcoat. Clutched in his hand, he carried a black hat, or biretta. Hart nodded at Crosse.

'I bet you a pound to a penny that that's our man who is meeting Halle. Clerically clothed and I'm sure a certain look passed between him and our lady in red as they passed by each other. Yes, it has to be him.'

Just then, the coffees arrived on a tray and they were placed on the table in the correct places next to Hart and Crosse. The waiter smiled and turned to leave, but Crosse had other ideas.

'Wait please. Please take this and keep the change.' She handed the waiter a twenty-euro note.

With a bow and a '*Grazie mille*', he was gone.

'Right, Max, all we have to do now is wait and watch and then leave whenever we want to without having to worry about the bill or its payment.'

'Spot on again, VC. I'm really glad you came along this morning, I was half asleep until I saw our lady.'

'I thought "Our Lady" was a term of reference to the Virgin Mary? This one is certainly not a Mary and I would bet my house on her not being a virgin either.'

'God, you're sharp this morning, I…wait look!'

The elderly man in black was being led to a table by one of the other waiters, but before he arrived there he was cut off by a smiling Halle, silver buttons glinting in the morning light, who shook his hand warmly and then led him to a table further towards the back of the room. With just one furtive look around, Halle offered the man a chair and then proceeded to sit down himself. Almost as a reflex action, Hart had bent backwards and out of the line of sight the moment that Halle had slithered in. The man in black's features meant nothing to Hart. He hadn't the slightest inclination as to who or what he was, other that he was very important and from the Vatican. Clearly the man was even more of an unidentified person to Crosse.

'What do you want to do about the photograph, Vicky, had we best leave now, after all we don't know this chap and sitting here any longer won't help us in that respect?'

'Come and sit here with your back to them, Max. Come on!'

Hart did as he was told without question.

'Now then.' Crosse sat down at his side and summoned the waiter she had tipped earlier.

'Excuse me, would you mind taking a photograph of the two of us please?'

The waiter was only too happy to oblige and took the camera from Crosse's outstretched hand, instantly holding it the wrong way round.

'No, let me show you,' Crosse smiled.

She had already calculated the correct angle between the waiter and themselves in order to be able to pick up Halle and Mr Vatican in the background and moved the waiter into the correct position. She then demonstrated which button should be pressed, turned the camera the correct way round and returned to her seat next to Hart. The pair of them sat there, gormlessly smiling at the ace paparazzo.

'Yes please.' *Click, click.* 'Good. Again…again…again and again, and one more final time! Thank you very much.'

'You're welcome, *signora*.'

The beaming waiter handed the camera back to Crosse and scurried away.

Crosse, quickly brought up the pictures on the camera that the waiter had just taken, and then whispered out of the corner of her mouth,

'*Perfetto*! And now we exit right, through the door over there. Our job here is complete. *Andiamo*!'

Hart grunted. 'Why are you whispering? They got super hearing or something?'

He stood with her and then with both of them shielded by the fronds of the various palm trees, they made an elegantly controlled exit from the room, Crosse's arm linked through that of Hart. They continued walking together steadily until they were outside on the pavement.

'I so much wanted to break into a run as we left there its untrue, Vicky.'

'Why do you think I took hold of your arm?'

She smiled at him knowingly and they continued to walk nowhere in particular, but in the general direction of the Basilica. In fact, anywhere away from this hotel and especially from the conference centre!

Chapter 66

Back inside the Hotel Turin breakfast area, the small talk between Halle and his guest had run its short course, with Halle's resources of smiles now almost running on empty. It hadn't yet affected his ability to fawn on his guest excruciatingly; however, a guest who within minutes of meeting him had quickly formulated his opinion of Halle as a peacock, full of his own importance, pomp and circumstance. Halle ceased twirling his moustache and continued the conversation that had paused while the waiter arranged their coffees on the table. Halle's cafe latte should certainly last the length of the meeting, which his guest was actually hoping would last no longer than his own ristretto.

'To come straight to the point, Doctor Halle, what I would like clarification on is the current availability of materials for stem cell treatment and also what that availability will be in, say, six months' time? Can we start there?'

'Yes of course, sir, but can I apologise first for *Signorina* Volpe's absence. Unfortunately, she had a previous meeting to attend. Very well, Africa plays an important role in this and in answering your question I will include some details from there if you don't mind. In Africa, things are progressing very well and we are now obtaining a ready supply of stem cell containing material from various sources there. Of course, the charitable actions of the church there in supporting my company as we provide basic run-of-the mill drugs at reduced costs and even at no cost at all to clinics, has been a great help in stimulating growth in our stem cell sector. A problem we have recently discovered is that at present, we are unable to substitute Caucasian stem cells with those from African biological sources, so the huge flow of stem cells appropriate for treatments globally that we earlier envisaged has so far not been possible. However, developments are increasing this possibility, I should actually say *likelihood*, daily.'

'But you realise where I have come from today and on behalf of whom I am making these enquiries? I need to be assured that this person will continue to receive whatever level of treatment is required. It will not have escaped your notice that one of the adverse events of maintaining and prolonging life is that the patient requires higher doses and more frequent treatment to sustain at least their stability. We are not talking of cure here, Doctor Halle, we are just talking about maintenance of a stable condition. I know that important people around the world are currently receiving these drugs, and at a considerable cost no doubt, but I need you to tell me that you have a patient priority list and furthermore that this person of interest will be at the top of that list. *Numero uno!* Do you understand? But I have one question. It is a question of logic, which your report raises in me and it is this. If you are unable to substitute Caucasian stem cells with those of a non-Caucasian origin when treating Caucasians, why is it apparently possible to substitute non-Caucasian stem cells with the Caucasian variety when treating non-Caucasians. A paradox no?'

Halle was becoming flustered under the scrutiny of this intelligent high-ranking priest from the Vatican and he stuttered as he made an effort to respond.

'Firstly, let me say that I totally understand your position, sir, and I can assure you that in terms of treatment priority you are indeed "*numero uno*". That is for sure and it is my promise to you. Now as you are aware, the person of whom you talk has a personal physician who has a direct line to appropriate people within my company, who will respond immediately to whatever request is made. In fact so important is this person to us that we have maximised as much of the drug as we can possibly store. You know it has a relatively short shelf life, but this full amount is standing by at all times. I can assure you that at no time will your physician make a request that we cannot fulfil immediately. Your second point, an excellent scientific question indeed if I may say so, is more difficult to answer. What you say does seem to be quite "a paradox". We are very aware of it of course and it is something that our scientists are exploring urgently around the clock. We do not yet have the answer, but we are very close.'

The priest cut his obsequience short.

'So, there are no foreseeable problems then, Doctor Halle?'

(Hart was Halle's only possible problem, but following his discussion with Volpe, Hart would be totally eradicated in the near future.)

'None at all, sir, I can assure you of that. We have a very full risk mitigation program which covers even the slightest possible incidents, even down to a shortage of paper clips I believe. Ha, ha, ha.'

His attempt at levity fell on stony ground.

Fool! thought the unimpressed guest.

'Thank you for that reassurance, Doctor Halle. You are aware that one of my Vatican colleagues takes a great interest in Africa and the state of its healthcare, yes?'

'Yes, of course, sir. Peter Mondo is very well respected throughout our company. He's a fine young man surely destined for high office and of course a family member of our esteemed owner.'

'Good. I like to think that I am the cardinal's friend as well as his mentor and, therefore, I am very close to him. Any concerns he might have now or in the future, relating to African health and medicines issues will no doubt be conveyed back to me. Do I make myself clear?'

It was not difficult for Halle to read between the lines.

'Totally understood, sir. In fact, regular updates on African medical and research issues could be provided to both of you should you find them useful.'

'Not necessary. Peter has his own, shall we say neutral independent sources. And now, Doctor Halle, I must take my leave of you and thank you for taking the time out of your busy agenda here at the conference to meet me.'

He stood and offered Halle his hand.

Halle was taken a little by surprise at the sudden termination of the meeting and rose quickly, knocking the table as he did so. He took his guest's hand and shook it gently.

'It was my pleasure, sir, and I look forward to meeting you again soon.'

For both men, it was a great relief that the meeting was over. The guest walked away wiping any remaining coffee from his mouth, whilst Halle remained wiping the spilt latte from his trousers.

Chapter 67

Sitting in a small green park close to the Basilica of Saint Anthony, relaxing in the dappled sunlight streaming through the trees, Hart and Crosse talked stress-free, about the comings and goings of the last few days. Clearly, they had done all, and more besides, of what their intentions had been in coming here. Hart would now have to apply some kind of logical order to the mass of documents that Crosse had faxed to Williams, even though by now as per Hart's instructions the previous evening, he would have probably split the documents into, however, many copies he believed to be appropriate and assembled them into separate piles. For Hart to collate the documents appropriately would involve nothing brain taxing at all; in fact, he was looking forward to the task as it would likely crystallise all the things together into a story that he would be able to capture in his report.

'Right then, VC, let's have a look at your pictures of Halle and friend back there in the hotel.'

'Actually, I had a quick look back there and they seem pretty good to me.'

She produced her camera from her bag, turned it on and passed it to Hart. The quality of the photographs was excellent.

'Good enough for you?'

'Yes indeed, well done these are perfect. The guy's face is really clear and his identity so obvious…at least to anybody who knows him that is! No really, VC, these are great. It's a pity you didn't use your phone, you could have sent them to me in Milan. I'm sure my friend Gianni would know him and if not would probably know someone who did.'

Crosse rolled her eyes.

'When will you ever learn? I will download these onto my computer and send them to your iPhone, so then you'll have them.'

'Thank you, VC, I wondered how long it would take you to figure out that one. I'll contact Gianni from the train and give him a little information and if I can manage to forward those pictures to him, by the time I arrive at la Stazione Centrale in Milan, he will most probably have the answer to who the "man in black" is.'

'OK then, Max, let's return to our hotel, pick up our bags and flag down the first taxi that comes along. I guess it will be the railway station first and then the airport, unless that is you've dreamt up more tasks for me to do, like ironing a shirt for you or polishing your shoes? If we go now, we will certainly be in good time for my flight and your trains are in any case pretty regular.'

Having reclaimed their bags from the hotel and with them loaded on board the taxi that they had flagged down outside of their hotel, it was a drive directly to the station as agreed. As it pulled into the station passenger drop-off point, Hart smiled at Crosse,

'Vicky, it's been very…interesting. Many thanks. I couldn't have done it without you. Have a great flight home and stay in touch.'

'Thanks to you also, Max, you've been amazing. Have a well-deserved break in Milan.'

They kissed briefly and off they both sped, Hart into the station and Crosse forced into the back seat of the taxi under considerable G-Force as it quickly accelerated away to the airport.

Chapter 68

Hart located the ticket office and bought a one-way first class ticket to Milan. His plan was to spend a few days of "la dolce vita" there and then fly home from either Malpensa or Linate Airport. His train was direct to Milan but with three stops on the way, those being Verona, Desenzano del Garda that he knew and really liked from his business visits to the hospital Santa Maria there whilst working in Milan some years before and Bergamo.

He looked at the departure screen and saw that his train would leave from "binario 2", platform 2, and proceeded there looking as he went for the ticket machine he would have to use to stamp his ticket with the time and date. He arrived at the platform and immediately saw the bright yellow ticket machine standing proud, which he engaged immediately. As he completed his "clocking in", he felt a warm breath on the back of his neck and moving no more than half a yard back from the machine collided with a fellow traveller who was standing close enough to dance with him. He turned round ready to pay some suitable comment to the person, even though he realised that none of his verbiage would likely be understood, and quickly saw that the person almost standing in his shoes was a priest. His potentially cutting comments were quickly modified to a brief 'sorry', and he walked away quickly further down the platform to where his train was standing.

He smiled realising that the train was of the older "corridor type", which equated with being spacious, luxurious and comfortable. To actually gain entry to the compartment once aboard, he had to slide open the full-length glass door, which opened as smoothly as silk. He nodded and offered a "*buongiorno*" to the only other occupant of the compartment, an elderly man who paused from reading his newspaper just long enough to nod his response, and then he hoisted his small case into the overhead rack. He had packed his now empty satchel inside the small case, having agreed with Crosse that she should take all the documents that had passed their scrutiny with *her*, as he would not be back in the UK for several days.

Hart loved these older trains. As he sank down into his sumptuous velvet covered seat his phone vibrated in his jacket pocket and interrogating it he saw that true to her word, Crosse had sent him the photographs of Halle and the unknown man. Without delay, he forwarded them to his friend Bossi with a few words of explanation and then responded to Crosse asking her to do the same then relaxed knowing that he had now completed all his tasks and had three days of relaxation ahead of him. From his seat once the train was in motion, he would be able to take in the views of the towns and countryside on both sides of the carriage as the train sped onwards towards its final destination in Milan. Hart's reverie was interrupted by the arrival of another passenger. It was "the bloody priest". The man of God smiled at Hart and his fellow passenger and sat himself in the seat nearest to the glass sliding door facing away from the engine. Hart's seat was by the window, facing the engine and opposite the elderly man. As he checked the time on his watch, there was a shudder from the carriage and the sound of the metal couplings taking up the strain and the train moved majestically out of the station.

Thinking of nothing in particular, his thoughts turned to an observation he had made earlier and which he confirmed now. The priest was wearing pink socks! *Ah well, everybody has to have some outlet for unusual aspects of their personalities, and being a priest is no exception. Wearing black every day must be a nightmare.* He returned to his reveries, satisfied by his own explanation.

Forty minutes after leaving the station behind, Hart decided to call his friend Bossi to ensure that he had received the text and to confirm dinner arrangements. He left the compartment and stood in the corridor looking at the fields, thinking of times past, as telegraph poles running parallel to the tracks flashed past. He hit speed dial and almost instantly heard his call ringing out on the other side of the ether. Almost as quickly his call was answered in Milan.

'*Pronto*?'

'*Ciao* Gianni, *sono* Max, come *stai*.'

'*Ciao* Max, I am very well, thank you very much. I have received the e-mail and I see a very nice girl in the front of the picture.'

'Yes, that's Victoria, but what about the priest at the back of the picture? Have you any idea who he might be Gianni?'

'Max, please! For me it is an impossible question. How many priests do you yourself know, or could recognise from a distance?'

Hart's spirits sank a little.

'But don't worry, Max, the face did look a little familiar to me in fact and so I sent the picture to my friend Bruno. Bruno has connections with the church here in Milano through a man called Luca Messi, who in his own way is quite a famous person in all Italy, especially with respect to his association with il Vaticano and il Papa, the Pope.'

'Ahh, the friend of a friend, eh? And have you had any reply from him yet?'

'Max, it was incredible. I send him the e-mail and after only ten minutes, he called me back asking for more information. He spoke to me like I'm a *criminale*. *Cazzo*! He demanded to know when, how, who, what et cetera, et cetera. So forgive me, but I have arranged for you to meet directly Luca Messi personally at his office in Milano centro. *E bene,* Max? Do you agree? We cut out the middlemen yes? His office is very close to il Duomo, so you are able to walk there from your Jolly Presidente hotel in a very short time. Allora, call me when you are almost arriving in la Stazione Centrale and I will meet you there.'

'Fantastic Gianni, thank you very much. I will see you later and explain some of the situation. I am looking forward to eating some fish with you, you know I can almost smell it from here! I will be hungry when I arrive Gianni, there's no restaurant car on this train. *Ciao* for now.'

'*Ciao, ciao,* Max. I am very interested to hear your story and am intrigued by your picture, but you must be thinking of English fish by the way. Here in Milan, the fish is far too fresh to smell from that far away! See you later.'

They both laughed as they completed their call and hung up. Once again, Hart noticed the strange echo and click on the telephone line as he hung up. He returned to his seat and taking a ballpoint pen from his jacket inside pocket, scribbled down some of the things Bossi had said to him on a small note pad he had removed from his hotel bedside table. He placed the notepad back in his inside pocket and the pen in his jacket outer breast pocket, noticing then that the train was slowing for its first stop. Verona.

It had begun to rain outside and looking through the rain streaked window he could see that the platform at Verona station looked quite deserted. He only saw three passengers climb aboard the train, but then as the final whistle was blown for it to leave, a fourth large bear of a man blowing and puffing under the exertion of his short dash, scrambled aboard.

As the train picked up speed and headed into the open countryside, Hart made an effort to take in the view he had been looking forward to seeing, but his vision was distorted by the rain now slanting down the windows. The sudden arrival in the compartment of the ticket collector caused much general rummaging around by all three passengers for their respective tickets and Hart half expected the badly shaven priest wearing pink socks to be summarily ejected from First Class. To his surprise, all was in order and he received a salute from the ticket collector as a bonus. As the ticket collector exited the compartment, his way was temporally blocked by the awkward passage along the corridor of the man Hart had seen just mounting the train at Verona. As he ambled by Hart's compartment, he glanced inside and for one moment there was a barely noticeable eye contact made between himself and the priest.

Some 15 or so minutes later, Hart found himself nodding off to sleep, an activity certainly not in his plan for making the most of his rail journey. Moving on another 15 minutes and he found himself nodding off once more. It was time to do something about it, so he elected to visit the washroom along the corridor and freshen himself up. The train was fairly hurtling along now and his shoulders made contact alternatively with both sides of the narrow passageway as he rock and rolled towards the WC. Once inside, going through the "comfort motions" proved to be quite a test of skill, but he coped and then washed his hands, splashing his face with copious amounts of cold water and drying himself on a bunch of paper towels pulled from the dispenser. He was ready to face the world again.

He unlocked the door and emerged into what was the wider area of the carriage, with exit doors on opposite sides. Immediately, he saw that the way back to his compartment was blocked by the very large man, who clearly had no intention of moving out of his way. As Hart was about to go through the necessary pleasantries in order to pass by, the noise of the train rattling along the track intensified considerably and he was hit by a great gust of wind. Looking to his right towards the noise and the wind, he was astonished to see that the exit door stood wide open and there next to it, with one hand firmly wrapped around the handrail to prevent himself from being sucked out into the rain and the darkening evening…was the priest!

'Excuse me, Doctor Hart.'

Hart looked inquisitively at the priest, but made no comment. How the hell did he know his name? He was frightened now, for clearly these two men were part of the "Halle show" and this scene was going to end badly for him. In a moment, he recognised that the main danger here was the large man between himself and the corridor. The small man was also obviously dangerous, but in this situation if he managed even to deal with the small priest, he would still be left with the insurmountable problem of the big man. Therefore, if it came to a test of survival, he should take out the big man first if at all possible, and see how things went from there. Above the noise of the wind, the train and the rain the priest spoke again.

'Doctor Hart, excuse me but it is time for you to leave the train now, but unfortunately, it will not be possible for us to bring it to a halt first.'

He gave Hart a bad-toothed grin, released his hand from the handrail and briefly motioned towards the open carriage door, before quickly taking hold of the rail again.

The wind suddenly lifted the priest's hat off blowing it across to the other side of the carriage. Drawing upon his much vaunted and well-practised negotiating skills, Hart addressed the priest as diplomatically as the situation warranted.

'You can go fuck yourself!'

At the same time, he made a swift effort to squeeze past the big man with the aim of recruiting some help. Unfortunately, the brick wall had been anticipating this move and in Hart hitting this immoveable object the equal and opposite force sent him staggering back towards the door of the WC.

'Please, Doctor Hart.'

It was the priest again, his cassock suddenly cracking like a whip under the influence of the howling wind.

'I say again, this is your stop, so please make it easy for yourself and just go quietly.'

He looked at his huge accomplice. 'Franco, *presto, andiamo!*'

The priest's aim was clearly to deliver Hart into the awaiting Veneto countryside before the return of the ticket collector. Hart's mind went into overdrive. As the big man advanced upon him, he raised his left hand and to both of them said, 'Look here, chaps, I'm a writer, not a fighter,' and to prove the point his right hand snatched his biro out of the breast pocket of his jacket.

The big man was totally unimpressed by that, most probably because he didn't understand a word of it, and opening both arms, he embraced Hart and lifted him from the floor. Squeezing him like a long-lost friend, he edged towards the in-rushing wind, clearly intent upon throwing him through the open door. In a sudden decisive movement, Hart gritted his teeth and drove his pen hard into the man's eye. The man screamed out loudly and put both hands over his eye, copious amounts of blood now running freely between his fingers as he released Hart from the bear hug. As the cyclops continued to scream and roll his head in agony, Hart seized the collar of the startled priest's coat and hurled him first against one wall, breaking his grip on the safety rail and then, maintaining his own hold on him, back again. On the backward traverse, the priest slammed up against the rail shouting out in pain. However, he sprang back from the wall, coming hard at Hart swinging a right fist which caught him on the side of his face. Hart staggered back against the wall releasing him from his grasp under the blow, but the glimpse of metal reflecting in the carriage lights and heading for his throat caused him to pull his head violently to one side and as he did he saw the blade of a knife miss him by inches and plunge into the plywood fabric of the wall. The knife sank into the wall almost to its hilt and despite the efforts of the priest to extract it, it remained stuck. Hart was very frightened, but anger held the upper hand on his emotions at this juncture and gripping his opponent by the collar once more punched him as hard as he could in the area of his throat. As the priest fought for breath gagging violently, Hart quickly stepped behind him putting an arm around his neck and holding him tightly.

The big man was still crying out in pain and bleeding profusely between his fingers and the pen, but blindly advanced towards the area where he had heard the scuffle and the priest's cries of pain.

Hart was now just feet away from the open door and the rain-soaked night. He held the priest in front of him with the bloody cyclops still slowly advancing blindly towards them both.

'Quickly, tell me and I'll release you. Who sent you?'

The priest ignored his question and despite his great pain and difficulty in breathing, managed to croak in Italian, 'Franco, he's here by the open door. Take him now!'

With a bellow, the cyclops removed his bloody hands from the bloody black socket that held his useless eye and charged like a mad bull in the direction of the voice. At the final moment before contact was made, Hart released his arm-hold around the priest's neck and summoning all his strength pushed him forward into the advancing man's outstretched arms, then within the following split second dived down onto the floor away from the embracing couple. The blinded man immediately enveloped whoever it was he had caught in his embrace, assuming it to be Hart, but being unable to check his momentum charged straight through the open door and into the night carrying his co-conspirator the priest with him. Hart's last view of the priest was a flash of his pink socks, now decorated with red spatterings of blood, as he was taken by the dark along with his blinded colleague. The last sounds Hart thought he heard from the couple, above all the other noises was the brief cry of the priest, followed quickly by what he believed must have been the terrible thud of body against wooden telegraph pole. He wasn't sure whether or not he had imagined the latter sound, but in any case the whole scenario was over in a couple of seconds.

Suddenly realising that the ticket collector could be back at any second, he dragged himself to his feet. Looking around, the floor resembled something of an abattoir with quantities of blood liberally spread around and in a corner he saw the priest's black hat. The wind was still rushing in through the open door as he very carefully edged over to the hat and picked it up. Holding on to whatever he could grasp on his way he edged back to the door and with a mighty throw hurled the hat against the wind, straight through it. Despite the effort of the throw the hat barely made it to the outside, but make it, it did and was quickly whisked away in the train's slipstream.

Holding on to the handrail previously used by the priest, he leaned out into the darkness, the wind and rain lashing at his face, and managed to take hold of the leather window strap being blown out horizontally by the wind, and pulled the door for all he was worth. It closed with a bang and once again he found himself on the floor. He looked down the corridor and saw the ticket collector only minutes away from him. A quick dash into the WC where he grabbed a handful of paper handtowels, followed by a very quick rub of the floor over the bloodiest parts with them and there was just time, as the officer joined the nearest compartment passengers in conversation, to put the soiled paper back inside the WC before he arrived on the scene. As the official walked into the WC area, he looked at Hart, who was now leaning against the exit window with his back turned against the wall covering the still protruding knife, and walking towards him raised an arm and signalled to the sign somewhere above Hart's head, which printed in Italian, English and German read, "Leaning against the doors and windows on a moving train is very dangerous and can result in loss of life and is, therefore, forbidden!"

'Too bloody right, mate!' He raised a thumb to indicate that he had understood.

The man in uniform continued on his way and Hart turned to the knife behind him. With an almighty pull with both hands, he managed to remove it, then opening the window slightly, he tossed it out. He stumbled back into the washroom on what felt like legs of jelly and for the second time that evening turned on the coldwater tap and washed his face in the cooling water. All things considered, all he had to show for his life threatening experience was a sore jaw, which he moved from side to side to ensure that there was no fracture and the smallest amount of cyclopean blood on his trouser leg. Now exhausted with the after-shock, he seated himself on the closed lid of the toilet pan and tried to concentrate on what to do next, because if his train journey was known to an enemy who had placed assassins on board, it was a racing certainty that there would be similar people waiting at the station in Milan to finish the job off where the other two to had somehow failed.

After only a few moments of consideration, he resolved to leave the train at Desenzano, which was the next stop, and travel to Milan by taxi. He checked his watch and realising that there were just 15 minutes before their timetabled arrival, he returned to his compartment and retrieved his bag. The elderly man in his compartment was now asleep, so no *arrivedercis* were required there. He returned to the fateful door of his earlier exploits and waited for the train to come into the station at Dezenzano. Should he exit the train and walk away as bold as brass, or should he somehow extricate himself from the carriage as secretively as possible and make for the station exit hiding in whatever shadows he could find? The train finally came to a screeching halt, metal grinding against metal, at which point his involuntary reflexes took control of the situation.

As he opened the door and descended from the train, in a mental blur he suddenly sprinted to the exit and out into the street. What to do now? He had used this station many times in the past, coming from, or going back to Milan. He remembered that there was a good bar close by where he could pause, have a drink and perhaps a bite to eat and decide how to deal with the rest of his journey to Milan and also how to deal with the next few days.

He found "il Bar Luigi" very easily, less than a stone's throw from the station and went inside, straightaway ordering at the bar and paying for his order before finding a quiet table to sit at. Having deposited his bag at a suitable table, he returned to the bar and waited for his medium sized beer and cheese and ham panino.

It didn't take him long either to decide that staying at the Jolly Hotel Presidente was now completely out of the question, as was his back up hotel the Michelangelo, opposite the central station. Most importantly, he now had to stay as far away as possible from his old friend Gianni. There was no way he could involve Gianni in this mess, but he did need some guidance from him now on how he could meet up with his "friend of a friend" Luca Messi. He took out his mobile phone, speed dialled Gianni and placed it to his ear. The usual dialling tone ensued followed by the annoying click and echo which seemed to be standard now and he waited for the number to ring through. After two rings, there was a continuous tone and his phone cut out. He tried again…and obtained the same result. He looked at the phone and saw that annoyingly the battery was completely flat.

'Shit! What now,' he said loud enough for the whole room to hear.

'*Signore*, if you need to make an urgent call, we have a public telefono at the back there. I can give you money in coins for it if you need them.'

The voice he heard came from a young girl clearing the tables of their used cups, glasses and plates and her English was good.

An angel in disguise!

Hart gave her a ten-euro note and with the change he received went over to the telephone on the wall and having dialled the number he wanted, began to feed it with coins. Eventually, it was picked up at the receiver's end,

'*Si, pronto?*'

'*Ciao,* Gianni, it's Max. I'm in a load of trouble.'

Hart briefly summarised the situation he was in to Gianni, emphasising that he needed to find a different hotel now and that he didn't want Gianni Bossi within a hundred miles of him from here on in. Unusually for him, Bossi, who was normally prone to Mediterranean melodramaticism and over-excitement remained very calm.

'Max, no problem, all is arranged. You must get the taxi driver to take you outside of Milano to the Opera district, where of course I live, and to drop you off at the Hotel Opera which is just five minutes from my apartment. Eat and sleep well there tonight and tomorrow I will call and pick you up at 4.00 pm and take you out of Milano to meet this Luca Messi. It will not be possible to meet him until 6.00 pm, but we have a little way to drive and in any case we can talk to each other then, *si*?'

'Look, Gianni, don't get involved. This is getting more dangerous by the day. Whoops, there go the pips and I have no more coins…'

'No worry, Max. Hotel Opera tonight and tomorrow we meet at 4.00 pm. *Ciao*, my friend.'

The line went dead. So, that sounded like some kind of a plan and all he had to do now was to locate a taxi driver who knew Milan…and he knew exactly where.

Chapter 69

Luca Messi was a man of routine. Every morning upon arriving in the area of his office, he would take a swift double espresso coffee in the small bar next door to the elegant office block in Piazza Filippo Meda near the centre of Milan, where he occupied a rather cramped office (due as much to his own body size as to the rows of cabinets, one large desk and one smaller together with chairs and other furniture squeezed in there) on the fourth floor. At 10.30 am on the dot, he would walk out onto the piazza and take a cappuccino and a large slice of the home made cake at il Bar Diana. Lunch was usually spent at la Movida, also on the piazza, at around mid-day when it was common for him to take a double-helping of the pasta dish of the day together with his currently favourite wine. At the moment, his wine of choice was the fairly local Corzetti Barbera, a beautiful aromatic red with overtones of deep black-cherry fruit and with wonderful background oakiness. It was his love of good food and wine, together with his sedentary lifestyle which had endowed him with his rotund stature. Standing some 5 feet, 9 inches tall, he weighed in at almost exactly 19 stone, which equated to a body mass index of 38.6, well into the morbidly obese range. For him, the main ingredients of a suitable office were, therefore, partly its size, but mainly it having a lift, especially as there were four floors to manage in his current accommodation.

On this day, he sat at his usual table with the large white serviette tucked well into the neckline of his shirt, enjoying his second portion of pasta whilst appreciating the wonderful sight of the one hundred and thirty five white spires and pinnacles and 1800 statues, which occupied the uppermost levels of the Duomo. The whole of this wonderful structure was overlooked from the highest spire by the beautiful golden Madonnina, the symbol of the city and the patroness of the Milanese people. Such a wonderful sight and just fifty metres away! This was a beautiful time of day, for as well as this there were the wonders of Italian dress sense to marvel at via the smartly dressed men and the so-stylish women going about their business. However, being in possession of a BMI of 38.6 did not lend itself well to smartness of dress and all he could do was appreciate it from afar.

Finishing his lunch, he wiped his mouth on the large serviette, paid at the cash register counter including his usual tip and went out into the bright sunlight waving at the smiling staff and responding to their farewell calls.

Chapter 70

When her plane landed at East Midlands Airport, the effects of the series of in-flight gin and tonics were just kicking in. Feeling nicely anaesthetised and just a little wobbly on her feet, Victoria Crosse followed the line of fellow passengers as she emerged from the shuttle bus which had brought her from the plane to the arrivals building. As the line snaked nearer to the passport control desks, she removed her passport clumsily from her bag.

'Next please.'

She approached the passport control officer smiling as she handed him her passport. He took it from her and swiped it through the machine and paused as she stood with outstretched arm ready to receive her returned document. But the officer didn't hand it back. Instead, he raised an eyebrow and nodded at the two men in plain clothes standing to one side by the exit to the baggage reclaim area. The man in possession of her passport finally spoke.

'Thank you, Ms Crosse. These two gentlemen would like a few words with you please.'

He indicated to the approaching men.

'What!?' This was all she needed.

Her fellow passengers in the line looked on with interest as the plain-clothed men approached her, one of who leaned in close and whispered,

'Ms Crosse. We would like to talk to you for a few minutes please.'

'Let's go somewhere a little more private if you don't mind, there's an unoccupied office over here.'

With that, they led her away to the office they'd identified, where once inside the apparent leader of the two men reached inside his coat and displayed his identity card to her. It had his name clearly printed on it and additionally in bold letters, "SPECIAL BRANCH".

It was as if a bucket of cold water had been poured over her and suddenly the effects of those gin and tonics were washed completely away.

'Shit! What's going on?' Then a little panicky, 'What's happened?'

She immediately thought of Hart.

Chapter 71

The very obese man crossed Piazza Filippo Meda and entered the large, rather ancient-looking door, whence he made his way to the lift. Upon arrival, he was met with a sign taped to the lift door, "Lift Out of Order".

He groaned. The 4th floor was a long way up for a man of his size, with many stairs to climb. Too many! Unsurprisingly, he was completely out of breath when he reached the summit of his own particular Everest and he paused for some minutes to regain at least some of his breath before pushing through the door and into the office. He had had to climb these stairs several times before and it certainly never got any easier.

The office was in a constant state of distress, the beige painted walls and high ceiling peeling profusely some twenty years after the paint brushes that had originally painted them had dried and been discarded. One obvious reason for the sad state of repair and decoration of what parts of the walls were visible, was the almost continuous line of bookcases in which every shelf was bowed in deference to the floor under the weight of the often-huge tomes positioned upon them. Four sets of filing cabinets were parked somewhat askew near what must be the centre of the room and an additional table, the size of Maria's desk, was piled high with papers and documents.

This so-called "Office of Catholic Affairs" was indeed an extremely cluttered and busy place. This office was the focal point for inundations of both official mail and documents of too sensitive a nature to be transmitted electronically, and because of the nature of their contents very little, if anything at all, was ever destroyed. In fact to underline this fact, much of the threadbare carpeting on the floor contained similar piles of freestanding unfiled paperwork. To one side, there was a smaller outer office which suffered from the same standard of disrepair and decoration and which also was a compendium of paperwork. It was in this small outer space that the largest free space of wall existed and much of this was taken by a metre square diagram of what resembled some kind of family tree going back to the early anno domini years. In this case, however, the "tree" represented the unrelated family of Popes who had led the Catholic Church from those early times. Each of the names was accompanied by an explanatory piece of information, the what?; when?; how?; how long?; bad?; good?; children?; secrets?; rumours? and so on. The final branch of the tree was occupied by the name of the present incumbent Pope, information as yet uncompleted but with plenty of space alongside the name for inclusion eventually of a similar summary of him to those summaries of his predecessors.

The lamp on Maria's desk was still burning.

His first thought was that it was odd to find the office unlocked, for Maria the secretary was always very careful to ensure security at all times, with all the sensitive and extremely confidential documents filed away, apart from the obvious mountains still stacked on the floor. He peered at her empty desk and decided that she must still be out at lunch, which was odd in itself as she rarely left the office at lunchtime. He approached the main desk and placed a small parcel on it, then moving forward through the full-length open glass panelled doors, he ambled out onto the small balcony, where placing his hands on the balcony rail, he breathed deeply still recovering from his epic climb up the stairs. He squinted against the sun and took in the vista. To the left, he had the wonderful view of the Duomo and to the right the spectacle of the front of the famous La Scala theatre. The piazza he had recently crossed was laid out below with stone flagstones and had a small non-functioning fountain in the middle. As well as the cafes and bars that he knew well, there were the occasional shops and stalls around the periphery of the piazza selling postcards, ice creams and mementos to tourists.

As he turned to return to the office, he was jolted out of his post-prandial reverie by the sudden presence of two nuns, standing side by side just in front of him, and who he thought must have really struggled through the four stories of stairs in their long habits. As he stood with his back to the balcony rail, his huge frame now blocked out the dazzling rays of the sun such that the two sisters were able to remove their hands from above their eyes as they stood in the shadow cast by his huge body. They both smiled at him benignly.

'Ah sisters, I'm sorry but you will have to return a little later as…'

'That's no problem, *Signore* Messi,' smiled the nun on his left wearing strangely, blue eye shadow and heavy mascara, 'our business with you will only take a minute.' Her companion smiled and nodded in agreement, her mouth slightly parted presenting perfectly glossed lips.

'But it's not possible at the moment. You see I'm—'

'Please, it is no problem,' said nun number two, wearing the lip gloss, and then offering her blue-eyed companion a knowing look they moved forward very quickly pressing their hands against his chest simultaneously in a well-rehearsed procedure and then on 'now' from blue eyes, they pushed hard in unison at the incredulous fat man. Taken totally by surprise, by the time he realised what was happening, he had already stumbled backwards crashing into the rail. Once travelling at such speed with such combined force his momentum, assisted by his bulk, sent him toppling over the balcony rail. The nuns followed through with their combined push until the man was over the balcony and heading for the stone slabs of the piazza below.

The fat man had only enough time to utter one scream before the sickening thud of his corpulent body on the stone slabs resonated around the square. He lay there spread-eagled and face down, his head split apart by the collision with the slabs now surrounded by a pool of thick red blood and brain tissue.

The nuns looked at each other and nodded. Glossy lips took out her cell phone from inside her nun's habit and hit a number. When a voice answered at the other end she responded with two words only,

'Job done.'

The two assassins then swiftly moved towards the office exit, one of them stopping on the way to look inside the smaller office space where she confirmed that the bound, gagged and anaesthetised Maria was still sleeping behind a high pile of documents, and then they made for the lift. Once at the door of the lift, the "Out of Order" notice was removed and the doors opened to reveal an empty rucksack. With the lift door closed, they each lifted their habits over their heads and stuffed them in the rucksack and pressed for floor zero.

When the lift door opened at ground floor level, out stepped two very attractive Milanese women, very smartly dressed and cosmetically made up, one wearing extensive eye make-up and the other a liberal amount of lip gloss and carrying a rucksack.

Chapter 72

Hart remembered that just down the street from the Desenzano station on via Garibaldi was a taxi office that would take passengers "anywhere at any time". He had used it on numerous occasions whilst on some of his visits, even to get him back to Milan when he had missed the last train due a little alcoholic over-imbibation. He just hoped that it was still there. Sure enough there it was, two cars lined up outside with their drivers obviously inside due to the still falling rain.

He entered the taxi office.

'Do you speak English?'

'A little.'

'*Bene.* I want to go to Milano.'

'When, tomorrow or this evening?'

'Now, *adesso.* I want to go now. OK?'

'It will be expensive.'

'I know how much it will be, you have taken me before. In fact, it was Fabio who drove me last time.'

'Fabio is in the back of the office. I get him for you.'

Fabio greeted him like a long lost brother, but Hart was fairly sure that he didn't remember him from Adam, and after a few hellos and how are yous, he led Hart out to the taxi, taking his case and placing it in the car boot. Hart climbed into the back of the car breathing a sigh of relief. The thought suddenly struck him that back down the rail track towards Verona lay two broken bodies. At that thought, he began to tremble, no doubt aftershock having its effect. The driver looked at him closely.

'Hey guy, you want I get a doctor or something?'

'No, I'm fine, just a little cold.'

'Why you no take the train? Is cheaper and faster than by taxi.'

'Look, please just bloody drive, will you? I like the car better, OK?'

He reached inside his jacket, removed his wallet and pulled out a handful of euros, which he waved at the driver.

'Money is no problem OK. Please let's go. *Andiamo!*'

'OK, OK, it is your money, so we go. *Presto!*'

He took his place in the driving seat, glanced into his rear-view mirror one more time to check on Hart's condition and then sped off towards Route 11, which would eventually bring him to the autostrada A4, the Autostrada della Serenissima and on to Milan. However, Hart's condition continued to worsen and within fifteen minutes, he really did have the shakes and with his mind racing with unanswerable questions relating to his predicament, his condition was becoming serious. The driver, noticing this during one of his glances through his mirror suddenly pulled the car onto the hard shoulder of the road, at which point, Hart panicked and made an involuntary grab for the door handle. The driver quickly turned round and leaned over his seat putting a firm hand on Hart's shoulder.

'*Calma, calma*, my friend, no problem. Look I have something for you.'

He put his hand in his trouser pocket and pulled out a hip flask from which he unscrewed the top before passing it over the seat to Hart.

'Come take some of this. Is very good for cold.'

Hart took the flask from him and took a drink, promptly going into a coughing convulsion. The man laughed and urged him to take more, which he did. The second time, he took a long swallow and felt the liquid burn the back of his mouth and then his throat as it went down, but once swallowed it had a marvellous warming and satisfying effect. He smiled at the concerned looking driver and handed him back the flask.

'It's very good, thank you very much, I'm feeling better already. *Grazie mille.*'

'Please, take, you have all, no problem.'

Hart took the flask back and lifting it to his lips emptied it. The driver was right, he did feel much better and the shivering had all but ceased. He handed the empty flask back to the driver (rather a strange object for a man driving for his living to have in his trouser pocket) who returned it to its place of origin.

'*Grazie*. Put it on the bill.'

The driver laughed. Of that there was no doubt, Hart would certainly pay for his drink one way or another, but at that moment, he couldn't care less.

'*Allora, andiamo ancora*. Let us go again. You try to sleep now, signore.'

The driver accelerated hard as the taxi regained the autostrada in a cacophony of blaring horns from cars coming up behind them, which amused the driver no end.

Hart remembered that he hadn't yet told the man where he wanted to go.

'By the way, I want to go to the Hotel Opera. It is in a place, a commune, called Opera just outside of Milano. About ten kilometres south I think, not far from Mirasole. Do you know it?'

'Of course. I come from Milano. I am Milanese. No problem.'

With those words of comfort in his ears, Hart soon drifted away into a fitful sleep.

He was awoken, by the sudden jolt of the braking taxi, followed by the obligatory sounding of horns of other vehicles. The taxi had stopped at a set of traffic lights and next to them he saw a welcoming sign.

'*Comune di Opera*, Milano,' the driver called to him,

'Five minutes and we are there, signore. At last eh!'

True to his word in slightly under five minutes, the car pulled up outside the Hotel Opera.

'Fantastic! *Grazie*. How much. *Quanto costa?*'

The driver scribbled a sum down on a piece of paper and passed it back to Hart, looking almost embarrassed at the cost of the ride.

'I'm sorry is high cost, signore, but Desenzano is far from here and—'

'No, no,' Hart interrupted, 'it's fine. I am very grateful for all your help.'

He reached for his wallet and took out the cost of the journey plus a 50-euro note and handed them both separately to the driver so that the tip he was giving was obvious. Not cheap, but all of this would eventually be paid for by Denis Williams.

As he handed over the note for 50 euro he smiled at the driver and said,

'Take this and get yourself some *decent* whisky, yes?'

'*Grazie, grazie*!'

He jumped out of the taxi and ran to the boot from which he took Hart's case, which he then put on the hotel steps. He opened the passenger door and with a slight bow ushered Hart out, taking and shaking his hand vigorously before he had even had time to stand upright.

'*Stai bene*, be well, *signore*.'

With that, he leapt back into the driver's seat and with a screech of tyres was off into the night once more.

Hart looked up at the welcoming sight of the hotel and picking up his bag trudged wearily to reception. The receptionist smiled as if expecting him as a regular patron of the place and before he could announce himself, Chiara said to him,

'Good evening, Doctor Hart, I believe?'

'Yes indeed, it is I. I think you have probably got a room booked for me for tonight?'

'Yes, sir we do, the best in the house.'

Hart completed all the usual formalities and she handed him the key to the room.

'The lifts are to the right, sir, you are on the third floor. Breakfast is from 7.30 am until 10.00 am in the morning and it is still possible to take dinner this evening if you wish.'

He thanked her and headed directly to the lifts and his room. Gianni had done well. The room possibly *was* the best in the hotel, large, elegant, with a small sitting room off to one side. He probably booked this place for a lot of his business guests. Hart dropped his case and slumped into a comfortable armchair positioned in front of the large TV screen. There were still lots of things for him to ponder before retiring for the night.

At 4.00 am he awoke, ponder-free and still in the chair fully clothed. Staggering to his feet, he proceeded to absently strip down to his underwear before crashing onto the bed where sleep immediately re-engulfed him.

Chapter 73

He awoke with a start at 9.45 am and looked at his watch.

'Jesus!'

Too late to shower and go down for breakfast, he telephoned down for breakfast courtesy of room service. He got out of bed and quickly splashed cold water on his face in the bathroom sink, drying his face on the bathrobe hanging on the door, which he then threw on. Looking around the floor, he saw his clothes from yesterday scattered around following his rapid dishabille at 4.00 am.

So what was the plan for today? Yes, Gianni would pick him up at 4.00 pm and ferry him to meet this Luca Messi, who he was dearly hoping would be the key to solving this mess he had gotten himself into, whilst filling him in on what exactly was going on. By the time breakfast arrived, he was feeling cool, calm and collected and tipped the room service guy handsomely.

Fed, showered, shaved, dressed and re-packed, he was ready once more for whatever the day had in store for him, but please God it was going to be an easy one! He had very little time to do much more than this as he had to vacate the room by mid-day and he decided to check out and spend the afternoon in the solarium on the hotel roof.

Checked out and comfortably seated in the solarium, a table close at hand holding his notepad and trusty pen, a similar one of which had proved indeed to be mightier than the sword on the train the previous day, with a large cappuccino being his weapon of choice this time, he began a memo list of events to help with his no-doubt upcoming lecture to Bossi and Messi. By the time he had finished and read it through a couple of times, it was 2.00 pm.

In getting off the train at Desenzano and electing to travel by taxi to this hotel suggested by Gianni Bossi, he felt more secure. One thing that disturbed him greatly though was the little item of the murder of two Italian citizens on board the train the evening before. For sure, the bodies would have been found by now and already investigations would be underway, with descriptions of a nervous looking Englishman with a possibly slight American accent being circulated nationally. Would the taxi driver hear of last night's events and spill the beans to the local police, or would the euro-50 note keep his conscience in check for a while? Having watched the television over breakfast, he was happy to see that news of it had not yet reached that medium.

When in doubt, order another coffee, which this time was an espresso to keep him wider awake. By 3.00 pm, he was becoming a little restless and was much relieved when a young porter coming into the solarium informed him that Doctor

Bossi was asking for him in the lobby. He gathered his possessions and made for the lift, smiling in anticipation of the meeting with his good friend once more.

At the sound of the '*ping*' the handsome Mediterranean-looking man with intense brown eyes, greying black hair swept back over the top of his head and neatly trimmed moustache, wearing an immaculate deep blue suit with startlingly white cut-away collared shirt with a perfectly knotted green printed silk tie held against it with a gold tie pin, and with a rakishly set green silk pocket handkerchief, turned and stood facing the lift in readiness for his imminent reunion.

As the doors of the lift parted, the two men moved quickly towards each other with arms outstretched, huge smiles on their faces. There followed a long embrace and much back-patting before the Italian pulled away and clasping Hart's hand warmly spoke through glistening pearl-white teeth.

'*Ciao* Max! I am so thrilled to meet with you again.'

'Gianni, it's so good to see you,' effused Hart, 'and you are looking so good. In fact so expensive!'

Bossi smiled. 'Of course, Max, it is the latest incarnation of Gianni. It is my new image.'

'Not a new lady then, Gianni?'

Bossi placed a finger over his lips conspirationally,

'Shhh Max, is a little secret we don't talk of, eh?'

Hart smiled, rolled his eyes and nodded. 'Same old Gianni.'

'But, Max, your hair is very short now yes and your face is errr a little tired?'

'It's my Americano look, Gianni, not to mention the fact that I haven't slept properly in a bloody long time.'

Bossi placed his hand over his heart.

'My God, Max, I am so sorry. I have not a lot of ideas of what you have been through over the last days, but for sure it must have been terrible I know. Please forgive me, my friend.'

'You'll be forgiven if we can have some delicious fish for dinner at il Ristorante Leo near that hospital in Milano.'

Bossi suddenly looked very serious.

'Please, Max, let us go to my car outside the doors here. We have much to say.'

'Shit! Sounds like no fish then.'

'Sorry Max, come, follow me.'

They exited the hotel and Bossi led the way to a red Alpha Romeo sitting directly outside. Bossi threw Hart's case into the boot and then they both got in. Bossi started the engine and drove a mere 30 yards into a deserted part of the hotel car park. He turned to Hart, serious lines cut into his face in the shaded car park.

'Max, this situation is very serious indeed.'

'For God's sake, don't tell me they've run out of fish, Gianni!'

'No really, Max, you are in great danger. We must go from here immediately and meet Luca Messi. On the way, we can catch up with our current lives. *Allora, andiamo!*'

He applied the gas roughly to the car and despite his air of "look over your shoulder secrecy" and the emphatic need for keeping a low profile, managed to spin the wheels of the Alpha throwing up a cloud of grit and dust as they sped out of the car park.

There was quiet in the car for the next few minutes as the car sped through the streets of Milan and eventually it was Bossi who broke the silence.

'So tell me, Max, what happened with your job at World. They are a very large and ethical company, so why you no longer work for them?'

'Oh, yes, Gianni I saw the window of opportunity there, but unfortunately they kicked me straight through it!'

The moment had been lightened.

'Max, I very much miss your English sense of humour, but please, please tell me the whole story.'

Over the next thirty minutes as the car raced along narrow streets and back-roads, Hart updated his friend on his fall out with World and his introduction to Denis Williams. At that point, Bossi raised a hand from the steering wheel and indicated Hart to stop his presentation.

'Max, I think we stop at this point in your story and save it until we meet Luca, otherwise I will get another reprise. *Capisce?*'

They laughed and as they left the city streets behind heading out into the countryside, Bossi first reminiscing over some of the more outrageous situations they had enjoyed together whilst Hart had worked with him in Milan years before, then updated him on his own most recent curriculum vitae. From there he quickly moved to his family at home and Hart could imagine in the dim interior of the car Bossi's eyes misting over as he spun the story of his wonderful family, consisting of his beautiful wife Leonora and their wonderful daughters, both now in their mid-teens.

At that point, another car had the temerity to poke its nose out of a side road and for its pains received a long loud blast from Bossi's horn.

Hart tried peering into the growing dimness of the passing countryside.

'So give me a clue then. Where are we and in how much time are we going to meet this friend of yours? Who is he by the way and in fact what is he?'

'I'm sorry, Max, but my instructions are to wait until we arrive, when all things will be revealed. He will tell you everything he knows. By the way, he is not exactly *my* friend, he is my friend's friend.'

The Alpha accelerated again as they picked up the Route 35.

'Max, I can now at least tell you that we are meeting Luca Messi at a particular place outside of Milano, which is for you, how you say, the safe house. It may be that you will have to stay there—'

'What'!?

'—you may have to stay there until some things are resolved. What they may be I have no idea. You know I have not been directly involved in any of this and, therefore, am not known to the bad guys who are after you. For this reason and for the sake of my family, Luca has told me that I must not get any deeper in the situation other than to bring you to him. Let me tell you this though, Max. Today at the office of Luca there was a very bad incident, where a man was...yes assassinated. The dead man was only delivering some mail or other, but he looked much like Luca, who has a special issue with body size. He's very fat! Reports say that he fell from the floor of Luca's office and died on the piazza floor.'

'Shit! That's really bad. You know I too was, or still am I guess, on somebody's hit list. Yesterday I, too, was nearly killed on that train to Milan.'

'Max, I will stay with you here for a time while you talk with Luca and will help in any way I can, if it's only for translation of language.'

'OK, so tell me, where are we going?'

'You should know this area.'

'Perhaps in the bloody daylight, but it's getting dark out there and there's mist rolling around. I may as well be wearing a blindfold. In any case, its years since I was here last!'

Hart peered out of the window again, screwing his eyes up against the gloom outside. They were certainly on the A7, a sign to that effect just flashing by, but where? Suddenly some way ahead in the growing mist, Hart was able to pick out an illuminated white building. As the car drew closer, he could see that what he had seen were the retaining walls of a much larger edifice and then he saw the flickering, the flickering of a multitude of candles. It was a cemetery. As they passed by, the high walls gave way to what was clearly the entrance, evidenced by two huge wrought iron gates, each one topped with a large gold cross. Almost in reverence, Bossi slowed the car to jogging speed, allowing Hart to pick out the row upon row of compartments, rising to a height of some thirty feet, each one illuminated by a lighted candle.

'So now you recognise this place, eh? You recognise this *cimeterio*, yes?'

'Yes I do. I remember now, we must be on the road to Pavia. We came along here often in the past to visit…what was his name? … Got it! … Professor Ronaldo.'

'Good Max, you have it.'

'And I remember along the route there are rivers, or dykes, where you used to fish, yes?'

'*Bene*. Good. I still fish out here, but the water starts just a little further down this road.'

A sudden very sharp S-bend loomed up in front of them and although Bossi knew the road well, he still had to fight a little to first pull and then push the car around the bends. As he did so, the mass of black oil that was the pool of road water came quickly into view, illuminated by the headlights of the car and by the light from a spotlight on the edge of the road illuminating an advertising board showing a large cup of Lavazza cappuccino. For a short while, the car planed on the water. Hart gripped the edge of his seat nervously.

'Whoa! Careful Gianni. I remember old whatsisname…Angelo somebody or other, took off on one of these bends and flew straight into the bloody water…and that was in bright daylight! What's more he was driving my bloody car at the time!'

Trying to keep panic out of his voice as he experienced the white-knuckle ride, Hart continued, 'So then, are we going all the way to Pavia, or are we stopping soon? I may just need to use a bathroom!'

'No, it's not far to go now and I am sure you will recognise it immediately when we approach.'

'Why is there all this mist, Gianni?'

'Ah, that is because of the water from the rice fields, plus the mist from, how did you call them the dykes along each side of the road and of course we are in the valley of the Po River and the effects of the heat of the day on all of them add up to make for these unusual atmospheric conditions. I have to say, though, perhaps unusual for you, Max, but for the Milanese quite normal.'

A couple of miles ahead, with the aid of the sudden appearance of street-lighting at the side of the road and the illumination escaping from its windows, Hart could make out the outline of a large building complex. Out of the darkness a road sign flashed by and in an instant Hart was able to pick out a name which immediately jogged his memory.

'It said La Certosa. It's the monastery Certosa di Pavia. Surely we're not heading there?'

Bossi smiled and nodded his head. '*Si si* Max, our destination lies immediately ahead. From the hotel to here has taken just 80 minutes. Not bad at all.'

Suddenly Bossi swung a tight left hand turn and the car raced into the dimly lit drive that led up to the beautiful building that was the monastery. As they approached, it was clear that beyond the treeline through which they were now passing, the facade of the monastery was illuminated. Looking upwards, Hart was amazed at the beauty of the building's white towers and spires caught up by the series of floodlights set at ground level.

The monastery of La Certosa di Pavia was a national treasure, four hundred years old and a museum rich in its many varied works of art. As the name suggested the Certosa, or charterhouse was, despite being closed down by Napoleon at one time, a monastery for Carthusian monks who committed themselves to a lifetime of silence and contemplation. In 1968, the monastery was once again taken over by an order of monks, this time the Cistercians, who continued to live there following the Cistercian way of life and supported by government grants and tourism. An additional and not insignificant income, and one which was a carefully kept secret from all except select members of the government, was that paid by a combination of the Catholic Church and the "Catholic Affairs Office, or the Office of Catholic Affairs", itself a virtual secret department within the church itself and one of the number of "special services" departments of the Italian government. This particular "special service" department was a lesser-known arm of the Italian Secret Service.

In return for the income provided by this "special service" department, the department was awarded secure, select offices and accommodation within the heart of the monastery's inner sanctum and it was here that Luca Messi patiently awaited the arrival of his "friend of a friend" Gianni Bossi and the man Hart, who for some reason appeared to be at the heart of the recent stirring up of the huge hornets' nest, which had brought such deadly outside forces to bear on their organisation.

Chapter 74

Bossi changed down a gear or two and drove his car at a speed in deference to the surroundings as he approached a substantial barrier, obviously there to prevent entry to unwanted or unannounced guests. The barrier rose automatically as they approached it, obviously programmed to receive Bossi, who continued towards the beautiful white edifice via the yielding gravel drive. When twenty yards from the front entrance to the Certosa, he turned left into a dark parking area, illuminated only by his own car's headlights, and killed his engine.

'*Ecco*, we have arrived, *andiamo*.'

Thus saying, he opened the car door and alighted. Hart did likewise from the passenger side and was surprised by the sudden appearance out of the darkness of two black-robed monks.

Bossi approached them and after a few words produced his identity card from his jacket pocket which they inspected using a battery operated torch and then handed it back to him. The conversation then clearly turned to Hart as there were deliberations and indications in his direction and after some moments he too was given "the hooded nod". Bossi turned to Hart.

'All OK, my friend. I had to show them my *carta d'identita* but they wanted to see yours too, but it is fine, they know now that you are English.'

'Ah, I guess you gave them the correct password then?'

'Yes of course. As soon as I say "English Prick", they understand totally and let us pass.'

More laughter, as the darkness was split by a segment of light as a door in the Certosa opened revealing another robed figure, who waved them to advance.

'Have you been here before, Gianni?'

'No, is my first time except as a local tourist of course, but clearly they are expecting us.'

The two robed figures who had inspected Bossi's identity card turned and walked ahead of them towards the open door. As the monk in the doorway stepped aside to let them enter, Bossi began to speak to him, but immediately the man raised a finger to his lips.

'We are clearly entering a no-speaking zone,' Hart added.

Another monk standing behind the huge oak door through which they had entered closed it with a loud bang, which echoed away in front of them down a dimly lit stone walled passageway. Lighted candles were positioned in small recesses at regular intervals along the walls on both sides of the passageway, but not regularly enough to create any greater light source than just "dim".

The monk who had greeted them at the door moved off ahead, indicating with his hand for them to follow him. Behind them, they heard the clunking of metal as the series of locks and bolts were operated on the oak door. The candle-lit passageway grew narrower as they progressed along it, amplifying even more the sound of their feet on the stone flagstones and Hart began to feel claustrophobic as he noticed that the ceiling too appeared to be lower at this point. For the first time that evening Hart was feeling decidedly nervous.

They walked on for some minutes before their leader made a left turn into another similar stone passageway, equally dimly lit with candles. Five more minutes later, the corridor began to grow larger and they found themselves arriving outside yet another large oak door. Hart glanced at Bossi.

'If this is the toilet, it's too late. I already went on the seat of your car. Such terrible driving!'

If Bossi had heard him, he did not react, for he too was now becoming distinctly nervous with the situation. Their guide reached inside his robe and produced a huge key, worthy of the size and structure of the door and with no little difficulty inserted it into the lock and turned it. The door opened slowly and they were invited to enter. Once inside, the door closed loudly and there was the sound of it being locked, this time from the other side.

The newly arrived robed figure looked first at Hart and then at Bossi and in perfect English began to speak.

'I'm so sorry. We are almost at our destination. You have to realise that you are now effectively in an area of very high security. I can assure you that these measures have been designed to benefit all of us in certain high-risk situations.'

During his short speech, his hand swept all the walls of the immediate area and beyond, where there were CCTV cameras pointed at every angle. The monk continued,

'We totally understand how you must be feeling gentlemen and although we are not familiar with the details of your recent trials, Doctor Hart, we do know what Doctor Bossi has indirectly informed us of and indeed what has recently appeared in the local and national press. So now, please bear with us for just a few more paces.'

The room in which they now stood was much brighter and it was obvious that they were in a small chapel. The vaulted ceiling was supported by a series of white marble pillars and the whole room was illuminated by two large suspended glittering chandeliers. It was clear to see now that the walls were completely covered with beautifully interpreted frescos in a myriad of colours and as Hart's lines of vision travelled to the ceiling he saw that there too the entire space was a riot of brightly coloured frescos. Directly ahead of the group of men, on the flag-stoned floor, was a carved wooden altar and a similarly carved wooden pulpit. The voice of the monk shook Hart from his reverie,

'It is wonderful, isn't it? Really, it is a most beautiful sight.'

Hart responded, 'It is indeed splendid, but some of its content needs to be X-rated I think,' and he pointed to a particular fresco on one wall where a woman kneeling in prayer was about to have her head removed by a bearded man holding aloft a large scimitar.

'Ah yes, it is the martyrdom of Santa Catherine, but please we go finally though this last door and then we have arrived.'

Ahead of them, he indicated the apparently final large oak door of this particular trip. On this occasion, he knocked gently on the door and without waiting for a response entered, inviting Hart and Bossi to follow him.

In only two strides, they quickly travelled from the 14th to the 21st century, for now they were standing in an office of the most ultra-modern design. The room was decorated in basic white, but in contrast to this was a deep, thick pile, dark blue fitted carpet. The walls were hung with an array of colourful abstract paintings amongst which Hart recognised a couple of Klees, a Kandinsky and two large surrealist paintings credited to Magritte. If the paintings were prints, then they were excellently produced, but Hart had the feeling that these could be originals. The room's illumination was provided by spectacular chrome and steel ceiling spotlights which were remotely electronically moveable along steel strands that also fed them with electricity. This source of light was supported by matching chrome wall lights, two on each of the room's four walls. From some unknown source in the room, there emanated a very low-pitched rendering of some classical piece that Hart couldn't put a name to.

Directly ahead of them was a massive white marble fireplace in which blazed a fire, fed by large logs of wood. However, the full view of the heart of the fire was obliterated by the bulk of an extremely fat man, who was seated at a king-size chrome-framed, plate-glass topped desk intently reading a document, his brows deeply furrowed. The desk was almost totally occupied by neat piles of papers and files, apart from one side where sat four telephones, and the central area where rested the keyboard and very large screen to a desktop computer, the works of which occupied a large area of floor beneath the desk.

If Hart had not known better, looking at the man seated behind the desk he would have sworn that he was in the presence of Luciano Pavarotti's younger, but even more obese, brother and he smiled as he thought of the noise previously generated by the closing and opening of the huge oak doors with their great brass locks… "nessun dorma" …nobody shall sleep! A second thought made his smile even wider as he saw the orange and yellow glow apparently emanating from the area of the seated man's lower back, but what was in fact reflection from the fire.

He must be on the side of the good guys, the sun is shining from his arse!

After what seemed like an hour, the man eventually looked up. What theatre! What drama! He then hauled himself to his feet, his huge body mass obliterating any signs of the fire burning behind him.

'*Ciao* Gianni, good evening, Doctor Hart, I'm so pleased and also so very intrigued to meet you.'

He offered Hart a pudgy hand to shake, which Hart took expecting a vice-like grip from a man of such stature, but to his unpleasant surprise found a totally limp handshake without any detectable presence at all of bones in the hand. It was as if he was holding hands with a soft, puffy, boneless fish.

'Please come and sit by the fire.'

He turned to the eloquent monk who had led them on this final stage of their journey.

'Prego Alfonso, please bring some wine for our guests here.'

As Alfonso nodded an obedient *'certo signore'*, the brother of Pavarotti aka Luca Messi, indicated to the three sumptuous deep blue velvet arm chairs to one side of the desk into two of which both Hart and Bossi gratefully sank. Then turning to Hart, he came straight to the point saying in very good English,

'Right then, Doctor Hart, let us see if we can untangle your story and see whether we can envisage any way out of this situation for you.'

It was music to Hart's ears. So much so that he could have cried with relief, for in that instant his previous self-preserving bravado completely evaporated.

Chapter 75

Denis Williams was seated in a well-worn armchair in the so-called "War Room" of his house in "The Park" in Nottingham. Opposite him sat Victoria Crosse in a less battered but probably less comfortable chair. The mood was grim.

'So, Vicky, tell me about your meeting with Special Branch.'

'Actually, Denis, to be totally accurate, they told me not to speak to anybody at all about this matter, but in no way could I not bring you totally up-to-date. You are aware of all the events of our trip to Padua and you have all the documents that I sent to you.'

Williams nodded.

'Our final act in Padua was to follow up on something overheard by Max whilst stuck in the air conditioning ducting at the meeting venue, directly over the heads of...let's call them "the conspirators". The fellow called Halle, who seemed to be the likely most senior member, and who by the way was responsible for Max's dismissal from World Pharma...'

'Oh I wasn't aware of that relationship.'

'That's for another time, Denis. Well, Halle said that he would be unable to join the crew for another important meeting on the following day because he had a very significant meeting himself with a person very much an essential cog in their organisation. As a result of hearing this, Max decided that we should try and track him down at their meeting, and make an attempt to obtain a photograph, or at least a reasonable description of this "important chap". This we did. We actually were able to obtain really good photographs of the pair of them together, which you have there.'

She indicated to the manila file that Williams was nursing on his lap.

'Yes, the priest. It seems like an odd duo to me.'

'That's the point, Denis. Later, Max had me e-mail the photographs to an old friend of his in Milan, who he believed might be able to identify Halle's lunchtime partner, or at least be able to put him in touch with someone who could.'

'And has he?'

'I really don't know. The last time I saw Max, he was bound for a train which would take him up to Milan from Padua. He had in any case arranged to spend a few days there after the Padua trip as he worked there for a spell some years ago and has Italian friends there.'

'Yes, Max called me the evening before you left and instructed me to assemble all the notes and documents we have, "evidence" he called it, and send copies of it to a whole list of different official bodies and organisations. He didn't mention Special Branch though, so where do they fit into the picture?'

'There was this couple of plainclothes men waiting for me at passport control at East Midlands Airport. They took me to a small office where they informed me that they were very much aware of the… "ongoing business" … as they put it. They then informed me that Max had agreed to extend our work in order to benefit the Italian authorities! In other words, they indicated that the Italians already had an inkling of "certain diverse activities", their words not mine, and that Max had volunteered to assist them further!'

'It does sound quite reasonable, Vicky. You know our biggest problem was always going to be how we could convert our knowledge, our evidence, into something more concrete that could be used against these people. We particularly needed some official organisation to prosecute our findings, hence Max's list of various possible organisations that he gave me to contact. It now sounds as if one of these groups has instead found us and instead of us leading the horse to water, the water has come to the horse. Surely that has to be positive …hasn't it?'

'Let me finish, Denis, and then see what you think. The thing that scares me is that fine, Max is working with whatever Italian authorities, but these Special Branch guys told me that I was under no circumstances to make contact or have any communication with Max until the work was finished. They said that he would be working in very difficult circumstances, possibly undercover, and that any distraction or external contact, i.e. by me, could have dire consequences on his continued safety!'

'Bloody hell!'

'They actually took my mobile phone from me, Denis, saying that if Max called me, they would be the ones who answered his call. I was told not to even answer my home or office phone until Max was back in the UK.'

'So what are you going to do?'

'I'm going to do exactly what they told me to do. I'm going to take some days off work and hide myself where nobody can contact me. I'm going to be bloody Howard Hughes, for as long as it takes.'

'That sounds a bit excessive, Vicky.'

'Bloody hell, Denis,' her voice was raised for the first time since arriving, 'if I'm not supposed to talk to Max for fear of getting him killed, how else can I do it? Every time a phone rings, anybody's phone, I'm going to be on edge. Should I answer it or should I leave it? At least if I'm away, I can just ignore it, as nobody will know where I am and I obviously won't be carrying a mobile phone. So that's it!'

'So when and where are you planning to go?'

'I'm going to disappear the minute I leave here. My case is packed and in my car. As for where I'm going, that has to be my secret, Denis, but I'll call you from some landline somewhere in a few days' time.'

Chapter 76

To Hart's astonishment, Luca Messi dropped down into the remaining armchair fitting so tightly that he was fearful that Bossi and himself would have to shoe-horn him out of it at the end of their meeting. Certainly there was much complaining from the chair's tortured springs as his mass landed and his girth noticeably pushed the chair's arms outwards in an effort to escape the pressure. Hart couldn't help wondering if this was the first time Messi had "relaxed" thus here in his office.

Hart and Bossi waited for Messi to begin the conversation.

'*Allora*. First let me thank Gianni Bossi here for passing on the information that you sent to him from Padova Doctor Hart, and also thank you very much for doing so. Believe me the details and photographs are of great interest to us.'

Hart smiled appreciatively, but his smile belied the anxiousness and the frustration he felt at the possibility of having to spend several hours here whilst one hundred bushes were beaten about. He was desperate for Messi to get on with it and cut to the chase, but he felt it important not to appear ungrateful or ungracious, so he decided to just sit it out and go with the flow...or "trickle" as he guessed it would probably be. Messi smiled and raised his pudgy hands.

'Please, Doctor Hart, I'm afraid that this will take a little time...'

'Groan!'

'...but first let me introduce myself. My name is Luca Messi and as Gianni has probably already informed you, I am a member of the office, sometimes called the Bureau of Catholic Affairs. Under any other situation, I would have to ask you to sign an agreement of secrecy. In truth, not just for *silencio*, but also for maintaining total confidentiality relating to this place where we now meet. It would be of the same level as your own Official Secrets Act. However, we are meeting here today and not at my official office in Milano because my own office is no longer safe. Whilst I will not enforce the Official Secrets signage, Max, can I call you that by the way...?'

Hart nodded.

'Thank you...it is very important that what is said here stays here and this place of our meeting remains only in your head. Now while I think about it, before we move on, you might wonder why an Italian organisation such as ours has an English title?'

Hart nodded again. 'Now you mention it, it does seem a bit strange.'

'Basically, it is in order to be taken seriously by America and the UK, both of which seem unable to understand any language outside of their own, sorry Max, and we are an important organisation looking over a religion which has the most Christian followers in the whole world, 1.2 billion at the last count, and so it stands to reason that we should use an international language, hence English. I have to say though that here in Italy it is not unusual for us to be referred to by the Italian version of the same name. In Italia we are called "il Ufficio degli Affari Cattolici" or the UAC. You can perhaps see now why we generally prefer to use the English version of our name.'

'Thanks for the explanation…and I apologise for my countrymen's lack of linguistic abilities.'

Messi continued seriously,

'As a result of my receiving your reports, Max, and of our pending meeting today, this afternoon an attempt was made on my life at my office in Milano.'

Hart gasped slightly. 'I'm so sorry about that. What can I say, Luca? All this has snowballed way beyond my understanding I'm afraid and—'

He was cut short by Messi's raised hand.

'No, please Max, there is no need for apologies. We have now entered a very dangerous game and I must warn you that your life too is in continual danger, but then I am aware that you already know that for I have read the newspapers and have seen the news of the death of two men presumed to have fallen, or have been thrown, from a train yesterday bound for Milano. One of them was a priest wearing pink socks I believe.' He forced a smile. 'Not typical footwear for a priest I must say.'

Bossi looked aghast at the revelation. 'Max I'm so sorry. I did not realise.'

Messi picked up a newspaper and tossed it across the table towards the two men. It was picked up by Bossi who read the banner headlines aloud, translating for Hart.

'**Traccia di Sangue**…Blood on the tracks. Then below it says, "Two men, one apparently a priest, have been found dead in, circostanze sospette, suspicious circumstances near the Venezia, Milano train line." Max, this was your involvement?',

Hart regarded his friend and then looked at Messi.

'I think we should decide at this point who tells what to who and just how much. I am also worried now at Gianni's involvement. He is totally innocent of any involvement at all so far, but now he might be at risk. I'm sure that the less he knows the safer he will be.' Then looking at Bossi, 'Sorry Gianni, it's for your own good.'

Messi nodded in agreement, but Bossi protested.

'No, Max, please, I am already involved. I bring you here to this place to meet Luca, so I am indeed involved. Please, therefore, proceed with your story.'

Messi scrambled himself out of the glove-tight chair and lumbered over to where Bossi was seated and placed an almost translucent hand upon his shoulder.

'Dear Doctor Bossi, Gianni, Max is correct, for in truth you know very little of this matter. A matter which goes much deeper than you could ever expect. In fact, in reality the same could apply to you too, Max. The fact is that you are placing, not just yourself, but all of your family in grave danger with the knowledge you have already acquired, let alone what I have not yet revealed. In which case, Gianni, as we share the same friend and as I like you,' he smiled, 'I cannot let you put yourself in jeopardy. I really would like you to leave us now please if you would, Gianni. Leave while you are still *relatively* safe at least.'

Bossi shot to his feet. 'Ma no! I protest Luca. Please at least let me hear your account of what is happening. That much at least you can surely tell me. Tell me that and I will leave for sure.'

Hart looked at Messi, who shrugged his massive shoulders in a show of resignation.

'Luca, Gianni, here is what I propose. I will tell both of you my story, going back over the past few weeks. Luca can perhaps fill some of the gaps there are in it, together with who he believes some of the characters in the drama are, and what he feels is going on. Then, Gianni, you go home and Luca can get me a taxi to take me back to the hotel in Milan. How does that sound to you?'

Hart looked at his friend who seemed content with the outcome of his protestations, but Messi was not quite so convinced.

'I agree, Max, but with one change to your proposal. Max, you must stay here at La Certosa for the time being. There is much to tell you, besides which you will be perfectly safe here. One thing is for sure, we have no priests in pink socks here, my friend!'

'But what about the hotel, they have a record of me staying—'

Messi cut him off with a raise of his pudgy hand.

'Please do not worry, Max, we are a serious and respected, sometimes feared, organisation and can organise everything. In fact, I am aware that already you have checked yourself out of the hotel. My agents have spoken with staff at the Hotel Opera and they have been sworn to state secrecy. In fact, your name has already been removed from their hotel register. I would guess that your clothes are already here at La Certosa in fact, in the boot of Gianni's car, *si*? So then, please tell me, are you content to stay with us a little longer, Max?'

Hart pondered the offer for only a minute. He trusted and actually quite liked this ungainly mountain of a man and felt there was safety in his memorably strange hands, whilst ensconced in the confines of the monastery.

'OK Luca, it's deal, I'll stay.'

Messi was happy. 'Bravo Max. Now wait one moment. *Aspetta*!'

He pressed a large button situated in the wall at the side of the fireplace. Within seconds, the door was opened and a robed monk entered. Messi spoke quickly to the man, who bowed his head in acknowledgement of his brief orders and retraced his steps out of the open door, returning almost immediately, carrying a large ornate tray on which sat a bottle of red wine and three large glasses, which he transferred to the table before turning and scurrying out of the room, closing the door firmly and loudly behind him. As the echo receded, Messi clapped his hands together and smiled at Hart and Bossi.

'There, it is done.'

For the first time, Hart noticed the Italian splendour of the man's whole attire, despite the challenges of his inordinate size. His green tweed jacket was complemented by equally voluminous green twill trousers and a green and white checked shirt topped off with a fine green and red handtied paisley silk bow tie.

The man's shoes were a light-brown fine leather, originating from the "Gucci stable".

He adroitly poured the red wine, equally into the three glasses and handed one each to his guests, who sipped it appreciatively.

'I see you approve of, how might you say, our little tipple, Max?'

'I do indeed. It's more than a tipple I believe? It's a Brunello, isn't it?'

'You are right, Max. Very good. *Si, un Brunello di Montalcino*, vintage 1995, a very good year I think no?'

Bossi clearly agreed with the analysis of the quality of the wine but had rather more basic, pragmatic questions on his mind.

'*Si, si*, Luca, it's a very fine wine. Very expensive! But where…who pays for all of this, this wine, this luxury, these things here?'

He passed his hand around the room taking in the full contents.

'Easy answer, my friend. It is you the taxpayer and of course also the church, but mainly you.'

Messi enjoyed baiting his new friend, "the friend of a friend", a little. In return, Bossi only shook his head and heaved a sigh. 'Bah!'

'It is only a joke, Gianni.'

Hart was liking this man more and more. Bossi still unsmiling, either not seeing the joke or perhaps not appreciating it, said in a rather hushed tone,

'It's no bloody joke, Max, this is Italy and this is the way things are done in high places.'

Hart addressed Messi.

'Right Luca, I will begin. I will relate all I know to you and all the things that have happened since the beginning of this affair. There are many things to relate and not all of them are bound entirely to just one or two countries. I will be totally honest with you and in return, I want you to be the same with me, even though I've not signed any secrecy document. I am also very keen to know how you might imagine I can extricate myself from this pile of manure.'

Messi waddled over to the sofa opposite Hart and unceremoniously dropped into it. Hart raised his eyes on pure reflex in the direction of Bossi as the big man came to land, half expecting springs and stuffing to burst forth from the tortured piece of furniture, but the sofa took his weighty bulk admirably and without any visible protest.

And so it came to pass that over the next two hours, Hart was able to describe fully the events leading up to the wonderful glass of Brunello, with occasional gasps from Bossi and a catalogue of questions from Messi. He began in fact, before the start of the affair with his premature ejection from World Pharmaceuticals at the hand of Robert Halle, which had led to his return to England and his introduction to the man in purgatory, Denis Williams. He related Williams' agonies which had culminated in the suicide of his wife in some detail.

To grimaces and intakes of breath, he relived his activities with Victoria Crosse at the Paddocks Hospital and added details narrated to him by Williams relating to the Paddocks' sister private hospital in Liverpool. He then moved on to his adventures with friend Klaus Grille in Greifswald, dwelling a little on his inquisition by Bettina Arben, "Greifswald's very own Doris Day". At that point, Messi gave a knowing nod of his massive head.

'You have heard of her already, Luca?'

'I have heard of her and from what I have heard she is far from stupid though, Max, and it would be dangerous to underestimate her.'

'It's a bit late for that, *mio amico*, I've already totally pissed her off as you will hear anon.'

Hart pulled the ties together which he believed linked the UK hospitals with the Gerhard Roscher Schmoller Institute (GRS) in Greifswald and the possible connection with Vita Pharma in Sicily and at this point began to talk of the theories he had relating to stem cells, especially those of unborn babies, at which once again a knowing smile crossed the lips of Messi. Hart decided that Messi might require a short lesson in stem cells, although he was aware that Bossi as a physician would already have this basic knowledge and so he ploughed on.

He gave Messi a resume of the many untreatable, incurable debilitating neurological diseases, along with spinal cord injuries and strokes et cetera, where symptoms have been alleviated via medication with human embryonic stem cells. He talked about the ready-made market with VIP customers already waiting in line for a successful treatment, whatever the price, and underlined the billion dollar market that awaits the first pharmaceutical company to come up with the first effective commercially available 'miracle cure' for those said conditions.

He added his and Crosse's conclusion that World Pharmaceuticals has made several major breakthroughs in stem cell research, some evidence being available already in published clinical studies, which have required a steady supply of suitable cells, but looking at the scale of their current international programs this steady input has most probably increased to more of a continual *stream* which is growing in volume and speed on a daily basis such that it is getting almost impossible to make that supply meet the current demand by usual, normal ethical routes.

'I firmly believe that already, VIPs in high office, or high in the public domain are *already* receiving stem cell treatments. Experimental treatments are being supplied at great costs, but unethically, and as I have just surmised I have to count World Pharmaceuticals as the lead player in this. There is a very large door of opportunity here, a door which offers the great opportunity to admit unethical and immoral activities for those so inclined, and my belief is that the door is now wide open to a great nefarious, *efferato*, trade.'

Messi fired a series of questions at Hart, some of which were answered by Bossi and more easily understood by Messi in his own native language. The room became heavy with gloom, before Messi moved for progress once more.

'So, Max, tell us about Padua.'

Hart launched into his story of events at the International Symposium that he and Crosse had attended in Padua, and his experiences in the GRS hospitality suite, which were again accompanied by frequent sharp intakes of breath and low whistles of incredulity and with no little admiration from his engrossed audience. At the point in his story at which he gained entry to the overhead ducting, Messi had raised a hand from his enormous stomach, and Hart paused for more questioning.

'So, tell me, Max, before you escaped into the roof space did you actually find any concrete confirmation that World are involved in multinational activities with stem cells?'

'Yes indeed. I actually saw in files there paperwork that identifies the countries that they are working with in this field, and the programs that are both running and that are planned. It seems that there will be a big push to develop research areas on the African continent.'

'Do you know where exactly in Africa they plan their biggest efforts?'

'Yes, Zimbabwe, Guinea and Angola are high on their list. You know a little bribery goes a long way in poor countries and authorities are always willing to turn a blind eye to inadequately controlled clinical programs and open drug testing. I have to say though in fairness, that there are some good works being done as well for the local populations. For example tested, ethical drugs are continually being laid gratis at the feet of government agencies. Of course how the agencies then deal with them is another question. I have this information not from my foray into the GRS hospitality suite, but from my own personal general knowledge of the international pharmaceutical industry which, even though I say it myself, is pretty wide.'

Once Hart arrived at the point in his tale of crawling through the ducting, he moved quickly to his enforced pause above the room in which the small meeting group were assembled and proceeded to first describe what he could remember of what was said before making an attempt to describe the attendees. At that point Messi became visibly excited. It was clear that he had knowledge and details of some of the people met there.

'Max, please describe to me as well as you can the woman with, how you say, the red head?'

Hart smiled. 'Ahh, that red hair. Well, she was absolutely stunning. I was positioned directly above her and got an excellent bird's eye view. Her red hair was long, with lots of curls, which hung down and framed a really beautiful face. She had wonderfully large brown eyes and a beautiful nose. Her blood red lips were provocatively perfect. Her legs, which she crossed and uncrossed several times were barely covered by her short skirt and were exquisite. But I have to report, gentleman, somewhat ashamedly I'm afraid, that her most stunning attributes were her most splendid breasts, which like her legs were barely covered by her clothing.'

There was a slightly embarrassed cough from Messi.

'Great tits is not something that we can file in a report, Max.'

There was a little disdain in Messi's voice.

Bossi smiled. 'Max, remember that Luca works for a church organisation and doesn't *theoretically* consider such…items. Luca, you certainly would have ended up providing misinformation in any report relating to the lady's chest area was it you hiding in that roof rather than Max. But seeing you climbing up there in the first place would have been an even better sight than those breasts. Ha, ha!'

Hart continued his voice becoming serious.

'Luca, you know her, don't you?'

Messi nodded. 'Yes I know her very well. In fatto I know *of* her, rather than know her personally. Despite her great beauty, she is most dangerous. Known by many as "the Red Fox" she—'

'*Cristo!*' It was Bossi's turn for interjection. 'Max, this woman is famous in all Italia. It is said that she leads one of the most brutal of Sicilian mafia cells. She truly walks hand in hand with death. *Cazzo!* Sorry for my profanity, Luca, but…*cazzo!*'

Hart looked at Messi and raised an eyebrow, 'She's as bad as that, Luca? You must tell me more.'

'*Si*, Max, I will tell you much more about the Red Fox and for sure I will certainly confirm what Gianni says. He is totally correct. The Fox, or to use her real name Claudia Volpe, you know volpe is in fatto also the Italian word for fox or vixen which is very appropriate in her case, is the leader of a very dangerous mafia cell. It is as Gianni says located in Sicily, but it is like a big tree with branches reaching out not just all over Italy, but also much further beyond. She is the first woman leader in what has always been a male dominated… profession, and she did not attain her position by being beautiful and having a nice body. It is often an additional benefit, *si*, but la Volpe has reached the point of being *la Capa* by being uncompromisingly brutal in her…management style…shall we say. Perhaps her gender has made it necessary to be harder and stronger than her male competitors? I don't know. She is not just *la Capa* though, she is I believe *la Capa di tutti Capi*, the boss of all the bosses.'

'You talk about "profession" and "management style" as if it's a normal business set-up. A family business set-up.'

'That's because, Max, in most ways that is what it is. Traditionally the position of *il Capo*, the chief, is passed on and down from generation to generation, it was always the case. However, many years ago the ruling family of the group, the Settimi by name, were all killed in a now famous bloody shoot out with another competitor mafia group in the north of Sicily. Their position now being vacant following their total demise was taken by the very strong Volpe family, and so it was for many years. However, there came a point when they too suffered a virtual wipe-out, resulting from a poorly staged and not very believable car accident in the hills around Palermo. You see there is more than just one mafia cell operating on the island and the competition to be number one was…*is still*…very fierce. One cell operated in the north of Sicily and the other in the south. Over the years, both groups have been intent on securing the position as the one, united, single cell on the island. Sometimes they have tried to come to an arrangement by discussion, but usually it has been through violent activities resulting in many deaths as was the case of the car crash. So, when the family were decimated in the car, it was actually a large people carrier, following discussions with "friends in the north", and when the loose ends had been tied off by additional acts of violence by their would be assassin supersedents immediately afterwards; it seemed that there would indeed now be one single cell on the island.

'However, nobody had taken account of the very young sister of the deposed family, Claudia Volpe, the youngest of six children. Like many famous names in history, although young, when she saw the confusion and likely forced abdication of what had been her entire family from her "family business", she drew upon her own reserves of juvenile female strengths and miraculously injected new life into what her competitors had believed to be an expired corpse. Her father was much too old and frail to take on the mantel of Capo, but he was still greatly respected amongst the mafia syndicate and it was he who urged and supported her in taking on the role of *la Capa*. Ordinarily, the position would have been passed to the next male family member in line, but of course this was no longer possible for the family Volpe. I don't know, Max, perhaps it was here that her amazing looks and vibrant personality took a part in the drama, because she travelled the island and beyond to the south of Italy for a long time, ceaselessly recruiting a veritable army of Mafiosi. She subsequently became *la Capa* and eventually *la Capa di tutti Capi*. In any case though, I can tell you that in the end her revenge on the group responsible for what had gone before was incredible. It was absolute and total. She has since then led the Sicilian organisation with wisdom and also with great ferocity at times when required. She is a very dangerous person, not to be angered or crossed in any way.

'Her bonds with local people in Sicily, the church and businesses, particularly the pharmaceutical businesses, became absolute under her stewardship, all these groups gaining mutual reward for their mutual associations. It was and is what one might call "a rewarding symbiosis for all".

'So that is the Fox and just a piece of her story. It is very important, Max, that you are also aware of other links and connections in the "Country of the Fox" and of that I will say more later.'

There was a quiet in the room, which was broken as Hart drew in a deep breath.

'Tally bloody Ho! One thing I should have mentioned, although I did allude to it earlier, is that prior to my disappearing act from the hospitality suite, not only did I view various seemingly sensitive papers I actually took the opportunity to photocopy a selection of them. This includes details concerning other countries where World have interests and these, together with some of their more public literature were faxed to a safe house in the UK on that same evening by Victoria Crosse. Oh shit, that means she is now probably in as much of harm's way as I am. That's all I need!'

He struck the arm of the sofa in irritation.

However, Messi put out a hand of consolation.

'Max, no, she is safe I can assure you. Please continue and then I will tell you more.'

'That's good. Let me continue then. The assembled group seated below me in the meeting room, together with our striking lady, discussed a further meeting planned for the following day. It seemed to be important, but my old adversary Robert Halle gave his apologies saying that he had a meeting with another important figure on the morrow and would not be able to attend. It was at that point that I made a mental note that if at all possible I would try and discover who this important possibly "new player" was. Going back to this meeting though, there was a fear in the room, especially amongst the physicians, that was almost tangible.

'It was very clear that a great deal of pressure was being applied to these doctors to get them to step-up the volumes of stem cell material that they were harvesting and passing on. It was also clear that our foxy lady had an enforcement role at the meeting and it was from here that the fear was generated. She was definitely there to keep the team in line.'

Hart finished this part of his story with a brief outline of the last stages of his descent from the ceiling cavity and his return from the meeting place to his hotel.

'Any further questions so far?'

Bossi was the first to speak.

'Ah, Max, this is an incredible story, but too dangerous and I fear for your safety.'

'You "ain't heard nothin'" yet, Gianni. What about you, Luca, do you have any more questions or comments at this stage?'

'No, Max. Not yet. All of this story is very interesting and I am building a better picture in my mind of the jigsaw I have been working with. You are doing very well in supplying many pieces for the gaps I have in the picture.'

'Not one for the ceiling of the Sistine Chapel I guess,' joked Hart.

Messi smiled. 'You might see the irony of your joke a little later on I think, my friend.'

'So where were we? Yes, I organised all the documents and copies which I had *borrowed* from GRS, which we should now refer to perhaps as World Pharma as they are the true owners of Vita, to be faxed to Denis Williams in England once I had arrived back at my hotel. I also spoke to him on the phone to indicate that a large fax was on its way and I additionally advised him to make an effort to contact whatever regulatory and law enforcement agencies were appropriate, although I'm pretty sure he won't have been able to sort out the wheat from the chaff in respect to that particular task.'

'Not a bad thing though, Max,' added Messi.

'OK, after I had contacted Gianni and arranged to meet him in Milan and sent the pile of literature to the UK, the next thing I wanted to do was to try and discover who Halle was meeting on the following day. I had overheard Halle's conversation with Arben earlier so I had a reasonable idea of where his rendezvous with person X was to be and it was simple for Victoria and I to turn up, keep in the shadows and take the photograph, which I then sent to Gianni, and then on eventually to you, Max?'

Both the other men nodded their heads in confirmation.

'And now we arrive at the drama on the train between Padua and Milan between myself, the gorilla and the priest in the pink socks, where things turned out rather nasty.'

The audience were all ears for the next part of Hart's story and gave him their totally unbridled attention as his recounting of the fracas on the train played out to the end, at which point Gianni sprang to his feet.

'Jesus Max, I never realised things had gone this far. You are in worse danger than I had thought!'

Messi struggled to his feet and faced Hart and Bossi.

'The truth, my friends, is that we are all three in very great danger, you and I Gianni by our association with Max. Let me remind you that the reason we are here in La Certosa today, rather than in my office in Milan, is that this afternoon my office factotum was murdered. Murdered in error I believe, for it should have been me laying on the piazza floor. Dear Massimo was in the wrong place at the wrong time, but more to the point he was in fact unfortunately the wrong shape and size. In all of Milan he was probably the only one man who from behind resembled me!'

'Bloody hell, I'm so sorry that I've got you on the hit list as well!'

'No please,' Messi raised his hands, 'I have already been on this hit list for some years now and only now things have taken an acute turn and they are quickly coming to a head. My big question is, how did these people, these would be assassins, learn that you were coming to Milan, Max and who you were coming to meet? That is the big question indeed. I already know who they were and who they were "representing". So who then sent pink socks and his friend? Well, I can tell you both that it was the Sicilian mafia. The assassins were some of the arms of the lovely Claudia, the Sicilian Hydra. You will not have seen the very latest newspaper headlines referring to the suspicious men killed on the train, but they were identified post mortem as notorious Mafiosi. You were very lucky indeed, Max.'

Hart was past the point where he could be shocked any further and merely shrugged at Messi's point, but there was a burning question he had of his own.

'Going back to the question of how they knew where to find me, the only person who knew my whereabouts and travel intentions was Gianni, who I made a call to.'

'My God, I told no one!'

'No, no Gianni, I am not saying for one second that you gave up this information in any way at all. Somehow it was picked up though. Was I overheard for example? I just don't know.'

It was Messi, who having struggled painfully to his feet had now taken to walking backwards and forwards stroking his chin in contemplation, who fired the next question at Hart.

'Tell me, how did you call Gianni? Did you use the hotel telephone, your cell phone, or some other?'

Hart paused and thought as hard as he could in this current pressure cooker. He had made several calls the evening before he left Padua. For some of them he used the hotel phone and for others he used his mobile, but which for which? Eventually he decided.

'OK. I used both my own mobile and the hotel phones...to spread the cost a little, but I'm fairly sure that it was my mobile phone that I used to call Gianni to tell him of my intention to meet him in Milan. All the other calls I made were using the hotel phone, I'm pretty sure.'

Messi was still parading. 'So let me see, could I look at your phone please, Max?'

He stuck out a short arm to receive it, reminding Hart of one half of Tweedle Dum and Tweedle Dee.

'Do your calls sound the same now as they usually have done in the past? The background noises or the actual voices I mean.'

'I'm not sure. The only thing I've noticed recently, and this has been for a little while now, is a faint echo, especially at the end of conversations, but this is normal I think with signals for international calls bouncing around off satellites here there and everywhere. Ah also, now I come to think of it there has been an occasional "click" when I terminate the call.'

'*Bene, videamo,* let us see.'

Messi's fat digits struggled gainfully over the small letters and numbers of the phone's dialling pad before finally releasing the plastic plate covering the battery and sim card.

'Ah interesting. Please look Max and Gianni and tell me what you see.'

He held out the dissected phone and the two items. Hart and Bossi moved in and closely examined the phone items as they sat on Messi's hand. Hart spoke first.

'OK, I see a normal cell phone, battery, wires, sim card, a connector of some sort...normal I think?'

'*Si, si,*' Bossi concurred.

'*Bene.* So do you see a small object that looks like a garden pea, *un pisello,* gentlemen?'

'Yes, that's the connector I mentioned.'

'Is true yes, it's the connector Max has seen.'

'Well, my friends, let me tell you that that innocent looking "connector thing" is in fact a microchip transmitter. What it does is automatically connect whatever number you dial out to a third person, allowing them to listen in to your conversation but unable to speak in it.'

'Fucking hell!'

'*Cazzo!*'

Came back Hart and Bossi's measured and controlled responses.

Messi continued the lecture.

'Sometimes these "baby peas" can also turn on to the "anonymous listener" when you receive a call. It's not only when you dial out. It is hard to tell outside of a laboratory, but one thing for sure is that all your outgoing calls at least have been monitored by somebody else. The echo you have been hearing is the second wave of sound during the additional transmission.'

'Hang on then, when I called Gianni on my cell phone telling him I was taking a train to Milan, they would have picked that up and hence the gorilla and his handler with the pink socks would know my train intentions and be able to join me. Now when I phoned Gianni to say that there had been a change in travel plans after the pair left the train early, my mobile phone battery was flat and I called him from a public phone in a cafe in Desanzano and, therefore, they would have no knowledge of any of that call. That is why we've seen nothing of them since my arrival. They would neither know that my arrival would be by taxi nor the change in my hotel arrangements.

'So now somebody must be wondering where the bloody hell I am. Wait a minute though, how did they do this? How could they contaminate my mobile with their device?'

'Gentlemen, first let me say that I think that Gianni is now relatively safe. Mine was the only name spoken in full, together with my address, so relief, eh Gianni? But you must now destroy your own mobile phone for additional security. Also, my strong advice to you is to go home and leave the rest to Max and me, there is no point in you getting in any deeper.'

Bossi began to protest, 'Max, my problem is your problem, we must—'

'No Gianni. I thank you for all you have done for me, but now you really must leave this to Luca and me. I could never forgive myself if anything bad was to happen to you or your family. As you have heard already, really bad things have already happened in this business and it's not over yet. This is not the time for unnecessary heroics. I am so very grateful for what you have done to help me so far, but now I urge you to please go back home to your family!'

Messi drew upon his most serious face.

'You really must leave, Gianni, Max is right. For it is futile for you to remain here and I am certainly not prepared to discuss another item while you stay in our presence. A brother outside the door will escort you back to your car.'

After one-half of an eternity, common sense prevailed and Gianni Bossi embraced both Hart and Messi in succession before making towards the door, a tear in his eye.

Hart called after him,

'Don't worry, Gianni, all will be fine.'

To which the response was,

'I'm not worried about you, I'm worried that I might get lost trying to get out of this bloody fortress. Sorry, Luca.'

The door closed behind him, leaving Messi and Hart alone.

'Tell me, Luca, how could my phone have been bugged?'

'It would have had to have been out of your possession for a period of time. Can you think of such a time?'

'No, I never leave it anywhere.'

'Think hard. Go back some days, or even some weeks. Think.'

'No, definitely, I'm sure. My mobile phone has never been out of my poss— wait one minute.'

Hart cast his mind back to his recent trip to Greifswald. Yes! The security guard there had taken his phone away from him while Frau Arben grilled him. That must be it. He excitedly related the story to Messi.

'Yes, and then there was a second brief time when Arben and friend took it once again when they caught me in the hospitality suite at the Sheraton in Padua! Sorry, Luca, I'm going insane. I completely forgot.'

'No problem, but that is excellent, I knew you would eventually remember something; it just had to be. You were bugged back in Germany and it was probably re-checked in Padua.'

'Fuck them! Fuck the lot of them!'

'Please, Max *calma*, calm down. You are playing a game against experts and this at least certainly proves that. We will take some more excellent wine now whilst dinner is prepared, over which we will decide how to proceed in the most perfect way. I will furnish you with more information that I have and we can discuss how best to put an end to all of this. *Bene?*'

'*Bene, grazie*, Luca.'

Chapter 77

Robert Halle sat at the desk in the small office area of his suite at the Sheraton Hotel, Padua, and punched out the mobile phone number of Claudia Volpe using his own phone. It had been some days now since their meeting and he was keen to receive an update from her on various outstanding items on his agenda, particularly those relating to Hart. The very thought of the man immediately raised his temperature several degrees and even now as the call rang out he was angrily drumming his fingers on the teak desk surface.

In one way, he now somewhat regretted the death sentence he had issued on him via the offices of Claudia's Sicilian "business associates". Since Frau Arben had confirmed that Hart had probably had access to sensitive details relating to their research plans and business activities whilst confined in the GRS/World hospitality suite, he had decided that it would have been of greater benefit to interrogate Hart thoroughly before disposing of him, with the purpose of discovering his affiliations, how much he actually knew of the plans and most importantly how much of his acquired knowledge he had passed on. It irritated him that his utter loathing of Hart had so over-ridden his own personal more sensible and logical thought processes. Without even knowing it, Hart had become Halle's Achilles' heel.

The call was picked up almost immediately, giving him no time to sip the water from the crystal glass he was in the process of raising to his taught lips.

'*Pronto,* Claudia. Claudia, its Robert here. I'm calling you for updates if you please. I need to call Alberto later today and try and put his mind at rest that things are progressing satisfactorily, although as you know satisfactorily is never enough for him. He seems nervous and if *he's* nervous, then I'm bloody terrified!'

'So then, let's start with Hart. How did it go? I presume he is dead by now and I am supposing that there is no way of connecting any part of his demise to ourselves?'

There was a pause on the line.

'Hello, Claudia are you still there?'

There was a second brief pause and then,

'*Si*, Robert, I am here, I'm sorry but the line is not good. Have you not seen the newspapers, Robert?'

'What? Of course I haven't. You know I don't speak or read any Italian. Tell me, Claudia, what should I have read?' his voice had risen in volume as further irritation crept in.

'There is no easy way to say this, Robert, but the likelihood is that my men have failed. I do not know exactly what happened, but their bodies were

269

discovered by railway workers this morning along the side of the railroad line about half way between Padua and Milan. There was no sign of any other body and although a body may turn up later, for now we have to assume that Hart is still alive.'

'Damn! I can't believe it. Hart is no fighter. He is basically a coward and I cannot see how he could possibly succumb to two expert assassins. Who did you send for God's sake, a couple of geriatric grandmothers? But he might still be dead, yes? It might just be that his body has not yet been discovered?'

'I am so sorry, Robert. He could be dead, but by now I think it is unlikely to be the case. The newspaper edition which carried the story was an early edition and only able to provide a short paragraph, apart from the glaring headline, but there was no mention of any other body and I have been scanning all subsequent news bulletins both on television news channels and on-line news agencies. There may be more in the later editions perhaps.'

Volpe heard the crash as Halle's fist hit the desktop, sending the crystal drinking glass down onto the marbled floor where it shattered.

'God, this is total incompetence, Claudia! Any suspicious thoughts Hart may have toyed with before this will now have certainly been irrefutably confirmed to him. He's many, many things, but he's certainly not stupid. The man's a veritable physical weakling, a chicken. One single blow should have been all that was necessary to terminate his pathetic life, but for two so-called professional experts to fail, and what's more die in the process, is utterly beyond belief. It is most important that we apprehend him as soon as possible! Do you hear?'

During his outburst, in which his voice doubled in volume and increased in pitch by almost one octave, it totally escaped Halle that his previous observation that his loathing of Hart was over-riding his rationale thinking, was being fully played out now to Volpe.

'I already have men in Milan, Robert. They are checking the Central Station where they will be with copies of his photograph. They will also check all the major hotels there. I know there are many hotels, but I have put many men on the ground. My men are circulating his photograph within our Milanese contacts on the streets and are offering a reward for suitable information on him. Milan is a big city, but if he is there, I am confident that we will find him. We also have men at Linate, Malpensa and Bergamo airports and at the larger bus stations and also at the other Milan train stations. The noose is very tight and for sure as a stranger to Milan we will have him very soon. We also have men at the dogane, the customs points, if he tries to drive out of Italy, as well as people on lookout at key autostrade toll booths if he is aiming to travel elsewhere in Italy by car.'

'Very well. What surprises me though is that he will certainly need help from somebody, somewhere, which means he will have to make at least one phone call. We have his phone bugged, but so far there has been not a squeak from him. It seems that we have been totally unable to track him. He may be re-charging his phone of course, but we must have a person in attendance listening in at all times, looking for him to make that call which will bring us down upon him. Now though, there is a change, Claudia, I want him taken alive if at all possible.

There is information we need to obtain from him before we dispose of him and I would very much like to be present if possible. Got that? I want to be there!'

'*Si, si*, I will undertake the interrogation myself when we have him, but I will ensure that you are summoned to be there also. I do want you to appreciate though just how many people we have on the ground in our hunt for Hart at the moment. Be assured that we are treating this matter very seriously indeed.'

'Yes, yes I get it, and so you should. Now then what about the conference? Was he attending it with anybody else do you know?'

'We have checked and it seems that he arrived with a woman from a UK university, but she is for sure a scientist and very interested in the presentations and exhibitions rather than anything else, and we are sure that her presence at the meeting was purely for scientific interest. It does seem that they had almost no contact with each other during the meeting.'

'Nevertheless, I want her checked out again. If as you surmise, she is not connected to Hart in his activities fine, we will leave her alone, but if she is connected, then she must also be disposed of, but intelligently, Claudia. Too many bodies will eventually draw too much attention to us. I want you to call me every two hours, if only for two minutes at a time, until this is resolved. You have no further room for failure here, Claudia, you are aware that far too much is at stake at many different levels. You know what I mean. Now go and come back to me next time with something positive to report. Please!'

'I understand all you say very well. Don't worry, I will not fail the cause.'

Halle ended the call with no farewells. As the thorn in his side, Hart, was getting deeper and deeper. Halle had a full agenda of internationally important issues to worry about, but at this moment his only issue was Hart who he wanted *really* badly! He wanted him captured and then interrogated as painfully as possible, for which Volpe would do the job admirably, and then he wanted him dead at his feet.

Sitting alone in Padua, Volpe was incensed. Halle had no real idea of what her position was in Sicily and also beyond there in other parts of Italy. He was only aware of titles and not what the titles actually meant to the more knowledgeable people...such as the whole of the Italian population! She was the *Capa di tutti Capi* for God's sake, a position that garnered huge respect and often fear from both her own mafia people and from the community at large, especially in Sicily. Halle had no right to talk to her in that way and she was really pissed about it! However, because of her very profitable association with World Pharmaceuticals, it was necessary for her to remain diplomatic with the Philistine Halle...for now at least, but her time would come!

Chapter 78

Dinner was set out on a glass-topped table in a part of the room that had been in partial darkness earlier. The hooded brother swiftly and efficiently laid out the table with cutlery, condiments, crockery and fresh wine and water glasses and then, when Hart and Messi were seated, proceeded to deliver the courses of food.

Hart was relaxed in Messi's company, bearing in mind the traumas he had endured of late and Messi too enjoyed Hart's presence, even if his conversation was occasionally a little blue or risqué.

The glorious grilled sliced vegetables with a liberal dressing of a wonderful olive oil that were the antipasti were helped on their way by a delicious white wine, an Ancilla Lugana. The main course, or *secondo piatto*, was shin and hind shank of veal prepared as osso bucco, served in a sofrito sauce with yellow saffron rice on the side, and accompanied by a full-bodied Barolo red wine. A simple vanilla gelato ended the most wonderful Michelin standard meal, cheeses having been refused before the arrival of the ice cream.

Few words were spoken during the meal other than 'wonderful', 'excellent', 'perfect' and 'simply the best', plus a dozen other superlatives, but finally Hart lay down his cutlery and looked at Messi purposefully.

'You know, Luca, I have come here to this place, your…shall we call it "office"?…with no knowledge of who you are and what body you work for and represent, other than its name. In fact, I know absolutely nothing about you. I do this of course because of the intercession of my very good friend and ex-colleague Gianni Bossi and your shared friend and because after the events of the last days and weeks I am traumatised, with no idea of what I am really involved in, what I should expect next, or what I might do to rid myself of this terrible "sword of Damocles" hanging over my head. For sure, a good many people would like that sword to do its worst to me. The bottom line is that I am here with absolutely no idea where I should go next and I seem to be, therefore, totally at your disposal.'

Messi looked back at him, his face clouded in seriousness.

'Max, let us leave the table and take the seats by the fireside. There is so much I need to say to you still.'

As Hart looked on, Messi placed both palms on the fragile-looking glass table and pushed downwards very hard. His legs did work in unison with his arms, however, and he successfully struggled into an upright position. Hart was relieved, as for one dreadful moment as Messi had applied his lifting pressure to the table, the glass bowed and Hart fully expected Messi to go crashing through it, but he was saved as his stubby legs took on the major part of the load.

He must do this death-defying exercise every day when he's here, he thought.

Messi waddled, penguin-like, to one of the fireside armchairs and crashed down into it. The springs groaned, complaining at their abuse once again. Hart, rather more elegantly, took a similar chair facing him.

'Where shall we start, Luca?'

'Well, first of all, I have to tell you that the table is toughened plate glass. OK?'

Both men laughed knowingly.

'Let me start then, Max. I don't expect you to know anything at all about my employers, The Office of Catholic Affairs, the OCA?'

'Correct, I've never heard of them before, unless it's for the procurement of questionable ladies for such as the brothers here, but I'm sure that that idea is wide of the mark?'

'Ah, I was warned about your humour. It's a nice guess but no it is not for that function. It's a long story, but I will try and be as brief as possible. As this may take some time, I have taken the liberty of ordering a little more wine for us.'

As if on cue, the heavy door swung open and the old monk returned with a bottle, two new glasses and a corkscrew, which he laid on a small table at the side of Messi's chair. Whilst Messi fiddled with the bottle seal and cap, the monk quickly cleared and wiped the table they had taken dinner on leaving the room at the instant Messi finally pulled the cork from the bottle.

'We continue with the Brunello I think. OK, I will tell you everything, but then of course once you know everything, I will have to kill you myself. Ha, ha, ha.'

He laughed until tears rolled down his flabby face.

'Nice one. I'll risk it, go on.'

Messi dabbed his eyes dry with a huge handkerchief which he returned to his jacket pocket, and re-arranging his posture for greater comfort proceeded with his explanation.

'So then, the Catholic Church is, no has always been in fact, a very big business organisation, not only in religious affairs but also in... *"business business"*, if you follow me.'

Hart nodded.

'These business interests are global and massive and you can imagine the incredible sums of money which are channelled down one path or another every day on behalf of the church. To help deal with all this, we have a massive system of banking matrices which makes all of this, at least a little, manageable. We are only human, however, and occasionally there are those within the organisation whose hearts are not quite as pure as they should be and at times large sums of money have been misappropriated by these miscreants. This is one area where the OCA is called upon to act. Of course in severe cases historically, it has been known that the mafia, together with certain members of our own church have maintained an...un-natural alliance and once again the OCA have been called in. It would be true to say that we are a semi-secret organisation on a kind of par with the Secret Service of the USA, or MI6 in the UK, but our main areas of activity are mainly ecclesiastical, with some politics thrown in and sometimes also some commercial issues when appropriate.

I give you the example of Vatican banker Roberto Calvi, "God's Banker", who in 1982 was found hanging under Blackfriar's Bridge in London, with bricks in his pockets and $15,000 US in his wallet. Not long before, there had been a huge scandal when the Bank of Ambrosiano went bankrupt.'

There was a flicker of recognition of the story in Hart's eyes.

'Ah yes of course, I remember now. There was potentially a huge scandal involving the mafia, the Vatican and God knows who else.'

'Yes you have it, in fact freemasonry was also involved. The Office of Catholic Affairs looked long and hard at that time into the involvement of the Vatican in that business and although it was made clear that the Vatican had no legal responsibility for the bank's downfall, following our investigation the Vatican acknowledged that they had had a "moral involvement" and paid $241 million US to creditors.'

Hart let out a silent whistle.

'I did wonder if the OCA existed to cover up scandals involving the Catholic Church but I would have been totally wrong. It sounds like the OCA certainly operated in a fair, balanced and impartial way, in that affair at least. Impressive.'

'Justo. Yes indeed, Max. Do you think for one moment that the Vatican would have offered such a high level of compensation had we not actually demonstrated their "moral involvement"? There are many other ways in which our OCA group now works in almost an internal self-policing role, which will become more apparent as I go on.'

'Hang on. You're surely not intimating that the Vatican and the mafia have worked hand in glove at times over the years?'

'To take some understanding of that, you have to understand the very nature of Italy, and it is not always easy for people from outside our country to do that. A school lesson for you I'm afraid.

'The whole of la bella Italia is a mixed bag of contradictions. For example, we are a very religious country, we are of course the seat of the Catholic Church, but in politics, we often elect godless communist politicians to high order. Fascists as well. We are very religious but we have the most beautiful prostitutes in the world. Prostitutes, who ply their trade openly in public areas. Many of these are also transgender, or part thereof, so the menu on offer can be very varied I am told. Sunday is the day for our people to go to church, but Sunday is also the day for Italy's third love, after the love of love and the love of cars, we have the love of football, when once again historic battles are fought out, but this time on the football field. It is these divergences that make Italia, Italia. Ah I say again, la bella Italia! I talked of the mafia earlier, so you are aware now that there has always been a firm connection between the church and the mafia, and not always for bad reasons, for often it has been a good connection.'

'You know these are completely new considerations for me.'

'Let me move on with my lesson. Now you probably believe that the Pope must be a man. There is one shocking secret that is still obscured by rival accounts and theories and that involves the existence of a female Pope. Pope

Joan was elected into office in the 1100s, as a very talented woman but dressed as a man. It was only after giving birth prematurely to a son after riding out on horseback that the subterfuge was exposed, after which she was tied to the tail of a horse and dragged through Rome before being stoned to death by a mob. The OCA was alive in those times and did much to keep as much scandal as possible from the public gaze. Obviously not preventing the stoning to death of a female Pope by that very same public has to go down as our complete failure.'

'Your church sounds like a great club to be in, but a shit to get out of. Remind me not to join, Luca. Now then, it's getting late and I'm starting to tire and to be perfectly honest I'm not sure where the conversation is leading other than giving me a history lesson and I really do want some resolution or at least some ideas of how to resolve this very dangerous hornet's nest, which I think I am responsible for stirring up. So please Luca...'

He spread his arms pleadingly.

'Please, Max, bear with me, it is very complicated but I promise you I am getting there and believe me, my friend, the wait will be worth it.'

Hart rolled his eyes towards the ceiling. 'Carry on then, but please cut out the history lesson.'

'Thank you, but when I am done you will surely realise how important the history lesson was. I carry on then. There have been many occasions over the years when things have come to the attention of the public that the OCA has been involved in working within the body of the church, but all the work done has been in secret, one reason being that of public confidence, for were the many OCA outcomes made public the vast number of people who depend upon the church for moral and spiritual guidance and support would be desolated.'

'Are you saying then that effectively, what comes to the public's attention through newspapers, television and other media sources is just the tip of the iceberg?'

'Absolutely. It is not the tip though, it's the tip of the tip of the tip! Probably the most thought provoking event that the OCA have been involved in within the last thirty or so years was the death of Pope John Paul I, who died just 33 days after he came into office. He was known as the smiling Pope. He read the Readers Digest and retired to bed regularly at 9.00 pm. There have been many great conspiracy theories concerning his death and a popular one is that he was murdered via a conspiracy between bishops and cardinals in the Vatican who were in league with the freemasons. Once again, the Vatican Bank was the central focus of the scandal and accusations. It has been said that he was about to go public on his knowledge of the corruption in the bank, but additionally the rumour was that he was about to give papal permission for the use of birth control amongst the Catholic congregations. It was said that his early morning coffee was poisoned... It was also said that Vatican officials lied about the circumstances of the death to avoid admitting that it was a nun who took the Pope his coffee in bed every morning.'

'There you are then, breakfast in bed...a capital offence if ever there was one!'

Messi continued unabashed.

'The OCA was extremely active with that incident and the real truth of the matter was that John Paul I actually died of an untreated embolism. There is one other, yes this is the last one in my presentation, much publicised incident I want to tell you about and this one brings us back to the present in that I believe it to be possibly related to our current situation. However, it is important that I place everything in the correct order so you can best follow and understand it, but for that I need you to go first through your own summary list of knowledge and events, but briefly eh.'

'At last! God really does move in mysterious ways!'

Messi smiled. He liked Hart and could even put up with his strange sense of humour. Was this really the great sense of humour that the English were famous for? Surely not?

He sat back, his hands now clasped over his huge stomach and closed his eyes in semi-meditation. Hart reeled off his list, counting each item by raising a different finger of his hands:

'One. You are Luca Messi and you belong to the Office of Catholic Affairs, a semi-secret organisation within the Catholic Church.

Two. It is a self-monitoring, self-regulating organisation within the Catholic Church, but is also responsible for the investigation of internal serious events and possible scandals.

'Three. It seems that there are close relationships, or at least there have been in the past, between the church, the mafia and freemasonry.'

Messi nodded his agreement, but added,

'But relationships still exist. It is not purely historical. Carry on, please.'

'Four. I will now talk about my own activities. Following contacts of a personal nature in the UK, I am following up on what I believe to be an illegal trade in stem cell materials. To be brutally honest, stem cells from illegally aborted foetuses.

'Five. Mine is a personal quest. I am not linked to any official department in any country.

'Six. I have traced a link in the harvesting and subsequent passing of stem cell material from England, to Germany, to Sicily.

'Seven. The laboratory involved in Germany is the Gerhard Roscher Schmoller Institute in Greifswald under the auspices of Bettina Arben.

'Eight. In Sicily, the laboratory involved is that of a company called Vita Pharma, based in Basiglio, but il Laboratorio di Scoperta Fondamentale, may also be involved.

'Nine. In Padua, I learned via documents seen and copied and a meeting listened in on, that World Pharma is up to its eyes in this illegal trade. In Padua later, a call to my former secretary at World confirmed that World Pharmaceuticals acquired GRS, Vita Pharm and il Laboratorio di Scoperta quite a while ago. This means that World Pharma is running the whole damn show!

'Ten. I also learned in Padua that this is now a global business with a large emphasis on Africa.

'Eleven. I've run out of fingers, but I established in Padua that a lead player in the trade and acquisition of stem cells for research is Robert Halle, a senior member of the World Clinical Development Departments.

'Twelve. I also learned in Padua that as well as international physicians being recruited to the cause, part at least of the Sicilian mafia are involved via Claudia Volpe, alias the "Fox", or is the "Red Fox"?

'Thirteen. It is being intimated to me by a member of the OCA that there is also Vatican involvement somewhere along the line, but for what reason remains unknown. Information yet to be received from Luca Messi!

'Fourteen. I've obviously pissed off these people who now want me dead and who have failed in at least one attempt using the mafia, on the Padua to Milan train.

'Oh yes, fifteen. I have photographed Robert Halle in conversation with a ranking Vatican priest in a hotel in Padua, on whom I now want further information from Luca Messi.

'So that's my story update in summary. I would really now like to know the following things:

'What is the relevance of the priest who I saw with Halle?

'Why are the Vatican involved? Surely not for money?

'What are the connections between World Pharma, the mafia and the Vatican?'

Hart nodded to Messi indicating that he had come to the end of his lists.

Messi nodded back appreciatively.

'Thank you, Max, now let's see if I can fill in some of those blanks for you. You certainly have a good snapshot of things as they are at present. I will now try and give you the bigger picture, although I too still have blanks, but it will involve a little history again I'm afraid.'

'Ughh!'

'You are right, Max, when you say that there is a lot more at stake than money. Every organisation you have mentioned has an individual stake in, or benefits from, bringing about the objectives of this business, but all also want success for *the whole* from the main plan…if that makes sense? Let me begin by answering your question as to who was the priest that your friend Halle was having tea with in Padua. His name is Francesco Negri and his is no ordinary priest.'

'You surprise me!'

'You will not have heard of him before. He is a cardinal in the Vatican and probably the single most important cardinal in the whole of the college. "College", by the way is the collective noun for a group of cardinals, especially those in the Vatican. Why so important? Because he is at the Pope's right hand. He is the one person who in all of this world is the closest to the Pontiff. He is Italian of course and holds the position of Prefect of the Congregation of Bishops, which enables him to advise the Pope on Episcopal appointments throughout the world. He has had a very successful career so far, although seventy years old now, and is currently deputy to the Secretary of State. This may not mean much to you, but his position gives him a key role as the Pope's chief of staff. As a successful career diplomat, he is a workaholic and a very determined person, famous for persevering with any cause he believes in until he comes out finally on top. Some say that he could well be the next Pope, but the general theory is that he prefers to work…behind the throne…'

'Pulling the strings,' Hart completed the sentence for him. 'I've known people like this in my own profession you know. People who are not prepared to take on the lead role, such as principal or chairperson, but who prefer to work in the wings, one reason being that if things turn pear-shaped they do not assume responsibility for it. I call these people the "Chairs of Hind-sight Committees".'

'*Justo*, exactly. Umm, I like that phrase. I must make a note of it.'

'But why would he be prepared to place his position at risk by being seen consorting with members of the mafia, or by being possibly involved with pharmaceutical programs considered to be of a dubious ethical nature by the church?'

Messi laughed out loud. 'Ahhh, the naivety, I love it. Listen to me. In Basiglio in Sicily, if we go back a generation or three we have three famous groups. Many members of the groups were friends from birth and close throughout their time of growing up. In that period, all of them often assisted the local poor people a great deal in many different ways, and I can tell you that there were indeed very many different ways. These famous groups represented the church, the mafia and there was way back also an entrepreneurial family that was also closely involved. Local families within these groups, whilst working for the poor, were also very close to each other, although their sources of help were very different.

The entrepreneurial family started out making medicines from local herbal remedies, which they made freely available to the poor and as time went on the family expanded and developed a very successful business throughout the region and later far beyond, whilst also becoming extremely wealthy.'

'Don't tell me it was the Mondo family?' asked a slightly incredulous Hart.

'*Si, si*, it was the Mondo family. They initially became very rich as a result of manufacturing products that they supplied to the armed forces during various wars, before they expanded far afield landing eventually in America, as you will now guess becoming super-rich in the process. The thing to understand, Max, is that all three of these families are as a single family, in fact an "unholy Trinity".

Francesco, or Franco, Negri is one of the Negri family who were very close to the Mondo's in friendship and activities. They were a family from which came many sons at different generation levels, many of who became priests of different levels of seniority. So then at our own generation level, or a little before, we have Alberto Mondo, Francesco Negri and the Mafioso father and brothers of Claudia Volpe, all of them very close friends.'

'Incredible!'

'No Max, quite normal in many parts of my country. Remember this is Italy, not some genteel Northern European society. There has always been closeness between the church and the mafia, especially in Sicily, where, as close friends they worked together for the good of the poor, but the thought that the mafia is some kind of Robin Hood organisation is a myth that should be discouraged.

They are criminal organisations regulated by unwritten iron-hard, often brutal, and inexorable rules. You know the mafia is one of the world's most enduring criminal organisations and one of the most serious problems confronting Sicily today…despite the Robin Hood effect! The group have murdered judges and also priests, despite the Negri connection, and worst of all even children, but the bond between our beautiful friend, the Fox's mafia group and the church remains solid. Before the murders which eventually placed the Fox at the Head of the group, the ruling council, or Cupola, was led by the Fox's father Alfonso Volpe whose nickname coincidentally was actually "the Pope"!'

Hart nodded. 'I see the tight connection between church, mafia and Mondo, but how the hell does this square with stem cell research? Surely this is a huge no-go area for Catholicism? And by the way, please don't tell me that Robert Halle has some Italian linked mafia ancestry or I will go crazy!'

'No, Halle is not connected in that way. But as for your other comment you are correct. The Vatican has stressed time and time again that it considers all research using stem cells from human embryos to be morally unacceptable. The Pope himself has spoken at length about this, even making direct approaches to the President of the United States. The taking of innocent human lives, including the killing of human embryos, even if carried out to help extend and improve the lives of others is absolutely unacceptable in the eyes of the church.'

'But you must realise that the huge potential for stem cells is tremendous, surely? Thousands of suffering people could be helped.'

'Yes, I do realise and I sympathise with those sick people, but you know Max at the end of the day I am a Catholic. I work for the church and I have a personal faith which must follow the current doctrine of the Vatican that "in the living resurrection of the Lord lies the greatest most effective remedy against these ills."'

'In that case you'd better put up with that headache until the second coming, Luca, there's no point in pissing off the Vatican by taking an aspirin! Sorry, I take that back, it was totally insensitive of me. I should respect your views, but as a scientist, I find it difficult to deny the obvious.'

'Apology accepted and the reason for your comment understood, but not all the Vatican believe in the "resurrection ideal". Within the Vatican are modernisers who would make great changes to the basic concepts and beliefs of our church if the possibilities were there. It is possible that those possibilities will arrive with the eventual choosing of a new Pope, which may not be so great a distance into the future. In these constantly changing times, it is likely that the next Pope will be quite different to our present Pontiff, in terms of personality, ethnicity and style, and it is likely that he will respond positively to these changes in philosophies. I cannot predict what the next Pope will be like…other than that it will not be a woman of course!'

'No, you missed your chance for that back in the 1100s when you allowed Pope Joan to be stoned to death. I still can't grasp what the link is between all these things though. What brings these opposites together other than for dirty money?'

'Well, money is certainly one thing. As you have said earlier, we are talking of billions of dollars, in fact billions of all currencies. Another, less spoken of thing, is very controversial. It belongs in the "conspiracy theory" drawer I would say for a majority of people, but for myself and also my organisation it is a concept that begins to ring more and more true and you will not be surprised to hear that it concerns the Vatican. Not necessarily, the Pope our leader of course, but other powerful forces within, linking with those without.'

'The more I hear, Luca, the more I realise just how small I am in this business, no microscopic, and how particularly insignificant I am when it comes to folk having me swatted as if I am an insect pest; however, I'm obviously a good deal more significant to them when it comes to the actual reasons that they want me dead. It makes me feel that even though I don't entirely know why, I must be rocking their boat considerably and I find that both terrifying and frustrating.'

'Let me add some more details, Max. Again I apologise, but a little more of our history is necessary. It is more recent history this time however. I have already spoken of "the Smiling Pope", Pope John Paul I, and his untimely death 33 days after taking office. Well, around that time after his death, the Vatican were desperate to regain some kind of order, more discipline, a more organised way of life kind of thing, or to at least elect a Pope who could survive for longer than a single season!'

He smiled at his own joke.

John Paul had suffered incredibly with Parkinson's disease and some say that it was a miracle in any case, whatever the outcome, that he had even lived as long as he did. In that short time and for some time before his election, he was actually able to contribute so much to the church and its future direction. You will remember that when he died, he was succeeded in fairly rapid succession by first one and then another new Pope, neither of whom had even the longevity of the "Smiling Pope" with the result that we were back in this quick turnover situation again. When our present Pontiff was elected, it really was an incredible event. Can you imagine…the first Black Pope!'

'Yes, I remember it was quite a sensation. It was obviously a lot harder to elect a Black Pope than a female one that is for sure!'

'*Si, si*, sensational is the right word. There was great excitement that this new black Pope…by the way I must correct myself here. He is not the first Black Pope. The first was Pope Gelasius I who ruled for four years from 492 to 496…'

Hart acknowledged the information. There was much to admire about Messi. He was clearly a devout man, and his depth of knowledge was absolutely incredible. Under different circumstances, Hart would very much enjoy dining out in his company, but the range of the food and quality of the wine would need to be on a much lower cost level if they were splitting the bill!

'Our current Pope was seen from the very outset as a man who could strengthen the appeal of the church in the third world, his own colour and ethnicity being an additional aide in that respect. He also had the unusual distinction of being baptised many years before by an Angolan priest, who he himself later beatified on the way to him being declared a saint. It has all worked very well, our support in the third world growing and growing year on year.'

'Hang on. World have poured a lot of money into Africa, but I would expect that their profits there have far outstripped their investments, so what links are at work there if any, between the church and pharma?'

Messi smiled. Hart was getting it.

'There are many more links than you could imagine. Our Pope actually comes originally from the very area where World have their main operations and African base in Angola. It was pressure from our Pope which swayed the local African government to accept World, where previously they had rejected all advances from other pharma companies. We weave a very twisted web, no? However, before the Pope felt that he could exert any pressure, no actually *advice* rather than pressure, I think, he felt it essential that he educated himself on all ranges of pharmaceutical activities and he really did examine in detail what a pharma company could add to the area. This Pope is such a good man, Max. Anyway, he received his in-depth education and much encouragement from a young man at the Vatican. In fact, it was a young cardinal who now sits at his right hand in many other things also, offering advice from a "younger" perspective. This excellent man is also silently sponsored by Negri, who clearly sees the good and the wisdom in him to the extent that many now believe that when the ailing Pope passes away, he will be a strong contender to replace him. He is young, he is well educated, he is very intelligent and he is a polyglot speaking English, Italian and French. By the way, it is essential for any Pope to speak Italian, as part of his title is Bishop of Rome. He is also very progressive in his views and attitudes to most things. His only drawback has been one of lack of experience, being comparatively very young, but as the Pope has recently recovered much of his former self from the ravages of Parkinson's disease, he has been somewhat of a mentor to this cardinal along with Negri. It seems that Parkinson's is the curse of the Catholic Church, but thankfully the Pontiff's slide into incapacity has apparently slowed of late. Either that or he is getting relief from symptoms by some form of placebo effect from schooling this younger man. If this man succeeds in impressing the Pope and the College of Cardinals over the next few years, I see no reason at all why, as Pope himself, he shouldn't lead the church for the next 30 or 40 Years.'

'It sounds like there's a Superman waiting in the wings.'

'You could be right, Max. The name of this cardinal, perhaps in waiting, is Pietro, or Peter. Cardinal Peter Mondo, the brother of your Alberto Mondo of World Pharmaceuticals!'

He finished with a flourish worthy of Agatha Christie's Hercule Poirot at the point of some incredible denouement.

Hart was speechless, totally taken aback. Eventually he was able to squeeze out a single word,

'Jesus'!

'Therefore, it now becomes clearer what the conspiracy theory I mentioned might be. It is that whilst the Pope's illness and symptoms have considerably improved over the last year, much against experts' prognoses, Pietro Mondo has flourished more and more. The conspiracy theory is that the Pope could have been kept not just alive, but in a significantly improved medical condition thanks to some new semi-wonder drug, a ground-breaking drug that is in fact being developed and produced by World Pharma.'

'Bloody hell, stem cells!'

Hart brought a hand down hard on the arm of the armchair.

'It *is* possible, but I can assure you that neither the Pope himself nor Peter Mondo are party to this and both are also completely unaware of this latest conspiracy theory. The Pope receives treatment by injection, but to his mind, and also I will probably add to the mind of his own personal physician, the treatment he is receiving is the standard therapy for Parkinson's. It seems that both the Pope and the cardinal are mere chess pieces on a huge chessboard with decisions and moves being contemplated well ahead of the game. There could be a new empire being planned around them completely without their knowledge, but remember, Max, this is only a theory.

'How can this be so though, the Catholic Church is absolutely against this type of therapy? It would be an incredible scandal that would not just rock the Church, it would send it spinning into orbit. What evidence is there that this is happening, rather than it being just a theory, Luca?'

'I have emphasised that *is* only a theory, Max. We do have a certain amount of evidence but it is mainly historical and circumstantial. The thing is we believe that it is likely that the current Pope is not the first Pontiff in recent years to receive treatment for a terminal illness which is deemed to be both unethical and sacrilegious. You may remember that back in 1998, two of the Swiss Guards and a woman were killed by gunshots within the Vatican City. The Swiss Guards, who by the way have been a presence at the Vatican for over 500 years and who are all sworn to lay down their lives for the Pope, were the commander of the guards Alois Estermann, his wife, and a young lance corporal, Cedric Tornay. This was a terrible bloodbath of a killing, but after only four hours and without any forensic investigation whatsoever, the Vatican announced that the 28 year-old Tornay had shot the couple and then turned the gun on himself in a "fit of madness". Later, more independent enquiries disclosed that the two men were in a sexual relationship with not just each other, but with the wife as well. Now we have believed, and we do have evidence to support this, that in fact one of this trio was linked to a larger group within the Vatican who were at that time actively involved in prolonging the life of the Pontiff using what have been labelled "unholy techniques" and when the other two discovered this, that is when the fight began. The two who had discovered the activities of the third had to be killed and it fitted the situation perfectly for the third member to be killed also, with the reasons given harmonising with their ménage a trois. We came across certain letters that confirmed our suspicions, together with certain treatment packs and syringes, but it was still not possible to prove things conclusively and conclusiveness is what is essential to us, because our mission is to protect the church and creating a totally unproven scandal through the actions of a small group of Vatican players would be absolutely counter-productive and counter to the status of the Church as the worldwide focus of all that is good. Can you understand our position in the business we have here right now, where we cannot proceed with any action at all unless we have 100% proof and our case is completely watertight, otherwise the very existence of the Catholic Church is in danger?'

'It sounds to me that it is impossible to obtain that 100% proof, and without that you and the OCA are not prepared to make a move, ergo the chain of misery goes on and people like me are disposed of with no chance of justice. Keep it quiet, brush it under the carpet and wait for it to go away. In the fullness of time, the Pope will die and Mondo will assume his mantle and all will be well. That is apart from myself, the people suffering the misery of losing an unborn foetus, others thinking suspiciously about unfolding events and most probably yourself, Luca, as an attempt has already been made on your life. What is needed is for the OCA to finally develop some balls, or do you and your colleagues believe Peter Mondo to be truly the best man for the job?'

'First, Max, we do have the balls to see this through. We do have a lot of circumstantial evidence that we want to convert into hard evidence. For example, we need the proof that Mondo is producing this treatment medication, that it is finding its way into the Vatican, and that it is there being given to the Pontiff. We also need to prove a relationship between Mondo, Negri our suspected Vatican link and also the Sicilian mafia. We do think that there is a way to do this…and this involves you, Max, but first let me answer your question as to whether I believe Pietro Mondo to be suitable as a "chosen one".

'My short answer is "yes I do". Not only has Pietro been groomed to perfection, it is important to realise that he is a fine upstanding cardinal in his own right and he is now so close to the Pope through the mentoring of Negri that his future is totally secure as our future leader. He *will* be the next Pope, but only if we fail to show the balls you mention. Because of the way that things have been organised and orchestrated he must never be the Pope, and that will be a tragedy. You see there is more than you know. Not only is he now the best contender for the papal position, he is the only contender for that post, for over the last four to six months certain other cardinals, usually in different countries, who would have possibly made the short-list for Pope have been systematically assassinated.'

Each time Hart thought he had reached his pinnacle of shock-ability, Messi came out with another example of some horror which set the bar even higher.

Messi continued, 'There is a long list now of tragedies that have recently befallen some of our finest, most loved, progressive young cardinals. A sudden heart attack here, a car crash there, a perfectly placed bullet in the head somewhere else and one future candidate even blown to pieces in a suddenly unmarked minefield. We have evidence of a carefully ordered, premeditated plan of assassinations. We actually have two assassins under lock and key and out of the public scrutiny until a proper complete case is in our hands.'

'This is all too fantastic. I cannot see for one moment how my own comparatively trivial existence can be allowed to continue in such a scheme. Persons desperately want me dead. How do we get out of this, Luca, and notice I include you too?'

'No! You are much more important than you can imagine. The information you hold, together with additional information that you may yet be able to obtain could very well bring the whole conspiracy crashing down, but you are correct in the respect that the knowledge you have makes it essential to them to ensure that you do not remain alive any longer than is absolutely necessary.'

'In other words, I'm a bloody dead man! I know little of these people, but what I do know is that they never rest until they get their man, for to borrow a quote from a "Harry Palmer movie", "their arm is long and their vengeance is total".'

Messi smiled politely, despite the capital punishment sentence that had just been passed on him by Hart and despite the fact that he hadn't a clue who Harry Palmer was or what Hart was actually talking about.

'We are not dead yet, Max and we now have an opportunity for the first time to go on the attack. In fact, it's our first and *only* chance. We cannot spend the rest of our lives in hiding, even in a beautiful place such as this. To do this though Max, as I hinted at before, we need your help.'

'Just pass me that cloak of invisibility and I will go wherever and do whatever, but without it I will be dead in hours and certainly I cannot live at the North Pole either for the rest of my life in order to escape their wrath. I would never be able to look at Santa's Little Helpers again without being suspicious. Which one of them was carrying the *real* gun?'

'We need more wine to finalise our difficult discussions I think. You joke, at least I think you joke, and sometimes I don't understand all of what you are talking about, but remember that even at the North Pole you must expect there to be mafia connections,' smiled Messi.

Within seconds, the door opened and the monk brought in another bottle of Brunello, which Messi uncapped and removed the cork from. A long sniff of the cork, a smile and a nod of appreciation and he poured the wine into their glasses.

Hart was a little bemused. Each time Messi had mentioned a bottle of wine, the monk had appeared from nowhere with a fresh bottle.

How did he do that? Perhaps he had a remote signalling button, with the wine bringer standing continually by on emergency wine call perhaps?

In any case the service was impressive. Hart had hoped that Messi would have been able to produce an easy solution to his predicament, but all he had done was to complicate matters immeasurably and suggest that the solution involved more, presumably dangerous, work for himself.

Chapter 79

Victoria Crosse was extremely worried, worried and scared. She was worried over the whereabouts of Hart, who she hadn't seen or heard from in days, and she was scared for her own safety. She had done what the men from Special Branch had recommended and was duly staying at an old friend's weekend retreat, stuck in a remote cottage in the wilds of North Yorkshire. Apart from a call to her place of work in order to cover her absence, due to some bug, she had spoken to no one. Her only touch with civilisation was her visit to a supermarket to stock up with food supplies on her way up from Nottingham.

She had expected at least one call from Hart, if only to put her mind at rest, even though Special Branch had told her that he was OK and would not be telephoning her. They had returned her own phone to her but there was no mobile signal at the cottage so she couldn't phone out or receive calls anyway.

Stupid! So he couldn't call me even if he wanted to. He may have tried already and be sitting pretty somewhere by now. God, this place really is remote!

Another downside was that there was also no television reception, so no news of the outside world other than via a resident crackly old radio.

Finally, her nerves got the better of her and she took a drive to a small hamlet some five miles away where there was a landline telephone box, and dialled Denis. The call was answered almost immediately.

'Hello?'

'Denis, its Vicky.'

'Vicky, how are things? Have you heard from Max yet?'

'To be honest, Denis, things are pretty shit! I'm on my own, miles from anywhere in a cottage with no TV or phone signal and I've not heard from Max since I left him in Italy, but then the chaps from Special Branch told me not to expect him to call...even if there was a signal. Knowing what a rule breaker he is, I did expect some contact though. I'm being irrational I guess.'

'I'm sure he'll be fine, Vicky. The last I heard from Special Branch he was being looked after by some high-ranking official in the Italian Catholic Affairs Office, or some such department, so we should expect him to be living high on the hog somewhere in Italy while things are sorted out I would think.'

'So Denis, what are you up to now? What is the current state of play?'

'No change really from our last conversation. I've handed all the documents we have, along with a summary of our thoughts, to the UK government agency, who in turn have updated their various contacts in the USA and Italy and God knows where else. I've been told to take a break from sleuthing and to let the authorities take it on from here.'

'And do you believe that they totally believe our story and will give it their full attention and efforts?'

'Yes, I actually do, Vicky. The guys I spoke with were very impressive and certainly convinced me that something positive would come out of all of this. Anyway, I actually scanned in all the important documents so we at least have electronic copies of much of the stuff, just in case.'

'Excellent! That's all quite reassuring. I can go back to the wilderness now with much more confidence. Thanks Denis.'

Where the bloody hell is Hart!

The same question was being asked some 1,000 miles away from Crosse's Yorkshire hideaway, in Italy's Padua. This time the questioner was Robert Halle and the person receiving the "hair dryer treatment" over the telephone once again was Claudia Volpe.

'Robert, we are trying our best to locate him, but he seems to be invisible. I am confident we will pick him up soon though, he cannot hide away forever.'

'You'd better believe that, Claudia. I'm returning to the US any day soon and I want to see Hart face to face for his final farewell before I leave. Got it?'

'Yes of course Robert we—'

He slammed down the hotel telephone cutting her off in mid-sentence, brushed his hair back with a hand and straightened his tie. He still had a particular image to project to the outside world even though things were not currently proceeding in his favour.

Claudia Volpe was left high and dry on her phone again, with the call with Halle prematurely terminated by him. She'd had enough of Halle. Tomorrow she would return to Basiglio and continue to orchestrate the hunt for Hart from home.

Chapter 80

'Luca, can we press on again please?'

'Yes of course. So then, what additional information do we need to support our evidence? Well, for one thing, we need to show that the refined stem cell drug is being passed from Vita Pharma in Basiglio to the Vatican, where a person such as the Pope's personal physician Doctor Luigi Agnelli is receiving and treating the Pontiff with it. I don't really think that Agnelli is our man though, it could be Negri himself or more likely some physician we are yet to discover.'

'Why not just open or scan all the Vatican mail? It will be clear where the package is from and in any case the drug will have to be transported in dry ice, which should be a really obvious giveaway?'

'Because once we have opened our first package, which will probably fail to discover anything anyway, we will have completely blown our intentions and also our cover. We currently have the benefit that our knowledge of their intentions is a well-kept secret from them. It is in fact our own "secret weapon". They know that you personally probably have a good idea of what is happening regarding the stem cells, but there is no way they can assume that you are aware of their grand conspiracy, which they have already begun to unfold!

'We are now sure that the "medicine" *is* being picked up and delivered by courier all the way from Vita Pharma to the Vatican. In fact, the courier used is one of the local businesses owned and run by *Signorina* Volpe and friends. One idea is that we station a series of official roadblocks on days when we believe the transport to be taking place. We have had the whole of the World complex in Basiglio, and that includes Vita, under careful undercover observation since we received your information and hope to quickly narrow down the days and times when the courier leaves the laboratories for the port of Messina. We plan to hold roadblocks and search their vans under the pretext of looking for certain escaping criminals for example. We are yet to confirm the final plans for this but we will do this for all transport on the Messina road, cars included, in order to complete the illusion. Messina is the ferry port from where the boats go to Reggio di Calabria, a short stone's throw away, and from there any packages in transport using the ferry would then be driven on to Rome and the Vatican. There are alternative routes from Messina of course, via Salerno or Napoli for example, but our most recent intelligence has confirmed that Reggio is their most likely their route of choice. It is also the quickest route, other than by air.

We will search the vehicle, find the packages and place an unobtrusive electronic tracker on them. As you observed, the medicine will need to be stored at an optimum low temperature and this will help our search. Once identified,

287

we leave the packages in place and follow the vehicle. Using the trackers, it should be no problem finding them when they arrive at the appropriate place in the Vatican. What do you think?'

'Honestly? Not a lot. Don't you think it's a bit of a thin story? I mean will your men really look the part? Will the courier really believe that they are actually policemen looking for a fugitive and do you really believe that they will be able to identify the packages correctly and place your tracking devices on them?'

'Yes and no. Yes: Our men will have the correct uniforms and official paperwork to show to the drivers before doing any search. All will be done as for the real thing. The problem is that we cannot use local policemen as there is very little secrecy between police and mafia in the area, the flow of information between the two groups being constant. We will have to bring in fresh faces from another region off the island and only inform the most trusted senior island police officials of the action. They will ensure that our men go undisturbed with no interference from the local police. No, we cannot guarantee that they will be able to identify correctly the medicine package and if that is the case the whole operation will fail. Therefore, we need someone to be part of the squad, looking like a policeman, but an expert in identifying the goods. We also need an expert to first update the small team of OCA agents we have in Sicily with details of how the stem cells procurement is being made outside of Italy and how they are dealt with in Germany before arriving at Vita Pharma. This will give the greater sense of importance and seriousness to the operation…and a translator will be available at all times.'

'Whoa, hang on, I bloody knew it, you expect me to be this so-called expert dressed as an Italian policeman, yes? You're bloody crazy. Take a look at my pale, wan face, fair hair and blue eyes. Do I for one minute look Italian? The answer is a big fat no, Luca!'

'One thing to remember, Max, the natives of Sicily are not typically Italian looking. Back in history, the island was invaded by the Vikings as well as other northern European races and as a result there are many tall, blond, blue-eyed true Sicilians living on the island. Really! I have already said that the network between church, mafia and Mondos there is very close. Confidentiality, using people from the island is impossible and finding a suitable expert from off the island equally impossible. You are really the best man to do the job. You definitely have all the knowledge and expertise to ensure that we bring this business to a successful end. That is I think the only way that we will both be able to live our lives once again without the fear of assassination.'

He poured more wine into their glasses and raised his own towards Hart. Hart raised his glass likewise.

'I propose a toast, Luca. Salute, *cin cin*, here's to the end of a beautiful friendship. You must be crazy if you expect me to be parachuted into that war-zone once more.'

'No, Max, I mean it, you are the only man, I repeat, the only man. One other thing to tell you is that the OCA has a small army of men that is on standby to enter and search, under warrant, the headquarters of la Fox in Basiglio and expose all things connected to Mondo and the Vatican. They will do this one week after we confirm the transport of medicines from Basiglio to the Vatican. Volpe will never expect such a bold action as a raid on her base and especially coming one week after the successful transportation of the medicine. All there will be calm, with the feeling of safety and untouchability as has been the case there for as long as I can remember. To make the raid before the confirmation of the medicine transport would undoubtedly cause the transport to be postponed for who knows how long and we would fail in our main objective. This really is a task which we must not fail in pulling off! The full reason why you should seriously consider doing this thing, Max, is that you and I and also your friends in the UK for all we know, are on the mafia hit list. They want us urgently and I fear that the only place that we can remain safe is here in La Certosa. Can we spend the rest of our lives as monks, Max, for as soon as we return to the outside world, we will be killed? Killed very quickly as the mafia are as we speak covering every manner of escape, especially for you. I have agents reporting those facts. You do realise I know in your heart of hearts that the only way we can live our lives properly is by bringing Mondo, Negri and the mafia crashing down. We can do this quite easily now, as we know so much. Please, Max, help us finish this for both our sakes but importantly also for the sakes of all the parents who are still yet to be put through the misery and heartbreak of premature child-loss in this immoral and evil trade.'

Hart stared into the fire, the personal story of Denis Williams and his wife Ruth once more occupying his thoughts.

'You really can tug at the heart strings. Tell me honestly, how difficult and how dangerous is this mission likely to be? It's not a "mission impossible" I hope?'

'Max, it is a piece of cake. We take you in with a group of our agents, you identify the medicine and ensure a tracker is attached to it and then you leave. It's as simple as that. Before that, you give a talk in the north of the island to my group of men to encourage them and give them extra reason and greater stomach for the mission, yes?'

After some moments in thought, Hart put Messi out of his misery.

'This is the deal then, you get me to the island where I meet your men. We get uniformed up and then very quickly we do the roadblocks. I want a quick hit on the package front. I don't want to have to keep stopping vehicle after vehicle, which will leave me more and more open to exposure. Also, I am not prepared to give your men a pre-action pep talk. I want to arrive, do the job, and leave within a couple of days. What's more, I need some security, some phone backup that isn't going to lead them to me like they did on the train. I tell you now, I will be looking out for pink socks every chance I get.'

He actually smiled in saying the final piece and his smile was joined by a laugh from Messi who also clapped his hands with glee.

'We have a deal, my friend! I will contact others in my organisation and make the plans for your journey to Sicily. By now, your face will have been circulated and distributed to all mafia connections in Milan and so it will be impossible for you to travel again by rail, or by plane from the airports of Linate, Malpensa or Bergamo and by car would take far too long.'

'Fantastic. Lucky I have wings of my own then!'

'We have even better than that in fact. Here at La Certosa we have our own private small plane and a runway, although it's a little err…uneven. Tomorrow, or more accurately now later today, you will be flown to Catania in Sicily where I will arrange for you to be met by one of our specialist agents, who will take you to a small house, which is one of our bases near Basiglio, from where the operation will be run. I will give you more details later after my telephone calls, but you may need to be there for a little longer than you prefer I think. Is that really a problem, Max, for you, what's a couple of days here or there when the final outcome is so important?'

'The problem will be more for your men I think. Total immersion in the English humour can be very confusing. I will need though, some clean shirts and underwear, otherwise the mafia will smell me coming!'

'No problem there, it will be possible for me to arrange that with the brothers here.'

He saw that Hart was about to speak and cut him off … '*Normal* clothes that is, rather than the uniform of the order here at the monastery.'

It was very clear to Hart that Messi had already anticipated a positive response to his suggested actions in Sicily, with plans already laid for his arrival and for his role there. It was a shame that the most important parts of the proposed visit had not yet been thought through enough to instil any confidence in him of them being able to obtain a positive outcome from the exercise. Those details included how the discovery of the stem cell packages would be properly made, proper details of the mode of their attachment to the tracking devices and how the unobserved shadowing of the vehicle from Basiglio to the Vatican would be successfully completed. A final major consideration was how Hart, clearly a northern European in appearance and with his photograph no doubt circulated widely, would be able to travel incognito on the island without being identified.

'*Bene*, just one more thing to deal with and then we can retire for the last few hours of the night and then meet again tomorrow. You mentioned having a secure mobile phone and I have just the one for you. First though, ecco, here is your *own* mobile phone.'

'Yes, the little bugger that almost got me killed. I think that I should smash the daylights out of it. What do you think?'

He took it from Messi's hand.

'Do *you* want to destroy it, Luca, or shall I?'

'No, no it may be a useful tool to have with you. You can keep it and if necessary use it to divert your opponents elsewhere. For example, if you are feeling a little claustrophobic due to their close proximity to you, call me and if you intend to go north tell me you are headed south, likewise you can tell me the opposite of any direction you intend to go in order to send them off in the wrong direction. That will confuse them somewhat at least as I'm sure they will be listening in again. Tomorrow, I will give you a phone which is not bugged and which is untraceable, on which you may call me at the touch of a single button at any time, day or night. That one will be your genuine phone.'

'Now, it is 3.00 am and I think we should get some sleep. You have an early start for Catania and a very interesting and scenic journey I believe.'

He walked Hart to the large oak door, which opened as they approached, (*How do they do that?)* revealing a monk waiting on the other side. Messi uttered a few words to him and then turned to Hart,

'He will take you to your room and then collect you in the morning. Your case is there and I surmise that you already have sleepwear, but if not some can be made available for you.'

Hart indicated that he didn't require anything and Messi continued,

'I'm sorry but the corridors are quite dark as the rule here is that lights are extinguished on the stroke of 11.00 pm, but stay close to the father and you will be fine. A *domani,* Max, see you tomorrow, *buona notte* and sleep well, my friend.'

'*Buona notte,* Luca. Oh and I expect to see some *proper* details of my excursion tomorrow before I make my *final* decision to go, not just the hair-brained off the cuff plan you told me earlier. OK?'

'Yes, of course, Max, everything is in hand. We will talk again in the morning when I'm sure I will be more convincing. *Buona notte.*'

Hart gave him a thumbs-up and stumbled off into the darkness close behind the "Father guide".

As for Messi, he still had calls and arrangements to make, for even at this late hour certain fellow members of the OCA would still be awake and awaiting his contact regarding the expected outcome of his long discussions with Hart.

The room Hart was directed to in the darkness was accessed as usual through a huge oak door, which opened into a chamber totally out of keeping with the regular monasterial surroundings, being laid out more like Messi's office with ultra-modern furniture, technological accessories and a splendid spa-bathroom. Hart entered the room and sat on the huge bed as he took in the palatial surroundings with thoughts of his impending journey forcing their way into his mind.

Suddenly he was aware of a gentle touching of his shoulder, which increased in intensity as his eyes slowly opened.

'*Buongiorno dottore,*' said the monk, who had apparently a few minutes earlier led him to his room. He rubbed his eyes and looked around. He was fully clothed, and looking at the mantelpiece he saw that the large clock thereon was indicating that it was 6.30 am.

'Oh shit! *Buongiorno Padre. Grazie.* Time to rise and shine I guess.'

Chapter 81

The surrounding rooms were quiet and still now, and here in his office the lighting was very subdued. In the semi-gloom, the distinguished-looking man spoke into the phone.

'Can you hear me?'

'*Si, si*, the line is very clear.'

'*Bene*. I have you on speaker-phone and I have with me Robert.'

'Hello Robert.'

'*Ciao* Franco.'

Halle stood with his back to the fireplace, in which logs flickered casting moving shadows across the room. As usual, despite the late hour, he was formally and elegantly dressed, as always in the same style. The man that had called him to the meeting was if anything more finely attired. For a man of his years, he was a designer clothes outfitter's dream…especially if one's name was Giorgio Armani. At the other end of the line, the recipient of the call was in standard Vatican black.

The two men who had been summoned to this additional meeting were nervous. Despite the calmness of the host, both men were feeling very uncomfortable as to what was about to enfold, particularly as their last meeting in Padua had been so uncomfortably difficult, where it had been obvious to both of them that neither man particularly liked the other. It had clearly been "dislike at first sight" when they had met at the Hotel Torino. Halle's expectation for this meeting with him, now back in the USA, was that the botched attempts to silence Hart and then track him down again would be the main agenda item. However, the "man in black" at the other end of the telephone in Rome, considered that the reason for his summons would likely be something ultimately out of his control and more in the hands of God. As things turned out, both men were wrong in their reasonings for the gathering this night.

The host waved for Halle to be seated.

'Friends, we have reached the milestone that I had never thought to be possible. We, or more accurately you Franco, have nursed il Papa for many months now using the medicines of the new technologies that World Pharmaceuticals have developed and advanced. We are indeed, I am proud to say, the world leaders at the cutting edge of a new generation of stem cell research and treatment.

'Through the good offices of il Papa and especially through his African roots, we have established a platform in Africa, not just to enhance our research, but also to push our pharmaceutical sales to a fantastic level. I can assure you both that both of these items are the envy of the rest of the pharmaceutical world. At the same time as this has been occurring, other things have been planned and progressed. A wonderful successor to the Pontiff has been schooled and groomed in all papal aspects. There have been many difficult times when we feared that the Pope's life might ebb away before we could bring our plans to fruition, but it is to the great credit of Franco, our specialist doctors outside of the Pope's own medical team and our scientists, plus of course our own considerable external resources and who is not to say God himself, that his holiness has continued in office, some would say appearing stronger by the day.

'However, my friends...it is time for the ultimate will of God to be done. The time has come to end all non-divine interventions. I do believe that our objectives have reached an excellent endpoint and it is time that the Pontiff was allowed to pass over with dignity. To this end, despite our ultimate love for il Papa, I want the treatment to cease at the end of this month. Is that completely clear to you both?'

The man in the Vatican was the first to respond, his voice very grave.

'That is so very sad, Alberto. I did not expect this quite so soon. I understand that there is one final delivery of treatment from Basiglio planned and then that will be the end of the precious cargo, at least for our use, unless you want the treatment to be stopped immediately that is?'

'It indeed a sad time, my old friend, but it is a time that we have planned and worked for. We have delivered much extra quality time to the Pontiff, but now it is time to leave his natural fate to God. However, we have worked to a strict plan and that includes this final delivery and so we should continue with the treatment right up to when that final supply is exhausted. When that stage arrives, we will sever all associations with the treatment manufacture and delivery, at least from the Vatican standpoint.

'The responsible team, including the laboratory personnel in Basiglio, will be dispersed to other of our development facilities and all transportation agreements with Claudia Volpe, from Basiglio to the Vatican will be terminated. So we will enter a new chapter with the work in this therapeutic area going forward at full speed, but with the teams enlarged and working in new and different cities and countries of the world.

'Now tell me, are you both confident for our next chapter and are you totally clear on our way forward? Francesco, tell me please.'

There was a pause on the telephone line during which time Mondo had to enquire whether Negri was still there, but eventually he spoke.

'So Alberto, in the *main* things are continuing to go very well. I have great sadness of course as we reach this particular juncture. As you well know, Pietro is well known and respected in all Vatican circles and is especially close to the Pope, who treats him these days rather as he would a son and for sure when the Pontiff passes Pietro will be very sad indeed. I would confidently say at this point that Pietro must be considered, even at his young age, to be the most favoured cardinal amongst his peers to assume the role of the new Pontiff when the time arrives...'

'But?'

'I'm sorry, Alberto, did you say "but"?'

'Indeed I did. You know me, Francesco, I can smell a "but" coming a mile away. What is it?'

Halle stiffened somewhat. He had been saying a small prayer of thanks as Mondo's agenda seemed to have taken a better turn than he could ever have expected, but the "but" word set alarm bells ringing in his head. Negri continued,

'No. No problem, Alberto. Just one small thing in that there has been some rumour along the corridors here that there may be some ongoing activity by the Office of Catholic Affairs, but this is just relating to some disturbance at the recent congress in Padua. Perhaps Robert can explain?'

'What a shit'! Halle was absolutely furious with what he believed was Negri's early card played in the game of self-preservation should the stuff hit the fan further down the line. However, always one of the straight poker face, he kept his cool, despite Negri's act of buck-passing and responded,

'It's really nothing, sir. We have an ex-employee "nobody", who believes he has an axe to grind against the company, who is either now working for himself or as a paid consultant for a competitor company, trying to find any dirt about not just ourselves but about any pharmaceutical company at all that he can use for personal benefit. To that end, he stole some World Pharma documents at the congress. These were not sensitive items and were in fact available to all delegates present at the congress anyway. We reported the theft to the local police and I think that is where this incorrect OCA rumour started. It's not important; in fact, it's over and done with now, even as I speak.'

'I believe you, Robert, but I am a little sensitive as you know as our strategy is far too important for even a "nobody" to cause a ripple on my pond. If the fellow continues to irritate you, and by extension he will of course be irritating me also, I want him out of the picture. Out of the picture totally, *capisce*?'

'Absolutely sir, you need have no fears on that level.'

'Yes, I know and trust you to do the necessary thing as always, Robert, thank you.'

Halle carefully held back a smile of satisfaction as he thought, to himself, *Slam dunk, Franco*, but true to type he gave Mondo a slight gratuitous bow and sycophantic nod of the head, with lips firmly pursed together.

At the other end of the line, Negri was quietly distraught at the thought of yet another life potentially being taken by the cause. This business would not just be the end of his great friend the Pope, it would be the end of him also. Thoughts of the likely eventual trade off of Pietro for the current Pope was all that kept him sane. His devout faith had long ago been traded in.

'Gentlemen, I feel we should end there. *Buona notte*, Francesco; good night, Robert.'

The line from Italy finally disappeared in a wave of static, '*Bu–a no–te,* gent–m–n.'

'Good night, sir.'

Halle turned and made for the door, thanking his lucky stars.

'Robert,' Halle stopped in his tracks. 'I was serious about this possible traitor in our midst. What is his name?'

'It's Hart, sir, Doctor Max Hart.'

'Very well. I want you to keep me fully updated on Doctor Hart and please be sure to inform me when this particular Hart stops beating...yes?' He smiled at his pun.

'You can be sure of that, sir.'

'Goodbye, Robert.'

Mondo turned his back on Halle, who was still incandescent inside with Negri, as he exited the room. He lifted his glass of red wine once again from the desk and absently swirling it, focused his gaze through it into the flickering embers in the fire-grate. His true destiny was soon about to come to pass, but he could not allow himself to rest for even one minute until that glorious day arrived.

Chapter 82

Hart threw off the clothes he was still wearing from the night before and headed with bleary eyes to the bathroom. The lights automatically illuminated as he entered the ultra-modern room that served as bathroom, shower room and spa. Towels of fine Egyptian cotton were in abundance as were a range of white cotton bathrobes on a rail. High on the wall opposite the bath was a 40-inch television screen and around the walls were arranged high quality speakers, able to deliver sound from the impressive music system positioned back in the bedroom.

Fifteen minutes later, showered, shaved and shampooed, he was back in the bedroom where he found his case open and a set of clothes laid out on a stand at the side of the bed. He noted too that there were several additional pairs of underpants, as promised the evening before by Messi, on display. He quickly dressed in what he assumed was the "monk's selection" of attire and decided to try and find his way to Messi's office/lounge/dining room of the night before. The oak door opened surprisingly effortlessly and he started through it to immediately discover one of the brothers apparently on sentry duty, awaiting his arrival on the scene. The Father nodded and smiled and indicated Hart to follow him.

They walked along the dimly lit corridor, Hart a couple of steps behind the leader, to the accompaniment of 100 jackhammers going off in his head, the after-effects of the long series of fine red wines that Messi and himself had demolished the night before.

They reached the office and the monk led him in and to the dining table on which was now spread all elements of a sizeable continental breakfast. As Hart located the coffee and poured some acqua naturale, the monk happy that he could now be left alone exited the room. Hart smiled as he noticed a bottle of ibuprofen next to the carafe of spring water and immediately un-capped it and downed three tablets. Part way through his selection of cold meats and cheeses, the door opened and in ambled Messi, looking as fresh as a daisy and beaming, he waddled over to the table and dropped down onto one of the sturdy dining chairs.

'Good morning, Max. I hope you slept well. We have very little time this morning, for you will be leaving in around 45 minutes on your journey to Sicily.'

'Hang on, Luca, we've not discussed any of this yet. I can't just fly off without a full idea and details of the proposed plan or do you think that once I am on my way it will be too late to change my mind?'

'No, no, forgive me for that is not the case at all. I do want you to be fully aware of the program that has been laid out for you before you leave. So, as I have said you will leave very soon and be flown to Catania in Sicily. Once at Catania you will be met by Federico, a colleague of mine and fellow operative of the OCA. He will drive you to a safe house we have on the outskirts of Basiglio, where you will stay during the short time that you are there. He will provide you with the appropriate uniform of the "Special Police" once you arrive at the house and you will wear this at all times when in public. By the way, I spoke with him after you had retired to bed this morning and confirmed what your size would be.'

'What are the Special Police?'

'"Special Police" is a division within the OCA, but really it is just a term. You see people in Sicily are traditionally not suspicious of men in uniforms, especially those with police connections. In fact they are very respectful. In Sicily the main problem can be sometimes from the police themselves, many of who have affiliations within the mafia, but don't worry for officially you will be on "special assignment" checking for particular criminals from North Africa, allegedly seen thereabouts. As for the work involved, you will be stationed on the road from Basiglio to Messina with Federico and at least two other uniformed OCA associates, just as we said last night. Don't worry, all of my men will speak very good English and be completely knowledgeable of the plan. Vans and small lorries that resemble courier vehicles will be pulled over and searched for the theoretical criminals, but you will in fact be searching for the presence of parcels and packages that look suspiciously like containers of biological materials, so obviously requiring low temperature storage during transportation. It will be essential to gain some proof that any suspicious parcel does actually contain biological materials, that is original stem cell material, and at best you might be able to confiscate some it, but if difficult then surreptitiously steal some of it, or at least photograph it. Photograph also the name of the person to whom it is being sent and also that person's address, which will likely be at the Vatican.'

'Confiscate? Steal? What are you talking about? I mean what will be the reaction of the people transporting the items to me just helping myself, and remember I will not be able to speak to them?'

'You can do it, Max. You see they will see you as the "Special Police" and they will respect you automatically, it is their way, it has always been like that. The fact that you do not speak will only intensify the feeling of your importance and superiority.'

Actually that bit made some sense to Hart, although much of the rest didn't, but nevertheless, it made him nervous.

'The *operation*, as I prefer to call it, will last no more than one week. We only have one chance to make this happen and if nothing has occurred within a week, then we will have failed I'm afraid. We do not know, but if they already suspect that we are thinking of the possibility of a conspiracy such as theirs, they could well call an end to the treatment distribution to the Vatican. They already probably know that the OCA is curious, and for sure they know about the now infamous Max Hart, so it is likely that we only have a very small window of opportunity. As for being kept up to date on things, and for information from me, it is best to keep telephone silence as much as possible and leave it to Federico to keep you informed. He will be as up to date as possible and will be happy to tell you all he knows about what is happening as the time runs down. At the end of one week, Federico will drive you back to Catania Airport, where your pilot will return you to La Certosa.'

'So what then is the optimum outcome you perceive from this exercise, which I have to say I still believe to be a wafer thin operation in terms of logic, do-ability and actual believability? Also, what will happen not just in Sicily to the Vita Laboratories and presumably the organisation of La Volpe, but also at the Vatican, when I leave? Finally, and I have asked this before, why does it need me to go to Sicily? Surely there are other experts amongst your own group who could do this job equally well? From how you have described it you could even do it yourself!'

'For myself and the OCA, the best outcome would be to confirm, with proof, that the Vita Laboratories are the end-stop of the line where the final production of treatment material is made from the stem cells, harvested from murdered foetuses, and that the mafia there is part of the scheme. Importantly, we need to prove that the medicine is transported from there to the Vatican specifically for treatment of the Pope. Of course we would expect to find much incriminating documentation at the Vatican as well as additional evidence of treatments.

'When we have confirmed this latter, we have trained men who will effectively raid La Vita and search it from top to bottom, arresting all who are leading the process.

'At the same time, another group of OCA colleagues will raid the headquarters of the Volpe Mafia organisation, once again searching the place from head to foot and taking all into custody. From these two places the volume of evidence should be significantly huge.

'So my optimum overall outcome would be to destroy the stem cell conspiracy around the Pontiff and nullify the whole of the kabal that is left, especially in the Vatican and ensure that not a single member of the conspiracy remains at liberty. Our scheme is certainly possible with some good luck and I am optimistic of a positive outcome.

'Now for you, Max, the big question: why you rather than another? You underestimate yourself. You are the key person in this in identifying accurately what the situation is on the ground. You will know immediately when you detect the treatment in transit and I am confident that you will do all that is necessary to obtain the proof we need when that moment occurs. Also, you clearly are able to think on your feet, which might be very important. One final thing, you are not well known to either the public or to the local mafia, although your photograph will no doubt have been circulated. If any of my men were recognised, our operation would be dead before it even started.

'A major additional thing here though, Max, is that you have a huge vested interest in helping this mission succeed, because your life and your freedom are at stake. For you this is the personal "grand prize", but never forget the hundreds of ordinary people you will be saving from the crime and resulting heartbreak of having their unborn foetuses taken away from them and being transformed into expensive treatments for those rich and famous people with enough money to pay for it. Remember too what you will be indirectly doing for the peoples on the African continent. I just know that you will do everything in your power to successfully complete the mission; after all, I too *need* to have this confidence in you because my own life is at stake as well. What better compliment to you. As to why can't I do this myself, having all the necessary knowledge, I have to take this as one more example of your sense of humour, unless you have problems with your eyes this morning and cannot see the fine, athletic example of manhood that is sitting at the side of you.'

Hart couldn't help but laugh at Messi's self-deprecation.

However, what Messi hadn't told Hart was that he was now "public enemy number one", with a large reward on his head offered for any information of his whereabouts being reported to mafia representatives the length and breadth of Italy.

'Come on, Max, it will be all over in a very short time. Remember it really and truly is the best way to extricate yourself from this web and actually save your own life. Remember also to always keep very alert, but try and enjoy the time while you are in Sicily and take in some of the beauty of the country, especially on your flight down there.'

'Don't patronise me please, Luca, I'm well aware of the personal dangers of taking on this operation and I can still see how hare-brained it is, but as you say, I can see of no other way of getting free from the constant worry of being killed; it's as simple as that. Now, what next?'

Messi fumbled around in a small cardboard box and removed the promised mobile phone, which he handed to Hart.

'So then now you have both the phones, the "good one" and the "bad one". Remember the "bad one" is your own old one and it still retains the bug placed there by our enemies. Don't forget that you might want to use it to send people on a wild goose chase after you in certain circumstances. The "good phone" has the single hit button which will connect directly to me and which is not bugged, use it well and sparingly. OK?'

Hart took a deep breath, which he held for some seconds before exhaling loudly.

'Right then, if it's time for "chocks away chaps", let's do it.'

Messi smiled, put his stubby arm around Hart's shoulder and then patted him on his back.

'I'll walk you back to your room so you can pick up your case. It has been re-packed by now by one of the fathers, who will also ensure that your room will be ready for you upon your speedy and successful return. All that leaves me to do now is to introduce you to your pilot. He is a very colourful character, Max, and may actually be the only other living Italian who will enjoy your humour. Come on, *andiamo*.'

Chapter 83

In the company of Messi, Hart picked up his small case containing a few clothes and his satchel from his room before following him only yards down the corridor to what was to be the final huge oak door, for this visit at least. Messi turned the thick iron ring, his pudgy hand just squeezing into the ring's aperture and eased the door open. They stepped outside into a warm, bright morning, the sky a bright azure blue, with just an occasional isolated wispy cloud hanging there. The sun, although on the lower heat range at this time of day, was never the less quite dazzling and Hart had to shield his eyes as Messi led him forward.

'It's a lovely day for a flight, Max, and there ahead is your transport to Sicily…and back of course. Ha, ha! She is a beautiful little lady, no?'

Hart peered ahead and sure enough there sat the plane that was to take him to God knew what events. It was indeed a "*little* lady", probably at best a six-seater.

'I don't see a pilot, Luca. As part of this "Luca Messi low cost airline", I suppose the instruction manual is inside the cockpit?'

Messi chuckled. 'No, no here he is now. Just don't forget that I told you he was a colourful character, for which there is no extra charge on this "Luca Messi low cost airline".'

He laughed out loud, proud of his newly developing sense of humour.

The pilot, clad in a one-piece sky-blue flying suit, appeared around the front of the plane, ducking smartly as he passed under the single propeller at the plane's nose. As he neared, Hart could now make out the "colourful pilot" more clearly. He was standing no more than 5 feet 6 or 7 inches tall and sporting the "de rigeur Italian pilot's badge". "The badge" or *lo simbolo*, being a wide and thick RAF-type moustache, curled up at the ends. He was a veritable Hercule Poirot of the airways…along with the other 20 or so thousand internal pilots in Italy! A crimson-red silk cravat around his neck was colour co-ordinated with his crimson-red Nike flying bootees and the whole outfit was topped out with a pair of Oakley Navigator sunglasses. His thick medium-length black hair was gelled close to his head and reflected the sun's rays at Hart almost as much as his sunglass lenses. As they drew near to each other, the pilot flashed a white smile that was almost as effective as the hair and the shades in reflecting the sun. When within range, he extended his hand to Hart.

'*Ciao Dottore* Hart, *piacere*! I am Luigi, your "peelot".'

Hart smiled back and shook hands with the aviator.

'*Piacere* Luigi, I am your "pissenger". But where is the stewardess?'

300

Luigi laughed. His English was very good and he had instantly picked up on Hart's amusement at his slight mistranslation of the word "pilot".

'I am sad to report dottore that she has decided to stay in bed today, so for you on this occasion I fly and I also make the coffee. OK? But no *other* extras!'

Messi had remained serious throughout the introduction ceremony and finally placing a hand on Hart's shoulder said,

'Max, you must please take care and keep your guard up at all times whilst in Sicily. Remember we are dealing with the most dangerous of people there. If you feel unable to discover and confirm the information we have spoken about, don't worry. Whilst we do need that information, we also need you to return here safely. Those are the most important things…stay safe and come back.'

Hart smiled.

'*Now* you tell me! Don't worry, Luca, I shall be back before you know it…possibly married to that Foxy Lady down there.'

Through pursed lips, Messi said, 'I cannot over emphasise how dangerous this woman is, she—'

'I know, I know,' Hart interrupted. 'I will see you soon,' after which he indicated to the pilot his readiness to leave and followed him to the plane.

'Max wait. Please take this…in case the mobile phones go out of action, *si*?'

He dropped what appeared to be a chain with a tag hanging from it into Hart's pocket.

As Hart neared what appeared to be nothing more than just a toy plane, he shaded his eyes from the sun and for the first time took in the plane's livery, comparing it to the "uniform" of his "designer pilot". The fuselage and wings of the plane were of the same shade of blue as Luigi's flying suit. The blue of the fuselage was offset by a red "bolt of lightning stripe" travelling from the area of the nose to the tail-plane. The picture was completed by the plane's red wingtips, red propeller tips, red nose cone and red tip of the tail. What a marvellous colour coordinated combination of pilot and plane!

Hart followed the pilot to the far side of the plane where a set of small wooden steps had already been positioned at the side of the aircraft. The small door was open and Luigi indicated for him to climb aboard. Looking inside, he confirmed what he had anticipated earlier. There were six passenger seats in two rows of three, but with an additional seat upfront at the side of the pilot. He looked back over his shoulder at Luigi.

'Where do you want me, Luigi?'

'Where you like, *Dottore*? Why not at the side of me. You can be co-pilot and take over when I fall asleep, *si*?'

'Fine.' He swung his light case onto a seat in the second row and squeezed into the front seat followed by Luigi on the other side, who slammed the plane doors shut and manoeuvred himself into the pilot's position.

'Fasten your seat belt please. We are cleared for take-off.'

He quickly ran-down the list of necessary pre-takeoff checks on a clipboard and satisfied that all was OK, replaced it in its small over-windscreen compartment. Leaning forward, he fired up the engine, which started at first push of the button.

'*Bene Dottore*, there is no need for you to push us after all, ha ha. *Andiamo*, let's go!'

Hart looked out of the windscreen somewhat apprehensive, but never the less in a strange way exited about his journey and the hoped for outcome of it. Like an Alice in Wonderland adventure, his was getting "curiouser and curiouser".

Chapter 84

The toy plane bounced down the swathe of grass which purported to be a runway, looking to gain sufficient speed to enable them to take off, whilst throwing both pilot and passenger around in their belted seats more and more roughly the faster it went. Hart, never a good flyer at best of times, gripped the dashboard with white knuckles.

'Bloody hell, Luigi, this strip is no better than a rough football pitch!'

Luigi smiled and nodded at the window on Hart's side of the plane. Hart turned his head to look out just in time to see a set of white football goal posts go flashing by.

The pilot just laughed and then he was slowly pulling back the joystick and the small plane was leaving the pitch below and rising up towards the sky…and then down towards the ground again…and then back up again.

'Air currents,' shouted the comandante above the complaining engine of the plane. 'Air currents and air pockets, but no worry, we will hopefully soon climb above many of them.'

Some way behind them and standing on the perimeter of a football pitch remained Messi, staring at the small plane as it made its way towards Sicily. He waved farewell to the disappearing plane for a long time after it had made its final bounce into the air, saddened by the fact he had sent the likeable Hart into the lion's den with, if truth was told, a strong chance of not returning.

As the plane continued to climb into the bright morning sky and the turbulence all but disappeared, Hart's appreciation of the wonderful view below them finally overtook his flying fears and he felt his body relax more into the bucket seat of the cabin. The plane had actually taken off in a northerly direction, to eventually swing round and fly south, so ahead of them Hart was able to see the sprawling city of Milan and behind it the wonderful sight of the snow-capped Alps.

As Hart began to relax, the plane suddenly banked to the right pulling him from his reverie in double quick time.

'Bloody hell!'

'I'm sorry, *Dottore*, I should have warned you in advance, we have to swing completely round in order to now fly south to Sicily.'

The view below was wonderful.

'Beautiful, absolutely beautiful, Luigi. How long before we arrive in Catania?'

'Ah, the children they always say, "Are we nearly there yet, papa?", and you are the same, *Dottore*. We have to travel some 770 kilometres, which will take us around four hours depending upon the weather.'

'There'll be time for some sleep then. For me anyway. By the way, Luigi, please call me Max, unless you want to tell me about a medical condition that is.'

'*Grazie Dottore*, err Max. That is better. So I tell you like on the big planes, we will be cruising at a speed of 195 km/hr, mainly at a very approximate altitude of 2,500 kilometres, depending on the weather. Our rate of climb when we took off, and drained all the blood from your face, was around 644 feet per minute. See I give it you in the English measurement.'

He laughed out loud, having recently re-read and now recited the American Flight Handbook to perfection.

'And here, if you are interested is our flight plan for today.'

He handed Hart a folded map in a plastic case, which Hart opened and looked at…trying to appear intelligent on these matters. It was clear from the map that their route, rather than being "as the crow flies", mainly followed the routes of the various highways, or autostrade, which from the altitude that they would be flying at meant that all would be visible to Hart. He sat back and allowed the panorama to unfold.

As the small plane followed the autostrada A1, he eventually picked out the city of Modena below, and then they flew onwards towards Bologna. Whilst still some distance from Bologna, the comandante banked abruptly to the right where he picked up the more southerly section of the A1, the route to Florence, at which point the scenery changed from the flatter plains rising to the Tuscan Apennine Mountains, an area crammed with many of the world's most beautiful towns and cities. The rolling landscape was of green hills draped in vineyards and punctuated with cypress trees and hillside villages of stone houses and cottages. The road that they were following below snaked through beautiful mountains and countryside, often disappearing into the many mountain tunnels, or "galleria", whilst at other times, crossing sections of deep mountain rifts over bridges supported on long slender legs planted in the valleys below.

The city of Florence is obviously a no-fly zone, but from his position, Hart could easily make out in the distance the terracotta roofs, the towers and famous churches and next to the famous Campanile, Brunelleschi's incomparable dome, seated on top of the Duomo. He saw the River Arno winding its way under the loping bridges and the hilltop balconies of the Piazalle Michelangelo and the Belvedere Fort. Wonderful!

Hart found himself involuntarily fondling the dog tag in his pocket where Messi had dropped it and taking it out read the inscriptions on each side before hanging it around his neck. The silver tag on the silver neck-chain bore the inscription, *"Buon viaggio. A presto!"* On the reverse side was Messi's private free-phone contact number. Messi's final instruction had been that should he need assistance of any kind at all, a call to that number would summon immediate help no matter where he was in any part of Italy. He must have known that Hart would finally accept the mission to have had the tag thus etched, but then realistically thinking, he probably had a drawer full of them in his office for other similar occasions!

'So much for confidence in the mission!'

Chapter 85

A quick look at the flight plan informed Hart that after Florence the plane was on a direct flight path to Grosseto, from where they would head out over the Tuscan Archipelago, heading southwest, taking the coastal route down to Sicily.

Once more, the views at this height were intoxicating as the mountains, hills and greenery gave way to the turquoise sea and the coastal resorts and beaches. As the landscape eventually gave way to a far more rugged mountainous picture, Hart worn out by reflecting on the sheer beauty below him and to almost the same extent by the exuberant conversation of the pilot, fell into a deep sleep.

He awoke to a view of just sea, but they had reduced their altitude and Hart could clearly pick out details of the many boats going through their individual functions below.

In response to Hart's assumed unasked question, the comandante informed him,

'We have not much further to go now. Just ahead are the Straits of Messina from where there will be a most magnificent view of Mount Etna, for which you *must* stay awake, Max.'

'No problem.'

Hart looked ahead and downwards and there lay the island of Sicily, set at the crossroads of the Mediterranean, a land of mountainous landscapes and a thousand mile coastline of sandy beaches, rocky coves, cliffs and hillsides. Many civilisations over the millennia had left their own impacts on the island. The Greeks, the Romans, the Barbarians, Arabs, Normans, Angevins, Aragons and Bourbons had all left traces of their respective cultures and none more so than the Vikings, whose blood line had led to tall dark and tall blond Sicilians with blue eyes.

'Ecco Max, look!'

The pilot dipped the nose of the plane and pointed ahead as the little mosquito began to descend.

Directly ahead of them was the currently slumbering giant that was the volcano Mount Etna. In truth, it was more of a dozing giant than a slumbering one, as even now plumes of grey steam could be seen issuing forth from its mouth and from its surrounding fissures.

As the plane finally touched down, the wheels squealing as their rubber tyres made contact with the tarmac, it rapidly slowed down to its taxiing speed.

Luigi turned to Hart, 'We have arrived in Sicily, Max…and I never even asked if you wanted anything from the duty free trolley.'

'Perhaps on the return flight?' smiled Hart.

He'd enjoyed his flight with this extrovert pilot and was already tentatively looking forward to a completed job and an equally enjoyable flight back to La Certosa.

Catania being a busy international airport, has its own separate terminal for small aircraft making internal flights away from the main concourse, and within ten minutes of landing, the pilot was steering the little plane past the huge Alitalia passenger aircraft and round the back of the airport to their appropriate internal arrivals station. Once in position on station, Luigi killed the engine and without further small talk, asked Hart who his contact was.

'It's an officer named Federico. Do you know him?'

'*Si*, I know him well. He should not be too difficult to spot I think. Let us disembark, or should I say de-plane?' smiled the pilot.

Hart reached back and took his case from the seat behind and exited through the plane's small door and down the short flight of three steps which Luigi had lowered to the ground ahead of him. As he took the final step, he turned round and came face to face with a good looking, olive skinned, man mountain, but not fat like Messi, instead this man was tall, solidly built and well-muscled, certainly not a person to fall out with. The man held out a hand.

'*Buonasera, Dottore* Hart, I am Federico. I am pleased to welcome you to Sicily.'

Hart smiled and extended his hand in greeting. Luigi had certainly been right in Federico not being easy to miss.

Luigi said his Hellos to Hart's new mentor and turning to Hart shook him by the hand.

'Max, it has been my pleasure to fly with you and I look forward to an equally pleasurable flight back in a few days. My colleague Federico will make the necessary arrangements when you are ready for your first class flight home. Enjoy your stay and let us hope that there are not too many eruptions.' He smiled ironically.

'Thanks Luigi, I look forward to the return ride too. Let's hope it's sooner rather than later. *Ciao*.' He glanced at Federico, who nodded in agreement.

Chapter 86

Hart's companion didn't speak as they made their way to the car, merely silently indicating to the anonymously looking Alpha Romeo as they quickly crossed the car park's rough stony surface. Suddenly as they reached it, in perfect English, which totally belied his looks, he spoke.

'So then, *Dottore*, may I call you Max?'

'Yes of course, and I will call you Federico as that's the only name I've been given. Is that OK?'

'Yes indeed, welcome once again to Sicily. Allow me to take your case and then I will tell you what I believe to be in store for you, or rather us, over the coming few days.'

He smiled as he took the case and put it in the boot of the car.

'Please, let's get inside.'

They both got into the car, Hart comfortably, but Federico clearly struggled to haul his huge frame through the door. He turned on the engine, placed his hands on the steering wheel and as he pulled away turned to Hart.

'Where we are going is only a twenty-kilometre drive from Catania Town. Near to the place we are headed to is the small town of Basiglio, which as you know is where the Mondo family originated from and of course the family still own property there. The World complex of factories and research facilities, which includes the Vita Laboratories and also the Laboratorio di Scoperta Fondamentale, are also near to there as is the safe house that we will stay in.'

'You speak excellent English, Federico, where did you learn it?'

'I learned to speak English whilst studying at Oxford University. I was a student there for three years.'

Hart raised his eyebrows. The response was so unexpected.

'I'm both surprised and impressed. What subject did you study there?'

'Political science and history and of course, English. I won a scholarship and was sponsored from the very start by the OCA. They are very good in that respect, but their sponsorship does require the student to spend at least the first two post-graduate years working for them, but that is no problem.

'So then briefly, what will we do for the rest of this week? Well every day we will position ourselves on Route 120 with my two colleagues, and we will stop all appropriate looking transport vehicles and check for a delivery that is bound for the Vaticano. I guess you already know this though?'

'Yes, but bloody hell, we surely can't stop every vehicle? Won't it look suspicious?'

Federico looked across at Hart and smiled.

'In America perhaps it would look suspicious, Max, but this is Sicily where although people are very suspicious of all police, there is a great respect for them and if we say it is official business it will not be questioned. Our cover was to be that we are "la Polizia Speciale" searching for dangerous criminals who have come into Sicily from outside, having escaped from a high security prison, but we may change that slightly and I will update you if we do. We will all of course be equipped with the "Polizia Speciale" uniforms. I think the blue uniform will suit very well your eyes,' he laughed, 'but I think Luca has already told you this, yes?'

'Yes he did mention it, but he didn't say anything about my eyes though.'

As for the number of vehicles we will need to stop, we will only stop those that we feel are appropriate, and we do have some inside information as to the type of van we should expect, plus a few others just for show and for the theatre of it. In fact, Max, there will be very few I hope.'

'But how do you know that we can expect to see the vehicle we are after over the next few days?'

'The person we have on the inside at the World Research Centre should know within a day or two when the next shipment will be dispatched from La Vita to the Vatican and at present he informs us that it will be this week for sure.'

'So let's get this straight. You stop the van, or whatever, I confirm the nature of the contents as best I can, collect any proof and identify their destination and then what?'

'Once you make the confirmation et cetera, we allow the delivery to proceed, but we ensure that we mark the package in whatever way is possible. We have specific small labels at hand for this and also to help track it we have electronic tracking devices that are almost undetectable to the eye that we must also attach to any parcels. Our major aim is to locate its final arrival at its destination inside the Vatican and take action against all involved, both at the Sicily end and of course at the Vatican end.'

'So, a big question here for you, Federico. How the hell will all this save my own skin?'

'Don't worry, if our plan sounds simple to you, that's because it is simple, and if it appears to be somewhat amateurish, I can assure you that we have agents embedded both in the World organisation and in the Vatican. Our initial team is small, but as soon as we have confirmation that the transported material has finally arrived at the Vatican, we have a small army that is ready to hit World, Volpe's mafia and the Vatican itself. It will be an incredible scandal, but major heads will roll, heads belonging to people in the highest realms of government, the church and industry. It will not just rest here in Italy of course, offices, hospitals and research bodies in many worldwide locations will be hit at the same time and all of this will be the result of your "simple" assessment of the cargo in a van here in Sicily. Now about your own skin, once the *merda* hits the fan, the people concerned will be too busy trying to save their own skin to bother about, and I hesitate to say this…the small fish that is Max Hart. Do you see, Max, that whilst you may be public enemy number one to them at this very moment, once the game is afoot, you will instantly become of no importance to the perpetrators.

In plain terms, you will be released from their need to eradicate you. Can you take any comfort from all of that? I do hope so. The very important aspect of all that Max is *timing*. It has been decided only today that all the "hits" I have mentioned really do have to happen at precisely the same time, no matter where on earth the perpetrators and all their associates are, for it only needs one group to inform others that things are going down and they will disappear into the night.'

'But what about global time differences?'

'It makes no difference, everybody involved will be hit at exactly the same time, so it might be at 7.00 pm here and 12.00 mid-day in America, or even in the early hours of the morning elsewhere.'

Hart nodded. Federico had done an outstanding job in boosting his confidence in the planned mission.

'Thanks Federico, you've given me great confidence. You've talked the talk very well, now let's try and walk the walk equally as well, OK?'

'Together, we will do this. We will succeed in our mission and bring down the whole rotten bunch. They are all bastards, Max, unfit to hold any office at any level and the world needs to know it, so sit back and relax for our short journey now.'

Chapter 87

'You OK, Doctor Hart? Do I drive a little too fast for you?'

'I'm fine thanks and by the way you must call me Max.'

'*Bene*, Max. I will tell you a little about our journey. We are approaching a pretty little place called Fontana Rossa, which is some 6km from Catania, which is a much bigger and much shittier place I must report.'

Hart laughed.

'From there, we go north towards Messina on the A18, but we will take a left turn before we reach there onto the 120. Randazzo is the place we are heading for, a very small village close to, but far enough away from our enemies', the Fox and the World factory and laboratories, location. We should be there in another thirty minutes or so…if I continue at the speed of sound that is.'

He laughed out loud and Hart grimaced.

As they sped on, Federico gave Hart an excellent detailed commentary on the area, the towns and villages and their local histories.

'Have you had any special education on this area of Italy, Federico?'

His guide laughed. 'Yes, of course I have, Max. I read it all in a travel brochure!'

At that moment, a car in front and to their right, shot out of a side road and careered crazily across all lanes and at the next bend spun entirely off the road. Federico braked quickly, whilst holding his hand down firmly on the car's horn, and allowed the out of control car to follow its ordained path to the scrap heap.

'Shit! Bloody crazy Catanese drivers! Still we only have 30 more minutes left and we will arrive at our destination. We will be able to eat and talk business then.'

'If we get there in one piece that is!'

Federico laughed and gunned the car's accelerator again. '*Andiamo mio amico*!'

Let's hope we'll both be laughing in a couple of days' time, thought Hart seriously.

Chapter 88

Robert Halle slammed down the telephone.

He was a different man of late. In sartorial terms, he hadn't been looking his usual impeccably dressed self. His physical aspects too had changed, for never a humorous man, his brow now bore even deeper furrows of worry and seriousness than was normal for him. His hair was looking decidedly greyer and less well kempt and his famous moustache, or "pet slug" as many regarded it following Hart's outbursts, was in need of a sizeable trim. He still wore the same trademark blazers and occasional suits, but of late, he had not carried them with the same formal elegance and there was a noticeable drooping and rounding of the shoulders. As for his famously tied ties, they no longer seemed to present with the same perfect Windsor-knot symmetry.

He was a very worried man and this worry and concern was being reflected in his whole outward appearance. Minions around the office who bore the brunt of his tattered temper had put this change down to the difficulties that the company was experiencing in obtaining international regulatory approvals for a key drug, but the true reason for his metamorphosis was down to one thing alone, or in fact down to one person, Max Hart.

Hart was still at large somewhere in Italy, "or even somewhere else in Europe for God's sake!" But whilst Hart's knowledge and activities were likely to be in the nature of a flea bite to World's huge empire and especially to its ongoing activities relating to the Vatican, they were to Halle a massive irritant and in fact there *was* always a chance that Hart was better informed than he anticipated. Added to this irritation was the sudden deathly quiet that had descended upon World's European harvesting operations in the stem cell field. In this, Halle was sure that Hart had had more than a flea-bite effect and he wanted him found and crushed as soon as possible. In fact he had wanted this for over one week now, but so far Hart had managed to remain hidden somewhere, but it would only be a matter of time and he, Robert Halle, would be there wherever it was to deliver the final deadly coup de grace.

With regard to this sudden "all quiet on the Western front" situation, it seemed that all of the key operatives in the various European clinics and obstetric units were suddenly either on vacation or not contactable. It was his latest series of failed attempts to make telephone contact with several of these key opinion leaders, followed by a very disappointing call from Volpe that had been the cause of him slamming down his telephone just moments before. It surely was too much of a coincidence that all of these essential experts and providers were sunning themselves somewhere on some exotic beach, or dutifully attending some vaguely important conference somewhere in the back of beyond? Worst of all, to add to these great woes, Alberto Mondo was becoming suspicious that all was not going so well after all.

Halle had tried his utmost to keep the lid on the activities involving Hart, dealing frequently and directly with Claudia Volpe, but Mondo was no fool and was becoming increasingly aware that something was "off beam" despite Halle's every attempt to divert and placate him. Halle's only respite was that the news from the Vatican continued to be good. Under the expert mentoring of Negri, Peter Mondo had become a confirmed "Vatican star" and was now the outright favourite to eventually replace his friend the ailing Pope.

Alberto Mondo was also suffering great emotional stress now that the mission for which he had planned and invested was almost at an end, having made the decision that the Pontiff should receive just one final series of stem cell treatments. The final shipment of tailor-made stem cell products being transported in the coming days from World's Vita Laboratories in Sicily to the Vatican would signal an end to a major part of Mondo's complex and convoluted strategy. The natural end to the life of the Pope upon the withdrawal of the treatment that had extended his time on earth by more than two years would be a tremendous emotional loss, but it had always formed the basis of his essential strategies.

As for Franco Negri, he was conflicted. He was sad because even though the Pontiff was his dear and close friend, he still held the strong belief that he had been working towards an endpoint that was for the eventual greater good of the church. Now, however, as an end was clearly in sight, with the future looking very positive for the Catholic Church with a new young leader, for some reason the end no longer held any appeal even though it did apparently justify the means. After all the months of expectation, caring for the old guard and nurturing the new he was feeling exhausted and worn out.

But Halle could not stop thinking about Hart. Hart, without even trying or most probably even knowing, was eroding Halle bit by bit. Halle was furious that this "World failure", this "Company reject", had been permitted to escape to God only knew where, but of one thing he was certain, whilst Hart's death was important to him, it was equally important to extract from him by whatever means all he knew and with whom he was working, before he breathed his last gasp. Once that information was obtained, he would be very happy for Hart to meet an as unpleasant a death as possible and he wanted to be there to witness it in person.

However, his most recent call from Volpe confirmed that Hart had not been located, even though all points of exit from Milan had been covered by her best people, with other points of departure further afield in many other parts of Italy being covered also. They were still no closer to his capture. The only single piece of solid information was that Hart was still in Italy. The mafia's contacts within the Italian transportation bodies on land, sea and in the air and also within the Italian Emigration Agency had established that fact for sure.

Uncharacteristically, in an open office at least, Halle clenched his fist and brought it down hard onto the oak desk, and through gritted teeth whispered the burning question, 'Where are you, Hart, where the bloody hell are you?'

Chapter 89

'We're here!'

Hart had caught sight of the Randazzo sign as they flashed past it along the deserted road, and it was confirmed a few miles and a few twists and turns later when his driver proclaimed their arrival.

Federico's earlier prediction of "just 30 *more* minutes" had translated from "Italian minutes" to 75 minutes UK time. The driver drove past the front door of the house, made a right turn on the gravel drive down the side of the dwelling and parked his car out of sight, before sounding his horn loudly and alighting, indicating Hart to get out also. As they walked back to the front of the place, the ancient rustic door of the ancient rustic house opened and an indistinct ancient rustic figure emerged. Federico raised his hand in salutation.

'Ah here is our team. *Ciao* Marta!'

Hart looked in disbelief. The "team" as Federico had put it seemed to consist of a single old woman of some apparent 90 years or so, clad in traditional black dress, black stockings and black headscarf.

'Bloody hell, Federico, did you say "team"?'

His colleague laughed.

'Of course. Marta is a *member* of our team. She is our mistress, but please do not tell her that.'

(The Italian name of Marta does in truth translate into English as "*mistress*" or lady).

'You know, Max, money and resources, especially human resources, are very scarce in our field of work.'

'So then, what is Marta's particular range of essential skills for this mission? Explosives, electronics, cellular biology, or perhaps she is a grand master of some form of unarmed combat? Surely she's not just here to make the pizzas?'

'No, Max, you are the biology expert in the team, but you are also correct in your assumption, for Marta is indeed our wonderful cook. She will keep our stomachs very satisfied during our stay here I promise you. However, I do joke slightly, for we do have more members of our, albeit small team who you will meet later. Now, please, come forward and say hello.'

He advanced enthusiastically towards the old woman and delicately kissed her on both cheeks, first the right side and then the left.

'Come on, Max, please!'

Hart approached the nonagenarian who looked at him with great suspicion from rheumy eyes located within a face as leathery and lined as the ploughed summer Sicilian fields.

He held out his hand. '*Piacere signora.*'

His hand was left hanging in space as the old woman gave him a barely visible nod. He turned to Federico.

'Looks like I've scored again. I'm always a great hit with foreign ladies you know.'

'Come on, Max, let's go inside.'

He led Hart through the weathered door of the house and into what Hart supposed was the main living room, squinting as his eyes adjusted to the dark interior from the brightness of outside. What he saw when his eyes finally became accustomed to the light came as a great surprise, for the interior of the residence in no way reflected the ravaged aspect of the exterior. He was reminded of how surprised he was upon seeing the interior rooms of La Certosa, but rather than that brand of wonderful modernity, this place simply exuded great rustic charm. Brightly decorated, it had several comfortable-looking armchairs set around a huge open fireplace. Although the floor was of basically simple flagstones, attractive hand-made rugs were scattered randomly around. In the centre of the room sat a large wooden table complimented by six wooden chairs. A simple chandelier hung from the ceiling over the table, illuminating the mass of papers and documents littered across the tabletop. Around the sides of the room were various rustic looking wooden bookcases and cabinets, the tops of which were adorned with locally fashioned ornaments. The walls of the room were hung mainly with paintings of a bucolic nature, befitting the house's surroundings. Over the fireplace hung a very large, wooden, ornate crucifix, from which was draped a long string of black rosary beads. In one corner of the room a large wooden open staircase ascended to the second level. To the left of the room an open doorway revealed the splendid looking farmhouse kitchen, through the window of which Hart could pick out Federico's parked car. Hart quickly poked his nose through an open door on the far side of the room that gave entrance to a smaller sitting/reading room which contained well-stocked bookcases of various sizes on the walls, a coffee table and three comfortable looking armchairs.

'So then, Max. You like it? We will all sleep upstairs—'

'Not in the same room I trust?' interrupted Hart, looking pointedly at the old woman.

'Mind you who knows what might happen after a litre or three of the local wine?'

Federico gave Hart a reproachful look for the tasteless comment.

'No, we all have a room each…and in any case we do not have enough wine for any likelihood of that situation arising! Do forgive me, I am getting as bad as you, Max, it must be a "bad taste contagion" I think?'

He turned to Marta and they spoke animatedly for several minutes, after which time he addressed Hart.

'Right Max, let us sit down here at the table. We have much to discuss and I can update you more on our plan and on the latest news that Marta has given me.'

As Federico sat down, he spread open his blue tunic for additional comfort and it was at this point that Hart noticed the gun that he was wearing in a holster, supported by his belt around his waist. Italian legislation stipulates and regulates the type of weaponry that may be used by the different levels of police for public control and restoration of public order, but there are no written regulations for weaponry used by the "Special Forces", of which Federico was a member, so whilst the standard Italian police handgun of choice tended to be the 9mm Beretta 92Fs, Federico's choice as a member of an elite police tactical unit, was the Glock 17, a sidearm also popular with the British SAS.

By comparison, Hart's own holstered "sidearms" consisted of two mobile phones, one for firing off live communications and the other for firing diversionary blanks.

'To begin with, Max, I have to tell you that it has not been possible in the short time available to obtain for you a beautiful official uniform like mine. Unless you feel you might fit into one of my spare sets you will have be a plainclothes officer I'm afraid. The other men on our team will be happy to share their uniforms with you, but they too are of strange sizes I believe and I guess they would be either like me too big, or like Marta too small, for you.'

'That's a blow, Federico, you know how the girls simply love a man in uniform. Still, I really am happy to wear my own clothes. I certainly wouldn't relish squeezing into Marta's black designer wear, but aside from that, you have hit on a problem that I have had from the start here. Why so few men for such an important mission and why do you personally need *me* particularly? Surely you have many people at your disposal who would be just as suitable as myself?'

'You must remember that the mafia are not seen as total criminals around here. They have done, and continue to do, many things which benefit the people at large. They employ many of the population for one thing. It is the big organisations that they concentrate their criminal activities on and they always ensure that there is some public benefit eventually at the end of it. Many people on this island would not hesitate to feed the mafia with any information that they felt would help them, or that would earn themselves some reward. The bottom line is that there are very few people here that the police can trust. In fact there are very few *police* here that can be trusted. It is one huge mafia extended family. Therefore, the men who have been picked for this important mission are the ones who can be trusted with information one hundred percent. Sadly this means that men have had to be brought in from the mainland. I am the only Sicilian in this unit. I have met the colleagues before of course, those who will join us later, and I have also trained with them, but always on the Mainland and my fingers are crossed that they have never been to Sicily before.

'As for, "why you?" Well, I believe that Luca had discussed this already at length with you and I have to say that I totally agree with what he has told you. Max, you are simply the best person to pull off this mission, there's no argument.'

'Thanks Federico, the plan sounds logical at least, and I am complimented by your personal comments. It does give me some confidence, but in any case I'm here now and all I want is for us to get the job successfully completed as quickly as possible, but of course we do have to assume that despite what you say about my anonymity here, my photograph will have likely been distributed far and wide.'

'Thank you, Max, I admire your sentiments and your little test. No doubt your face has indeed been circulated, so we will ensure that we do not advertise you too much. Don't worry, we *will* succeed and succeed very quickly I am sure. We should now eat a little I think.'

Marta arrived shortly with a tray containing a large plate of mixed antipasti, a carafe of local red wine and a bottle of Aquafina mineral water, plates, glasses and cutlery, which she placed in the only clear area on the table. She leaned over and whispered a few words in Federico's ear.

'Please, help yourself, Max.' His colleague indicated to the tray.

'We will likely have no uniform for you, Max, but the good news as you already know is that we do have a source inside the World complex, which includes Vita Laboratories, and this mole has reported to us just now that the day after tomorrow could be the final shipment of the "low temperature controlled treatment material" that will be made to the Vatican. We joked a while ago, but in fact Marta is the contact to whom the mole reports. If that information turns out to be true, then you have arrived without a moment to spare. Tomorrow, six other colleagues will join us here, in uniform of course, and we will rehearse our procedures for stopping the traffic on the road leading away from Basiglio towards Messina, and also practice how we will effectively conduct the searches. We will especially need to practice just how you will comport yourself, Max, in performing this exercise as you are not fluent in the language. We will have to set out our stall early and be seen stopping vehicles that we are already sure of being totally innocent so as not to appear suspicious as the day progresses. Ahead of this, probably this evening and then throughout tomorrow, OCA agencies will be responsible for putting out news bulletins on local radio and television alerting the public to the fact that two dangerous men are being sought in the area and that accordingly road checks are being made in order to take them back into captivity. I actually think that people having heard the news will be pleased to see our police presence on the roads.'

Hart nodded approvingly, trying to appear to be treating this deadly game with more respect than he had so far shown, but sometimes some people cover their fears with excessive humour and Hart was one of this group.

'Actually, Federico, the number of men that you have told me will arrive is greater than what Luca Messi indicated and that can't be bad.'

'Yes, things change, Max, and Luca is not always completely up-to-date. Anyway, we now know from our mole that the delivery will leave the Vita factory at around 2.00 pm on the day after tomorrow and we must be there to search the vehicle accordingly. I emphasise, we *must* be there on that road and at that time, ready to carry out our plan effectively. Once the vehicle has been identified as our target, you will enter the back of it with myself and examine the contents, whilst our colleagues divert the attention of the driver and anybody else with him by checking his documents and looking around and under the vehicle. His documents will confirm where he is from and interrogation by our colleagues will confirm where he is heading. I think you have been told already that the transportation will be in the hands of Volpe's men, *si*?'

Hart nodded affirmatively.

'Our actions at the van will not be seen as suspicious activities, as they will be expected by the driver under the circumstances, after all he will have absolutely no knowledge of the importance of the load he will be carrying. So Max, as I have said, I will accompany you in your inspection and of course I will do all the talking, but you will do all the searching and most probably do the tagging of the articles as well, but tell me, what exactly will you be looking for?'

This surprised Hart, for in truth he hadn't laboured too much on exactly what he would be looking for, he just knew that he would know what it was when he saw it. He focused his mind.

'That's a very good question and a question that I am unable to give a definite answer to, other than to say that I will know it when I see it. I would expect though that biological materials will be in plain sight, especially as the factory people will have no reason to hide or camouflage any parcels. To them they are just standard biological packages, requiring to be kept at a lower temperature during transport, which itself will not be out of the ordinary to them as this is commonplace with all biological materials. The key thing here is that of temperature and I'm pretty sure that dry ice will be required within the packed articles to ensure a constant low temperature, otherwise the temperature will rise and the materials will be rendered useless. An expensive waste, but not just that, so much depends upon the consignment arriving at its destination in pristine condition that I would expect that no expense will have been spared in creating the necessary temperature conditions. Certainly no effort will have been made to hide it in any way, as the visibility of it is paramount in ensuring its continued biological viability. I would be very surprised if the packages were not labelled as containing dry ice and that a constant low temperature was imperative. In other words, the packages should speak to *us*… "Here we are"…rather than us having to play hide and seek with them. I am very confident that if they are there, they will indeed be very obvious. Of course it depends also on their size, and if the materials occupy a large volume I would expect them to be transported in metal containers or even hardened polypropylene boxes or bottles. We will know it when we see it I'm sure. I'm sorry that I can't be any more specific than that, but that's it, so let's see how we go and keep our fingers crossed, although I'm sure that when it comes to the crunch crossing our fingers will not be necessary.'

He finished his short lecture exuding confidence, but despite his final words, his fingers were crossed as he touched the wood of the table to double his luck!

'Oh and a couple of other things. I will certainly attempt to apply the tracking device, which you need to demonstrate to me today or tomorrow, or in fact you could do that yourself if convenient and I will try and photograph the labelling. I think the chances of "acquiring" any of the samples is both remote and also pointless though, as once it reaches ambient temperature the material will likely be destroyed anyway. We'll have to play it all by ear, Federico.'

Federico nodded.

319

'As soon as you have a positive outcome in detecting the specimens, Max, I will notify my OCA colleagues who will be waiting on standby and they will swing into action with the appropriate plans for the eventual co-ordinated visits to World and the mafia here in Sicily, the Vatican and everyone else connected, even outside of Italy. You know the OCA have been speaking with overseas authorities about this situation with World and our overseas colleagues are also very keen to make appropriate visits to their own local centres which are involved. I am becoming more optimistic by the minute that within two days our work here will be successfully completed and the whole international mission will soon be brought to an end. Let us drink to it, Max.'

He raised his glass of red wine and clinked it against Hart's raised glass.

'Salute and Cheers!'

'So then when my colleagues arrive here tomorrow afternoon we will rehearse as arranged, but in the morning, Luca Messi asked that I take you to Basiglio to give you a view of the outside of the World complex and Vita Laboratories for your general interest.'

'Why?'

'You see, the town owes so much to the Mondo family for all they have done for the whole area over the years. Not only the Mondo's though, the church and the local mafia have helped the people considerably. In fact, there is a museum in the town of Basiglio and much of it is based around the history of the Mondo family and the way in which the company has grown from its very humble beginnings to the global pharma company that we see today. There is in fact a whole section of the museum which is devoted to the Mondo family tree. Luca was keen for you to see it as you were personally quite important in the company yourself when you worked for them in America and he feels you will find it interesting.'

'Fine.'

Having outlined and confirmed the plans and activities that would occupy them over the next few days before Hart's return to Catania Airport and his flight back to La Certosa, Hart and the affable giant of an OCA agent Federico dined on typical Sicilian country fare, which was turned out of the all mod cons rustic kitchen by the apparently permanently angry Marta. The meal although basic was absolutely delicious. The two courses were washed down with the local Etna Rosso and there was plenty of the red left at the end to help dispose of ample portions of local pecorino cheese and the remains of the ricotta salta (salted ricotta) used in the pasta dish. The bread baked in the kitchen oven and drizzled with local olive oil was absolutely delicious.

At around 10.00 pm, Federico having delivered his case from the car, Hart decided to call it a night and thanking his hosts he retired to his room, and to his extraordinarily large and comfortable bed in which he immediately fell asleep.

Chapter 90

Hart woke at around 7.00 am with the early morning sunlight streaming through the paper-thin curtains at the window. He lay for a while with the hope of obtaining a little more sleep, but once awake his mind began racing over the job that lay ahead in the next couple of days and in the end, with those thoughts going through his mind now joined by the sounds of reveille from a waking cockerel, plus the barking of at least a couple of dogs somewhere outside, he rose and took a long hot shower in his en suite bathroom, followed by a shave.

Assuming that an adequate police uniform wouldn't be forthcoming, he went to his trusty bottomless case and came up with a pair of dark blue chinos and a lighter blue polo shirt. Suitably dressed for the day, he arrived down at breakfast at 7.45 am where he found Federico, looking smart and elegant in his uniform of the "Special Police", consisting of…dark-blue trousers and light-blue shirt with red embroidered logo on the breast pocket. Seated at the large table eating his continental breakfast, he looked up and waved Hart forward.

'*Buongiorno*, Max. Oh, Snap! You have a very fine uniform after all. Please take a seat and have some breakfast. Marta will be happy to bring you whatever you want, just tell her and she will understand. There's coffee here already if you wish to take some.'

'*Buongiorno*, Federico, just fill me a cup with some black coffee please, I'll consider chancing Marta's wrath over a breakfast request later.'

'*Bene*. Later the rest of our team will arrive, but first I would like to take you on that brief trip to Basiglio I talked about last night if that's OK with you?'

'Just give me fifteen minutes to give my blood glucose a gentle hit and I'll be ready to go.'

Hart swiftly drank his excellent coffee and savoured a couple of the pastries and a thick slice of the previous evening's bread spread liberally with butter and strawberry compote, wiped his face on a serviette and returned to his room where he located his satchel and checked that the contents included his wallet and passport, his two mobile phones and the small flat camera that Messi had given him. It had been thought that with the possible complication of him having two mobile phones, it would be safer to use an actual camera for any photographs that he was able to take. Complete now with his bag, he went outside to join his partner, who was now seated on a wooden bench smoking a foul smelling black cheroot. He nodded, indicating that he was ready to go and quipped,

'Remember, I expect a non-smoking flight.'

Federico smiled and extinguished the cigarette, rising as he did so, and walked over to the car.

'Let's go then, I'll give you the commentary en route again.'

At the end of the winding dirt track from the house, Federico finally gunned the Alpha out onto the main road and headed in the direction of Basiglio. The Basiglio sign at the entry to the town was partnered by a large white marble statue representing the crucifixion. Beyond these, the town proceeded in earnest, with rows of neat well cared for white rendered houses on each side of the road. Hart noticed the orderly procession of TV aerials and telephone wires on the buildings, totally unlike the chaotic mess of wires, aerials and overhead electricity cables that had been evident in Catania the day before. As the car drew closer to the town centre, the road narrowed significantly and narrow streets came into view leaving the main road on both sides, but still having similar rows of houses as those on the main road. As they pressed on, at a much-reduced speed now, the road gave way several times to small squares, piazalli, some of which had the benefit of attractive fountains and others statues of what looked like Roman, or perhaps Greek, characters. One statue, however, was glaringly different. It was a larger than life figure of an elderly man holding what appeared to Hart to be a kind of laboratory flask or retort, into which he was staring intently. Federico pointed to the statue and confirmed what had already crossed Hart's mind.

'That is an un-named representative of an early family member of the Mondos working in the laboratory.'

Looking at the statue, it was confirmed that what Hart had always believed was true. No matter what the status of the person, or how lofty and important a position the person held, in the eyes of the fowl of the air all were equal when it came to crapping on their statues, all being treated with the same degree of reverence.

The road continued through the centre of the town, each side of it lined with attractive traditional shops selling the whole gamut of typical Sicilian quality high street wares.

Of particular note, Hart saw a rare charity shop, run on behalf of the Mondo organisation, with money going to a myriad of worthy causes, but only local ones. The shop was extremely busy. This was another example of the Mondo family, or at least their organisation, working for the benefit of the local people and that instance finally affirmed to Hart that whilst the local populous might respect the police, in no way would they ever do anything which worked against the Mondo name. Moreover, Federico confirmed that people would go out of their way to report to the Mondo offices any activities that were either suspicious or considered to be counter to Mondo's welfare.

Federico directed Hart's gaze ahead of them down the cobbled palm tree lined road, which had suddenly widened by some four or five metres, to where he now saw the high fronted beautifully domed Baroque masterpiece that was the Basilica of San Giorgio. Within the small piazzale in front of the basilica, were wooden benches, which even at this hour were being fairly well used by the locals, who all appeared to be greatly animated in discussing whatever issues of the day there were.

'Federico, I have noticed that clearly we are the focus of attention by the locals as we drive through the town and I'm aware that I must stand out like a sore thumb. I would expect that my description has been circulated pretty widely by the local mafia here. You know, fair hair and handsome with distinguished pale looks sort of singles me out. I would feel better if I could at least cover my head. Do you have a spare officer's cap that I might use?'

'For sure back at the house, but you can borrow mine for now. Of course it will bury you, although I tell you, Max, not to worry too much as we will be close enough to the Fox's lair in this place for her to be able to smell your aftershave!'

Hart reached into the back of the car and picked up Federico's peaked police officer's cap and placed it on his head.

'Actually it's not too bad a fit.'

'You seem to know so much about the island and particularly this place, and I'm positive that it isn't from travel brochures, and so I'm wondering if you were born here...oh and were you joking about our distance from Volpe's headquarters?'

'No, I wasn't joking about that and no, I was not born in this town, but I *was* born in Sicily, in a small town called Oliastrello, but I have mainly worked well outside of Sicily so I am certain that nobody here will recognise me. But look, we are arrived near to the museum that Messi wants me to show you.'

Federico parked the car on the road in a "no waiting" space, the police insignia of his car giving ample immunity to any overzealous traffic warden, and indicted that they should proceed forward. Within several minutes, they were standing at the front of the small museum, its title translated as "The Museum of the Lives and Times of Basiglio". Although small, its frontage was classical Greek in the syle of the famous temple at Agrigento, some 180 kilometres away on the southern Sicilian coast. Hart removed his borrowed cap and followed Federico up the steps and through the two huge pine entrance doors.

Chapter 91

The telephone rang out noisily in the still of the Princeton night and the handset was immediately snatched from its cradle by a tired and dishevelled man wearing a dark blue blazer. His usually immaculate shirt was untidily unbuttoned at the neck and his striped tie was untied and creased.

'Halle speaking,' his voice full of irritation.

'Robert, it is Claudia.'

'Speak Claudia and for God's sake tell me you have Hart under lock and key...*prego*.'

'No, Robert. I am very sorry but it is as I told you yesterday, we do not yet have him. We have so many of our people still out looking for him and still paying even larger sums of money for relevant information on him, not just here in Italy but also over neighbouring borders, that all we can assume is that he went to ground when he arrived in Milan and he has stayed there ever since, afraid to come out of his hiding place. The minute he does, I can assure you that we will have him and will bring him here to Basiglio where the local law is...much more flexible to our activities shall we say...and we can do with him exactly as pleases you best.'

'Claudia, you sound like a needle stuck in an old record groove, always repeating the same thing. What "pleases me best" is to have him in captivity, no more no less. The very endgame of our whole mission is now in sight and while-ever Hart is at liberty, I am anxious that he will do something to screw it up. Things have been happening that, whilst it is not possible to prove them to be directly attributable to his inference, are just too much of a coincidence to be anything otherwise in my eyes. I will admit to you that I have had to be less than honest in my updates to Alberto Mondo, so I will repeat what I said to you yesterday and the day before and the day before that, I want him taken! If you are not successful within the next few days, I will have to consider using some of your competitors to do the job and if that happens, you must realise that it could be the end of the special World-Volpe relationship. That is how serious this is now!'

Volpe was chilled by Halle's threat. All the years of hard work, not to mention the loss of the lives of near and dear loved ones, together with the excellent symbiosis formed between the "Holy Trinity" would be lost and crumble to dust. She could not let this happen...she could not be seen as the one, the first woman mafia leader, to be responsible for this apocalypse. She needed to be harder, stronger and if necessary more brutal in pursuing her goal and especially in delivering her quarry Hart very soon.

'I understand you, Robert. Give me a few more days only and this man will be delivered at your feet. This I promise you.'

'Very well, Claudia, I will give you that time, but it is borrowed time only. You are correct though in assuming that I still want Hart delivered at my feet, preferably alive…at least for the time being, that time now being very short. I need you to contact me the minute you have him, for I still intend to make the journey over there. Do not fail me!'

Halle put down the telephone firmly and stared into the distance. He must not let Hart continue to get under his skin. His own general mental health was certainly suffering of late since his nemesis appeared on the scene.

Volpe heard the connection between them come to an abrupt end and she too stared into the distance. She had never met this man Hart and wasn't convinced of any effect he was possibly having on the greater mission, but clearly his very existence was having a deleterious effect on Halle and that must be remedied. She would meet with her senior leaders in the morning and discuss additional ways forward, bearing in mind that this Hart could be two thousand kilometres or more away in a different country.

The great irony was, however, that unknown to Volpe, Federico had been absolutely correct moments earlier whilst speaking to Hart when he told him half-jokingly that Volpe was "possibly within smelling distance of his aftershave".

Chapter 92

It was some minutes before Hart's eyes became adjusted to the darker, softer lighting of this inner sanctum. Likewise his ears, for the clammering of the outside world continued to buzz on inside his head for quite some moments before the velvet silence replaced it.

Federico waited giving time for Hart's senses to auto-adjust and then ushered him further into the double-vaulted room that was the museum, a tranquil place producing almost reverential sensations in its visitors. He directed Hart past the reception area where there was seated the museum's uniformed "keeper", who broke off his conversation with a visiting priest to eyeball the two visitors at some length. No words were exchanged between the visitors and the "keeper". Federico whispered,

'Entry to this museum, built to the glory of Basiglio and to the Mondos, is gratis, Max.'

With eyes now totally acclimatised to the low-lit room, he took in fully the view before him. The room appeared to be quite small at some 400 feet square, and immediately in front of him stood a life-size bronze statue of Francesco Mondo, or as Federico whispered in Hart's ear with some irony, "this is Mondo the 1st". Francesco Mondo, the founder of the now pharmaceutical giant World and the original benefactor in Basiglio, stood before them with one arm outstretched in welcome to visitors about to see his family history, with a benign smile on his lips. His other arm was stretched to the side of him where his hand was entwined with that of a female, also cast in bronze, his wife Margherita.

'Here we have Francesco and Margherita Mondo, the founders of the Mondo Empire,' Hart's personal guide informed him.

Beyond the statues was a double row of large floor standing exhibit cases. As Hart strolled around them, he saw that they contained many original items from past times. The first case contained what purported to be the original workbench of Francesco Mondo, containing mortars and pestles and a series of glass jars containing what Hart assumed were meant to be medicinal herbs and other such compounds. His guide tried, but struggled, to translate the Italian descriptions.

'Max, slow down please, it is very difficult for me to try and translate at this speed.'

'Don't worry, I'm getting the gist of it all anyway thanks. I tend to take in this sort of thing using broad mental brushstrokes rather than fine-point brushwork. In that way I don't get bored quite so quickly.'

'*Va bene*, go at your own speed then.'

A large second case contained a laboratory bench on which were positioned other tools of the herbalist trade back in the day, such as the obligatory glass retort on its wooden stand, complete with some form of spirit burner below it and seated at the end of its long pointed nose an ancient form of receptacle. Once again, bottles of powders and herbs littered the bench. As Hart moved on the contents of the cases became more modern in terms of laboratory equipment, until in the final case there were large photographs of some of the latest factory and the laboratory equipment in current use. Within that case, in addition to the photographs, Hart was interested to see a list of worldwide factory and laboratory names and places of World's main named companies, plus similar information for its subsidiaries. He quickly saw his own former place of work in New Jersey, but his excitement grew when he saw the names of Vita laboratories here in Sicily, but then his pulse raced when he saw the name and location of the Gerhard Roscher Schmoller Institute (GRS) in Greifswald, Germany. Finally, on the wall rather than in a glass case was a large map depicting the world and on it, illuminated in red flickering lights, were all the global offices and factories associated with and owned by World Pharmaceuticals. It was a truly impressive sight, with red lights only missing from the outposts of Russia and China and the North and South polar icecaps.

'Tell me, Federico, where are the true relics of Basiglio, those left by the Greeks, the Romans and the Vikings, to name just three of the races that have lived here from almost time immemorial?'

'There are some further along in the next small room, but remember there are much larger museums on the island dedicated to those very important ancestors. This is just a small museum in the main dedicated to the Mondo family who have done so much for this town.'

At that moment, Hart became suddenly aware that they were not alone on their journey through "Mondo space and time" as he caught the stare of "the guardian of the grotto". It was the uniformed man they had passed at the entrance and who was now no longer in conversation with the priest. They both turned and faced the man, who smiled nervously and speaking to Federico,

'Are you happy with our little production, or do you have any further questions that I might resolve for you?'

'No we are fine, thank you,' Federico responded.

The man gave a slight bow and smiling looked intently at Hart, '*Grazie signori*,' before retreating to his position at the entrance.

Hart returned to the bronze statue and this time proceeded to look at the wall directly opposite the bronze couple. The whole of the wall was covered with the Mondo family tree, starting at the left hand side and continuing to the right, with names, dates and most interestingly photographs. The tree extended along the whole width of the wall and onto the adjacent one, where it occupied a least half of it.

'You said that Luca wanted me to see this place and made particular reference to the family tree right? Do you have any idea why?'

'No, I'm sorry. What he said was to direct you to the family tree if we came here, and that you would find something, let me think of his exact words here… "of tabloid newspaper interest to you," but you would have to look closely.'

'Interesting.'

Hart moved in close to the family details. It was apparent that the "tree" with its associated "pictoral biography", although no doubt in full bloom before the arrival of Francesco Mondo, only blossomed at that particular point on the wall, his predecessors being covered in a single plaque with the statement that the family had been present on the island for as long ago as could be documented and that these family members had been sons and daughters of toil, being very poor, impoverished and scratching a living off the land.

As the family's depiction began in earnest, with grainy brown photographs of Francesco and family members, a description was given of the family of fifteen children, two of which died in early childhood and another who reached adulthood but died in unspecified circumstances. Mondo had virtually no schooling and by the age of ten years was working at whatever he could lay his hands on to secure money for the family. The pictures then jumped forward to the introduction of Margherita Conte to the family group, with faded creased photographs of the wedding of Francesco Mondo to Margherita Conte. Other photographs depicted the couple working in their early married life, cultivating medicinal herbs as well as vegetables for the table at the back of the house in which they lived. The next line of sepia photographs depicted the young couple working in their kitchen preparing remedies which they bottled and handed out to local people. Mostly, there was a low cost involved, but as most of the people were virtually destitute much of the handed out medicine was given free of charge. A further selection of photographs showed Mondo in smiling groups of people, sometimes shaking hands, sometimes embracing and sometimes staring seriously at the camera as was generally the pose then.

Suddenly, one picture bounced off the wall at Hart. It was a photograph of a trio of obviously close friends all smiling happily at the camera. For once, the subjects of the photograph were identified in the text. They were Francesco Mondo, Gianni Negri and Alberto Volpe. The headline, which required no translation, read "The Three Friends of Basiglio, working together for the entire community".

From there, the pictures moved on to the war and the arrival on the island of "soldier of fortune", Giuseppe Garibaldi and his 1,000 strong army of "red shirts". It was in this era that the business really took off with the Mondos making good use of the anti-lice compound that had in fact been handed down to Margherita through generations of her gypsy ancestors, which they had supplied to both the "red shirts" and to governments further afield eventually to help in other wars. One large photograph depicted the pair of them waving off a shipment of the powder, with smiling troops looking on.

As boredom began to set in, Hart switched his interest in the information on show to his "broader brushstrokes" coverage and quickly zoomed through the Mondo rise through supplying the Italian forces in their ill-fated foray into Abyssinia; the tragic deaths of two of Francesco and Margherita Mondo's children before attaining one year of age; Francesco's death on the day of son Luigi's 10th birthday; the many local philanthropic achievements such as new roads, new public buildings including a fine library, medical dispensaries and a meeting hall; reports and photographs of Francesco's funeral; the onset and benefits of World War 1; Alberto Senior's birth to Luigi and his wife Ilaria; photographs and reports of the Negris and their great involvement in the church; the surprising and bold emigration of the immediate family Luigi and Ilaria, to America in the early 1920s; the concession to the US by changing the company name from Mondo Farmaceutici to World Pharmaceuticals and Healthcare ('Healthcare' being dropped from the company name some years later); greater wealth via the re-match of Italy and Abyssinia under the auspices of Mussolini; the advent and profit from World War II; the marriage of Alberto Senior to Claudia in 1940, with the early birth of Alberto Junior; the sudden return to Basiglio from America, bringing with them their faithful retainer Lorenzo and two housemaids, Lucia Grimaldi and Agata Ricci, to rekindle old friendships as Alberto Senior's health seriously deteriorated; the birth of another son to Alberto Senior, despite his poor health, in Sicily, and named Pietro; Alberto Junior's marriage to Barbera Ferraro, the daughter of another important Sicilian family; Alberto Junior's return to America with his wife.

It was clearly a great and virtuous company, with a truly great history of endeavour and success and under other circumstances, Hart would have been proud to have worked for them, but things had soured totally for him and he now believed them to be unethical, vicious and murderous. Sometime, somewhere, something had gone terribly wrong inside this great Company.

He glanced at Federico, 'They will soon need to extend the wall to accommodate all their family and achievements.'

He had come to almost the end of his tour of the museum and had seen absolutely nothing of the "tabloid newspaper scoop" that Luca Messi had hinted at to Federico. His one last act of boredom was to scan, for one last time, the part of the wall which contained the extensive branching Mondo family tree. There they all were, dating back to Francesco Mondo and coming right up to present day. He looked at the names of Luigi and Ilaria, considering what a giant step it was for them to move to the USA in the 1920s and forward to Alberto Senior and Claudia's sudden return with their family for their Sicilian sabbatical and the birth of another son Pietro to them. The line of Alberto Junior was yet to be added to the tree in any detail other than that of his marriage to Barbara Ferraro.

'Fine thank you, Federico, I've done here…hang on though,' he returned his stare to the family tree. 'Is there any chance of there being any mistakes here?'

'From what I have read from the travel brochures there are no mistakes. All is perfectly correct.'

'OK, thank you. I think I see what Messi was hinting at. *Andiamo!*'

Chapter 93

'So then, Max, did you enjoy our little excursion to the museum?'

The pair, seated in Federico's car, were now taking the back-road a short distance out of Basiglio for the second part of the trip, a ride out to see the World factory and laboratory facilities, including Vita Laboratories.

'Yes, thank you, it was both educational and enlightening. As a past employee, I never realised the hardship that the Mondo family suffered and what great entrepreneurial skills they had, with help from the Negris and Volpes of course.'

'And did you spot the tabloid piece advertised by Luca?'

'Possibly, but I will have to ponder on that one a little more.'

Federico accelerated hard, spinning the car's rear wheels and kicking up clouds of dust on the Basiglio back-road.

'Did you notice anything about the curator back there, Max?'

'He seemed to be interested in our visit and he did offer some assistance I suppose. Who pays his wages?'

Federico laughed.

'The mafia of course. He's one of their lowly minions, of that there is no doubt. He was there obviously to protect the exhibits, but also to watch out for "people of interest" who might wander round. People like us, a man in police uniform accompanied by an obvious Northern European.'

'I never made that association, but now you've mentioned it I'm worried. Are you worried too?'

'Max, this town is run by a mix of Mondo, church and mafia, all are the same. To go into a shop or a bar for a beer is to buy it from someone connected with that Trinity. There is no escaping it no matter where you go, so it is better not to worry.'

'How can I not worry?! I'm on the hit list of some of those bastards, the mafia members working for Mondo for sure, and they've already come very close to removing me permanently from the scene. Also, they will have my card marked for killing a couple of their close associates and will be just waiting for a second crack at me!'

Federico merely shrugged his broad shoulders and for the next ten minutes, they drove in uncomfortable silence. Then, as they rounded a bend in the road, leaving the final scattering of houses of Basiglio behind them, he pointed ahead.

'There it is straight ahead, the World Pharma factory and Vita Research Laboratories. I will drive past it without slowing down, so take a careful look. You will have heard also of "il Laboratorio di Scoperta Fondamentale" and that company was absorbed into Vita some years ago, although it still markets certain chemicals locally under that long trade name. It roughly translates as Laboratory of Fundamental Research, but we believe that of all three companies, that one is not involved at all in any of the stem cell treatment developments, only Vita and of course World.'

The World complex began as a low line of single storey buildings, spread over an area of around five acres.

'Here we have first the laboratories, then the factory areas and finally the office section.'

This latter appeared as a series of four or five-storey very modern-looking buildings, of steel and smoked glass. The whole of the complex was surrounded by steel fencing, about eight feet high, topped with razor wire. Spaced equidistantly along the boundary fence were a series of warning "Entrata vietata" and "Divieto di Entrare", "Keep Out" signs. The next bend in the road brought the car past what looked to be the main entrance for personnel and visitors to the complex, consisting of double lifting barriers guarding both entry and exit. At least six security guards appeared to be on duty at that point, stationed in small huts adjacent to the barriers, there no doubt in order to both check entry permits and to ensure that nobody was escaping from the complex with the World crown jewels secreted upon their person. Hart glanced away from the site for a moment and then back again.

'I hadn't imagined that the place would be so big here, after all the head office is in the US and has been there for a good many years.'

'*Si*, but remember this is the Mondo original place and there still exists a great relationship with the town. It still is like a great family and even now there is barely a single family living in Basiglio whose ancestors did not benefit for their very existence from the Mondo family and of course often from the church and the mafia. You mentioned earlier that you were worried, Max, because you are personally at war with the mafia here and also with World…but I think not with the church though. However, what you should seriously consider instead is that you are at war with the whole population of Basiglio! Just think, over 3,000 people are currently employed at this complex alone, not all from Basiglio of course, but they will be loyal to their employer, plus most of them still carry the gratitude of their ancestors. Therefore I think the total number of your enemies has risen somewhat.'

'Shit! I hadn't considered that. It's a good job we're almost done here. Suddenly, I feel an urgent need to catch the flight back to La Certosa.'

'So now, Max, we drive on, but I have to tell you that there is no way out of this road by driving straight ahead. We reach the end and then we turn around and we drive back. However there is a bar near the end where we will take a coffee.'

'You mean there's not even an even smaller road that we can take?'

'Unfortunately not, but in some ways it is fortunate because it means that when we hold the roadblock tomorrow, we can be sure that the van we look for can only come down this road. It cannot go any other way. This road leads to all other routes in Sicily, whether it is Catania, Messina, Palermo, or any other place and this will be very good for us.'

Hart nodded appreciatively.

They drove on past the last of the Mondo buildings and it was at that point that Hart saw the official exit for company vehicles carrying manufactured drugs and medicines etc. It also served as an entrance for the delivery of chemical constituents and other items that would go into the manufacture, packaging and labelling of goods.

Fifteen minutes down the road, they came across the bar that Federico had mentioned and they pulled up in its un-made-up car park, alighted from the vehicle and entered. The place was surprisingly busy and when their drinks arrived, Hart scanned the place for a couple of seats. Federico however, downed his cafe ristretto in the millisecond of time that it took Hart to reach for the sugar for his cappuccino. He raised a slightly surprised eyebrow as Federico placed his empty cup back on the counter of the bar.

'Same amount of coffee, Max, but you take an additional litre of water with yours. *Andiamo.*'

Five minutes after arriving at the bar, they were retracing their way back down the dusty road, once again passing the World complex, only this time seeing it from the opposite side of the road.

Completing the guided tour past the World facilities, Federico drove back out onto the road and finally back to the safe house. For Hart, it had been an enjoyable and eye-opening drive.

Some distance before they arrived at their residence, they had been able to pick out the flashing blue lights of the three official police cars that had arrived with the men who would complete their team.

It was immediately obvious from the assembled men standing between their cars that their team of six extras had dwindled to five extras as the quintet stood in a circle comparing weaponry. Hart was impressed with at least the look of the men's armaments, although his knowledge of firearms didn't stretch much further than the .22 air rifle that he had won a doll with at a local fair in his youth. Whilst all the men carried holstered Berettas, three of them also shouldered Beretta PMX submachine guns, light and with ambidextrous controls these weapons had full automatic capability as well as select fire control.

Federico smiled and greeted them all and turned to Hart.

'Well, what do you think of our team now?'

'Well, they certainly succeed in loosening *my* bowels, that is for sure.'

Federico shook hands warmly with the five men, who he clearly already knew, and then went through the formality of introducing them to Hart, who true to form forgot their names instantly.

Federico half-whispered instructions into the ear of one of the team who quickly disappeared into one of the cars, re-emerging with a handful of what looked to Hart like white table tennis bats with red circles in their centres. He passed them around to the eager troops who then excitedly went through the process of waving them in the air, rather like directing an aeroplane onto its stand. That's almost exactly what they were, for indeed they were the highly sophisticated instruments for directing the roadblock! Hart nodded appreciatively at Federico and to the smiling team.

'Who's brought the balls and net then?'

'Max, I am going to ignore you. We will now spend some time rehearsing our mission and then after we will take lunch. We will then wait to hopefully hear from our mole inside the factory as to when we should expect the van, or whatever they use, to leave World for the port of Messina.'

With those words, Federico turned to the Italian members of the team and with much gesticulation, described what was expected of them and where exactly on the road they would put their mission into action, after which he said to Hart,

'As for you, Max, you wear a cap, si, as a small disguise. You say nothing at all once we have stopped any vehicle, just follow me to the back of it and I will get the driver to unlock the doors if necessary, after which I will ensure he returns to the front of the van. I will then open the doors and you and I will get inside, where hopefully we, no you, will easily identify what we are looking for. You will remember that once you have identified them to me, we will both photograph the packages, and especially the addresses on them, and also attach the trackers to them. If it is at all possible, you are to extract a sample of treatment material from one of the packs and I will later send it to Luca Messi. I will give to you some trackers later. All clear?'

'Perfectly.'

He then passed an additional small camera to Hart, who confirmed to him that he also had the one given to him by Messi…just in case of problems. It all sounded quite a simple operation, the only thing Hart was unsure of was his ability to open a package and remove a sample without creating any suspicions, but in any case that was a non-essential part of the mission.

'Max, from now until we complete the job we must be completely serious at all times. No more jokes. Yes?'

'Of course.'

Federico had been correct when they had earlier discussed Hart's idea of wearing a borrowed uniform from one of the team. Of the five men, three were almost as large in stature as Federico and the remaining two a good head in height less than Hart, so in order not to create the appearance of a circus clown Hart decided to remain in the clothes he was wearing and just take the borrowed cap.

At that moment, Federico's mobile phone rang out. He quickly raised it to an ear.

'Si, pronto.'

He looked grave as he closed the phone.

'That was our mole. A white transit van will depart the World complex for Messina in only forty-five minutes from now. It is much earlier than he originally told us so we must move immediately. I want us to be seen stopping at least one, preferably two or more other vehicles before the white van appears on our radar in order to hopefully lessen any suspicions.'

As the Italian barked instructions to the other members of the team, Hart felt the knot in his stomach tighten. This was the moment! Following Federico's instruction, he went and sat in the passenger seat of his car and as an afterthought checked the contents of his satchel. The five additional members of the team likewise took their places in their own three cars and all four cars then pulled away in line, at speed, with Federico in the lead.

Chapter 94

The cavalcade of four police vehicles sped down the dusty track from the safe house and onwards towards the point in the highway that Federico had decided was the best place for the roadblock.

He had chosen the junction of the main road into Basiglio and the road leading past the gates of the World complex. This place would allow them access to all vehicles departing from the complex, whilst also giving the appearance of having the potential of blocking the road itself into Basiglio. It was smoke and mirrors of course, the only vehicles of interest being those from World Pharmaceuticals.

Turning left into the World access road, Federico stopped his car on the right hand side. The second car in the line followed him and parked on the other side of the access road, both cars with blue lights flashing. The third and fourth cars parked up on either side of the Basiglio main road in positions just past the World turn-off. This arrangement would allow vehicles coming from the complex and turning in the direction of the port of Messina to be stopped and would also give them the opportunity to stop anything which slipped by Federico et al and turned onto the main highway. The officers positioned themselves as per Federico's previous instructions, one each side of the Basiglio highway at the side of their "blue light flashing cars" with the remaining three officers joining Federico and Hart. Federico indicated for one of his colleagues to take up position next to the car on the opposite side of the road to himself and Hart, and for the other two to join himself and Hart facing down the road towards World. Hart was instructed to take up position just behind Federico on the blind side of the driver of any approaching vehicle from the World complex and then he raised an arm indicating to all that they were in their correct positions. Hart's body tensed in anticipation of his "great expectations" of the next fifteen minutes or so. He harboured no thoughts of failure in his mind, just an overwhelming need to see the job over and completed successfully.

The day had turned round suddenly for Hart, from one of semi-relaxed tourist mode, to one of high alert, with the main game about to be played out in earnest. Although nerve racking, this pleased him, as it signalled a likely shorter stay than he had previously anticipated here in Basiglio.

The seven men waited, five of them holding the "table tennis bats" in nervous anticipation and all of them armed, the three on the World approach road holding the strongest argument in any discord, in the shape of the Beretta sub-machine guns.

With the team in their final positions, Federico signalled to the two officers on the highway into and out of Basiglio, to stop a vehicle on each side of the road, a planned diversionary tactic to hopefully distract the attention of passing vehicles from their true intentions. Within minutes, a van and a truck had been stopped, their drivers spoken to and the interiors of their vehicles sparingly searched, after which they were allowed to drive on, their drivers now aware that dangerous criminals were at large.

At the position on the "World road", an oncoming vehicle was spotted by Federico and his three officers. This vehicle was identified as a yellow transit van, not their informed vehicle for attention, but nonetheless, the two officers standing together moved forward a few paces and waved their bats indicating the van to slow down and pull over. Federico stood, with legs slightly apart and hands clasped behind his back, rocking gently backwards and forwards on his heels. Out of the corner of his mouth he said to Hart,

'I will speak to the driver and then indicate for you to accompany me to search the back of the van. OK?'

'OK Federico.'

For Hart this had the dreamlike quality of some old wartime movie, with Federico playing the pompous self-important Italian army officer. He was only acting a role of course.

As the yellow van came to a standstill at the side of the two officers with sub-machine guns, Federico strode up to the driver's open window and leaned in close. Identifications were asked for and duly shown, followed by Federico's explanation of why the vehicle had been stopped and supplemented with questions to the driver as to whether he had seen any suspicious characters on his journey whilst travelling to the World complex and if he had left his van unlocked for any period of time. He then indicated to the driver their intention to search the inside of the van, whilst at the same time nodding to Hart and beckoning him forward. With the two armed officers now in close proximity to the driver and the third crossing the access road to join them, Federico strode to the rear of the van, Hart at his shoulder shielded from the stares of the driver, and clasping the door handle, with a sharp twist of the wrist flung the door open. There was little inside the van other than a couple of boxes, but the pair made an extravagant show of moving them around in search of the invisible criminals. The search completed, as Hart closed the van door Federico marched back to the driver, thanked him and allowed him to drive away.

'A good rehearsal I think,' said Hart, congratulating all around him.

His comments were received with grunts and nods of agreement. The leader barked out words to the effect of "back to your positions" and the game was in play once again. They were ready for the next customer. This next customer appeared coming around the bend from the direction of the World complex just ten minutes later. It was identified by the eagle-eyed officers, assisted by small binoculars, as being a white van with markings along its side and they noted that the driver had an associate sitting alongside him in the front passenger seat. At the order of their leader, all re-addressed their positions, bats and machine guns at the ready. Hart's heart rate noticeably increased, he could almost hear it, *Could this be the one?*

As for the previous van, on Federico's mark his two officers started the process of flagging down the white van whilst he assumed the legs apart, bouncing on the balls of his feet with hands clasped behind his back position. Once again, Hart stood back, out of sight behind his shoulder. As the van slowed, it was overtaken by a motorcycle, causing the two officers to glance at their leader who shook his head indicating that it was not important. Further back down the road, out of sight of the police group, a second motorcycle pulled into the side of the road and stopped.

As the van stopped at the side of the two officers, Hart immediately noticed the World Pharmaceuticals' logo and livery along its side, and his nervousness increased even more.

This surely had to be the one.

If Federico was at all nervous, he showed no signs of it and confidently approached the window of the van, now flanked on both sides by his machine-gun toting colleagues, with Hart off to one side at his rear. The driver, who was accompanied by an aggressive-looking companion, slid back the door window and glared at him.

'So what do you want?'

Federico flashed his credentials and in turn requested to see those of the driver. With those checked satisfactorily, he next took on the stare of the passenger and firmly requested to see his identification card, la carta d'identita. Grudgingly, the man produced it and held it up to Federico. Next, Federico explained to them the reason for the roadblock and the necessity to check the inside of the van. At this, the driver protested.

'Look, I can assure you that we have no stowaways in this van and furthermore we are carrying very important medicines from the Vita Laboratories, which need to be kept at a very low temperature. If you open the door, the temperature will rise and the medicine will be destroyed.'

'I understand completely, *signore*, but I have my orders and I am giving you yours. Is the back unlocked?'

'*Si.*'

'Very well, we will be very quick and the temperature will not be affected. *Grazie.*'

A glance at Hart, who had pulled the officer's cap low down on his forehead, and the two moved quickly to the back of the van where Federico briskly opened the roller-door and both men jumped inside. The van was the equivalent of the British "Luton" type and allowed both men to stand comfortably once inside, even Federico. Various cardboard boxes were stacked around the floor, but at the far end of the goods space was an article that Hart had not envisaged. Up close to the partition separating the goods space from the driver's cab was a chest freezer with the capability of storing its contents at minus 20 degrees centigrade. The freezer was labelled with large signs which informed one that it contained biological materials in transit and not to open it. Hart smiled and nodded at Federico and opened the unlocked lid of the freezer. Inside were packed together several cardboard boxes. Hart counted eight of them, each labelled with; "Attention: Urgent Biological Materials in Transit". In addition, each box clearly held a label containing the address of its destination and whilst Hart couldn't read much of it, the words "Il Vaticano" stood out from the print. He looked at Federico and nodded indicating that these were indeed the materials they were seeking and pointed at the address. Federico nodded back and gave him a "thumbs up", then quickly joined Hart in photographing the boxes and their labels. Within minutes, the "photofest" was complete and they had all the snaps that they required, Hart taking photographs using both of his cameras. The OCA man then quickly opened a small purse attached to his belt and from it took a handful of yellow stars measuring some 30 millimetres point to point.

'Here Max. These are the "trackers". You will see that they have self-adhesive backing, just peel away the protecting paper and stick it on. Remember we must be sure to attach one to every box. They are already turned on and active.'

Hart took roughly half of them and in no time at all the men had attached one to each box, Federico placing the unused ones back into the purse.

It was now clear to Hart that one of his objectives was impossible. It would not be possible to open up any one of the boxes and remove a sample of the medication and close it again properly, as this would clearly give the game away down the line. In any case the sample, if taken, would certainly not survive in its present form for very long at outside temperatures, but this was unimportant now, they had everything else they needed. Quickly, he closed the lid of the low-temperature freezer and checked the temperature gauge on its front. It had increased by barely two degrees during their investigation of it.

'Perfect. We are done, Federico,' he whispered.

With that, both men jumped down from the vehicle and whilst Hart closed the roller-door, Federico returned to the driver and informed him that all was in order and to proceed, but to be aware of any suspicious men he might see along the highway and to call the local police station should he see anything out of the ordinary. The driver growled some words in response and with a spin of the rear wheels moved off, turning left at the junction towards Basiglio and the port of Messina. Hart, keeping out of the sight of the driver, had caught the full dust-storm as the van accelerated away and for some moments coughed and spluttered, before finally looking at the grinning Federico.

The two men embraced and then shook hands warmly.

'It is done, Max. We did it.'

'I can't believe it went so smoothly, Federico. You and your men were superb.'

'I agree, Max, but without us having the confidence that you had the knowledge of what we should be looking for, although it was fairly obvious as it turned out, we could never have made the plan in the first place.'

'Well, you have Luca Messi to thank for that.'

'Exactly, and that reminds me, Max, I must speak with Luca and then my men, and then make my arrangements to move on to Rome for the final chapter of the story. We must also send the photographs of the boxes containing the

338

treatments, together with their labels, to Luca as soon as possible. Luca will already be involved with the OCA people who are tracking the boxes. It was interesting to come face to face with the Volpe Mafiosi driver and his companion. They did look a little pissed off with me, but I expect that it's the first time that they have been stopped doing their regular run to the Vatican. Ahh, molto bene, I feel very content with the day's work.'

He laughed happily and waved to his men at the road junction, who immediately got into their cars and joined him at the primary assembly point. He called over the other members of the team, who had wandered slightly away, and together with the other two arriving colleagues they celebrated loudly and expansively, with much back-slapping and hand-shaking. After some minutes, Federico turned back to Hart.

'So then, Max, I have told my men to return now to the house and enjoy a long lunch and a little vino, which Marta will be preparing, before departing back to their home bases. There will be a debriefing meeting with everybody present, except you of course, in a couple of days when the excitement has worn off somewhat. What I suggest for you and I is that we take lunch together, but not until we have sent the photographs to Luca, eh. I will also contact Luigi, who has already arrived at Catania, and make arrangements for your flight back to La Certosa.'

'That all sounds very good, especially the lunch part of it, I'm famished!'

With more handshakes and thumbs up, Federico dispatched his men back to the safe house. There were final waves and '*grazies*' to Hart and the three cars containg the five OCA officers, this time with blue lights extinguished, sped off for their appointment with the lovely Marta. In the wake of their dust and exhaust fumes, Hart and Federico climbed into his car.

'I would feel a lot better now, despite my elation, if you could e-mail those photographs to Luca please, Federico.'

'Absolutely Max.'

He removed his laptop from the rear seat, logged in and downloaded the pictures. Then eventually finding Messi on his e-mail list he sent off the pictures from all three cameras, together with a short summary of the mission's success. Within seconds, the response pinged back from Messi. He was ecstatic and fulsome in his praise, promising both men grand celebrations when they next met. Federico closed the lid of his laptop.

'*Allora*, Max, *andiamo*, let's go and take some well-earned lunch.'

He turned his car round, headed to the road junction and turned right down the road towards Catania.

As they left the turn off to the World complex behind them, the second motorcycle that had parked way back down the road towards the complex pulled away.

Chapter 95

The restaurant Federico took Hart to for lunch was only a stone's throw along the highway leading to Catania and specialised, as did most of the restaurants in this area, in Sicilian rustic food. He pulled up at the end of a line of parked cars and the two men alighted.

'Max, I chose this place especially for you. It is called L'Ultima Cena, "The Last Supper".'

'Very apt.'

'Come on, let's go inside.'

The building was a single storey effort predominantly made of large timbers and over the door was hung a rather faded representation of Leonardo da Vinci's 15th century fresco of the "Last Supper".

They seated themselves in a corner at the back of the room, which gave them the opportunity to keep a ready eye on the rest of the restaurant, although that was probably unnecessary at this stage of the day's activities.

'Max, let me order for both of us yes? I promise you will enjoy it.'

'Yes, you go ahead, place the order and while we're waiting we can get our minds clear on where we go from here.'

'*Perfetto*. However, I can confirm immediately that after taking you back to the house I will drive to the airport at Catania, leave the car there and then take a flight to Rome where I will join other colleagues of the OCA to discuss the next steps. As for yourself, Max, Luigi will pick you up from the house and fly you back from Catania to the football field of La Certosa. Messi will await your arrival there and probably the next day will join the OCA in Roma. You, my friend, will then fly from Malpensa back to England. You will be free from this business…at last! All you will need to do then will be to read the newspapers and watch the news channels on the television to see how things will continue to unfold, if censorship allows it that is!'

Before Hart could comment, the waitress arrived at their table and Federico ordered the full gastronomic Sicilian lunch, including dolce and wine. As they ate, Federico interrogated his phone for incoming messages and ticked off some of the other points of interest for Hart's benefit, following their successful earlier activity. For him, the mission would probably give him quite a hike up the promotional ladder.

'Oh yes, you'd better keep my two cameras, Federico, they will be excess baggage for me from here on in. By the way, don't you think the OCA will have done their, sorry *your*, masters a huge disservice in exposing the Vatican in this business?'

Federico gave him a wink and a knowing smile.

'Please, Max, do you really think that the media will hear any of this? They will hear rumours and speculation of course and no doubt there will be some investigative journalism on the topic as there always is. In fact, as there always *was* as it has been throughout our history whenever there was any hint of scandal. The OCA, whilst in search of the truth, is here to protect the church not to bring about its downfall.'

'But Luca told me of many conspiracy theories that have come into the public domain over the many years. There was no cover up possible in those cases.'

Federico laughed.

'Of course there was, Max. None of those happenings were ever proven to be factual. They were only in the minds of the writers and storytellers, for even if true do you think for one moment that the faithful would believe them for a single minute? Much of it was stranger than fiction and although possibly true it only took a few words from high members of the church, including the Pope himself, to rubbish the stories. If we do smell something rotten, we will do our best to root it out, but we will manicure the way the story is told to the people. You see, the people need the church so much and they need to believe that all is pure within it, so they will overlook many of the shortcomings, and be only too pleased to accuse reporters and journalists of being… lowly muckrakers.'

'So the OCA will work towards uncovering corruption and unethical goings on, but you will only report these issues internally whilst solving, or let's say cleansing, the situations. In other words, it seems that your mission is to keep everything under wraps and away from not just the sensationalist tabloid news media, but also away from the quality news reporting organisations?'

'Well done, Max, you have won the jackpot. You are completely correct, if a little naive, which is a compliment rather than an insult. But please, let us stop this discussion right there of the OCA's raison d'être and its modus operandi, to mix my languages, for we should now be celebrating our short but very successful mission together.'

'You're right, Federico, you and your men, and Marta of course, have done an absolutely magnificent job and I raise my glass to you all. Cheers, salute!'

The two men raised their glasses and clinked them together.

'And our meal here was fantastic, thank you.'

'*Cin cin*, my friend. We will finish our drinks and then if you don't mind I will pay the bill and take you straight back to the house, otherwise I will miss my plane.'

'Perfect. I am already getting withdrawal symptoms from the absence of the lovely Marta, so thank you for a great lunch and let's hit the road.'

In the fifteen minutes that it took to arrive at the track up to the house, the men spoke little. Hart was feeling very contented, a combination of success and an excellent meal, and was in the mood for an afternoon nap before the arrival of Luigi. Federico was also feeling very contented, the success of the mission contributing much to the condition, but also because of the professional kudos that would certainly accompany it. For him the standard of lunch was normal, although perhaps usually taken with less wine.

'OK, Max, we are arriving. Home sweet home.'

'Thank you, Federico. You have your bags already in your car right, so just drop me off and you can get straight off to the airport for your flight to Rome.'

'Thank you, Max, I will do that if you don't mind. I see that our colleagues have already left before I could give them final thanks, so I will leave you with the lovely Marta. Once again thank you for all your help and of course for your understanding.'

The two men shook hands warmly.

'Thank you too, Federico. I'm hoping my life will return to something like normality as things progress from here, and thank you also for the tourist information, I've learned a lot from my visit.'

Hart picked up his satchel, but left the officer's cap behind, and stepped out of the car onto the now empty parking frontage of the house and waved as Federico pulled away. Federico sounded his horn a couple of times, which would no doubt rouse Marta, and was gone in an instant. He stood there for a moment letting the outcomes of the day sink in, and then rather wearily trudged up to the house door. Indeed, a short sleep before departing with Luigi would not go amiss.

Chapter 96

Hart turned the door handle and entered the house.

'Interesting', he thought, 'that this be would the first occasion of him being alone with Marta.'

They would no doubt both speak fluently, but only in their own native tongues. He called out loudly into the kitchen where he most expected the old lady to be.

'Ciao Marta. Sono Max. I am here. Sono qui'. Then louder, 'Ciao Marta, it's Max, I'm here.'

Silence.

He walked to the kitchen door, pushed it open and walked in.

'Ciao Marta. Sono Max, sono qu...Jesus!'

In front of him lying across the kitchen table was Marta, her eyes wide open as if in astonishment, her mouth set in a horrific rictus grin of death, with fingernails bloody from where she had scratched at her attacker in her final seconds. The cut, or rather slash, had been made across her throat almost from ear to ear, nearly severing her head completely. Through the gash and the huge amount of blood from her carotid artery and jugular vein, he could see the severed windpipe. Her head rested on the table in a spreading pool of blood and the clothes on the upper part of her body were saturated with it.

In a state of shock, he walked out of the kitchen and into the rear sitting room where he intended to sit down and pull his thoughts together. As a physician, he had witnessed copious quantities of blood and associated death several times during his hospital employment and wasn't traumatised in the slightest by the physical nature of the sight he had just witnessed. His trauma came from the sheer bloody callous murder that had taken place. He was suddenly very afraid.

As he entered the sitting room, his eyes moved to the window and looking through it he made out on the drive behind the house four police cars parked neatly in a row, out of sight from the front entrance. He suddenly became very confused, but his confusion turned to horror as his gaze met the bloodied corpses of his five former colleagues. They lay at irregular angles on the flagstone floor all with a similar look of shock on their contorted faces to that of Marta. It was clear, however, that these men had been shot unceremoniously and at close range. Their heads had been smashed by a cascade of bullets and their clothes were torn by the passage of lead. Where the bullets had hit other parts of the bodies gaping holes were evident and huge chunks of flesh had been lifted from muscle and bone. This was a slaughterhouse! The walls and parts of the ceiling of the room had been honeycombed by the sheer volume of ammunition that had been fired at these men, who clearly had had no time at all to remove their own weapons and return any fire at their attackers. He moved quickly to the prostrate men and checked each one individually for any signs of life. There were none.

A sudden thought came into Hart's spinning head. There were four police cars outside. There should only have been three. The five men had arrived in three cars, not four. Angered by the slaughter, shocked by the frenzied violence of the attack, confused by the additional car outside and…suddenly agonised by the sickening blow to the back of his head, Hart collapsed heavily to the ground, with blood pouring from the head-wound down his neck and onto his shirt. Then all was black as he was enveloped painfully and ferociously by unconsciousness.

His considered afternoon sleep had come in a very different form to that which he had only just recently imagined.

Chapter 97

The Sicilian mafia under the leadership of Claudia Volpe had grown strong. With their first female head in place, they expanded into many business areas, always taking care to appear as partial benefactors to the populace of the island. Volpe, despite her striking appearance, was not just a figurehead of the organisation. Her meritous university educational background, which covered combined higher degrees in politics and business and an additional honours degree in Sicilian history, provided her with all the necessary qualities to help her make the most shrewd business moves, whilst her stance against all apparent odds, her unbending determination, her qualities of leadership and her ferocious dealings with those unfortunate enough to cross her, set her up to reign supreme as la Capa.

She had seen the importance of the organisation diversifying in as many ways as were possible and consequently had instigated dissemination into areas of business such as waste management, construction and carpentry, wind farms, real estate, high-end restaurants and pizza bars, night clubs and traditional pavement bars. A huge, relatively new and important area of involvement was fish, for as well as controlling actual catches and their buying and selling, this had given her a foot in the doorway of actual port management. This meant that nothing came onto the island or left it without her total detailed knowledge of it. The significant thing which pulled all of these activities together, however, was the means by which money could be laundered.

This evening, Claudia Volpe was seated in her office within the main building of her waste management empire when the phone rang. She started slightly, but picked up the receiver, noting the name of the caller which came up on the small screen.

'*Pronto. Ciao*, Robert, I was just about to call you.'

'I'm sure you were, Claudia, I'm sure you were.'

'Yes, Robert, I was about to call and tell you that we have Hart in our custody.'

She smiled slightly to herself during the following pregnant pause as Halle collected himself. Whilst she was empress of all she surveyed in Sicily and on much of the Italian mainland, she also had certain influences in other parts of Europe, but despite all of this, she was still nervous in her dealings with Halle and careful not to irritate or fall foul of him, as the World contacts between them were potentially global and of a very powerful and profitable nature. Upon hearing her news, Halle's tone of voice changed perceptively.

'That's very good news, Claudia. I presume that your people took him today? Did they manage not to kill him as I requested?'

'Of course. He was located here in Sicily not far from the World complex, by a very astute member of the team that recognised him from one of the photographs that we have circulated. He was in disguise and in the company of police officers, from whom we relieved him with a minimum of effort. Now, Robert, you have expressed a wish to travel to wherever we held him and meet him face to face as soon as possible. Is that still the case, for I have to tell you that the two men he killed on the train to Milan were particularly well liked by our colleagues here who would like nothing better than to deal with him in as painful a way as possible? What are your thoughts at this time?'

'I have to say thank you for a start, Claudia, and a special thank you to your man on the spot who recognised him. I can understand the strong feelings against him there, but I cannot say in strong enough terms that I must see him and see him alive. Your men may have some sport with him if you feel that is necessary for their morale, but I am insistent that Hart will be in a fit condition to talk intelligently to me when I meet him. To that end, I will organise a flight from Philadelphia to either Catania or Palermo, preferably Catania, for as soon as possible. I will have my PA send you my travel details as soon as they are available and you can make whatever arrangements are necessary for my ground transportation and hotel.'

'Of course, Robert, once I have your details I will make all necessary arrangements and it goes without saying that I will be in the car that picks you up at whatever airport is the most convenient to you.'

'Thank you, Claudia, I look forward to meeting you very soon and of course to renewing my acquaintance with Doctor Hart, so for now I wish you good evening.'

Chapter 98

Imagine a black page:

Imagine letters appearing...... one at a time.
Then, eventually ....
coming together
to form meaningless
................words,
which eventually.........................
take on some meaning.................
finally fitting together.....
to make........ actual....................
understandable sentences,...
**.....but feeling in the stranglehold of confusion, fear and above all
else............
PAIN!**

That was the way Hart finally returned to wakefulness in the room in which he found himself bound tightly to the chair into which he was collapsed. As he mentally examined the various parts of his aching body, he was firstly aware of his head, hurting like hell from the blow he now remembered receiving from behind him in the house and the accompanying ache which was currently spread all around and inside his head. His body felt as if it had been used as a football, which in fact it had been following his initial assault. Of the four men carrying out the bloody assassinations at the derisory "safe house", two of them at Volpe's explicit choosing, were both friends and family of the two Mafiosi sent to murder Hart on the train from Padua to Milan. As Hart had hit the floor, they began a frenzied attack on him using both fists and feet. Without the eventual intervention of the other two men, Hart would have undoubtedly died there and then, but Volpe had received instructions from the American that he must continue to live, at least in the short term.

Eventually Hart's self-examination moved from his damaged head, which included a bloodied nose, a split and swollen lip and aching cheek bones, via the bruised and possibly cracked ribs, to his aching and no doubt bruised thighs where several of the flying boots had also made contact and ended at his ankles, where the pain emanated from tightly pulled ropes, which bound him to the chair. His wrists were likewise tightly bound to the chair.

Self-evaluation completed, he cast his mind, now coming back into some kind of order, back to the house and the sight of the old woman and the five OCA officers brutally and bloodily murdered. These latter thoughts brought a feeling

347

of tremendous nausea over him and he vomited slightly down his dirty bloodstained shirt and onto the floor.

With his half-closed eyes looking dizzyingly around the foreign room, it was obvious to him, even in such a wreck of a condition, that the chances were that he would never leave this place, wherever it was, alive. He frantically peered around through his blur for some form of exit, but even if an open door was presented to him, he was so tightly bound that he would be totally unable to make any use of it. The room was clearly part of an old office of some kind, illuminated by a trio of ceiling lights. A large window was visible to him to his front, but on each side of him were walls. He had no idea of what might be behind him. Around the room in front of him, he could just pick out rows of large boxes stacked in front of what appeared to be a panelled wall area. Close by his left side was an ancient desk and screwing up his eyes and peering at the desktop, he finally made out next to some ornate object which he assumed was a paperweight, his satchel, which had contained his personal documents and the two mobile phones given to him by Messi. By now, he expected that the bag would be emptied and the contents a source of some future questioning of him.

He was suddenly aware of sounds coming from behind him on the other side of what must the door to the room. It was clear to him that it would be in his greatest interest to try and play for time and as he heard the door unlocked from the other side he let his head drop onto his chest as he feigned continued unconsciousness.

Claudia and her trusty lieutenant, Giorgio, took no time upon entering the room in taking up position in front of the faux unconscious Hart. As an afterthought, Claudia indicated to the door and Giorgio duly responded by quickly locking it before returning to his position. In turning to her lieutenant as he locked the door, the Capa almost lost her footing, skidding in Hart's vomit on the now slippery floor. She looked at the lieutenant as if he was personally responsible and he immediately took a large handkerchief from his pocket and handed it to her, nodding nervously. With the white handkerchief grasped firmly in her hand, she leaned over, bending her knees very slightly, and rubbed at her lime green Louis Vuitton "Horizon Sandals", both across the narrow leather foot-strap and underneath her toes. She snapped her fingers and magician-like her man conjured a handful of tissues with which he wiped the floor, throwing the soiled tissues into a heavy cast iron waste bin near the desk.

Despite the 51-gun salute going off inside his bloodied head, Hart allowed his heavy eyes to flicker apart just far enough to take in the vision before him. There, some two and a half feet in front of him was the "Fox", her long luscious red hair moving in synchronised motion with the hand that was cleaning the shoe. Despite his advanced condition of physical damage and wretchedness, through squinting eyes, Hart was struck once more by her overpowering physicality and beauty. Eventually the scent of her wonderful perfume was able to percolate though the snot and clots of blood in his damaged nose and he smelled the combination of bergamot, fig and orange. The perfume Balade Sauvage by Christian Dior, was Volpe's particular perfume of the week and it had certainly scored with the A&E patient bound and trussed in the chair in front of her.

As she stood up, Hart closed his eyes tightly, importantly focusing on playing semi-conscious, an easy role in his current condition. Volpe cursed as she became aware that now attached to her wonderful perfume was the additional fragrance of vomit. She addressed the minion.

'I want him awake and standing. No bindings, understand?'

'But, Claudia, are you sure, it may be dangerous to untie him, knowing of his history?'

Volpe raised a hand before he could speak further.

'What are you, Giorgio, a man or a mouse? Look at him, he's pathetic. Are you telling me that you are afraid of this…half a man? He's a doctor you know not a bar room brawler or professional boxer. Get on with it! We need the information he has and we need it quickly before Halle arrives and takes over the interrogation. Why can't people stick to the jobs they were trained to do? We have Hart assuming the roles of secret agent and assassin and Halle the would-be Capo and interrogator, and I am becoming very pissed off with it! When I have the required information from Hart, I will be happy to let him die in whatever way you prefer.'

A grin spread across Giorgio's pock-marked face, scarred from a lifetime of fighting battles for the cause, and today from the rakings of the dying Marta.

'Sorry Capa, straight away.'

Hart's teeth were gritted. It was abundantly clear where his painful future lay with these people. The bottom line was that he actually had *no* future at all and within the next few minutes, he must formulate some kind of rapid escape strategy. The problem was that Volpe was totally correct in her assessment of him. He must try something at least to escape, but would most likely die in the attempt. His vision was a little less blurred now, but still the room looked as it did at first glance…an old regular style office. One thing he noticed, however, was that beyond the large windows was a large and noisy factory-like sorting area, with conveyors travelling along, sideways and upwards. It occurred to Hart that the factory was possibly an addition to the outside wall of the old office in which he was captive. The locked door to the office, which he felt did not open into the factory area directly, was behind him, so was there another door which led out into that area? All Hart could see were stacked boxes in front of a wooden wall panel, but the panel had what looked like a metal bar somewhere along the mid-line of it.

Could he rush the window and launch himself through it in an attempt at escape?

Chapter 99

With three rapid cuts, using a knife of surgical sharpness which he removed from a sheath on his trouser belt, Giorgio released Hart from his bindings.

Hart moaned and his chin dropped onto his chest. Volpe was not impressed.

'Come on, Doctor Hart, you need to be awake and standing for my purposes.

She issued a command to her assistant, who put his strong hands under Hart's armpits and then in one swift movement hoisted him to his feet. He then quickly changed his position such that he was now supporting Hart still from under the armpits, but now from behind him so that Hart and Volpe were face to face. She moved her face to within one foot of his on the verge of delivering a final ultimatum to him, but overcome by the terrible smell of the vomit on his breath and his clothes, she swiftly moved back out of range. Her hands, however, were still within striking distance and she slapped his face repeatedly in an effort to keep him awake and focus his attention. In trying to put on the greatest performance of his life, he rolled his eyes and moaned in order to support his envisaged semi-comatose status.

'Oh my God, my head! Where am I? Have I been in some kind of accident?'

'Please, Doctor Hart, don't make this an Oscar-winning performance, just cooperate and I will ensure that you are suitably taken care of.'

Hart opened his eyes and stared into hers.

'Welcome back, Doctor Hart.'

He opened his mouth to speak but she cut him off, her voice aggressive.

'Don't waste my time with any idle chatter, which I do realise is a particular forte of yours. I know that you are involved deeply now in a business that doesn't concern you and I need to know in this instant what that involvement actually is, what you know and who you are working with?'

Hart took a deep breath, deciding to divulge some of what was required whilst re-focusing around the room and finalising his foolproof plan of escape.

'I'll tell you everything I know, which is not a lot in fact. It all started for me when I returned from the States…'

'Yes, yes, I know you worked at World in Philadelphia for Robert Halle.'

'So when I finally returned to the UK, I was appointed to a small local company working on stem cells.'

Hart looked at Volpe. At this point of his story at least, she looked interested and, therefore, it was perhaps a good time for him to have a sudden dizzy spell. He rocked backwards and forwards on the balls of his feet, closing his eyes as he did it. He was wrong! Without warning the "lady" struck him violently with the back of her hand across his face cutting into his cheek with the large emerald in her ring.

'Come on now wake up! Don't piss me off, Doctor Hart, I grow impatient.'

'Jesus! You fucking bitch!'

Not the best bridge-building statement in the circumstances. His face was now stinging from the slap and hurting intensely from the gouging cut. He was hurt and angry, but in this lose, lose, situation it was important not to antagonise his enemies any further, at least not just yet, but the time was nearly there. It was too late for conciliatory thoughts though, as a similar slap quickly followed up and hit him on the other cheek, this time without the added pain of a cut. At the same time, Volpe nodded to her assistant who short-jabbed him hard at his side and under his ribs.

As the clenched fist struck his ribs, he heaved and retched in the general direction of Volpe. Whilst part of the contents of his stomach had already been discharged earlier, in spasm he began to vomit again. Volpe's eyes widened in disgust and she barked at Giorgio,

'Cristo! Use the bin, take him to the bin!'

She pointed at the metal bin close to the desk and Giorgio accommodated her request by dragging Hart over to it. As Hart's head was forced down towards the bin, he heaved the last of his lunch directly into it. He continued to retch and gag and added to the vomit bitter tasting bile, which he spat out noisily, saliva running down his chin. During this episode, the fingers of his right hand, out of sight of Giorgio, who was now diverting his view from the sight of more vomit, wrapped around the heavy ornate paperweight on the ancient desk and suddenly in one swift movement he rose up and smashed it hard against the temple of the unsuspecting Sicilian. There was a crack as his skull fractured, followed by a copious amount of blood, and Giorgio went down like a large sack of Italian potatoes, totally unconscious if not killed outright. Volpe was frozen in shock at Hart's sudden violent explosion into life, her eyes wide and her beautiful mouth open. Continuing the move, he applied both hands to the heavy iron bin, lifted it quickly and brought it down hard, open end first, over her head. It was a tight fit with her volume of hair, but fit it did allowing the dazed mafia boss to feel and smell the vomit and paper tissues mixing with her hair. Once for luck, Hart struck the bin hard with the bloodied paperweight, the reverberations from which sent Volpe's head into an even greater spin. He spun her round and applying his foot to her backside propelled her across the room and over the desk, where she landed in an inelegant heap on the floor.

Without taking any further glance at his adversaries, Hart snatched up his bag, which he hoped still contained the phones and his documents, lined up the wall with the window and ran at it as hard as his seemingly disconnected legs would possibly allow him. As he neared the window, he launched himself off the ground, leading with both feet, but not at the glass. In that final rushed moment, it clicked with him what the likely metal bar along the wooden panel might be and, therefore, instead of aiming himself at the glass, he aimed for the panel. As his feet struck the metal emergency release bar, there was a loud clatter and the door burst open, completely off its hinges from the violence of his contact with it. He had correctly assumed that the wood panel was in fact a long unused emergency door. In fact, it dated from the time before the factory extension was built on to the old office and had been forgotten for years. Hart himself landed awkwardly on his backside, but in this adrenalin powered moment not appearing to suffer any major injury he dragged himself quickly to his feet and scrambled over the cardboard boxes, that had followed the door in its flight from its fixings in the office door frame and which had likely contributed to breaking his fall.

He was free from the office and from Volpe and Giorgio for now, but time was short and he had to make a quick decision as to which way to run. The golden rule of "TV thriller chases" being that when pursued by bad guys, always escape either on the level, or by going down, characteristically Hart chose to go up in the building!

To be fair, the only immediately obvious way out on this level was a large entrance directly across the far side of the vast, busy, noisy factory area and to arrive at that point, he would have had to navigate through a throng of work people, who he was sure would have no compunction about dragging him down to the ground and therefore back into imprisonment once more.

Looking to his immediate left, he saw a wooden-framed glass door and through it he could make out a short corridor with a rising staircase. With the limited selection of freedom exits at his disposal, this was the route he quickly chose. For a man in his present physical condition, he covered the distance to the door very quickly, aware that he would be followed imminently by Volpe and other cohorts of hers, and without looking back opened the door and headed straight for the metal staircase. Once at the staircase, he surprised himself by taking the stairs two at a time, the sound of his shoes on the black iron treads ringing out in the stair well. As his adrenalin kept him moving as well as he could expect, he quickly considered his next options, either to enter one of the corridors on the higher floors or to continue to what would likely be the roof of the building. Not wanting to submit himself to the possibility of running into more gentlemen of the mafia, he decided to keep going upwards and hope that his energy would hold out until he at least arrived at the top of the building…and also that the number of floors was few.

He had already rejected the first floor option by the time he caught the sound of the screams and curses from Volpe below. He had gained a little additional time on her as she dithered outside the office, having first finally removed the bin and its horrible contents from her head before pondering which way he had gone. She eventually chose to first check with the body of workers on the factory floor of this dry waste processing plant that he hadn't gone in their direction. Having thus learned of the direction of his flight, she was now in full cry, happy in the knowledge that he was heading for the roof where she would undoubtedly be able to round him up with the help of her colleagues very quickly. She kicked off her high-heeled shoes and hoisted her lime green skirt to mid-thigh level ready for the sprint ahead and with four of her men now in tow followed Hart up the staircase. Upon reaching the second floor, Hart afforded himself a glance back down the stairwell at the oncoming vixen and her small pack. She was charging up the stairs, her men behind her having difficulty in keeping up with her. With his rapidly improved vision, Hart was now able to pick out the adornments of vomit soaked tissue in her mass of tousled red hair but more worrying for him, the Beretta pistols clutched in his pursuers' hands.

He took a deep breath and continued upwards. One advantage he had was that his pursuers were unsure at each floor whether or not he had ducked out down a corridor or continued with the climb, but in order to consolidate this, he had to tread more lightly on the metal stairs to discourage the noise of his footfalls. Happily for him, from the second floor onwards the stairs were carpeted, representing the more "executive" areas of the building where men and women in offices worked not just on paperwork associated with waste management, but with the administration and clerical work associated with the firm's many other functions outside of waste.

He gained the third floor still miraculously holding his lead, wondering just how many floors the building had. A sudden irony struck him as he continued to climb. For once the hound (himself) was being pursued by the "Fox" (Volpe)! His legs were aching tremendously now, burning as the lactic acid began to do its worst, and he made the decision that he had no option but to exit the stairs into the corridor upon reaching the fourth floor. As he approached the door to the fourth floor, it opened gingerly and a short swarthy man edged out, a holding a Beretta pistol in his outstretched hand. Hart had expected this to happen as he had arrived at each previous level and was prepared. As the arm preceded the man, who helpfully peered carefully in the wrong direction (i.e. up the stairs), Hart grabbed his wrist and yanked him out onto the staircase and maintaining the momentum heaved the surprised man over the banister into the void, his foot added purposefully to the man's body applying even more urgency to his downward departure. Such was the surprise of the mafioso that he had hurtled through space for one whole floor before he eventually had the presence of mind to let out a cry of despair. Volpe and her crew now approaching the third floor held up abruptly seeing the man dive past, assuming that he had gone over the stair railing at this floor and proceeded cautiously. They weren't even sure at that stage whether or not it was in fact Hart himself who had taken the dive and consequently Volpe dispatched one of her team back to check upon the identity of the fallen man, where he had now come to rest on the ground floor.

Hart changed his mind about leaving at the fourth floor and continued upwards, *Surely the end must be in sight?* He was now beginning to gasp for breath and his legs were turning to jelly, but he had to imagine that the people behind him were experiencing similar effects to himself. He was after all a weekend jogger back in the USA!

Suddenly the staircase came to an end, along with the plush fitted carpet, at a door which was clearly an emergency door to the outside, most probably, roof space. He stood momentarily to regain a little of his breath before opening the door.

All was black! He had lost all sense of time, of whether it was day or night. He had fully expected to be met by daylight upon emerging onto the roof, but as it happened he was wrapped in the blackness of night. He carefully pushed the door back closed, hopefully not giving away any clues that he had finally made it to the roof and looked around.

Chapter 100

After several seconds, his eyes became slightly accustomed to the darkness. There were no lights on the roof of the building and as the roof was above most of the others in that area there were no secondary light sources. If there *were* any other buildings out there of similar height, they apparently had their lights turned off. The cloud covered sky didn't help any either, blotting out any possible illumination from the moon and stars.

Left or right?

He chose left, his quick appraisal of each alternative having returned the same result. Nothing!

Thus chosen, he ran crouched low and scurried across the rooftop, occasionally tripping over items left strewn across the floor and finally colliding heavily with the side of a building of some sort. With the breath momentarily knocked out of him, he paused and looked around. He could make more out of the roof landscape now, aided by the occasional shaft of light now visible coming up from the street below. The low building that had interrupted his flight was a small outhouse of some sort, probably used for the storage of maintenance items. Looking around, he could make out a low, perimeter wall marking the edge of the roof, but his hopes of coming across any fire escape were looking to be slim to say the least.

Suddenly the dark was pierced by light emanating from the door through which he had emerged onto the roof and he was able to see four characters emerge. There were three of the mafiosi together with their leader, Claudia Volpe. They knew that Hart's chances of escaping the roof were slim, especially as only one of the two fire escapes was currently serviceable, the second one being under reconstruction. Volpe closed the door behind them, automatically locking it from the outside. She had the only key which would permit their re-entry. The quartet stood in discussion for a couple of minutes, Volpe indicating who should go where on the roof. Like Hart, their eyes were initially unaccustomed to the darkness and their progress in the directions indicated by their chief somewhat slapstick as the trio clumsily collided with each other and tripped in the darkness amid constant cursing. Eventually following a hissed instruction from Volpe, they realised they had torch facilities on their mobile phones and with much swearing they awkwardly accessed these modes, their three individual point sources of light appearing almost simultaneously. Volpe of course already had her torch accessed. The functioning fire escape stairs were off into the now partial darkness to the right and two mafiosi funnelled in that direction upon her command. She sent the remaining mafioso straight ahead and he showed his appreciation by immediately falling all his length over some building materials left there by the construction workers. She herself decided to take the left of the roof space where she proceeded at some speed.

'Shit!'

Hart moved out from the side of the hut and proceeded forward as fast as he dare. It was obvious to him that the source of light from Volpe's torch was approaching his position rapidly and he decided to throw caution to the wind and change up a gear. Unfortunately for him, the roof was randomly littered with much builders' debris and soon after his decision to put more wind into his sails he struck a rock and sank. In fact, he tripped over a pile of bricks and did a perfect forward roll, hitting his head on the rubble and ending up on his backside up against what looked like a partially open skylight. Peering through the window he was surprised to see that beyond the glass was a void that wasn't filled until it met the ground floor, where the separation of dry waste materials was noisily taking place and where a couple of people were dragging away one very deceased colleague.

He dragged himself to his feet, bent on sprinting into the darkness that remained to his left.

'It's a long way down, Doctor Hart, yes?'

The smiling Volpe was suddenly standing no more than three feet away from him. In her hand and pointing at his stomach, she held a Beretta handgun. She doused the torch on her phone and slid it inside her skirt pocket, where it nestled next to the key to the fire door.

'Here we are together again. All this excitement and my people below work on oblivious to everything. Tell me, Doctor Hart, why did you kill my men? You know I will lose face now if I let you live.'

'Look here, Miss Volpe, I never wanted to kill anyone. I have been trained to save lives not to bloody well take them! You know very well that had I not killed your men, they would have killed me. They were assassins and what I did was in self-defence. Surely you must see that?'

'Yes of course, you had no option and by the same token I too have no option, for you would surely kill me also if it was your only means of escaping from here. Because of that, Doctor Hart, I am going to shoot you.'

Even at this likely late stage of his life, Hart couldn't help but be impressed by her savage beauty, vomit and tissues included, but he wasn't going to go down quietly. Hart indicated to her right.

'Why don't you keep your hands clean and get your man here to do it for you?'

In the split second it took for her to glance sideways, Hart dived forward grabbing the wrist of her hand which carried the gun with his own two hands. She fought wildly, her un-held hand striking at Hart's head and her finger nails drawing bleeding red furrows down his face. He shook his head away from the razor-sharp nails and quickly transferred a hand from her gun hand to her other wrist. She was screaming and spitting at him now trying fiercely to free her hands whilst kicking his shins and attempting to bring her knee up sharply into his groin. It was at this point, as her knee came up and his own knee moved over bringing his thigh in front of his groin, that the pair of them lost their balance and entered into what suddenly became a dance of imminent death in which they were both locked. As they struggled, they suddenly tippled sideways in the direction of the skylight and it became obvious to them both in that instant that they were destined to crash through the glass and plummet to the factory floor below. Hart let go of her gun-hand and caught hold of the lower part of the window frame as Volpe's back smashed through the glass, but he managed to retain a grip on her free hand. There they were temporarily frozen in time and space, Hart on his knees gripping on to the raised fascia below the window frame with one hand, whilst with the other holding Volpe's wrist as tightly as he could, as she dangled in space below him some five storeys up from the factory's concrete floor.

'I can save you. Throw away the gun and grab my other hand and I will try and pull you up, otherwise we can call your men to help us.'

She hung there swaying slightly and smiling, whilst pointing the Beretta Pico 0.38, semi-automatic handgun, at Hart's head. In the next moment, several things happened simultaneously. Suddenly Hart's knee gave way and his upper body involuntarily dropped to one side. At that same instant, Volpe, whether by design or by reflex action to Hart's sudden shift in position, pulled the trigger. The report was deafening and as Hart automatically leaned quickly to one side he saw the leather on his satchel tear open as the bullet passed through it and with the sudden impact came a sudden deep pain. All the while his hand, wrapped around her wrist and holding her above the void, had been slowly slipping due to the sweat that was being generated by them both.

'You've fucking shot me! Now you're slipping. Get rid of the gun and take my other hand…quick!'

Through the pain, he saw her smile and raise the gun to fire once more. It was at that point that Hart, driven by pain and the fear of an encore shot, decided very reluctantly that she had been hanging around for long enough and with great regret released his grip on her. As she began to fall, a quizzical look now on her face, she fired off several more rounds of bullets in his general direction, but this time he had anticipated this likelihood and had already ducked away from the line of fire before the first bullet was fired. From his almost prostrate position, he heard the sickening sound of her body striking concrete and the resultant commotion below. Before retreating once more into the darkness and before the arrival of her henchmen, he peered quickly down at the floor five storeys below taking in the terrible sight of the beautiful Volpe laying there broken, bleeding…and dead.

The three men on the roof had been told by their boss to hold their allocated positions and to take Hart into captivity again if the opportunity arose, but otherwise to wait for her return in the expectation of her completing the kill. It was some time, therefore, before the penny dropped with them that not all was well and it was only then that they decided to leave their posts and investigate the situation, by which time Hart had had the opportunity to move further into the darker more welcoming areas of the roof.

He knew that before much longer the roof would be swarming with enraged mafiosi, all intent upon exacting the worst kind of revenge on him, so it was absolutely paramount, therefore, that he found a way off the roof as soon as possible…"but how and where?"

Chapter 101

Below him all was chaos in the building since Volpe's fenestration, with both workers and mafiosi running around colliding and cursing, but with nobody knowing exactly what to do next. Female workers were screaming and then cries went up for somebody to fetch a priest, but only a full blown miracle could help the broken Claudia Volpe now. It was clear to all that the Englishman was responsible for perpetrating this act and word was spreading rapidly that he was trapped on the roof and probably unarmed. Like soldier ants, the queen's men began to swarm up the stairs, pistols drawn, with terrible vengeance at the front of their minds.

Meanwhile, Hart continued to track across the roof in the direction he had started out on, whenever possible dodging behind various structures that loomed up out of the dark for cover whilst keeping as low as possible. He was surprised at the so far non-appearance of any of Volpe's gorillas in his vicinity, but across the other side of the roof he heard chaotic shouting and the occasional report of gunfire and also saw its associated muzzle flashes, as his nervous hunters began firing at shadows. The torches held by the men didn't help them a great deal in the blackness, in fact they were more of a benefit to Hart as they illuminated their positions, confirming their lengthy distance from him.

His shoulder was hurting like hell and putting a hand over the area under his satchel where the bullet entered, he felt something wet and sticky. Suddenly he made another collision and upon closer examination discovered that he had run into the small wall which marked out the perimeter of the roof and in fact was the roofs end. He now had no option but to follow the edge around the side of the building. He ducked quickly as a couple of bullets ricocheted off a metallic chimney nearby. He anxiously looked into the darkness, but the torchlights he saw were still quite some way off. In an instant, the roof area on which he was standing was bathed in a soft low light. In the dark, he had not been aware of any buildings of similar height close-by, but now it was obvious that there was a building across the other side of the road and his guess was that the result of the frequent gunfire had been to rouse its occupants, who had switched on their apartment lights.

In that instant, he saw that the roof of the building in the same row as his next door, was on the same level as the one he was now on and his heart leapt. However, upon closer inspection, it became obvious that the distance between the roofs was too far for him to cover, even with a good run-up and with him one hundred percent fit. Could a badly beaten up man with a bleeding gunshot wound make the leap successfully? He leaned out and checked the distance once again.

'No bloody chance! Surely there must be some other way of crossing the space between the two buildings' roofs?'

Minutes before he had collided with the last wall, the other obstacle that had contributed to more skin being scraped from his shin was yet another pile of builders' materials. Looking quickly amongst the empty cement bags, bricks and tools in the semi-light, he spied and felt several metal scaffold poles. With his mind now racing in overdrive, he dragged one of them free of the rubbish and fed it out into the night across the void between the two buildings in the direction of the other roof. With no length of pole left to play with at his end, he laid it down. Then, the big question…would it fall down to the alley below, being too short to cover the distance, or would it find harbour on the other building's own parapet?

Answer…success! Unable to walk a tightrope, he quickly delved into the rubbish for the metal pole's partners and came up with two more, which he put through the same bridge-building process. When finished, he had three substantial poles laying side by side across the gap, some eight or nine inches in total width. Whilst better than a tightrope, it was still narrow and unstable, but he would have to attempt to traverse this "bridge" he had fashioned in very poor light, if he was to have any chance of escape. He stood and looked at the combined width of the metal poles and the distance to the alley below. Did he have the nerve to attempt a crossing? Another couple of ricocheting bullets nearer this time made up his mind for him and before he knew quite what was happening he found himself up on the wall and edging gingerly out onto the poles. He was terrified that the poles might roll apart as a result of his weight upon them, but he had no choice. He looked straight ahead and started out on his skywalk, feeling with his feet for the poles each fairy step of the way. He was almost past the halfway mark when, as he had feared, he froze stuck in space, but a swift recollection of the gruesome state of his colleagues' bodies that he had found at the so-called safe house was all the extra adrenalin he needed to propel him forward again. His last few fairy steps rapidly converted into a sprint as he overcame the final few feet of his makeshift bridge and he finally stepped off the poles onto the low wall of the next-door building. Happiness was pole-shaped! For his next trick, he pulled each pole across to his own side and carefully, not too noisily, dropped them onto the roof. At the end of this exercise, he had successfully navigated himself over to the roof next door, whilst hopefully removing the possibility of his hunters following him using the same method and at the same time not drawing attention to his position by the noise of dropping metal poles.

He still had to find the fire escape from this second building though, but buoyed by his success he set out as quickly as he could. His theory was that as the fire-stairs were clearly not on this side of the building, they would likely be on the far side, which he would access by hugging the roof's perimeter wall, keeping low and using any resident structures to help shield his back. He was thankfully correct in his assumption and having travelled the full length of the wall on the street side, in following it as it turned left at the far end, where once again an alleyway ran alongside it, he saw a standard metal fire escape which zig-zagged down the building's side to the alley below. Once he had arrived at the stairway, he looked back at the roof of the Volpe building, which whilst still in darkness had the pencil beams of the men's torches criss-crossing everywhere. Many men were still running randomly around like a disturbed ants' nest, but shouting and swearing, together with the occasional gunshot sounds with the accompanying flash from the guns' muzzles.

Hart checked that he still had his bag, gripped the handrail of the stairway and started his descent.

'Buona notte a tutti!'

Chapter 102

When Hart finally reached the bottom of the fire escape and his additional adrenalin surge had dissipated, he realised how much the recent events had taken their toll on him. His shoulder was agony, although a quick feel confirmed that the blood had now stopped flowing and had indeed dried on his shirt. He hurt from head to foot, on top of which he felt totally exhausted, both physically and mentally. The image of Claudia Volpe's last few seconds would haunt him for a long time. Now was not the time to rest though, he must press on and put some safe distance between himself and the Volpe Mafia and then attempt to call Luca Messi, who would hopefully advise him of the steps he should take to obtain his freedom…and also update him on what the hell was going on in terms of the raid on the mafia and on the particular office within the Vatican.

He correctly realised that he must look a horrific fright, torn, tattered, lacerated and bloody and rapidly considered the pros and cons of either keeping to the back streets out of the stares of the public or staying on named streets with some decent level of street lighting. He was all at sea in terms of his location, but decided to take his chances on the main streets rather than in the labyrinthine backstreets where he risked walking in circles. One thing was for sure, he certainly had no energy to accommodate circular tours of the district! He reached the end of the alley and peered out right and then left, half-expecting to see the street flooded with mafiosi, but he saw no suspicious persons at all.

In looking left once more, however, he saw in the distance the illuminated church that he'd passed with Federico earlier in the day when visiting the Mondo Museum. Finally, he had a compass bearing of sorts as to where he was. He edged out of the alley and hastened along the illuminated street in the direction of the church, all the while staying on full alert for hostiles. Once there, he would re-gather his thoughts and decide upon his next move. He was in the loneliest of positions, a stranger in a strange land with nothing to his name but what he stood up in and his small bag and with only a passing knowledge of the language this dirty, bloodied creature must surely stand out like a sore thumb. Once he had travelled a further block down the street from the waste office, he crossed over and took the first street on the right. Now that he knew the direction of the church, it was not so essential to have such a well-lit route. As he rounded the corner, he was surprised to see a large group of people milling around in the piazza in front of him. His instant thoughts were that this was a large congregation of the mafiosi, about to divide up and hunt him down in the town, but he was relieved when upon closer scrutiny of the assembled people he realised that these were ordinary people met up to take part in some collective activity of celebration.

Hart saw a couple of fly-posters on the ground. His limited Italian was enough to inform him that the "Acireate Festival" was taking place that very evening.

Hart had heard of this before, it was probably the most famous of all Sicilian festivals and had Federico been there he would have no doubt told him that according to the tourist guides, 'This was the pre-Lenten carnival, a brazen fusion of Christianity and paganism which was so characteristic of most Sicilian festivals.' In this particular case, the event had begun with a fair in the main town piazza and now continued with processions, dances and concerts. By chance, Hart had stumbled upon the place that was being utilised as the "backstage" dressing and group organisation area, albeit in the open piazza. Looking around, he saw people holding large, string operated puppets, plumed ponies hooked up to small decorated carts and people carrying variously shaped tall figures carved from beech, olive and lemon wood. Most of the assembled people were dressed in multi-coloured costumes of reds, blues and yellows, traditionally echoing the islands oranges, lemons, sun and sea and celebrating the meeting of the sacred and the profane elements of Sicily. Many of the people were also wearing traditional Acireate Festival masks, some of an angelic nature and others absolutely hideous. For Hart, coming to this scene after his recent harrowing experiences, the whole thing was totally surreal.

He was abruptly dragged back to reality, however, at the sight directly across the piazza of a half a dozen obvious mafiosi searching through the crowd. Far over to the left, he spotted three other men similarly employed. Back the way he had come, he saw three more of their colleagues. Time to panic!

As he looked for the easiest and least attention drawing exit for him from the piazza, his attention fell upon a pile of costumes which had been dumped randomly on the cobblestones. Swooping a hand down, he snatched up a large red and yellow cloak, which he immediately draped around his shoulders. Best of all, in the spot where the cloak had laid he spied one of the hideous looking masks, which he quickly covered his face with, courtesy of the attached rubber band and at the side of *that*, a blue and yellow top hat which he grabbed and tried on. It was a perfect fit.

Now moving forward into the throng he next spotted a pile of multi-coloured paper garlands on the ground and these too he swept up thus completing his Acireate ensemble. Waving and swirling them maniacally, he melded into the crowd of similarly attired and performing locals. He was now one of them and from his hunters' viewpoint unrecognisable. He decided to accompany his newly found comrades as far as was necessary to relieve him of the immediate burden of the hunt, nestled under his newly found cloak of invisibility and together with the crowd of revellers moved away from the piazza. Some of his newfound companions were singing, some were dancing and some were drinking alcohol from glass flagons, but all of them were waving their multi-coloured garlands. Hart continued to try to copy the crowd but he was in too much pain from his shoulder to facilitate little more than a ripple rather than a full wave. He really should take a closer look at his damaged shoulder as soon as possible.

Then surprisingly, the crowd slowed to a standstill, accompanied by a deathly hush. A blast on a whistle pierced the evening air, followed by a raised arm at the front and a shout from the man who appeared to be leading the procession.

'*Avanti tutti! Andiamo!*'

A great cheer went up from the multi-coloured ensemble, and they moved forward once again, this time showing even greater fervour. Once again, Hart saw small groups of men, obviously not there for the celebrations, scanning everything in sight. Shop doorways, alleyways, kiosks, bars and food stalls all received their attention. Some of them continued to walk within the crowd, all the while looking for signs of the Englishman who had killed their leader. Hart tried hard not to pay them too much obvious attention and concentrated more on the festival procession and on mimicking the antics of his neighbours in the crowd, but unable to resist he glanced momentarily to his left where he saw two suited men no more than a couple of yards from him checking the contents of one of the carts drawn by a plumed pony, no doubt looking for a stowaway. The search appeared to be frantic and the attitudes of the men severe, clearly not entering into the spirit of the evening!

Hart was afraid once more and worse still his whole body was hurting again and his head was pounding, not helped by the nearby incessant drums.

A street drink fountain suddenly caught his eye and moving to it took off his mask and hat and quickly washed his blood, snot and vomit covered face, drying it on his cloak then replacing his mask and hat. Feeling a little better already, he checked his watch. It was now forty minutes since he had donned his costume and sought refuge in the celebrating mass of parading people, a parade which had moved along considerably from their starting point in the piazza where Hart had joined them. Now, however, it was clear that breakaway groups were forming and dispersing in different directions. Hart knew that the time was close when he would have to leave the group himself and strike out, but when and to where he hadn't a clue. For sure, he had at least one urgent call to make to Messi with respect to finding out what sort of deliverance was being proposed or orchestrated for him from the mess he was in. He also needed to know how much Messi knew of the events of the day, including the demise of Claudia Volpe, and of course what the overall state of play now was with the mission, for he had witnessed none of the activities against the mafia base that Messi had predicted. Perhaps it was too soon? However, none of these updates could be given or discussed from within the ranks of a chaotic celebratory party which was being watched by the mafia, that was obvious.

To Hart's mind, he had two alternatives, either head to Catania and the airport, or find the way to the Port of Messina where he might catch a ferry, crossing the narrow strait to perhaps Regio Callabria, but he needed guidance and instruction…urgently. One thing was certain though, whichever path he chose to take would be infested with Volpe's grieving cohorts bent on his painful extinction.

As it turned out, the decision was taken out of Hart's hands by the small group of inebriated revellers who he had kind of fallen in with in the crowd. For once his very basic knowledge of the Italian language paid off as he was included in a conversation between an angel and a devil.

Angel, 'When are we leaving the parade?'

Devil, 'Soon.'

Angel, 'Where is the bus stop?'

Devil, 'Just along here, the bus will arrive soon.'

This was music to Hart's ears, so for now he must stay close to both angel and devil. Then,

Devil, '*Ecco la fermata.*'

Hart's mind, *Here's the bus stop.*

Excellent, but which direction would the bus take? Basically it didn't matter a jot, the important thing being that he could put some distance between himself and his hunters, and hopefully reach some place where he could then make some attempt to get off the island. He was thinking a little more clearly now and he realised that jumping a ferryboat would be immeasurably easier than catching a flight for at least one hundred reasons. Suddenly without warning, the angel and the devil, together with another six of their host, peeled away from the crowd and staggered and sang their way to the bus stop, with Hart in tow. The devil put an arm around Hart's shoulder and saying something to him of which Hart didn't have a clue, raised his carafe of wine to Hart's mouth. Hart raised his mask, smiled and drank, allowing the red wine to run down his chin and then replaced his mask.

'*Grazie mille.*'

'*Niente,*' came the reply, 'nothing', and the devil tightened his hug.

It crossed Hart's mind that he didn't have a ticket for the bus, nor did he have any currency in fact. Looking around, he was relieved to see that this bus operated via tickets bought from cafes and news-stands and that such valid tickets were accordingly fed into an automatic punch slot machine on the bus. As for most ticketed journeys of this type in Italy, none of the passengers mounting the bus had any ticket at all and just passed on down the aisle. Also as usual, the driver couldn't care less and at this time in the evening all he wanted to do was to finish his shift and go home. The magnificent.....nine... squeezed into three seats at the back of the bus, which soon filled up with other drunken party poopers. Hart elected to sit by the window, with the angel and the devil at the side of him with their remaining compatriots positioned three in front of him and three behind. He believed that being surrounded by locals was probably the safest seating formation for him were any mafiosi to board the bus. Being next to the window would also afford him a reasonable view outside and hopefully enable him to obtain some idea of where on earth the bus was heading to. He looked around at the other passengers who were all animated in conversation or singing and being dressed appropriately for the festival, he felt quite at home sat in the middle of them.

His fear and expectations were justified just ten minutes into the journey as two suited members of Volpe's taskforce stepped out in front of the bus and waved it down. The driver cursed and sighing slowed his bus to a halt. This could be a long night.

'*Cazzo!*'

The party animals on the bus went very quiet as the men talked briskly to the driver, who underlined his responses with a considerable amount of hand movement. Hart felt his stomach turn somersaults and he let his head fall onto his crossed arms which he had positioned on the back of the seat in front of him, so that his face was completely hidden. The men asked the driver if he had allowed a strange or different-looking man onto the bus in the last hour or so and despite his response in the negative they decided to see for themselves. At the point of entering the bus, their path was suddenly blocked by a man who was desperate to get off, vomiting in the attempt. This was all too much for the mafiosi one of who turned to the other,

'*Tutti sono sbronzi!*' (They're all pissed!)

His colleague took him by the arm and they quickly left the bus, waving the driver to proceed, leaving the man vomiting in the gutter.

The angel put a hand on the Hart's arm and in perfect English said,

'It's OK they've gone.'

Stunned, Hart replied,

'Thank you. I won't go into the reasons that they seem so keen to find me, other than to say that if they had, my evening would have ended rather prematurely and certainly permanently.'

'I can imagine. These men are *bastardi*, but you should be OK for now at least. Where are you going?'

'You tell me. Wherever the bus is heading is my destination.'

'Well, the bus is heading to Messina, if that's OK for you. We have another forty-five minutes or so before we arrive there. Our stop is the last one. It is the terminus.'

'Perfect. Is the ferry far from the terminus?'

'Ten minutes *sempre dritto*, straight on, when you get off the bus.'

'*Grazie mille.*'

The angel patted Hart on the shoulder.

The devil re-joined the angel in conversation and Hart let his head sink back down to rest on his folded arms on the back of the seat in front. Even the raucous singing and joking, which had started back up immediately upon the departure of the two mafiosi couldn't prevent Hart from dozing off, despite the pain he was in. He looked up with a start some thirty or so minutes later in time to see the sign indicating that that they had entered the town of Messina drift by the window, quickly followed by a poster on the wall of a building picturing the front end of a boat advertising ferry crossings to Regio Callabria and Napoli. At this point of the journey, the majority of passengers, still in fancy dress, had spilled out of the bus at the various stops en route leaving only the "magnificent nine" waiting for the terminus. The wait lasted a further ten minutes only and then they arrived. The driver called out that it was the end of the road for these last dregs, who dragged themselves to their feet and shuffled off the bus, wishing the driver a '*buona notte*' as they descended to the pavement.

Hart's travel companions paused "and the angel spoke to him".

'You must go forward and ahead and you will arrive at the port in ten minutes. We will now go the other way. *Buona fortuna*, good luck. We hope your getaway is successful. You know, we know what the men looking for you are like and you really must do your best to evade them. At all costs yes?'

'Yes, at all costs and thank you all so very much for your help. *Grazie mille.*'

In unison, the rest of the group responded with '*Buona fortuna*', then turned and trudged away in the opposite direction, looking very spent from their night's wild celebrations. Hart waved and turning away started out for the port. It was a strange feeling to have made such good acquaintances, especially with an angel and the devil, without ever seeing any one of their faces. Likewise, he had remained totally anonymous to them also. Reaching a lighted alleyway in the street, he ducked in and within seconds had removed his cape and mask and disposed of them, together with his hat and the multi-coloured garlands which had waved their final wave almost one hour ago, in one of a series of refuse bins stationed there. He now went through the painful procedure of examining his gunshot wound. He winced as he removed his busted leather satchel.

'Time to man up!'

Lifting his shirt, he ran his hand over the wound area and jumped abruptly as he touched something protruding from his flesh which was sharp. It was quite small but he was able to grip it between his thumb and forefinger and with a quick pull, accompanied by a suppressed cry, remove what under the streetlight was revealed surprisingly to be a sliver of plastic. He quickly examined the contents of his satchel. The bullet had torn a ragged hole in it upon entry and had continued its journey passing through his passport and other documents and also through both of the mobile phones he had. Turning the satchel round, he saw a smaller ragged hole at the back where the bullet had finally lodged, forcing the sliver of plastic from the shattered phones out and into his shoulder. With great relief, he realised that he didn't have a direct bullet wound after all, for the combined effect of the contents of his bag had saved at least his bacon if not his life exactly.

'Phew!'

He reassembled the contents of his satchel, adjusted his shirt and lit out again in what he hoped was the direction of the ferry. A few yards further on, he saw with satisfaction a sign indicating a left hand turn to the ferry and he took it, immediately gaining the wonderful sight of the water, the Strait of Messina, and a solitary ferryboat anchored there. Across the water, he could actually see the lights of Regio distinctly and peering at the coastline to the left he could see lights running all the way up the coast to what was presumably Naples. With just a single boat on show, his choice of transportation was clear cut, with traffic for it queuing from its open loading doors back down the road to almost where he was standing. The vehicles were in two lines, one line consisting of cars and SUVs and the other of commercial vehicles, such as vans, small lorries and trucks. It was loading up time, although at present the vehicles were stationary waiting for the starter's flag. It then became disturbingly obvious that the area and especially the commercial vehicles were being unofficially searched and policed by at least one dozen non-uniformed men. It was the *local* mafia's last line of defence in preventing his escape from the island.

He needed to try and talk to Messi immediately and doing an about turn he returned to the alley where he had dumped his disguise items and where he hoped to find some seclusion, if only for five minutes or so.

Chapter 103

Upon hearing of the final taking of Hart in Sicily, Robert Halle was absolutely elated. Worn ragged over recent days and weeks as Hart continued to remain at large, he was now able to relax in the knowledge that quite soon he would know the full extent of Hart's knowledge and involvement in any activities hostile to the "Great Plan", after when this this thorn in his flesh could be removed once and for all. For Halle, it was a no-brainer that he must be there in Sicily to witness at first hand Hart's presence "at the pleasure" of Claudia Volpe.

Halle's journey to Sicily, organised by his PA, required him to take a flight to London's Heathrow from JFK and then on to Catania by BA. Upon arriving at Catania Airport, Volpe and a car would be there to meet him and from there speed him to Hart's place of imprisonment.

Upon arriving in London and hearing a call out for him over the tannoy, he contacted a member of BA's groundstaff. When he was finally able to take the "urgent call" in a private British Airways office, he was thunderstruck and consumed with rage to not only hear of Hart's escape, but also to hear of the demise of Claudia Volpe. It seemed to Halle that whatever the bad news, Hart always seemed to be in some way tied up in its cause. The bearer of the infuriating news was one of Volpe's most trusted lieutenants and the person who was probably now in pole position to take over from her as *Capo di tutti Capi*, the boss of bosses, Claudio Vespa. With the skill of a second-hand car salesman Vespa assured Halle that Hart's re-capture was imminent and that by the time he arrived at the office in Basiglio, they would have him once again.

'For you know, Doctor Halle, this Hart is playing on our turf, on our island, with nobody to support him. He only has the clothes in which he stands up and likely no money in his pocket. Yes, I estimate that he will be in our hands once more by the time that you arrive here. It will be I who meets you at Catania Airport now.'

'Vespa, stop bull-shitting me. Listen to me and I will tell you exactly what I intend to do now.'

'*Si, si*, of course, Doctor Halle, please tell me.'

The exasperated Halle explained.

'I shall now hopefully check into the Heathrow Hilton Hotel, where I will take an executive suite. Once there, I will wait until I get confirmation from you personally that Hart is indeed once more under your control at whatever place. At that time, I will take whatever flight is appropriate and available and join you there. Vespa, I give you a maximum of 3 days to deliver Hart and then I shall return to the States. In the meantime, I shall not only consider your own personal future, I will consider the future of the whole of your organisation, *capisce*? There must be no more bungling. Now go and find me Hart!'

He hung up the phone before having to listen to anymore of Vespa's pathetic salesmanship.

Later, successfully ensconced and settled into his Hilton suite, he dressed for bed and took a couple of sleeping tablets to help him on his way and despite his agitation and anger he drifted into fitful slumber thinking of Hart and his miraculous survival from all that had been thrown at him. It just had to be more by luck than by skill or judgement?

'Surely, his time must soon be up?'

Chapter 104

Hart soon arrived back at the quiet alley where he had disposed of his festival disguise items and by the dim glow of a streetlight searched through the satchel he had been guarding throughout his flight from team Volpe. With great relief, he put his hands directly onto the two mobile phones that he had been given by Messi back in La Certosa, one for "genuine" calls to Messi and the other for "red herring" calls to him. He recognised immediately which phone was which and also realised immediately that the phone for his "genuine" calls had been smashed beyond repair, and certainly beyond any use, by the first bullet fired from Volpe's Berreta Pico. Indeed, his shoulder still hurt considerably as a result of the sliver of plastic from that phone that had pierced him. With his worry mounting, he examined the second phone, the "red herring", as closely as he could in the restricted light. That too showed catastrophic signs from being struck by the same bullet. He turned the phone on and waited. After what seemed like an eternity, it finally became illuminated, but the illumination was sporadic and limited to only some areas of the face of the instrument. Suddenly the sound of music, apparently being played under water, became apparent as the final sequence of its switch-on procedure was completed.

'Ahh shit!'

The speed dial button which would connect him directly to Messi was not illuminated. In fact it never would be as the bullet had clearly damaged that particular area of the keypad.

'What now? Think carefully.'

He had one useless phone, which he might as well now throw away and a second severely damaged phone with which he was unable to speed-dial Messi. He didn't have Messi's telephone number even if it had been possible to dial him directly using the individual undamaged keys on the keypad. Hart took to walking backwards and forwards tapping his head, as if that would knock an idea or two into his brain. A sudden twinge in the area of his shoulder wound caused him to wince sharply and he slid his hand under his shirt and gently massaged the wound, now covered with dried blood. As he increased the area of his shoulder under massage one of his fingers suddenly caught on something. He carefully examined it further with all of his fingers this time.

'Yes!'

It was the silver chain that Messi had given him as a departing memento from La Certosa and still attached to it his fingers located the dog tag. He yanked the chain free from his neck and held the dog tag closely in front of his face. There, sure enough was the number inscribed on it that would connect him directly with

Messi…if the phone still worked in those areas of the keypad. He hit the send key and instantly heard a dialling tone. He read the numbers out loud, tapping the corresponding keys on the wounded phone and waited…

Eventually through a crackling and hissing background he heard the accepted numbers dialling out. He closed his eyes willing the phone to be answered at the other end, daring to imagine the large man ambling as quickly as his hulk would allow him to get to his own mobile before going into voice mail. Then….

'*Pronto*, Messi speaking.'

Hart could barely believe it.

'*Ciao*, Luca, *sono* Max.'

'Max… Fantastic! You are still alive yes? How are you? Where are you? I have heard already through my sources of the murders of my OCA colleagues and of your capture by Volpe. I have also just learned of her death during your escape. You play a deadly game my friend, but luckily you play it well.'

'Look, Luca, I am stuck in Messina, I have no money and I need help urgently. Where were the police back at Volpe's base when I was there? I saw absolutely no swoop on the place as you predicted, and I am feeling to say the least, abandoned! What is happening? Also, before you respond, Volpe smashed my genuine phone and so I am calling you on the "red herring phone", so you had better consider your comments well.'

'*Va bene*. Look Max, don't worry about anything, all is well.'

Had they been using the other phone, Messi would have been able to tell Hart that when news came out of his escape and of Volpe's death, and it came very quickly from one of their people undercover at the Volpe base, it was re-confirmed by Messi's superiors that they could not commit to a raid on the mafia base until the arrival of the treatment at the Vatican was confirmed, when all raids organised internationally would take place simultaneously and *now* additionally until the next Sicilian capo was appointed. At this moment, it looked like a man called Claudio Vespa would likely be the capo ultimately, but until that was assured Messi's superiors believed that it would be a waste of time to make a move on the base with no new line of management yet in place.

'What do you mean all is well? That's not bloody…'

Hart stopped speaking, suddenly remembering that any details exchanged at this time would most likely be picked up by those listening in, which would screw the whole plan totally.

What Messi was also unable to tell Hart was that all had gone remarkably to plan. The treatments had been successfully tracked in their delivery right up to the point of their collection at the Vatican. They now knew who received them and where they, and remaining treatments there, were stored. At this point, it would be easy to catch the arm of the octopus, but by waiting his superiors were sure that they would catch the remaining arms… *and* the body, as well.

Luca Messi continued to speak,

'I'm so sorry for this, Max, as you have done such an excellent job for which you now appear to be stuck in a very dangerous situation in Sicily. But don't worry, I have worked out a plan by which you may escape the island and be taken in by friends of the OCA from where you will be brought back to me here at "La

C" very quickly. I promise you that all will be well. Remember which phone we are speaking on, *si*?'

'Look Luca, fuck the phone, nobody will be interested in listening in now, they are all out searching for me. Tell me what I should do next. I am at the port in Messina looking at two lines of traffic about to board the ferry to God knows where. Shall I try and board or not, and if I do where the bloody hell will I arrive at and how can I make contact with one of your friendly faces? Come on speak quickly and convince me that you really do have a plan, because *this* phone will probably die very soon, as will I if you don't do something positive.'

Hart was very angry and very scared. He suddenly believed that Messi had no plans at all that he could put into play to rescue him, probably having reasoned a while ago that he was by now dead. Much as he wanted to rage at Messi down the line, a level of self-control was necessary to keep his gradually raising voice level from the ears of his searchers, plus the fact that there was probably not enough life left in the battered phone for him to have a major explosion down the line.

'Max, please calm yourself, if only a little. I have here now a list of all ferries leaving Messina this evening and the one you mention is destined to cross the Strait to Reggio. It is a 30-minute trip and it costs just euro 3.50, *bene*?'

'Thanks Luca. Shall I wait here for you to send me the money by post for the crossing then? I have already told you that I have no money, nothing, *niente*!'

'OK Max, all you have to do is hitch a ride with one of the truck drivers in the line, or better still as you have very little Italian, try and get into the back of any vehicle if it is open…be a stowaway! This should pose not much of a problem as many of the trucks will be open, carrying fruit and vegetables and that kind of thing.'

'Brilliant!'

'Now listen carefully, when you dock in Reggio make for the church that you will see from the port there. It is very close and it is named…'

There was a rustling of papers down the line.

'For Christ's sake, come on, Luca, we have a problem here, my phone is all but dead!'

'It is called la chiesa di Santa Andrea, the Church of Santa Andrea. The padre there will be expecting you. You will be fed and clothed and after a night's sleep you will be collected by OCA agents and brought to me here. I look forward very much to meeting you again tomorrow Max and *buon viaggio, ciao*.'

'*Ciao* Luca and…'

Just before the phone finally gave up the ghost and died, Hart heard the second click on the line and the slight echo that he recognised from before when his calls had been monitored from elsewhere. As he had said to Messi, with the whole of the island's mafia out looking for him, it was doubtful whether anybody would be spared to phone-sit.

He quickly put the two dead phones and the dog tag back into his bag, stepped back out of the alley and walked towards the line of queuing vehicles, which by now had almost tailed back to the point from where he had just made the call, and began searching for a truck with an open back end that might allow him to stow away for the 30-minute ferry crossing. He walked in the shadows along the line of trucks and small lorries all the while looking for one which would obviously afford him an easy welcoming entry, whilst attempting to stay out of sight of the drivers who were in their cabs impatiently revving their engines and in so doing adding both noise and copious exhaust fumes to the night air. Suddenly, the line of vehicles began to move slowly forward towards the drive-on area of the dock. At that same time, he became aware that some dozen or so vehicles in front of him, groups of men were walking up the line having words with drivers and then making searches of the trucks and lorries.

'Shit!'

The need for a suitable truck for him to hide himself in for the crossing had become *really* urgent. As he continued to watch the line, the traffic flow stopped and he became aware that ahead of their respective "interviews" with the mafiosi, drivers were leaving their cabs and doing cursory brief inspections of their vehicles' contents themselves. The relatively small truck just ahead of him however was an exception, with its driver remaining in his seat. The back end of the truck had a raised wooden panel across it of about two feet in height, but above that was open space right up to the roof. What the contents of the truck were was of great importance, as he would need to hide behind or under something once in place, if indeed he decided to make a dash for this particular vehicle. At that moment, the driver of the truck following this smaller vehicle decided to leave his cab and check his own truck's storage space for signs of any interlopers and accordingly opened the cab door and descended to the road. As he walked towards the back of his truck, Hart made an instant decision to make a dash for the small truck and once the other driver was past him and out of sight round at the rear end of his vehicle he sprinted as best as he could under the pain of his injuries and also as quietly as possible. Placing both hands on the top edge of the wooden base panel, he heaved himself over it into the bowels of the rear compartment. He succeeded in doing this out of sight of the driver from the following truck and as the engine was running noisily also out of earshot of the driver of his chosen truck, who for some reason had chosen to stay in his cab listening to music on the radio.

Hart landed on something that felt initially like a moist fur rug, quite a comfortable touchdown in fact. It was then that the attack came. It was an attack on his nasal senses and it was an onslaught to great effect.

'Jesus Christ!'

He heaved and retched, the malodour was so appalling and he re-tasted the bitterness of bile that his heaving had dragged from his empty stomach. The smell was so bad and so overpowering that he was unable to stop his guts from contracting involuntarily and his resulting retching caused his eyes to stream and the muscles of his stomach to ache. Through all of this, the truck's engine sputtered on and the music played out with the driver oblivious to the agonies taking place in the storage compartment behind him.

Feeling around the floor in the darkness, Hart realised exactly what the cargo was that he had opted inadvertently to travel with on this ferry across the Strait of Messina to Reggio Calabria. He had actually born witness to such a truck on

374

one occasion before, whilst working in Caserta, a town close to Naples. Some years before, he was being taken out to be wined and dined as a semi-important pharmaceutical company visitor when the car in which he was a passenger became stuck behind a small truck, which they had no option but to follow for almost one hour. At the end of the story, they just had to pull back and away from the disgustingly smelling vehicle and sit at the side of the road for a good hour whilst he and his companion driver Ciro, recovered from their terrible experience. After recovering physically, they were still unable to rid their clothes of the noxious smell and their fine dining ended with a take away pizza and copious amounts of Coca-Cola and water. It had been a hellish nightmare of Dante proportions and so far this evening's brief experience was in the realms of one thousand times worse.

The smell *then* and the smell *now* was the smell of multiple death and putrefaction. Hart was laid back in the bowels of a truck containing the corpses of several hundred putrefying animals, most of which were cats, but with an additional selection of dogs, rats, mice and other small rodents. Not all was death here, however, for amongst the decay was life, and much of the mass of putrefaction was moving like the ebb and flow of a calm sea, the current being provided by large volumes of seething, feeding maggots.

The truck was on its usual monthly run between areas within Reggio Calabria and Sicily, where the job of its driver was to scoop up from the roads, streets and alleyways the multitude of mostly feral animals that had died or been killed in the course of the days (although mainly nights) and hoist them into the back of his truck, which he would then eventually return to Reggio where the disgusting remains would be incinerated. Feral cats and dogs abounded in these areas, living wild and foraging for whatever scraps of food they could find and with so many restaurants at their disposal the scraps were not always of particularly small sizes. The monthly collection of the corpses stretched over at least one week, which meant that the majority of the bodies were in a late stage of decay and putrefaction when the truck at last started on its journey across the Strait of Messina back to Regio. Tonight, Hart had landed on a particularly abundant collection of festering corpses.

Hart felt maggots crawling over his hands, which were resting on a semi-liquid mass of cadaverous meat and he heaved again. He had a great urge to abandon this ship of putrefaction, but to do so would land him straight into the hands of the mafiosi patrolling just yards away outside and so he resolved to stay the course and ride out what would be a torturous sixty minutes or so. Sitting at the back end of the truck, he would be in plain sight of the advancing men of the mafia and so he had no option but to crawl through the sticky, furry, fetid mess towards the front end of this mobile necropolis directly behind the panel separating the driver from his cargo, uncertain whether breathing through his mouth would serve him better than taking in the vile smelling air through his nostrils. In the end, he decided to let his body decide involuntarily what to do in that department whilst he concentrated on maintaining his concealment. As he crawled, he was aware of his hands penetrating the maggot infested decaying animal bodies and at times started as he placed a hand into an open mouth of one of the animals, feeling its teeth in death rake along his fingers and hands.

The music coming from the cab was finally extinguished and he heard voices as the driver spoke to the mafiosi. It was time for Hart to submerge out of sight and he dragged what bodies he could grip over his legs, stomach and chest. Then, leaving it until the last possible moment, he pulled his shirt up over his face and buried it in the seething mass of putrefying corpses and maggots, blindly brushing heaps of them over his head with his hands and then plunging them too into the rotting mass. He lay there for an eternity feeling the movement of maggots all over him, paralysed by the disgusting smell. The maggots made their way successfully through the weave of his polo shirt and he felt them crawling over his face and then worst of all up his nostrils. This final insult was too much for him to bear and he had to blow down his nose sharply to remove the wriggling lodgers that had moved in. If he managed to survive this night, for sure these actions and experiences would be the stuff of nightmares for him for a very long time to come.

Lying in his seething tomb, it became clear why the driver was the only person in the line of vehicles who had not dismounted and checked his payload when the mafia had first appeared on the scene, for who in their right mind would subject themselves to sharing the literal "bowel" of the truck with so much vile filth. But now with the advent of the searchers, the driver finally got out of his cab and led the two men to the rear of his truck and pointed inside. The men took one breath and one look at his cargo and turned to him.

'*Cazzo*! What a shit hole!'

'*Cristo*! For fuck's sake drive on!'

The driver chuckled and scurried back to his cab. One of the searchers heaved and the other pulled him away to the next lorry in the line. Whilst Hart was not aware of the exact reactions outside his torture chamber, he assumed the message was that he had passed the inspection as the truck revved up and moved off, accelerating to catch up with the vehicles in front. He emerged from the morass of rotting animals in a rush, like a drowning man emerging from under water. He tried to maintain quiet, but crawling away from the vicinity of the back of the driver he could not hold back on yet more retching and heaving and blowing fetid air back down his nose in order to clear it.

But he was now past the inspecting mafiosi and he suddenly felt the bump of the truck and heard the sounds of tyres on metal floor plates as the truck mounted the ramp into the hold of the boat where it received the shouted instructions of crew members, who's job in the case of this truck was to try and manoeuvre it into a position on board where it would cause the least disgust to other customers and passengers. He saw the headlights of other lorries as they too came to rest in the hold and heard the slamming of doors as drivers dismounted and trundled off together to another part of the boat, no doubt where they could find coffee and food and swap stories of the evening's events during the short crossing. Hart lay there until he could hear no further sounds of arriving trucks and dismounting drivers and then decided that it was time to say farewell to his companions. He stood as best he could in the confines of the truck, shook himself and batted himself down as well as he was able and slipping and sliding in the semi-fluid fetid mass, finally dismounted onto the iron walkway which ran the length of the line of vehicles, leaving that particular level of Dante's Hell happily behind. He immediately took in a great gulp of the fresh night air. Never had fresh air felt so good! However, he had passengers of his own still and in a rush pulled off his shoes and poured out the writhing contents that were the maggots. He batted down his socked feet before replacing the loafers, which although free of intruders no doubt still carried their smell. Next he opened his bag and poured the whole contents onto the walkway separating the living contents from the personal documents, the dog tag and the two mobile phones. Having given the bag a good bash to remove any reluctant-to-leave larval life, he then replaced documents, dog tag and phones. He swiftly pulled his shirt off over his head and through a combination of shaking it and twirling it in the air managed to disperse many more of the would-be blow flies, quickly putting the garment back on when he was satisfied that he had done his best to remove the infestation.

'What next'?

He certainly had to find a bathroom and toilet if possible, but it was equally certain that he could not venture into any place where members of the public were, unless of course he wanted to cause a severe public disturbance. A shower and a change of clothes were what were really necessary of course, but he would have to make do with whatever crossed his path. He knew that ferries such as this one continued to make return trips across the water for virtually twenty-four hours each day and that the seagoing boat staff would have their own areas for eating, sleeping when necessary and importantly washing and showering etc. and it was obvious to him that it was to this area of the boat that he must gravitate. He didn't expect it to be too difficult to find these areas from where he now stood, as the location of ships' non-white collar personnel was always well below decks on these boats as they too were not expected to mingle with fare paying passengers. He waited another twenty or minutes and watched the heavy metal ramp rise and clang shut in an upright position ensuring a watertight seal against the sea and creating a barrier between himself and the world outside.

The vehicle parking area was now virtually empty of all drivers and boat's crew that had remained in position until the ramp was securely located in place, with the boat now ready to sail. Hart calculated from the information that he had picked up in his brief recent conversation with Messi that he would have no more than one hour in total to do what he had to do to produce a look of at least passable humankind in himself and he headed back urgently down the iron walkway.

He hadn't walked far when he arrived at a large heavy iron door on which was emblazoned, "*Uso Riservato al Personale*", "Use Reserved for Personnel", which he opened and passed through. The massive door groaned when it was opened, making a deafening clang when he closed it. It was clearly imperative that he maintained his concentration and remembered the way back to this door for the next stage of his "stow-awayed" journey. As he walked on, he became aware of a disgusting odour permeating the corridor and looked around anxiously momentarily, before realising that it was himself that he could smell. He rubbed

377

his hair roughly being suddenly aware of movement there, and sure enough discovered other stow-aways as they fell to the floor. He pressed on looking for the tell-tale signs for a toilette, WC or bagno and sure enough he soon came across such a multi-language sign bearing appropriate logos indicating that he should proceed straight on, but interestingly, there didn't seem to be any delineation between men's and women's. At the sight of the sign, he quickened his pace and two minutes later, was standing outside the room that had been signposted, his courage stalling slightly with regard to entering.

In the end with the "brass neck" in mind, he strode forth confidently into the bathroom-cum-WC. In this case, fortune did indeed favour the brave and he found himself in an empty medium-sized room, consisting of a small shared changing area, two separate shower cubicles and four WC stalls. Of particular interest to him was a large bin with a flip-top labelled, "*Vestiti Sporchi*", which he recognised as being a "dirty clothes" bin, obviously for personnel to dump the dirty work-clothes that their company had issued them with in. Of greater interest, however, was the bin labelled "*Vestiti Puliti*", "clean clothes", but when Hart excitedly flipped open its lid he found it to be empty. Flipping the lid of the "dirty clothes" bin, however, revealed quite a selection of dirty and sweaty tee-shirts and over-trousers, which Hart rifled through eventually selecting a tee-shirt and over-trousers which were of approximate wearable size and not too filthy. In any case, anything at all would be better than the putrid, foul smelling clothes which he currently stood up in. He would have to forego wearing socks and underwear though, but that was a small price to pay.

He arranged his "new clothes" on the changing bench and began to undress, using hands made stiff and crusty with the dried semi-glutinous fluid of animal decomposition which had become adhered to him during his nightmare fumblings in the back of the truck. Whilst undressing, he considered the second part of his journey, that was to the church of Santa Andrea in Reggio, but decided to shelve that until showered and re-dressed. A sudden thought that he had omitted one additional item from his consideration…a towel to dry himself with…elicited the usual expletive from him.

'Shit!'

He scrambled through the dirty clothes bag once again, searching for even a used towel, but failed in his quest. In the end, it was obvious that he had to sort out some of the cleaner, softer, dirty clothing items and use them to dry himself with, which he quickly did piling them up next to his "new'" clothes. He rolled his own disgusting clothes into a ball and placed them under the other garments at the bottom of the dirty clothes bin and feeling that in this less than human state he could wait no longer; now naked, he entered the shower cubicle. He instantly spotted a plastic bottle of liquid soap suspended from a hook, and turned the shower jets on full blast. He ran the shower hot and on high power, luxuriating as his body returned to life under the hot soapy jets of water. He held his head under the water for a long time and worked up a soapy lather in his hair, which he rinsed away during another long period under the jets of hot water. When he looked down at the basin, he saw that the flow of water down the plughole was constricted by more maggots which he had flushed from his hair. He bent down and using a finger forced them, one by one, through the metal strainer until he was finally alone, his demons temporally flushed away. He looked at his body, which now resembled a black and blue patchwork of bruises, and he winced. For the first time he was able to look at the wound to his shoulder made by the sliver of mobile phone plastic aided by Volpe's small Beretta 0.38 and felt a little embarrassed with himself for having made so much fuss over such a minor incision.

He could have stayed under the hot water jets forever but was jolted back to reality upon hearing the door of the bathroom open and then close followed by the sounds of a man undressing, presumably for a shower. Indeed it was a man who was also preparing himself for a virtuoso concert whilst under the jets of water, as whilst he undressed, he warmed his vocal chords with a very flat rendition of "O Sole Mio". Upon taking his stance inside the shower cubicle, the high pressure of the water had little effect on the quality of his voice, but when he switched his aria to "Your Tiny Hand is Frozen", Hart did notice a definite improvement. Hart decided that it was now the time for him to leave the cubicle before the man decided to take his bows to his imagined audience and step out of the cubicle, and he set about using his hand as a squeegee to remove as much water as possible from his body, leaving less work for the substitute towels to perform. The pain incurred in carrying out this simple activity was intense and underlined to him the brutal treatment he had received from the mafiosi both when "in" and "out" of consciousness.

He turned off his shower and stepped out, making a bee-line for his "towel garments" and his change of clothes and in doing so noticed that the newcomer to the bathroom had left a sports bag on the changing bench. Unable to resist peeking inside it, Hart saw that the man actually had two towels, a blue one and a pink one ("his" and "hers" perhaps?) and in that instant, he decided to borrow the pink article and he quickly dried himself with it. Having completed that process, with the tenor (sounding more like a "fiver") now massacring Nessun Dorma, he neatly folded the towel and returned it to the bottom of the sports bag. He quickly pulled on the DFDS company tee-shirt ("Det Forenede Dampskibs-Selskab", alias "The United Steamship Company", the largest ferry company in Denmark working internationally) and the too long, but tight enough, DFDS over-trousers, the legs of which he rolled up slightly, then put on his own shoes, picked up his trusty bag and minus socks and underpants exited the steam-filled room at the very moment that the other man struggled up the musical scale to hit the final strangled note of the aria…missing it by quite some distance, but nonetheless, bringing an entertaining performance to a close.

It was easy for Hart to work his way along the corridor to the door through which he had entered this part of the boat and it was with some relief that he heard the massive door once more moan as he opened it and then clang shut behind him. He was back on the iron walkway which led past the parked trucks and lorries and his task now was to choose one suitable for hiding him safely for the last couple of miles between the port of Reggio and the Church of Santa Andrea in the town, where hopefully some kind of sanctuary awaited him.

He walked slowly past the parked trucks and lorries, carefully looking for one which had a suitably unlocked goods space at the rear and most importantly, after his recent visit into hell, a storage hold that was more appropriately filled. The presence of fruit, vegetables, general foodstuffs and especially decaying biological materials was out! He looked at his watch and by his reckoning, he had fifteen minutes to get comfortably sorted in a truck before the drivers began to drift back to their cabs. He hadn't walked far when one truck caught his eye. It had an up-and-over roll rear door which was slightly ajar and clearly not locked and sported the logo on its side of a winged chair with the inscription "La Sadia Volante", which likely meant "The Flying Chair", and below it "Mobili Transloci Piu Presto!", which to Hart's mind was most probably a reference to "speedy furniture removals". There was no need for any brain hurting translation however, as a quick look into the back of the truck through the small gap between the raised door and the base did indeed reveal a hoard of poorly stacked furniture, which was obviously in transportation.

Sorted!

Hart quickly looked around and seeing nobody close by, although there was a group of men assembled at the far end of the level, as quietly as possible raised the truck's up-and-over door just enough to permit his body to squeeze through the gap into the storage area. Once inside, he carefully eased the door back down leaving a gap wide enough to allow sufficient illumination from the deck's dim lighting to enter to aid him to move around. His movement was assisted more by his sense of touch than by that of sight, but nonetheless, this was adequate to enable his identification of most of the pieces of furniture that he quietly barged into. He felt more than saw a couple of tables, several chairs, two sofas, bookcases and wardrobes, and at least three sideboards, none of which he felt with any confidence would provide him with a half decent hiding place was there to be any kind of search. Moving carefully to the back of the storage area (i.e. towards the front of the truck), his hands rested on probable wardrobes but then he had a Eureka moment when he tripped over what turned out to be a wooden ottoman of sorts. He lifted the hinged lid and stepped inside, lowering his backside to its floor and then stretched out his legs.

Almost.

He was *almost* able to fully stretch out his legs, but was not uncomfortable with a slight bend at the knees. The next thing to try was closing the lid, thus ironically incarcerating himself in what was a virtual coffin. The lid closed perfectly. His place of concealment was decided. One additional thing though. On his approach to his newfound sanctum, he had briefly placed a hand on a number of cushions and it was to these that he now returned. Then, clutching hold of two of them, he returned to the ottoman. He would at least have the basic comfort in his confinement of something soft to rest his head on that wasn't a dead animal. Now lying prone in his coffin, with the lid slightly raised so that he could keep both visual and audible tracks on any proceedings outside the truck and also to minimise any mild claustrophobia, he might feel he awaited the departure of his hearse.

He didn't have long to wait, as what only seemed like minutes after resting his head on his cushions he heard the loud voices of men outside together with much laughter and then the movement at the front end of the truck as the driver put his weight on the step to his cab and swung into his driving seat. This was followed by the sound of the engine being turned over a couple of times…

Please start!

…and then the mild explosion at the self-ignition of the diesel gas with the resultant rattle of the exhaust pipe as the engine burst into life. There was a revving of the engine and the crashing of the gears as "first" was selected…

Ahh, for a bit of synchromesh!

…the sound of a ratchet as the handbrake was disengaged, and the truck moved forward towards the disembarkation ramp.

The truck shook as it moved forward causing the unanchored, freestanding furniture to collide and rub against each other. The vehicle trundled forward in line with the others, up and over the metal ramp causing more disturbance of its contents, and down onto the dockside. Hart heard the engine rev louder and even from his tomb, he was able to feel the truck accelerate forward. Suddenly there was a squeal of brakes and the truck shuddered to a halt. Inside the storage area at the back there was carnage, as items of furniture were hurled forwards and backwards, then sideways, bouncing off whichever items were in their path. Wardrobes and bookcases that had not been fastened to the walls crashed down and it was Hart's bad luck that one such item landed squarely across the lid of his place of refuge.

Up front and outside the truck, a veritable melodrama was enfolding. Members of the mafia had stationed themselves on the dock area on the mainland side of the Strait of Messina and were pulling up vehicles at random. One such pair of mafiosi had taken it upon themselves in a last second decision to halt the truck in which Hart was a passenger and had stepped out in front of the vehicle at the very moment that the driver had depressed the accelerator causing him to slam his foot down hard on the brake, with the resulting effects on the truck's cargo. The furious driver wound down his window and gave it to the two men at full blast.

'What the fuck are you doing? I could have killed you.'

The men ignored the ill-conceived outburst and instead shouted to him,

'Have you been approached by a man looking for a lift?'

'No, I have not!'

'Have you seen any suspicious persons on the boat?'

'Only you two!'

'Get out! We need to search your van.'

Cursing, the driver opened his door and scrambled down to the men.

'It's a truck, not a van!'

'Come on, open up the back.'

The driver was now having a change of heart, realising who the men were that he was being difficult with and of course what they could do, and he scurried ahead of them. As he passed the logo on the vehicle's side, he looked back at the men and pointed at it.

'Look, very high quality furniture removals. I could do you a special deal, very cheap.'

'Just get on with it!'

He rounded the back end of the truck and shielding the fact that it patently wasn't locked, fumbled and rattled the padlock hasp and then hoisted the door. He looked inside aghast.

The two men burst out laughing and before reaching actual hysteria one of them slapped the driver on the back.

'Quality furniture removals, did you say? All you are going to have left in here when you've finished your *quality removing* is a pile of shit that is only good enough to burn on the fire.'

They burst out once again in a fit of uncontrollable laughter.

'Flying chair? Crash-landing more like!'

The driver was severely pissed off with these mafiosi, for had they not suddenly stepped out in front on him in the first place, there would have been no "crash-landing" inside his well-ordered truck. Still, they were clearly mafia people and as such they had to be respected and definitely feared, so he merely smiled nervously and muttered,

'*Si, si,* you are right'.

'I think we have wasted enough of our time on this heap of rubbish. Look, if you go straight through town, you will come to the City Tip, where for a handful of euros, they will take this load of crap off your hands.'

Again there was uncontrollable laughter during which one of the men indicated with a hand for the driver to roll down the door, and then still laughing waved him to drive off. This had been wonderful light entertainment for them on what was a grim and heavy night, although the demise of the beautiful but fearsome Claudia Volpe had clearly done little to dispel their humour.

Once again, the driver took his seat in his cab and once again he fired the engine into life. It started first time on this occasion and Hart felt the accompanying shudder of the van, or rather "truck" as the driver had insisted on it being called. With a crash of gears and a jolt as the handbrake was taken off, the vehicle moved off, heading towards the centre of Reggio.

Hart was aware from his brief conversation with Messi back at the dock in Messina that the Church of Santa Andrea was not a long way from the Reggio ferry centre and as soon as the truck was steadily rumbling along he set about lifting the hinged lid of his coffin. However, it wouldn't budge by more than a couple of inches, being now held down by the fallen wardrobe. After much straining, he managed to raise the lower half of his legs and put himself in a position where both knees and toes were pressed hard against the lid. Then, with both hands also placed up hard against the lid, he contrived to exert as much pressure as possible using all limbs simultaneously. Happily, the fruit of this labour was that the lid of his sarcophagus opened completely.

Once his Houdini act was completed and he was standing again in the back of the truck, he took a deep breath and after a quick massage of his aching lower back threaded his way to the up-and-over door and lifted it.

Outside it was dark, but he could make out the lights and shapes of cranes at the ferry port that they had left behind and also the lights of houses on what must be the road into town. There was no sign of an illuminated church however, as he had been told to expect by Messi. The Church of Santa Andrea was of semi-cathedral status and so illumination of at least its dome, if it had one, or its frontage was his minimum expectation.

As the truck slowed for traffic lights, he leaned out trying to spot any signs of the church. The truck went straight through the red lights and as it did, Hart suddenly saw in the distance the illuminated white edifice of what he calculated was the church he was heading for. Unsure whether there would be any further indication whether this was the correct church or not, he decided that he had no option but to go for it. He quickly pushed up the door and as the truck slowed to walking speed for more traffic lights, he was ecstatic to see a sign indicating that la Chiesa Santa Andrea was indeed down the road to the right.

Hallelujah!

He sprang out of the truck before it could "run" *these* red lights and rolled into the gutter. He lay there for a moment surprisingly feeling no ill effects from his brief flight and subsequent quite hard landing from the "Flying Chair" and then stood up. As a reflex action, he automatically batted himself down, thinking with irony that it would indeed have been a complete tragedy to make any mess at all of either his soiled DFDS tee-shirt or his over-trousers, adjusted his satchel over his shoulder and took the road towards the illuminated church, feeling extremely bruised and battered, but relieved.

The road was very quiet with little or no traffic on it, but this suited Hart, as he was still acutely aware of not wanting to be conspicuous to any mafiosi, who he believed were still likely to be on his trail. At a fork in the road, a people carrier stopped and disgorged about ten men, who Hart decided from their work-wear, which was not too far removed from his own, were men from the dock who having completed their shift were now being dropped off on the way home. A couple of them looked at the strange sight that was Hart and nodded, obviously impressed by the man wearing no socks (or underpants). Hart returned the nod and took the opportunity to tag on at the back of the group, hunching his shoulders and forcing his hands deep into his pockets as they ambled towards the town and its highlighted church. He had been wise to remain cautious of a mafia presence, for sure enough before his group had walked another fifty yards, a couple of obvious mafiosi appeared from inside a bus shelter and eyed the group carefully as they passed by. Before reaching them, Hart had merged quickly into the centre of the group, where he was afforded some level of visual protection from them, and had placed his arm around the shoulder of one of his surprised newfound chums whilst at the same time turning his head away from the "searchers". The group passed by the two mafiosi, progressing without any confrontation at which convenient time, Hart removed his arm from the man's shoulder, smiled and offered him a 'grazie mille'. The man looked at him and shrugged his shoulders. Clearly the tramp that had joined him temporarily was "one sandwich short of a picnic", or however that translated into the local dialect. With Hart now focused on the illuminated church, in the closing distance, there were no further interruptions in the group's forward progress until the road forked once more, one way leading towards the illuminated town and the other way to the illuminated church, at which point Hart peeled away and continued on his own, now quickening his pace at the glorious thought of the safety that awaited him fifty yards ahead.

Minutes later, he was climbing the wide, steep, stone steps at the church's front and heading towards a relatively small wooden door, which in fact formed part of a much larger and grander portal set into a splendidly carved stone surround. He had finally arrived at the entrance to the Church of Santa Andrea. He stood and looked up at the illuminated building, absorbing and admiring the beauty of the stone edifice that he had travelled through hell to reach. Finally after a short pause, he turned the large iron ring, pushed the door open and entered the much-welcomed place of worship and sanctuary.

Chapter 105

The door opened surprisingly noiselessly and he tentatively stepped inside, pulling it closed behind him. The church was lit with the soft glow of hundreds of flickering candles and perfumed by the heady smell of incense. This was a world of silence, reverence and meditation and at present that world was empty of people except for a solitary priest at the front of the church, knelt in silent prayer in front of the ornate alter, behind which hanging down from the roof of the building was a crucifix bearing a dramatic life-sized image of Christ.

Hart made his way down the aisle towards the priest, who rose to his feet at the sound of the tired footsteps and turned to him, smiling. He looked to be very young to Hart, probably in his mid-thirties, with good looks which would no doubt work wonders on increasing at least the female numbers in his congregation, although Hart guessed that some of the more elderly women would have reservations about opening their heart of hearts to one so…attractive.

'Hello Father, I'm—'

'Yes, I know. You are Doctor Max Hart,' the priest interrupted, still smiling.

'Welcome. I'm so very glad you made it here. As you must know, you are fully expected. You look very tired and somewhat…interestingly dressed, Doctor. Please follow me. By the way, please accept my apologies for my English, which is not so good I'm afraid, but I do believe a typical English comment should be "you look like shit". Am I right?'

Hart laughed, amazed at the priest's use of such a basic expression.

'Perfectly correct, and more like shit than you could ever guess. If there's time, I will explain more later.'

'Yes, later indeed, Doctor Hart, but first we must offer you our shower facilities, some proper clothes and of course some food and drink.'

'Thank you, Father. Yes, some food and clothes would be very welcome and although I managed to take a shower not very long ago today, it would be nice to have what we could call a "proper one", with proper towels.'

Hart was led out of the precincts of the church nave and along a corridor to what he anticipated would be some meeting area for the Fathers. They finally passed through a large and heavy wooden door and indeed there they were in a room that was definitely a relaxation area for priests, although his new companion was the only priest apparently on duty. With stone walls and furnished in keeping with the age and nature of the building and with its numerous lighted candles, together with an amount of electric soft lighting, it looked to be very relaxing. A long central table surrounded by a dozen chairs was set for just one person to dine at.

'Please take the seat with the plates, Doctor Hart, and begin. It's not Michelin star standard, but you will find it welcome I'm sure. By the way, it *is* remiss of me, my name is Achille. I am Father Achille. You will find a tourine of soup sitting on the food heater together with pasta, meatballs and a typical sauce. There are also cold meats and salad on the sideboard and also wine and water if you wish.'

Hart sat down and helped himself to soup and bread and then worked his way through the menu. He couldn't remember his last proper meal...oh yes, it was the "celebration" with Federico after they had completed their mission. God! Some cause for celebration that was, looking back now!

'In case you are wondering, Doctor Hart, I must tell you that I am not a member of the OCA. My priestly vows forbid it, but let me say that I am on the side of good and I am happy to help out when necessary against what I see as the forces of evil.'

'In that case, I'm indebted to you. Thanks once again. Your English is excellent by the way, where did you learn it?'

'Oh that's easy. I learned it from the TV gameshow, "That's my Line",' he smiled.

Hart laughed.

'It's still business as usual here in the church to everyone tonight, but when you have finished eating, Max, I will show you to the bathroom and to a small dressing room where you will find the clothes that I will lay out for you.'

'Thanks Achille, but I will need socks and underpants as well I'm afraid.'

'Fine. Did you know that we Fathers actually wear socks too...and surprisingly also underpants? It's where we keep our testaments you know.'

'Oh, and I thought it was to prevent you from looking down on the unemployed!'

Hart was a little surprised at the level of the priest's humour, but of course he was still young and most likely represented that face of the modern church that appealed to the youth of the day. In any case, it was a face that suited him too and he found him really easy to get on with and comfortable to speak unguardedly to.

'We have a veritable shop full of clothes back there, Max, so write down some sizes and while you're showering I will see what I can get hold of. I would expect medium should cover the items sizes though, but don't expect them to be new.'

Hart polished off what food he wanted, which included some of the delicious soup, salad, spaghetti with meatballs in a tomato sauce and filled himself up with some of the cold meats and a little cheese. In other words, a portion of everything on offer! He washed it all down with a couple of glasses of red wine and water. When finished, Father Achille led him without any preamble to the bathroom facilities where he took his third shower of the day, but under far less stress than his last one and in the knowledge that drying himself would be less of a hit and miss affair this time. There was no live operatic accompaniment this time though. On the edge of the sink, he found an unused toothbrush and toothpaste and was very happy to use them to brush away the remaining after-taste of the last couple of days from inside his mouth. What simple luxury!

Showered and dried, he found the dressing room and inspected the clothes he'd been given to wear. He'd done very well. There was a pair of blue denim jeans, a navy blue polo shirt, boxer shorts, blue socks and a pair of Nike training shoes. Most *were* new, despite what Achille had said, and all in all, they all fitted him very well. Feeling refreshed, and for the first time in some hours adequately dressed, he made his way back to the room in which he had eaten and where Achille would now be waiting for him. There would no doubt be much to talk about.

Opening the door, he walked in, ready to talk about the arrangements for his return to Milan and La Certosa. The sight that met him was a seated, forlorn-looking Father Achille, the colour completely drained from his previously hearty-looking face. A voice from behind the door had a similar effect on Hart's own disposition.

'*Buonasera*, Doctor Hart, I see from the table that you have already eaten. I was hoping that you would take your *final* course with us, but no problem, we can still arrange that. In fact we can make it your *final,* final course, ha, ha.'

Hart felt sick with shock and his stomach churned as the man's words hit him. Looking to his left, he saw the speaker, a stocky man of medium build with an early 1960s style pencil moustache, its colour matching his black slick-backed hair, wearing a black single-breasted suite and black open-necked silk shirt. Interestingly, he was wearing black patent lace-up shoes. A white silk handkerchief hung out of his jacket's breast pocket. His left wrist was adorned with a Longines Vintage 18-carat gold watch with gold bracelet and around his right wrist he wore a thick, elaborate gold chain. In his pierced left ear, he wore a single small black sapphire. In addition to his various jewellery, in his right hand, he sported a Beretta M9 semi-automatic 9mm pistol with a silencer attached, which was now pointed directly at him. The man was smiling and nodding in a self-congratulatory way. Opposite Hart, and out of his line of sight as he had entered the room, were four other men, two with guns pointed at the head of the priest and the other two pointing their weapons at Hart, with arms outstretched. The man spoke again,

'I will not kill you yet, Doctor Hart, as you have been personally responsible for my rather rapid recent promotion within our "Company" and for that. I feel I owe you some kind of thanks. As for the priest, I bear him no grudge, for I would guess that he is only fulfilling his priestly duties in feeding you and making you look presentable for my colleagues and my arrival.'

Father Achille looked hopelessly on, trying to convey his feelings of regret to Hart and hoping that he didn't believe that he had baited and lured him into this trap.

'Now whilst my colleagues bind your hands, Doctor Hart, if you will excuse me for two minutes, I have a call to make.'

He gave his men their orders to tie Hart's hands behind his back with the rope that he produced from his jacket pocket and with one final look to ensure that all was secure, he left the room. Unusually for Hart, so far he had been too stunned to make any of his infamous smart ad-libs to his captor and suddenly he felt very tired, and depressingly that for him the game was now almost completely over.

Chapter 106

Robert Halle's fitful, sleeping pills induced sleep, at the Heathrow Hilton was finally rudely interrupted by an urgent thumping on his door. For several minutes, he lay there in his bed and stared at the ceiling wondering where the hell he was, and then he remembered. He was sleeping off his jet lag, the second reward to add to his already chalked up air miles for his transatlantic flight. He threw the Hilton Hotel dressing gown, which lay across the bed, around himself and staggered to the door, looking at his watch.

'Yes? Who is it?'

'Room service, sir.'

'What do you want?'

'Sir, you have had two urgent telephone calls which you have not answered and the caller has phoned the hotel switchboard to ask that we ask you to respond urgently please.'

Halle was confused. He had been in his executive suite the whole time since his arrival and would surely have picked up on any phone calls, but then he realised the reason for his non-responsiveness. Immediately upon arriving he had taken his usual cocktail of sleeping tablets, but on the occasion of hearing of Hart's escape, he had doubled up on the doses in order to assure himself of a sound sleep whilst waiting for further news of his hopeful re-capture and had clearly been completely out for the count as a result. He opened the door and glared down on a young boy of no more than sixteen years of age.

'Well then? Who called? Do you have any details for me?'

The young man handed him a list of written details relating to the caller and nervously added,

'The caller said that he would phone again in fifteen minutes, sir, and for you to please be ready to receive it. He was calling from Italy I believe, sir.'

'OK thank you…and wait.'

He returned to his bedside table and removed a bill from his wallet and handed it to the messenger.

'Thank you.'

Suddenly the room phone rang and he jumped. It had been a very short fifteen minutes. He picked up the receiver,

'Hello, Robert Halle speaking.'

'Doctor Halle, it is I, Claudio Vespa, speaking, I have news for you.'

'Go on then, don't keep me in suspense all night!'

Halle was irritable in the extreme in dealing with Vespa and gathered himself ready to fire off another salvo of insults and threats at the man, who it seemed had become Volpe's successor. He prepared himself for the next batch of excuses and reports of failure.

'Good news, *Dottore*, we have re-taken Hart and he is our prisoner once more.'

Halle couldn't quite believe what he was hearing. Had this band of incompetents truly re-caught his nemesis?

'Where are you at this present moment, Vespa?'

'I am in Reggio Calabria with four of my best men and we have Hart bound here in front of us.'

'Is he alive?'

'Very much so, Doctor Halle. He is alive and looking in reasonable health, although he is clearly very pissed off at being once more in our grasp.'

Halle was delighted to hear this news but didn't want to appear over enthused with Vespa and his team's performance after the multiple debacles that had preceded it. He thought for a moment and finally expounded his decision.

'Vespa, as you know I am currently at the Heathrow Hilton and my intention is to fly out to meet you and Hart as soon as there is a suitable flight. I suspect that I will be unable to fly there directly however, so I want you to keep Hart under very close observation at all times until I am able to join you. I do not want you to give him the slightest opportunity to escape again. Do you understand me, not the slightest opportunity? So tell me, do you have some office or other where he can be held securely in Reggio? Remember, I do not want him to be transported any further than is necessary from that town.'

'Yes, of course, sir, we have an office and warehouse here in Reggio that backs directly onto the water's edge of the River Crati. We will take him there and await your arrival.'

'Thank you. As soon as I have flights booked, I will contact you with the details. Once I have done that, I will expect you to arrange for me to be picked up at whatever airport I fly into and brought immediately to wherever you and Hart are.'

'Yes, of course, sir, that will be arranged as soon as you inform me of your flight arrangements.'

'Very well. Finally, just confirm for me that you realise how important it is for me to meet Hart and how he must be in a fit state for me to interrogate him. He will most probably have key information that will inform me of just how much of our plans are known by outside policing bodies and I am the only person that will likely be able to make any sense of what he says. He's a smart-arse, Vespa and you should expect some slippery talk from him between now and when I arrive in Reggio, but keep calm and cool and don't let him drive you into making any mistake that could result in him getting away again.'

'Si, si, Doctor Halle, I understand all those things. He will be here in a perfect condition for your interrogation when you arrive, but I have to say that so far he has not revealed to me any of his "smart-arse" talk.'

'He will, Vespa, he will. I will see you soon I hope, so goodbye for now.'

'Goodbye, *Dottore*.'

Halle hung up the phone, then immediately called the hotel reception and via the 24-hour business service reserved for people staying in the "executive suite", was able to book the next available flight to Reggio. Unfortunately, there was indeed no direct flight and in the end he opted for an Alitalia flight from Heathrow to Rome Fiumicino and thence, via a connecting flight, to Reggio Calabria's Tito Minniti Airport, a total travel time of around six hours.

Chapter 107

When Vespa returned to the room in which Hart and the priest Achille were being held at gunpoint, he was met with total silence. Both Hart and Achille had remained in a nervous silence since his short absence, awaiting the judgement that was obviously being finalised on them. Hart looked across the room at the priest, whose handsome tanned face now wore a mask of pallid fear and gave him a reassuring nod and smile. Vespa too smiled, but for a different reason, profoundly enjoying his moment of power, and spoke to his two captors.

'Gentlemen, as I said before, the priest is free to go but only after we have left this place. For your actions, no grudge will be held, but note, Father, your card has been marked! As for the doctor, your future is not quite so rosy. We will leave here and assemble at our office here in Reggio, where you will be interrogated and then afterwards dealt with as will be considered to be the most appropriate.'

Finally Hart spoke,

'So tell me, how did you know where I was here in Reggio, I thought I'd made a reasonable job of keeping under cover?'

'I have to say that you have done an excellent job of staying out of sight, but your problem was that we knew where you were heading to before you came anywhere near this place.'

'The telephone call?'

'Yes, of course. It was the call you made from Messina. The phone reception was very bad for some reason and we were only able to pick up pieces of your conversation. One of these pieces was the name of the church that you were advised to head for, but we missed the name of the town. We looked at the ferry crossings from Messina and the only two places you could have travelled to were Napoli and Reggio. We then checked out all the churches called Santa Andrea in both places and bingo, the only one close to any ferry port as described by your telephone friend, Messi, was this one in which we now stand. All we had to do then was to wait for you to arrive. I probably came over from Messina on the same ferry as yourself, Doctor Hart, so that I could be here especially to welcome you. So you see, you gave the game away yourself in your conversation with Messi, or rather *he* gave it away. Oh yes, and by the way, we did spot you between the ferry and this church, but preferred to let you arrive here rather than cause any public disturbance. You remember walking alongside the men from the boat and putting an arm around one startled fellow when my team arrived on the scene? Well, my men knew who you were even at that point and just wanted to check that you were confidently coming here. My men even stood in the shadows and watched you as you stood at the door of the church, looking up and admiring its beauty. At that point, they called me at the port, where I was having coffee, and confirmed your arrival here and ecco, here we all are.'

He beamed another self-satisfied smile, revealing an over-white, perfectly shaped set of teeth.

'So you're not as dumb as you look then.'

Although it would likely end in a painful response, Hart began his now regular ploy of needling the opposition in the knowledge through recent experiences that a needled opponent can make mistakes which might just unlock that window of opportunity to escape. Vespa continued to smile.

'Doctor Hart, I would remind you that you are the one that has been caught once again, so how dumb does make *you* look?'

Vespa addressed his men indicating that they would now depart, taking Hart with them to their riverside warehouse, but leaving the priest here at the church. This caused a little dissention amongst his troops however, one of who was not happy at leaving any live witnesses. Annoyed by this show of insolence in front of the other men so early in his promotion, he stormed over to the dissident.

'I'm your fucking leader and you will do as I say. If you don't like it, you can always leave us. I'm sure the undertaker Giuseppe can supply us with a coffin here at very short notice!'

He waved his gun at the priest indicating him to be seated and then taking Hart's arm manhandled him through the door, followed by his men. Before leaning back and closing the door, his final words to the priest over his shoulder were,

'We're leaving now, Father, but remember what I said, you are free now but your card is marked against any future activities against us. *Capisce*?'

He slammed the door shut and then between them the five men pushed and pulled Hart roughly through a side exit to the outside, where a black Mercedes-Benz GLE SUV and a black Alpha Romeo Julietta were parked. Vespa bundled Hart into the rear seat of the SUV and took a seat beside him. A second henchman took the seat on the other side and with one of them at the wheel and another in the front passenger seat the final mafioso was left to take the Alpha. With wheels spinning on the gravel drive, the two cars shot forward and took the route that would lead them to the warehouse cum office, where Hart's "interview" would be conducted in depth upon the arrival of Halle.

'Wait! Wait!'

In response to Hart's urgent cry, the driver applied the brakes of the SUV hard causing all the unbelted passengers to shoot forward in the vehicle, the man in the front passenger seat hitting his nose hard on the dashboard. When he lifted his head, blood was pouring down his face and onto his white shirt.

'*Cazzo*!'

'What the hell are you doing, Hart?'

'You pulled away and my seat belt wasn't fastened. That could have dangerous results you know. Statistics have shown that…ouch!'

The passenger with the bleeding nose had reached back over the seat and slapped Hart hard across the face and was about to repeat the treatment when Vespa placed a hand on his arm and with some strength held it down.

'*Calma.* We must expect this type of thing from this man. He is a *pirla*, but we must stay calm with him. You know well that our American colleague needs to be able to interrogate him freely and with a damaged face, his replies will be difficult. Please hold your anger until we are finished with him and then I will be happy for him to be fed to the sharks, or yourselves, whichever is the most painful.'

For the first time that evening, the party relaxed as they laughed at Vespa's little joke. Ten minutes of high speed driving through dark streets later, the cars turned sharply left into the courtyard of a large blacked-out building. As they skidded to a halt, the large electrically operated gates behind them which shielded the yard from the street outside, closed. Vespa quickly threw open his door and got out of the SUV, his gun trained on Hart.

'Out! Now!'

A sharp dig in his back below the ribs in the area of his kidneys by the other rear passenger was encouragement enough for Hart to comply with the command. There was a slamming of car doors and now Hart was surrounded by five armed men, ready to lead him inside the place of his forthcoming "interview". There was a slight chill in the night air and Hart thought that he could smell the sea. It was in fact the smell of the River Crati, which had been caught on the evening's gentle breeze and wafted under his nose, a river which flowed closely past the rear of this warehouse finally ending its journey in one final surge into the sea of the Strait of Messina.

Hart was marched across the courtyard to a door illuminated by a single bulb set in a fitting above it. Vespa announced himself using the electronic speakerphone and within seconds, there was the metallic sound of bolts electrically snapping back. Vespa opened the door and pushed Hart roughly inside. The last man to enter was the one with the handkerchief covering his bleeding nose and there was much baiting of him from the man who had come to meet them at the door. This went down like a lead balloon with the blood-stained man who raised his clenched fist in response, but a few sharp words from Vespa nipped the situation in the bud. Ahead of them stretched a long corridor, dimly lit by naked low wattage bulbs suspended from the ceiling. Everywhere other than directly below the hanging bulbs was dark, but the over-riding play on the senses was the damp smell of must. As they proceeded along the corridor, Hart being unceremoniously prodded forward every few yards, there was a very noticeable drop in the temperature up to the point where the temperature became so low that Hart began to shiver. Where he could make them out, the walls looked wet and slimy. He knew that he was still at ground level, but the whole feel of the corridor was more akin to a very damp cellar. As he slowed his pace to ensure a secure footing, once again he was urged on by the hard prod of a Beretta pistol in the small of his back. In the gloom a staircase rising to the right was in evidence, but it was straight ahead that he continued to be pushed towards what appeared to be the final door in the corridor. As he neared this door, there were sounds of riotous laughter coming from the room beyond it.

Vespa stormed forward and threw open the door at which point all laughter eventually ceased, but not before Hart had witnessed a most surreal and bizarre scenario.

Chapter 108

The heavy door had opened into a much more brightly lit room to reveal four quite young men in suits who, for want of a better word, were *playing*.

Two of them were wearing on their heads what Hart recognised as plastic bedpans and each armed with an aluminium walking stick were fencing with each other with some vigour. The other pair of "knights" was also helmeted with bedpans, but these combatants were mounted. In this instance their "trusty steeds" were in the form of electrically operated wheel chairs and in this game aluminium crutches served as lances.

Vespa exploded! In a tirade of angry abuse, Vespa's face turned scarlet as his voice rose to ear damaging levels. The four men like naughty children, although contrite, could not stop themselves from continuing to grin uncontrollably which increased Vespa's volume and his roseate face to even higher levels. Eventually, the four men removed their "helmets" and cast their "swords" and "lances" to a bench running the length of one wall. Following a further bout of uncontrollable laughter, with a resultant further tirade of abuse from their leader, they retreated from the room closing the door behind them. Hart gave Vespa a long look.

'You have my ultimate admiration. Your men are fearless and I would be very happy to have them standing next to me on any field of battle. You must be very proud.'

'Shut up! I will not tolerate their sort of behaviour. They will be punished for it.'

'Don't be too embarrassed, they are only children and as we say in England "boys will be boys". I have a question though. Are we in a medical supplies warehouse or a madhouse? I must admit, it's difficult to tell.'

'I warn you, Doctor Hart, not to say words that you will later regret. You are a coward, always running and afraid to face us, but now you are here to stay… until the end.'

'You forget that fighting is not what I was trained for. I am a medical doctor and as such charged with helping to make sick people's lives more tolerable and where possible to save lives. In the cause of self-preservation and despite not being a fighter, I have managed to dispose of your two assassins on the train and also your feared leader, who you are now happy to take over from. So do you still see yourselves as "world class" or "world beaters", because in my eyes, you come over as total amateurs?'

Vespa spoke to the four colleagues giving them a resume of Hart's short soliloquy and finished with orders as to how he now wanted Hart's stay here to proceed in view of Halle's predicted arrival. One of them then set about removing Hart's binding from his wrists, releasing his hands from behind his back. Vespa turned to Hart.

'I warned you about regretting careless words, Doctor, and I hope you will consider this during your stay. We will be leaving you alone for a while soon, but before then there is one more thing...'

He smiled momentarily and then suddenly without any warning sent a clenched fist crashing into Hart's stomach. Hart, gasping doubled up desperately trying to suck in air, his eyes bulging in their sockets. A sudden blow to the kidneys from the man with the bleeding nose standing behind him brought his body back upwards and he howled in pain, only for a second blow to be directed at his solar plexus, this time sending him toppling to the floor urgently gulping for oxygen. As he lay on the floor in a foetal position, he was suddenly aware of a shoe coming towards his unprotected ribs travelling at many miles per hour. He quickly moved his arms down to offer his ribs some protection by taking the kick on his forearms, in which action he was partially successful.

'Aspetta! Aspetta! Wait, wait,' Vespa cried as his men continued towards frenzy level in their attack on Hart. 'Not the face!'

In that instant, Hart rolled away, but only in time to see another antagonist send an equally aimed foot once again towards his stomach. This time he was unable to parry the kick at all with his arms and he took the full force of it in the area that it was aimed at. Vespa smiled down at the wide-eyed, gasping Hart, now holding his stomach where the bleeding nosed man had made contact with his size-42 brown Gucci brogues.

'Basta, basta. Enough, enough. We must not incapacitate him too much or else he will be unable to speak sufficiently well when our guest arrives, and we must certainly not kill him...not yet at least. OK, my friends, we will hold him in this room until then. When all is completed, we will dispose of our trash in the usual way. The river is always very grateful for our little contributions, or at least the fish are.'

There was much laughter.

'Now then, let us get him into the chair.'

Vespa stood aside as two of the men each placed a hand under Hart's armpits and dragged him backwards along the floor to one of the electrically operated wheelchairs. Once there, they heaved him up and dropped him onto the seat. Hart was still moaning, gasping for air and writhing in pain, but he was fully conscious and aware of what was happening and he intended to do whatever minor thing he could that might possibly assist him in another escape from a certain death situation. The man with the now no longer bleeding nose quickly scanned the bench along one wall of the room and finding a couple of rolls of tape, used for sealing up the boxes containing the range of medical items and disability and mobility aids that were the "front" for their organisation in Reggio, he tossed one to his cohort. With the other two men holding Hart's hands in position on the arms of the chair directly behind the two vertical handles which guided the vehicle, they quickly wrapped a good section of the roll around both his wrists, thus binding him there. During that activity, Hart attempted to stretch his hands away from the chair arms hoping to give himself some small range of hand and wrist movement. As for his legs, these now fairly lifeless appendages were likewise taped at his ankles to the front legs of the chair, with his feet positioned on the chair's footplates. That done, they had a little fun pulling back and pushing forward the guidance handles on the chair and driving Hart around the room. In truth they had a great deal of fun. Vespa, who had been watching on for reasons of quality control, was content with their work.

'Well done, men. Now let's go to my office and have a celebratory drink. We will leave Hart safely locked in this room and I will station one of the team outside the door. We will rotate every two hours and there will be no entry to the room by any of our team for whatever reason during that time until Halle arrives. If there is a fire, then we present Hart to him as toast, but we do not go into the room even to ensure that he is brown on all sides, OK?'

His men laughed. '*Va bene*, Claudio.'

'Let's go and relax then. Matteo, you will stand the first watch on the doctor.'

As they left the room, they had a long look at the pathetic twisted body taped to the chair, knowing full well that in no way could he escape this time. Vespa patted each man on the back upon leaving and then locked the door behind them leaving Hart, beaten, bruised and alone.

Chapter 109

Hart was slumped forward in the chair now fully conscious, but still gasping to draw in vital oxygen and acutely aware of the searing pain in his ribs. What could be next on the evening's agenda of entertainment? Eventually his breathing returned to something approximating normality and he was able to draw himself upright in the seat, wincing with pain, but getting a proper look at the rest of the room…having already had a close inspection of the floor!

It was obvious that the room was a storage area with various items of medical support equipment strewn around. He'd already witnessed the walking sticks, crutches, bedpans and the electric wheelchairs, but along the wall were stacked boxes of other items. On the bench that ran the whole length of one wall were various unpacked items, including the tape used to bind him to the chair and the "toys" used in the mafiosi's games. Squinting at the sealed boxes, he was able to discern indicative pictures of their contents via labels which were adhered to them. He saw arm and leg splints, Zimmer frames, abdominal corsets and even a series of prosthetic limbs. There were also various types of bandages and surgical equipment. It was highly likely that the warehouse represented an outlet for these types of medical equipment, thus representing the bona fide face of the company, whilst covering the nefarious mafia activities. Such a place, with a no doubt easy access to the river, would of course also be an ideal location for the initial distribution of said medical items by boat, but would also be ideal for the distribution of less bona fide items such as drugs…and the disposal of an occasional body or two.

A sudden cold blast of salty air drew his attention to the area of the room directly in front of him, where the floor sloped down ending at a combined wall and door section. It had a window at head height and a wide concertina door which covered at least two thirds of the remaining space. The room was mainly quiet, but he was under the distinct impression that he could occasionally hear the lapping of water outside, perhaps the river? As he gazed at the window, he saw the lighted topmast of a passing sailboat and heard the single cry of an itinerant seagull.

In his condition, he knew that in terms of energy, he was running on empty, but his will to survive remained strong and his mind refused to shut down from examining all possibilities that might lead to his freedom once again. He did realise though that his situation was very grim indeed, worsened by the tape binding his wrists and ankles. He heaved his wrists against the binding of the tape and although he had stretched his wrists against it when it had been applied, he found very little give in it. There was a little movement though. Perhaps he could bite through the bonds if he could lean far enough forward? He started to lean in order to test his theory, but shot back upright as the burning knife twisted in his ribs once more.

Shit! Shit! Shit!

Unfortunately, the utterances of those three magic words failed totally to have any impact whatsoever on his situation. There was no way in this world that he was going to be able to free himself from these bonds.

As he wallowed in his despair he heard the lock on the door click and then the door creaked open and in walked his presumed chaperone. This minder was a very young man in his late teens or early twenties Hart guessed, and like his colleagues he was dressed in a black suit but unlike them he sported a black tee-shirt under his jacket, an obvious sign of youth differentiation. He edged around Hart's chair spitting verbal abuse at his captive, occasionally emphasising a point with a little clip across Hart's face. It was clear to Hart that the death of his former leader was burning away at him and that he could expect no different treatment from any of the group apart from Vespa probably, who actually owed him a debt of gratitude as he himself had alluded to earlier. Eventually, the young man's eyes rested upon the control panel of the chair and upon the directional lever by which the chair was instructed to move and his eyes lit up. He smiled malevolently at Hart and placing his feminine-looking hand upon the lever gingerly pushed it forward.

The chair jolted and moved gently forward. The young man nodded knowingly and moved the lever into the slow-reverse mode at which the chair stopped and then followed its new command. It was clearly mafioso playtime again. Next he moved the lever to the left at which point the chair, guided by the front wheels and driven by those at the rear, began to turn in a slow circle, pinioned by the stationary left rear wheel. Hart was not amused at being the play thing of his young guard, but being still in the recovery stage following the vicious beating that ensued his last "smart-arse" comment, he chose to remain quiet. With the chair turning circles, Hart's tormentor looked around for additional toys with which to entertain himself and smiled as his eyes picked out a suitable item amongst the disorderly pile of equipment on the bench. Hart peered at him at every revolution of the chair and watched him open a box and take out an article which flashed briefly as it reflected the light from the ceiling bulb.

'Fucking hell, he's gotten hold of scalpels!'

The young man took out two of the surgical scalpels from their box and positioned himself in front of Hart's chair with both arms outstretched, a scalpel held in each hand pointing forwards in a space level with Hart's head. With each revolution of the chair, he moved a little closer, so that eventually he was close enough to Hart's head such that on each pass of the chair each blade gently nicked his face, causing trickles of blood to run down onto the collar of his recently acquired navy-blue polo shirt. Hart was scared now. This young idiot was capable of cutting him to ribbons just for laughs. What should he do? He decided quickly that his best option was to try and summon attention from one of his other captors, preferably Vespa who had left explicit instructions with his

400

men that they needed Hart alive and in a relatively good condition to speak. Whilst giving his men almost carte blanche to do with him as they wished, he was adamant that Hart's face at least should not be touched or show any signs of violent actions upon it.

As Hart reached the point of crying out, the chaperone suddenly moved forward and pushed the chair's lever into the hard left position. The effect of this was to cause the chair to lurch and rapidly pick up speed, throwing it into a chaotic high-speed spin in circles around its rear wheel. The young man whooped with delight and moved in to take up his position once again, with the scalpels once more held in the hands of his outstretched arms. Never one for fairground rides, Hart's head was spinning faster than the chair causing him to feel totally nauseous. Then at the point at which he passed, his tormentor for the umpteenth time, not for the first time day vomit exploded from his gagging mouth. On this occasion, his stomach contained ample projectile material, having worked his way earlier through the entire menu on offer at the church, and the projected vomit struck the idiot guard exactly where it hurt him most...bang on his designer suit! He was in receipt of wonderfully mixed proportions of minestrone soup, green salad, spaghetti with meatballs and tomato sauce, a selection of cold meats, a small amount of gorgonzola cheese and two glasses of red wine. This wonderful cocktail hit the man directly in his chest, clinging there momentarily to both his jacket and tee-shirt before slowly starting on a downward journey to his trousers.

At first impact, the young man screamed and leapt back from the spinning chair, but then moved back in again in an effort to stop it spinning as Hart continued to vomit in spiral patterns on both the man and the floor. As the young gangster continued to shout his disgust at the ruination of his suit and as Hart's chair took on a loud whining sound as it continued on its dizzying course, the noise from the room travelled to where Vespa and his off duty guards were relaxing. Vespa sprang from his sofa and raced down the staircase and along the corridor to the storeroom, where he flung the door open and charged in with pistol raised, followed by four of his retinue. He had fully expected to see his young colleague in some dire peril from the squeals he was making, but what greeted him was a scene from some cinematic farce.

Vespa stood there rooted to the spot as the Laurel and Hardy epic unfolded in front of him. Two of his colleagues made a dash for the circling chair in an effort to take hold of it and slow it down, but all that they succeeded in doing was to slip and slide in the vomit on the floor, ending up with both of them in a heap, the expensive suits demonstrating an amazing absorption quality as they efficiently soaked up the vomit. It was up to Vespa to finally calmly lean in and flick the control lever off before not so calmly attacking the young man about the head whilst simultaneously hurling abuse at him. Looking at the pathetic sight of Hart drooling at the mouth with numerous bleeding cuts to his face, and with Halle due in three hours' time expecting to see a prisoner in a fit state to be questioned, he completely lost his temper again, striking his young colleague repeatedly about the head whilst screaming obscenities at him. The young man fell to the floor, not hurt physically but with his dignity seriously bruised, and burst into tears. Hart looked up groggily.

'You should be selling tickets for this bloody fiasco.'

His comment went unheard, which was probably in his best interests under the circumstances.

Vespa, as leader of the group of circus clowns, selected men to fetch buckets of water and mops and get the floor clean. He physically threw the young man out of the room, taking care not to come into contact with any of Hart's stomach contents and then set about cleaning Hart up and treating the cuts on his face with great care and faux compassion. His own future would be at stake when Halle arrived and there was still plenty of time to salvage it from the current mess. The room was quickly cosmetically made-over to look something like decent and Hart was now sitting in what appeared to be a semi-comfortable position, still taped into the chair but looking a little cleaner and less the worse for wear for the beatings he had endured. He barked more orders to his men.

'Better. Things are looking better. Here is my latest change of plan. We will leave Hart alone here locked in for thirty more minutes after when I want Angelo to first check on him and then wait outside for a further one hour, after which I want Nicolo to take over for the next two hours and then Angelo again to repeat the process. Is that clear?'

There were nods from the group. Vespa wasn't satisfied with their responses,

'IS THAT CLEAR for Christ's sake!'

This time everybody responded almost in unison.

'*Si*, Claudio.'

'Then let's go.'

As the men exited the room, Hart made a sorry sight. He still felt as dizzy as hell and still was only prepared to stare at a single point on the floor, afraid that any further eye movement would send his head spinning out of control once more with the resultant induced vomiting. How he could do with a drink of water!

Thirty minutes later, when Angelo dropped in on him, he felt much more stable and was able to ask him for a drink of water. Surprisingly, he obliged without any comment and held the glass of water to Hart's lips so that he might drink, after which act of mercy, he left the room, locking the door behind him. Hart now had one hour before "the changing of the guard" to try and work a miracle on the tape binding his wrists and ankles.

Chapter 110

As Hart's eyes finally left the safety of the floor and started to re-scan the room, a movement at the far end caught his bleary eyes. Focusing as best he could, he established that the movement had come from outside the window in the end wall. There was somebody outside. Suddenly, there appeared a full face framed there and despite his condition, Hart was able to identify the features as those of the priest Father Achille. Making eye contact with Hart, the priest raised a finger to his lips indicating that silence should prevail and then he disappeared as quickly as he had arrived. Time seemed to drag on and Hart wondered whether Achille had himself been captured, but no, back he came giving Hart the thumbs up and waving what looked like a metal bar, before once again disappearing below the outer edge of the window. Hart could now hear metallic noises on the outer part of the wall at the point at which it came into contact with the concertina door. To his alarm, the noise of the scraping of metal on metal grew in intensity, and he expected at any moment some member of the mafiosi to discover the priest's presence. Suddenly there was a snapping noise and the concertina door parted from its contact point very slowly. Father Achille forced his body through an as small an opening as possible and quickly crossed the floor to Hart. He certainly looked most un-Fatherlike, out of uniform and wearing black jeans, black jumper and trainers.

'Doctor Hart, please do not try to speak. I have levered the padlock lock off the door and it is now free to open, but for now we will leave it only slightly ajar. Now let me look at your bonds.'

Seeing that the bonds were of tape rather than rope, he realised that it would be necessary to cut them and began scrutinising the bench for a suitably sharp instrument.

'Check that end of the bench farthest away from me, Achille, I have definitely seen a box of surgical scalpels there somewhere, in fact if you look at my face you will see that I have already sampled a couple of them.'

'Mamma mia! Wait, here they are.'

Armed with one of the scalpels, he set about cutting through the tapes securing Hart's ankles to the chair.

'The river is right outside the sliding door, it goes up and down with the tide and when at full tide it can be a torrent, so we must try and get you out before then. At present, the tide is low and there is a concrete slipway that we can walk on.'

He managed to cut through the tapes on Hart's ankles quite quickly, but the wrist binding was proving more of a challenge. He chose to make his cut on the underside of the chair arm so as not to run the risk of slicing through Hart's flesh, but it was in an awkward position.

'When I have freed you, we will leave through the door and across the slipway and then on to a small church down the river past the next bridge from here. I'm hoping that you will be able to walk sufficiently well despite your terrible looking condition, for we will have little time for our escape. You should be safe there…safer than at Santa Andrea for sure…and we can make arrangements for your quick departure from there back to Milano.'

Hart sucked in a long breath of air and with difficulty croaked,

'Good. There is a guard outside the door behind me and in forty-five minutes' time, he will be replaced by another of his team who will probably look in on me, so the time at our disposal might be short.'

The tape anchoring Hart's left wrist suddenly pulled apart.

'*Bene*. Now for the other wrist.'

Father Achille began his work with the scalpel on the other wrist sawing and cutting as quickly and as safely as he could.

'Achille, I would prefer it if you could choose quickness over safety please, we don't have the time to follow health and safety regulations at the moment.'

'*Si, si,* I understand.'

Achille speeded up his cutting to the point that the chair itself began to shake and rattle but then suddenly he stopped. Both men had picked up the sound of approaching voices in the corridor outside. It quickly became apparent that the approaching men had reached the door and were gaining the guard in conversation.

'I must return outside to the slipway until we have an "all clear", *Dottore*, for now would be a bad moment to be caught. Don't worry I will return as soon as is possible. At least you now have both legs free and one free arm.'

With that, he skipped across the room and out through the narrow gap between the wall and the concertina door, gently sliding it back into position after leaving. Hart in the meantime flattened down the severed tapes around his ankles and made the best he could of holding the cut tape from his left wrist in some sort of position that appeared to be binding. He had no sooner finished when he heard the key turn in the lock and a new mafioso face entered. This one carried a wooden kitchen chair, which he positioned on the floor in front of Hart, but away from the marks left by the cleaned up vomit, and then sat upon it whilst looking closely at Hart. Some minutes later, with his inquisitiveness about this non-fighting man who had managed to cause so much turmoil satisfied, he fumbled a rolled up magazine from his trouser pocket and began to thumb through the sexually explicit photographs in it.

Bugger! thought Hart.

Oh dear! thought the priest.

It was evident that this new man on the scene was also planning on staying for a while, again counter to the instructions that Vespa had delivered earlier. The priest groaned inwardly. This could be a long waiting game and all he could do was keep out of sight, ready to go back in at a suitable time and complete the job on Hart's right wrist. Hart was worried. In the end, there may be neither the time nor the opportunity for one final dash for freedom, but with the man engrossed in his magazine, he carefully worked the bound wrist backwards and forwards and side to side, hoping to weaken the bond.

A whole hour dragged by during which time Hart recovered somewhat from his earlier ordeal and importantly began to think clearer again. He was still working his right wrist in an effort to release it and it was now feeling very sore with little to show for it. Exactly on the hour, the lock was turned in the door and another name on Vespa's list of guards was ticked off as a new man entered and took over the role as watchman. No words passed between the two men as the one arrived and the other one left, but the relieved mafioso took care to ensure that his magazine went with him, with many photographs still left un-ogled for his lonelier moments.

The new man took his place on the vacated chair, sparing Hart only a cursory look as he lit up a cigarette and opened a newspaper he had carried in under his arm. Hart had expected all his minders to remain outside in the corridor, which would have allowed the priest to fully complete his job, but as this was apparently not now the case he had to work even harder at removing the final strips of tape and he even resorted to using his freed hand to assist in this, but this was dangerous as once seen by his guard, all hell would break loose again.

Yet another hour went by and another guard assumed position in the room. It was at this point that Hart saw the face of the priest once again at the window. Father Achille gave Hart a thumbs-up and then by making the sign of waves with one hand and pushing up with his other hand indicated, or so Hart thought, that the level of the tidal river was rising quickly. Why the rising river was a cause for a thumbs-up was beyond Hart's comprehension, but perhaps the priest had perceived some advantage in it. In fact, the truth was that he was trying to indicate the need for him to retreat to higher ground as the waters were now swirling up the slipway, a definite cause for concern for both of them!

Time moved on and eventually Hart began to doze involuntarily. The sudden loud bang of the door being closed startled him awake and two men approached him.

Chapter 111

'My God, what a mess in here! Hart looks totally out of it. I hope for your sake that he is compos mentis enough to answer the questions I have for him.'

Hart recognised the booming, bombastic voice immediately and a chill ran through him. As the door to the room had opened, icy cold air had been dragged in under the bottom edge of the concertina doors, off the now racing river, so now he felt doubly chilled. He shivered and raising his head lifted his heavy eyes, confirming the identity of the wearer of the blue double-breasted blazer, the pristine white oxford shirt and of course the striped company tie, tied in the famous Windsor knot. Robert Halle smiled and leaned forward ensuring his image filled Hart's entire field of vision.

'Good evening, Doctor Hart, it's a tremendous pleasure to meet you again after all this time.'

He had definitely aged since Hart had last seen him and although wearing the same uniform, he looked somehow less kempt and the senior military officer air was no longer in evidence. This at least pleased the battered former member of staff. In a matter of a few weeks, Halle's meticulously kept ridiculous moustache had become flecked with grey, as had his greasy combed back hair, or perhaps he had foregone the process of dyeing them of late?

'I've come a long way for this reunion, Hart, and I really do hope it will be worth it. In any case, I'm sure that I will glean much pleasure from it in one way or another.'

He screwed up his eyes and cast them over Hart's vomit-stained clothes and over the stains on the floor and smiled again in his smug and confident way that made Hart, alias "the writer not a fighter", seriously want to smash him in the face!

'It's a bit of a mess around here, old chap. It would seem that our five star treatment has not been entirely to your liking,' then turning to Vespa, 'Claudio, I think you can leave Doctor Hart and myself alone now thank you.'

'But *Dottore* Halle, he is a dangerous man you know and—'

Halle raised a hand stopping him in mid-sentence,

'I know exactly what our friend here is, and looking at him now, it would be foolish I think to believe that he was going anywhere other than to meet his maker. No, *grazie* for your concern, but it really is the time for the doctor and I to be alone together.'

Vespa nodded in compliance and left the room closing the door behind him, the door from which Halle had removed the key as he first entered and which he now returned and turned in the lock.

'Alone at last. I thought he would never leave.'

He placed a small Gladstone bag on the bench and took up a position in front of Hart, who stared at him, drained of both energy and confidence! He didn't just look at Halle, however, his eyes also focused on the bottom of the concertina door under which water from the swollen river was now advancing.

'As I was saying, I have come a long way to see you and we have much to discuss. You really have been a pain in the backside to our whole organisation, Hart, and I have important questions to put to you, which by hook or by crook, you will answer.'

He briefly looked at the Gladstone bag, as if this Pandora's Box contained key items that would no doubt enhance the questioning.'

'I don't see why you would want to do that, Halle. It must be fairly obvious to someone of even your level of understanding that all that I've tried to do is go about my gainful employment working for a devastated client back in the UK, and all that you and your group of morons have done is to try and put me out of commission for some bloody reason or other. Why are you and your team of half-wits treating me like this for God's sake?'

Bluff was always going to be his first line of defence, or rather attack.

'Nice try, Hart, but what exactly *is* your gainful employment and exactly *who* are you working for? I'm intrigued to know who pulls your strings, who your bosses are and what your objectives are. I also want to hear what you think you know about our…World's…current business plan.'

Hart was amazed at Halle's response. He and his cronies really did have him tarred with completely the wrong brush. They really did think he was part of some other major company's spying and espionage activities. He was being treated like this under completely false assumptions. However, he continued to bluff away.

'As you are aware already, I'm working for a small biotech company in the UK, specifically in the area of stem cell research. I went over to the stem cell congress in Padua to try and pick up as much of the latest research and competitor information as I could, including if possible details of work that is not yet in the public domain. The next thing I know, after an enjoyable couple of days at the conference, I find myself being attacked on the train to Milan.'

'But come on, Hart, you're missing something out. What about your previous little foray in Greifswald in Germany?'

'That's fairly obvious, Halle. As you well know the GRS Institute there, is very well known as an important place for stem cell research and the opportunity arose for me to go there and see it first hand, so I did.'

'So let us forget for now your…loss of way…while you were there and move on a little. Why did you make such an arse of yourself in our hospitality suite at the Padua conference?'

So far the questions were easy to respond to with no associated threats and despite his flagging condition, Hart felt well up to dealing with them.

'I was there on genuine business as I have already told you. The opportunity arose to learn more than was being divulged at the scientific presentations and so by staying back in the suite at closing time, I was able to access some additional trials' data.'

'Yes, illegally, Hart. What you were doing amounted to industrial spying and that is a very serious matter…especially when you are spying on research and global plans that are so very sensitive, as is the case here.'

'You have to take your chances,' Hart cut in, 'when I eventually found another job, I had to demonstrate my ability to climb the ladder there as quickly as possible and hence my keenness to become expert in stem cells as soon as possible. You know, Halle, it's important for me to get my quality of life back to approximately similar levels as it was at World quickly, for as you are no doubt pleased to hear I have fallen a long way.'

Halle gave a brief smile,

'Yes, it was indeed a joyous day for me when I saw your arse disappear from my office for one last time, and your face…oh my God, the look on your face!'

That touched a nerve with Hart and despite his perilous position, he couldn't restrain his resulting comments.

'Halle, you always were and still are a totally predictable twat! You never did have the necessary qualities or mentality to plan and manage. Importantly, you have never had the capability to do essential detailed risk assessment of the work you are doing, let alone actually *mitigate* for things that might go wrong, and that is now becoming obvious. I suspect that you were responsible for what happened on the Milan train, and you must also hold yourself responsible for the death of the Queen of this group of mafiosi idiots that you are working with. You and your team are frightened to death of what you think I might know about your global stem cell activities and I include the Vatican in that. Do you think for one moment that I have any expectation at all of leaving this place alive after Claudia Volpe died, who by the way turned out to be just as useless as you, but far better looking of course! Why don't you come straight out with it and ask me what I know about the OCA and the plans you have for the Pope?'

Harts voice had risen in volume as he had adopted this aggressive, challenging posture.

Halle didn't speak for several moments but instead, in a move which was very un-characteristic of the man, without any warning, he slapped Hart across the face with the palm of his hand and as the face turned with the impact, he brought his hand equally hard back again, so that on its return it was the *back* of his hand which made contact. Surprisingly, Hart felt no pain at this effort. Halle led a delicately easy kind of life, being in no way particularly physical in any of his activities, so that when his soft manicured hand made contact with Hart's face it was like being firmly brushed by a silk glove and it was clear to Hart that the hand was stinging more from its swipes than was his own face. He looked at Halle contemptuously.

'You really are unfit for this type of work, Halle. You're much too soft. Surely, you must realise what a joke you are back at the New Jersey office, with your perennial blue blazers and that bloody striped tie. The hair under your nose is a ridiculously poor representation of your manhood, and as for your breath, your breath is so foul that it's discernible on the next floor of the office, it's horrific! No doubt you've brought the infamous "freshener" with you that never leaves your side? I can tell you one thing for sure at this interview, whatever it costs you, it's not worth the money, but then manure is not an easy smell to successfully mask.'

Hart's repartee was finally too much for Halle to compete with verbally and raising his clenched white-knuckled fist he drove it at Hart's face. Hart had half expected some additional retribution so that when the telegraphed blow arrived, his face rode with it as best he could manage and he ended up taking the glancing blow on his cheekbone. The look on Halle's face revealed that the strike had visibly hurt his soft hand, which he shook with the pain. Hart, despite his utter vulnerability, continued with his taunts.

'Pathetic! You talk to me about the illegality of industrial spying, whilst at the same time you've been trying through your inadequate contacts to have me assassinated. You talk utter bollocks, Halle. Take my tip, forget interrogation and vengeance and fuck off back to your cosseted life in the USA.'

Halle paused, collecting his thoughts and trying to calm down a little. Finally, with the smarmy smile back on his lips he spoke,

'As usual, Hart, you have become verbally aggressive and foul-mouthed, but let us say that we *are* interested to know exactly how much you *think* you know and who you have shared that information with. Interested enough to make what's left of your rather tragic life very painful for you if you do not co-operate with us. It's you who are the one tied to the chair and I am the one in the position to pass judgement on you and decide where you go from here.'

In his mind, Hart was wondering, even at this late stage, whether some kind of trade off with Halle might be possible, but could he trust him? Absolutely bloody not, under no circumstances! However he needed time, time at least to try and finish the job of working his way out of the final binding holding his right wrist down on the chair arm.

'OK, Halle, I'll tell you everything I know.'

Halle raised his eyebrows.

'That's a shame, Hart. I was really looking forward to having to give you some additional "encouragement".'

He moved to the chair close to Hart and sat down, sitting close enough for Hart to pick up on the bad breath for which his nick-name had become the not too subtle "Doctor Halletosis".

'So tell me, let's hear it all and we will consider how we go forward from there.'

Hart drew a long breath, turning his head away from Halle's breathing space as he did so and began.

Chapter 112

Hart gave Halle a drawn out mixture of truths, half-truths and downright lies, trying to satisfy some of the questions that he presumed were on Halle's list. His hope was that whilst talking, he could continue to work away at twisting his right wrist hopefully wearing down the tenacity of the tape, which was now definitely showing signs of wear.

He lightly covered aspects already spoken of briefly at different levels to both Arben and Volpe, and also to Halle again now for his second time of hearing, concerning his trips to Greifswald, Padua and Sicily. In talking of the murder of the OCA operatives in Basiglio, it became obvious by the look on his face that Halle was not fully informed on the depths to which his mafia friends had descended. He went back even further, to the very beginning and talked of Williams and the fate of his wife and the initial suspicions, that were now close to the *proof* stage, relating to the methods of obtaining foetal stem cell material from European and possible African maternity clinics. All the time, he attempted to grow the story of his employment with the small biotech company and how by gaining knowledge in current stem cell research he could further his own professional future.

At Halle's direction, he returned to the OCA, relating an insignificant part of his meeting with an un-named senior executive of that group and the man's promise to relieve him of the death sentence he was under from the mafia, no doubt working for the team of which Halle was a senior member, if he could help them in some slight way in Sicily. He talked of the Vatican and the likely need for processed stem cell material for the treatment of the Pope and of course the Mondo connection in all of that and in the end the billion-dollar opportunity all of this presented to World Pharmaceuticals.

When he had finished, Halle sat there and smiled.

'Thank you, Hart. I score you three out of ten for that, and that includes presentation and content combined. Funnily enough, I actually believe much of what you have told me. What it shows to me, however, is the level of your naivety in this business. Despite what I feared, you are a mere pawn in this game, or in this business I should say, that has a strategy far too complex and brilliantly conceived for you to ever comprehend and I must say that it gives me unparalleled pleasure to pass sentence on you here and now.

'Doctor Max Hart, I sentence you to death at my hand in this place, today. Ha, ha, ha! However, personal pride prevents me from dispatching you before I have made the effort to fill in the glaring gaps in your knowledge and you will see how misplaced your earlier accusations were that I lack planning and risk assessment abilities.'

The good news was that Hart would learn the whole protocol of the plan. The bad news was that unless he removed the final piece of tape, he would take the information with him to the grave. He needed more time still, and the possibility of a way to gain that time came to mind. It was a question that he had considered when talking to either Janet or Victoria Crosse.

'Halle, to be fair to you, you never used to be like this. You were always as straight as a die, upstanding and very moral in your outlook on all things in life. You hated my laid-back approach and especially my habit of polluting the air with the more than occasional expletive. You recognised all the rules relating to clinical investigations and the ethics that governed them and then suddenly you completely changed. Even the staff you work with noticed it. World staff at all salary levels have commented on it I hear. Tell me if you can, just what did bring about the changes in turning you from Mister Upright to Mister Lowdown. What happened in your life to create this Jeckyll and Hyde effect?'

A terrible sadness and anger showed in Halle's twisted face and raising his fist, he approached Hart once more, but then at the final moment, he halted and looked away. He was silent for a couple of minutes and then lowering his fist addressed Hart.

'You are going to die today, Hart, of that there is no doubt, and so I will tell you what I have never ever spoken to anybody else, bar one, about.'

'Come on then, let's hear it and I really hope it's worth it. Your life has for sure been strictly black and white and pretty one dimensionally boring, so I am intrigued.'

Halle ignored him and continued,

'My father was diagnosed with motor neurone disease some years ago. Towards the end of his life, he begged to be allowed to either take his own life or to place himself with some group who would do the job humanely for him, even if it meant travelling abroad to Switzerland or some other country to get the job done. As a family, we fought against his wishes and in the end, he died in great pain having lost all vestiges of dignity and hating us all for it. The "all" being myself, my two younger brothers, our wives and our mother. You might have thought that we would have learned a lesson of some sort from those experiences, but no. Not very long after he had died, my youngest brother began to develop certain of the symptoms. Now there is evidence of a one in ten probability that the disease can be famial, or hereditary, with genetics obviously being a major contributor through demonstrated gene mutations. Therefore, as it is not difficult to obtain genetic testing for motor neurone and other neurological diseases, my two brothers and I, including the sibling showing the early symptoms, underwent genetic screening. The relevant affected gene sites are well documented, some of them being more virulent than others and the results of our screening were that my youngest brother had the most virulent form, whilst my other brother had a form with medium virulency and I had the least virulent form. My youngest brother's symptoms advanced very rapidly and as in the case of my father we as a family were not prepared to step outside of the

411

recognised standard forms of treatment that were given to my brother. Towards the end of his life, he too expressed a deep wish to be allowed to die, but once again the family, including his wife, over-ruled any consideration of the issue of assisted death and he subsequently died suffering almost as much as our father.'

'Jesus, Halle, I never guessed—'

'Let me continue while I can. In the meantime, my mother suffered a severe stroke and died. My remaining brother now has early symptoms of the disease. This time, however, I decided not to consult family members about his treatment, but instead consulted…Alberto Mondo.'

'Bloody hell!'

'Through my involvement in our "Great Plan", which in any case I am thoroughly supportive of, I am able to obtain treatment for my brother, based upon the very stem cell extraction work that you have an interest in, and he's doing well. Further down the line, I too might require a similar treatment should my genes take a turn for the worse. So you see that for me, my total active immersion in the whole stem cell business and the "Great Plan" is a no-brainer.'

'I disagree, you can't—'

'I've not finished! You can imagine what all this has done to the family and much of the work done in finding the best people to contact in trying to improve the disease prognoses has been done by my wife, who is a scientist herself. Now for the difficult part. In working through a short list of suitable physicians and interviewing those who seemed to be particularly outstanding, she met a young specialist who was extremely bright, very outgoing in nature, gregarious even, popular with his contemporaries, very amusing, kind, good looking, a bon viveur, perfectly turned out for any occasion…the list of positives goes on, although as a negative he is rather prone to outbursts of vile expletives I am told. Anyway the upshot of it is that just under one year ago, she upped and left the Halle residence to start her life again with this…perfect man!'

'Shit!'

'Shit indeed, Hart, but the worst thing of all the shit I have described to you so far is that it seems that this Superman bears a very close resemblance to yourself in all those things described, and I hate you even more for it! In fact, I bloody well despise you and having destroyed your professional life of late, I now intend to kill you!'

'But that has absolutely nothing to do with me!'

Halle's eyes were bulging and sweat was pouring from his forehead and down his face.

(*He's gone mad, totally mad.*)

Suddenly Halle shook his shoulders, and like the turning off of a switch seemed to come out of the self-induced trance-like state he had been in. He showed absolutely no signs of being aware that he had poured out his heart to his nemesis and he continued as if he had never spoken of, or even mentioned in passing, his family life. He looked around the room and removed a small table from under the bench, which he positioned ahead of Hart and closer to the concertina door, which now had water from the river flowing copiously under its lower edge. He placed his chair next to the table then reaching for his Gladstone bag from on top of the bench placed it on the table. He opened it and after peering into it for several seconds nodded his head and removed from it a syringe, a syringe needle and a small bottle of clear liquid. Hart was alarmed! Halle smiled at him and clasped his hands together, his eyes now firmly back in their sockets.

'Fancy a short ride, Hart?'

He approached the wheelchair in which Hart was seated and after perusing the drive mechanism on the chair arm slowly pulled it forward until the chair began to move. Hart's eyes widened in dismay wondering what Halle planned to do next, but it wasn't a great deal, for as the chair reached the side of the small table just a few feet further forward, he eased back the drive handle and brought the chair to rest.

'Right, Hart, that's much more suitable. I am going to tell you the most amazing story, after which with the help of a small amount of injected chemical…' he indicated to the glass vial, '…you will tell me everything you know, this time in its entirety and with no untruths or misdirection. After that, with a little more of the chemical, you will sleep the long sleep and I must admit I will be most happy. My Italian colleagues, who you have already met and who you hold not a lot of respect for, have requested that they may perform the final act in your passing. That will be burial at sea. Well, not quite, more a burial in the river, you see the river is a short distance from this door…' he looked at the bottom edge of the door where water was flowing in, '…in fact, I see it is trying to claim you already. It is the resting place of so much local rubbish and detritus, Hart, so you will finally be at home. The team here sees it as payback for their beloved Claudia, although they do feel somewhat short-changed as under the circumstances they really did want to make you beg to die at the end. But we'll see how I feel after injection number one, and who knows, I might change my mind and give them a treat.

'But enough of that, now for the story of stories. We have already talked of the billion-dollar market that is waiting for the right drug to come along for the treatment of the long list of currently untreatable neurogical indications and spinal injuries. Well, World now has such a drug, which has been proven to be effective, albeit in small patient number clinical trials, but also certainly in tests performed under laboratory conditions. It has been demonstrated to be beneficial in all cases where patients were afflicted with advanced diseases such as Parkinson's, stroke and even dementia. We have even jumped the approvals processes in many cases where patients are sufficiently desperate and most importantly sufficiently wealthy, and have treated them directly, privately, with outstanding outcomes.'

'Don't forget to mention in your self-congratulatory speech that this has been done totally unethically by illegally taking the unborn foetuses of innocent pregnant women through induced abortions. Can't you imagine the terrible misery that you are responsible for?'

'Yes, of course I am aware of that, but a little pain is necessary when it results in a huge gain. The restrictions on stem cell work in the USA and Europe have been responsible for what has been termed the "dark discovery and development". We have an ongoing unmet need for this human material and

413

hence we have had to obtain it in such a way as you describe. To give you some idea of the scale of it, we are also in the process of stepping up supplies from the African continent where things are a little less formal and restrictive. To firm up our African process, it has been necessary for World to invest heavily in that continent, but with the certain knowledge that the resultant rewards will be great. The initial problem was getting a substantial foothold there, but Alberto Mondo came up with a brilliant strategy. The Pope is the first black African Pope, he's from Angola remember, and that is where we set up our first development plant. In the end, all it needed was some local, well-advertised charitable work done on behalf of the company, plus some Christian philanthropy and of course our "factor X".'

'What the hell is "factor X"?'

'Family ties, Hart. Family ties. Peter Mondo, that is Cardinal Peter Mondo, the brother of Alberto Mondo, who in all innocence has very effectively sold World Pharma as a benign benefactor to the Pope. You see he is very close to the Pontiff and moves very much in those tight circles of important people within the Catholic Church who have the grand ambition of bringing third world countries forward into our present-day world, if only to initiate a process of curing their current medical ills. Through Peter Mondo, together with some well-placed support, we have been able to focus our efforts on the Pope and are exceeding our most optimistic hopes on the "Dark Continent". Umm, "Dark Discovery and Development on the Dark Continent"…nice one!'

Halle liked that strap-line.

'But Peter Mondo is no fool. Surely he will realise how he is being manipulated in all of this, and by his own brother too?'

'He is a revered and respected young cardinal in the Vatican. Revered for his work in Africa by both his peers and now especially by the Pope himself, with whom he has grown so very close. A potentially great problem to the Great Plan, however, has been the continuing failing health of the Pope and it has been essential not only to just keep him alive, but alive and active in his papacy. As you probably are aware he suffers from an advanced form of Parkinson's disease. There are two major reasons that it is essential that he keeps heaven waiting. The first reason is to ensure that all ethical and governmental approvals, rights and processes are in place for our African dream to reach fruition and secondly, well let's say that when the Pontiff passes over it would be extremely convenient to the cause to have a…friendly face…sitting as his successor, if you get my drift. It's also something that Alberto longs for, his brother as Pope.'

'Bloody hell, you want Peter Mondo to be the next Pope so that he can, in all innocence, help you continue your immoral activities!'

Halle laughed.

'Right in one.'

'But it can't be as easy as that, Halle, the Pope is elected by the College of Cardinals in Conclave. It's an election, Halle, not a bloody lottery!'

Halle laughed again. After a shaky start, he was thoroughly enjoying this now.

'It's only a lottery if all the balls are in the hat. Do you imagine that we could allow all the prospective candidates to remain in that hat?'

'What you mean you've....'

Hart was incredulous, their suppositions were indeed true.

'Yes, we've removed them, or at least all the other serious contenders to Peter Mondo's possible promotion to Pope. They are all now residing in a "higher place" and will no doubt be reunited with the present Pope in the near future.'

'You're fucking mad, Halle, and so are the others in this crackpot scheme, including old man Mondo himself!'

Halle connected the syringe needle to the syringe and removed the protective sheath. He then unscrewed the aluminium top from the vial of clear fluid and pushed the needle through the rubber cap into the liquid below.

'On the contrary, Doctor Hart. This has become a game of stupendous strategy. A game which has at certain times, been almost screwed by an insignificant foul-mouthed amoeba. Of course I'm referring to you, Hart. You've always been trouble for me, right the way through your working life at World and right up until this present moment, but now you will repay me by assisting me one final time. You know, despite your story, there are many details that you are hiding and just one little prick will reveal them all. I also need to know the level of involvement of the OCA and any other similar international bodies in this and the level of their combined knowledge, which I'm sure you are privy to. Now then, prepare yourself for that little prick and things will be much better for all of us.'

'That little prick is you, Halle, you bastard!'

Halle moved closer.

'One little prick, Hart, and then you can sleep forever. The world will suddenly be such a wonderful place.'

Hart wondered if Halle really had gone totally mad, he certainly acted as if he had, but it was now irrelevant, his own time was almost over and he had to do something urgently.

From his seat, Halle pushed up Hart's shirtsleeve and examined his arm for a suitable injection point.

'Ah, there we are, Max, my boy.'

'You're fucking crazy. Totally fucking crazy!'

He picked up the syringe and with it on its way towards his chosen vein, he paused and placed it back onto the table.

'I tell you what, Hart, why don't I be a sport? Why don't I let you say a prayer first? You know the church has so much involvement in this matter that it seems ungracious of me not to allow a proper conclusion...for you at any rate...so go on, I will allow you to say your final prayer.'

Hart was stunned. He didn't have any prayers in his memory bank, but he needed as many final moments as he could get to finish off the final layer of tape.

'OK Halle. This is the only thing I can think of to say at this moment. You'll no doubt remember the Blade Runner and the dying lines of the Replicant Roy Batty, model number N6MAA10816.'

Halle looked at him quizzically, obviously not having a clue what he was talking about.

'You can say what you like, Hart, but you have just sixty seconds to say it in. Ha, ha, ha.'

Hart closed his eyes and repeated those famous words.

'I've seen things you people wouldn't believe... Attack ships on fire off the shoulder of Orion... I watched C-beams glitter in the dark near the Tannhauser Gate... All those moments will be lost in time, like tears in rain....Time to die.'

Indeed in that instant Hart *was* ready to die...but suddenly Halle's phone rang out and kept on ringing. Cursing, he looked at the name of the caller and somewhat to his horror saw that it was Alberto Mondo and it suddenly struck him that contrary to Mondo's strict instructions, he had failed to call him even once in the past 48 hours.

'Shit! I'll have to take this, Hart. Don't go anywhere. Ha, ha.'

With that, he stood and turned his back to Hart walking slightly away whilst talking to Mondo in totally cringing sycophantic tones. Hart picked up lots of "Yes sirs" and "Sorry sirs" as Halle responded to his boss.

This had to be Hart's final last gasp chance to remove the tape. Quickly, he took his left arm off the chair arm, something he had been unable to do whilst being observed earlier, leaned his head over to his right wrist and plucked violently at the tape with his incisor teeth, all the while checking that Halle's back was turned to him. The teeth did most of the necessary work and by the time Halle was facing him again he had his right hand back down on the chair arm...unbound!

Halle sat on the seat and checked the position of his favoured vein in Hart's arm once again.

'Yes, there we are. Lovely.'

That done, he picked up the syringe and moved his head towards Hart, who could smell his fetid breath as his face neared him.

'You know, Hart, this really is the end of an era...thank God!'

'You know, Halle, this really is the end of this charade. However, in this instance it has to be "Tails you win Heads you lose".'

Halle looked up quizzically and as he did, he briefly caught sight of Hart's forehead coming rapidly towards him on a collision course with his aquiline nose. He had no time and no chance to avoid it as it smashed into its target. There was a crack as Halle's nose broke and a cry from him as blood welled from the resulting two-inch long open gash and cascaded down across his mouth and chin. The syringe dropped to the floor as his hands went to his nose. The blow had also caused much bleeding inside the nasal cavity of the once regally aquiline nose and together the dual sources of blood rendered his face a bloody, sticky mess.

Hart dare not let this element of surprise and pain that he had created go to waste and summoning all the hatred and revulsion he carried for Halle sent his clenched left fist crashing against the side of Halle's head in the area of his temple. With a groan, he went down onto the floor, the blood from his newly shaped broken nose mixing with the spittle from his mouth and with a small amount of sudden vomit formed a revolting cocktail. He put his hands down on the floor and pushed himself slowly upwards in an effort to get back to his feet, but Hart having now ripped away the last of the tape that bound his hand used that hand to offer another crashing blow to the other side of Halle's head in almost a mirror image place of his first punch. Halle was not yet down and out, however, and Hart dragged him to his feet and then hit him low with a telling right hook. There was a whoosh as the air was forced out of him and Hart caught the corresponding foul smell of his breath as he doubled up. As he went down again, Hart took him by the lapels of his famous blazer and lifted him backwards into the chair that he himself had occupied until some minutes before. Quickly eyeing the bench, he spotted the reel of tape which had been so effectively used on himself and snatched it up. He wrapped the tape tightly around Halle's wrists and ankles, cutting each piece in turn using the scalpel which he had also lifted from the bench. Halle was beginning to cry out incessantly now out of both pain and fear and Hart gagged him, once more using a strip of the omni-useful tape. It did cross his mind for all of one second that Halle might choke on his own vomit, but he put that thought immediately to bed.

Fuck him!

So now he was relatively free, but with no idea of what to do next. His first thought was to open the concertina door and explore the possibility of leaving via that way, but as he slid the door wide open a wave of river water surged in. The river was running high and flowing very quickly and with no moon visible this made for a dark night by the riverside, with only the dim lights from the warehouse providing any light upon the oily waters. Therefore, this option was not well considered by Hart. Halle had locked the door to the inside of the room himself and not knowing whether or not his guards were still stationed outside in the corridor, Hart dragged himself back to the door and pressed his ear against it listening for signs of the enemy. It was pandemonium out there!

Halle's cohorts realising that something was badly wrong inside the room were shouting through the locked door to Halle and also to each other in their confusion. Hart decided that his possible second option of escape had scored even less than his first option. The men on the other side of the stout oak door decided that their own best option was to kick it in, but several kicks and bruised toes later, their change of plan had Hart diving for the floor as bullets began striking the door. As the door began to splinter under the continuous impact of the rain of lead, bullets started to penetrate and enter the room pinging and ricocheting off everything in sight. As the bombardment eased off slightly, he crept back down towards the open door, with the river now approaching the chair in which Halle was just coming to his senses. Suddenly the barrage stated again and the room was full of bullets flying in all directions through the last flimsy remnants of the door. It was still too firm to be kicked open, however, and during a slight pause, as the kicking was re-enacted, Hart hurried for the river only to be caught up in another round of flying lead just as he passed Halle, taped in the chair. As he ducked down low, he witnessed the back of the chair tear as a bullet impacted on it, but its occupant was unscathed. Instead, the emerging bullet struck the vertical drive mechanism handle of the chair pushing it into its forward drive mode. As the chair moved forward towards the river, Hart made an effort to stop it, but another fusillade of lead sent him scurrying against the wall where he sat watching Halle advance towards the water.

Another lull in the shooting and Hart decided to take to the water himself and ran as best as he could through the open door and down the concrete ramp into the river just as the full moon emerged from behind cloud. He made it to the water slightly ahead of Halle and looking back saw the abject terror in his wide and bulging eyes.

Some moments later, as both men were totally engulfed in the raging, ice-cold river, the door inside the facility finally gave in to the kicks of the size 42, top of the range, brown Gucci brogues and a number of mafiosi tumbled into the room still firing their weapons in all directions. Hart was now some yards out in the water but looked back in time to see Halle's head disappear below the surface as the men rushed towards the river. He too ducked below the surface of the water so as not to be seen by the men and remained there not too far away from Halle as bullets whizzed and fizzed through the water around them. The current began to pull him away and in yielding to it, he took one last look back at Halle, now visible in the light afforded by the lights from the warehouse and the moon. At that very moment, he witnessed Halle's head explode in a crimson cloud of blood, raked by three bullets which fizzed through the water, all homing in on Halle's head in close succession.

Hart turned away and swam in panic, being forced quickly to the water's surface with his lungs bursting, to gulp some air before descending into the murky depths once again. On his next exhausted visit to the river's surface, he decided that he was far too tired to swim any longer and hoped that if he could just tread water, the strong current would carry him to safety.

After some five minutes of paddling, he suddenly collided in the water with a dark object floating near to him.

'Christ, it's Halle again!'

This was a cause for more instant panic, but happily in this case in death Halle had metamorphosed into a large piece of driftwood and Hart gratefully grabbed hold of it, clinging on for dear life, totally spent. In his now semi-conscious state, his mind drifted back to Halle and what were probably his final words...

'This really is the end of an era....Thank God!'

'Thank God indeed!'

Chapter 113

As the two pairs of strong hands dragged Hart onto the stony shore, he blindly thrashed out in all directions, his tired body functioning on newly found adrenalin and pure reflex activity alone. Within seconds, he was totally spent and submitted to the welcoming blackness that enveloped him once more.

He awoke to find himself lying in a huge wooden framed bed. Pain shot through his arm as he pushed himself into an upright position. The hand he used to get a feel of the painful arm detected a heavy bandage. He moved his body further and pains shot everywhere. His worst symptom, however, was dizziness and apart from this the aches and pains, although many, were actually manageable and under the circumstances of what had happened he had to conclude that he felt generally in reasonable order.

Where could he be? Looking further than the outline of the bed, he noted that the room was large with a high ornate wooden ceiling and dark panelled walls, which were inlaid with figures of cherubs and angels. On the small table at the side of the bed, he noticed a pile of clothes on top of which was a note, which he picked up and read.

"Max: Shower across the room. More clothes for you! Ring the bell when you're dressed Father Achille."

Hart looked and saw a brass school bell next to the clothes.

With an effort, he eased his naked body out of the bed and limped across the room to the open-doored bathroom where he took a long hot semi-rejuvenating shower. He still ached all over, but bearing in mind he'd survived potential death by beating, shooting, stabbing, lethal injection and drowning he couldn't grumble in the slightest.

Showered and dressed in the latest borrowed clothes, he rang the bell loudly.

Within minutes, the large door at the end of the room opened and in walked Father Achille and none other than Federico and Luca Messi. Messi waddled at speed to Hart and embraced him warmly.

'Max, it's so very good to see you again.'

Father Achille and Federico each shook his hand enthusiastically. It was Achille who spoke.

'*Ciao*, Max. Welcome back. I think you have had more comebacks than Frank Sinatra, yes?

It was then the smiling Federico's turn.

'*Ciao,* Max, once again I see you have been in the wars. I remember you once told me that you preferred to make love rather than war…sorry Father

419

Achille…in which case looking at the state of you, I never want to meet your lovers…please!'

'Father Achille, I really can't thank you enough. I'm sure it is you who I owe my life to.'

'*Si,* Max, I pulled you out of the river, but without the help of Federico here, you would have by now reached the sea. He really did arrive out of the blue after I had come to the warehouse and he later came with me to find you. We fully expected to find your lifeless body, but instead we saw you in the river tightly embracing the branch of a tree. We followed you downstream to the bend in the river where we estimated the tree would come closest to the shore and plucked you out.'

'You're both wonderful "pluckers" and I will be forever in your debts, but where are we now? Not in the Church of Santa Andrea I guess?'

'No, no, we are in a very safe place. This is a bishop's house who is currently on sabbatical. I can assure you that there is no way that the mafia will find you here…even if they believe you still to be alive. Also I think that Federico has news that will make you feel much more secure. Federico?'

'*Si grazie padre.* After you escaped from the warehouse, Max, myself and a group of specialist OCA operatives paid a visit there in order to make arrests and in the course of that operation there was huge resistance from the mafiosi there using firearms. In the course of the fight, unfortunately two of my men were slightly wounded, but with regret I have to inform you that all the mafiosi there were killed, including their recently appointed new leader Claudio Vespa. To add to that, at roughly the same time that we went in at the warehouse, another group of specialist OCA operatives moved in at the waste recycling offices in Basiglio and made various arrests. Many of the mafiosi there too were also killed. Once again we had two slightly wounded officers. Those there who could be considered as the next leaders of the Volpe group fought the hardest, no doubt to impress their colleagues when it later came to selecting a new leader, and amongst those killed are all those who would probably have wanted to be Capo at some next stage.'

'So who is left now to hunt me down and try again to kill me? Halle is dead for sure and he alone was pulling the mafia strings here and if you are telling me that the mainstays of the Volpe group are either dead or arrested, then I must be free. Yes?'

Messi, bursting to speak, took over.

'*Si,* Max, you are correct, *nessuno, nobody* here is left to hunt you…or me down.'

'Tell me, Federico, how did you know to go to the warehouse?'

'I knew you were here in Reggio and that you were planning on seeking out the Church of Santa Andrea following contacts by Luca and Father Achille. In fact, Luca told me to fly down to here from Rome to greet you, but unfortunately, I arrived too late I'm afraid. It was in the end Father Achille who advised me of all the details of the warehouse and its "owners" and here we are.'

Hart looked at Messi, who was clearly somewhat overcome with emotion.

'Luca, I really appreciate you flying down here like this to meet me. I guess there is much to tell me?'

'Yes indeed, Max, much to tell. I think that now my emotion has subsided a little so I will tell you all…if you feel ready that is?'

'Luca, I'm dying to hear it all….almost literally.'

'OK, let's all sit. Father, I'm sorry but you will have to leave us while I update our friend here.'

'Fine, I will see you all later.'

He left the room smiling and the remaining three sat down in the very sturdy-looking wooden chairs which were grouped together. This time Hart had no fears as for Messi's safety as he dropped down. Messi undid the buttons on his excruciatingly tight beige linen jacket and loosened his beige and blue spotted tie and breathing a sigh of relief began his report.

'First, Max, I must say that it's so good to no longer fear the sword of Damoclese hanging over my head. I will be in your debt forever. But now let us tell our stories.'

Chapter 114

At his New York apartment, Alberto Mondo was experiencing two of what were for him unusual emotions. The first was unease bordering on worry, for Robert Halle had been very strange of late. The usual arrangement they had for Halle to call Mondo every 48 hours at this crucial stage of the great scheme had faltered of late, with Halle often being remiss in keeping to the 48-hour limit and then sounding rather manic when contact was finally made. Mondo had grown tired of waiting for Halle's last call and had ended up phoning him himself. When contact was made, Halle sounded on the one hand very apprehensive and on the other almost jubilant for some unknown reason. Halle had actually seemed a little unstable during that conversation and all Mondo could do was to put his behaviour down to the stress that they were all feeling at this time, which Halle did not appear to be dealing with very well at all.

Added to his unease over Halle, he was beginning to feel let down by Claudia Volpe. He was aware of her constant contact with Halle as she attempted to keep them both updated and singing off the same hymn sheet, but of late she too had been remiss in contacting him directly. Again it was easy to pass this off, excusing her by putting it down to her current great burden of work, but it added to his unease and he wasn't used to it.

To add to his woes, Franco Negri had been very short with him in their last telephone conversation and since that call he had heard nothing from him in the whole of the last four days.

He opened a fresh bottle of red wine, a particularly expensive wine from his favourite area of Sicily. A sniff of the cork told him everything. This was the third bottle of his favourite wine that he had found to be "corked" this week!

'*Merda*!'

With a huge major social event looming up, to be held at his country house near Mount Olive in New Jersey, in order to promote World's latest grand act of African charity, the building of a new 3,000-bed hospital and associated clinical research centre, it would be a total disaster if the wine did not come up to scratch!

The event would be an evening with a difference, because for the first time he would be taking a back seat and allowing his wife Barbara, or "Bobo" to friends, to organise and run the show. It was a huge responsibility for her, but he was totally confident in her abilities and was sure that it would be a great success.

'Now where are those damn phone calls!'

Chapter 115

Eventually, it was Hart who kicked off first with his side of the debriefing, and he explained everything relating to the events in Sicily and his experiences in Reggio, right up to his escape into the river and the sight of Halle's exploding head. His graphic explanation was punctuated frequently by his listeners, who administered a variety of 'aahs, oohs, Madonnas and *mio Dios'*. Messi was particularly keen for Hart to provide and then repeat the full details of the method of his escape from Messina in the dead-cat wagon and his amusing experience in the shower-room on board the ferryboat. It was evident that whilst being aware of Hart's difficulties, he had previously had no idea of the level of traumas that Hart had endured, or of the semi-miraculous escapes that he had fashioned. He was aware of the deaths of Volpe and Halle however, and these un-orchestrated events put Hart on an unshakeable pedestal in his eyes, as these were the key events which now meant that they could count themselves as most probably being totally free from mortal danger. At the end of Hart's tale, Messi could only applaud.

'Bravo, Max, bravo! If all of this were not such a great secret, a secret which would be for sure denied by all the authorities and a secret that will and must never be divulged, it would make a very good book or movie. Yes, I see very clearly Tom Cruise in your role. Ha, ha, ha. You have suffered the trials of a true saint and I have great sympathy for all your pains, but your work has indeed been a major success and I can assure you that your name is held in very high esteem in very important high circles.'

'For all the good that makes, if nobody will ever be allowed to hear about it! Anyway high circles make me dizzy.'

'True, but you did it for a very just purpose and that purpose was not to gain fame, *si*?'

'Yes of course, you're right.'

'Just to underline things, Max, in coming to Sicily and then on to Reggio you have made yourself safe, and me too as far as that goes. I know that you have some doubt at the back of your mind, but remember what is left of your mafiosi aggressors firmly believe that you are dead. I know this for certain from a contact within their remaining group. They believe that the blood they saw in the water as a result of their indiscriminate shooting, by the light of their torch, was yours not Halle's. The fact that they saw no body rise to the surface confirms this for them, for you see that very last time they saw you, *you* were tied and seated in the electric wheelchair so it was you who they shot. It is also a convenient story for themselves, but as for Halle he is missing for sure, but so far he has not been reported by them as being dead…only missing, disappeared. Perhaps returned to the USA? The thing is that so many of the key people and leaders are either dead, and Claudia Volpe is particularly important here, or arrested that there remains very few of the group left on the ground and it is only a matter of time before the mafia group from the north of Sicily will take control of all. All previous battles and hostilities will, for the short term at least, be swept under the carpet and the remnants of the Volpe group will be amicably absorbed into the new group, but there is nobody worthy to take over from the Fox in Basiglio, that is for sure.'

'It all sounds too easy and cosy to me. These are a bloodthirsty bunch that would let nothing get in their way, I've seen and felt their brutality first hand remember.'

'Bloodthirsty? Yes. Brutal? Yes, but in the end they are simple men, who love their mammas and her pasta and who often have close ties with the church. They like to relax on Sundays and drink wine, eat simple fine foods and listen to the football on the radio. Pardon me, Max, but the quality of their simple lives is way above that of most other people, even in the rest of Italy. But now for the details of the stem cell trail.

'Federico with the other small team travelling in two unidentified cars soon picked up the transmissions from the trackers that you had placed on the consignment. The van with its special contents was already tracked by helicopter very soon after you had met with it and so it was no problem for its location to be passed on to Federico and his team, who then carefully and anonymously proceeded on up to the Vatican itself and to the private medical centre of the Pope, where they found the latest delivered medication together with existing identical forms of the treatment. There was never any question that the consignment was not destined to arrive there and from then onwards it has been very important, no, vital in fact, that things should be seen to carry on there as usual. As you know, it is essential that we do not scare away the big fish in the scheme for the sake of arresting the, how do you say…the minnows. Ah *si*, the minnows. I like that, it's a beautiful word.

Allora, anyway, what we then did was to replace the Pope's chief physician, together with the small medical team attached to him, with our own equally expert medical people. As I have said, there could be no information released either to other members of the Pope's team or to the general public, so it was seen publicly as a straight forward change-over of staff. Certainly there were hints of scandal and disgrace running through the Vatican, which was the last thing we wanted, but we did manage to dispel most of the rumours. This was indeed a very difficult situation for us to explain adequately to the various Vatican departments, agencies and committees though. We had the choice of saying that the physician and his team had moved to another high profile role, although in truth none could be higher than the one they already had, or of doing "something else". In the end, we chose to do "something else".

'This "something else" was, I think, very clever, even though I do say so myself. We decided to remove the whole medical team into isolation and put out the explanation that a very serious mini-epidemic of gastroenteritis had overtaken the team. This was in fact a double-lie, because we first told the team itself that there had been contamination of the treatment material with a virulent strain of hepatitis C. This was a very astute idea as it happens, and I look forward to your comments, Max, when I have finished my explanation, because whilst the common way in which the virus is transmitted is through exposure to blood containing the hepatitis C virus, perhaps via being stuck by a needle, in 40% of cases it is not possible to identify the source of infection at all. Furthermore, it can also be transmitted by sharing personal items and this team work very close to each other, that is for sure. However, the jewel in the crown of this ploy is that the virus can be transmitted by sexual contact of course. Can you image word getting out that the Pope's personal medical team has been isolated because of an outbreak of a serious sexually transmitted disease? Keeping this quiet has been very easy, therefore, as no member of that team would want the public or press to learn of their situation, their situation invented by us that is, for the very shame and disgrace of it and that is why they agreed very readily for us to release the news of an outbreak of gastroenteritis instead. The great irony here is that the American NIH, the National Institutes of Health of course, recommends the use of condoms during sexual intimacy to combat any transmission of the virus. I love it! The whole action we now have in place will only go on for a maximum of two weeks and so it will be easy to inform the medical team at that point that the hepatitis C results were false positives, the reason being a faulty batch of assay materials, which I understand can and does happen occasionally, and inform the press and public that the gastroenteritis outbreak was isolated, treated and eradicated. How does that sound to you? It sounds perfect to me…everybody happy and we are covered for the duration of our actions with our own medical team. In this time though, we also have to discover how much members of the original team have been involved in the "Great Plan" of Mondo and whether we have to arrest them, but not of course until the "big fish" are landed.'

Hart was fulsome in his praise of Messi's brilliant smoke and mirrors method of surreptitiously exchanging the Pontiff's medical team.

'I must admit, Luca, I do have to commend you on your ploy, it's very clever indeed. Just remember though that the time window for diagnosis, treatment and recovery from gastroenteritis won't stretch much wider than the time you have given yourself to wrap the business up, although an additional week here or there would easily be explained I suppose.'

'Ah the Royal Approval of Sir Max! Indeed an honour, ha, ha, ha! I'm glad you like it. One more important thing with the original medical team, we have had to insist that there is no communication by any of them to people outside. We have taken care of informing friends and family et cetera about the gastroenteritis and will continue to act on their behalves throughout the whole time of their isolation. They are keen themselves not to allow news of the hepatitis C to get out. We have also hinted at a "special bonus" for them. The thing is that we cannot allow any warnings to be transmitted to those who might be part of the Mondo scheme.'

'What about Negri?'

'Well, he is under house arrest, also in theory having been brought down with the dreaded gastroenteritis. A little more difficult for us in his case as a man

425

of considerable seniority and position, but of course he too has been stripped of all methods of communicating with the outside world. One word from him could turn all our endeavours completely pear-shaped! There are also some other senior figures in the organisation that we have had to treat in the same way and we hope very much that it causes not too much suspicion.'

'So, Luca, here is the biggest question of all…who is "the biggest fish" and what are your plans for landing him?'

'Of course the biggest fish in our pond is Alberto Mondo. If he gets one hint that his plans are undone, he will disappear off the face of the earth I'm sure, for you know this type of person always has an escape plan in position. Do you think for one minute that a man capable of devising a scheme such as this one will not have devised an equally audacious means of escape?

'So to continue, the Pope will now no longer receive the treatment that our church regards as sinful.'

'And he will die,' Hart interrupted.

'Yes indeed, as we all do eventually, he will die. Not immediately though, he will now die as and when his body is ready, but that will be at the will of God and not at the end of an immoral extension of a life that has no doubt already over-run its course, albeit a very good Christian, noble life serving his people and his church to his greatest abilities all over the world. It has been a life-extension implemented and executed totally unbeknown to him, using a medication that has been developed with the aid of almost terrorist actions on certain members of the flock that he serves. Mind you, Max, he will still continue to receive treatment for his condition, but of course this will be of the more standard type.'

Messi's voice had hardened and Hart thought back to the tragedy that had introduced him to this total nightmare. The illegal taking of living foetuses from desperate women and the resulting suicide of Ruth Williams following such actions and he suddenly felt guilty of his own hypocrisy and his all too frequent flippancy whilst pursuing the case.

'Hang on, Luca, what about Peter Mondo, for without his existence and position in the church there would never have been a "Great Plan" I'm thinking?'

'That is yet another very difficult problem, Max, because there we have a good and innocent man who has been caught-up unknowingly in a web of sin and intrigue at the hands of none other than his own brother. He is totally blameless in these matters and has always only acted in the best interests of everyone. When this business is over, along with the many others, he will be totally unaware of anything out of the ordinary that has happened with respect to the Pope. As for his brother, however, that will be a different thing altogether, but for sure, there will be no way that any connections will be able to be made by anybody to the Vatican.'

'So you will complete a grand cover-up then?'

'Yes of course, there is far too much at stake with the future of our church. I spoke to you during the evening at La Certosa of some of the strange histories associated with our church and how they had needfully been "covered up" and this will be no exception.'

'But what about the involvements of World Pharmaceuticals in the rest of the world? What about the continued existence of the global criminal clinics involved in this and what about their African ventures, where thousands of people are now dependent upon them for support.'

'As you know, Max, I am strictly for Italy. My remit is only for my "mother country" and I am unable to step outside of that remit. More important than that though, I can say that I am strictly for the Catholic Church and especially for the Vatican. That is my job, I have no alternative and so my involvement stays here in Italia and nowhere else. However, what I can tell you is that through national security services and law enforcement agencies linked with international health agencies and organisations throughout the world, but outside of Africa, using much of the documented details and information that you have provided, the people working at the clinics participating in this evil trafficking of both living and dead foetuses have been identified and taken into custody. However, once again so as not to cause the flight of the biggest fish, this has been done under great secrecy. Criminal physicians and nurses have, as far as can be organised, taken last minute "holidays" away from the clinics and units where they work and they will remain "on holiday" until the "big fish" is in our net. When that has happened, and not before, and I'm afraid that here decisions have been taken by those senior to me, there will be a great many arrests most of which will take place publicly. I'm afraid it will become very political at that stage with many politicians attempting to climb on board the bandwagon in an attempt to gain some kudos from it. As for Africa, I do not really know, but Peter Mondo is such a great man that I would expect him to do much to expunge the evil of his brother's work and find some other way to ensure that the people on that continent receive other forms of additional benefits and recompense.'

'So when do you anticipate that Alberto Mondo and his associates will be taken by the forces of law?'

'It is very confidential, but I do know…and I will confide it to you, Max, that in one week's time, Alberto Mondo is hosting a gala dinner at his country home. There will be very many people there, but strictly by special invitation of course. At that occasion, Mondo will take the opportunity to announce his company's latest investments and philanthropies in Africa. Everyone who is anyone will be there, including of course the key members of his executive team, African dignitaries and dignitaries of the Catholic Church, no doubt including Peter Mondo. There at that event we will see all the prize fish swimming together.'

'A veritable shoal of bastards! Will you be there, Luca…not as a fish of course?'

'If it can be arranged, yes, I, too, will be there to witness the taking down of this most evil Cabal.'

'And what are the chances of—'

'No Max! The answer, before you even ask, is no. Myself, the OCA, the law enforcement agencies, the various international health organisations and authorities and the medicines regulatory bodies are all indebted to you for what you have done and what you have been through, but now for you the matter has to end. It is the perfect situation to be in, the business is ended and you are alive

427

and under no threat from any outside people. Please, just relax, sit back and see how things come to a final conclusion. Watch the endgame from behind a newspaper or via the satellite news and I believe that later,' he winked knowingly, 'you might receive a very special surprise…but that too is a secret, *si*?'

Hart shrugged, pursed his lips and meekly said, 'That's fine by me, I've had enough excitement to last two lifetimes at least. But it will be no good hoping to read of the outcome in a newspaper or of seeing it on the television news, because as you have already told me as far as the public are concerned none of it, outside of Mondo's criminalities, ever happened!'

'Ah yes, unfortunately you are right, Max.' Then changing the subject, 'But Max you have had almost as many lives as the cat in this business, *si*?'

'Yes, but probably not those cats in the truck though, Luca. Look, I have an urgent question relating to my friends in the UK who I have been unable to contact for what seems like one hundred years. You told me a while ago that Victoria Crosse and Denis Williams were safe. You know Denis Williams was the sole reason I became involved in this affair. What is their situation now?'

'I promised you back at La Certosa that I would inform them regularly of your condition and I have done so. As for their own situation, Max, you need have no worries. They too are safe and have been throughout your "extended stay" in la bella Italia. Signore Williams has remained at his home address, but since her return from Padua, la Crosse has been living in a small country cottage. Both of them have had round-the-clock protection from the English police, who have been in constant communication with your UK Special Branch. So all is well in those departments.'

'Whilst I will be happy to put my feet up, read my newspaper and smoke my pipe, I have just one problem.'

'*Problema*? Which is?'

'Only the minor inconvenience of having no passport, no credit cards and no money of any sort, otherwise everything is *perfetto*.'

'Ah, there is no problem there, Max,' he smiled and patted the area of his jacket under which was his inside pocket. 'I have here for you your new passport, with a slightly unofficial photograph, oh but you didn't tell me that your middle name was Leonardo…'

Hart winced at the exposure of the dark secret he kept. Messi continued,

'… Two credit cards in your name and a suitable number of euros to help you to while your time away pleasurably.'

Messi placed a hand inside his jacket and removing the wodge of money, documents and cards, handed them to Hart.

'You won't need them just yet.'

'Right then, my friend, I will do as you suggest for the sake of my health and my sanity. From here on, I think that a little rest and relaxation, is the order of the day.'

He smiled at the *comandante*, who suddenly slapped his hands on the arms of the chair in which he was tightly wedged, and pushed himself into a standing position.

'Right, *Dottore*, I think we should now make the most of the bishop's kitchen and wine cellar and join Father Achille for a celebratory dinner. *Bene*?'

'*Molto bene, mio amico, molto bene. Andiamo.*'

'Very impressive, Max, just fifty more years here and you will be talking almost like a native. Ha, ha, ha!'

Accordingly, Hart, Messi and the unusually quiet Federico left the room and joined Achille in the outer room, where a veritable feast had already been prepared and laid out for them. All the talking and explaining had been completed, for now at least, and it was time for total immersion in food and wine, during which Hart would also have time to consider his plan of action for the coming days.

Chapter 116

Considering the circumstances of the recent traumas, dinner was a light-hearted affair, the food excelling Hart's expectations in all departments. The wines presented and paired with the various courses all accompanied the food perfectly. Hart turned to Father Achille.

'Achille, I must congratulate you for providing us with such a wonderful, and to be honest unexpected, meal. It's fantastic.'

'Thank you, Max. It was prepared by the same Father who prepared your meal on that first evening with us and it is a special celebration dinner in honour of the three of you. Our Three Musketeers.'

'Actually, Achille there were in fact four Musketeers and you are certainly our fourth. You must thank the Father on our behalf though, Achille, but how did he learn the skills by the way?'

'In another life, Max. In another life.'

Federico added,

'Actually, he read it all in a travel brochure, Max. Ha, ha, ha.'

'Luca, before I totally forget everything, as well as the passport etc., I will need a new mobile phone, preferably one that is not connected to the Kremlin or the CIA if possible.'

'It is well that you remind me, Max, as I do have a new one for you but I forgot to give it to you earlier. Remind me again a little later please and I will ensure that the KGB is cut out of the contact loop.'

They eventually vacated the table and took their places in separate armchairs where more red wine was taken, and where for some time there was small talk mainly around the subject of food and wine. Eventually, Hart brought up the subject of his departure, which hit the ambience like a bucket of iced water.

'I suggest you use the house phone here to make all your arrangements, but Max seriously, after you leave and after the business is complete, we will meet again in La Certosa at least one more time for final up-dates and outcomes, so your departure from here will by no means mark a final farewell to you. There will be much still to discuss and relate and who knows…there might be another proposition to you for your help in another situation.'

Messi smiled and winked at Hart.

'Luca, I would consider the prospect of sticking pins in my eyes and drinking my own urine currently to be more acceptable than sharing the back of a van with a pile of rotting dead cats and writhing maggots.'

There was laughter all round and Messi raised his glass.

'Gentlemen, I would like to propose a toast. To all of you here who have contributed so well towards neutralising the "Great Plan", although the work is not yet complete, and especially of course to our friend Max Hart, who, if I can paraphrase a famous split infinitive, "has boldly gone where no man should ever have to go, or even dream of going!" Seriously though, Max, I never envisaged when you accepted this mission that you would be put through so much hell, so for your bold activities *plus* your continued very dubious sense of humour whatever the situation and of course for your nine lives, I sincerely thank you. Salute *tutti e cin, cin.*'

'Salute!'

'*Grazie,* Luca. I did it all of course in the vain hope of glimpsing the wonderful breasts, sorry Achille, of la Volpe once again, but this time in greater close-up than previously. In the end, my charms worked like magic and she ended up really falling for me'.

Embarrassed laughter followed and Father Achille feigned disapproval, but this was a time for the relaxation of ultra-polite discourse as well as a time for celebration. Hart continued.

'I still have a few light-weight questions for you, Luca, if I may?'

'Certainly my friend, go ahead and ask.'

'OK. What is the situation now in Germany with the Gerhard Roscher Schmoller Institute and Frau Arben et al.?'

'In Germany, their authorities have acted more strongly than elsewhere, although they did wait and acted at a time to coincide with our other international activities. The regulatory body responsible in Germany is the Federal Institute for Drugs, the so-called BfArM organisation. They have moved into the GRS Institute and have actually closed it down. The clinics working there have also been closed and through tremendous organisation as you might expect of our German friends, have re-located all patients attending there to other clinics as close as possible to that place. A really difficult task, which they have succeeded well in accomplishing I believe. As for Arben and her cohorts, they have been taken into custody, not by the police, but by the German Federal Intelligence Service. This organisation, the BND, is subordinated directly to the Chancellor's Office and based in Central Berlin. Arben and friends will have no contact with the outside world, and I include access to solicitors, until our job is complete.' It was now Federico's turn to ask a question of his *comandante.*

'So what is the situation in the USA and the UK, Luca?'

'In the USA, the FBI, the CIA and the regulatory body the FDA are working together to bring this business to a rapid and successful close. They are holding back until making a dramatic appearance at the special event being held at the country home of Alberto Mondo in around one week's time. After then, all hell will break loose as raids will take place globally and especially at World Pharma locations of course. There you go, Federico, you've plied me with drink and now I have revealed a close kept secret to you. I might just have to kill you now, ha, ha, ha! In the UK, the Medicines Control Agency, the MCA, are working with Special Branch and will co-ordinate their actions with the USA...despite the differences in time-lines. There are no direct comparisons of enforcement agencies between the UK and the USA, but roughly speaking, MI5 is approximately the same as the FBI and MI6 approximates to the CIA. Both these UK organisations will also be involved at some stages of the proceedings.'

Hart had just one more point to raise though.

'Excuse me, Luca, I have one final question for you. With the end now firmly in sight, can you honestly say that you have been totally open with all the information you have? Have you shared *everything* with us, or at least with me, or have you left out a few, shall we say "extra" secret points?'

Messi looked long and hard at Hart, and the two other men were also suddenly all ears to hear what he had to say.

'In all honesty, Max, I do have to say that there are small "extra sensitive" points which I have neglected to add in my discourse, but to be fair, the knowledge of these things would not have altered or affected your actions in any way and certainly wouldn't have affected any outcomes. They were simply points that were not necessary for you to know. There is no harm done I can promise you that.'

In return, Hart looked hard and long at Messi.

'An interesting response, Luca. What would your reaction be if I told you that I too had information that I have not yet divulged to you? Information that I gleaned whilst in Basiglio, and likewise information that will not alter your own future actions or their outcomes. Points which may or may not be necessary for you to know, to re-coin your phrase.'

The onlookers felt an uneasy game of chess developing.

'I would say that I am familiar with the game of "you tell me yours and then I'll tell you mine" and it doesn't really impress me, Max. I am sure that at this stage of the business, whatever I have not told you will have no bearing on the outcome as far as you are concerned, and certainly what you may not, I repeat *may* not, have told me will have absolutely no effect whatsoever on the final outcome either.'

'In other words, you are not at all interested in what I might have to say additionally?'

'Correct. I have no interest whatsoever in what information you *think* you have to exchange with me.'

'OK, fair enough, at least the offer was there and there are no hard feelings… Salute!'

The 'Cheers' rang out once again as the four men downed their wines and re-charged their glasses.

'No hard feelings, Max, but it was a good try on your behalf. Good health!'

The drinking, talking, joking and laughing continued for another hour and with all the men now almost asleep, it was decided that they should retire for the night. Messi held back as Federico and Achille moved out of the room waiting to accompany Hart. Putting his arm around Hart's shoulder he said, through a breath saturated with alcohol and garlic,

'Max, I will miss you greatly. I feel that meeting you has been somewhat of a milestone for me and I really do hope that you will return to Milano and La

Certosa very soon, in fact I know you will because there will be much to say once we are completely finished with the "Great Plan", *si?*'

'I'll miss you too, Luca. I feel I have learned such a lot whilst in your excellent company and I will surely see you again very soon. In fact, hopefully it may be sooner than you anticipate. *Buona notte.*'

'*Buona notte mio amico.*'

Chapter 117

The following afternoon before booking his flight, there was just one call that was necessary for Hart to make. Messi had put his mind at rest with regards to Williams and Crosse and assured him that they had been updated with his own safety status, whilst at the same time assuring him of their safety also. That just left him considering the Barnes. If his absence and lack of communication had upset them, then flowers, champagne and dinner on him would no doubt turn things around…again!

He looked at his watch and did a quick calculation estimating that in New Jersey it would be around 10.00 am.

'Just right.'

He strolled along the corridor to the small office of the bishop's house, where Messi had indicated that it would be fine to use the landline to make an international call, and took a seat at the ancient wooden desk. The bi-colour plastic telephone looked to be antique too. He picked up the receiver and hearing the dialling tone slowly dialled the number that he knew by heart…and waited.

After what seemed like a week, a voice answered at the other end of the galaxy, stirring a whole cocktail of feelings inside him.

'World Pharmaceuticals, how may I help you?'

He paused momentarily, his nerve ebbing slightly before giving the receptionist the name of the person who he wanted to speak to.

'Putting you through, sir, have a nice day.'

He waited as the ring tone sounded, hoping that it would be picked up by the person he needed to speak to, and then…

'International Clinical Development.'

'Good morning, Janet, how the devil are you?'

Janet had assisted him when he had called her during his fairly recent visit to the congress in Padua and now her help was even more essential to him if his next plan of action was to come to fruition.

'Is that you, Max?'

'None other, Janet. It's lovely to hear your voice again and to see that you are still gainfully employed with World.'

'It's lovely, and also a great relief, to hear you too, Max. You know we heard that there was a strong chance that you had died.'

Her voice broke on the end of the line, but then there was a slight cough and, professional to the end despite the high level of emotion she was suddenly feeling, she continued,

'Are you really OK?'

'I'm as right as rain. I can't imagine where that rumour came from. After the Padua congress, I decided to stay on in Italy for a while mixing some business with pleasure. I was approached by a governmental agency here and asked if I could help them out with an international pharmaceuticals issue, so here I am. It's a wonderful place, friendly hospitable people, great food and wine and fantastic countryside.'

There was a slight pause.

'So you've not heard the news of Doctor Halle then?'

'Halletosis? No, I've heard nothing, but then one wouldn't expect to see much in the local Tuscany Times. What's happened to him, finally disappeared up his own arse has he, or has he had a respiratory accident with one of his breath fresheners?'

'No Max, he's dead. He was involved in some accident in Italy by all accounts. It has been made official now.'

'That's a bit of a coincidence, me being here at the same time, still I guess there's not too many tears being shed there.'

Hart wondered just who had organised the "accident" news story? He would take it up with Messi later if he remembered, but then thinking that it might raise the obvious questions relating to his call to the USA he decided to let it go.

'No, but it has still come as a great shock to everyone. The rumour, although obviously not confirmed, was that you were involved in the same accident.'

Well, the truth was *somewhere* inside the right ballpark at least!

'Well, I can assure you that I am alive and well and fighting fit, although today I'm feeling a little the worse for wear following a rather splendid dinner last night.'

'No change there then, Doctor Hart.'

'What about our old friend Ken Rogers, Janet? I've not spoken to him in ages. Is he well?'

There was another pause, longer this time, before his former secretary replied.

'Yes, I would say he is fine, Max, but he's definitely different these days.'

'I guess he must be missing me tremendously, that's what it is.'

'Not exactly. Since your departure from the company, Doctor Rogers has done very well for himself and as a result he has changed a lot, especially his overall persona. He is no longer the old Ken we used to know.'

'What do you mean?'

'Well, as you might already have guessed, when you left us he was eventually promoted to take over your own vacant position and from there he has become quite an important player in the company.'

'How important?'

There was a little worry entering Hart's voice now.

Again the pause.

'Well, he has become very close to Doctor Halle and also, something you might not have guessed, he has become close to the "great man" himself.'

'Not Alberto Mondo, surely?'

'I'm afraid so and what is obvious to all of us is that Ken will now step straight into Doctor Halle's shoes.'

'Bloody hell! First the dead man's boots and then I expect he'll be wearing the blue blazer and striped tie. Before you know it, he will arrive at the office one morning with a hairy slug inhabiting his upper lip, just like his past master!'

There was a brief uncomfortable silence on the other end of the line.

'So then, Max, it's wonderful to hear from you, but the last time you phoned me was from Padua and if I remember correctly I ended up doing something for you so tell me, what can I do for you this time?'

'Straight in as usual, Janet. Ahh, I love it!'

She sensed the arresting smile in his voice even four and a half thousand miles away.

'Well, now you come to mention it there is one little thing I was hoping you might help me with.'

'And that is?'

Hart juggled the words he wanted to say in his head, trying to arrange them in an order which would be the most acceptable to her.

'I believe that Alberto Mondo is holding a seriously significant bash at his place sometime in the coming days?'

'Yes, it's next week. It's seen as a very important international evening which has garnered a lot of publicity. High-ranking international people from medicine, research, regulatory bodies and even foreign governments will be in attendance and I understand that our leader will make some very important announcements. The TV and press will be there, but by invitation only. Security will obviously be very high and attendance will be strictly by ticket only.'

Once more, Hart found the need to juggle his words.

'So then, Janet, how can I get in there as a bona fide guest with the proper ticket? Could *you* assist me in this I'm wondering?'

'What! Come off it, you must be crazy! There is no way you could crash this event.'

'I expect Halle was on the invitee list, wasn't he?'

'Yes of course, but—'

'So why can't I use his ticket then?'

There was another pause. So far in this telephone conversation the length of the pauses was rapidly approaching the time actually taken in speaking.

'Janet, forget Halle, let me say it like this then, would it be possible for you to procure for me, in whatever way you find is appropriate, an entry ticket or pass or whatever else is required for me to gain entry to the Mondo beano?'

'Max, if I did this and was found out they would dismiss me immediately I'm sure. They would also, no doubt, find some clause in my contract negating my future pension, which by the way is not too far away now.'

'Look, Janet, I can assure you that you would never be associated with obtaining a pass for me should things go pear-shaped. I am working with a very high-ranking governmental department in Italy and they would immediately own up to getting me into the soiree if necessary, of that you can be sure. Also, as far as folk are concerned, I am out of the country, out of touch, out of contact and possibly even dead, so unless I disgrace myself, nobody will be aware of me being there. So how are you fixed?'

Once more the dreaded long pause and then finally.

'Very well, Max, I will do it. It won't be easy though! I will get you an official invitation, which might have to have someone else's name on it, but how on earth can I get it to you in time with you being in darkest Southern Italy?'

Another pause as the cogs turning in Hart's head almost made themselves heard down the phone.

'Listen, do you still visit the bench at the golf course?'

He knew full well that she would, for he was well aware that she visited it for some minutes of contemplation at least once every month. It was a wooden bench placed there in memory of her late husband William, who finally departed this mortal coil in what would have been his most preferred way. He had played the game of golf for forty years and in all of that time he had never shot a hole-in-one, but on that particular sunny day in the middle of a high level "seniors match", on the seventh hole, one of the course's two short holes, he drove the ball high into the sky and as he cupped his hand over his eyes to keep out the sun he saw to his astonishment and huge delight the ball bounce onto the green and roll straight into the hole. His arms went up in the air and as they came back down so did he. Game over.

'Yes, of course I do.'

'In that case would it be possible for us to meet there this coming Sunday at say around 3.00 pm? You could give me the pass then if it's convenient.'

'Three o'clock will be fine for me, Max, it will be lovely to meet you again.'

'Lovely for me too, Janet. I will see you on Sunday at three.'

'Bye Max.'

Over the following forty-five minutes, he organised the flights which would take him back to the USA for his Sunday rendezvous with Janet Blane on the golf course, and then for what would likely be for him three days later, the climax of these tumultuous recent events, the evening soiree at the country home of Alberto Mondo.

He booked a one-way business class ticket from Calabria's Tito Minniti Airport by Alitalia, to London Heathrow, from where after a short stopover he would fly with BA, again business class to JFK airport in New York. He also booked a limo to meet him at JFK and take him to his own home in Princeton.

All that done, and with his increased adrenalin levels now joining the remaining alcohol and it's derivatives in his system to impart him with the most incredibly throbbing headache, he retired to bed for the rest of the afternoon.

Chapter 118

The four men met for a light supper of cold meats and cheese at 7.30 pm and it was only Messi who dived once more into the wine. The talk was convivial and everyone took the opportunity to state how much they enjoyed the company of the others and how they should met up again when the business was completely over. Messi took the opportunity to remind Hart that the pair of them at least would be meeting in Milan in the very near future to discuss the whole of the action that had taken place as they had perceived and experienced it and he and Hart agreed that they would sign a joint document summarising all that they discussed at that Milan meeting and the conclusions that they came to.

Hart thanked everyone for keeping him alive over the past weeks and for coming to his rescue more than once. He also thanked Father Achille for the two complete changes of clothes he had provided him with and hinted that another complete change was due pretty soon. The padre smiled and nodded knowingly.

The gathering broke up at 10.30 pm with them agreeing to meet one last time for breakfast at 7.30 am, but not before Messi had explained that transport for Hart and himself was laid on for the morning and that they would travel together to the Reggio Airport where they would each take planes to their individual destinations, Hart to New York and Messi to Milan. On this occasion, Messi would be flying Alitalia as Luigi was otherwise engaged, Federico had a "company car" on loan from the Reggio OCA office which he would drive to Rome and Father Achille of course was already home. After this it was one final '*buona notte*' and then off to bed.

When Hart reached his room, he discovered on the dressing table a pile of clothes for the morning and for the first time since his arrival a pair of pyjamas. He smiled, having understood the knowing smile he had received from Achille when he had mentioned a new set of clothes over dinner. They had already been delivered to his room.

He slept well that night and woke at 6.30 am, feeling better than he had done for some days. He showered and shaved and put on the new underwear, blue jeans, green polo shirt and green socks, enjoying the change in colour scheme of his new apparel. With the sledgehammers now completely gone from inside his head, he walked to the dining room where he found his three colleagues, Messi, Federico and Father Achille drinking coffee and generally killing time waiting for his arrival before setting upon the breakfast that had been laid out on the large dining table.

Breakfast was a quiet affair, rather like supper the evening before, there being a mixture of sadness and eagerness between them. A degree of sadness because in the short time spent together they had become good friends and would miss each other's company, and eagerness because they were keen to get on with their normal lives and without doubt "when you gotta go, you gotta go".

One final short speech of thanks, once again, from Messi to everyone and a final round of embraces and they were ready to depart.

'Oh Max just check you have the passport, and money et cetera, et cetera, *si?*'

Hart patted his pocket.

'*Si, si,* Luca all in place thanks.'

'And don't forget the phone.'

He handed a new mobile phone to Hart.

'And one final thing from us, please accept this as our thanks.'

He reached under the dining table and withdrew an exquisite Gucci leather over-night case, which he handed to Hart.

'Please look inside, my friend.'

Hart clicked open the caches on the case and the lid flew open to reveal a series of items of clothes exactly like the ones that Father Achille had laid out for him that morning. Underneath the clothes he discovered a hardback book. It was in English and entitled, "'Information on Italy that the Travel Books Never Tell You". Everyone burst into laughter at Federico's joke, now well known amongst them. Messi had supplied the case, Achille the clothes and of course Federico the book. Hart was almost speechless, but not quite.

'Gentlemen, I can't thank you enough for these gifts, which mean so much to me. It's mainly down to your good selves that after the stresses and strains of the last weeks I have been able to recover well, stay sane, or as sane as I will ever be that is, and find such great friends as yourselves. This is not the last time we will meet, but thank you so much and *arrivederci tutti*! Goodbye to all of you…and keep monitoring the news!'

It was time to go.

They waved Federico off in his car, wheels spinning up dust as he accelerated away and then Messi and Hart took their seats in the car that was to take them to the airport, their luggage now stowed in the car's boot.

Father Achille was left alone standing outside the "bishop's residence" and he waved as they sped down the drive commencing their fifteen minute journey to the airport.

'Max, I won't get out of the car with you when we arrive at the International Departures Building as it is quite a hike from Domestic Departures, so I will say my goodbyes once more here. You know we could never have pulled this off or got so far without you and next week at the Mondo evening affair it will for sure be the finale. The mission will be brought to an end in a blaze of publicity of some sort at least, that I assure you. However, unfortunately as we have said before the details, especially those involving the Catholic Church, must remain secret. This is a secret that has been imposed and underlined by all our governments so neither television nor the newspapers will report the true facts of the case…but true enough for the public consumption I think.'

'OK Luca. Now then, this is your last chance to exchange any further secrets with me no matter how small. Yes?'

Messi laughed.

'Game till the end, eh Max, but no *grazie*. It is as I said the other night, all is done and dusted and any more knowledge, secret or not, would alter nothing…even if you did have something extra up your sleeve, which I am sure you haven't. It was just a bluff I think to glean a little more information from me, but well done for trying. I will miss you my friend. *Ciao*!'

'*Ciao* Luca, *buon viaggio*.'

Chapter 119

Hart's Alitalia flight of slightly over two hours from Reggio to London Heathrow passed very pleasantly and most importantly uneventfully, as he relaxed in his seat in the business class section of the plane and took advantage of the copious supply of champagne and "nibbles", with the added pleasure of a light meal.

Once at Heathrow, leaving the Alitalia plane behind he headed through the "connecting flights" area where he learned that he had a wait of two and a half hours before boarding the BA flight to New York, which he spent relaxing in the business class lounge considering his next steps upon arriving home. When his flight was finally called, he eased himself at a very leisurely pace to the gate.

As he boarded the 747 plane, he looked outside through the slight gap between the Jumbo and the passenger boarding bridge and smiled as he recalled an interview with a senior executive of Rolls Royce some years ago.

Interviewer: 'Tell me. If you have such confidence in your planes that have just two engines, why do you always travel to America in aircraft that have four engines?'

Executive: 'Because we haven't yet got any aircraft with six engines in service on this route!'

The stewardess looked at his boarding card and indicated the winding stair that led up to the upper deck.

'Seat 50B, Doctor, an aisle seat as requested on the upper deck. Please feel to spread yourself out, we don't have any passenger in seat 50A today.'

He sipped the offered champagne, nibbled the proffered nuts then eventually when the flight was underway wined and dined amply. Eight hours later, the plane touched down at JFK.

Having a permanent resident card allowed Hart to both live and work in the USA and consequently he was able to enter via the USA residents channel at the passport control, a great bonus as the "European and Other Countries" lines were each about two hours long. Within forty-five minutes of his feet touching US soil, he had cleared all the formalities of immigration and customs and having satisfied the border control officers that he was not a secret agent, an assassin or carrying drugs, a gun or a banana, he was headed for the exit and the "arrivals hall". As the double doors slid back, he was met by a forest of arms, held high and holding placards bearing the names of fellow travellers from his flight and from two other flights that had landed at close intervals to his. Wading into the forest, he finally spotted his own driver, also holding up a placard, but in this instance looking unlike all the other waiting people. The man holding up the placard on which was written "Doctor Max Hart", was well over six foot tall, wore a neat single-breasted black suit, white shirt and black tie and sported a pair of Nike black framed sunglasses which were pushed up and resting on his forehead. He knew Hart from previous occasions and as Hart made eye contact with him he smiled and raised his arm.

'Hi, Doctor Hart, nice to see you again. I'm just parked out front, shall I take your case? We'll have to be quick though, the parking guys are red hot today.'

'No, I'm fine thanks, let's just get out of this madhouse.'

Hart tagged on behind his driver and five minutes later, he was seated in the deep black leather rear bench-seat of the man's black limo.

'Home then is it, sir?'

'It is indeed, thanks Frank. How's business at present?'

'Ah, it's a bit slack at the moment.'

The driver, Frank Davies, worked for a company that over the last few years had done a lot of work for World and consequently could often be a useful source of company information. The intriguing thing about Frank, however, was that when chauffeuring jobs were scarce, rather than working for the FBI as his appearance suggested, he was actually employed in "funeral guest transportation" and accordingly, today he was driving his usual black funeral limo.

He pulled away smoothly and orderly into a line of exiting traffic and looking at Hart in the passenger mirror dived straight in.

'Say, Doctor Hart, I was sorry to hear of your split with World, it sounds like a really bum deal. You OK now? You put those bastards in their place?'

'Yeah it's a long story, Frank, but my arm is long and my vengeance will be total!'

'I did hear, Doctor Hart, that that man Halle has copped it. It couldn't have happened to a nicer guy, he was such a pain in the ass. You know he reported me twice to my boss for driving too fast and for what he called ungentlemanly conduct.'

It was Hart's turn to laugh now. Frank continued,

'So I guess you're still at 171 Johnson Street, in Princeton yes?'

'I am for the moment, but who knows what the future will bring?'

'So then, do you wanna talk or do you wanna sleep after your long flight, Doctor Hart?

'It depends. If you've got any juicy World information to pass on, I'll be all ears, but if it's the weather and baseball you want to discuss I guess I'll probably just doze.'

'Nah, *yourself* is the only piece of info I've got, so it looks like you'll be napping. There's iced water in the refrigerator back there if you want it.'

'Thanks Frank, wake me up when we hit Johnson Street then.'

'Oh yeah, there is one thing, Doctor, your old big boss Mondo is having a huge party at his country place on Wednesday evening. It's a very plush affair with all kinds of important people going, many from overseas I hear. You oughta get your ass over there and crash it. They say the food and drink that's gonna be handed out is gonna be fantastic.'

'Sounds like a not bad idea, Frank, I'll have to consider it. If I decide to go, can I book you to take me?'

'Sure thing, Doctor Hart, you got my number; just give me a call. A lot of the guys have already been booked by World to do the ferrying backwards and forwards, but between you and me I find a lot of these people real pains in the butt and I declined the offer to do the run, but I'll be happy to do the trip for *you* if you really want to go.'

'Tell you what, Frank, let's take it as booked then. I'll get my dudds on and go. How about you pick me up at my place at around seven thirty?'

'Wednesday at seven thirty it is then, you're booked. There's no going back on it now, Doctor Hart.'

'Johnson Street!'

Hart awoke with a start at Frank's reveille call.

'Now where is this house you're aiming for, 171 you said? I know I've been here a dozen times before, but they still all look pretty much the same to me.'

'It's a certain sea of similarity that is for sure. My place has *one* sore thumb though that makes it stand out from the others. See the bright red letterbox, that's mine.'

The limo pulled smoothly to a standstill at the side of the sore thumb. Hart had already paid on line for the ride and included his traditional good tip. He picked up his presentation Gucci case and made to open the limo door.

'Whoa, hang on, Doctor! Are you forgetting the booking you made with me before falling asleep earlier? You know the one where I get to pick you up here at 7.30 pm on Wednesday?'

'Oh shit yes. Sorry it slipped my mind…but only for the moment. Yes, I'll see you at 7.30 pm on Wednesday.'

The driver smiled and gave a little salute as Hart got out and closed the limo door.

He ambled up to his front door, case in one hand and mail in the other, and suddenly realised that all his keys had been lost or taken somewhere along his various tracks of the last few days.

'Shit!'

But *nil desperandum*, once again he could call upon his spare door key at least, and he congratulated himself on its novel hiding place. Placing the case on the drive, he looked down spotting the small piece of slate resembling the sun on the gravel close to the end wall of his house. He then counted the third stone from away it and turned it over revealing the key to the door.

'*Et voila*! The third rock from the sun.'

Once inside his house, he headed directly to the bedroom where he threw the fine case onto the bed, before stripping off and taking a long, hot, revitalising shower.

Showered and comfortably dressed, after an early evening spent drinking Californian cabernet sauvignon and devouring a "Ming Garden, Delivered to Your Door" set meal for two, he retired to his favourite arm chair with a notepad and pen and made a list of "things for consideration":

1. Contact credit card company
2. Check new driving licence requirements/application
3. Check cash in hand
4. Passport OK?…Messi
5. Arrangements for meeting Janet. Sunday
6. Contact Ken Rogers before Wednesday evening?
7. Wednesday evening … MH agenda?

When he reached item number 5, he considered two options for getting to his meeting at the golf course with Janet, his own car or a cab? He decided to take a cab and to use the credit card that Messi had given him. For item 6, he would first run the idea past Janet and get her opinion on it, as she knew best what Rogers' current persona was like. Finally, for item 7, he would just have to play it by ear on the night, whilst ensuring that at the end of it he was satisfied that he had returned the compliment to the one person who was responsible for his pain, his suffering and his fears, plus of course he had his little secret to consider.

Although still quite early by US time, for him it was six hours later in the evening allowing for the time difference and after a small brandy he retired to bed where he "slept the sleep of the innocents".

Chapter 120

Hart was awoken by the sunlight dancing through the venation blind at his bedroom window and flickering across his face. He checked his watch.

'Bloody hell!'

It was 10.30 am. He'd slept for almost fourteen hours. He got up and showered and shaved, and for the first time in he didn't know how long he was able to peruse his own wardrobe of clothes, picking out what he considered suitable apparel to be seen on a golf course wearing. A straight jacket was out of the question of course! He decided that chinos paired with a similar coloured polo shirt would likely suffice at the Princeton Forest Golf Club. Suitably attired he decided that a little breakfast was in order and as 'his cupboard was bare', he decided upon the short stroll to the Green Park Diner, five minutes' walk away. He placed his door key in his trouser pocket…

'Item 8. Get key copy made.'

….elected the matching Lacoste wind cheater and followed his nose towards the hearty breakfast.

Before leaving home, he checked the TV news, where as expected there was no mention of activities relating to his exploits. He had breakfast and then had a post-prandial stroll back to his house where he ordered a 2.30 pm taxi pick up. At 2.30 on the dot, he heard the sound of a taxi horn outside.

'Princeton Forest Golf Club please, driver.'

'Ain't you forgot something, buddy?'

'No I don't think so, like what?'

'Your friggin' clubs man, your friggin' clubs. Ha, ha, ha.'

'Nice one. Listen, it sounds a bit odd but I'm meeting somebody near the seventh hole, so what's the best way to get to it from the clubhouse?'

'Easy. Go in the pro shop and take a look at the map of the course they have hanging in there on the wall.'

Arriving at the club, he paid the driver and headed for the pro-shop where within minutes of entering, a fish totally out of water, he had located the map of the course and identified a footpath that led directly to the "rest area" at the top of the hill halfway down the seventh fairway. In stepping out, he looked around at the players coming and going and was pleased to note that he blended in as a fellow golfer quite nicely…apart from not having any "friggin' clubs" of course.

A few minutes along the path, he noticed it rise, peaking as a hillock on the top of which he spied a bench with a solitary person seated on it. As he drew closer, he was able to identify the person as Janet Blane, sitting there in peaceful repose gazing out across the seventh fairway.

'Excuse me, have you seen my ball?'

She turned her head smiling broadly and looked up at him.

'I'm sorry, sir, but I have left my microscope at home.'

She stood up and the pair embraced fondly. Hart stepped away.

'Janet, you look incredible! How do you do it? You must be keeping well to look so good. Either that or you've got some horribly ageing painting of yourself up in the attic!'

'Yes, I'm fine thank you and you look err...*different* in some way.'

'Yes, of course I do, I'm twenty years older now than when you last saw me three months ago, but don't ask me to go through the "whys and wherefores", suffice it to say that I've found myself in some very interesting and sometimes "hairy" situations of late, but I *am* fine now and that's the truth.'

Janet indicated for them to sit down on the bench.

'I told you that Doctor Halle had drowned somewhere in Southern Italy.'

'Yes indeed, in fact I did hear that the Italian Ministry of Health put out warnings of river pollution due to contamination with foreign bodies, or at least one foreign body.'

'That's a bit unfair, Max.'

'You are probably right, Janet, but he treated me very badly and to quote Sun Tzu, "If you wait by the river long enough, the bodies of your enemies will float by." Very apt in this instance I think.'

'Enough!' She nudged his arm gently. 'Did I tell you that I was leaving World? Yes, after 30 years I've decided to retire.'

'That's a great decision, Janet. Based on information I have, I would advise you to do it as soon as possible. You see, there is a large amount of excreta that is about to collide with the air cooling system, so now is the best time for you to do it if it's your intention.'

'Sorry?'

'I said, the shit's about to hit the fan big time at World, and there will be a lot of casualties I think, but please don't let this go any further just yet. But tell me about Ken Rogers.'

'Yes, I mentioned the recent great change in him. He really is a different person to when you were with us. Doctor Halle took him under his wing and within a very short time of you leaving, he was even attending meetings with Doctor Mondo himself!'

Hart groaned inwardly again as he had done the first time she had told him this over the phone yesterday. This was not the news he wanted to hear confirmed. He had actually felt quite close to Rogers, but the news of his close association with Halle and Mondo could only mean that he had likely been roped into the stem cell "Great Plan". In fact, it was almost certain that he was now involved, as there was no way that he could be that close to these men without having some knowledge and involvement at some level in their agendas.

'So how then has Halle's death affected Ken, exactly?'

'Well, for starters he no longer has an office in our building. He has moved into the executive building D10, with a new office that is very close to that of Doctor Mondo.'

'It sounds very much like he must now be part of Mondo's "special family" then?'

'It would seem so and he now treats us mostly as if we don't exist and when he does recognise our existence he treats us like dirt. The terrible change that has come over him is awful.'

'That really is a shame, but try not to upset yourself too much because changes are certainly on the way at World and very soon. I was actually wondering about calling Ken for old times' sake before the Wednesday bash. What do you think?'

'My advice to you would be no, don't do it. You would find the changes in him very upsetting I'm sure.

'Yes, things will probably be different after Wednesday night any way, but please that is for your ears only.'

'Of course.'

Hart looked at the brass plaque set into the middle of the backrest along the top edge of the bench on which they were seated.

'In loving memory of William Ernest Blane, who so much loved this course. 'Straight Down the Middle Bill!''

Janet really did have a great sense of humour, even in such sadness.

'So you obviously continue to come here often, Janet?'

'Yes, regularly. It helps a lot you know, Max. So then, tell me exactly why you need the entrance pass for Wednesday?'

She tapped her bag, indicating that the object of his current desire was sitting inside it.

'Over the last weeks, I've been through a hell of a lot, both in physical *and* mental terms. If I was to give you exact details, Janet, you would honestly find my story very difficult to believe. I've been knocking on heaven's door just too many times and this Mondo soiree might just provide a fitting climax to the whole business. As I told you before, I am working with the Italian Office of Catholic Affairs primarily, but other indirect contacts include the FDA and NIH and the CIA and FBI over here, and abroad similar organisations in both the UK and Germany. This is a huge and complex matter and Wednesday's soiree will have a much greater impact than Alberto Mondo could ever imagine…likewise for those others who stand with him, hence my queries relating to Ken.'

'Sounds very cloak and dagger to me.'

'Cloak and dagger it truly is and secrecy is the key thing to remember.'

She gave him a disapproving look and undid the clasp of her bag, thrusting her hand inside it. When she withdrew it, she was holding a sealed envelope embossed with the World Company logo, which she handed to Hart.

'By the same token you must not…'

Hart completed the sentence for her.

'…mention this to another soul. Uhm, nice envelope.'

He squeezed his little finger under the edge of the flap and carefully ran it across the full width of the envelope, pulled out the elaborate-looking card that was inside and read to himself the gold leaf message that was printed on it.

'You know already what it is of course, Janet. It's a summons from his holiness "the Mondo" to join him and his wife at a gala reception at the Mondo country residence etc., etc., etc. Ah shit!'

'What's wrong?'

'It's a bloody black-tie do, which means that I will have to hire a penguin suit and the rest of the trimmings at really short notice.'

'Is that all? Look, please feel free to say "no", but I do have an almost new evening suit and as you say, all the trimmings, hanging in a wardrobe at home. They were bought by William especially for the golf club's annual dinner, but of course he never had the chance to wear them. You do look to be about the same size, but come back with me and try the trousers and jacket on at least. If it fits and if you promise to take great care of it you can borrow it, together with the bow tie.'

Hart smiled at her. It would actually be an honour for him to wear her late husband's evening suit whether it fitted him perfectly or not.

'We could go back now if you like for a fitting. Are you in your car or did you come by cab?'

'I took a cab.'

'Very well then, I'll give you a lift. It's best we do this as soon as possible in case it doesn't fit and you have to hire one after all.'

'That would be excellent thanks.'

He slid the invitation into his jacket pocket having taken one last look at it.

'Hey what's this? This invitation is addressed to a Doctor Harrison.'

'All invitations are personalised. As I couldn't really put your own name on it, for I'm sure they will have a checklist of who to admit and who to turn away, I chose to use the name of an English doctor who was travelling in from somewhere in Canada, but who cancelled only on Friday last. OK?'

'*Perfetto!*'

'Come on then, your coach awaits.'

The drive to the residence of Janet Blane took fifteen minutes and within five minutes of arriving, Hart had been ushered into the guest bedroom, where Janet shortly joined him carrying her late husband's dress suit hung on a padded coat-hanger and enveloped in a clear plastic suit cover. She passed it to him.

'There, now go ahead and try it on. There's a full-length mirror over in the corner. I'll be waiting in the lounge, but you don't have to put on a fashion parade for me, just put it back on the hanger after you've tried it on and either take it with you or leave it if it doesn't fit.'

There was sudden slight embarrassment in her voice, for having your much younger ex-boss stripping off in the spare room was definitely a novel situation for her and having delivered her instructions she turned and scurried out shutting the door firmly behind her.

He quickly replaced his own chinos with the trousers belonging to the dress suit, fastened the button fly and the waist button, and walked over to the mirror.

They were a perfect fit, both around the waist and in the length of the trouser legs. He donned the double-breasted jacket and fastened the two buttons. The jacket also fit him like a glove. William Blane must have been almost the same size as himself. He walked out and into the rather chintzy lounge where Janet was seated.

'So then, I think it's a pretty nigh-on perfect fit. What do you reckon?'

Despite Janet's earlier insistence that she didn't want to witness a fashion parade, he did a mock-catwalk twirl.

'It really *is* a perfect fit, Max.'

'In that case, if you would like to gift wrap it I'll take it, thank you.'

Within two hours of him arriving at Janet's house, the cab had dropped him back home and he was in his own bedroom hanging the splendid Pierre Balmain dress suit in his wardrobe. The next time he would wear it would be for the "main event" and he shivered a little in nervous anticipation of it.

Chapter 121

On the Monday and Tuesday following his Sunday meeting with Janet, Hart did very little. He called his cleaning lady and informed her that he was back and that she could start again the following week and he also caught up with the mass of mail he had picked up from his glorious red letterbox, most of which was junk. He visited the local supermarket and replenished his refrigerator and pantry and spent a long time perusing dress shirts in the variety of designer label shops in the nearby mall. He wanted a shirt that would do justice to the Balmain suit that Janet Blane had lent him to wear at the Mondo bash and he finally obtained one that he thought was the perfect accompaniment. He also bought a white silk pocket-handkerchief, which for its size was ridiculously expensive, but which added to his new shirt would fit beautifully with his ensemble.

Working down the list he had put together, he confirmed the validity of the new passport that Luca Messi had presented him with and filled out a form for the replacement of his "lost" driver's licence. The final box which he ticked was the afterthought relating to having two new front door keys cut and he did this whilst shopping for the shirt.

This meant that he could now relax right up until the evening bash at the Mondo's residence, so on the actual day of the said event he merely pottered around the house and garden and had one of his luxuriously long hot showers ahead of getting dressed for the gala evening.

He stood in his bedroom admiring his reflected image in the full-length mirror.

'Not bad, not bad at all. You'll do.'

He was showered, shaved and shampooed and wearing with pride, the whole of his dinner regalia most of which belonged to Janet Blane, or at least to her late husband. The elegant Pierre Balmain dinner suit consisted of a double-breasted jacket with velvet edgings to the lapels, to the leading edges of the pockets and also to the leading edges down the front and round the sides of the entire jacket. The black self-supporting trousers, free of turn-ups, were also trimmed with black strips of velvet down the outer seams of the legs. The shirt he had spent so long searching for was a brilliant white silk Boss dress shirt, with winged collars and horizontal pleats across the region of the chest. At the turn-back cuffs he wore a pair of 22-carat gold cufflinks. Around the neck, he had tied the black bow tie lovingly lent to him, and had made a very decent job of it with the help of a short movie on YouTube. The white silk handkerchief was posed rakishly from the breast pocket. Around his waist covering the top of his trousers, he wore the borrowed black silk cummerbund with the narrow horizontal pleats and his "look" was completed by black silk Boss socks and a pair of not quite so new black church lace-up shoes polished to look like glass.

He strutted his stuff in front of the mirror and remembered the solemn promise he had made to Janet.

'Janet, I swear I will look after the suit as if my life depended upon it and I promise you that any lipstick, wine, food or vomit will be dry-cleaned completely away before I return it.'

Looking at his watch, he saw that there was just fifteen minutes to wait before Frank and the limo arrived. The unexpected sound of the limo's horn made him jump. Jack was fifteen minutes early. He picked up his wallet, checked himself one last time in the mirror and headed out to the limo.

'Evening, Doctor Hart. You ready for the beano then?'

Hart seated himself on the back seat.

'As ready as I ever will be. In fact, I've half a mind to ask you to head off in the opposite direction.'

'No, no, we can't have that. You'll be fine once you've gone in and had a couple of drinks. You'll enjoy it. By the way, I apologise for being a little early for the pickup, but I just dropped a fare down the road and thought you wouldn't mind me arriving here a little ahead of schedule.'

'I don't mind you being early, Frank, but I still don't intend going in until 8.15 pm at the earliest, so do you want to take us there by the scenic route?'

'No problem. We can always park up for a while once we arrive if you wanna to kill a bit of time. Congratulations on the turn out by the way, it's like having royalty in the back of the car.'

He pulled slowly away from the curb. Hart was tense, but nervousness was part of his make-up and he knew that once he was at the event he would quickly relax and slip into his normal (for him at least) flippant mode, but he wasn't sure how he would respond to meeting Ken Rogers again however. As for Alberto Mondo, he wasn't too worried about him as they had never met before and so he would be able to circulate pretty much at will. He was looking forward to meeting Messi again and couldn't wait to see the man's face when he saw that he had been able to crash the event after all…against all advice. He still had no plans for what he might say or do controversially at the soiree, but for sure things would not be the same at the end of the evening as they were likely to be at the start. If they were, he would have failed in his duty.

Chapter 122

At the country residence of the Mondos, Alberto had been in an unusual state of nervousness and anxiety the whole of the day, heightened by the fact that neither Negri nor Volpe had been in touch with him. The accidental demise of Halle was unfortunate, but he was replaceable.

The evening event was yet another very important affair for him, in fact the most important for some time, because the invited guests would be in his home for the first time. What added an edge to the guest list was that apart from a select band of people that he had insisted on attending, all the other guests were at the suggestion of his generals, namely Halle, Rogers and a sprinkling of others rising through the ranks. The result was that he knew and would be able to recognise only around one quarter of the people who were attending, and likewise their partners.

Another reason for a little nervousness was that his wife Barbara would be adopting an unusually high visibility role in the proceedings. Usually at these types of gatherings, her role was that of the quiet reserved wife, smiling and nodding in all the appropriate places, a veritable dependable rock behind the head of the Mondo dynasty. However, this evening in her own house she would be meeting, greeting and welcoming the guests as well as ensuring that the distribution of the drinks and canapés was perfectly co-ordinated. She had instructed the waitresses and waiters that no glass was to be under or over full at any time, not an easy job in a room of some 250 or so guests. At 5.30 pm, she was still running through final checks with the head steward, which included the timetables for the separate performances of the string quartet and the harpist, but at exactly 5.45 pm, she removed herself to her bedroom to prepare herself for the evening ahead as the wife of one of the most successful men in America. If one included his European, South American and African businesses there was good evidence to argue that he was indeed one of the most powerful men in the world, outside of the Presidents of the USA, Russia and China. Tonight, however, things were different, for tonight even though her husband was to announce some major activities for World Pharmaceuticals, this was for the first time ever *her* show. She had taken on the responsibility of organising the whole shebang, apart from choosing the wines of course, a job that Alberto was adamant about doing himself.

Barbara Mondo had an undeniably majestic, regal bearing. She was tall and slim, with black hair not yet yielding to any greyness. Her elegant facial features were classically Italian and if anything, were actually enhanced by the occasional smile-lines around her large hazel eyes. Her faultless figure did not betray in any aspect the fact that she had born four children, all of whom much to the consternation of their father had demonstrated complete antipathies to the family business. Tonight, she just had to look stunning in the way she presented herself to the assembled guests and adding to her looks the exclusive cosmetics and couture at her disposal it was a foregone conclusion that she would knock them all completely out of the park.

At 7.30 pm, she was standing in her room with her dresser and beautician cum make-up artist at her side, critically examining the almost finished item. "Stunning" she was aiming for, "absolutely stunning", was what she achieved. Some days after the event "The Tatler" magazine described her couture as follows:

"…and her most beautiful dress was from the Giorgio Armani 'Prive' collection, a diamante, white, strapless evening gown featuring a mesh of luminous white crystals that silhouetted a floral motif. The gown was accentuated with a hemline that exploded into a tulle and organza underskirt."

A little later, closer to the arrival time of the first of their guests she took from the bedroom safe a diamond necklace, a diamond bracelet, diamond drop earrings and a matching ring with an absolutely huge single diamond centrepiece. The whole ensemble of jewellery was completed by a simple diamond tiara. She was assisted in adorning herself with these complete contents of a small diamond mine by her dresser, who upon finally anointing her head with the tiara stood back and placing a hand on her heart breathed out,

'*Che bella*! So beautiful! You look absolutely amazing!'

The beautician followed suit in recognition of what really was the most beautiful of sights.

Barbara "Bobo" Mondo really was at this moment at her most regal and beautiful and she was finally ready to take centre stage and totally steal the show. However, there was another show about to run in the same theatre, but as yet the "cast of one" had not yet arrived.

Alberto Mondo was in his study dressed in his very fine dinner suit for the evening, but unlike "Bobo", he was pacing back and forth going through the bon mots he would be letting drop spontaneously throughout the evening together with his carefully rehearsed ad-libs! This was indeed a very important evening with many people present who he was keen to impress. He had even prepared a short speech in case the need arose and this too he had memorised and rehearsed avidly. In his more fanciful moments, he had pondered the possibility of being awarded a Nobel Prize by the Royal Swedish Academy of Sciences for his support of the ground-breaking work in medicine that his company were pioneering in solving the huge problems associated with the disabilities related to spinal injuries and to Parkinson's disease. There was also the great humanitarian and philanthropic work he was supporting on the African Continent. Surely, he should be considered for two Nobel Prizes? A family with a Nobel Prize winner and a Pope as members! Such heady thoughts and tonight he would be pushing discretely for both of those cherished outcomes.

However, reality and fantasy can be mutually indistinguishable.

Chapter 123

As expected, the limo took 45 minutes to make its way to the Mondo residence, or at least to the impressive black wrought iron gated driveway. The gates were supported by two large brick pillars, one on each side, on the top of which were set single huge stone globes (Worlds) of the earth, each one illuminated by a pair of spotlights positioned at ground level. Built into each pillar at car window height were the obligatory intercoms, which connected with the small security building, which also controlled the CCTV cameras dotted around the whole of the house and grounds in appropriate places. This single position was manned by two security guards 24/7. Tonight, however, the electronic opening of the gates and their surveillance was made redundant by the presence of two very smart gorillas, who were strangely dressed as penguins! Tonight it was their job to scrutinise guests' invitations and if necessary to politely invite them to go elsewhere. Frank slowed and halted Hart's limo twenty yards before it was necessary to enter the campus.

'Last chance, Doctor Hart. If you really don't wanna go in we can turn around and duck out. It's all the same to me, but it seems a shame now that we're here and being as you've gone to so much trouble to look the part...'

'Drive on, Frank, my feet are just itching to dance the night away and in any case I have a chip the size of one hundred potatoes on my shoulder that needs disposing of.'

'Go to it, Doctor Hart.'

Waiting in line, Frank finally stopped at the side of the first man on the gates, who facially looked like he had come out a distant second best of a few rounds in the ring with the late Muhammad Ali, and opened Hart's electrically operated window.

Without speaking, Hart handed the man his invitation, just a little nervous that some problem might be found with it and waited. The man scrutinised it closely for some moments, as if having a problem reading, and then handed it back to him.

'Thank you, Doctor Harrison. Have a nice evening.'

'I will. Thank you.'

Hart was a little taken aback at his name check, but quickly remembered Janet's explanation of the nom de plume. His only concern was Frank the driver, who visibly reacted upon hearing the wrong name called, but thankfully said nothing and drove forward.

'So then, you've changed your name for tonight, have you?'

'Shush! It's a long story, but thanks for keeping quiet back there.'

'No problem. Discretion is my middle name, Doctor Doolittle. Ha, ha, ha.'

The limo continued on up the winding drive and Hart looked back over his shoulder seeing the line of headlights behind them catching up as Frank kept their speed quite low to kill a few more moments of time. The drive wound its way up through heavily wooded areas and rolling grassy plains. It was illuminated periodically by what appeared to be gas-fuelled streetlights, but which were most likely good electric impersonations.

'Looks like they own half of the state, Doctor Hart-Harrison.'

'I wouldn't be at all surprised, Frank.'

It was a good five minutes before Hart and the driver were able to pick out the illuminated grand mansion ahead. The driver whistled as they came within visual range of it in the fading light.

'Jeez, that's really some place. In my job, it's great seeing these places, but the problem is I then have to describe them to Mrs Frank when I get home.'

The house was built in the style of the Venetian designer, Andrea Palladio, and, therefore, based on the formal temple-type architecture of the ancient Greeks. "Mrs Frank" would no doubt have been mightily impressed seeing all that white marble and colonnade frontage!

'What about the pick up when you're done here, Doctor Hart?'

'I'm actually expecting to meet some people here who will have their cars with them and they'll expect me to leave with them I think, thanks. I've no idea what time I'll want to bail out though. What's the latest you'll be available to pick me up, just in case?'

'Look, here's my business card, it's got my contact number on it so feel free to call at whatever time you like. I might even smuggle "Mrs Frank" in to feast her eyes on things. No, I'm only joking, you really wouldn't want to see her in her night attire and hair rollers after midnight.'

Hart laughed and taking Frank's card slipped it into the breast pocket of his jacket.

'It looks like guests are being met personally as they leave their vehicles, Doctor Hart.'

'More torture!'

Slowly, but surely, the limo neared the awaiting red carpet. As it approached, it swept past a series of ornate white stone fountains, illuminated by spotlights placed below the water line. Hart was not too impressed.

'Tacky! It looks more like something on the Strip at Las Vegas than a high society mansion. It seems that they have a steward who will open the limo door, Frank, so at that point I'll just hold my nose and jump out into the deep end. I'll no doubt talk to you again very soon.'

'Thank you, Doctor, I can't wait. You have a great time now…and behave!'

As the limo arrived alongside the red carpet, Hart's door was indeed swiftly opened, not by a member of the same simian species as those at the gates, but by a handsomely dressed elegant footman, who smiled and welcomed him to the soiree and indicated for him to pass along the red carpet and up the carpeted steps into the house. In not so many words, he also quietly told him not to break ranks in the queue, but to patiently wait his turn for the official welcome and possible handshake. As Hart complied with the instructions, he looked around furtively, half expecting someone to instantly recognise him and have him immediately ejected from the place. In truth, however, whilst there were many within the World organisation who were aware of "the idiot-comedian-plan-wrecker Hart", only a small number of them were actually aware of his appearance, although his photograph had been well circulated to the armed security men circulating amongst the evening's guests.

As he neared the next check-in stage, the volume and density of guests increased noticeably. The man to satisfy at this point was also dressed as a footman, but this time he was checking the invitations of guests with a bar code reader. Hart had never even realised that there *was* a bar code on his invitation. Perhaps there wasn't? Perhaps it had been omitted in error by whoever had forged it for Janet?

'Bloody hell! Open the gates, one uninvited guest coming through!'

When he was just yards away from the footman, he noticed a pleasant looking elderly woman who appeared to be on her own and looking apprehensively at the man and the procedure awaiting her. It was time for him to exude a little charm.

'This is quite a performance, isn't it, but essential I guess under the circumstances with all these important people...or should I say with all *we* important people, ha, ha?'

'Yes, it's not quite what I expected. Isn't this what one has to do to gain entry to events at Disney World?'

'Probably. I've not actually been there, but I have heard quite a lot about it. It *is* efficient though and it does get people inside quite quickly I believe.'

'Do I detect an English accent?'

'Indeed you do.'

'What is your connection with the family here?'

'I first met Alberto at a dinner at Buckingham Palace in London some years back. We sat at the side of each other in fact.'

'Oh, how very interesting. So what do you do, what is your particular skill?'

'Well, I'm an international medical consultant for advanced clinical trials, but at the time I met Alberto, as well as doing my daytime-job, I was assisting Diana in her patronage of a charitable AIDS clinical study.'

Hart felt sure his nose had just put on one inch in length!

'How absolutely marvellous! We must speak more of this anon. Oh I do hope we get the chance to meet Barbara Mondo, you know tonight is a great moment for the "International Women's Movement".'

By now, they had reached the footman with the worrying bar code reader. Hart turned to his new friend, a diversionary tactic of some sort being required.

'Would you like to give me your card and I will get it swiped along with mine? It will save you squeezing through the crowd.'

'How kind of you.'

She drew closer to Hart and passed him her card, linking arms with him as they reached the footman, then as Hart passed her card to him she called out,

'Look here, my man, clearly we're together. It's quite ridiculous having to go through this tiresome rigmarole!'

Somewhat shocked by the verbal attack, the young footman was momentarily thrown off balance and definitely "hand-bagged" by the elderly lady, the result being that he only swiped her card and didn't even ask for Hart's.

'Yes, of course, that will be fine. Please move along. Next please.'

Hart leaned over and whispered,

'Perfectly executed.'

She was happy to have shown this "mover in British royal circles" that she too carried some weight and prestige with lower mortals.

'It was my pleasure. I will see you later when I expect you to invite me onto the dance-floor, young man.'

'Yes of course, I will look forward to it.'

Hart was now already metaphorically looking for the fire escape, but instead he found the hostess Barbara Mondo! As he moved forward slowly in line, his new companion spied some friends off to the side and made a beeline for them, leaving him to proceed alone. A dense knot of guests directly in front of him suddenly dispersed and he found himself standing directly in front of the hostess. For Hart, it was love at first sight, for the sight of la Mondo had an even greater effect on him than did his first aerial view of Claudia Volpe in Padua. He was totally bowled over by her sheer beauty and elegance and was struck virtually speechless. She looked at him, offered him her hand and smiled. Hart didn't realise how lucky he was, for with around 250 guests arriving, the hostess could only greet a small fraction of them personally and offer her hand to an even smaller fraction. The others would have to walk on and admire her from a distance. Hart's lady friend, however, didn't even achieve the "pass-by at a distance" option, as in diving off towards her friends she had totally missed out on her most coveted aim of the evening, that of seeing the beautiful lady up-close.

'Good evening, I'm Barbara Mondo. It really is my great pleasure to welcome you to our home. I do hope you will enjoy tonight's get together. Thank you for coming, perhaps we will meet again later.'

That was all he got, but Hart was like a sixteen-year-old, totally overcome by her presence and totally unable to respond to her, and here he was in her home tonight, hell-bent on bringing down her whole household, starting with her husband and most likely laying waste to all that she had dreamed and aspired to.

As he moved away from the amazing woman in white, sparkling with diamantes and diamonds enhanced in the spotlights, he became aware of the oohs and ahhs of other guests who were now catching sight of her and being bowled over in exactly the same way as himself. Had he been sixteen years old he would have sworn never to wash that right hand again…ever! The fact that she was a lady in late middle age was absolutely of no consequence!

As he stood there, he was accosted by a young waitress holding aloft a tray on which sat an array of charged glasses.

'Champagne, sir?'

'Yes please. Oh and may I also take one for my friend who has just been pulled into conversation over there?'

He pointed to his new elderly friend who at that very moment looked his way and raised a hand in acknowledgment to him…as royally as she could muster to the close friend of the ex-Princess of Wales.

'Of course, sir. Please take two flutes. Thank you, sir,' and then she moved on.

Finding a small space in the milling crowd close to a large aspidistra plant, he became aware of the music flowing through the room and for the first time, in studying his surroundings, he saw a small temporary stage that had been erected in the opposite corner of the room on which were seated a female string quartet playing classical pieces into the night air. The part of the entrance area where he was standing was illuminated by two enormous crystal chandeliers, which cast light upon Wedgewood blue walls from which hung a series of large gilt framed portraits. Whilst most of the faces were unknown to him, there was one that he knew very well and which was 50% larger than all the others. It held the face of Alberto Mondo, and seated in front of him in the portrait was the most regal looking of women, the one who he had just met, Mondo's wife Barbara. The paraphrased words of an English comedienne came to mind,

So then, what first attracted you to the ageing billionaire Alberto Mondo?

Not to be outdone by the portrait, a life-sized bust of the current family head stared out proudly from its position on the top of a fluted Greek-style plinth.

Everything about the room was pure elegance, from the vertical marble columns rising from the deep-piled, plush purple carpeting to the ornately sculptured friezes bordering the plastered ceiling, which carried wonderful frescos of life in ancient Sicily and where the presence of Mount Etna was somewhat of a give-away to their location. The walls too, in areas that had not been accommodated by the portraits, exhibited beautifully colourful frescos of ancient life in Italy.

Hart was aware that the noise levels were rising in the room as more guests were funnelled in having passed the bar code test, and were congregating in small groups chattering excitedly. A waiter appeared with another tray of drinks and Hart helped himself to a single flute of champagne and proceeded to inspect the other guests in his immediate vicinity.

That the majority were very wealthy was without question. All were expensively clothed, from the ladies in their designer ball gowns, to the uniformly dressed men in their black dinner suits, where the only difference seemed to be whether they wore a black tie or, more risqué in these circles at least, a white tie.

It was then that he noticed a contingency from one of the southern areas of the African continent. In a group of around one dozen, both men and women were beautifully dressed in vibrant coloured clothing. The women were wearing either brightly printed materials or block-patterned fabrics, accessorised with rings, wristbands and anklets, whilst on their heads the married members wore the iconic hats called izicolos. Not to be outshone, the men were wearing traditional Batik silk shirts, also adorned in bright colourful prints, a le Nelson

Mandela, with colourful baggy trousers, the whole topped off with bright typira cloaks and the occasional handmade Dashiki hats. As for ornamentation, gold was the colour of the evening, the men all being adorned with enough gold jewellery to weigh down a small ship.

Another waiter came by and another flute of champagne was taken by Hart. This time, he sipped it slowly and gaining in confidence decided to move towards the source of the music on the stage. He'd not moved far when he saw an alcove, not visible from his previous position, in which tables were laid out with wonderful canapés and desserts. He couldn't resist them and moved in scanning the tables for a canapé that particularly caught his eye. In truth they all did, which made his decision rather difficult. During his consequent contemplation, he was interrupted by a voice behind him.

'Well, well, hello Max, I'm very pleased to see you again. I've tried many of the canapés of course and all are totally delicious.'

Smiling Hart turned round.

'*Ciao*, Luca, it *is* really good to see you. I'm not at all surprised to see that you managed to make it tonight. I was very much hoping that you would.'

Looking at Messi, Hart was a little wide-eyed as his friend seemed to have adopted a dress code all of his very own. Instead of the traditional black evening suit he had opted for cream. Cream suit and waistcoat, cream bow tie and cream cummerbund. All these items seemed to be straining against the bulk from within, which was stretching their elasticity to the limit. The only items on him that weren't cream were the black buttons on his white dress shirt.

'Well, Luca, despite your need for anonymity and secrecy you don't seem to have chosen battle fatigues that will blend particularly well into the forest of black here. You do look very elegant though.'

'Thank you. I'm hiding in plain sight, Max. I know I *shouldn't* be surprised to see you here, knowing you as I do by now, but surprised I am and you must tell me later how on earth you managed to conjure up a valid invitation for the most exclusive event of the year. Listen, if you leave the big room here by the door on the left and go a few metres down the corridor, there is another small room on the right, meet me and my colleagues there in fifteen minutes please.'

With that, Messi turned and left the food area, accompanied by a couple of men whose muscles almost visibly rippled under their tight suits and whose unsmiling faces were as cast in stone. Hart had looked around quite closely at the assembled crowd during his time under the aspidistra plant and up until this point he hadn't spotted a single person who smacked to him of security or government agents. He felt his stomach churn slightly as he considered how many more men with the capacity for potential violence were likely circulating amongst the guests. Before obeying Messi's instructions to head for the small room down the corridor, he decided to get closer to the stage and inspect the musicians. He was five yards from the front of the stage when the music faded and stopped. The audience applauded politely and the four musicians smiled and bowed. At that point as the music had faded so did the lights, leaving the room in almost total darkness. As the guests began to murmur, the lights were brought up again and there in the centre of the stage was the smiling Barbara Mondo.

There were appreciative noises relating to her wonderful appearance and also to her dramatic arrival in the spotlight and a ripple of applause passed through the room. Soon the ripple became a swell and it took la Mondo herself to gently request the applause to cease. Hart looked closely at her, so very easy to do, and saw that there were no mini-microphones attached to any part of her dress (of course it would be sin to desecrate such a divine ensemble), nor were there any floor standing upright microphones around her (another possibly sinful action that would interrupt the perfect view of her from the audience). Looking above her at the ceiling, however, he spotted a couple of booms with microphones attached and now looking around the room noticed a series of speakers hanging on the walls. The lady was going to speak. She coughed slightly to clear her throat and a deathly hush fell over her rapt audience. The anticipation and excitement were electric.

'Ladies and gentlemen, honoured guests, welcome to our home. My original intention was that tonight I would greet every guest personally upon their arrival, but as the numbers swelled to over two hundred, it became clear that this was not possible. It would probably have taken one whole week, by the end of which my right hand would have likely resembled that of Minnie Mouse!'

Polite laughter filled the room.

'As it turned out, I was only able to greet a few of you up close upon your arrival and for that I apologise. I have to point out that I did this purely in a random way, just like some of our clinical trials I am told.'

Another round of laughter.

'It is a great pleasure for me to welcome you all here tonight and for a change we have a little "woman power" in the organisation of it.'

Spontaneous applause from the *ladies* in the audience followed and there were also a few most unladylike 'whoops' and 'yeahs'. Barbara Mondo was relaxed and in control of her audience and she was enjoying it. There were also many audible complimentary comments within her audience, for they too were enjoying it.

'In mentioning "woman power", many of you are already aware of my leanings in that direction and bearing in mind the announcement that will be made tonight relating to the next stage of World Pharmaceutical's move towards global philanthropy I would like to begin my short welcome with a quote from Ban Ki-moon, who you will no doubt remember as the South Korean 8th Secretary General of the United Nations not too long ago.'

She had spoken so far without any visible notes or prompting devices and Hart was interested to see how long that would continue.

'So then I quote him: "Saving our planet, lifting people out of poverty, advancing economic growth…these are one and the same fight. We must connect the dots between climate change, water scarcity, energy shortages, global health, food security and women's empowerment. Solutions to one problem must be solutions for all".'

The audience applauded wildly. Hart too was really impressed. Here was a woman with apparently little previous experience of public speaking, absolutely "wowing" this international audience of business people and politicians.

Furthermore, she had quoted Mr Moon without referring to any written prompt whatsoever. It had clearly been delivered "from the head" and more than likely also from the "heart". Hart was now fairly convinced that she was in total ignorance of her husband's activities and his "Great Plan". If not, then she was both an incredible actress and a monumental hypocrite. The applause continued for minutes rather than for seconds from the somewhat surprised gathering and their comments grew louder.

'Hey Fran, where's old man Mondo been keeping this lady, she's an absolute star?'

'Jack, did you hear that? You could do with her on your upcoming political platform, she's a show stopper!'

'There you go, Bruce, this lady has got everything. What a winner!

Eventually the clamour died down and she continued,

'I want you all to enjoy tonight, so please feel free to indulge, or should I say over-indulge, yourselves to your hearts' content in whatever food and drink appeals to you?'

More laughter.

'There is an important part to the evening, however, which I alluded to earlier. As you know, through the World Board and my husband Alberto's good offices, the company has been bringing to the fore new and successful treatments for many illnesses and diseases that even two years ago were un-treatable.'

There was a slight pause for applause that wasn't forthcoming. Her first miss so far. She continued,

'It has not been generally publicised to the general public, but much of this work has been in very poor parts of Africa, and through World's charitable trusts medicines and new treatments have been made available, often with the great help of the Catholic Church, and distributed at little or no cost to the sick people requiring them.'

This time she scored a bulls-eye and received the round of applause that was expected.

'I am very excited to announce to you this evening that the company has recently agreed to commence a new development in Southern Africa.'

She paused, teasing her audience a little.

'World have agreed with the local African government departments to build a 3,000-patient hospital and alongside side it a state of the art clinical research facility. This means that—'

Loud and sustained applause erupted. When the room had once more become quiet she continued,

'This means that free medical care will be available to all in a centre of excellence and additionally people will benefit from on-the-spot drug research and development. By taking part in this research, they will be able to help develop new drugs through clinical trials and subsequently be the first patients internationally to receive those life-enhancing treatments. I thank Alberto for giving me this opportunity to meet and speak with you this evening, for I do have to tell you that life has been rather boring for me since I finished knitting his last sweater—'

More laughter and loud applause.

'—and I look forward to having greater personal involvement with World in the coming months. Finally, we couldn't have a World soiree without a quick appearance of the man himself. Ladies and gentlemen. I give you my husband, Alberto Mondo.'

Hart was now feeling disappointed the way her short speech had turned and was having second thoughts regarding what she actually knew of Alberto's darker global activities. She had certainly talked a good talk about it for one left in the dark over the less palatable issues!

As the applause rang out, Barbara stepped back out of the spotlight that was quickly filled by her husband, presumably having taken the same route to the stage as herself, leaving behind him in the shadows a handsome, olive-skinned, young (by church standards) man dressed in ecclesiastical scarlet. The shared genetics between Alberto and the cardinal were obvious. The man he had left off-stage was none other than the now famous Peter Mondo, Pontiff in waiting.

Hart was close enough to the stage to get a really good look at the man who until a few months ago had been the name and figurehead of the company that he himself had devoted so much skill and time to. Mondo looked pretty good, his portrait in oils having caught his true likeness very well. He looked lovingly at his wife and then with a kiss on the cheek he took her hand and they both exited right. The show, for now at least, was over. There were a few cries of 'Brava Barbara', and 'Brava Bobo', but the crowd quickly settled to loud discussion of what they had just seen and heard.

Hart was certainly impressed with her on-stage presence and her obvious authority. Her delivery of amusing one-liners was excellent and what's more she did indeed do it all without the need of a script. He had to wonder how long this entertainer and public speaker had been kept frustratingly cooped up inside the dutiful wife. Suddenly, he remembered his assignation with Messi for which he was now twenty minutes late, but surely Messi would also have been held up in watching and appreciating the star performance that had just concluded.

The room that Messi had indicated to him was in fact a small sitting room with the door closed and when he opened it and entered, he found he was its sole occupier. Within several minutes, however, the door opened and Messi, looking very much like "the man from Del Monte" and still accompanied by the two presumably agents entered closing the door behind them. Messi smiled and he shook Hart's hand warmly. Hart still had problems holding his dead wet fish of a hand, but nevertheless shook it just as warmly.

'I'm very pleased to see you here, Luca.'

'Indeed, Max, but let me introduce you to my two colleagues here. Not by name of course, but by the organisations that they represent, those being the FBI and the CIA.'

'Hi there, chaps. First though, Luca, I assume you caught the presentation by *la signora* Mondo? What did you think?'

'*Si*, I caught it, Max. I thought she was absolutely incredible. A good talker, she held the audience in the palm of her hand, but not the hand of Minnie Mouse eh, ha, ha, and she was amusing. But I tell you, Max, she was the most beautiful woman I have seen in some time.'

'I totally agree with you, Luca. I was one of the few who shook hands with her on the way in you know.'

'Then surely you will not wash that hand for one whole year, *si*, ha, ha, ha?'

'Exactly! You and I have the very same thoughts about this lady. I believe she even put la Volpe in the shade tonight, despite her advancing years. But what of your colleagues, what were their impressions?'

Hart looked directly at them. One of them responded,

'We are not allowed to have opinions, Doctor Hart. We are focused purely on the job in hand.'

'Just as I thought. Bravo, gentlemen, you give me much confidence and faith in your abilities.'

Messi scowled at Hart for his sarcastic response. These men were indeed very stiff and apparently bereft of any humour, but it was important for him to maintain a good relationship with them. One of the agents spoke,

'OK, Doctor Hart, I'll give it to you straight. You need to stay right out of any action that goes down tonight. Understand? We cannot permit you to draw any attention to us, or for that matter to yourself, which from what I hear about you and what I have already seen tonight is a nigh on impossibility. We cannot allow you to screw up our plans. Now is that clear, or do we have to escort you off the property?'

'Crystal. Although that would rather blow your own cover, don't you think?'

The agent only took note of the first word of Hart's response, allowing the rest to pass him by.

'Good! Then enjoy the party, relax and leave everything to us. It's our turn to kick ass tonight.'

Messi was a little embarrassed by his agent colleague, who despite his words had no real idea of what Hart had gone through to remain alive for this night's "party", as he had put it.

'Max, I'm sorry for my friend's abruptness but he is right, nothing must interfere with tonight's plans.'

Hart shrugged his shoulders.

'That's fine by me, but how did you and your colleagues manage to infiltrate tonight's proceedings without raising any suspicions. You don't look like run of the mill guests, you must agree?'

'Remember we are the OCA, the FBI and the CIA. Our ingenuity for an occasion like this can be almost limitless. We actually have many more of our people in the crowd as you have probably imagined, as have the security people on the Mondo side of course. My advice to you is to go and mingle a bit and enjoy the event, but my tip is to keep your eyes open if you want to witness Mondo's surprise of surprises. It will occur very discretely so as to cause the minimum of fuss amongst these important people.'

He turned to leave the room, but turned back to Hart pointing to the glass of champagne in his hand.

'And remember, Max, the wine can be a turncoat, first the friend and then the enemy so please slow down with the drink and keep a clear objective in the head, yes?'

He turned again and left the room in the company of the two agents.

Hart was left alone in the room, the naughty schoolboy in the headteacher's study following a firm telling off. Still, at least he felt more comfortable knowing that there was a reasonable presence of "good guys" on duty there that night, and taking Messi's advice, he decided to make the most of this splendid evening in the company of the glitterati and the movers and shakers of the worlds of business and politics…but this feeling of comfort was dampened somewhat at the thought of having to dance the "monster mash" with his new elderly lady friend to whom he had lent his arm when they first arrived.

Chapter 124

Hart moved out of the room, lifting another glass of champagne from the tray of one of the floating waiters, and began to circulate amongst the glitterati. Neither Messi nor the representatives of the authorities with him wanted him under their feet as they put whatever plan they had into operation, but he had a burning desire to be there when Mondo was taken to task by them. If he couldn't hang on to their shoulders whilst waiting, then perhaps he could get a birds-eye view by hanging onto the shoulder of Mondo, but first he had to find him again.

Moving amongst the guests, it was clear that this group of well-heeled movers and shakers were drawn from all areas of business and the political and social spectra. He now recognised many of the faces from past newspaper articles and TV appearances, and although unable to put names to their faces, he was intrigued to note how differences and political leanings had obviously been dropped for this occasion. Republicans rubbed shoulders with Democrats and people of strongly different religious persuasions laughed and joked with each other, the best of friends. Hart smiled to himself in his semi-inebriated condition, whispering under his breath,

'Everybody's pissing in the same pot tonight, that is for sure!'

He ambled smilingly across the wide corridor, noting that certain areas had been roped off for the evening including the ornate staircases, and walked into another reception room. This too was beautifully decorated and with the same crystal chandeliers pouring down light upon the ensemble. He stood in the entrance and gazed around bouncing slightly on the sprung floor. It was here that Hart envisaged dancing would take place later in the evening…Messi permitting.

One thing that still concerned him, being something that he should have taken up with Messi just now, was that with the media being represented by both the written word and now the television here tonight, how on earth would they be able to keep the lid on whatever events unfolded later on? Additionally, how could the expected events be kept from being broadcast by word of mouth by the very important attendees at the soiree? Obviously, Messi and his associates had all of these things covered and he would no doubt discover all for himself later.

Whilst testing the springing in the wooden floor, Hart continued with his appraisal of his surroundings. Two enormous wall mirrors, one at each end of the room, reflected brilliantly the crystal ceiling lights as well as the gathered guests, who he was able to study indirectly. Along the whole of one wall and taking up one half of another were more tables, extremely attractively decorated and containing the absolutely, almost "too good to eat" spread, which included some of the most enticing and artistically fashioned desserts that Hart had ever laid eyes upon.

Looking back down the corridor, he was aware of a small gathering at the foot of a staircase and perched on the lowest step addressing the adoring crowd once again was the man responsible for his nightmares. Hart moved closer but was unable to get close enough to hear complete sentences from Mondo, although phrases kept filtering through the court that Alberto Mondo was holding. Phrases such as '…and therefore ending the misery…' and '…tackling the poverty…' came through, along with, '…decimating disease…' and '….in a dynamic brokerage with the church…'

As he refocused his eyes, he suddenly picked out one guest at least, on the periphery of the group, to whom he could attach a name and who was continually nodding his head in agreement and calling out an occasional 'hear, hear' and 'bravo'. Hart quickly threaded his way through the crowd, excusing himself on the way, until he arrived at the guest's shoulder. The guest was standing in front of the open door to what was clearly a library devoid of other guests. Hart placed a hand on his left shoulder and scooped him into the empty room, closing the door behind them.

'Hey! What's going on for fuc—? Max! What the hell are you doing here? We thought you were dead!'

Hart smiled and tilted his head sideways.

'Hello, Ken, or should that be "*Sir*", these days? Of course you bloody well thought I was dead and so did your cronies. Mind you it wasn't for the lack of effort on the part of your partners in crime! No, as you see I am very much alive…and enjoying this soiree very much, but thanks for your concern though. You seem to be doing very well for yourself, Ken, and moving in very high circles now I hear, in fact *stratospheric* is the appropriate term I believe.'

'Well, you know…come on, Max…you left the company and well…I saw the window of opportunity…'

'And you dived straight through it, right?'

'Ah shit, Max! Why am I apologising to you for seizing the opportunity to make something for myself from the bloody mess you left behind. You *left* the company, get it, L-E-F-T the company. You crashed out a bloody failure…a loser, Max. What did you expect me to do come running after you? No, you blew it and you got your just desserts!'

Hart had envisaged the possibility of this meeting with his former friend and colleague Ken Rogers and had decided that above all else he would remain calm and collected were such a meeting to take place. Well, here he was, and his planned coolness had lasted all of sixty seconds following their "reunion". He angrily pushed Rogers against the wall. Rogers' eyes widened both in surprise and with a little fear and he looked around for help, but the room remained empty apart from themselves.

'So then, Ken, just how deep are you in it with Mondo, eh? It seems like you're pretty close to him to me. Peas in a pod, or should that be grubs in a rotten apple? Are you aware of what's going on here with Mondo and his *Great Plan*? Are you part of it?'

Rogers shook himself free.

'Part of it? Part of what? I can tell you that I am proud to be part of the team orchestrating this great research program, if that's what you are intimating at?'

Hart was taken aback by Rogers' demeanour. Janet had previously presented him with a rather uncomfortable description of the changes that had occurred in Rogers of late and her portrayal of him had been correct. He was a different man to the rather humble being that Hart had befriended and helped out when at World and was now seemingly infected by the same virus that had terminally affected the late Halle.

He verbally waded into Rogers holding nothing back in hitting him with known details of the stem cell research program, the illegal abortion of foetuses from unconsented parents, the huge shortcomings in the proposals for their African program and the attempts on his life.

Rogers tried his best to defend absent ethics in those plans, but the most telling response referred to the aborted foetuses.

'What's the fate of a few unborn foetuses measured against the cures we are able to make and the hope that we can give to thousands of people? The truth is, Max, we have finally cracked it. We have finally been able to come up with a treatment that is close to mass production.'

Hart continued,

'What you have done, and continue to do, is contrary to all the rules of ethics, reason, and morality. The ethical rules and regulatory regulations are there to protect these very people that you are violating, but you are disregarding these ethical standards purely for your immediate gain. You have no concern at all for the lives of ordinary people, only those wealthy enough to afford the treatments you have illegally turned out.'

'You're right. Of course, I don't have any concern for those people. They are weak and hopeless. They contribute absolutely nothing to the world in which they scratch out a living, only existing on what can be handed to them by governments and charities. They are a drain on the economy and should be expected to make *some* form of restitution at least. Don't you see, Max, that is why you have always been and will continue to be, a total loser.'

Hart stepped up his attack, bringing up the likely artificial prolongation of the life of the Pope and the need for the Pontiff's blessing in obtaining World's foothold in Africa.

'Are you aware of this, Ken?'

'Of course, I'm aware for God's sake! It's a brilliant scheme. We keep him alive, he keeps us in Africa, and he's none the wiser for doing it.'

'But what about the Great Plan, are you in on that too?'

Rogers looked at him quizzically.

'I don't understand what you mean. What Great Plan?'

'I mean, how do you imagine that the Pope has been influenced to help your bloody company? From inside the Vatican, that's how.'

'Oh, you mean Alberto's brother, Peter? Of course he has helped majorly in this, but like the Pope himself he has had absolutely no idea of any of the details of the plan and is totally innocent of any wrongdoing. He is guilty only of total naivity.'

'But here's the million dollar question to you, Ken, does he know how he has arrived in his current position at the right hand of the Pope, as the one who is best positioned to replace him when he dies? Is he aware of how, out of the long list of contenders to fill the Pontiff's shoes, he has risen to be the favourite? You could in fact say a "shoe-in".'

'I'm not talking about it any further, Max. We are supported by large global institutions and we can only win whereas, you are a perennial loser. '

'I'm not a loser, Ken, I pace myself. You see life is a marathon rather than a sprint, for those who manage to live long enough that is, and I think you may have hit the front rather too soon. I've been able to survive through these recent weeks with the help of the Italian Office of Catholic Affairs, who are very well aware of the minutest details of your plans and activities both with the Sicilian mafia, with the people inside the Vatican and with the names and locations of the global clinics where you ply your works of horror on the unborn.'

Feeling that he had made his points quite well, Hart was totally phased by the reaction his short soliloquy brought out in Rogers.

'Ha, ha, what a joke. The OCA has worked with World for years…even as a team on occasions. They even accepted help from Alberto in getting the Sicilian mafia to do a little work on their behalf on one occasion. All is a front with them, for behind their mask of pompous Italian importance and piety they are as corrupt as the very bodies they would pursue and bring to justice. So your blockbuster news of the OCA's involvement, far from giving me fear-filled chills, actually fills me with great confidence that we will succeed. You are a total fool, Max. All your efforts and escapes from the recent life threatening events will amount to nothing. You *should* have gone for the sprint, Max, you will have no time now to complete the marathon, as you put it, and I must now make the decision as to how and when you will be finally "retired", old friend.'

He laughed once more, shook himself free from Hart's now relaxed grip and adjusting his tie and jacket, opened the library door and joined the people in the corridor.

Hart stood for some moments trying to comprehend what Rogers had just told him about the OCA. This surely could not be true of Messi? If it *was* true, why would he have bothered with the Sicilian expedition which had resulted in the deaths of several of his own team members? Why provide him with all that information, information that Rogers had basically acknowledged to be true. Messi was a friend of a friend of his own good friend Gianni Bossi for God's sake! Was this the secret that Messi had intimated at in Reggio as "not being important enough to know of and having no bearing on the outcome"? One thing for sure was that Rogers was a fool in not realising that the American FBI and CIA, the German Federal Intelligence Service and British MI6 and MI5 at least, were involved in pursuing prosecutions in the matter of the *Great Plan* and he was pleased that he had kept this detail from Rogers, detail that had been passed to him by Luca Messi. He felt uneasy. He liked Messi a lot and hoped to God that he turned out to be totally genuine in his activities. He decided that he would only know the truth of Rogers' accusations when Messi made his final move later that evening, if indeed he was still intent on making such a move. The only way to be there at that time was to locate Alberto Mondo again and stick to him like glue until that moment of revelation. He adjusted his own tie and proceeded into the corridor and the guests, leaving the empty library behind him.

As the door closed, the high-backed swivel chair at the end of the room that had been turned away from them during their confrontation swung round to face the door, its occupant's face grim and ashen. Rising slowly from the chair, the red-robed Peter Mondo picked up the book that he had been seeking a reference in prior to being interrupted by the scuffle between Hart and Rogers and replaced it in its slot in the bookcase.

As he walked towards the ballroom once more, Hart's mind was focused on the last thirty minutes and his startling conversation with Ken Rogers. He was stung by the pure vitreole and hatred that had poured from Rogers and shocked by the man's almost Nazi views on the rest of ordinary mankind, but nevertheless, he felt a little guilty that he had reacted badly himself in exceeding the limits of his behaviour that he had earlier promised Luca Messi and friends to uphold.

Still, the bastard deserved it!

He decided that before stalking Mondo again he would savour some of the excellent canapés and confirm that the champagne was still up to standard. As he re-entered the crowded ballroom, he saw Alberto Mondo on the far side of the room in apparent deep discussion with Rogers and two of his minders.

As Rogers leaned in close and talked into Mondo's ear, he passed him a single-page document that he had hastily put together. As Mondo scanned it his face took on a look that began as angry and went through enraged to absolutely furious. It was at this belated point that Mondo first learnt fully of Hart's recent activities and the details of his international involvements that had been completely concealed from him by his "associates". His face became as black as thunder and after a quick word to his "heavies", he spun round and walked quickly and purposefully out of the room and directly up the flight of stairs roped-off and out of bounds to guests, situated opposite the room. In these past few minutes, Mondo had finally been updated on details he should have known of for weeks. He was incensed.

At least Hart now knew where Mondo would be, so he could concentrate for a short time at least on the food before him.

He hadn't been scanning the spread for long when he became aware of two presences at his shoulder. Mondo's minders had latterly retraced their ungainly steps down the stairs back into the ballroom and now stood behind him. Hart turned round and smilingly addressed them both.

'Hi guys, you do look smart.'

He bent over and leaning forward feigned to inspect the rear ends of the men.

'But tell me, chaps, just where do you tuck your tails in those very tight outfits? Anyway, forget that, perhaps you could help me…'

(*Where the fuck is Messi when you need him?*)

'….I can't decide which of these canapés to go for here.'

He waved an unsteady hand around the area of the food.

'Do you think I should choose the salmon, or the anchovie?'

Each man took one of his elbows and one of them said,

'We want you to come with us now…please!'

'Oh no, did I make the wrong choice? How about the *fois gras* then?'

The men began to guide him through the crowd, smiling at the guests who interrupted their conversations to stare at the unusual turn of events.

'Hang on, guys, those prawns look absolutely terrific!'

Suddenly a voice rang out and the men stopped.

'Hey you two! Leave some for me. He is with me you know and he owes me a dance or two!'

It was the lady with whom he had entered the soiree. Hart turned to her,

'Don't worry, as soon as they've had their dance, I'll be back for *you*. You could do me one favour though while you are waiting.'

'Yes, of course, my dear.'

'Could you as a matter of urgency please, find the rather plump man who is somewhere in the crowd dressed completely in cream, and inform him that I have been invited upstairs by these fellows for an audience with Alberto Mondo?'

'If it gets you back here quicker, I'll do it right away.'

'Thank you so much.'

As the men pulled him away, he called back to her,

'Don't forget me now, I'm depending on you.'

'No chance of that, honey. I'll see you later.'

By those actions, Hart had ensured that his two abductors were aware that he was now known in the room, with people having witnessed him being escorted away by them. The cause of any failure by him to return would subsequently be laid at their feet. His most important action however had been to ask the lady to get the news to Messi of his current serious set of circumstances.

Chapter 125

Hart was escorted up the flight of stairs mounted earlier by Mondo and Rogers, his two "minders" keeping a firm grip on his elbows.

However, the last moments of Hart's forced march up the stairs had also been witnessed by another important member of the household. *Signora* Mondo upon seeing the mini-fracas broke off her conversation with a small group of admirers, excused herself and followed them. She was so intent on tracking the trio ahead of her that she ran headlong into another family member, also intent on joining the meeting in the room at the top of the stairs. Peter Mondo had a grim look on his usually smiling face.

'Oh sorry, Peter, I wasn't looking where I was going. Are you alright, you look rather fraught?'

'My fault, Bobo, I was miles away. Yes, I'm fine thank you, but I'll be hopefully a lot better when I've spoken with Alberto.'

'It looks like we may be going in the same direction.'

Her eyes moved towards the flight of stairs.

'Yes, I think we may be.'

He took up a position at her side as they climbed the stairs, both stopping upon reaching the landing.

'I believe that Alberto may be in the cypress room.'

Outside the doors of the room Mondo's "minders" stood closely to attention at their approach barring their entry. Peter Mondo responded with a grim smile.

'We're going in, thank you.'

The minders had other ideas.

Chapter 126

The cypress room was a particular favourite of Alberto Mondo and it served as his main relaxing area in the evenings when he drank his favourite Sicilian red wine and smoked the occasional large Cuban cigar. It was also the room where he frequently made and received his most important business telephone calls and it was from this sanctuary that he had run the *Great Plan*, with what he now finally saw as very selective inputs from Robert Halle, Claudia Volpe, Franco Negri and latterly Ken Rogers. He felt deceived, undermined and very angry.

Inside the room, some minutes before Bobo and Peter Mondo's arrival outside, Hart had been thrust forward, coming to a standstill directly in front of the 'great man' himself. Mondo wasn't alone however, as standing behind his left shoulder was a severe looking Ken Rogers. Standing behind the pair of them were two virtual doubles of the men who had brought Hart to this room. As soon as Hart was in position for supplication, Mondo had dismissed the two escorts, who leaving the room, had taken up positions on either side on the outside of the door.

Hart spoke first,

'You rang m'lud?'

'Silence! You will only speak when I address you, is that understood?'

Mondo's face hardened and following a slight nod to his two men, who had now moved to the rear of Hart, they each planted a large fist hard into Hart's kidneys.

He cried out in pain and went down on one knee. Rising painfully, he stared into the face of Mondo. When Mondo spoke again his voice was low and controlled and now showed no trace of anger, but none-the-less carried an air of total menace. Hart, however, had been through far too much over the last weeks to feel any intimidation at all by this man, even though he would have appreciated the presence of Messi in the room at that moment.

'Well, Doctor Hart, we finally meet. I have heard so much of you and your exploits recently that I have come to believe that I have known you for a very long time. I am certainly very pleased to now have this opportunity to meet you in person.'

'I worked for your company for quite some time, obtaining for you a considerable number of new drug licenses which have resulted in large amounts of money coming your way. Am I here to receive my bonus?'

Always playing the flippancy card, Hart almost always received the punitive riposte and this time it was no different, as once again he was pummelled from behind on both sides with more blows to his kidneys. This time he did go down, but only as far as to his knees, where he remained trying to recover from the pain and resulting breathlessness. Mondo continued.

'The question is, Doctor Hart, what are we to do with you now? It seems that you are a walking time bomb ready to go off at any moment, in fact it may be that you have done so already. He waved the single sheet of paper, quickly put together by Rogers itemising Harts most recent "crimes" against the "Great Plan", and ran his eyes quickly down it again. Let us talk for a few moments about what you think you know exactly and we can take it from there. Who knows, perhaps we can correct some of your *misunderstandings*.'

His voice was as smooth as silk and confident, very confident, a man in full control of all about him…or so he presently believed.

'For fuck's sake, do you know how many times your people have said that to me recently? Both Volpe and Halle asked me the very same question and always I have given the same answer. Oh yes, and Rogers has also ask me that question. What's wrong here, are you employing slow learners or something?'

Once again the flippancy was rewarded with the same riposte from the men behind him. This time, however, they had to stoop to ensure that their fists arrived at the required anatomical place. He cried out in pain once more and fell forward. He was now lying face down, hurting and feeling sick. He recovered sufficiently to complete what he wanted to say, hoping it would be without punishment this time.

'Surely you must realise by now that it is not just me who has a total insight to your activities, to what you have done and why you have done it? Your crimes are known internationally with all those appropriate international authorities taking all necessary actions. Why do you think I'm here tonight…just to taste the canapés? Think about it! I'm not a single time bomb as you put it, I'm part of an army of people now bent on bringing you to justice. The game is finally up.'

The "minders" moved in to hand out a further dose of "correction" but Mondo raised his hand stopping them in mid punch. For the first time, his composure was ruffled and he looked very worried. Additionally hidden from the knowledge of what was happening with respect to outside regulatory bodies and law enforcement agencies, first by Halle and to a degree by Volpe and Negri, for fear of personal repercussions from him, the truth had finally been revealed to him by Rogers and its true devastating magnitude had finally dawned upon him. Suddenly there were raised voices outside and the doors were thrown open…

'Messi! Thank God the cavalry has arrived at last!'

…and in strode Bobo and Peter Mondo.

'Shit!'

The two new entrants looked down at Hart and then at the sheepish looking Mondo and Rogers. It was Bobo Mondo who spoke first,

'For God's sake, Alberto, why were we not allowed in here just now? What is going on and who is this poor man? We have important guests downstairs and you are spending your time up here with these…gangsters!'

Mondo produced a dreadfully sickly smile for his wife,

'Associates, my dear. These are my associates.'

'And is this man on the floor an associate too? I have definitely seen him around amongst the guests tonight. Who is he and why is he on the floor looking so distressed?'

Mondo smiled his smile and opened his mouth to speak,

'And I don't want to hear any bullshit, Alberto, I want the truth!'

'My dear, he is just an ex-employee who we recently fired and who has since born a grudge against us. He came here tonight to embarrass us as much as possible in front of our esteemed guests.'

His eyes locked briefly with those of Peter Mondo on their way to those of his wife, in the same fawning way a child might do when caught out lying.

'I said Alberto that I didn't want any bullshit and the room positively reeks of it, so now speak up and tell me exactly what is going on here!'

At this juncture, Hart, still shaken by the violence enacted upon him, struggled once more to his knees. Gasping out his words, he addressed the whole room.

'Well, that's not exactly true, Alberto, is it? I came here tonight to witness how the great World Empire is able face politicians, benefactors and the church, with its visions of philanthropy and wonderful deeds in the third world when I know for a fact the true amoral details of those deeds. I know the pain and the misery that really accompanies these acts of wonder.'

'That's enough! This man is a terrible liar and trouble maker and I intend to have him thrown off the premises immediately.'

Hart had not finished though,

'That would be very convenient for you, wouldn't it, but surely *Signora* Mondo and His Most Reverend Eminence would like to hear the rest of my story before I disappear from here…'

He paused for added drama…

'…perhaps never to be seen again?'

'This is ridiculous. The man is drunk and full of hate for our company. Barbara and Peter, please leave the room now and let me deal with this business in the way I feel is the most appropriate. I will meet you again in the ballroom in a few minutes time.'

He looked pointedly at the "minders".

'Escort my brother and my wife downstairs immediately.'

The men paused, unsure where this was leading and whether this family issue was out of their remit, but Mondo was adamant.

'Do it now!'

He took his wife's arm and attempted to lead her to the door. Peter Mondo had remained silent so far, but decided that it was the time now to intervene in this pantomime.

'Stop right there, Alberto.'

He stepped from behind Bobo and standing beside her raised one hand against the oncoming "heavies" and with the other removed Mondo's hand from his wife's arm. He addressed the room,

'You will all stay exactly where you are and not lay a hand on either *Signora* Mondo or myself. Doctor Hart will be allowed to recount his story and we will judge its veracity.'

Mondo was stunned temporarily into silence. He had never seen his brother in this mood before and clearly the "minders" were also taken aback, for he was after all a high-ranking servant of God, a cardinal no less and one deserving great respect. As for Rogers, this turn of events was way above his comprehension and he stood transfixed not knowing what to say or what to do to help resolve the apparent impasse.

'No, I cannot agree to that. The man is a drunk with a grudge against our company. Even now, he is probably receiving money from some unscrupulous competitor to start malicious rumours against us.'

'Alberto, I have spoken. We will hear what this man has to say, for to tell you the truth brother I was in the library earlier this evening, when totally unbeknown to them I overheard a very disturbing conversation between Doctor Hart and your associate there. A conversation that it is imperative for me to learn the whole truth of.'

The blood visibly drained from Mondo's face, leaving the previously distinguished tanned visage suddenly drawn and pale.

'My dear, Pietro, it was nothing, just two former friends now antagonists, saying more than they really believed or meant. They meant only to hurt each other with words. It was a spat, it's forgotten already.'

'On the contrary, Alberto, it is not over and forgotten as far as I am concerned and I am guessing that it is not over either in the eyes of Doctor Hart. I need to hear it in full from the mouth of Doctor Hart and then decide for myself whether or not it was indeed as you say, "a minor spat".'

'And so do I, Alberto.'

Bobo Mondo added her own demand to the conversation, but the decision was about to be taken out of their hands, at least for the time being, for the gravity of the moment was suddenly suspended by the sounds of more loud voices outside and within a few seconds the doors flew open once again. It really was the stuff of French farce, but in this case a farce of the Italian variety, for framed in the doorway were Mondo's two very large "minders" from outside the room and in front of them the two even larger agents that had accompanied Messi. Then, both pairs of men parted and through the middle of them strode a short, very rotund man, dressed all in cream. All that was missing was for somebody's trousers to fall to their ankles and the farce would be complete. Messi saw Hart on the floor and addressed him,

'Max, despite our wishes, you decided to begin the party without us and you must, therefore, take responsibility for whatever has happened to you in this room before our arrival. You have the elderly lady to thank for our arrival here, even though we are late, but we are here now so please stand up. Lady,' he bowed slightly, 'and gentlemen, my name is Luca Messi and I am Director of the Italian Office for Catholic Affairs. That is in Italy of course, but I carry an international role working across national borders, and always with the agreement and approvals of appropriate government departments. Let me introduce my

American friends here. Without awarding actual names, with me we have a very senior member of your FBI and likewise a very senior member of the CIA. They will officially introduce themselves to you and then explain the purpose of our presence.'

'This is outrageous. You are in my own house remember,' complained Mondo. 'My lawyers should be sent here immediately, for I know for sure that they are in the house at this very moment tonight.'

Ignoring the outburst, Messi turned to his two large companions and indicated for them to introduce themselves to the assembled group and then to proceed with the business as they had previously agreed. The two agents accompanying Messi were un-phased by the imbalance in the numbers of "heavies" in the room and after limited introductions, it was the FBI agent who directed his comments to Alberto Mondo.

'Alberto Mondo, I am here this evening to take you into custody, initially for first and second-degree murder together with conspiracy to murder, but also for accessory to murder in company with illicit criminal organisations, the planning and direction for the murder of unborn human foetuses, abuse of the unborn child, the planning, illicit manufacture and use of unlicensed, illegal forms of living biological compounds for medical treatments, together with an even longer list of additional associated crimes with which you will be charged in due course. For now, though, a cover-all charge of first and second-degree murder will suffice for us to get the ball rolling. I should also inform you that your many international associates are also going through this same process at this very same time in countries outside of the USA, including France, Germany, Spain, the UK and countries within the continents of Africa and South America. In those countries, the proceedings are being led by national agencies such our own in the USA. Now you have mentioned that your lawyers are present here tonight and I suggest that in due course you call them together to escort you to the eventual place of internment and interrogation. I would also suggest that somebody packs a suitable case for you because under the circumstances of our warrant I don't expect that bail will be an option for you. I would advise you however not to say anything that might go against your defence in court. Do you understand?'

Mondo's mouth opened, but no sound came out. He was in a state of total shock. Rogers pushed a leather armchair up to the backs of his legs and he dropped down into it. Rogers then sought a similar chair into which he too dropped, equally in shock. Barbara Mondo broke down in almost hysterical tears and was consoled as much as he could by Peter Mondo, who was himself in a state of great shock. Hart, too, was in a state of shock, but shocked that Messi had been able to pull this off, flying directly in the face of the comments Rogers had made in the library relating to the likely level of corruption of Messi and the OCA. Mondo's four "heavies" stood on their elected spots, their brains totally incapable of computing exactly what had just occurred but realising that the total level of shock in the room could probably significantly enhance the US National Power Grid.

Hart finally dragged himself into a standing position, the joy of the most recent events having had a wonderful placebo effect on the pains he carried as a result of the blows from Mondo's "heavies".

'I thought you would never get here, Luca. I was thinking that perhaps you had been waylaid by a large inviting tray of canapés and desserts and a bottle of the delicious champagne. Either that or you had stolen my dance partner and were too busy tripping the light fantastic with her.'

'Max, if you had stayed on piste rather than ad-libbing, you would not now be feeling the pains in your back. But *allora*, we are where we wanted to be and that is truly an excellent place to be.'

'Excuse me, gentlemen.'

It was the distraught looking Peter Mondo, now disentwined from Bobo having been able to reduce her previous sobs to mere sniffles.

'As you three made your dramatic entry, Doctor Hart was about to explain his story of this whole affair to us and I would still like to hear it as I seem to be very much involved, in part at least and albeit in an involuntary fashion. *Signora* Mondo would also like to hear his explanation I believe.'

Bobo sniffled and nodded in agreement.

Messi considered the request for some moments and then responded,

'Personally, I have no problem with that if Doctor Hart is in agreement, but Alberto Mondo has been charged and as such will no doubt feel unable to hear the story without having cause to reply, which could affect his charges and his defence in the case, but let's see how the two of them feel.'

Mondo welcomed the opportunity to dispute Hart's accusations and Hart was happy to purge himself of his saga for one *final* time, but the two agents were a little unsure for the reasons that Messi had suggested, in that statements by Mondo could later be used in evidence against him. In the end, it was agreed by all that Hart should present the facts of the affair as he knew them, but keeping them as brief as possible. Chairs were drawn up for all and Hart's summary presentation began.

Chapter 127

Hart stood for his presentation and looked at the expectant seated ensemble. Could this really be the final scene for Hart? The final, final scene?

He took some minutes to collect his thoughts, considering what to emphasise and what to leave out in this latest version of his story and finally having decided, he dove in starting at the very beginning.

'First of all, I have to tell you how important it is that you remember throughout my explanation that as a scientist myself, I judged every piece of evidence I gained on its own merits and not once did I jump to conclusions that had no basis in truth.

'OK then. Some months ago, after leaving World Pharmaceuticals…'

'After you had been fired you mean!'

'Yes, after I had been fired, if you prefer, I decamped to Nottingham in the UK for some relaxation and recuperation at the home of some friends. My relaxation didn't last long, however, as I was soon introduced via a scientist friend of theirs to a man whose wife had recently committed suicide following the death of her unborn baby…'

He continued describing fully the tragic story of the Williams that had drawn him into the investigation and his visit to the Paddocks Hospital and its outcome, including the details of IVF premature abortions there compared to national averages.'

'What nonsense! Of course they were worse, you were talking to patients already at risk of such events. That's the very reason that they were attending this clinic for related specialist obstetric treatment. Their outcomes were bound to be worse than the national average!'

Mondo looked satisfied with his interruption, but Hart ignored him and continued with a description of his visit and discoveries in Greifswald relating to the processing of human embryonic material followed by its transportation to Vita Pharma, in Basiglio, Sicily, where the final processing was completed. He highlighted the benefits of using different laboratories for those processing stages enabling World to keep its name completely out of the loop.

'I keep saying World, Alberto, but I might just as well say Mondo, because you were at the very heart of the arrangement, together with your ex-subordinate Halle and more recently his replacement Rogers here.'

Alberto Mondo looked at Rogers' sheet of paper again and responded,

'Totally ridiculous! You all realise that this man was caught on camera illegally roaming around a secure area in our German facility, where he was apprehended and questioned?'

'Thank you for confirming your German facility relationship, Alberto.'

'Yes, but then he was also caught red-handed alone in the World hospitality suite at the International Stem Cell Congress in Padua, rifling through filing cabinets, having gained illegal entry there also.'

Once more, Hart ignored Mondo's comments, prompted from the paper, and continued with his account,

'Once I had demonstrated the links of certain companies not at that point confirmed to be World affiliates, with the probable illegal foetus terminations and the processing of the materials, my scientist friend came up with the information that there was an International Stem Cell Congress imminent in Padua, Italy and seeing from the pre-meeting details that World's German arm had a marketing stand there as well as sponsoring several of the speakers, we decided to register and join the other delegates.'

He went on to discuss his aims at the congress and then moved into more sinister waters.

'It is important to note that at around this time a program of assassinations, developed by Alberto Mondo, project managed by Robert Halle, his then right hand, at the main facility in New Jersey, and delivered by the mafia team led by Claudia Volpe based in Basiglio, Sicily was underway.'

There were gasps from Peter and Bobo Mondo and continued silence from Rogers who so far had been unable to contribute in any way on Mondo's behalf.

'Ab-so-lute rubbish! How could you possibly know anything of this? It is pure invention!'

Hart smiled at Mondo.

'It is not I who has that information and detail, Alberto. All of that was well beyond my remit in the affair. No, the person with all that detail is our friend here Luca Messi. Luca, could you add a few words please for the benefit of our listeners.'

Hart looked at Peter Mondo. The OCA was known by reputation to all who moved in Vatican circles and the cardinal now clearly understood the importance of Messi being there in the Cypress room and the undoubted veracity in what he was about to relate.

The rotund Italian in the cream suit rose and pushed out his chest in an attempt to increase his air of importance, adding another item of stereotypic behaviour to the drama of the tragic farce, and addressed his audience.

'Yes of course. I can present to you the names of young cardinals who one would expect to be short-listed to replace the Pope upon his death, together with the dates, places and the modes of their assassinations. It was the belief of the OCA that these murders were carried out via the mafiosa cell of Claudia Volpe at the expressed wishes of Alberto Mondo and Robert Halle.'

Alberto was on his feet instantly.

'I deny it all.'

'As I was saying, this was only the *belief* of the OCA, with not a lot of evidence, but recently raids on the Volpe offices have taken place and documents have been found and removed that describe in great detail all the arrangements that were made at that time for the killings. In addition, we have discovered actual recordings of conversations between *Signore* Mondo and Claudia Volpe in which these very items were discussed in detail. It seems, sir, that la Volpe did not trust you so very much and made the recordings to trade with law enforcement agencies in return for either her freedom, or at least for a more favourable judgement and sentencing should the need arise. Not only that, since we arrested the mafiosi in Volpe's office in Basiglio and also members of her cells on the Italian mainland, as they say here in America it has been impossible to stop those birds from singing. We have irrefutable proof of who ordered the killings and the details of when they took place and now I propose to read the list out to you...'

With that, Messi put a hand inside his jacket and retrieved a folded paper from which, with much dramatic effect, he read out the names of all the assassinated cardinals together with the organisational details of the killings. At the end, he refolded the paper and with a grand flourish replaced it inside his jacket, slowly taking his seat looking at all the solemn and ashen faces in the room.

Peter Mondo buried his head in his hands and when he looked up again there were tears running freely down his face, as there were likewise for Bobo Mondo, whose smeared expensive make-up was resisting very poorly the constant effects of her salt-water tears.

'But why was it necessary to kill these men? Who could possibly gain from it?'

She called out the question, looking round at Hart, Messi and her husband, desperate for an answer, but it was Peter Mondo who was the first to respond,

'Let me answer that, Bobo. It was seen as necessary because there was a possibility that any of these men could be chosen eventually as a new Pontiff and the people who needed me in that position were not prepared to take any risk of me being beaten to it. So the short answer to your question, "who could possibly gain from it?" is me, Peter Mondo. I would then, and up to this moment, certainly have gained from it.'

Hart was keen to keep his explanation on track and interjected,

'Look, although that was a very valid question, let us keep to my order of events if we can please. I can assure you that we will come back to the reasons for Peter's assisted elevation in the Vatican ranks in due course. Let me tell you what happened in Padua at the Congress. I did indeed search through filing cabinets in the Hospitality Suite of World's German affiliate, where I found lists of World's global associates working on stem cell research projects, together with details of work being carried out at their facilities in Germany and Sicily. Some of the associates on the lists were working in the clinic that I visited in the UK and there were actually photographs of some of them. These were associates who had been condemned by the patients I had interviewed and importantly by the man who involved me in this affair in the first place. All of these people condemned World's associates as having deliberately caused their wives to miscarry and lose their foetuses. In addition, during this visit to World's affiliate hospitality suite, I happened to witness a meeting chaired by Robert Halle and attended by Claudia Volpe and various World associates from certain of the clinics, including a senior physician from the clinic visited by me in the UK. It was obvious that pressure was being applied to these associates by both Halle as director and Volpe as enforcer, to increase the falling yield of foetal material for stem cell extraction.'

Mondo was incensed.

'How dare you say that! Are we really expected to take the word of a petty thief here?'

By now, enough evidence had been presented to render Mondo's constant protestations an embarrassing irrelevance and the show continued without anybody paying him any attention.

'The next day, together with my scientist friend, I witnessed a meeting between Halle and a priest in the lounge at Halle's hotel. This was a meeting that Halle had told the assembly on the day before was too important for him to miss for the sake of the second planned meeting, which would instead be chaired by Volpe. My friend took photographs of the two men in conversation. The priest who Halle was so keen to meet was later identified to us as Francesco Negri.'

Cue protestations from *Peter* Mondo this time.

'What are you saying? I know Franco Negri very well. He is a very good and devout man, and as well as being a close friend of our family he has been of great support to me in the Vatican, in fact in many ways my mentor.'

He ceased speaking suddenly, as the inferences from what he was saying relating to his effortless rise through the papal hierarchy sounded an alarm in his head.

'My God! I am so naive!'

Alberto was up and raging once more.

'These are all lies. Doctor Halle is dead and there is no way that he can defend himself against these vile suppositions and innuendos.'

Hart continued,

'Having established the links between World, the mafia and the Vatican in the process, I considered my job to be done and left Padua bent on spending some time in Milan. During my train journey to that city, I was accosted and an attempt was made on my life. Fleeing the scene, I made it to Milan and with the help of an Italian friend was brought into contact with Luca Messi, who himself had had an attempt made on his life that same day. I put it to you that these were mafia attempts instigated by Halle, working on behalf of his chief Alberto Mondo. Information since collected, and more importantly from my point of view from direct face-to-face conversations I have had with both Halle and Volpe, has proved this to be true.

'Luca Messi convinced me to go the Basiglio in Sicily, the place where the final stages of the processing of the stem cell material was taking place and to confirm with the help of a small team of OCA operatives, that the final processed material was being then transferred from there, the Laboratorio Vita Pharma, by road to the Vatican or more specifically to the medical team who were being organised under the auspices of Franco Negri. By identifying the stem cell materials in the transport van and labelling and electronically tagging them, it was possible to track them directly to the Vatican where the rest is now history.

The objectives of this piece of work were achieved, but not without the horrific murder of most of the OCA agents on our team by the Volpe Mafia and an attempt made on my life by Claudia Volpe. Later, in Reggio Calabria, having escaped the Volpe Mafia in Sicily, I was recaptured and interrogated by both the mafia and by Robert Halle himself who before he died, to borrow the same American term used earlier, sang like a bird to me telling me all the details of the *great* Mondo *plan*. Even tonight in the library, Ken Rogers re-confirmed to me the nature of the plan and demonstrated to me the complete disregard for human life that this group under Alberto Mondo has. I think Luca can continue now. I have summarised all the activities as they are known to me. Luca, please.'

Messi cleared his throat.

'Firstly, I have to inform you that as well as Robert Halle, Franco Negri is also unable to defend himself in these matters. You see he was arrested earlier today during an OCA raid on a particular area of the Vatican and he later took poison, committing suicide. He is now deceased.'

Peter Mondo made the sign of the cross and lowered his head whispering a silent prayer to himself, but other than that the room was silent, the silence broken only by the occasional tinkle from the crystals of the chandelier as they were gently caressed by the cool air arriving from the air conditioning system. Finally, unsurprisingly Alberto broke the silence.

'Lies! These are all lies typical of this man and his colleagues, for I know for sure that Franco is alive and well. He must be!'

Peter Mondo spoke,

'In my eyes, Franco is a fine and honourable man who is esteemed throughout all Vatican circles and also beyond that in the greater body of our church. He is a great friend of the Pope himself and I would have thought that had he died, I would have been informed during the evening. However, I do trust Luca Messi and if he insists that Franco is dead, then I have no option but to accept the fact.'

'Thank you for your trust, Father. I have absolutely no reason to lie to anyone on this tragic issue. Following his arrest in the Vatican, he was taken to a cell in the police department where he subsequently took a very quick acting poison, which he must have carried secreted on his person in case of that very event of being arrested.'

Alberto also seemed to now accept the terrible news and he too made the sign of the cross and whispered a silent prayer to his old friend, associate, confidante and accomplice.

Hart looked at Messi nodding for him to continue.

'*Allora*, I think I should now try and explain to you the role of the Pope and Peter Mondo in all of this. I must say from the outset that Peter has been completely unaware of what has been occurring on his behalf in this business and how his future was being manipulated by others. Alberto Mondo was desperate to become the major pharma player in Africa, the reasons being money, fame and importantly the ability to trial new un-licensed and previously un-tested drugs in desperately poor and highly susceptible countries, leading of course eventually to even more money flowing into the company. A major unwitting key to World's acceptance by governments on that continent was the Pope himself, an African who had been born in Angola, in fact in the very first town that World had chosen to deposit its benefaction upon. But the Pope is dying and there still remain key things that need to happen whilst he is still alive to cement World's prime position in Africa. These key things include agreements between World and local ethics committees in return for brown envelopes stuffed with money in order to encourage them to turn blind eyes to the lack of adequate safety data for the drugs used in trials, together with similar arrangements with government officials and health committees. Upon completion of clinical trials, flying in the face of normal ethical standards for the continued provision of free "compassionate medication" to patients benefitting from the drugs, World have recently been charging high prices for such continued usage of efficacious drugs. In addition, official bodies have been effectively bribed to allow the company to supply, as far as possible, most of the drugs that are on national pharmaceutical lists for the huge population, when necessary actually re-branding other companies' products and reselling them at significantly higher prices. In this way, World has cornered the market and virtually killed off all competitors.

The costs of the free drugs handed out by World are potentially a drop in the ocean compared to the income that would be generated later upon a successful cessation of the trials when patients would then receive new and expensive replacement drug therapies. There has also been a plan afoot to recycle out of date drugs, by repackaging them and allocating new expiry dates to them. All it has taken once again is for an occasional brown envelope to land in the right pocket. Cheap drugs have also been repacked and given different brand names and re-circulated at greater prices. I understand that the latest ethical crime is that World are packing placebo treatments under a newly locally registered brand name and selling them as active treatments. It has all truly been a licence for World to print its own money so far and as long as there is an, albeit innocent, connection to the Pope and the Vatican the business will continue to develop and thrive.

'In addition and very importantly, the great indigenous population there will provide almost limitless supplies of foetal material from illegally terminated pregnancies for the production of stem cell treatments for neurological disorders and these outrages will in the main go un-contested and largely un-noticed. Max, please continue. I'm sorry, Peter, but I have not yet reached what your role is in this plan.'

Hart took over the explanation once again,

'In order for these things to fully come to pass, it was decided in Alberto Mondo's *Great Plan* that he would organise a process by which the Pope's ebbing life could be extended. With the Parkinson's disease from which he suffers being so severe, by rights the Pontiff should have been dead many months ago, but Alberto has been successful in his plan so far and the Pontiff has not been allowed to die. The Pope has been mothballed using the very stem cells obtained by Mondo's colleagues that have been extracted and processed from the aborted foetuses of women desperate to have a child. His clock has been kept ticking by the serial injection of these drugs by a specialist Vatican medical team co-ordinated by Franco Negri. That whole team has now been taken into custody, but of course, their leader will not have the ignominy of going to public trial. I must underline for you finally that the Pope himself is completely unaware of these activities that have been carried out as is Peter Mondo, of that there is absolutely no doubt.'

There were cries and sobs from Peter and Bobo Mondo, but Alberto and Rogers remained still. Alberto realising that he had come to the end of his denials could only half whisper,

'I need my lawyers and I need them here now, it is my right.'

It was the FBI man who had arrived with Messi who responded to him,

'You don't have no rights here yet, buddy. You've been charged, but you are not under any official interrogation. The comments you have made, and I have to say made contrary to my advice, have been purely voluntary. You can talk to your lawyers before we leave the house, if as you say they are here tonight.'

Messi resumed the explanation,

'And so we come to you, Peter. You see, Peter Mondo, schooled and guided by Negri, has become very close to the Pope. Peter's stance and opinions on traditional Catholic values and actions are very liberal and would seem to be very popular amongst the younger members of our church. He also has a great interest in Africa and without doubt upon the death of the Pope, were he to succeed him, he would most likely not only continue the work now ongoing there, but would try and expand it considerably. As Pope, his brother Alberto, together with his mentor Negri, would be able to influence and manipulate him with deeds of great African benevolence, but benevolence that was only superficial my friends. Benevolence that was really a tremendously cheap investment for the massive returns it would make in the future. For such a future to arrive though, Alberto Mondo had to be sure that the Pope lives long enough for his brother to move through the papal ranks and be in a position where he would be a veritable shoe-in when the Pontiff passes away. For this reason, Alberto Mondo could not in any way afford to let there be any serious threats of competition for the prime position from Peter Mondo's contemporaries, for if there were and the next Pope was not Peter Mondo but someone perhaps less liberal and traditional in his views, the likelihood would be that all his investments and plans in Africa would be money down the drain. His vice-like grip on the continent would be lost. Hence the serial assassination of the competition in as un-suspicious circumstances as possible.'

Bobo Mondo was uncontrollable once more in her sobbing and Peter drew her to him, himself totally shattered by Messi's summation. Alberto Mondo was silent and looking extremely grave, for whilst much of what Messi had outlined was true he had genuinely very close feelings towards his brother and although he had used him as a pawn in this game, in the end he did indeed want Peter to be made Pope whether he Alberto controlled the major share of pharmaceutical business in Africa or not and he needed to try and explain this to him, even though his brother now clearly despised him.

He stood and walked across the room to where his wife and brother were huddled together, each seeking solace from one another. He touched Bobo's shoulder and she pulled it sharply away from him. Crouching down with his face level with that of Peter, he began to speak.

'Peter, much of what has been said is true, but I still believe that at World we have developed stem cell treatments that will eradicate so many life threatening conditions all over the world. One day, the world will thank us for that. One day, we may even find ourselves elevated to Nobel Prize winning levels of appreciation when the world comes to realise that to attain the impossible, sacrifice is necessary. Unborn foetuses have been arrested in their development that is true, but the great prize has been that people in pain and dying from neurological diseases have benefited beyond all our dreams.'

Peter Mondo lifted his head and looked at Alberto through tear-stained eyes.

'But your whole edifice for the effective treatment of medical conditions deemed impossible to treat has been built on sand. You have murdered to arrive at the place you are now at. You have cured people with no previous hope of being cured, wonderful, but what a price you have exacted from others who have had to pay for this. Parents distraught, mothers so lost in grief that they take their own lives, whole families emotionally destroyed. To have progressed this far through proper ethical means would indeed have been a wonderful achievement that even I as a Catholic priest would have applauded despite our church's current general antipathies to many types of stem cell experimentations. At the end of all this I ask myself why? Why do you do this for me? I understand how my position as leader of the church would benefit you, but I have the feeling that you probably *did* want this for me. For me to have the honour and the glory of being Pope, but if so why?'

'Pietro, in these treatments, in these stem cells, we truly have the seeds of empires. The seeds by which our family would be heads of the greatest institutions in the world. With you as the Pope and me as the most successful pharmaceutical leader in the world, our family would head the greatest of modern day Empires. All that was needed was for the Pope to keep heaven waiting a little longer while I established you in the position to replace him when the time was right. You are still young and would rule as Pontiff for a great many years. Peter, I wanted this for you because you are my brother, my own blood.'

The time had arrived. Hart approached the trio and gazed into the eyes of the priest.

'Peter, I listen to your brother's explanation of why he has perpetrated this long list of atrocities and I feel that I've been transported to Nazi Germany in the late 1930s and early 1940s. The worst part for me is that he shows absolutely no mea culpa or regret for his actions. It is an undeniable fact that your brother and certain of his subordinates have planned and orchestrated some of the worst crimes imaginable, crimes both physically and theologically abhorrent and I know that this must be almost too much for you to bear, but there is another reason he has wanted you to be the Pope. A reason formed out of a disgrace that has been buried under many years of family history, but ironically something that far being a disgrace by today's standards has become all but normality.

'You see, on my short visit to Basiglio recently' I took time out to visit the museum. The museum is a great monument to the Mondo family and the whole of the family line is there, depicted across two walls. The family tree is amazingly honest, for upon inspection one can pick out a tiny branch with the name Luccia Grimaldi inscribed on it.'

Hart heard a sharp intake of breath from Alberto still positioned close to him.

'The line of Luccia Grimaldi is not actually connected to any family member in particular, but its proximity to Alberto Mondo Junior is sufficiently close to indicate that there was an illegitimate product of the aged and febrile businessman's young son and Grimaldi, the young family maid, which was a son. I have been able to confirm this simply by making a couple of telephone calls to friends in the genealogy trade since my return to the US. It is indicated in the museum that your family, who had previously moved to live in the USA, moved back to Sicily whereupon Luccia gave birth to this son, whence the aged businessman's wife Claudia brought up the child as her own. Any thoughts that the son was the product of Claudia and Alberto Senior were risible as the old man Alberto could barely lift a pencil at that time, let alone any important part of his reproductive anatomy. The son born of Luccia Grimaldi was named Pietro. Peter, Alberto Mondo Junior is not your brother, he is your father.'

There was a stunned silence that was finally broken by a shattered Peter Mondo.

'No, no, this is all too much. There is only so much that a mind can deal with.'

He put his head in his hands, his mind filled to bursting with never previously imagined details of his brother, Negri, the Pope and now his own birth.

Barbara Mondo put her arm around his shoulders. She too did not know where to start in beginning to take on board all the dreadful information that had emerged over the last hour, let alone believe that all this could have happened with her in total ignorance of it.

The last hour or so had been totally life changing for both herself and Peter Mondo. There was so very much to consider, the disgrace being immense and all brought about and orchestrated by her husband!

On a sudden impulse, Alberto Mondo dived at Hart screaming in his ear,

'You bastard! You fucking bastard! I'm going to kill you!'

The FBI and CIA agents pulled Mondo away and Hart smoothed down his dishevelled jacket with his hand. He was done here. He could take no more of this rotten business. He walked towards Messi, who looked totally bemused at this most recent turn of events and spoke to him.

'Luca, that is my secret that you would not allow me to broach to you in Reggio. I guess your secret was that the OCA worked in cahoots with both the mafia and World some years back, yes?'

Messi nodded.

'Yes, it is true, Max that there were certain occasions when it proved better for the OCA to work alongside the mafia in Sicily and with World also, in order to obtain certain required results, but I can assure you that murder was never a part of any of that co-operation. I can also assure you that that was many years before my time with the OCA, in fact I was probably only a baby then. So yes, that was my information that I found not necessary to divulge to you in Reggio.

As for your own piece of extra knowledge about the Mondo family line, I have to tell you…I was already well aware of it and have been for a long time! It was absolutely no surprise at all to me, after all I too have visited the museum and traced back the family line. Remember it was I who arranged for you to visit the museum in the first place. No, the "tabloid newspaper scoop" I intended you to find there was far more straightforward. If you had looked more closely at the dates when the Mondos supplied their medicines and lice powder to the Italian army for their invasion of Abyssinia in the late 1800s and then again around the year 1900 or so, you would have seen that in fact the Mondos actually supplied the Abyssinian army with the *same* wares, but at least one year before each of the attempted invasions, which would more than likely have assisted in the ultimate failure of the Italian army in that first campaign. They also advised the Abyssinians on how to stockpile the items whilst keeping them all viable, as it was common knowledge that a second Italian invasion was likely to be in the offing sometime down the line. The Mondos, therefore, could have been accused "in tabloid speak" of "making their dirty money through national treachery!" The early Mondos were famous double-dealers, supplying to anyone at all who was prepared to pay them for their products. Of course the town of Basiglio and its people also benefitted very charitably from the double-dealing and so who were they to rock the boat?'

Hart was totally stunned and felt like a total idiot. His precious golden nugget of additional information was composed of no more than "fool's gold". He looked at Luca, embarrassment written over his face.

'Thanks for that, Luca. So now feeling like a prize idiot, I'm going downstairs to get pissed on that excellent champagne. In any case, I can do no more here, it's yours and the two agents game now, I'm utterly finished…wiped out.'

'Bravo Max,' was all Messi could muster as Hart moved to withdraw from the room, leaving a total Hell of indescribable, distressed human emotions in his wake.

As he began his descent of the stairs towards the ballroom, his last impression was the sound of Alberto Mondo shouting,

'I will go no further without speaking to my lawyers. They are here in the house and I intend to go and find them and bring them to you, for I believe that you have considerably overstepped the boundary of your authority here this evening thus giving me cause for much redress.'

Hart painfully took the remaining few steps two at a time, his back aching acutely where he had been punched, anxious to leave the hustle and the shouting once and for all behind him.

'For God's sake put a sock in it, Alberto, it's time to dance!'

Chapter 128

Hart strode over the rope barrier at the foot of the stairs and made directly for the table of food and drink in the ballroom. He downed his first glass of champagne in one and whilst sipping on the next one perused the wonderful desserts still lying untouched on the table. In the background, the second harpist of the evening played on.

'Careful with that drink. If you intend to dance with me, I need you to be at least able to walk in a straight line.'

It was Hart's elderly lady friend.

'Hello there, many thanks for informing the plump man in the cream suit of my whereabouts, it really was important. As soon as I've dispatched this drink, I'll be ready for that dance. Did you say walk in a straight line? Line-dancing is it?'

His friend laughed.

'No indeed, but we have to first wait for the harpist to disappear and be replaced by the band.

The polite small talk was suddenly interrupted by gasps of alarm from the surrounding guests and he heard somebody say,

'Look he has a gun. We should all leave. Quickly!'

At that point there was a sudden stampede of guests towards the exits, their voices raised in alarm. Hart turned to see Alberto Mondo standing in front of him, his arm raised and pointing directly at Hart he held, what a confidential report would later describe as, an "S&W Bodyguard 38 concealed carry-gun". Hart addressed his lady-friend calmly.

'Do me another favour, will you? Please go to the window exit behind the stage area as quickly as you can and leave the room. Don't go with the crowd, it's too congested. It should be a "quickstep" if possible.'

Not needing to be told twice, the lady literally flew across the dance floor, undeterred by her advanced years, to the safety of the outside patio from where she proceeded to observe the unfolding drama within.

Mondo looked dreadful. His usually well-coiffured hair was a tangled mop-head and he had sweat pouring down his face. He had snatched away his bowtie and his shirt was roughly unbuttoned and wide open at the neck. His eyes resembled those of a man not in full control of his senses as they flicked rapidly from side to side on constant lookout for anybody who was brave enough to attempt to disarm him.

'You fucking bastard! You've ruined my whole life tonight. My business is finished, my wife disowns me and my son, yes I said it, my son wants nothing to do with me. On top of that, the authorities here want to lock me up and throw away the key, but if I'm going down so are you, you useless piece of shit.'

Behind him, Messi and the government agents, Bobo and Peter Mondo and the hapless Rogers were in close proximity. It was his wife who made the first of the pleas.

'Alberto, please put down the gun. You will only make matters worse and there is no need for anybody else to be hurt. Please, I beg you!'

Mondo remained statuesque, his gun still trained on Hart. It was now the turn of Peter Mondo to attempt to talk him away from the edge of the precipice.

'Alberto, for the love of God, please put away the gun. Don't you think there has been enough death and pain already? Come on, we can resolve our differences eventually I'm sure. Surely this is not how you wish to be seen and known in the press and amongst all these people here? This cannot be your final lasting legacy after all the good works you have done. Come now, please!'

Throughout the imploring and beseeching, Hart had been concentrating on Mondo's trigger finger. Suddenly with a scream Mondo jerked his finger back on the trigger and Hart, simultaneously with the explosive sound of the gun's report, dived downwards towards the table. At that point, events appeared to go into slow motion and Hart saw the floor coming up at him whilst at the same time hearing a crash and feeling a tremendous pain in his head. The wild Alberto fired off another shot in Hart's direction and again he felt the force of the bullet, this time in the area of his recently injured shoulder. As his eyes misted over, he now saw standing behind Mondo the comical looking figure of Messi, but this was far from any joke as Messi cried out to him,

'Stay down, Max, stay down!'

With a great pain in his head, Hart passed out and being away with the fairies missed the utter pandemonium that followed. The government agents threw themselves towards Mondo, who proceeded to spray his remaining three bullets (the S&W bodyguard pistol has a five-bullet chamber capacity) in random directions. The other members of both Messi's and the agents' teams broke cover from their "waiting on", stewarding and band-member roles, as did the covert men of Mondo's security force and war broke out between them as they all began firing their, until now concealed weapons, hopefully at the enemy. The noise of the gunfire was ear-splitting and adding to this level of sound was the sound of the shattering of the crystal chandeliers which under the barrage of the gunfire managed to fuse the house electrics, plunging the room into darkness. Mirrors shattered and plaster flew from the walls as the many stray bullets smashed into them. It seemed in fact that *most* of the bullets were strays as everything in the room suffered damage under the intense badly directed firepower. Faces in the oil paintings were shot to pieces and the large table of food also took a sustained barrage of bullets. The guests who had been unable to escape the room in time screamed in panic, with many of them diving in the darkness onto the broken glass covered floor. Others, unable to avoid the maelstrom of lead, lay there either wounded or killed outright under the onslaught.

Suddenly, it ended just as quickly as it had begun. The lights flickered back on revealing a post Armageddon scenario. The room was a total wreck. The air was heavy with gun smoke, and the pungent smell of nitro-glycerine resulting from the guns' discharges filled the entire room causing the assembled wounded and lucky escapees to cough violently. There were unmoving bodies on the floor and those wounded and prostrate were dragging their bloody selves to their feet, having been raked by gunfire and lacerated by shattered glass. In the middle of all this stood a solitary figure, miraculously completely untouched by the violent altercation that had just taken place. Messi, from his central standing position, looking as immaculate as he had done at the start of the evening, scanned the floor through the smoke and called out Hart's name, fearful for his friend's life.

When Hart came to, he heard his name being called but he was in a state of total disorientation and, therefore, unable to see from where the call came. He remembered the terrible pain in his head as Mondo's gun was fired and he dived towards the floor and indeed the pain was intense. He felt unable to breathe, the muscles in his chest unable to take the necessary actions and his legs felt paralysed. He tried to move them, but they just wouldn't react to his orders. His worst symptom though was that intense head pain he had, for certainly he had taken a bullet there. He managed to raise an arm and place a hand to his head around the area of his wound and recoiled immediately at the feel of the sticky substance he felt. Suddenly the assumed blood and tissue began to move down his forehead and face until it eventually touched his lips. At that point, in panic feeling that he was about to taste his own blood, probably mixed with brain tissue, he gagged and vomited the entire contents of his evening's indulgences over his coat and trousers. But what was that smell? What was that odour that he picked out above the pungent smells of nitro-glycerine and his vomit? It was a smell that he was able to attribute to his agonisingly painful and leaking head…

It was coffee!

He raised a hand once again to the wound on his head and scooped up a little of the stickiness he felt there and gently touched it with his tongue…

It was tiramisu for God's sake! He hated tiramisu! Translated as "pick me up", there were a good many people lying on the dance floor who would require considerably more than a pick-me-up to get them moving again this night. The multitude of random gunshots had obliterated everything laid out on the food table with the result that the wonderful looking desserts were now pooling on the tabletop and leaking down to the floor. Trifles (now Hart *did* like trifle), panacotte, fruit salad…and tiramisu, were all now in downward free flow, but it was the tiramisu that had had Hart's head marked out for a landing place. As Rogers had prophesied earlier in the evening, 'Hart had got his true desserts.'

With his head, which he had actually struck on the metal leg of the table in avoiding Alberto's first bullet, intact he moved on to his breathing condition, which he now registered as being restricted due to the weight of a body on his chest. Carefully moving the body round his breathing immediately improved, but to his absolute dismay he ascertained that the limp body was that of Peter Mondo, whose sad wide-open eyes stared upwards and unblinking. A neat dark bullet hole in the middle of his forehead was the obvious cause of his death, with the contents of his cranium spilling down the back of his neck following the line of the emergent bullet. There was certainly no smell of coffee there!

Gently moving the body completely from his chest, he was able to concentrate his efforts on resolving his inability to move his legs. In his quickly recovering state, it was soon very obvious to him that his lack of leg movement was due to another body stretched out in that region. Reaching down, he was able to ascertain that it was a female, and moving his fingers around her throat region soon found signs of a very much-reduced carotid pulse. He moved forward and lifted the woman off his legs. To his horror he discerned that this body was that of Bobo Mondo, but she was still alive, hanging on by a thread. Her greatly reduced carotid pulse rate indicated to him that she had likely taken a bullet somewhere and was bleeding at a rapid rate from it. It didn't take him long to find the source of the blood loss. From the position of the bloodstains on her dress he quickly located a gunshot wound just off centre of her chest. In other words, very close to her heart. He desperately began to scratch around for something with which he could apply pressure to the wound and thus staunch the flow of blood. It then occurred to him that he was lying under one of the food tables and stretching out his arms and feeling in all directions his hand quickly located several linen serviettes, which he placed over the wound applying as much pressure as he dared to, and shouted out loudly for help!

Messi heard his cries and headed towards the area where he had seen Hart go down as quickly as he was able, a large white silk handkerchief now held over his nose and mouth to keep out the offending smoke, dust and pungent smells. He quickly spotted Hart on the floor and with a great effort went down on one knee at his side.

'Max, how are you, are you hurt?'

'No, I'm fine thank you, Luca, but we have two very unfortunate casualties here. Peter Mondo lies there dead…'

'Oh no! *Mio Dio*!'

'…and under my hand here is Bobo Mondo…'

'Dead?'

'Not yet, but she is seriously wounded. She has taken a bullet to her chest and I think that it is in close proximity to her heart. Her pulse is very weak, but I am applying pressure to the wound and we need medics here immediately or she too will be gone.'

'*Si, si. Dio*!'

Exercising even greater effort than when he went down, he forced himself into a standing position and bawled out into the room at large that he was with Bobo Mondo who was gravely wounded and needing urgent medical attention. Within seconds it seemed to Hart, two paramedics appeared and immediately went to work on the stricken lady of the house.

Whilst one of them substituted Hart in applying pressure to her wound, his partner covered her nose and mouth with an oxygen mask and proceeded to talk gently to her.

'It's OK, Mrs Mondo, breathe easily now, we'll get you out of here in no time at all. You're going to be fine.'

The stopping of the blood loss and the additionally applied oxygen brought her into semi-consciousness and she moaned, in obvious great pain.

Very soon, two more paramedics arrived with a stretcher and with no little difficulty they managed to lift her onto it, a process that she obviously found very painful.

They left immediately, leaving Hart still on the floor and Messi standing in the middle of what had been a veritable war zone. With an effort, Hart stood up, the room suddenly revolving around him, and he staggered. Messi caught hold of him and he stood erect again, the room having come to a standstill.

'Are you all right, Max? You know I should get you checked out by one of the paramedics.'

'No, I'll be fine thanks. I guess we won the war in the end tonight, did we Luca?'

'*Si*, the fighting was very heavy but in the end, you know our men are especially trained and Mondo's security are just…come se dice, how do you say? "Disco bouncers". It was really no contest.'

'So what are the total casualties so far including the guests?'

'At the end of the story, Mondo lost eleven men dead…'

Suddenly there was a cry and a large shape rose from the floor nearby brandishing a gun in his hand. Messi very swiftly put his hand inside his jacket and withdrew a pistol, then without taking any aim shot the man clean between the eyes. The "bad guy" dropped on the spot, where he twitched once and then expired. Without showing any emotion whatsoever, Messi carried on talking, disregarding the small disruption.

'Sorry, Max. At the end of the day, Mondo lost *twelve* men dead and four badly wounded. Both the agents I brought with me survived the battle. As to the men we had under cover nobody was killed, but five of them were slightly wounded.'

'How on earth were you able to get so many of your people inside the soiree without raising any suspicion? So far I make it that you had seventeen men floating around.'

'That was easy, Max, we had men as stewards and waiters and in fact five of them came as one of the bands for the night's entertainment, although I have to say that if they had been called upon to play it would have been very embarrassing as none of them can play a note! We had three women agents as well, who I'm sure you took at least one glass of champagne from and who are also unscathed.'

'And the guests?'

'That was not so good I'm afraid. Fifteen guests were killed and another ten suffered serious injuries.'

'Bloody hell! Another nail in Mondo's coffin. Is he still alive by the way?'

Messi nodded in the affirmative. 'Not a scratch.'

'Isn't that just bloody typical! He fired off several rounds before he was, I'm guessing, overcome. I assume that it will be possible to discover if any of the fatalities came from his own gun?'

'Yes, it will be important to learn whether he was directly responsible for anyone's death here tonight and that we will know after post mortems have been carried out. You know in the end, he survived the battle due to the quick action of the two FBI and CIA agents who brought him to the ground soon after he had fired in your direction, but not soon enough I'm afraid to prevent him from emptying his pistol's whole chamber of bullets. He is still in the house being interviewed by the agents I believe, but will be taken away quite soon I expect. You know after you hit the floor following his shots, both Bobo and Peter Mondo rushed over to check out your state of health and it could be that pathologists and surgeons will find bullets from his .38 calibre pistol in both of them. That would be a terrible irony indeed!'

With a start, Hart suddenly remembered another member of the group that had assembled in Alberto's private office…

'Any idea what happened to Rogers, Luca?'

'No, I've not seen him.'

'In that case perhaps we should look around the floor.'

Both men set off searching the floor in the gloom, the lights not yet working to full capacity. They hadn't been looking for long when Messi called Hart from the far side of the room in the area behind the low stage.

'Max, here! I think I have found him.'

Hart strode quickly over to the stage and looked down at the body staring up at him, a body that had apparently died whilst playing a harp. Ken Rogers had obviously not been playing the instrument, he had merely tried to use it as a shield, although to expect any cover at all from a harp in a storm of bullets showed the absolute desperation that Rogers must have felt at that time…not to mention stupidity. As Hart stared down at him, he remembered what he had said to him earlier that evening in the library,

'Life has to be a marathon rather than a sprint for those who live long enough, and I hope you haven't hit the front too soon.'

Rogers had chosen the sprint and he had indeed reached the end, crossing the finishing line first.

'Yes it's Rogers, Luca. He was a fool to throw in with Mondo, but perhaps he had no other choice. What a terrible day!'

At that moment, on the other side of the ballroom, the FBI and CIA agents appeared, one with an arm in a sling, the other with Alberto Mondo handcuffed to him. Messi walked over to the three men and informed Mondo that his brother was dead and that his wife was gravely wounded. Upon hearing the news, he staggered and then howled like a dog. At the end of what had been a truly disturbing night, Hart gave him five minutes grace and then walked over to him looking at him in disgust.

'Please, Hart, save my wife. Please at least save the life of my wife.'

Hart glared at him for several seconds and then to round off the totally surreal evening he said with true venom in his voice,

'You utterly unfeeling bastard, Mondo! You've ruined Janet's suit, so you can go straight to hell!'

He vigorously pulled at the light stuffing protruding from the ragged hole in the shoulder of the jacket where Mondo's bullet had entered, whilst sweeping his other hand across the areas of the jacket and trousers which he had soiled with his vomit, Barbara Mondo's blood and of course the mixed desserts from the table. Then turning to Messi,

'I'll be waiting for my lift home from you when you're ready, thank you Luca, I need to sleep.'

With that, he spun on his heel and headed to the library leaving Messi, the two agents and especially Mondo, looking totally bemused and confused.

Chapter 129

Messi arranged for Hart to be driven home and then set about co-operating with the American security services to put some "official spin" on the evening's events. This included a long session with the many representatives of the media who had been at the soiree for totally different reasons. Heads of the various media outlets were summoned and having provided them with the "official story", it was indicated to them amongst much protestation, that due to the serious and sensitive international security aspects surrounding the evening's events for the time being at least an effective gagging order was being imposed limiting all media reportage to the short prepared statement.

The statement ran that "the principal owner and Chairman of the Board of Directors of World Pharmaceuticals, Doctor Alberto Mondo, had been charged with serious international breaches of law and taken into custody. In the course of the arrest there had been over-reaction to the events by the in-house security section of Doctor Mondo's staff resulting in a serious incident during which firearms had been discharged resulting in the injury of several of the evening's guests, two of which were Doctor Mondo's wife Barbara and his brother Cardinal Peter Mondo. Further details would be released at a press conference in twenty-four hours' time. There would be no questions permitted at this time and under the instructions of the official gagging order, for now none of the Mondo household employees could be spoken to or interviewed."

Messi finally arrived at Hart's house together with the dawn chorus of birds, as daylight was just breaking looking very tired, but still sartorially elegant in his "creams". Hart was still up, the events of the previous evening having driven all thoughts and physical possibilities of sleep from him and conducting Messi into his lounge area sat him down in the most robust chair in the house and proceeded to ply him with large quantities of Lavazza espresso coffee. The initial pleasantries were quickly dealt with.

'So how are you feeling, Max, you know I really feared for your life back at the mansion when Mondo fired his first two shots at you?'

Hart, seated and still wearing the disgusting-looking suit that Janet had kindly lent him and which he had promised to return in the pristine condition, gently rubbed the lump and small gash on the side of his forehead.

'Just tired and traumatised, Luca. The bang on my head is fine, it's amazing what healing effects a little tiramisu can deliver. You still look just as immaculate as when I first saw you at Mondo's mansion by the way, it's uncanny.'

Messi had apparently miraculously navigated through the gunfire, the smoke, the choking fumes of nitro-glycerine, the blood and the flying trifle avoiding all of them, leaving his cream dinner ensemble just as spotless and unadulterated now as when he had first arrived at the mansion.'

'God *and* Messi move in mysterious ways, Max.'

Both men smiled and spent the remaining hours of the early morning discussing in detail the events of the previous evening, when Messi informed Hart that as well as the arrest of Mondo, eighteen of his guests who were on the FBI and CIA list of backers of his *Great Plan* were also taken into custody.

It was almost breakfast time when Messi finally dragged himself up from his seat and returned to his hotel in the official car that had dropped him at Hart's and then waited outside for him.

In the end, it had been determined that the bottom line as things currently stood, was that World Pharma was in total disarray and with the morning's breaking news things would only get worse for the company. By then, with Mondo behind bars and cut off from all but his lawyers and now residing in a world from which he would likely never return to normal life as a free man, the various federal and healthcare agencies would have their official cases against Mondo completed. Already emergency meetings of the company's various international boards of directors and shareholder groups had been hastily set up worldwide as it became apparent that the company was truly in meltdown. All around the world in World offices, many key affiliate directors had either been arrested or were about to be. Great pains had been taken by international authorities to act at precisely the same time of day or night, according to their time differences, across the globe to prevent felons in those subsidiaries from fleeing ahead of their questioning and investigation. The coming day would also see major activities in the global clinics in which World had contracts, in the shape of arrests and immediate sackings.

As for the media, both the press and TV were beside themselves with frustration at the prospect of being unable to carry detailed news on such an important worldwide incident which included the involvement of most probably the Catholic Church, the mafia and a major pharmaceutical company. Apart from the violence of the previous evening, all they had outside of the short official statement was rumour and conjecture, however more details had been promised by the official government agencies twenty-four hours down the line and various strident alternative headlines had already been prepared by editors to cover most of the possible scenarios which would be eventually revealed to them.

Hart thought about all these things much later that morning following his late morning ablutions and a change of clothes, over a full cooked breakfast which he decided to take at his favourite local café. There he drank more coffee, pondering on just how much of the truth the media would be allowed to run, with respect to the massive scandal inside the Catholic Church. It wasn't until his third espresso with his caffeine levels now running at excessively high levels that he finally erased the associated smell of coffee with his tiramisu/shot in the head event, which had been the cause of some personal embarrassment, even though he was the only person who would ever know about it! He knew from Messi's own lips that previous massive scandals within the Catholic Church had been relatively easily buried by church authorities and by the OCA, who paid Messi's salary. Messi had warned him that there was a strong possibility that he would be impelled to sign various countries' and national organisations' official secrets acts and policies, but this didn't worry him as long as he could relate most of the events to the people nearest, and perhaps dearest, to him. These were the people who had also been in involved or helped him in some way, and who he thought deserved at least some small final explanation.

They included his former PA Janet Blane, his good friend in Milan, Gianni Bossi who had first introduced him to Luca Messi, and most importantly his "partners in exposé" Victoria Crosse and Denis Williams. Not to divulge the details of the saga to those two would be criminal…although was he to sign any official secrets document beforehand it would officially be a criminal offence to actually tell them anything at all! That firmed up the need for him to talk to them as soon as possible, before his signature ink dried on any document. He would spill as many beans to them as were necessary likely later that day when he would telephone the UK. He also owed some form of explanation to his good friends the Barnes, who had kindly put him up when he travelled to Nottingham, what seemed like a lifetime ago and who he had rather let down by going AWOL in very secretive circumstances. The Barnes would be content and forgiving he was sure, were they given the opportunity to digest just a minor portion of the tale, bearing in mind that they were responsible for introducing him to Crosse and ergo Denis Williams in the first place. He would call them also that afternoon, once he had decided upon a suitable time difference between their locations.

His most immediate alarm bells though, signalled his need to call Janet as soon as possible and make an excuse for being a little tardy in returning her precious dinner suit, but that might prove difficult as the suit he had promised to take care of with his life was all but totally ruined during the evenings fracas. Still, there are no such things as problems, only opportunities and he had an opportunity here to successfully resolve where one could obtain an exact replica of the probably "one-off" Pierre Balmain dinner suit she had loaned him.

For sure, at some early stage Hart would be compelled to attend a series of interviews with various high-level authorities, both at home in the USA and also abroad, so at least they could feel that they were completely au fait and aware of the bigger picture of the events as seen from *his* viewpoint. Messi would be responsible for the sensible, official, detailed report, even though he had viewed Hart's work at the coalface of the mission from quite a distance for much of the time. To this end, the two had set a date to meet again very soon when their many notes would be compared and no doubt much wine would be taken. In the end, Messi would combine their notes in some form of single document which once agreed, both men would sign off as being a true representation of all the events.

His final job now on this sunny morning was to order more coffee.

One hour later, seated at home in his study, Hart pondered for some time over the options for calling Victoria Crosse, Denis Williams and the Barnes in the UK.

In the end, he typically opted to call Janet Blane. He thanked her profusely for the loan of the suit, which he told her he had decided to return to her dry-cleaned, and he set a date with her for a couple of days hence when they could meet, at which time he would update her on some of the goings-on at the Mondo mansion and of course return the prized unblemished suit. He lied about having the suit dry-cleaned of course, as the local drycleaners had already declared it impossible to clean the trousers and repair the jacket effectively.

He subsequently made frantic calls to various charity shops and gentlemen's outfitters in a desperate attempt to find another such suit, but repeat bespoke one-off editions are not easily found, a clue lying in the phrase "bespoke one-off". In the end, one helpful outfitter whispered in secretive tones that there was a back-street tailor on the far side of town who would hand-make a suit to whatever specifications, in whatever time one wanted it…for the right amount of cash of course. Yes, cash only. He then kindly gave him the telephone number of "Mr Bobby", before finally totally flooring him with an estimate of what it would cost him…cash!

'Have a nice day, sir.'

Hanging up the phone, Hart immediately called "Mr Bobby's" number. After an unbearable wait, the phone was finally picked up and answered by a voice of certain Chinese origin. Despite the expected language difficulties, "Mr Bobby" finally confirmed that he would be able to make a one-off Pierre Balmain look-alike, double-breasted black dinner jacket, with black velvet edging, together with matching trousers and have them ready for pick up the following evening. It was arranged that Hart would take a photograph of the present suit for reference purposes, the suit itself being in too much of a disgusting state to take with him, and take the picture over to "Mr Bobby" that same afternoon and yes, leave a sizeable cash deposit with him. As he prepared to hang up, Hart suddenly remembered that the suit would need to have labels bearing the name Pierre Balmain sewed into the appropriate places. On that score, "Mr Bobby" was initially completely stumped, but after some moments thought, he suggested that Hart could remove the labels from the suit he had in his possession and take *them* along with him when he delivered the photograph. Perfect! A final haggle over the price and Hart finally hung up having agreed to pay the tailor the price of a small car for the suit that would never be worn again. Still it *was* priceless to Janet.

With the suit photographed and armed with the printed pictures, the cut-out suit labels and of course a note of the all-important required suit dimensions, Hart set off to find the emporium of "Mr Bobby", but with a stop-off to pick up a "wodge" of cash on the way. Two hours later, he was back home feeling very satisfied with both his trip into "the third world backstreet" and with the final discount that he had been able to obtain from the delightful tailor. He squashed Janet's original perfect, but now sorely abused, dinner suit into a black plastic bag and dispatched it to the outside waste bin.

'Next!'

For his next job, he had decided to phone Victoria Crosse. His plan was to say a few 'Hellos' and 'how have you beens' and then give her a short briefing of the events as they had finally concluded, but to ask her to arrange to meet with Williams the following day when he would call her again and have a longer more in depth conversation, with the telephone set to "speaker phone" so that all three could take part.

Hart had not expected the degree of emotion that was expressed by Crosse when answering his call. Her relief that he was safe was delivered in bucket-loads, her sentences being interrupted by occasional sobs. Both she and Williams had been totally fine whilst Hart had been on his "mission", with Special Branch occasionally informing them of Hart's continued safety and well-being. Special Branch was of course trained in many things, being able to lie convincingly being high on the list.

Their conversation lasted for nearly one hour and ended with Hart revealing that he was in the process of booking flights to the UK and would arrive in Nottingham in a couple of weeks' time, where he would book a hotel room for the duration of his open-ended stay. This was music to Crosse's ears and upon finally hanging up the phone, she excitedly called Williams with the great news, arranging the time when she should arrive at his place the next day for the greater in-depth call with Hart.

Hart felt a little drained after the call to Crosse and hit the caffeine trail once again before dialling the number of his good friends Alix and Jason Barnes, also in Nottingham.

As Hart had expected, they were very happy to hear from him and extremely content with his excuses, his apologies and his plans to visit Nottingham again in the very near future with his secret business now almost at an end. They were the most contented, however, to learn that he would be staying in a local hotel in Nottingham this next time during his visit!

As he hung up the phone once more, it rang almost immediately. He picked it up gingerly, having been expecting an avalanche of calls from the press, not to mention a small island of news people camped outside his house, but perhaps it was early days for this. He probably had that pleasure to come.

'Hello?'

'*Ciao* Max, it's Luca, how are you?'

'Bloody hell, you've only just left my place! I'm older thanks. I'm still wondering how you can keep last night's events out of the news. There must have been a couple of hundred people there who ended up fleeing for their lives and who have been just dying, no pun intended, to get their stories out about that evening.'

'Yes, indeed that is very true, but of those people, it was only those who were in the ballroom who were directly involved. I can assure you that all of those people were interviewed by agents on the night and given appropriate counselling, but all would have been asked to keep a lid on the events and in fact I know for sure that they were all asked to sign a secrecy document. You know many of the people were government people anyway and used to secrecy, but they would have been told of the need to wait until an appropriate statement had been prepared before speaking to the press and you already know what *they* have been told.

'It used to be called a "D Notice" in the UK.'

'*Si*, it's a similar thing here in America and also in Italy. The relatives of those who were killed will have been given all necessary support, which will of course continue, and they will have been asked to hold back on discussing the events due to the possible serious effects it might have nationally. You know how patriotic the Americans are. Of course other countries are not so patriotic and news will soon flood out from there, but it will no doubt be dealt with as rumour and conjecture.'

'We'll see about that. This must be the biggest truly international news item that has broken for years and I'm intrigued to see how long it can be kept under wraps.'

'It might only be a matter of hours in truth, Max, but in the end you can be sure that a cosmetically treated, sanitised version will be the one that is officially released.'

'Hey ho. So much for the freedom of the press in the "Free World".'

'You know, Max, I do have some very important things to tell you. Oh yes before I forget, there was the elderly lady who you nearly danced with last night? She was very keen to discover how you were as she says you saved her life. She has been told that you are totally fine and that you will no doubt be in contact with her eventually.'

'Bloody hell! Thanks for that!'

'So then, my important items. First of all, I have been asked to pass on to you the thanks and congratulations from the Vatican. As you know this will be the most secret part of your exploits in terms of the outside world being informed of the details. In fact, I would go so far to say that you would get more uncensored coverage in Communist China than from the Vatican. Also, the government and health agencies that have spoken to me so far are very impressed with the outcome of the mission and although they have very few details yet, they also want me to pass on their congratulations to you. You know there is one common thread coming from all these people and that is how can three amateurs, that's Williams, Crosse and yourself complete what no high flying, top of the heap agency have been able to do? What is the secret?'

'Let's just say beginner's luck and my nine lives!'

'*Justo*, most probably it is. I also have news that *la Signora* Mondo is now awake and able to speak at the hospital. It seems she is making a very rapid recovery and she too wants to thank you for saving her life. It is also rumoured that with World in meltdown, she will eventually step into the shoes of the disgraced Alberto and be the company figurehead once he has been confined to the rubbish bin of history. It is also rumoured that she will need someone of outstanding merit and virtue to lead the company in the most honest and ethical way in order to drag World back to the pinnacle of pharmaceutical research excellence and respect, which is actually important to the US government as well as World. Max, seriously I have already heard your name mentioned for the role of this new Mr Clean as a possible candidate for World.'

'What! You must be kidding. Haven't they heard about my outrageous flippancy problems?'

'No, I'm not kidding. In fact the OCA is also keen to talk to you after some vacation time regarding having some role with them, or should I say us.'

'Better make that a *ham roll* then, Luca. Can't you see the irony of what you are saying? I become a big cheese at the ailing World, whilst also working for the OCA. Brilliant! That would be World and OCA working together for at least a second time then…if your undisclosed secret is correct, that is?'

There was a short silence at the other end of the line and then,

'I am only telling you the latest that I hear on the grapevine. It is the end of an era and people are looking to a bright new age. You should stand up and be counted.'

'Luca, I'm too tired to consider fairy tales at present, I need a holiday. Look, I'll see you later, *ciao*.'

'Think about it though, Max. Oh, and finally I mentioned a possible little surprise for you when we said farewell in Reggio; well, be ready, the surprise is on its way. *Ciao*.'

'Hang on Luca, wait. What surp—?'

The line went dead as Messi hug up.

Hart spent most of the rest of the day doing absolutely nothing and went to bed at 10.00 pm.

Chapter 130

Hart rose early the following morning and strolled down to the local restaurant for what had become his now normal breakfast, taking a newspaper from the stand on the way which he quickly scanned. There was no mention at all of the previous evening's events.

He had e-mailed Crosse before retiring the evening before indicating that he had decided to call them at 3.00 pm his time, meaning that she would have to be with Williams and ready for his call at 9.00 am UK time. After that call, he would have to drive out to "Mr Bobby" the tailor and collect and pay for the Balmain suit forgery and then back home once more before driving out to Janet's house in order to feed her with some details of the saga and to present her with the "good as new" if not better, dinner suit.

The meetings with Messi and the various government and regulatory bodies would no doubt follow over the coming days, weeks and months, but at present no formal dates or times had yet been confirmed and his upcoming visit to the UK was for him now set in stone.

By the time that 3.00 pm had arrived, he was ready to make the call to the UK. He dialled Crosse and she answered on the second ring.

'Good afternoon, Max.'

'Good morning, Vicky and Denis. Denis, I spoke to Vicky yesterday and she insists that she is fighting fit, so how are you, it's been a little time?'

'I'm fine, thanks Max. In fact I'm a damn sight better now than I have been for a long time and it's thanks to you and also Vicky here for all you've done in prosecuting the outrages that were being perpetrated before you became involved in the matter. Thank you, Max, I really haven't the words to thank you enough.'

'No need to thank me, Denis, really, you'll have me crying into my afternoon tea. Shall I do the honours and relate the whole story to you from the very start? You can feel free cut in and ask questions whenever you want.'

'Agreed, Max, off you go.'

'OK. Well it all began when…'

Two hours later, Hart drew his explanation to a close. There had been many questions fired at him during his presentation, but when he came to the end there was absolute silence, which was punctured finally by Crosse.

'Max, we are both stunned here by your story. It's almost too fantastic for words. Thank you so much.'

'No problem. Look, I really do have a mountain of things to do, but I'll be in touch soon with details of my trip to Nottingham, so bye for now, folks.'

In unison from the UK, 'Bye Max, have a safe trip over. Bye.'

Click! The call was finished.

'What next? Oh yes, the suit.'

Suddenly, his doorbell rang out. Answering the door, he saw a uniformed man holding an envelope.

'Good afternoon, sir, I have a letter here which you have to sign for.'

'Er, yes of course.'

He signed the man's form and the letter was duly handed to him.

'That's it, thank you, sir. Have a nice day.'

He touched the corner of his peaked cap in salute and returned to his small delivery van. Hart went inside his house and examined the letter. It was a slightly padded envelope but there were no clues as to what the obviously important missive might contain. He carefully peeled back the serrated opening strip and pulled out the formal looking document inside, then sitting down in an armchair he began to read.

'Bloody hell!'

The letter was the "little surprise" that Messi had reminded him of. It was the formal notification from the Italian Office of Catholic Affairs that for his selfless actions in pursuing and bringing to an end the criminal and immoral activities….blah, blah, blah…he was to be awarded the Medal of Honour, the date and time of the presentation in Milan to be agreed at a later date.

The Medal of Honour was a particular Italian award to members of their Secret Services who had made outstanding contributions to ensuring the continued excellence of the political, constitutional or juridical order of the country. It was of course an honour that Hart would be unable, to discuss and share with anybody other than with Messi, but it was a demonstration of thanks which he was actually delighted to receive. Messi would have been very instrumental in pushing all the right buttons to enable Hart, a foreigner, to receive this most distinguished decoration and that thought made Hart feel even closer to his rotund friend. He would call Messi with the news of the delivery of the letter and arrange for them to have a suitable celebration.

Hart's final task now was to collect the suit and go and meet Janet.

Arriving at the tailor's, he found "Mr Bobby" already standing behind the counter holding up the suit with a smile from ear to ear, revealing that alternate teeth were missing and those remaining were a dentist's nightmare shade of yellow. He must have been waiting in great anticipation for Hart's car to arrive in the rutted unmade-up car park.

'I show you now.'

"Mr Bobby" gently removed the suit from inside the protective cellophane and proudly displayed it to Hart. It looked magnificent and when he indicated the official Balmain labels which he had sewn into it, Hart was ecstatic and generous with both his praise and his consequent tip. What a find "Mr Bobby" had been.

Hart now dashed back home, had a quick change of clothes and then drove his car sedately to Janet's home. Upon opening her door, they embraced fondly and she invited him into the sitting room.

'So then, tell me how it all went the other evening. Was it a glittering success?'

'Janet, it was a great success, but success often comes at a great cost and in this case the cost was in human lives.'

'My God, can you tell me about it?'

'Only you, Janet, would be knowledgeable enough to ask that question, realising that there could be a "non-reporting notice" on it. Have you not heard any whispers at all of what occurred?'

'No, none at all.'

'In that case I will reveal all to you.' …

And he did.

Like others who he had related the story to, she also remained silent and shocked.

'It's quite unimaginable, I can hardly believe it.'

'But the most unbelievable aspect of it, Janet, when all is said and done, is that it looks that I may be in line for a top flight job offer from both Bobo Mondo, when she recovers from her wound and takes the reins of the company, and also from the OCA who want me to do some work for them, presumably undercover. All very James Bondish.'

'And what will you do?'

'I can't face talking about it yet *Mish* Moneypenny, it's far too early and in any *cashe* it's only an early rumour. I can't quite see me doing either though to be honest, both are far too serious!'

Janet nodded, clearly unimpressed by Hart's impression of Sean Connery's Bond.

'Let's wait and see then. I told you last time that I was considering retiring from World, yes? Well, I handed in my notice last week and am now just playing out my final three weeks with them.'

'Good for you, although if hell freezes over and I'm offered a job there, there'll be an immediate invitation in the post for you to re-join as PA to the new, dashing, young, company saviour.'

'In that case, expect me to drive a hard bargain, my pension is pathetic!'

'Deal!'

'OK, I have to go out to the car.'

Two minutes later, Hart returned with a bouquet of flowers in one hand and the pristine dinner suit, wrapped in its original cellophane and hanging on a padded wooden coat hanger in the other. She went to the kitchen and placed the flowers in water and then returned for the suit.

'The flowers are lovely; thank you, Max.'

She took the suit from him, removed the wrapping and held it close to her, looking at the jacket and the trousers lovingly, her eyes lingering over the beautiful fabric.

'See, Janet, I've had it dry-cleaned. It looks just like new.'

(*Only someone as trusting as Janet would never consider for one moment that the aged suit might be a brand new forgery!*)

'Max, it looks wonderful; it's as if it's never been worn.'

(Only Max Hart would fail to realise that the original suit had two jacket buttons not three and the trousers had a button rather than a zip fly!).

'I think we should celebrate this moment with a glass of champagne, Max. What do you think?'

'I think that's a wonderful idea. Would you like me to open it?'

While Hart removed the foil from the neck of the chilled bottle, Janet placed two champagne flutes onto the small drinks table. The cork finally popped, or rather "sighed" as Hart preferred to call it, and he poured the fizzing liquid expertly into each flute. They raised their charged glasses and clinked them together.

'Thanks for all your help, Janet, I really couldn't have done it without you and without the suit of course. Here's to the future. Both our futures!'

'Thank you, Max. May a new broom sweep the "World" clean. To the future.'

'Cheers!'